BLIND SPOT

The Covenant's Forfeit

Thio Isobel Moss

AUDACITER
PRESS

ISBN (Paperback): 979-8-9933896-5-3
Library of Congress Control Number: 2025923466

Cover design by Thio Isobel Moss
Published by Audaciter Press
Kansas City, MO
Website: www.thioisobelmoss.com

Dedication:

This book is dedicated with love to
Bill, Coo, Oz, and Kendi.
Your insight, support, and faith
brought this story to life.
Thank you!

In memory of Ty —
the first person to hear this story
and a funny, generous,
and thoughtful friend
for many years.
We miss you.

Table of Contents

Prologue

Kenny: January 29th in Parkville, Missouri

"...reckless, irresponsible, idiotic, and selfish!"

Evelyn Vine, my beloved sister, was in rare form.

Her condemnation, declaimed with stentorian flair, failed to provoke me...much. I had calculated the risk of my current venture. In a place with only bad choices, this was the best.

Ignoring Evy's histrionics, I traced the nurse's path as he prepped the room. His movements were graceful and economical. There was something reassuring in his competence – the fluidity of purpose.

Swathed head to toe in generic teal scrubs, there was little to see of the man underneath. He was several inches below average, dark-eyed, with only brief flashes of brown skin revealed at the neck and cuffs. If I had not already known who he was, I would not be able to recognize him again.

The dopp kit he'd been holding hit the metal cart with a resonating clang, bringing my gaze up to his. Evidently, he wasn't keen on being the object of my attention. My mouth twisted in wry amusement. It was possible that he wanted to be here even less than Evy did. We hadn't exactly warmed to each other.

"No! This is...," my sister continued, choking on her fury. I had some concern that she might inadvertently damage herself. Or advertently. It hadn't occurred to me that she might until now. "This is insanity! After what happened to Dad...you can't let her do this!"

My eyes traveled to where my mom sat, serene in stone-washed jeans, a black blazer, her pixie cut perfectly imperfect, with her dog as the final accessory. The Belgian Tervuren stood at parade rest, guarding her. It was the perfect ensemble to launch a criminal enterprise. Although her expression seemed frozen — a steely veneer concealing...I wish I knew what.

A wave of guilt beat at me. I had miscalculated this moment. I'd thought choosing a direction would bring us a sense of purpose, if not peace.

Mom endured our strange tableau without her customary smile. Her smiles were a language, a barometer of her mood, and as habitual as breathing. They were her sword and shield. Its absence flummoxed me. What did it mean? There were no more illusions, no comfortable lies, no polite assurances?

A goose walked over my grave.

It hit me. This was real. My mother, her dog, my sister, and my best friend would serve as my witnesses and custodians. A blanket of surreal dread smothered me, stealing the oxygen from my lungs. All my scheming suddenly seemed like a bad joke.

"I don't let her do anything, my darling. Neither do you. Kenny knows what she's risking."

Did I?

"Our task is to trust her," my mom rebuked, as she stroked Mel's dark head.

Was it?

I suppose it would be too easy if she had said, "She's doing the right thing."

Beside her, Mel remained alert, one ear cocked toward the door and both eyes locked on the stranger in our midst. He was oblivious to my existential crisis. He hadn't reacted to my sister's ranting, either. He knew neither of us presented a threat to his familiar.

I envied the simplicity of his task.

With a grimace, I returned to watching the nurse as he unzipped the leather bag and slid a sharp, slender tool from its sheath. One by one, he laid out an impressive array of scalpels, serrated forceps, delicate clamps, and oddly shaped scissors on a white cloth. Objectively, they were beautiful — in a utilitarian sort of way. Subjectively, it was difficult not to theorize on their functions.

Holding up a scalpel so that it winked in the light, the nurse sterilized the pristine implement. In the mirrored surface of one of the wider tools, I caught his notice. Seeing the unfiltered fire in his liquid brown gaze, his expression was easy to read — rank suspicion accented by a softer strain of contemplation.

A smaller, slighter figure, equally aqua and anonymous, banged through the door and scanned the room with a gimlet eye. Everyone jumped, except for the dog.

"You want to do this here?" she demanded, appalled.

I surveyed the garage. Pegboard walls, dust-blanketed machinery, and a damaged workbench stacked with dingy tools and cardboard boxes surrounded us. Broken fishing rods lounged beside rusting lawn furniture, clothed in cobwebs. The ceiling was unfinished, with exposed insulation, well past serving any purpose. In the cold, stale air, everything looked tired, brittle, and hopeless. It was eminently suitable.

The lighting was dim, so we had arranged half a dozen mismatched floor lamps to brighten the ambiance...or, at least, mimic a clinical glare. They circled a second worktable draped with old sheets. An operating theater it was not, but it would do.

"Yes," I confirmed.

"It's not sanitary," she remonstrated — as if the state of the small building indicated a personal failing rather than an environmental concern.

"It is," I corrected, wriggling my fingers.

She regarded me skeptically, then shrugged. "It's your funeral."

An unfortunate choice of words. Evy found her second wind.

"Please, stop this, Mom," she begged, her voice hoarse and thin. I felt another twinge of guilt until she added, "She's not mentally stable!"

That was uncalled for.

It was true, perhaps...probably, but rude!

The nurse's brows lifted in surprise. He hadn't expected to agree with anyone associated with me.

I gave him a vicious smirk. Don't kid yourself, buddy. If I'm unstable, what does that make you? An upstanding member of the Community associating with an unstable practitioner? Heaven preserve us!

"Enough," my mother barked, two tears breaking past her resolve.

Something cold and hard formed in my throat. Her mask had slipped, and one trembling hand curled around Mel's collar. She was dangling over the abyss, and I had pushed her there.

Evy crumpled. The blaze that had sustained her died in an instant. She really believed that I was going to die — if not here and now, then soon after, and Mom refused to save me. I shut my eyes. Cowardly, perhaps, but I couldn't back out. I had to do something!

My lips flattened, a grim fatalism wicking away the dread. I had to do something. Once I accepted that, everything else fell away.

"On the table," the nurse grunted.

I did as instructed, kicking off my flip flops and lying back on the hard surface. My robe did nothing to protect me from the frigid worktop. My headlights were on bright, and my backside was stiff as a board. We should have brought a space heater.

The nurse's gloved palm twitched as he reluctantly took hold of my arm and sterilized a patch of skin near my elbow. He needn't worry; what ailed me wasn't contagious.

A second later, I felt the pinch of a needle. He taped the IV in place and turned back to his cart. The surgeon was busy scouring her hands and arms up to the elbows at the rusty sink. I felt oddly detached as the nurse prepared a syringe...as though all of this were merely a scene from a play.

I suspected myself of dissociating.

"I can't do this. I can't watch this...lunacy," Evy rasped, charging out the door with a sound somewhere between a sob and a bellow.

I shored up my resolve but couldn't keep from glancing over at my mom once again. She closed her eyes for a long moment but said nothing. Nore silently emerged from the shadows hugging the walls to stand beside her. She took one of Mom's hands between her own. Her mild expression betrayed nothing, but she offered me a slow blink from fathomless, black eyes and a single nod.

Four witnesses would have been better, but three would do.

"This is the point of no return," the nurse growled, unaffected by the drama. He held up the hypodermic needle. "Are we proceeding?"

A memory unfolded in my mind, like a paper crane being unmade. Warm, golden light splashed through a window and over the sink, staining the counters and the hardwood floor, catching on a bowl of apples. The familiar, comforting scent of fresh lemons and baking soda enveloped me.

A younger me stood on a step stool beside the marble countertop and explained the finer points of sandwich-making to an invisible audience. I was pretending to host my own cooking show. My ingredients were arranged in a row, along with a plate garnished with carrot and celery sticks. Mel listened from the floor as I crafted the pinnacle of peanut butter and jelly perfection — sliced diagonally.

The image fled as quickly as it had come — a mirage, quicksand. Even at eight, I had known my place in the world. The point of no return had come and gone twenty-two years ago. More recent events had merely underscored the inevitable.

"Do it."

"Glasses," demanded the nurse.

I swept them off and handed them over, closing my eyes to the searing light and stray visions my brain conjured. Although I didn't observe what followed, I swore I heard the scrape of rubber against glass as the plunger of the syringe depressed. Half a moment later, ice slid beneath my skin.

"Sleepy yet?" asked the nurse, apathetic.

"No."

"Count backward from ten."

"Ten," I began. The swish of fabric sliding against the sheet-covered table whispered in my ear. The ting of metal striking against metal pierced the air as I imagined hoarfrost creeping deeper into my veins.

"Nine," I murmured, trying not to fight the anesthesia. I didn't like being helpless.

I took a deep breath...and another, filling my lungs with cold, sour air. I wasn't alone. If I did pop off, I would be avenged.

The thought pulled a smile to my lips.

"Eight..."

Hours, weeks, or months later, I awoke...floating in a sea of dazzling light. The slow, persistent motion of glacial water, lifting my body only to fall again, made me queasy. Fighting the clinging lethargy, I opened my eyes, and two sharp blades speared through my skull. I shifted, trying to evade the pain.

"Where do you think you're going?" grumbled a voice from far, far away.

Heavy hands pressed my shoulders back down against a hard surface.

A few more synapses flickered back online, and I remembered — the operation. The voice belonged to the nurse. And his question was the closest he'd come to a friendly overture. He'd even managed to sound relieved that I was alive and awake.

Desperation did funny things to people.

As my awareness solidified, the iron-laden odor saturating the now humid air imposed itself.

Ignore it. Refuse to think about it.

A metallic film coated my mouth. I could taste it. My body heaved —
once, twisting inside, then a second time. Gulping air, I shoved the feeling
back, timing my inhalations and keeping my eyes clamped shut.

Don't think about it. If you think about it, you'll convince your body
that it's going to happen.

"You've been out for a little under six hours. The surgery was a success.
No surprises along the way, except for the return of your sister halfway
through. You'll experience some vertigo and nausea, so for everyone's sake,
stay still," the surgeon informed me with ambiguous satisfaction.

I didn't bother nodding but continued counting. I heard the clatter of
metal tools, and instantly, a blue cloth stained red and brown manifested in
my obliging imagination. I rattled my brain, hoping a distraction would fall
out.

The tap was running, and I pounced on the sound.

Focus on the pure and neutral sound of water flowing.

The hushed murmur was textured with the splashes of someone
washing their hands...washing off all the bl...

Focus on the sound of the damned water, Kenny!

A piece of tape was ripped off my arm, and I hissed, popping one eye
open to glare in the general direction of the nurse. A frisson of electric
agony was the predictable result. Reclamping it, I was forced to assume that
I had successfully communicated my displeasure and resumed listening to
the tap flow with violent determination.

I hadn't noticed that Florence Nightingale had also removed the IV until
the stiff sensation of a needle buried in my arm began to fade. He pressed a
cotton ball against the puncture site and applied a new piece of tape to hold
it in place.

The water cut off, taking my salvation with it. I shoved my attention
back into counting breaths.

A few minutes later, my stomach unclenched. I pressed my elbows
against the table, the cold burrowing into my bare flesh. The world wasn't
spinning yet, so I pushed myself up slowly. I made it six inches before my
stomach lurched and gravity dissolved. After five long beats, things
stabilized.

It was hardly the stiff-backed rise from a coffin traditionally depicted.

"Glasses", I hissed, trying to hold my head up without it rolling off my
shoulders.

"Idiot," the surgeon diagnosed.

Someone perched the frames on my face, and I opened my eyes. The light was still harsh, but manageable. I didn't study the new stains on my medical team's scrubs but looked past them to where Mom sat. She still didn't smile, but there was a gleam of triumph in her baby blues.

It was done.

Mel hadn't budged, still on duty.

Evy paced back and forth behind them, her expression just this side of murderous. Faded mascara circled her puffy manic eyes, and the state of her blond mane suggested she was coming off a week-long bender during which copious amounts of recreational substances had been used with unprecedented results. Retribution would be swift and terrible for putting her through this.

Nore contented herself with a small Mona Lisa smile.

"May I see a mirror?"

The nurse pulled a hand mirror with whorls etched into a pink plastic frame from the lower shelf of the cart and handed it to me. My fingers felt clumsy as I peered into it, slightly surprised that I recognized myself. There was some swelling in my cheeks and mouth, but otherwise, nothing had changed.

I grimaced, inspecting my teeth. They were all present and accounted for, if a little gory around the edges. Mentally, I searched for tiny muscles that never appeared in anatomy textbooks...and found them. With a gentle snick, a pair of slender fangs shot out from under my gums and glided over the slick contours between my lateral incisors and canines.

They were a perfect color match.

"The material is home-grown," the surgeon explained woodenly. "There is nothing artificial in your head, no stitches that need to be removed, nothing major left to heal — but maybe wait a few hours before brushing your teeth. The Agency could autopsy you tomorrow and be assured that your cold, lifeless corpse belonged to an unfortunate but upstanding member of the Community."

Charming. More to the point, liberating. The Community outlawed 'witchcraft', but vampires were welcome.

The nurse made a sharp, sudden movement so that the glaring light and empty shadows engulfed him in equal measure, painting him in Rorschach blots. A yank on his mask and his own much more prominent bicuspids were beautifully silhouetted.

"Congratulations on your rising," he purred softly.

Suddenly, he was looming over me. I hadn't seen him move.

"We have upheld our end of the bargain. Your turn."

I smiled at my reflection, turning my head left, then right, inspecting the craftsmanship. My fangs were flawless.

"Indeed."

Unwillingly, I set the mirror aside and took off my glasses, bracing myself. The world fractured into chaos — a meld of gloom and glow, solid objects stretching into impossible shapes and mind-numbing panoramas overlaying the garage. A sheen rippled off gossamer webs connecting everything real and unreal, each thread pulsing with energy. It took a few moments for my mind to make sense of it.

When it finally did, I noted that one outer-world resident stared, for lack of a better word, back at me. He was gargantuan, naked to the waist, and the acres of bare, clammy, gray skin on display were textured with ritualistic scarring. His head was missing a face. His dank hide stretched over where eyes, nostrils, ears, and a mouth ought to be. Yet, somehow, he was aware of us. He followed every stray noise on our end of existence, swaying as though curious — even though sound couldn't...shouldn't...travel between planes.

A dull ache blossomed behind my right eye, a reminder to get a move on. Dabbling in the beyond was not without risk — it was more than the human mind was designed to accept. And attempting to manipulate the ley lines when I hadn't even gotten a handle on the post-op drool was exquisitely stupid.

I took a deep breath and lifted my hands, weaving to create intricate patterns as ley energy began to curdle around me. The movements were unnecessary — just window dressing. Practitioners, conjurers, sorcerers, diablerists — whatever word you fancied — we understood the inherent magic of the theater and capitalized on it. Mystique was just another shield.

I was rewarded for my efforts when the real vampires' jaws dropped. My eyes had lit with white fire, causing the throb in my head to strengthen. I'm photosensitive. External light was bad enough; internal light was simply masochistic. The choreography was familiar, though, and I needed familiarity for what I was about to attempt.

A radiance rolled under my skin, erupting into a million will-o'-the-wisps fluttering through my veins. My dreadlocks came alive, floating around and coiling over each other like luminous snakes. Working the light show, I rose to the tips of my toes, ascending until I was cradled two feet above the floor, basking in the splendor of my special effects.

It was a ridiculous waste of energy.

I plucked at the ley lines, priming them with my own power, while keeping the hand jive on overdrive. Magic wasn't all that magical. It's a mechanical process that every living creature participates in. Cause and effect; launch the right program, pull the right lever, and abracadabra! No one ever wills something into being. If that were how it worked, we'd have been overrun with ponies, sand fairies, sky bison, and regal rangers with broken swords long ago.

Once I'd spindled enough juice, I took a deep breath and started excavating a tunnel through the bowels of the beyond — or, more accurately, constructed a temporary transplanal bridge. Easy-peasy. I had managed it four times. I'd been assured that it would get easier with practice, as all sequences did. With sweat dripping in my eyes and an immense pressure crushing my chest, I doubted my handler's promises.

And then, stuck between an arcane rock and a hard place, I hesitated.

Ley manipulation attracts attention — the Community relied on Agency warlocks to hunt, subdue, or exterminate any magic-twisting vermin. To prevent uninvited guests, we'd warded the garage so thoroughly it felt like a null zone. Unfortunately, wards only operated on this plane. My skills were unique on Earth but not in the greater existence. Gritting my teeth, I pushed past my anxieties.

I'd made a promise.

Sooty vapor unfurled from thin air, reaching out with nimble, greedy fingers. It curled around and between us, stalking us, eager to swallow us whole. Between one breath and the next, the lights were snuffed out. I couldn't see my hand in front of my face. I checked.

And then, the clicking began.

Vaguely metallic, there was a soft shush and then a hard click. It repeated, getting closer. The heavy energy buzzing through the circuit built upon itself, the sensation potently addictive. Reality receded the more deeply I became enmeshed with the beyond, the visual noise lessening and with it, the ache behind my eyes.

Above the operating table, a sphere grated into place, plate by plate — composed of ley energy, time, space, and whatever useful bits of matter had existed between me and my goal. The clicks graduated to a roar as the portal stretched.

"What have you done?" the nurse shouted.

I didn't bother replying. He wouldn't have believed me.

Turbulence whipped against my skin, informing me of what I could not see. The attack never landed. I was too deeply cocooned within the field of magic.

A mildly hysterical cackle bubbled up within me, but I wasn't safe. I needed to hurry.

The sphere tore open — a lipless mouth, taller than the building, yawned wide and warm, fetid breath beaded on my flesh — revealing a shadowed and jagged pit beyond. Existence stretched grotesquely to accommodate the construct, warping the roof and floor.

The faceless spectator, having drifted to the left, grinned with an uncomfortable stretch of skin. His chest rolled as he laughed, fading out of view. There was no other visible presence, but as I anchored my gate, I knew I wasn't alone.

The watcher. Every time I attempted a working, there he was — as if to weigh my raw and naked soul before the cosmos. My breath rattled in my throat, my palms grew slick, and my muscles refused to obey. I was small in the vastness of creation; insignificant. Perhaps it was by that token that I'd managed to survive thus far.

I forced myself to exhale. He was here, and he wanted me to know it. Inhale. Fine. He could watch, judge, and leave. Exhale. It made little difference.

Something massive whipped past, inches from my face, distracting me from my feelings of inferiority and impending doom before whistling by again. Screams cut off as the metal mouth liquefied and sealed — sated. The word rang loud in my mind as the gash on this physical realm smoothed without a scar, leaving us in a stinging well of silence.

Exhaling again, I dared the Watcher to do something. Was he going to reach through the primordial nothingness and pluck me out of existence — again?

I rammed the intrusive question into a mental box, welded it shut, and chucked it into a conceptual ocean. I didn't know his purpose. I didn't understand his interest. He'd only interfered once, and I had survived.

Shaking, I forced myself into action, scrubbing the building of magical fingerprints. As the magic broke down and was funneled away, the room returned to its former brilliance.

My right eye socket throbbed, hinting at imminent mutiny.

Almost done. Just sweeping the lint under the carpet...

Stepping down from the tangle of lines that had held me aloft, my bare feet found the gritty concrete floor. The flickering lights writhing under my skin settled down to hibernate. Some residual energy in my hair snapped at me. I squeaked, rubbing the current from my palm, and forced myself to slow down. Power took time to spindle and release safely. Carelessness would only lead to unwanted attention from threats on this plane.

The rest of my weavings collapsed in a whisper as I funneled the energy back into the lines, like tired party decorations. The quiet became natural.

Looking up, Mom regarded me with resigned humor.

Mel looked bored. Nore issued a delicate snort, and Evy, slumped against the pegboard wall, muttered, "Drama queen."

I stuck my tongue out at her.

I'd never told them about the Watcher. There was nothing they could do about him except forbid me from using my gift and worry when I refused.

My medical team was conspicuous by their absence.

"A promise kept," I murmured, the charged air giving a final crackle as I stepped back into my flip flops. I mentally checked off step one of my master plan; unfortunately, step two — winning over and leading a cadre predisposed to loathe me — was rather complicated.

Baby steps.

Clapping my hands, I barked, "All right, everyone, grab a lamp."

Chapter 1: Time's Up

Ten Years Later: February 26th at the Agora in Chicago, Illinois

"Senator, they're ready."

Rufus Balbay glanced up from his pristine desk and nodded to the aide. He signed the document in his hands and placed it in the out tray before rising from his chair. It was a delicious combination of toffee-stained oak and supple leather that gave a little whimper as he stood.

He donned his suit jacket — bespoke and British — and checked his reflection in the marbled enamel mirror that hung on the opposite wall; a severe face took his measure — dark hair touched with gray, olive skin, forbidding brows over deep-set eyes, and a meticulously groomed beard. His mouth twitched — a futile stab at warmth before turning to the door. Even he recognized the futility of such an exercise.

With a flick of his fingers, he signaled for his companions to follow. The soles of his polished wingtips slapped against the stone floor, flattening the motif of flowers and vines. It was a long way from his office to the lower levels of the Agora, and the glass and gilt lifts presented a fine view of the snow-dusted city — a quiet moment to ruminate, were he inclined to indulge, which he was not. No corner of his mind was available for idle thought.

Eventually, the ground rose and swallowed him. A few seconds and sixty feet deeper, the cabin doors slid open. The sophisticated veneer of the Agora's public face had vanished, leaving behind pale gray walls and dim, outdated lighting — buzzing as a bulb began to fail.

"Fix that," he snapped.

"Right away, Senator."

A dark gray carpet, accented with vaguely geometric patches of maroon and chocolate, softened the impact of his tread. He entered a room lined with monitors, inhabited by three people, and a one-way window.

"Rufe, excellent. We were just about to begin," a slender blond woman in a charcoal pantsuit informed him, pressing a small, green button on the wall. "Unfortunately, the Director won't be joining us."

"You were going to start without me, Isolde?" he inquired. The curve of his mouth was gently mocking, but the weight of his gaze communicated a warning.

Senior Special Agent Isolde Gerahty's answering smile was sweetly venomous — her specialty. "Of course not. That would be brazenly naive."

"It would," he agreed, studying the sullen, young man and sole occupant of the cramped room beyond the window. He sat on a plastic chair, elbows on the metal table, hands fidgeting as he waited. The boy was pale as death, with limp sandy hair and sunken, empty eyes.

"Name?"

"Levi Wilton, seventeen, son of Frank and Jenelle Wilton, cadre affiliation — Ierning Aldor. He was caught on camera speaking with Talia Davis ten minutes before the abduction. He didn't come forward, so we extended an invitation. He has reluctantly obliged us."

An agent, lean and dark, entered, setting a folder and a pen on the table before taking a seat. "Mr. Wilton, I am Special Agent Benning. Would you care for a glass of water? Tap only, I'm afraid — waste policy."

Mr. Wilton glanced up, his eyes void of emotion, and returned his attention to his hands. Benning smiled, called for water, and sat, clearing his throat.

"They'll arrive shortly," he assured the boy. "You spoke with Talia Davis before she was grabbed — a three-minute, forty-three-second exchange. Would you please describe that conversation?"

Levi studiously picked at his nails. Special Agent Benning waited patiently, undisturbed by the silence. After knocking, a second agent entered with two glasses.

"Thank you, Petry." Benning smiled at the agent's retreating back. "Talia's parents have not heard from their daughter in over seventeen hours. No ransom demand; nothing to direct the search. Her chances are dropping like a rock."

Mr. Wilton yawned, unmoved.

"You're a good kid, Levi — grades, volunteering. You're service-oriented. Anything you know — Talia's mood, her worries — now is the time to spill. Even crumbs could help."

Mr. Wilton scratched some old tape off the table but remained silent.

Quietly, Special Agent Benning murmured, "If she's murdered, consider how you are going to feel, Levi. How will your parents feel? They're watching this interview."

Levi glanced at the mirrored window, his eyes flickering with life but his lips firming in a straight line. He went back to the grubby tape.

"It may be in your power to prevent a tragedy," Benning coaxed.

The boy didn't look up, but his mouth spasmed. It was there and gone in a fraction of a second.

An exultant smirk crinkled the corners of Rufe's lips. He'd recognized the flutter of muscles for what it was. A smile could mean anything, but it was enough to convince the Senator that Levi Wilton knew something. Rufe tapped on the glass.

"Time's up," the special agent sighed and rose.

The Senator continued to study the boy for a moment, considering his next move.

"What? Are you waiting for permission? Serrecold's given you free rein," Gerahty exclaimed, waving a hand at the door.

Chuckling silently, he nodded and exited. The good Senator was aware that his popularity was not universal. Isolde Gerahty and others of her ilk resented his interference and questioned his motives and methods. They could not argue with the results, however.

A moment passed before Rufe appeared on the opposite side of the window.

"What a prick," Special Agent Gerahty mumbled with vehemence. Those with her wisely remained silent, however much they might agree, even when she demanded, "What does this have to do with Internal Investigations, anyway?"

A fair question.

Mr. Wilton had launched an in-depth analysis of the structure of a callus on his palm. With equal fascination, Rufe repositioned Benning's chair and, moving in a blur, hammered his fist down on the center of the table with enough force to buckle its metal legs, sending the two untouched water glasses flying. Glass shattered.

Levi's head shot up, and he stared at Senator Rufus Balbay. The boy's pupils expanded, a horrible understanding entering his expression, until his face went slack.

The Senator's grin was slightly apologetic, his manner brisk.

"Start at the beginning, Mr. Wilton. Tell me everything you know about Talia Davis," he encouraged.

"All rise."

Her Honor, Judge Mara Dietricksen of the Heliaia — the High Court — swept in, her gray robes billowing like a wraith. The room went silent. The lady had earned her reputation — her judgment was fair but flinty, and a sense of decorum was advisable.

"Your Honor, a petition has been entered to admit observers to this hearing," stammered the little clerk.

Rufe's brow quirked up in surprise, and he sat up straighter, a hunter's smirk tugging his mouth.

"This is a closed courtroom, Ms. Andreassen," her Honor replied, claiming her chair.

"Representative Jones, your Honor," the woman whispered, keeping her eyes lowered.

Dietricksen cackled.

"You certainly didn't waste any time, Ms. Montgomery. Very pragmatic."

Ms. Montgomery's eyes flared ruby-red before subsiding as she rose to stand beside her client. "The defense did not request the attendance of any Angel of Mercy. My client is innocent."

"Indeed," Her Honor replied curtly, smothering her amusement and mulling the matter over. "Very well. As Representative Jones is a member of the Quorum, I'll spare her five minutes in my chambers to justify her request."

Her existence, more like.

For the brief moment her chamber door was open, a shrill, savage roar echoed from deeper within the skyscraper, accompanied by the sound of something ripping — a gentle reminder of the consequences for any who dared attempt evading the court's justice.

Rufe made an indistinct noise, clearing his throat.

It could not have been humor — the man would break if he laughed. Although if he had, watching the Community's elite squirm after hearing the last remnant of the Wild Hunt take their tea would doubtlessly tickle it.

Ms. Andreassen click-clacked to the courtroom's broad doors and stepped aside to admit a most peculiar young woman — one who had obviously arrived posthaste via the Peregrine Gate. Attired in a white tank top and jeans — both liberally adorned with sawdust — Representative Jones stepped barefoot into the historic room.

Rufe appeared to be in actual pain, poor chap, as he observed the lady. He swallowed thickly, fully dumbstruck. No doubt, he slept and showered in a suit to avoid such an embarrassing situation.

Ms. Montgomery's jaw worked, scandalized by the Representative's slovenly appearance, while the prosecuting attorney, Mr. Li, was not quite clutching his pearls, but it was a near thing. Those closest to him readied themselves to assist, should he succumb to the vapors.

"This way," murmured Ms. Andreassen, her kitten heels skittering.

Jones followed in a resolute stride. Despite her inappropriate garb, she seemed immune to the curiosity her appearance excited. From the crown of tea-colored dreadlocks to the flex of her ankles, every detail was absorbed and dissected. Her mahogany skin, her mesorrhine nose, and the way her flashing eyes assessed the room in one sweeping glance.

Ms. Andreassen ushered the Representative back to Her Honor's rooms before returning to her station. She had just enough time to slouch in her chair and draw a deep breath before Judge Dietricksen's head emerged from the passage.

"Ms. Andreassen, a moment."

Eyes comically widened, the little clerk scrambled up and scampered after her.

For several minutes, only soft inhalations and the ticking of an old pocket watch were heard in that hallowed hall. Then, causing a second fervor, Ms. Andreassen reappeared.

"Ms. Montgomery, Mr. Wilton's presence has been requested. Please escort him through."

"Ms. Andreassen, I must protest," Mr. Li proclaimed, rising from his seat.

"Judge Dietricksen requested me to explain that the boy is not going to kidnap her from the Agora, Mr. Li, and while these circumstances are unusual, they are lawful and not without precedent. As it stands, Mr. Wilton is only accused of a crime — not convicted. He still retains all the rights and privileges of a registered member of the Community, so sit down."

Mr. Li, as surprised as anyone at her commanding tone, sat.

Levi Wilton, after a nod from his attorney, hesitantly rose from his chair and followed Ms. Montgomery.

Exactly one minute and eleven seconds later, the entire group returned.

"Representative Jones has requested permission to observe the hearing. She has presented excellent reasons for doing so, and I am inclined to accede to her request. Mr. Wilton, do you have any objection?"

Mr. Wilton appeared to have found his courage somewhere between the Judge's chamber and the courtroom. He met Judge Dietricksen's glacial scrutiny with striking composure before his gaze roved over to Representative Jones.

"No, Your Honor."

"Mr. Li," she inquired, addressing the prosecution.

"None, Your Honor, barring the irregularity of the situation."

"Excellent. Representative Jones, please find a seat and let's begin," Judge Dietricksen said brightly, reclaiming her own. "Levi Wilton, you stand accused of warped practices. As you have confessed before a member of the Quorum, and due to the serious nature of the crime, this matter has been recommended for immediate trial. Ms. Montgomery, I conclude that your client wishes to present a defense?"

Chapter 2: Good Talk

Kenny: March 3ʳᵈ at Sullen Creek Farm

The silence continued on unchecked and progressed from uncomfortable to agonizing. I sat, elbows propped on my knees, fingertips braced in the shape of a Gothic arch, nestled within a cognac-colored, amphiptere leather wingback by the fireplace, striving to look trustworthy.

It wasn't working.

My facial muscles were stiff from maintaining an impartial mask. I had to say something, but what? What did they already know? A misstep could be catastrophic. If we were exposed…lying was as habitual as breathing and as vital for survival, yet words clogged my throat. Even breathing was hard.

I swallowed and croaked, "No."

The girl, maybe eleven and of South Asian descent, narrowed her eyes. "No, what? No, he's not a demon, not a vampire, or vampires aren't demons?"

The boy, a bit older and Latino, pleaded silently for absolution.

How did I get into these situations? They needed a shrink or someone at least slightly qualified for this mess — Déjà, Maggie, or Davy. Even Nore would have been a better option, but she was otherwise occupied, and woe betide any and all who disturbed her.

I murmured a prayer and pushed on.

"No to one and three. Milo, you're not a demon. Becoming a demon doesn't happen overnight. Becoming a vampire can. They're not inherently evil, though. Most are just regular people. The…"

Traumatizing cosmic accident that led to this crippling shift in identity? No, I couldn't say that. The twist of fate that will define the rest of your life? Probably not?

"The…experience you've described is typical for how the Strigoi and Incubi are usually created."

The Eliberarea Demonului ritual, the only other method, wasn't worth mentioning. Forced vampirism had only worked seven times and required a lost Romanian artifact — the broșă de creuzet, and lost knowledge since its creator, Corvin Hofer, was slain by warlocks in 1637.

"What the what?"

18

Mouse, as the girl chose to be called, was a natural communicator — a budding orator or a great poet. She shifted her legs, perched on the back of the sofa. If Nore had been here, her eyes would have been laser-focused on the dirty shoes grinding filth into the dark green velvet upholstery. Me? I was occupied with trying not to sweat visibly.

"Vampire is a catch-all term that covers hundreds of incarnations...," I noticed two sets of furrowed brows and amended my words, "types that fit into four subtypes — Strigoi, Moroi, Dhampir, and Incubi or Succubi."

"That's five," the girl informed me. By her tone, it was obvious that she had decided I was either an experiment in artificial stupidity that had succeeded beyond what was considered remotely possible or a very poor but pathological liar. I shifted my glasses and considered whether she might be on to something.

"Incubi are male, and succubae are female, but apart from sex, they're the same — so, four. Strigoi and Incubi are made, not born."

Incubi didn't feed off sex or a human's life force, but I deemed that unnecessary information. Folklore was full of legends that took a kernel of truth and smothered it in the worst possible interpretation, buoyed along by perverted flights of fancy.

"You'll need upkeep — regularly incorporating blood, pheromones, or some other component into your body. Replicator cells copy the essential material and produce enough to keep you healthy, like vitamins. The upside is you get superpowers — speed, strength, and the ability to mesmerize others for short periods. Cool, right?

The boy, Milo Pereira, hung his head. His shoulders were shaking, and I concluded that between crying or laughing, the former was more likely.

My pitch had evidently flopped.

Mouse rolled her eyes. "Good talk, but we really need Emmy."

Crud.

"I get that you trust Emmy more than you trust me. She's earned it, and I haven't. Fair enough. If she could, she would already be here. Right now, though, we're stuck with each other. Next question?"

"Is she in danger?" they demanded in stereo.

The intensity of the question slicked my palms and caused my heart to race.

"She's safe. Her team will keep it that way. That's all I can say."

A swirl of vertigo threatened to bowl me over when they nodded, accepting the sparse explanation. Emmy must have prepped them. My word alone wouldn't cut it.

"What are Moroi and Dhampirs?"

"Born vampires. When two Strigoi... If a..."

I held out my hands and fumbled. My interactions with children were somewhat limited, more so with children raised by norms. I'd never spoken to any child about the birds and the bees and had no clue how much they might know. As runaways, their upbringing was hardly typical. My own was even less so. I couldn't remember how old I'd been when my parents had explained sex and reproduction.

"You mean when a Mommy Strigoi and a Daddy Strigoi love each other very much, have sex, and get pregnant, the baby is a Moroi or a Dhampir?"

Wow. That sarcasm was sharp.

It would almost be worth hauling Emily out of storage so that she could deal with this crap. No. No! I was a big girl. I could handle this.

"The offspring would be a Moroi, the same as in a union between a Strigoi and a Moroi. The Moroi don't require blood, though they do benefit from the practice. A Moroi that doesn't will essentially be a norm."

"A norm?"

I stared at Mouse's face for half a second, confused, until I realized that she hadn't asked the question. Milo had. Perhaps I hadn't botched this yet.

"Uh — so, a norm...or norma...is slang for humans without hereditary magic. There's also the uninitiated, the mundane, half-sighted, numb, di—...um...others that are considered rude."

Milo nodded.

"A Dhampir is the offspring of any vampire with a partner from any Origin outside of Vampires — the Dverg, the Fae, Therianthropes, a Hybrid, a Norm, or theoretically, a practitioner. Dhampirs have a slight strength and speed advantage over norms, but are otherwise indistinguishable. They don't require blood and wouldn't like it."

"Practitioners?" demanded Mouse.

I wondered if she knew how to ask a question without making it an order.

"Practitioners, usually referred to as the Warped, the Shunned, or the lost Origin, are those who practice ley manipulations."

"Those words actually mean something?"

An involuntary smile slid onto my face, and the two kids looked at me as if I had set a ventriloquist's dummy attired in a Victorian suit on my knee and introduced him as my longtime boyfriend, Mr. Boliver Bubbles, Esquire.

I snatched my key ring off the table and fiddled with it.

"Practitioners use magic."

"So, they're witches, wizards, sorcerers?"

"In the modern vernacular, sure. The Shunned call themselves practitioners, though. 'Witch' used to be reserved for those accused of serving evil. The Community reappropriated it for an ancient smear campaign. These days, people pretend that practitioners no longer exist...or they're a weak shadow of what they used to be."

Mouse nodded, like this made sense. Go figure.

"So, the other Origins killed off the witches because they were powerful and evil?"

Soooo not what I'd said. This kid hadn't even been raised within the Community, but she was slurping the Kool-Aid through a twisty straw.

Leaning back in my chair, I pulled my hands, along with my keys, inside the trunk of my oversized sweater and, by feel, popped the buttons on the little silicone fox attached to the ring, in, out, in, out, in, out.

"Ca...ca..." I forced myself to pause, take a breath, and slow my speech to the point of sounding sleepy. "Can any one group of people — babies and children, as well as adults — be deemed wholly evil, right d...down to the last individual? Isn't it more l...likely that the most frightened, the most confused, the most ambitious, and the cruelest in any society will use the worst of one group to condemn the entirety of that group?"

Aha! Another awkward silence. I'd thought we were overdue.

"So....anyway," Mouse mumbled, her eyebrows raised, "how much will Milo need to drink?"

How much...? I mentally retraced the conversation, dismissing an image of the dark-haired boy chugging a bottle of single malt from my imagination. "You mean blood or pheromones?"

"Duh," she drawled.

In theory, I liked kids. In reality, there were children that I loved, some
that I got along with, and others that annoyed the crap out of me. I
understood Mouse. I understood her animosity. Life hadn't been kind, and
she'd constructed a shell to protect herself. Scorn had proven a solid
building material, if a bit inflexible. Now, Mouse was an expert in her craft
— a savant — and a little asshole.

I pushed my arms back into their sleeves, dropped my keys into an agate
dish, and snapped up what looked like a decorative red glass ball from a
bowl on the coffee table. It was a pod of Elixir — branded and
commercially produced blood.

"Well," I murmured, my fangs unfurling as I held the little sphere up for
their inspection, "one of these staves off the bloodlust for four days —
when I can't get anything fresh. Blood is nutritionally dense, so the murder
sprees are kept to a minimum."

I punctured the fat, little globe with both fangs and gave it a hearty
slurp. Cherry juice trickled down my chin — delicious!

My intent was to intimidate — not very nice of me, but there it was. I'd
been up all night and was cranky.

Ironically, Mouse grinned, revealing her own sharp, little teeth.

"Sweet! She'll be like your surrogate grandma, Milo!"

Milo, his horrified gaze locked on my mouth as I licked an errant dribble
from my bottom lip, vomited all over my pretty rug.

Chapter 3: A Start

March 12ᵗʰ in Chicago, Illinois

Veritas jolted awake, the solid timbers of the Phantom Dancer shivering and shaking beneath him. A groggy tick passed as his sleepy brain sparked, and he ripped the curtain from the window. Sheets of implacable rain beat the sides of the ship as she struggled against the wind.

Yes!

He scrambled over to his ceiling-mounted maps — gray for ore, green for flora, brown for fauna, blue for... Blue! He yanked the blue tab and studied the weather map. Zooming in, he traced the storm system northwest, eyes glinting like struck flint, adrenaline tightening his veins.

This was it!

Spinning, he barked his shin on the desk's curved leg, swore like a seasoned dockhand when the injury registered, and lurched toward the transmitter. Unfolding the speaking horn, he put the receiver to his ear and yanked the cord to signal the helm.

As soon as he heard the telltale buzz of the line being picked up, Veritas ordered, "New coordinates, Mr. Maitland. Make for the Mulberry with all possible speed."

"Aye, aye, Captain!"

Dressed and scrambling to the main deck, he saw that the crew had redirected the rudder and adjusted the sails. Maitland's bellow cut the tempest, his vibrato mocking the howling gale. "When the sky turns to gloam, hold the line."

Golden tendrils unspooled from the ether, shimmering like molten wire against the shifting, lightning-limned haze.

"A storm's a-brewin' — hold the line," the crew roared, sails snapping taut. "Light the lanterns — hold the line! Warlocks come for the Shunned! Man the guns! Stem the tide!"

"Where hate is free to roam, hold the line," roared Maitland.

The gilded threads sped down the length of the ship, weaving a protective cocoon before fusing at the stern with a snap. Instantly, the sounds of the storm were muted. Light pulsed once, twice, thrice — as blinding as Medusa with bedhead!

"A storm's a-brewin' — hold the line," the crew chanted, their voices melding in a defiant chorus. "Light the lanterns — hold the line! Warlocks come for the Shunned! Man the guns! Stem the tide!"

The flash of magic mellowed, and Veritas could, once again, see beyond his sails. He studied six dark specks on the horizon, satisfied, despite the increased fervency of the squall. The ley lines had flung them five hundred miles northwest.

"Rise above it," he shouted in Maitland's ear.

His first mate shoved a large, brass lever adjacent to the helm. Ochre wings rattled free, catching the wind. Veritas planted his feet and gripped the rail as the ship climbed through the roiling clouds, protected from the wind, rain, and lightning by their opulent cage.

"'Til the helots are freed, hold the line."

"A storm's a-brewin' — hold the line," brayed the crew. The Dancer emerged from the tumult, and a luminous sunrise bathed her decks.

"Well done, Mr. Maitland," Veritas applauded.

Telescope up, he scanned the horizon, finding a series of jagged smudges breaking past the cloud cover — the Star Stairway, and floating above, the guild city.

"Right fifteen degrees rudder, steer zero-five-five — the Seba Rewed is in sight."

"Aye, Captain."

Veritas returned to his berth and caught his reflection in the mirror. His habitual garb would not work. The black brocade coat and the tricorn hat weren't too bad, but the death's head mask — a thin plate of hammered iron resembling a moth's face — was too distinct.

Veritas clicked on his inventory. No. No. Meh. Too gaudy; he wasn't begging to be robbed by his own guild — cutthroats, every last one! Too plain; he'd sooner eat bilge than look like a noob. Lantern light fell on a fold of black leather, supple as sin.

"Oh, yes," he purred, snagging it.

Three minutes later, the molded armor was strapped tight, and he reviewed his swords.

"If memory serves," he murmured, picking up a short longsword with an upturned hilt. It wasn't canon, but he didn't care. He tested its weight before twirling it in a figure-eight.

Utter perfection!

Veritas had the tender put him off on a crumbling pier, bypassing the Mulberry's commercial harbor. Rain-slicked boardwalks stretched through the floating city, and shops cobbled together from wrecked hulls loomed like silent giants. Intimately familiar with every plank, he darted over moon bridges, vanished into narrow alleys, and emerged again from a shadowed doorway opposite the Cocoon, the guildhall of the Saturniidae and a piecemeal tribute to economy.

Warm, luxurious light pooled across the promenade outside the mullioned windows. With an eager hand already on the door, he froze.

"Your name, idiot!"

Cursing himself, he pedaled back into the darkness and tapped options. He switched to alias mode and, on the third try, landed on an unused username. Satisfied that he had considered everything, he slithered back to the door.

The tavern was half-empty; unusual, but irl, it was the asscrack of dawn. The gentle thrum of a lute accompanied a bard lamenting the slaying of a warrior queen while a party of kobolds lavished unwanted attention on a morose wizard. Cozy as a thief's den.

"Brother," a voice slurred in a poor imitation of a Lacertian accent — a cold-blooded lizard race. "Me sixth looong-lost brother 'as finally found 'is way 'ooome!"

Veritas started, turning to the bar, from which the unprepossessing vocalization — and accompanying hiccups — issued.

Six of his square-jawed siblings held an amber-eyed court with a lion, a witch, and a wendigo. Ger3, Rivalt_of_Geria, Ralt424, Gerald1987, Ger*de*Rive, and TheWitchster79 guffawed and waved him over.

What were the odds?

The haggard and male bartender had been renamed Yenefire51 for the occasion — mod humor.

"Rivien83, grab a pint," hollered Ger3. "Tell us a tale, lad."

Veritas smirked but said, "Another time, brothers. I'm near the end of a hunt."

"On the Mulberry? Which one? Griffin's Tail? Queen's Folly?" pressed Ralt424. "They're rolling out updates, so forget all you've heard about that vamp queen."

"This is my quest, not yours. You must let me finish it."

"Ooooo," his audience hooted, recognizing the adapted quote.

"Not just a pretty face," chortled Ger*de*Rive.

Bowing, he slipped down a torch-lined corridor, delving into the labyrinthine halls. Navigating away from any activity and checking for any monster-mincing facsimiles stumbling about, he palmed the guild leader's door. It unlocked after a series of clicks.

An auxiliary login page jumped onto his screen. After entering his credentials, he maneuvered through the system, digging into its framework, and sailed through streams of code, humming to quell the guilt gnawing in his guts. Usually, he was as law-abiding as anyone…but extraordinary situations called for extraordinary measures. Breathless, he granted himself access to all guild members' personal information. Mentally apologizing to the powers that ruled Egress, he searched for Weaver.

Seventeen hits popped up, nine of which were active. There — the original.

Hello, Kenny Jones.

It was always Jones — Indiana Jones, Jessica Jones, Jughead Jones… Not important. He rifled through her contact details, copying the listed address, email, and phone number before moving on to settings — all on default. Weaver's history was absurd — nearly a decade of flawless quests, raids, ambushes, and coups. It was statistically impossible.

With a grimace, Veritas moved on. He'd figure her out eventually.

She was good. Everything appeared just as it ought; only one detail offered a flicker of hope. Weaver auto-recorded gameplay, with a link to Hooligan. Nothing odd there — he had a channel — Phantom Lights. Sponsors and AdShare had provided stability to his once feast-or-famine career. Weaver was a high-level pirate sorceress, captain of the dreaded Wicked W'yatch'ch, and one of the Saturniidae's founding members, and he had never heard of her channel, Ship's Log. Knowing everything there was to know about Egress was the backbone of his career. If Ship's Log had ever been publicized, he would have been her first subscriber.

It was a secret, then, and she was hiding something.

Wiping his tracks — the Dancer's movements, logins, code changes, everything — he melted back into the shadows.

It was a start.

Chapter 4: Trash Fire

Kenny: March 15th in the In-Between

Highwayman, all 263 pounds of him, hit the stone floor like a sack of wet bricks. He slumped against the wall, yanked his mask off, and used it to mop sweat from his light brown hair.

"Remind me...why don't we bring a keg on the bridge?" The dwarf's voice was as rough as a gravel road.

Nebthu handed him a water. "No booze on duty, you lush. Besides, even Snake Venom would be too weak for this trash-fire... Speak No Evil, six-point-five."

The burly shifter braced the wall, his head dropping against the raw stone, shoulders rippling as he exorcised the demons clawing inside his skull. I averted my eyes. Nebthu was a former SEAL and our rock — only Oscar might out-tough him. If something stuck with him, we didn't need the details.

We all had our ghosts.

I pulled my glasses from my quest tote and put them on, feeling indecent relief as I listened to Oscar bark at his aids.

It was funny. The big horrors often made little impact. The small shit — a show of defiance, a nine-rayed sun scratched into a wall a thousand times, a plate of food next to a starved corpse — those set up camp in my brain and gatecrashed my dreams. The unanswered questions were clingy imps.

"Time Bandits," I volunteered, stretching out on the floor. "More cages over bottomless pits — yawn. Four."

Deathblade nodded emphatically, coaxing a snicker from Finiel.

"Clockwork Orange," Tellus muttered, curling into herself. "Nine."

Nebthu slid down beside her, arm out in invitation. The curly-haired brunette accepted the comfort, tears spilling despite her shaky smile.

Highwayman sniffed, snooty and nasal. "Insidious; a two, if I'm generous. They capitalized on the color scheme but failed to evoke the unpredictability of the film."

We shut up, glad to be alive but craving distance from this crap.

"Everyone's breathing, the B-teams got to sit it out, twenty-two retrieved, and we're off dungeon duty for sixteen weeks," Oscar grunted, stitching up wounds with spelled thread. "Apprentice picks are next."

My gut twisted like I'd swallowed a gearshift.

Good effort, shitty prize — training newbies to wade through depravity's deep end. Candidates were often chosen years in advance; it was just the sales pitch that remained. It was a prestigious gig, but no sane parent wanted this life for their child. I've never regretted my choice of career, but a part of me always hoped my invitations would be declined.

"Incoming," Kukri hissed, nodding to the wall. The stone undulated like a drunk puddle, and a dark pinprick swiftly bloomed into a large gopher hole. "Any guests RSVP?"

"My plus-one," I yawned, climbing to my feet. The floor had proved comfier than expected.

The portal twisted into the entrance of an ancient temple framed by apple-green pillars ornamented with carved animals. A tall figure in black fatigues — masked, gloved, and with her utility belt jingling — emerged. She marched forward, telegraphing discipline with every stride, and, without so much as a hello, thrust a zip drive at me.

"Thanks," I said, sarcasm switching on, and traded the drive for the one in my zippered pocket.

Arms tight to her chest, the newcomer signed: *Nineteen's awake and drilling holes through your thick head.*

A spike of adrenaline shot through me. Every retrieval had been dosed with the same potion; they all ought to be down for the count. I replied in kind: *Intriguing development. Please alert the relevant parties.*

She gave a sharp nod before disappearing through the portal. The gate shrank, the chrysoprase lightening like pulled taffy, leaving behind only the rough gypsum of Orion's bridge.

I waited until the ancillary corridor was gone, then clapped my hands. "Break time's over, kids. No rest for the wicked," I chirped, fake as a three-dollar bill. "Tellus, seal the first two doors."

"Sure, boss," she groaned, wiping at her swollen eyes and bounding up. Her hands danced. *Trouble?*

I nodded, grateful that my people weren't loudmouths.

"Kukri, Orion, Jax, Onyx, since y'all are fresh as daisies, crack open a few doors so we can drop our guests off."

Kukri rose, creating a physical barrier between me and the make-shift med ward. I signed: *Nineteen's awake. Minimize targets. One door at a time; seal if she blinks.*

"Here I was thinking I wouldn't have to work tonight," lanky Onyx whined, ditching a box of bandages and his gloves.

"I've only done a cursory exam on the second half," Oscar grunted from the other end of the room, occupied with repositioning a broken arm. "They aren't ready for transport."

"One through eleven are," I insisted, pushing my glasses up on top of my head.

Oscar froze, recognizing the soft sound, and studied his patients as I walked over, the containment ward sliding over me like thick Jello. It lit with a flash of green fire; I tweaked it so that Nineteen's view of what my colleagues did was obscured. Hopefully, it wasn't already too late.

Doing my best to ignore the stench of filth and blood, I scanned the lines; they looked like the same, old, glittering spaghetti — overlayed with capering donkey-birds on a distant plane.

Nineteen's wealth of dark hair spilled like ink over the sheets. She lay so still, I watched her chest as it rose and fell. There was something peculiar about the ley lines feeding into her reservoir. They were thick and mangled. It took a moment for me to understand; I'd never seen such a phenomenon before — more energy was flowing into her body than out — a slow, guaranteed death sentence unless it could be fixed. I needed a closer look.

I stitched protection charms over the other patients, edging toward Nineteen. It wasn't a jinx, hex, or curse. The lines looked and behaved naturally until they delved into her core. Three had somehow been grafted onto parallel ley lines.

"They'll live," Oscar agreed, patting his pockets. He'd mislaid his glasses.

"Then we'll get started."

He nodded, grim. "Thirteen and eighteen are wrecks. Twenty is a clinic case."

Oscar's aides gave him big eyes but didn't dare contradict him. Eighteen and twenty were about the same as most of the others — undernourished but alive. Compared to thirteen, they were in the pink of health.

"Do what you have to," I replied, winking to confirm his guess. "We can work around you."

The light bulb went on for Bea, the senior aide. She paled, but when Iosephina opened her mouth, she gagged her with a hand and shook her head.

"We'll get them stabilized. They should take precedence," Oscar grumped, sending both aids scrambling with a gesture.

Nebthu hefted himself up and offered Highwayman a hand when I headed their way. I signed: *Glasses on, watch the lines. Guard, but don't jump unless Nineteen goes active.*

The bridge hummed with activity. While everyone worked, I considered how to handle Nineteen's ley saturation. There was a chance that I could help, but it would be risky and painful. Still better than certain death.

Nebthu caught my eye and signed: *Charms.*

I glanced at the patients. My protective weavings had loosened. Technically, they were still functional, but ineffective.

I replied: *Watch and wait.*

Two minutes passed before I saw it — the slightest of feathering in a line tickling at my weavings. We had ourselves a practitioner. The question was what motivated her? Did she belong to a rival coven? Was she an Agency warlock or a solo act?

We let her carry on; if unknotting my work kept Sleeping Beauty occupied, then so be it. In short order, fourteen patients, our less experienced operatives, and the aids had been ushered off the bridge. As they prepped the last patient, I was tempted to chuck a ward around Nineteen. But…would it hold? Her excess of ley energy concerned me. Could she supercharge her spells? Or would she let us fling everything we had at her, shielding until we were drained, then kill us?

"Weaver," Kukri whispered, breaking my reverie.

"Mmhmm?"

She pushed on the remaining bed — patient fourteen's — but it didn't budge. Ley lines clung to the wheels like cobwebs. Nineteen was a multitasker, too. Fantastic!

I stowed my glasses and tapped the foot of her bed.

"Is fourteen special, or did you finally clock us?"

A man's voice, suave and smug, poured from her petal-lipped mouth. "I only require ten."

I nodded like this — Nineteen being awake and juiced, having a cosmopolitan male voice, and her reasoning — made perfect sense. She was a helot, a practitioner subjugated to another's will. It explained the voice — her body was possessed. And ten...people? Patient fourteen and Oscar made ten.

"You have stolen from me on six occasions," the voice chided me, "Impressive but, alas, quite annoying. Here's my offer: I will allow the patient, and only the patient, to be evacuated from this...charming cavern, or you and three colleagues. Everyone else is mine to do with as I like."

Something pricked my memory. It was on the tip of my tongue...

"Batman Forever," Oscar grunted, taking the opportunity to run another battery of tests on Fourteen. "One-point-five. Low effort distraction with a perverse desire to see us betray each other."

"I almost had it," I snapped.

"I was stuck on The Dark Knight," mused Nebthu.

"Make your choi... Wait, which one is Batman Forever?" demanded Nineteen, her nose wrinkling adorably.

"Val Kilmer, Jim Carrey, Tommy Lee Jones..."

"Weaver has a crush on ol' Tommy Lee," Nebthu stage whispered.

"Traitor," I grumbled. "He's a great actor, okay? And I think, for an older man, he's...compelling. Now, when he was a few years younger..."

"Quite," Nineteen conceded, looking crestfallen, "The Riddler's trap. Hmmm."

"Originality is a myth, but the 'impossible choice' isn't common. Too hard to pull off," I assured her, setting my ward a split second before Nebthu, Kukri, and Nineteen released theirs, trapping Nineteen with me.

"Weaver," Nebthu barked.

I ignored him, settling into a fighting stance. Martyrdom didn't hold any allure, but while I wasn't our best fighter, I was our best practitioner. I had only one idea how to handle Nineteen, and I was the only one equipped for it.

A deep, mocking chuckle rolled from her mouth as she hopped off the gurney. "I suppose we're all predictable."

"Usually," I agreed, sending a nip of power into a swirl of embroidery on my sleeve and slinging the bolas that manifested in my hand. The length of weighted rope wrapped around her, pinning her arms to her sides.

I tapped a diamond-shaped emblem at my wrist and charged. Ikita Kawaki, the Living Thirst, an ice-white kunai, flared in my hand with an eerie light. I thrust the weapon into her chest, just below her sternum. The pyramidal blade burrowed into her reservoir.

She roared, trying to shake the artifact out, and fell. Her wide eyes met mine and, for a moment, I saw her and not her warden. Malice bled back in, and a fist of power punched me into my own ward. My personal protections shielded me, but even so, my right shoulder crunched, and my hand went numb.

Nineteen freed herself and clawed at the kunai, desperate to extract it. But her hands slid through it. The artifact was finicky about who handled it.

Screaming, she started flinging spells at me — fast, sloppy, potent. Untrained or overwhelmed, she wasted fistfuls of magic.

Shielding, I edged closer. Tethers bound her mind, subtle and thorough. It spoke of experience. Even within the Community, helotry was illegal...but the practice continued.

"Who tugs on that chain?" I wondered.

Nineteen screamed and flung raw energy at me. There was no control, just animalistic fury. I hooked the blast as soon as it left her hand and twisted my intent through it. The brutal wave dissipated, but she flung more, driving me back against the aegis.

The kunai pulsed. The blade was nearly full.

Nineteen, a degree of sanity returning, noticed and considered the artifact with pinched brows. Either the kunai had the speed and capacity to drain her, or I'd be fighting for my life. Either way, the matter would soon be settled.

My team roared as their wards unraveled. It would only take them a minute or two to break mine.

Nebthu glanced at me and flashed his fangs, half shifted to his other form, and beyond livid.

"Why?" he demanded.

Before I could reply, his eyes went wide. I heard it and turned. My vision filled with black flames.

Chapter 5: Mirror-Mirror

March 15th at the Agora in Chicago, Illinois

If a room mirrors the soul that manufactured its arrangement, it could be assumed that Darragh O'Brien, Chairman of the Union of Seers, was a man of great reticence and modest demands. The small corner of the Agora that he had claimed for his own was sparsely furnished — a set of barrister cases replete with heavy tomes and yellowed maps, a desk and a cushy chair, two opposite for visitors, and a small settee shoved under the window like an awkward cousin. Each piece was an antique, handsome and well-made, although mismatched and probably pilfered from a wizard's garage sale.

It was an unpretentious space — tranquil, comfortable, and ideal for cerebral pursuits. O'Brien was, himself, reserved, at times austere and self-effacing — despite having received, in both face and form, every gift of masculine grace. Above and beyond all his charms, however, Darragh O'Brien was clever — a far-sighted and erudite man. A man born to greatness-

You're doing it again.

"What am I doing?" inquired the reticent and erudite man, unruffled by the heckling voice in his head. O'Brien carefully set the ornate mirror he had been peering into face down on the desktop before flicking his eyes up to the amorphous intruder standing across the desk from him.

Was standing the correct word? Floating? Manifesting?

Special Agent in Charge John Dorrit casually leaned against the oak-paneled wall with his arms crossed over his chest. His body held a suggestion of color but was entirely see-through.

Preening.

The moody lighting of the room, isolated from the rest of the world by the darkness pressing in at the windows, gilded O'Brien's ardent, agile countenance and the dark, careless curls that crowned him. And he knew it.

"Mine is an arresting visage, John. Byronic. Even I am not immune," he replied, his lilt oozing charm.

Dorrit, equally compelling in his own way, refrained from commenting on O'Brien's excess of vanity. He even managed not to roll his eyes — a shocking show of restraint.

Bad news, sir. I'm afraid-

"Ah, you've heard. A sad day. Senator Francis Dal Park, pride of the Unrelenting, assassinated." O'Brien sighed heavily, a flash of pain etching his face. "The press has been ghoulishly giddy – calling Serrecold every five minutes for a statement."

Assassinated?

One eloquent eyebrow arched. "You don't know? Four hours ago, Park posted a video confessing to blackmail, kidnapping, torture, and murder, culminating in the triple homicide of his wife and children, by way of a suicide note. It's already gone viral within the Community."

Dorrit's intangible form lost its definition as he grappled with this news.

I'm sorry, sir. That's horrible, particularly about his family. But suicide isn't assassination. Regardless, I came to rep-

"That's not the end of it, John. The APA found a noose hanging in Park's living room, sure enough, but the man himself wasn't dangling from it. Park had gone down to the corner store and called me on the clerk's cell, claiming innocence. While he was on the phone, an unknown assailant fatally shot both Park and the clerk in the head multiple times. I've seen the recordings — a professional hit. Tidy, efficient, and ruthless."

O'Brien absently traced the relief on the back of the mirror with a finger, his mind perturbed.

Why kill a man who's intent upon checking out? Why didn't he use his phone?

"Why, indeed," murmured O'Brien, gazing out on the dark city. "Without the right seer's gift, we can but speculate. Perhaps he crossed the wrong person. Perhaps it was because he was one of my best assets within the Unrelenting camp — and a friend. Perhaps it was because he wore yellow socks with dinosaurs on them last Thursday. His cell mysteriously disappeared. It wasn't on him or in the penthouse."

John Dorrit paced the parquet floor, his footsteps eerily silent. Arriving at a decision, he faced the other man.

I can spare two agents.

"Bollocks!"

I cannot go myself. Until your favor has been repaid, Serrecold won't allow it. We need someone we can trust heading that investigation. MacDonnell and I must remain in Snohomish for the postmortem. Ridel will organize an observation post in Austin. Sarduy...has been injured and is recovering at the clinic. That leaves Hatter and Blake. I have every confidence in their abilities."

"Austin! Postmortem? Don't tell me," groaned O'Brien.

Silhouette Martin was found dead last night in her apartment — multiple shots to the head. We suspect a sound ward was used to keep anyone from hearing the deed, but no trace of magic has been detected. The place was scrubbed. The failure of Martin's wards alerted us. All exits had been under constant surveillance. She was the only person to enter or exit the apartment that evening and for the three days prior. It was not suicide, and there was no struggle.

O'Brien flopped backwards in a practiced swoon, as if all his strength had fled in the face of this new dilemma. The wear in the upholstery exactly corresponded with the Chairman's outspread limbs.

"How many does that make?" grumbled O'Brien, lightly chewing on his plump bottom lip.

Seven.

"Eight, then — three on our watch," corrected O'Brien, covering his eyes with his forearm and slumping so low that his derriere was in danger of sliding off the seat. "Olivine Brent, Sylvia Ewens, Nevaeh Howard, and Martin — shot at home. No evidence besides the bullets. Dunia Azan is comatose from a 'crash'. Desiree Abara, Novia Walls-ffrench, and now Emily Caterham — plus two foundlings — all vanished into thin air. How does he get there first?"

He runs a successful international crime syndicate with more resources, better underground connections, and fewer scruples.

"That does about cover it. As soon as we initiate contact, they die. The victims must contact their handlers. How? Not a phone call, not the internet... The handlers then handle them in the most efficient way possible."

How do you suggest we proceed?

O'Brien sprang from his chair, running his hands through his hair, mussing his silky curls. He paced up and down the short room twice before committing.

"We must change the game. Would they hesitate to eliminate her, though? She's not like the others — not isolated, not a pawn..."

Sir?

Resting an elbow on a large, crystal ball, he finally clued Dorrit in, waving to a file on his desk. "Representative Jones, John. Remember? We were discussing the Sheta Djew the other day — the entrepreneurs with the Midas touch? Jones is their representative, and she's the one I've been eyeing for our side project. She's connected to this. In what capacity, I don't know, but her name pops up in unexpected places. As such, I've delayed mentioning her."

Dorrit flicked the relevant folder open and, a scowl tracing his features, studied Jones's photograph.

Information gathering, infiltration, or protective custody?

O'Brien internally debated the issue for some minutes, wandering back to his desk.

"The first. Observe her at a distance for a few weeks — learn the lay of the land and conduct a background check — go deep. We'll discuss strategy once we determine how she's involved. Don't bother with Senator Park — Serrecold has assigned his case elsewhere."

Is there a connection to Senator Park?

O'Brien shrugged. "Impossible to say. The murder method on its own doesn't justify any leaps in logic. When ballistics come back, we may revisit this conversation."

You seem preoccupied, sir.

It was only then that O'Brien seemed to notice his hand was once again toying with the hand mirror.

"Rather," acknowledged O'Brien, gingerly removing his fingertips and rubbing them as if something sticky and unpleasant clung to them. "It's sixth century, you know."

The back of the mirror was laboriously wrought silver depicting sly beasts and anguished faces, blackened by an ancient patina, and set with jet and moonstone.

It's ugly.

"It is that — forbidding. The tools of truth frequently are," O'Brien agreed with a morbid chuckle, then inquired, "What happened to Sarduy? How was she injured?"

A drunk driver. MacDonnell's fine, but...it was a close shave for Sarduy. She'll recover.

"I see. Luck only goes so far, John. There have been a few too many close shaves recently."

We know, sir.

The Chairman let it go with a distant nod. "About Jones... She's not a naive or vulnerable bystander who got tangled up in something she didn't understand." He tapped the desk twice, punctuating his words. "She's dangerous — an ipseitatum dualis. She knows how the game is played. Innocent or guilty, she'll have her own agenda and won't hesitate to cheat if it serves her ends. Tread lightly."

<h1 style="text-align:center">Chapter 6: Shitty Prize</h1>

Kenny: March 16th in Biloxi, Mississippi

"Here," Dhairya Patel said, pulling over.

The house was a squat mint green bungalow with peeling paint and visible rot. The yard, corralled by a chain link fence — more rust than metal — was littered with sun-bleached toys. The grass was patchy and brittle, mainly due to the homeowner's mean-looking mutt marking its territory. I opened my door, provoking the dog to growl and snap its teeth.

Ignoring the menacing guardian, I climbed out of the car, fingers sliding under my cuff to stroke the puckered scar on my wrist. A few sagging strawberry plants grew in split milk jugs, weighed down by overripe fruit. Several had fallen, looking like pulpy blood stains on the concrete steps.

After I'd regained consciousness — a mere sixteen hours ago, studying the textured skin had become a habit. Nineteen's captor had delivered his message — he would break his toys if he couldn't keep them. Seventy percent of my body had been covered in burns. I had no memory of it, but Oscar and I'd had a rough night. He had worked miracles but left the scar as a reminder that I was part of a team. Every time I touched it, I saw Nineteen's face wreathed by black fire.

"Tank don't like strangers," a voice called from the corner — an olive-skinned, rough-edged man. His buddies snickered, elbowing each other and exchanging ribald comments. Their spokesman appeared to be in his late thirties, an inch or two below six feet, attractive in an angry-at-the-world way, and dressed in worn jeans and a tank with an unbuttoned shirt thrown over it.

"Tank particularly don't like entitled pricks steppin' into his territory," the neighborhood busybody added, sneering at Dhairya's gray suit and my mallard green ensemble with a feather-adorned fedora.

It was a bit much. And sweltering.

Still, if I was going to be cast as the villain of the piece, then I was going to look the part. Better than being the failed hero.

Across the roof of the car, Dhairya grimaced. "León Botero. My apologies, Doyenne. I should have warned you."

"No matter," I murmured, crouching sideways a few feet away from the agitated dog. Murmuring to him, my fingers grazed a ley line — cool like river water and humming faintly — and plucked it. The canine quieted, and the gate swung open. Dhairya and I moved toward the house.

"What the hell was that?" Botero's voice spiked, his swagger checked. His associates appeared equally disturbed.

Not practitioners, then. Pity.

Tank whined and bumped his broad head against my leg, begging for a scratch. I obliged him as Dhairya skipped up the crumbling steps and rapped on the door.

"You freaks better get off my turf," Botero barked, puffing out his chest and stalking into the yard. He'd convinced himself that he hadn't seen what he thought he had.

"This is not your turf, Mr. Botero," I said, turning to face him. In my heels, I could look him in the eye. "And we are not here for you. I'd advise you to accept that for the gift it is."

He lunged closer, but Dhairya blurred into his path.

Who said chivalry was dead?

The angry man paled, then doubled down.

"How do you know my name, bitch?"

"We've got your whole life on flashcards."

"León Izan Fernández Botero; five-eleven; two hundred seven pounds. Born on February 5, 1988. You work part-time delivering pizzas and as a bouncer at Cielo Azul," recited Dhairya, crowding the other man. "Elena's told you she's not interested. Leave."

"Step up or shut up, suit!"

The two men glared at each other from inches apart, neither willing to back down. Botero's friends stilled, collectively holding their breath. I studied the combatants, a growing suspicion ruining my bad mood.

"Who are you?" a quiet voice cut through the tension. A slender woman with extraordinarily high cheekbones, smooth brown skin, and soft curling hair observed us from behind the screen door, her gaze sharp and wary. She balanced a fussy toddler on her hip and wiped the little girl's mouth with a napkin. Petite as she was, the child looked substantial enough to topple them both over.

Dhairya turned his head a fraction, unwilling to give Botero his back. "Elena." An endearment and a warning rolled into one.

One word, but it clinched the matter.

Elena Romero and I sighed at the same time.

My companion had a more personal interest in his former student —
and said student's family — than I'd been aware. More fool me. It was
tempting to be irritated, but Dhairya's romantic entanglements were none of
my business. Unless he got me involved in something I wanted no part of.

"It's all right, León," the annoyed damsel informed her gallant knight.

Mr. Botero glanced up at her and reluctantly nodded. "I'll just-"

"Thank you for looking out for us, León. My guests are nothing for you
to worry about. Go home. Enjoy your day off. You work too hard."

He nodded again and, after giving Dhairya and me a final glower, let
himself out of the yard.

I released the ley line that I had unconsciously primed and let the energy
dissipate. This was educational. Informative. I was on edge, and I couldn't
trust Dhairya's judgment.

"Xiomara made conchas. I'll bring some by later," Botero called from
the sidewalk.

I nodded appreciatively. He'd check in on Elena after we'd gone and pay
for the privilege in homemade pastry.

"I'll look forward to them," Elena answered with a smile. She swung the
screen door open and stepped aside so we could enter. "She's gotten very
skilled."

Botero acknowledged her with a wave and rejoined his crew.

"I'm sorry to drop in unannounced, Lena, but the Doyenne will only be
in town a few days," Dhairya explained, his dark eyes apologetic as he
allowed me to enter first.

Elena Romero gave no indication of having heard him, praising the
overgrown pup instead. "Good girl, Dulce."

Dulce? Tank was more intimidating, I supposed, but Dulce could make
herself understood, despite the name.

Mrs. Romero's living room was small but tidy, with two young boys
playing a game on the floor. They sat up straight, tensed to move at a
moment's notice, even as they continued. Their mother made a small
gesture, and the children instantly scampered.

"Would you like something to drink?" she offered, stepping toward the
kitchen and, consequently, further away from us. "I have water and iced
tea."

"That's kind, but no, thank you. I'm here to see Colt," I explained.

She closed her eyes for a long moment, looking tired and anxious. A breath later, it hardened into determination.

"Why?" demanded a new voice. "Hello, Mr. Patel. Who's your friend?"

A rangy young man emerged from the pocket-sized kitchen and, placing a comforting hand on his mother's shoulder as he passed, neatly stepped in front of her, blocking her from view.

Colt Ebersol had grown. He was all of six feet, maybe an inch above, yet made a rather insufficient obstacle. He'd fill out in a few years. His skin was warm like his mother's — the nose was hers, too. Slack, ashy brown hair, a little on the shaggy side, fell into hazel eyes — inherited from his late father. He had a long, animated face, with a wide, agile mouth meant for smiling. His mouth and eyes crinkled at the corners, and he had all the confidence that good health, youth, and knowing that he was both loved and needed could bring.

It was a far cry from the last time I'd seen him. As I reacquainted myself with his features, I removed my sunglasses and smiled. "Hello, Colt. It's been a minute."

The kid's eyes widened, but he didn't move a muscle. It was as if the very sight of me had turned him to stone.

"How do you know her?" his mother whispered in a small, strained voice, taking her cue from Colt and remaining stock-still. "Who is she?"

The toddler in her arms began to wail, reacting to the atmosphere. Dulce mooned at me with reproachful eyes. I had fallen in her estimation.

Elena bounced the toddler on her hip and cooed, her eyes tortured whenever they flashed up to meet mine.

"The same way you know me, Mrs. Romero. It's been a long time — nine years — but your son made the Covenant a promise. I've come to collect."

"You can't have him," she informed me, her voice strangely calm as she tried to force her youngest into her oldest son's arms. Power spindled around her, hot and plentiful — more than should have been available to her. My scalp prickled, reliving yesterday's skirmish. But Elena Romero wasn't chucking death curses at my head.

I stretched my senses and investigated, discovering that I'd made a mistake. I'd kept tabs on the family — certain behavioral patterns had become evident. Elena Romero encouraged men to act as protectors and providers, or so it seemed. I'd dismissed her as a practitioner because I viewed her as an opportunist. Perhaps I was right, but the woman knew how to set a trap. She'd known that trouble would find her family again, and it would be on her to protect them.

I'd picked a hell of a time to wear null contacts.

Her weaving was exquisite, the construction subtle. I couldn't see her work; I could barely feel it — a numbing chill and a dull buzzing the only clues, testifying to the years invested in perfecting the hex. She'd built an Ahaztuta — a ley prison — in her living room. The word meant 'forgotten'. It would use my energy to trap me; difficult, time-consuming, fussy magic — an inspired choice. Polishing it must have become second nature — a self-soothing response to stress and fear.

It wouldn't hold me long...a few days — less, if Dhairya chose to help, but Elena would disappear with her children. A practitioner was never more dangerous than in her own home.

Under other circumstances, I would have tried to recruit her.

"I do not doubt that you have done many a brave and foolish thing to protect your children, when necessary," I said carefully, making certain that I didn't accidentally tug on a line. Any show of aggression would be seen as a declaration of war. Tempting, though. I wanted to see the Ahaztuta work.

Colt, once again, put himself in front of his mother. "It isn't necessary, is it?"

"No."

"I'm sorry."

A smile stretched across my mouth, and a tempting trickle of euphoria bled into my veins. He couldn't leave his family — not with only Elena and Botero for protection. But...it was still too soon to feel relief.

"Don't be."

I turned to Elena Romero, who was beginning to realize that we weren't going to kidnap her son. Somewhat embarrassed, but still suspicious, she tucked her power away.

"This is for you. There are no strings attached, no conditions or exceptions. We'll see ourselves out. Your Ahaztuta is splendid."

Colt's head jerked up, sighting on me. He hadn't known about his mother's hex.

I removed an envelope from the inside pocket of my jacket and passed it over. Her hand trembling, Elena accepted the heavy vellum sleeve. She passed the baby off to Colt as Dhairya opened the door for me.

Dhairya was not happy. I could read it in every line of his body as we returned to the car.

"That's it?" he hissed, outraged. "Everything, every decision that boy has made, was so that he could earn his place as an apprentice. He did everything that we asked of him, and you're just going to leave them here?"

Oh. Now it was about Colt Ebersol.

"The dreams of a ten-year-old boy aren't always compatible with the realities of a nineteen-year-old man," I replied, opening the passenger side door and silently willing him to move his butt. "I require complete commitment, and, by his own admission, Colt cannot give me that."

"Fine, but abandoning them in this dump? Even if Colt isn't willing to be your pet project, you could do something for them. Do you have any idea what she's endured?"

Better than he did. And the neighborhood had grown on me.

"Because the Covenant's resources are so plentiful, and I'm permitted to indulge every whim? Why stop with one family? Let's revitalize the whole street!"

I spared Dhairya a pitying glance over the top of the car door.

"If they stay here, it's by their own will."

Dhairya did not find that a sufficient response. He glared at me as I climbed into the car. I arched my eyebrows and gazed back pointedly. The standoff lasted several seconds longer before he muttered something vaguely insulting and slammed the door. He had made it halfway around the vehicle when the screen door whined as someone in a tearing hurry bashed their way out.

Damn Dhairya.

I rolled down the window. The car wasn't on, and the windows weren't manual, but magic had its uses.

"Is this for real?" Colt demanded, bounding down the steps with the letter clenched in his fist.

"Yes."

He staggered to a halt and bent forward, resting his hands on his knees as if winded. The letter, crumpled in his white-knuckled grip, betrayed the fine tremor in his hands. When he spoke a moment later, though, his voice was calm and deliberate. "If the Covenant will have me, I will honor my promise."

Elena Romero stepped out onto the porch, hot, angry tears streaming down her face.

"I won't thank you," she informed me with quiet dignity, an emotion too controlled to be called fury radiating off her. "The Covenant saved our lives, but now you've claimed his."

I acknowledged the truth of her words and, for my sanity, tossed away the fallacy.

"You have two days to change his mind," I said.

She laughed mirthlessly and shook her head.

"Kenny Jones?"

I nodded.

She struggled with something but disappeared back into the house without saying another word.

Colt straightened, not looking back but listening, tracking his mother's path.

If Elena came back… If she begged him, he would stay.

As we waited, my fingers drifted to the strange new texture on my arm. Helots and teenage heroes. There had to be a better way than this.

Colt's shoulders loosened, and his attention landed on me, still sitting in the car.

"I can't tell you that this is the right path for you. There are times we have to be cruel —tear our souls apart. For me, it's worth it. That may not be true for you. Two days, Colt."

Chapter 7: Lich Hockey

April 5th in Chicago, Illinois

The silver moth mask allowed Veritas to expire with some dignity, despite the bare-assed pixies farting in his ears.

He saved, although there was little point.

It was impossible. What she had accomplished was...just...fundamentally impossible! Sure, it was a quest well above his skill level, but he was fifteen up on Weaver and still eating pixie dust!

The timer went off. Veritas rocked forward and heaved himself off the low sofa. He shuffled into the kitchen, the untied belt of his robe doing its best to fell him. Heat mugged his face as he opened the oven door. Infinity gauntlets protecting his hands, he pulled out the crusty loaf, sniffing appreciatively, and set it aside to cool. He selected an Albarino from the wine fridge, settling the bottle in one pocket and a stemless wine glass in the other.

Veritas extracted a tray from the pantry. He turned off the heat on the stovetop and served up scallops in white sauce, roasted lemon pepper asparagus, and a grilled watermelon salad. Two slices off the loaf and a dab of orange saffron butter completed the meal. He'd save the black cherry panna cotta for afters — with coffee.

Loot in hand, he returned to the media room.

After organizing himself, a sip of wine, and a bite of scallop, Veritas shuffled through the multitude of pages he had transcribed. Kenny Jones's channel on Hooligan was invitation-only — not that it had been an issue.

Veritas frowned.

Getting in should have been more of an issue, actually. When he'd hacked the system, it had been familiar. Perhaps their chief programmer had worked for Egress before Hooligan. The code in both systems used a dialect that he'd never seen before. He distrusted coincidences.

Ship's Log was shared between players — Thekwane, Highwayman, Asibikaashi, Deathblade0716, OGGimli, Lady Gelsemine, Oscar, Tellus, and Tainlong were familiar to him as long-established members of the Saturniidae. Brigand and Changeling were unknowns.

Veritas, however, only had eyes for Weaver.

She was the only member of the Saturniidae to have never failed a quest or died since the dawn of Egress. She'd been beaten and poisoned by dire platypi, burnt to a crisp babysitting chubby baby dragons, and more heavily lacerated than a cabbage destined for coleslaw — a lich cultural enrichment program gone wrong — all without shuffling off Egress's coil.

No, she pulled out a plate of steaming calamari; smeared herself with ley-charged aloe and summoned a monsoon; or invented lich hockey, enabling the undead to express their tribal rivalries through competition. Bottom line, she survived.

On team quests, not a single player in Weaver's party had ever bitten the big one, except her first year. Even if Oscar wasn't among the party, she'd somehow managed to heal them. Well...she kept them alive, even though her healing skills were suspect at best. She always happened to have the right potion, amulet, or scroll at hand for whatever the enemy threw at them.

The real mystery, though, was that Weaver, with so much success over so long a history of gameplay, had only made it halfway up the guild's leader board. She played regularly, participating in individual quests, player versus player, and group raids. Several members of the Saturniidae often worked together — those that shared the Hooligan account and a few others. Each was a solid, rank-and-file member, but without a star among them.

Their exclusive little group rarely invited new members to join. They weren't motivated by glory, loot, or other rewards. They logged on, did their dailies, a few raids, the occasional quest, and logged off. They racked up experience like a well-oiled machine, yet they hovered on the board. And they only communicated in Blue Tongue — the Saturniidae's internal language.

Even Veritas wasn't that...committed? Consumed? Obsessed? Not to say that he hadn't learned the language. He had. He was fluent in all the major conlangs: Klingon, Dothraki, Quenya, Newspeak, Lapine...and a few less typical. Lingua Ignota. Leerish. Dritok. He didn't like to brag. People had the most unaccountably adverse reaction when he did.

Reciting Elvish poetry at parties never won anyone friends.

Veritas pondered the riddle the Ship's Loggers posed, gnashing a chunk of watermelon to pulp. Weaver was cheating. It was the only way to win so consistently. But why if there was no reward? Veritas had transcribed Weaver's equipped weapons, her inventory of spells and potions, and every move she made in some of her more notable conquests.

He'd calculated Weaver's average in-battle rate at ninety-four command phrases per minute. Sure, battles were typically over in five to fifteen minutes, and even the most elaborate dungeons were cleared in under an hour, but that speed was insane. Veritas's personal best was seventy-eight ppm sustained for sixteen minutes, and he was no slouch!

Weaver knew where to stand. She anticipated her opponents' movements. She knew what weapon to use and what spells to cast. She made strategic decisions and translated them into commands flawlessly. It was a symphony of tactics, timing, dexterity, and talent. Watching her was...an experience.

He wanted to believe that she was truly that adept — that she had done these extraordinary feats! It was possible for a single quest...perhaps even several in a row, but she had been active and flawless for the entire nine-year span that the game had existed. She had improved over time, absolutely, but even at her worst... It just wasn't humanly possible. Every player had died at least once. It was part of learning the game, a rite of passage. Veritas had died seven times.

Kenny Jones was a computer.

Had to be.

A whine made Veritas glance down. An angular, snow-white face with a broad, impish grin leered at him coquettishly.

"No, Russell. You've already had yours. These are for me," Veritas explained firmly.

The pittie-mix howled mournfully, stalking over and leaning against Veritas's leg. He remained strong and resisted the puppy-love.

Russell, in response to such hardheartedness, reached deep and bawled. When Veritas failed to relent, Russell dropped to the floor and rested his head on his owner's slippered foot.

"Good boy," observed Veritas, leaning over and rubbing the good boy's tummy.

He sipped his wine, cogitating over the possibility that Weaver was a computer.

It didn't fit.

He'd heard Weaver speak — in Blue Tongue and, on the rare occasion, in English —through Skype numerous times. AI had made great strides, but he'd yet to hear of a platform that could imitate a human's cadence, spontaneity, and mental dexterity and then couple it with humor, emotion, and occasional fits of childish behavior. He knew he was called Ferret-Ass behind his back and that she'd started it.

So...not a computer. The remaining possibilities were that Ms. Jones had developed a program that assisted her with the game, or the game designers intentionally manipulated the game for and against her. Or, Ms. Jones was some kind of augmented human, an alien, or a sorceress.

Probably one of the first two.

Probably.

There was something here, though — something...odd.

"Come, Russell. Let's mix you up a batch of biscuits. This conundrum requires further contemplation."

Chapter 8: Eat Your Duck

April 6th in Chicago, Illinois

"I called in Holly Hildebrand to look at the crime scene."

"Class-nine sensitive," O'Brien recalled, chopping shallots. "Did she find anything?"

They were in the Chairman's kitchen, all gleaming wood cabinets and proofing drawers, and he was in chef mode — braising a duck, reducing wine, marinating vegetables. Outside the Agora's illustrious walls, his own came down. O'Brien was never at ease, but keeping his hands busy helped. He flew from one task to another while listening to Dorrit's report, absorbing it without apparent effort.

"She did. We were lucky; the echo of an enchantment was cresting. She traced it to a moon-shaped lamp."

"After...twenty-six days? That's..."

"One hell of an echo," said the agent.

O'Brien sampled the sauce he'd been stirring, his mind whirling. There were two ways to track magic — by turbulence in the ley lines or the echo that rebounded after the fact. A skilled practitioner could calm the lines after a spell, removing evidence of what they had done and why, as well as their unique signature. A skilled sensitive, level four or better, would know a scene had been scrubbed because the lines would be too quiet. Dorrit was level seven.

There was no way to prevent an echo. The ley lines were connected; what happened to one affected all — like dropping a rock in a pond. A subtle wave would expand from the site of the manipulation, traveling out until it met resistance and bounced back. Echoes were devilishly tricky to predict and even more challenging to glean information from...unless a level nine sensitive was on hand. There were only sixteen in the world.

"And?"

Dorrit grimaced.

"Martin activated a beacon. The Curator knows when to act because the victims alert him."

49

"Must be quite a charismatic character," O'Brien observed. "These contractors aren't stupid, or world-class museums and auction houses wouldn't have hired them. The Curator doesn't risk leaks…so, why the dedication?"

"Enough shop talk, boys," a feminine voice called from the hall.

A moment later, a tall, strawberry-blond woman of Japanese descent appeared in the doorway. Smiling, she headed straight for O'Brien and, bracing her hands against his chest, kissed him soundly.

Not being a complete fool, he wrapped her up and reciprocated.

"You promised," she murmured against his lips.

"I promised," he agreed, a tender smile molding his mouth before he glanced toward the agent. "Rena would appreciate it if we avoided all talk of politics, assassinations, and intrigue for the evening. She wants a nice, quiet dinner."

"I've no objections," Dorrit agreed. "How are you, Rena?"

"Thriving, not that you would know," she pouted, pecking his cheek. "So, let's hear it. What's your excuse? I haven't seen you in two months, and I know you've been invited over."

Dorrit's eyes flicked to the Chairman, who was absorbed with plating his culinary masterpiece. The aroma was intoxicating.

"You love him," she chided, flicking his shoulder, "or you wouldn't work with him."

"There's no accounting for taste."

"I'm right here," huffed O'Brien without looking up. "John, eat your duck. Rena, love, would you select a wine?"

Rena obliged.

Despite the extravagant fare, they settled in the breakfast nook rather than the formal dining room. Minutes passed in silent decadence as they savored the offerings O'Brien had provided. Slowly, after their plates were half empty, conversation resumed. Once the usual topics — food, music, travel — had been exhausted, they arrived at that convivial lassitude that follows a good feed.

"You didn't ask what he had in the box," questioned Dorrit, caught somewhere between surprise and incredulity.

Rena shook her head, tears leaking down her cheeks. "I thought — excuse me — I thought he was trying to surprise me," she wheezed, ending in a wail.

"Oh, I surprised her," chuckled O'Brien, his lilt having matured into a brogue after the third bottle.

"He put it in the fridge," Rena continued, barely comprehensible. "He was acting sly. I wanted him to think he was getting away with it. Then, when I was making breakfast the next morning, I peeked."

"You didn't."

"She did."

Rena, still crying, mouthed, "I did."

"If I'd turned the blighted things in immediately, Lester, who was director then, would have had to arrest the Bader twins. I knew they weren't guilty — creepy, you bet — but not guilty," O'Brien explained with a shrug. "I popped a preservation charm on the pests, stuffed them in the fridge, got a good night's sleep, and was set to turn 'em in not twelve hours later. Went off without a hitch...until Rena opened that dratted box!"

"Puckwudgies! Sixteen tucked into tiny, little bags like they were camping! Three of them woke up and vanished," Rena hiccupped, almost calm. Then she lost it again. "I thought he'd made Canelés de Bordeaux for our anniversary!"

"We were infested with the little buggers for months. Tried everything to get rid of them."

"I understand why...but what possessed you to bring sixteen magical constructs into your home?" exclaimed Dorrit. "They're knots of malevolent magic — there's no reasoning with them. And you didn't explain it to your girlfriend!"

"Couldn't. It was an open case," O'Brien shrugged. "Who's for coffee and dessert?"

As he hustled back to the kitchen, Rena surprised Dorrit by seizing his hand. "I'm breaking my rule, John, but I need to know — has something happened to Darragh? Has he confided in you?"

Startled and affected by her earnest concern, he searched for an answer. "No, he's not said anything. I know the investigation is eating at him. What has you worried?"

"Rena, before I forget, could you defragment the laptop after dessert? It crashed right in the middle of something," O'Brien called from the kitchen.

"Of course...or you could learn how to do it. It's not hard," she yelled back, shaking her head. "He's not been sleeping. When he does, he dreams. He's always on his laptop..."

Dorrit's mouth twisted in a wry, indulgent grimace.

"Rena, he would be micromanaging me if it were serious. You know how he gets."

"He's been baking!" Her whispered words were sharp, and she bit her lip to leash her frantic thoughts. "He's baking and not just the odd quiche. More than when we were watching The Great British Bake Off. More than when Kohler lost the election! He's attempted phyllo dough twice!"

Dorrit fell silent. This was troubling.

"He trusts you more than anyone. John, don't make that face — he does, yes, even more than me! He can tell you things that he isn't allowed to tell me. It's more than that, though, and you know it. He's known you longer and, don't hate me, but you remind him of his son."

Dorrit gave her an exasperated look, causing her to laugh.

"You know what I mean. He loves you. He doesn't like to be vulnerable, but don't doubt it, John. You humanize him."

"Not doing very well, am I?" he muttered.

"Better than you realize," she returned. "Please ask him. Don't let him carry this alone."

He couldn't refuse her. There was something fine about Rena Amano. Although she was capable, those around her felt it; she awakened protective instincts.

"I'll ask, but he may not be able to tell me."

"It will be enough. Thank you."

O'Brien returned, pushing a tea trolley. "We have raspberry, lemon, and frangipane tartlets; pistachio and orange madeleines; and a chocolate praline gateau," he announced, setting a plate with three exquisite miniature desserts before each of them. "Coffee with cream, no sugar for Rena, and cream with coffee, two sugars for John."

Rena stared heavily at the immaculate patisserie.

Dorrit squeezed her hand.

"Very pretty, sir," he said with a studied lack of inflection, taking a bite. His eyes closed involuntarily, but he quelled any further indication of rapture. O'Brien was quite vain enough.

After the sensory overload abated enough for the shutters to rise, Dorrit started.

"What the... Did you... Is that Puckwudgie?"

He thrust a finger at the decorations topping the gateau and slid down the banquette in the same motion.

Rena's eyes popped even as she shrieked, searching the spread for tiny imps. When nothing moved, vanished, or reappeared, she swatted him.

"Don't do that!"

Kenny: April 8th in Parkville, Missouri

The circle glowed, melting with color, as the sun dipped behind the Wyoming peaks. Colt stared, unblinking, at the sleepy subdivision. I understood the awe — workshop dust and toolboxes on one side, wild glory on the other.

"Hedge-jumping's a lost craft. Elke Durchdenwald, the last known, was executed on December 7, 1831, for unnatural behavior."

Bet poor Elke wished she had stuck with knitting. But then, magic was addictive.

"I read up after…" Colt trailed off.

"After we met."

The night the Saturniidae entered the subversion business, the night Colt's father died saving his family. Ten-year-old Colt pledged to earn his place as my apprentice, learn my craft, and save others.

That vow nearly broke me.

We'd thought we were ready; just eighty-three seconds to connect to a marked location, seventy-six if I'd been there. After months of training, Evy and Nore nailed every door. We had a former Navy SEAL therianthrope, a bard, a vampire med mage, and combat-trained practitioners, plus the element of surprise; what could go wrong?

Seventy-six seconds was an eon in a fight, and our opponents had been playing this game much longer. Our arrogance cost Isaac Ebersol his life. Colt disagreed — Elena Romero never blamed us either — but ever since, we all kept a mental tally of lives lost against lives saved. Keeping a healthy perspective was difficult.

My apprentice stood silent for several seconds, caught in grief's web, before shaking free.

"Where's that?" he asked, nodding at the gate.

"Rawlins, Wyoming — seat of Carbon County," Oscar grunted, elbowing in with steampunk-esque rifles — brass knobs, scopes, gears — that came in handy in some strange situations. "Home to Jason Cleary and family."

Oscar dropped the guns and nodded — everyone was set. Operation Orientation was a go; time to set this trainwreck in motion.

"And Jason Cleary is?" Colt prompted, eyeing me and the healer. He caught our silent exchange but didn't push.

"Oscar, Colt. Colt, Oscar Mendoza—my défteros and second," I said, eyes on the portal. Technically, they'd met before, but we'd reminisced enough already. They sized each other up.

"Jason Cleary: husband to Kathleen, father to Zach and Matthew, Little League coach, and fireman," I said, stressing the stakes. "Two days ago, he saved a pregnant woman and her cat from a burning building. It collapsed. They walked out unscathed — no smoke inhalation, not a scratch on them."

"He's a practitioner," Colt deduced.

"No."

"The woman?"

"Jason Cleary's a norm. Erynne Stone is a Hybrid. She reported her hero for warped practices four hours after he saved her, her baby, and Lilibette the cat. He doesn't know what he did and probably couldn't repeat it. He's never heard of the Agency of Preternatural Affairs, he's unaware his world's gone, and that his family will have to adapt fast to survive."

My phone buzzed, blaring Joan Jett's lack of concern for her notoriety. I silenced it.

"That's our signal. Watch, but don't interfere."

Colt blinked, his brows scrunching.

"Your job is to watch and obey," I said.

Oscar stepped up and crossed his arms, giving Colt the full weight of his attention. At five-seven, he shouldn't have been intimidating, but what he lacked in height he made up for in attitude. Looming was a particular gift.

Still confused, Colt nodded and turned to the gate.

In Rawlins, a dark sedan pulled up to the Clearys' raised ranch, disgorging two suited men. They strode up the steps, telegraphing government muscle.

"Who're they?"

"Agents," Oscar sneered.

"So I watch. What're you two doing?"

"Providing a safe learning environment," I said. We had gone through variations of this song and dance many times; going to the dentist was more fun.

"You're not—"

"Watch," Oscar barked.

Zach Cleary opened the door, but was swiftly replaced by his mom. The agents flashed badges, spoke briefly, and she disappeared. A moment later, Jason came to the door. The badges were flashed again — one showed a warrant, the other yanked him out of his home, tased him mid-breath, and allowed Cleary's body to tumble down the stairs.

"Why aren't you stopping this? Isn't that what the Covenant is for?" Colt snapped, hands trembling.

"Watch," Oscar growled.

The kid charged the portal, but we caught him after two steps. Although it wasn't an active gate, Colt was a practitioner. Instinct or some other force might carry him through. It had happened before; we'd learned from our mistakes.

"No! Do something," he shouted, thrashing. "Help them! Please-"

His cries garbling, Colt stiffened under my hex. I hated freezing someone I liked. He was still awake, alert, and facing the gate, and he'd thaw faster than my guilt.

Eight suits emerged from the deepening shadows — four with guns on Kathleen Cleary, holding her boys back from the brave defenders of the Community: four covering the first two as they loaded a cuffed, bloody Jason into the car.

Two identical vehicles pulled up, and seven agents piled in. The last threw some words at Mrs. Cleary. Desperation holding her taut, she hugged her children and nodded. The agent spat at them, then climbed into the last car.

Oscar began dismantling the portal, and I turned to Colt, still paralyzed.

"This wasn't meant to test or torment you," I told him. "Your mother accused me of claiming your life; I will do my best to keep you alive, but the things you witness will claim you — they'll become your obsession."

I couldn't tell if he was listening.

"Most folks can't handle this work; we must determine if you can. That takes exposure. What you feel right now — the anger, fear, and desperation? Use it. When you want to quit, remember this. Decide if preventing another atrocity is reason enough to keep going. Lives will depend on you, so you'll need to convince us that you're ready."

Tears streaked down Colt's face, fists clenching as he regained bodily autonomy.

"This was designed to be a brutal lesson, and it isn't even the worst. If you continue, everything — your loyalty, strength, ethics — will be tested. Rushing in without a plan kills people. What would have happened if we'd grabbed Cleary before the APA?"

"He…wouldn't…have…died," Colt rasped, twisting his neck.

"Jason's alive, Colt," I promised. "Think. If crazy people kidnapped you, claiming the government would arrest and brainwash you, leaving your family ostracized, would you believe them without any proof?"

I sensed the warp in reality swirl into existence behind me, rippling the lines and compressing into a chrysoprase passage.

Each practitioner's magic manifested in unique ways — mine usually featured clockwork, Evy's a historic library, Oscar's a gory display of sinew and bone. Even knowing that, the jubilant green corridor startled me — more so because of its weaver.

I tilted my head to the new door. "That leads to a manifold bridge — connecting multiple locations and creating a temporary pocket plane. If you follow us, please remain silent. We'll answer your questions when we return."

The kid glared with no indication of whether I had reached him or destroyed his trust. With orientations, it could go either way.

The passage led into a vast, silent room hung with vines, cut by slender streams, and supported by lofty pillars. Shimmering wards protected four zones, keeping the noise from becoming overwhelming. We queued, waiting behind other mentors and apprentices. Colt studied the quadrant where invisible operatives opened and closed portals. In a smaller section, robed figures distributed supplies to the newly exiled.

Over half the temple-like space was set up as a medical ward — refugees to one side, injured practitioners on the other.

A tall woman, clad head-to-toe in unrelieved black, masking her identity, motioned us forward and guided us down a row of gurneys. Jason Cleary was sitting on the side of a hospital bed, flanked by his sons. His wife, dry-eyed but shaky, occupied a stool, one hand on his knee to assure herself that he was alive.

A man in a white Oxford and slacks stood nearby, guarding the reunited families. He nodded to us, his expression grim but satisfied. I returned the gesture as our escort led us back to our gate.

Once we'd returned home, Colt, his voice hoarse but steady, asked, "What'll happen to them?"

"They'll be taken somewhere safe to recover and learn to avoid tapping the lines. Once they've mastered that, they can choose between receiving new identities and leaving or taking the Covenant's oath and learning ley manipulation. Most leave, but some stay. Some even become operatives."

Oscar, meeting my gaze, gave me a pointed look.

"I don't like how you did this," Colt murmured, "but I understand. It makes an impact."

"If you think of a better way, I'm all ears."

Orientations were a drain; seeing the kid harden inch by inch was watching a slow-motion tragedy. Reminding myself of the good things in life — a swing on the porch and a cold beer while Milo and Mouse played with the farm's animals — helped.

"How'd it go?" hissed a sibilant voice. Maggie landed in the swing opposite mine.

"He hasn't left."

"He won't. He's nauseatingly earnest, like you." She mimed vomiting on my boots. "I thought Arlo was bad, but he, at least, rebels occasionally. You're Colt's knight in tarnished armor, and he's your devoted squire."

"Thanks…I guess."

"Just wait. He'll look up your previous apprentices' stats and shred them. He won't even have the decency to be smug, thinking that's what he's supposed to do."

I snorted at the picture she painted, believing it. Colt hadn't been told how to earn an apprenticeship, so he overachieved at everything. By now, it was routine.

The screen door clattered as Milo, Mouse, and a baker's dozen of pets, goats, and brown bats rushed in.

"New arrivals," Mouse announced, dropping onto a swing. "There's a little boy with Davy."

"That's Eli, her son, back from visiting his grandparents."

"He lives here," Milo reasoned. "In our room?"

"Here, yes; your room, no — he has the loft in Davy's suite."

The screen squeaked again as Eli, with his mother's heart-shaped face and tousled black curls, bounded in — stopping short when he saw Milo and Mouse. His mother followed at a calmer pace.

"Welcome home, Professor," I said, offering a hug.

Eli flung his arms around me, never looking away from the kids.

"Thanks, Aunt Kenny."

"Glad you're home. Eli, meet Milo and Mouse. Guys, this is Eli."

I wasn't clear on what was socially appropriate for children, but ours were clearly defective.

After three beats of silence, Davy, grabbing a beer and taking a perch on the hearth, instructed, "Eli, stop gawking and say hi. Why don't you show Milo and Mouse your telescope?"

A flash of irritation scrunched his face, then smoothed as he surveyed his new friends. "Hi."

Mouse remained silent, eyeballing the interloper. Milo grimaced and waved.

"Whatever," Mouse grumbled, dragging Milo outside. I debated whether this exchange warranted a talk about manners.

Unperturbed, Eli hugged Maggie and launched into a detailed account of his adventures in Wenen.

I caught Davy sneaking glances at me.

She set her beer down and leaned in, asking, "Did Colt survive orientation?"

"Seems like."

"Good. He's hooked then — yours to corrupt," she grinned, tipping her bottle to me, taking another pull.

Yes, fantastic. Another soul in the ledger.

Chapter 10: Empty Fort

April 12th at the Agora in Chicago, Illinois

"You've reached the office of Representative Wes Pavlica. This is Carol. How may I assist you?"

"Carol, this is Mara Dietricksen. I'm returning Wes's call from twenty minutes ago."

Dorrit's transparent eyebrows climbed his forehead.

"Oh, I'm so sorry, Judge Dietricksen! He just left for the airport. I'm afraid that he'll be out of the country for the next few weeks! I can transfer you to his voicemail, although emailing might be a better option if it's urgent."

"I see. That is a pity. Well, I'll leave a message in that case."

Dorrit opened his mouth, but O'Brien scowled and silenced him with a sharp gesture.

"Of course, Judge Dietricksen. I apologize for the inconvenience."

A beep followed a few clicks. A man's gruff voice invited Her Honor to leave her name, number, and a brief message.

"Hello, Wes. This is Mara. I'm so disappointed that I missed your call. I'm even more disappointed that you failed to present Cora before the court today, as requested. You are now considered fugitives from the law, and your cadre has been handed over to Senator Amspoker for review. The Garrán Dorcha are not happy. Keep a lookout for some old friends — I've released the Hounds. There's a slight chance they won't rip your magic from your living flesh if you cooperate. I'll see you soon!"

O'Brien tapped one long, elegant finger on the top of a plain gold cube, ending the recording. "She's still single, if you're interested."

Astonishing. May I say, sir, that it has been an honor to serve with you. You will be sorely missed, but rest assured that your murderer will be fully exonerated by the Quorum, due to the lady's high status, and that your friends will be too pragmatic to avenge your excruciating death.

"That was beautiful, John. Mara can be creatively brutal, but she plays by the rules. In the eighty years she's stood on the Heliaia, she's been investigated twice. Both times, she eventually found out. Everyone involved is still alive, in full possession of their inherent magic and all their appendages. I checked."

Dorrit was all approbation for the Chairman's due diligence.

60

Is she a suspect?

O'Brien shrugged noncommittally.

"After Wilton's trial, I did some digging. In the past year, seven different Quorum members, APA officials, judges, or senior marshals requested access to closed trials. Each request was granted for undisclosed reasons, and all seven defendants were convicted. For Levi Wilton's case, Jones was admitted after a brief private consultation with Judge Dietricksen. It's very odd. As an Angel of Mercy, Jones's services have been requested 96 times, never refused, but she's only observed five of those trials, four as a material witness."

Is it possible that nothing hinky is going on?

"It's the Community, John. The day nothing hinky is going on will be the day after the apocalypse! Maybe. I wouldn't put it past some of these cockroaches to survive. Nothing hinky may be going on that involves Judge Dietricksen. We shall see. How are matters progressing?"

The Snohomish team has pursued several leads with no luck. They've been reassigned. The Austin team has been unable to locate the tote bags the two children were seen carrying. None of Ms. Caterham's possessions appear to be missing.

O'Brien's nod was grim. Their best efforts had uncovered depressingly little.

Any advances in Senator Park's murder?

O'Brien's countenance contorted like he'd bitten into a particularly sour lemon.

"I don't know! Once it was established that the gun used didn't match the one that killed Martin, Serrecold cut me off. I know that Hildebrand took a look at the body, and Park's mental autonomy had been compromised. He was intentionally released before death. Someone wanted to punish him, show him what he'd been forced to do. They wanted him to hang himself in despair — waste of time. Park hated drama. Anything on Jones?"

Dorrit grimaced, inciting a level of curiosity he had not intended to raise.

"Something bothering you, John?"

Dorrit scratched discontentedly at his chin.

Everything.

"Oh! Not much hope there, I'm afraid. Something slightly more specific we might have remedied..."

Are you familiar with Jones's history?

"Not very. Why?"

Dorrit paced the length of the room.

Mendoza, only three decades into his political career, decides to step down and, out of the blue, a young prodigy — skilled as a military strategist, a diplomat, an entrepreneur, a philanthropist, and a politician — appears just in time to replace him. That stretches beyond wildly improbable.

"Yes...multi-talented individuals are often annoying."

Dorrit was invulnerable to O'Brien's sarcasm.

I don't understand Jones' motives. There've been enough personal challenges, assaults, and biased legislation to prove she's a contender. The Sheta Djew is an ambitious financial juggernaut, yet Jones is a homebody, defending but never attacking. Their membership has stalled just below 1,800 for three years; just 200 more would raise her vote an entire tier. Why doesn't she pursue a senator's seat?

"Where are you going with this?"

The Empty Fort Strategy.

O'Brien's silence was eloquent.

Zhuge Liang. Romance of the Three Kingdoms. Knowing that he was outnumbered, Liang had the city gates thrown open and sat on top of the walls playing his guqin when the enemy strolled up. Liang had a reputation for strategy, and the opposing army, suspecting an ambush, retreated.

O'Brien's ears perked up in interest. "Go on."

Jones's meteoric rise to power was too clean. Almost staged.

"Ah ha."

Perhaps she encouraged or even hired challengers.

The agent stopped pacing and glanced up. O'Brien, chewing on the notion, nodded for him to continue.

The Sheta Djew's farm includes a beer hotel. Housemates, guests, day-trippers, staff, and delivery vehicles come and go daily. Their security appears to be lacking. The land is potent with magic; she has strong, layered wards, but their purpose is unclear. They haven't kept us out, but they react when crossed. And the house... Look up Punk Bunks.

The Chairman did so.

"It looks like a well-kept haunted village. What style would you call that? Not Craftsman...not industrial... Fairytale villain meets modern, rustic, industrial, neo-Victorian? Is it a faerie mound?"

It's not underground, so no. It's the Modern Witch aesthetic — there's a giant twig broom sticking out over the brewery's doors. Jones is advertising to anyone who's watching that she's a Correctionist with an open-door policy.

O'Brien swiveled where he sat, settling his feet on the tufted arm of the settee. "Brewers used to do that when illiteracy was the default — the broom, I mean. They used them, and it became a recognized symbol. Originally, they had nothing to do with practitioners, but some fool — a teetotaler, no doubt — decided the ladies who brewed the beer needed to be persecuted, and the connection was forged."

O'Brien continued to study the gallery of images. "Jones is a Correctionist but not an activist. She gained status as an ID by funding archaeological digs at suspected covensteads. She handed over every grimoire unearthed — eighty-something of them — but was permitted to keep most of the other artifacts, after they were deemed inert. It's worth noting that she didn't sell the artifacts even though they would have brought in a packet. All things Warped are en vogue."

Dorrit did not comment.

"All right. Suppose she did invite challengers; why?"

To build a reputation quickly. The Sheta Djew absorbed three local cadres after unprovoked attacks. The Community was buzzing about instability in the region for months, but Jones is a lover of peace. Now, the Sheta Djew is on excellent terms with their remaining neighbors, and no one has challenged her for over five years.

"Biding her time?"

Possibly. Her wards are unique, custom, and intricate...but she rarely demonstrates her ley talents. When she does, her work is stable but unambitious; she avoids the spotlight. What if Jones isn't as gifted with ley manipulation as is believed? Perhaps she learned how to activate an artifact or made a deal with an old power. Why didn't the Unrelenting object to those digs?

O'Brien bucked so violently that he nearly bit his tongue in half.

"Object to it," he choked. "My dear John, they lobbied for it! The Unrelenting are not anti-magic; they're elitists. They love her because she amuses them. A Correctionist who's executed as many convicted practitioners as you have — possibly more? They were delighted with the digs. It saved the Quorum an enormous amount of time, money, and liability. Covensteads are well-defended, even after the warped are gone. Cost seventeen lives, and another sixty-three were injured, including Jones! The Quorum seized what they wanted and left her enough tchotchkes to make her happy."

You're inclined to dismiss my theory?

O'Brien stood and dusted himself off.

"No. It's the Quorum's stance that none of the old powers remain; I disagree. I think they've lost interest in life; reinventing ourselves gets old eventually. A new mask, another thin shell," he mused, sounding fatigued. "Good thing, too; the eldritch practitioners make the Hounds look like fluffy bunnies. If Jones has met one, then they own her. They don't deal with their inferiors; they chain them. No, if anyone were inclined to humor her, you and I would already be cold in the ground. I could believe that she's managed to unravel the complexities of some artifact, however. Intriguing notion."

He pondered the riddle Representative Jones posed a moment more.

"There is something odd about her — magnetic. She's stood before the Quorum, a powerful speaker. Do we have people in her hotel?"

Blake and Sarduy have visited. They've set up a few cameras in outdoor spaces. We haven't made it into the hotel. The place is booked solid until late autumn. Hatter is finessing their system. Unfortunately, it's proving unusually resilient.

"Really? That's unusual..."

We've secured a loft over a music store catty-corner from the Sullen Creek Brewpub. There's good visibility of the bar's front and side entrances, as well as the lot down the hill where Jones habitually parks. We've tagged the household vehicles and installed cameras around the perimeter of both the farm and the pub."

"How's the beer?"

What?

"It's a valid question, John. Far better to find out now if you like it or not than wait until your life depends on convincing the lady you're a connoisseur and not a stalker."

Blake and Sarduy are fans. I haven't had the opportunity to sample the wares.

"Make an opportunity. All work and no play makes John a dull boy. Make some new friends in town while you're at it!"

Chapter 11: To the Bone

Kenny: April 13th at Sullen Creek Farm

"Facultates supra rationem?"

Colt, eyes closed and forehead wrinkled, recited, "Functions — no! Abilities beyond reason."

He quickly corrected himself, flapping like an agitated bird auditioning for Swan Lake, before continuing. "The Facultates describe a set of hereditary talents: Far Sight, seeing the distant future; Fore Sight, glimpsing the near future; Second Sight, perceiving present events, often triggered by glamours; Hind Sight — also known as psychometry or psychoscopy — revealing the recent past; Remote Sight, uncovering the distant past; and True Sight, seeing the ley lines."

One eyelid opened a slit and locked on me.

"Why didn't those kids leave with the group? Who are they?"

I quirked an eyebrow, and his lid clamped shut. He bobbled again, but with a little more chicken dancing, all was well.

"Correct," Oscar grunted, ignoring Colt's question. He generously overlooked the kid peeking, saving the lecture for when it would really hurt — like when the kid had a 'study session' with Davy's pretty apprentice planned. "Pros and cons?"

"Pros: You might know more than you used to. Cons: precognition involves probabilities, not certainties — except for a Bean Sídhe, whose visions guarantee a dirt nap within three days — but seers can't help reacting to the visceral intensity of their visions. The future, being fluid, shifts when a vision is shared, even if it's dismissed. Seers feel driven to act according to their moral code. Most eventually go nuts, yet the gift persists, and the madder they become, the more they cloak their words in cryptic riddles."

Oscar's attention flitted to me, but I waved him off. He tended to fuss.

"Milo and Mouse are runaways from a norm foster home. They know little about our world, and Milo recently rose as a vampire. We're trying to ease them into things," I explained, tinkering with an ether-safe prototype. Anything could be stored in the in-between, but it wasn't secure — until now. Eventually, someone would figure out how to bypass the locking mechanism — probably Clan Haigh, but they'd have to find it first. "Mouse is preternatural but doesn't trust us enough to discuss it. Mind what you say in front of them. They're inclined to view practitioners as inherently evil. Mouse thinks I'm two hexes away from turning green, growing warts, and flying around on a broom. Ehlidantus's Theory of Accidental Magic?"

"That's rough. Ehlidantus argues that accidental magic stems from humanity's instinct to recognize and repeat patterns, making anyone who observes a manipulation — even unknowingly — far more likely to tap a line by accident."

"Seers with True Sight," Oscar prompted.

Colt took a breath.

"True Sight seers lose the script faster than others. Historically, blinding them delayed insanity, allowing them to sense ley lines without seeing other planes. Only twenty-three genuine True Sight seers have been recorded. The practical applications for the gift are limited; they're basically over-juiced sensitives prone to madness."

I smothered my cackle. Both Oscar and the kid were watching me — the former concerned and the latter perplexed.

"Don't mind me," I murmured. "Gallows humor."

Blinding seers was, thankfully, no longer a thing. My adoptive parents chose a different path, funding a massive research effort with the few remaining biomancers, morphogists, and histomancers — ley scientists — to find an alternative. After several failures, they developed null glasses. A decade in, the first viable pair emerged. They were life-altering. I enjoyed a month free of headaches, auras, jaw pain, and eye strain, with even my reflux abating.

Insanity suddenly became a distant possibility instead of a bleak cloud of attention-seeking doom. The null glasses bought me decades, maybe even a century, before my mind broke.

"Milo and Mouse are from Austin," I said, changing the subject and jiggling the ether lock's door. It fell open even though it had been locked. I sighed in disgust. "They're keen to be reunited with the operative that took them in. Unfortunately, that's not possible."

"Did the operative die?" Colt softly inquired. Even with his eyes shut, balanced on the thick cable stretching the length of my workshop, he managed to look somber.

The glass garage door had been rolled up, inviting the cool evening air inside. It was drizzling, the sound a soft patter. Oscar had hoped a stiff wind would add a layer of complexity to tonight's physical challenge, but the breeze was smoother than a sigh.

"Uh...no. She was...reassigned. It's complicated. I'll explain more when we get deeper into your training."

Flesh golems were a bit controversial — easy to misuse, hard to trust, and the debate on whether they were alive or not was always hot.

"Is that your way of saying I'll understand when I'm older?"

His tone was polite — even teasing, but there was a whisper of ire buried there. Finally! I flicked the ether-lock's door back and forth in quiet celebration. If an apprentice never felt frustrated, I wasn't doing my job.

Oscar and I exchanged a smug look, and I snorted, remembering what mentoring Oscar had been like. Name-calling had escalated to shouting matches, ending with him biting me just before I turned him into a toad. It took time, but after we put the literal and figurative fires out, we found our way.

The experience with Colt was very different. He eagerly accepted the daunting reading list and cheerfully rose at four to assist me with chores. A handful of instructors pounded a dozen subjects into his head, and there were ridiculous exercises to complete every hour. He learned how to fall. He learned how to think through pain. He learned survival skills. If he was lucky, we allowed him five hours of sleep each night. The curriculum was a purposeful grind for the first twenty-four weeks, but Colt had managed to get ahead of the schedule.

I smiled as I tightened the ley screws on my project.

"I'm sorry if I was patronizing; just know, we never see the full picture. Once you take your oath, you'll know more, but even then, information stays limited in case of capture."

Colt made an indistinct sound and, arms fluttering double-time, involuntarily stepped off the cable.

Oscar's grin was pure evil. A tumble meant starting over.

"How long?" Colt demanded, swiping his sweat-dampened locks out of his eyes.

"Six months. Sometimes longer, sometimes shorter. Sometimes, apprentices get reassigned," I said, throwing down the gauntlet. "Training never stops. I train. Oscar trains. Personnel in non-combat operations train. We can never be fully prepared, but we do our best."

The ether-lock snapped shut on my finger, and I screamed, trying to pull myself free. My hand moved; the first knuckle on my index finger did not. The bone was crushed.

"What did you do?" Oscar roared, suddenly there and cradling my hand and the rabid safe. "Numbskull! You're never happy until you've found a new way to kill yourself."

"It fucking hurts!"

"Of course, it fucking hurts! You've amputated a finger using the in-between as the knife!"

I looked away as Oscar pried the thing open, uneager to view the damage, and met my apprentice's open-mouthed shock. Ignoring the pissy messages my nerves were sending my brain, I tried to think of a joke — something to reassure the kid.

I was free. Without thinking, I looked at my hand, numb yet blazing with cold fire. Oh, it was gross — bloody matter dripped on the floor. Maybe the lock was a little too tight?

"Not…what I meant when I said…unghh…we'd work your fingers to the bone," I mumbled, leaning my head on Oscar's shoulder as he worked on the ruined finger. The numbness started to fade.

"Right." Colt nodded, watching Oscar work. "I heard Derringer got a new cookbook."

Huh?

"He's trying to distract you," Oscar explained.

Oh.

"Yeah… He wants to brew kombucha. He thinks our diet doesn't include enough fermented foods."

Five minutes later, Oscar interrupted our discussion on the merits of sauerkraut. "How does that feel?"

I tentatively experimented. Good as new.

"So…six months," murmured Colt, nodding.

Without even a grunt from Oscar to spur him on, he flipped upside down into a handstand, indifferent to the filthy floor. My second, eyebrows high, held up a tenner and shoved it in the betting jar, mouthing, "Five and a half."

I wrote it on the blackboard, reveling in my recovery and adding a five beside my name. "How can you fuel a spell?"

"Reservoir energy; twining reservoir energy with energy from the lines; priming a spell with reservoir energy to avoid creating a vacuum but otherwise relying on ley line energy; and the forbidden method, tearing energy from the lines."

This kid didn't need to be pushed — he'd overtake a caffeinated jackrabbit. I added a ten to the kitty.

"Oscar," the kid prodded, red-faced and dancing on his hands.

"Where do seers fit into the Community?" Oscar quizzed, rolling his eyes as he and I cleaned bloody sawdust off the floor. Sometimes, it was impossible to read him, and sometimes it was easy: this kid's too earnest and it's annoying.

As if intuiting my thoughts, Oscar winked. A smile snuck onto my face as Colt continued to regurgitate his homework.

"Seers aren't a distinct Origin, as potent soothsayers exist across all subsets. Officially, the Quorum doesn't classify seeing as a warped practice, since it doesn't disrupt the flow of ley energy. Unofficially, their value drives the Quorum to use the insanity excuse to funnel every diviner into Agency service. There's at least one seer attached to every warlock team."

Chapter 12: Seer Season

April 13th at the Agora in Chicago, Illinois

"Let the record state that at three minutes after eight on the evening of April the thirteenth, the Committee on Intelligence was called to order with Dumitru DeWitt, Magister of the Quorum, presiding," the ancient gasbag crooned before hammering a gavel on the podium with startling force. With his thin greasy hair, waxy powder-blue complexion, and long spindly fingers ideal for strangulation, he wasn't merely a relic; he was a revenant. How he passed in mixed company was a mystery. "The Committee recognizes Senator Hersch. Senator, the floor is yours."

The light dimmed over the Magister's diseased countenance and brightened on the south side of the chamber where the Unrelenting's chosen voice box waited. The harsh light limned the long, graceful lines of the Senator's figure, draped in an excess of midnight blue velvet. Evening garb was not de rigueur for the Committee, but to each her own.

The dark poisonous flower that was Acacia Hersch rose on her whisper-thin stilettos and swept the fall of jet-black hair behind one shockingly bare shoulder. Candlelight shimmered along her pale skin, luminescing like the cold white scales on the belly of a deep-sea serpent.

"Thank you, Magister. On the question regarding the rising prices of precast spells manufactured in Sanctuary, our investigation has revealed no malpractice or violation of ethics as defined by the Charter-"

Senator Balbay, sitting opposite, made a derisive sound through his teeth, without looking up from stirring his coffee.

"Yes, Rufe? Would you like to add something?" she purred, seductive as a rusty razor blade.

The Speaker for the Correctionists was unmoved.

"Only my astonishment that you can utter those words with a straight face, Acacia."

"So noted. Moving on, the cost for a decent precast spell will continue to rise as a natural, if unfortunate, consequence of the Cleansing. With the old powers done and dusted and the pervasive ignorance among the residents of Sanctuary, it is our expectation that, even as the expense soars, the quality will plummet. Nothing to be done — unless we elect to educate the residents of Sanctuary on the very practice that led to their convictions. That said, more registered Ipseita Dualis will likely opt to manufacture their own. This will inevitably encourage members of the Community to dabble in ley manipulation. Measures to prevent such criminal activity should be discussed when the Quorum is assembled."

"Are you feeling poorly, Acacia? It's unlike you to miss an opportunity to gather up more inmates for that pit of a prison," Rufe inquired with false solicitousness.

"It is not a prison," corrected Chief Justice Irit Jackson.

Where Senator Hersch enticed, the Chief Justice remained aloof. The lines of her ultra-modern pantsuit were so sharp, they looked lethal.

"There are no barred cells, no wardens, no restrictions on where the residents go within the city limits or when." Her powerful voice echoed, creating the sensation of divine intervention.

O'Brien allowed his head to fall back and gazed up at the curious starburst pattern repeated in the millwork gracing the ceiling. "Chief Justice Jackson, they cannot leave. By definition, that is a prison," he groaned, knowing he was allowing himself to be sucked into the oft-repeated debate, yet unable to help himself.

"Gravity prevents me from floating off into space, Chairman. I do not view Earth as my prison but my home," retorted Senator Hersch, rolling her protuberant eyes. "Will anyone argue that the laws imposed by nature are to our benefit? The boundaries of Sanctuary benefit the warped. They can live in peace and comfort, and the rest of us can sleep easy. If you want to go back to lopping off heads, I'll vote for that!"

"Exactly!" exclaimed the Chief Justice, thrusting her hands toward Senator Hersch as if this logic were beyond contestation.

"It's mind rape and slavery," returned Rufe, toasting the ladies with his mug. "And very lucrative to investors. Irit, don't you own a few shares?"

There was a hideous shriek, a pulse of red eyes, the blur of movement that even the preternatural eye could not track, a spine-liquefying snarl, and a sudden wash of air. Quite invigorating! When O'Brien's vision settled, everyone was in their assigned places. Only now, Balbay was smirking as he sipped his caffeine fix.

"We could argue semantics all night, but some of us have real jobs," Her Honor, Judge Dietricksen, interjected...with only a hint of impatience as she tapped her bloody claws on the table. It was not by accident that the movers and shakers of the Community were allowed to see her silver-gray fur recede into creamy, smooth skin as she squirted hand sanitizer onto her palm. "We must be pragmatic. The fact of the matter is that necessary evils exist and cannot be avoided. Certainly, Sanctuary's denizens are not guilty in the usual sense. However, we cannot contain practitioners without the measures in place. If we cannot contain the warped or execute them, then they will destroy the Community, and Earth will descend into chaos. Shall we move on?"

As the silence lingered, everyone looked to the podium.

Dumitru DeWitt was draped over the lectern and drooling as he sawed logs.

Her Honor rolled her eyes and barked, "Magister! Shall we move on?"

The decrepit vampire sprang upright, twirled, and, catching himself on the wooden stand, scowled at the lady in question.

"Judge Dietricksen, for shame! I will have order within these walls. That means no shouting, young lady! Behave yourself or I shall have you expelled!"

Without so much as a snicker, Rufe held out a handkerchief to the living dust-collector.

"Thank you, Senator Balbay," DeWitt muttered, accepting the square of fine lawn and dabbing away any evidence of moisture from his chin and cravat. He blew his nose, folded the abused cloth, and handed it back.

"Keep it. I insist," murmured the Senator, his expression stoic.

The Magister bowed graciously before turning to consult his notes.

"The Committee recognizes Minister Pendragon."

The spotlight over the Convocation of Dverg's table illuminated, and a stocky bearded man in dark robes rose.

"Thank you, Magister," he began, his booming voice ringing off the chandeliers. "Ladies and gentlemen, as head of the subcommittee on wild construct control, it is my duty to report an unfortunate turn of events. A team of Oxford sensitives has conducted a comparative analysis of ley activity recorded over the last century. Their findings suggest that the amount of energy in the lines is growing and, until we find a way to vent that energy, will continue to grow. Therefore, wild construct sightings and attacks will continue to rise."

"Nature gave us a way to vent the lines," Adam Bell, president of the Therianthrope Council, observed in his quiet, steadfast way, "and we declared war on them. This is the direct result of the Cleansing."

"That hasn't been proven, nor is it relevant," spat Chief Justice Jackson.

"Of course it's relevant," countered Balbay, laughing at the assertion. "If we fail to understand why this is happening *and* fail to correct the problem, the situation will not fail to get worse. Denial is not a solution."

"What is the solution, Senator? Necromancy," Judge Dietricksen inquired acidly. "We agree that the cause warrants an investigation, hence the formation of the subcommittee. However, we need to determine a way to deal with the problem now, regardless of its cause. I move that we draft an amendment to the budget reallocating funds from the National Preternatural Park System, the Anti-Detection Network, the Eldritch Care Program, and Cryptid Encrypted to the tune of two billion dollars to launch a new program within the Agency of Preternatural Affairs dedicated to training agents to hunt and destroy wild constructs."

Director Serrecold smiled almost apologetically and said, "I second the motion."

"Motion carried," the Magister rasped, hammered his gavel, and proceeded to have a violent coughing fit lasting three full minutes. When finished, he consulted the agenda. "The draft will be presented to the Quorum in three weeks. The Committee recognizes Chairman O'Brien. Sir!"

"Thank you, Magister. Senators, Representatives, it is my privilege to inform you that the famed Seeress, Melisande Waites, has had a series of visions."

He paused for the collective groan, humming a little under his breath as he ticked off the seconds.

"Yes, seer season is upon us once again! I know you've all been eagerly anticipating the long-awaited return of The Riddlers. Wait no more! In the first of three episodes, Ms. Waites chronicled — in iambic pentameter — the climactic pilot for Call of the Wild, a matchmaking show that sets up a lovely mundane lady with six preternatural suitors and follows the twists and turns of their romantic adventures. Will the maiden tame the beast? Or shall hunger prevail?"

He preened when Her Honor snorted.

"Chairman, recall yourself," she pleaded.

"Of course, Your Honor. In the second vision, Ms. Waites played a long game of charades with her handlers, acting out the part of a gushing fan at a book signing, losing her cool, and involuntarily shifting forms in public. The esteemed Ms. Waites was very insistent that it be noted how compassionate the mundane author was and that the other attendees thought it quite good fun."

"Chairman O'Brien, is there some point to this, or are you merely poking fun at the mad ramblings of a once-great and now pathetic mind? If the former, please get to it, and if the latter, remember — your time will come."

"Yes, thank you for that PSA, Senator Balbay. There is a point — and please forgive me if I celebrate my sanity and humor, while they are both still intact. The loss of either is tragic, indeed," he retorted.

"The third prediction is still in the process of being translated. As luck would have it, one of the nurses who attends Ms. Waites is a gamer and recognized the fictional language known as Blue Tongue. It is the secret language of the Saturniidae, a guild of pirate witches," O'Brien savored the committee's reaction to the controversial w-word before continuing, "in the popular massively-multi-player-online-role-playing-game, Egress."

"And?" coaxed Gilles-Eugene Serrecold, with a tiny, mischievous smirk lurking around the corners of his mouth.

The director of the Agency of Preternatural Affairs, a typical beautiful and otherworldly fae, was an odd duck. His white hair was cut short, stubble hugged his square jaw, and his pale laughing eyes missed nothing. Clad in jeans and a cotton tee, a blazer his only concession to the formal surroundings, he embraced the current age. To use the modern vernacular, he seemed pretty chill. He wasn't. The director was cheerfully ruthless. Serrecold could be friend or foe — possibly both — on any given day.

"What has been translated thus far is the dialogue of an interview between a mundane reporter and the warlock Ghost, for some sort of documentary. Ghost's participation was not entirely voluntary, it seems."

"The point?" chided Rufe.

"Well...isn't it obvious? Whether any of these prophecies come to pass or not, the possibility that knowledge of the Community's existence will be leaked to the uninitiated must exist in the here and now."

The cacophony that followed was everything he'd hoped for and more.

"This committee ruins everything," President Bell howled, jabbing at his phone. "I've canceled my Egress account."

Kenny: April 17th at Sullen Creek Farm

"Saturation wards...blanket the... hu-uh...protected area...where everyone who enters...hu-uh...is monitored. In the event...hu-uh...of a transgression...the ward may eject...hu-uh...the perpetrator...from the area...hu-uh...disable...or kill them."

Startling me, my phone buzzed across the workbench, blaring *A Little Wicked.* Colt dropped from the bar with a thump, face blank. He'd cracked the song's significance in under a week.

The kid was too disciplined to beg. He didn't need to. His posture as he awaited the inevitable dismissal, hazel eyes gleaming as his brain whirred — calculating the odds that he would be allowed to stay with rapid-fire precision, did all the begging for him. Instructing him to leave was like kicking a well-mannered puppy.

I passed the welding torch to Oscar, ditched my hood, and grabbed the phone.

"Pull-up pop quiz will need to wait," I murmured, scrolling. The new quest was a smash-and-grab, low-risk, perfect for Colt's intro to fieldwork.

Oscar glanced up from his cell, eyebrows raised. I nodded. His mouth twitched — a lightning strike of a smile, then scowled again. We'd agreed the kid could observe if a good opportunity arose.

"Don't speak, move, or touch anything unless told," Oscar growled — menacing, yet endearing. "Observe only. If we say leave, run, or hide — do it."

Colt's jaw dropped, realizing the healer was barking at him, not me. Oscar, in the role of fairy godmother, often had that effect. The kid swallowed and nodded at the shorter, scarier man. My second glared at him for a full five seconds, driving the message home, then grunted in approval.

Colt remained at attention, his loose stance replaced by rigid apprehension. Young practitioners were generally taught just enough about manipulations to avoid attention. He'd seen me do a few small magics, but this would be his first time seeing a full-fledged working.

I stashed my welding gear. Oscar tossed me my quest tote from the gear garage. I pulled out fatigues and unzipped my coveralls. Colt flushed and turned as Oscar flung him a uniform.

"Tank and leggings," I said. "If I go commando in the boilersuit, I get weird looks — besides, my thighs chafe."

His face was a wash of crimson.

"She's kidding," Oscar snapped. "No one notices when she's weird anymore. You can change in the bathroom."

Minutes later, Colt returned in a black uniform. The fit was okay, but in a few weeks it would be snug. We'd need to call the commissary soon.

"Your uniform comes with fun accessories," Oscar explained, prodding an eye-shaped appliqué on Colt's sleeve. The kid started as he disappeared, the red toolbox behind him visible. Oscar poked it again. "Now is not the time to play with them."

"When we're done, check them out," I said, handing Oscar my glasses. Lesser crafts didn't need bare eyes, but constructing a door through time and space did — even if it meant that some planar oddity peered over my shoulder.

The gentleman in question — possessing four bronze faces and appearing male — set aside some complicated device and watched us keenly. Behind indigo robes, two sets of wings fluttered; from underneath the hem, a pair of cloven hooves peeked out. He stood on a terrace in a glorious garden, littered with scientific instruments and surrounded by undulating grasses.

Focusing, I stitched a circuit within a ley line, creating a simple engine, and primed it. Ley energy throttled through it, crackling and snapping, faster and faster. Before it burst, I stretched the circuit toward our marker, forging a connection.

"Whoa," Colt breathed as the warp in reality became visible to mundane eyes.

The appearance of constructs fluctuated according to mood and purpose. My default portal feathered out from nothingness, vapor condensing into a circular metal mass floating in astral fog. It was difficult to see — clouds and shadow drifting in a landscape of machinery and cords. Indistinct sounds, or the echoes of lost causes, added an ominous percussion. Roaring gusts of bracing breathable air swirled around before being swallowed up by the beyond. Cosmic backwash, if you will.

Energy and matter merged incrementally, and a knot formed. It smoothed and shaped itself into a small ring with hundreds of translucent membranes folded inward, protecting the center. With one final push, gears crunched and the lacy wings bloomed, revealing a copper circle covered by a thin, transparent film. The aperture was tiny, perfect for sneaking a cheeky peek.

Reconnaissance first — so sayeth Oscar. Those who failed to abide by his rules were taken out of the field — myself included. That was the deal he had brokered in exchange for watching our backs and patching up our boo-boos.

I anchored the opening and stepped back.

"Look," I told Colt, taking my glasses from Oscar. Slipping them on was like whipping off my bra at the end of the day. The ache behind my eyes receded, and light suddenly didn't seem so hostile.

He hesitated a bare moment, then approached the arcane product. "It worked — there's an exhibit! It's extraordinary."

Oscar white-knuckled the worktable, his jaw tensing; he was about to say something unfortunate. I tapped his forearm, snapping him back from a dark place.

Hard eyes glared at me as old shadows haunted him.

I shook my head. His mouth closed with a click of his teeth. His issues were not Colt's, nor should they be. The relics, mere trinkets now, represented a legacy he'd once shrugged off. It was a sore point — stinging more deeply for the converted.

"Indeed," I responded to Colt. "I'm going to dismantle the door. Watch closely."

"Why?" Colt squawked, almost angry.

Dabbling with magic was risky unless contained and scrubbed clean — turbulence was an open invitation to the Agency's warlocks and death or servitude. Wasting magic was, therefore, the greatest of sins.

"Because when I reconstruct it, you're going to wear these," I explained, pulling out a pair of deep-sea goggles from the reinforced pocket on his tote. They had a black, plastic frame and a single thick cloudy lens. Sexy was not in their vocabulary. Aggregate specs were expensive, so only early prototypes were issued to apprentices.

"I don't understand."

"You will. These babies are a royal pain in the ass, but you're going to need them. Prepare yourself. Your mind is about to come under siege, and the sensation can be disturbing."

"Uh-huh," he responded, doubtfully examining the specs. Colt's voice turned skeptical. "What do they do?"

"They reveal ley lines," I explained. "You'll see what I do as I explain it."

With that marketing wizardry, he slid them on, scanned the room, and toppled like a felled tree. Oscar and I caught him inches from the floor. He hadn't even put his arms out to catch himself. Shaky and bewildered, he yanked the specs off, staring at the concrete.

"I'm okay… I think I'm okay. Is it normal to…"

"See outer-world residents? Sure. That's Chauncey. You'll see worse before mastering this."

"Okay," he murmured weakly. "Wait! You know his name? You've communicated with him?"

"Nope, he just looks like a Chauncey. Parallel planes never cross, but they peek through sometimes. It's unlikely you'll see the same fellow twice."

Colt considered my reply for a moment. "I have...questions...but I don't know where to begin."

"Questions are good. We'll do our best to answer. However, we have work to do. Put your glasses back on," I told him, taking my own off.

Colt's hazel eyes narrowed, wrestling with his goggles' elastic. He froze — as if he'd been slapped with a kraken.

"You have true sight."

"Mmm-hmm."

"That…sucks."

A snicker escaped me as I unwound the anchor and siphoned the energy back into my reservoir. "The greatest gift can be a curse, and the worst curse can be the greatest gift," I told him, quoting my mom. "It's what you do with it that matters."

Colt was my seventh apprentice, but the quickest to acknowledge the onus of true-sight. Despite my mother's wisdom, it did suck. I wouldn't trade it for anything.

Still resting on the floor, Colt wrangled the glasses back on and watched. They magnified his eyes, leeching them of color. He looked like a Latin James Veitch.

I reversed the current in the ley circuit, forcing the delicate lamina to fold in. Clouds of vapor swirled back into existence. When it cleared, the copper ring was gone. Colt had remained engaged, even throughout the cleanup. That was good. Good housekeeping would help keep him alive.

I plucked another line and started anew. Once the peephole was in place, I stepped back so that Colt could take another gander, nearly tripping over poor Mel.

Where'd he come from?

Mel was not allowed inside the shop, but pesky things like rules, safety, and locked doors never stopped him from performing his duty — ostensibly, acting as my bodyguard but really spying for my mom. She rarely acted on any information Mel provided, so I tolerated him. Also, he was adorable. I sidestepped as if I'd known the floofy boy was there the entire time.

My loyal-ish canine companion stared at me, not fooled.

Oscar snorted. Mel never missed a quest. I ought to accept it.

"You're up," I announced, only mildly desperate to reclaim my glasses.

Colt clambered to his feet with Oscar's assistance, his face traveling this way and that as he examined the beyond. Together, my companions made the perilous six-foot journey. My apprentice peered through, and for several seconds, the only sounds came from the air conditioner.

"The Covenant hasn't built a museum, have they?" he inquired, the words subdued.

He understood — the objects beyond were practitioner-made.

When we didn't answer, he turned, expression bleak.

"They weren't stolen," I said.

It was the usual assumption. The Community abhorred practitioners — those they didn't own — but we fascinated them, too. Believing those with enough knowledge and skill to oppose them had been decimated, few within the Community would hesitate to claim our treasures.

"I don't understand," Colt whispered.

"The Covenant wants freedom; Lex Talionis, revenge; most covens want to be left alone. There are practitioners, though, that are fine with how things are," Oscar grunted, taking my glasses when I handed them over yet again.

Every preternatural, whether they cared to acknowledge it or not, was a practitioner. Every living person carried the potential to be one.

I stepped around Colt and peered through the eyelet. The room beyond was an airy mélange of white marble, soft gray walls, subtle gold accents, and shimmering velvets. Three-story windows flooded the space with light, highlighting twenty pedestals carved from stone or exotic woods.

"No one yet," I reported.

No one I'd seen, at any rate. If someone unseen had noticed a floating eyeball, we wouldn't hear them. The membrane muted sound both ways.

Unlike a fully anchored door, the peephole's single tether flexed slightly. I didn't see our prize, an orrery, so I pushed against the weld, stretching and turning to see the space directly behind the eyelet. I rose on my toes, raising one leg for balance, and tried not to rest my weight on the ring.

Nothing doing.

"Behind the portal, maybe," I murmured, glancing around for ideas.

I couldn't hear Chauncey tittering at my contortions, but I saw him. Either that, or three of his faces were sneezing violently. Probably the fourth, too. Allergies — they spared none.

Turning a cold shoulder on the alien being, I grabbed a stool and placed it in front of me. I was about to try again when the back of my neck tingled.

"What?" I demanded.

"I didn't say anything," objected Colt.

"Not you. Oscar. I can feel the caustic waves of his judgment beating on my back."

Mel grumbled under his breath. He felt the waves, too.

"The stool will slide," my défteros pointed out. "Use your apprentice. He can contribute."

Yeah… I didn't want to faceplant on a sawdusty floor.

"Colt, stand there," I directed. "Plant your feet. I'll be pulling and pushing. Got it?"

"Yes, ma'am," he replied, moving into position.

The next question in my head stared back at me from his eyes. Could he remain stable? Despite the eight inches he had on me, I probably outweighed him.

Colt's expression steeled. I wasn't going to doubt him.

I locked the peephole to my eye, stretched it, and leaned, a hand on Colt's chest. He tensed, counterbalancing as I twisted left. A blur of movement whizzed out of sight. I angled to chase it, straining, and found the floor. A series of overlapping gold rings circled a pink ivory pedestal. Above, sat the orrery, all gleaming gold clockwork; glass orbs of billowing, magenta smoke; and twelve spider-like arms languidly dancing, each trailed by a system of satellites. The beast was six feet wide, eight high — breathtaking, unless you knew its history.

"Found him," I chirped. The peephole snapped back, smacking Colt's chin. He winced but stood firm.

"Oops."

"No worries. Now, I can tell Katie that I was injured on a mission."

Oscar snorted. "You've been working too hard, but if your first thought is to impress girls, I'm not going to worry."

I chuckled, easing off Colt.

Our source had come through; everything was just as it should be...

Chauncey was doubled over in my peripherals and trembling sporadically. It wasn't allergies. I was used to astral spectators, not mimed commentary.

"Glasses!"

Oscar handed them over.

"The orrery's guarded by ring wards — gold inlay," I informed him, nose wrinkling. The Community was fascinated by magic, but not the philosophy of balance that underpins every practitioner culture around the globe. "I saw the sigils for gravity, withering darkness, lightning, and black fire. I couldn't see the others."

"Don't show off," Oscar warned, eyes sharp, handing me a snag-bag and slapping a sticker on my neck.

Mel glowered — as if Oscar's ire weren't frightening enough.

I opened my mouth, but he continued, tagging Colt with another sticker. "Nothing complicated is required. Don't give the Agency any information you don't have to."

"I'll behave," I exclaimed, handing him my glasses. "Have painkillers ready."

"You heard her," Oscar growled at Mel. "If she's lying, you back me up. I'm not sitting through another of Padŭ's lectures."

With a roll of his eyes, Mel flopped over and played dead.

Chapter 14: Frizz

April 17th at the Agora in Chicago, Illinois

O'Brien paced from one end of his office to the other, pulling up a contact on his cell so swiftly his finger blurred.

"Ghost," a deep voice answered curtly.

"Are you anywhere near upstate New York, per chance?"

"No. I'm tailing Jones through the River Market in Kansas City."

O'Brien's face pinched. It didn't make sense. But if Dorrit had her in sight… "You have her in sight? And you're certain that it is her? You're following her scent?"

"Yes, yes, and yes," replied John Dorrit, a trace of amusement shaping his words.

O'Brien dragged a ginger nut from a baggy in his pocket and demolished it in three bites, spice filling his mouth. He was missing something — unless Jones could be in two places at once.

"Pity. Cannon Blom's estate was broken into late this morning, and every ward, snare, and trap surrounding his private collection was activated. That wing of the house — what remains — is currently hell on earth."

Dorrit hummed in acknowledgement, but when he replied, his cadence was distracted. "Was it an inept burglary attempt or is Blom compensating for something?"

"The latter. Blom's never met a bell or whistle without ordering a round dozen. We haven't been able to conduct a proper sweep of the room — there's still an ice spike storm in progress, six feet long on average — but the early indications point toward something inanimate and non-magical triggering the wards."

What if she could? What if she'd found a way to be in upstate New York and, at the same time, in a very public, open-air, ginormous farmer's market full of bustle and, more importantly, witnesses?

"What do you mean?"

"They've found what used to be a pomodoro, some sort of sticky residue that might be the remnants of rubber bands, a half-melted crystal ball — Blom's own, most likely, wood ash, and other bits and bobs."

After an incredulous pause, Dorrit quietly exclaimed, "Someone MacGyver-ed it?"

"That is the consensus. No suspects, no indications of where the perpetrator entered or exited, at least twelve million dollars in damages — soon to be more if the magic zipping around isn't drained — oh, and a one-ton orrery has vanished. Blom's been alternating between tears and terrorizing the APA agents," O'Brien chirped. "You're certain that you haven't, at any point in the last four hours, lost sight of Jones — even for a moment?"

"No, sir. We've had a full day; Representative Jones has been fully occupied pricing home decor. We've been to three flea markets, a rug shop, stopped for lunch at an Ethiopian restaurant, froyo for dessert, and now we're at a custom upholsterer's. Oh, I picked up an antique silver brush to go with your ugly mirror."

"John, that was thoughtful...but I have curly hair. I apply conditioner and comb it in the shower — otherwise, I frizz something awful. I don't suppose they had a silver comb? Never mind... What has Jones purchased?"

"Not a visual I needed," Dorrit mumbled, "Nothing as far as I can tell, despite a good deal of negotiating. If she's picking out furniture, though, it would be delivered."

"Perhaps. Are we wasting our time?"

Dorrit chuckled, a smug, hungry sound.

"You read the files I sent? The shipping records? They don't make sense. The Sheta Djew owns or is invested in at least half a dozen businesses that the Community relies on — Crimson Elixir, Shifteeze, Battle-Plan — but where are the factories? The warehouses? They should be as rich as Croesus, but their bank accounts show only a modest balance. Where's the money? Jones may not be the mastermind, but she has them on speed dial. My bet is she doesn't get her hands dirty."

"Hmmm... Run anyone she spoke with through the registry. Any other activity?"

"Possibly. I've seen one shy sort of fellow several times throughout the day. He's made no attempt to get near Jones. It may be a coincidence."

"Let's not gamble on the possibility of coincidence. Keep me updated. Stay safe."

"Will do… Oh, Jones just spotted a birdcage. Think she could use it and a hairpin to rob a bank?"

<h1 style="text-align:center">Chapter 15: Egg Drop</h1>

Kenny: April 17th   at Sullen Creek Farm

"Uhhh-ah," I yawned, stretching back in my squishy office chair, careful not to disturb Mel, who'd plopped his ruffled head on my foot in a rare show of camaraderie.

"Nanandi seylombet," I groaned triumphantly. *Package retrieved.*

Crickets.

"Tetreel kendim. Tinni dahl, Padŭ," Oscar asked. *Quest complete. Copy, Padŭ?*

"Yes, I heard," Muma Padŭrii replied smoothly in Blue Tongue. "Blom's off the quest board. Where's the orrery?"

"Workshop," I sang, peeling off the neck sensor with exaggerated relief as I logged out of Guardian. I hated being watched.

"Complications?"

"None," I snapped. New quest, same old question.

"No one was there," Oscar added, cutting off the usual spat.

"I know — I watched in-game," Padŭ explained. "Weaver's Rube Goldberg setup confused the programming. We'll know soon enough whether it was a glitch or active interference. It's stirred up a storm of speculation on Egress; we locked the server, but enough players saw the fire at Halberd Krog's palace. It was visible all the way in Tresling. More cleanup for Arlo and Evelyn, assuming they're cleared of aiding and abetting this disaster."

Oscar's head swiveled toward me like a marionette.

"Oh," Padŭ said, driving another nail in the coffin, "the APA arrived ten minutes after Blom's wards triggered; they've been wrestling the chaos for six hours now. If they're paying attention, they'll connect the incident to Egress. We'll have to fall back on the secondary system. It isn't ready, so the Mulberry would be running missions blind."

Some people were born pessimists. I'd followed Covenant policy; if they found my actions excessive, they needed to rewrite the rules.

"Weaver," Oscar rumbled, his tone soft but insistent.

His doubt stung like acid, but I met his gaze.

"I didn't use my magic," I said. "Blom's security failed to read the fine print when they designed their wards — I just exposed the flaws. It was a deathtrap. I had to do something!"

"He stacked apántisi wards, not knowing they burst outward," Colt snarled, backing me up — furious at the lack of trust my colleagues had in me. "Leaving them untouched would have killed people, violating our core beliefs. Weaver put lives ahead of convenience."

The unspoken 'so get off her case' hung awkwardly in the air.

I ripped off my headset, struggling to breathe. A molten river surged through me as my emotions tumbled over each other, too quick for me to identify. I stormed out, leaving Mel grumbling under the desk, and splashed cold water on my face in the bathroom, counting breaths to keep from lashing out at an innocent wall.

Padŭ always got under my skin. Her loyalty was absolute, but old wounds skewed her perspective. The irony? She'd say the same about me.

Colt had schooled a doyenne! That happened. A grin crept over my mouth, followed by a cackle. Padŭ's face as he laid into her — priceless. There were…seven people, maybe, who might have gone toe-to-toe with a doyenne on my behalf — eight now. My eyes stung, but no tears followed. The unexpected loyalty speared deeper than anything Padŭ could chuck at me.

But apántisi wards? We hadn't covered them in his assigned reading. If he was studying independently, when did he find time to flirt with Davy's apprentice?

With a sigh, I marched back to the game room, jammed on my headset, and cut Padŭ off mid-sentence.

"We don't answer to you, Muma Padŭrii," my voice somehow steady. "Take it to the elders if you have a complaint. I have faced the judgment of my peers before, and when their eyes searched mine, they saw only themselves gazing back. I'm ready to face them again. Meeting's over. Sheb ylmoora fohsha." *The river flows.*

"Sheb ylmoora fohsha," Oscar echoed, smirking. "Log off, kid. You did well."

"I didn't do anything except watch," Colt protested.

"You didn't do anything except watch well."

The orrery had no visible screws. The magically reinforced gold withstood my sawzall. More accurately, it broke my sawzall. We'd tried blow-torching it — a ward in place so we didn't accidentally burn down the workshop. The orrery remained infuriatingly intact. I'd thought dealing with the monstrosity would be an admirable way to vent my frustrations, but it only fed my fury.

"What's next?" I asked Colt, who was sweeping up the ashes from a hunk of beadboard I'd forgotten to move.

Mel looked up at my apprentice and waited patiently for the kid to dazzle us.

"You've only tried physical means, so ley energy?"

"Yes, although ley energy is physical, even though most people aren't sensitive to it." I held a hand near an orb, allowing angry ley needles to prick at my palm as it passed. Soon, you'll be free, I promised. We're not giving up. "Do you know why I didn't start with it?"

"The orrery's magical in nature," he said. "We don't know how it will react to a ley attack."

"Correct." If it were feeling pugilistic, heaven help us. "I'm setting up another ward. An artifact like this will have its own defenses. If something goes wrong, obey Oscar — no heroics. Do not try to save me from my stupidity. Capiche?"

"Yes, ma'am."

"Wear your glasses," I said, removing mine. Breaking them wasn't an option.

Colt eyed his pair with dread.

Behind him, Oscar crossed his arms and loomed.

"I get it," I told him. "It's weird knowing other planes are that close — beings watching us on the toilet. But to craft gates, you need to see the lines. Remember, they know we have VIP seats to them petitioning the throne, too."

He nodded, put them on, then ripped them off, stumbling toward the door, vomiting spectacularly.

That was the reaction I'd expected earlier, when he first tried them on. Confused, I looked around, noticing that I now shared space with a very large something — a giant, winged centipede, laying its slimy, softball-sized eggs in the flesh of a mangled corpse on a neighboring plane. A sickly web of membrane inside each egg pulsed rapidly...until it burrowed deeper into the meat.

Mel whined. Me, too, Mel; me, too.

"Give it twenty," I muttered, patting Colt's back.

Oscar, rather unfeelingly, handed him a mop.

May 17ᵗʰ at the Agora in Chicago, Illinois

"Another one?"

"Another two," O'Brien corrected, smiling as the breeze ruffled his curls affectionately.

Rufe's scowl deepened, his bloodshot eyes and drooping mouth radiating weariness and strain. Poor fellow worked too hard, and it showed. He would never lower himself to fidgeting, per se, but he did swirl his ice cubes rather more than necessary. Sunlight would do him good; even vampires need vitamin D.

"You're sure Ms. Waites is warning us of a potential leak?" he asked, lowering his voice as patrons passed by. Holy Water, the sleek rooftop bar atop the Agora, buzzed for one p.m. — mornings and evenings were its usual peak times.

"Yes. We had a devil of a time interpreting the fourth episode," O'Brien confided. "Melisande used sign language and, at four hundred, she has a distinct tremor. It was some YouTube channel whose schtick was fake ads for comical products used by preternaturals — delousers and the like. Once her handlers realized the vulgarity was deliberate, things sped up considerably."

"In the fifth vision, Sandy sang a one-woman opera — a superb soprano, you know, despite the quaver. I was fortunate enough to witness that one. The story followed a young woman, cruelly abandoned by her therianthrope lover when she fell pregnant. She sued him, presenting eight Cocker Spaniel pups to the court — supposedly his offspring. The lady thought all shifters were wolves and that the puppies would pass as cubs. Her former lover, however, was a selkie. Case dragged on forever. Turns out even water fae can drown in enough stupidity."

O'Brien sipped his whiskey before continuing. "Seers aren't infallible, but for these episodes to occur, a leak must hold a significant probability. The compulsion's clear — Sandy drives herself beyond her physical limits. It's better now that we've caught on; we record the episode, then suggest she's seen a possible leak, she nods, and goes to rest. There can be no doubt, Rufe."

"No other seer has reported similar visions?"

"None. Few are generalists — most of us track one or two people at most. No one alive today could hold a candle to Sandy at the height of her powers. She remains formidable, even now. And visions are coming faster; we're running out of time."

"What would you suggest, Chairman? I can speak to Director Serrecold, but without a name, occupation, or something to indicate the culprit, I don't know what good it will do. Give me even a suggestion of evidence and I'll raid Irit Jackson's office within the hour," Balbay begged. "Until we know what direction to take-"

"Senator Balbay, Chairman O'Brien, sorry to cut in — there's a message for you, Chairman."

The server set a silver plate on the table and melted into the crowd. O'Brien, studying the mark of a Crann Bethadh on the creamy envelope, frowned and cracked its seal.

"Your plan for a quiet meeting's not going well," Rufe noted dryly. "What?"

O'Brien had paled, his breath hitching, as he read the note. Shaking his head, he crumpled it.

"Nothing," he said, tossing it on the table with the straw wrappers. "A project with an unexpected setback."

The words hung awkwardly between them, only fading with the burn of whiskey as they nursed their drinks.

"I'll impress the importance of the visions on Serrecold," Balbay promised. "But we need a na-"

Thwack.

Two tables exploded into shards, nearly pelting them with debris. Chairs scattered like pins. A wall of curious patrons materialized and pressed in from all sides.

"It fell from the sky!"

"How did it get past the wards?"

"A body!"

"What the-"

Both men surveyed the blue sky, staring as a monstrous creature — nine feet tall, with a crocodile head atop a humanoid body, pupilless eyes glinting with malice — passed overhead. It was held aloft by a pair of pale bat wings and covered with fine translucent fur and a loincloth. A second Hound, with an eagle's head, landed lightly on taloned feet and slung the corpse over a muscled shoulder.

"Cora Wells," O'Brien breathed, recognizing the dead fae.

"Ah… Dietricksen's fugitive," murmured Rufe, gulping reflexively. "No marks. Mara wanted an object lesson."

Seven Hounds followed the first, the last hauling a quivering mass — presumably Wes Pavlica, although the former representative was unrecognizable.

"Excellent; a little rough for the wear. Still, he's alive. Take him to his cell and deposit that in the morgue."

The serene voice of Judge Dietricksen cut through the din, earning a jump from the onlookers. Turning on a heel, she stalked to the bank of elevators, the Wild Hunt falling in line behind their mistress.

"Please! Help me!" the captive shrieked, shrill when all else was silent. "They killed her! Fed on her energy! They'll feed on me! Please!"

No one moved until the elevator doors had closed, cutting off the screams.

"What? No time for autographs?" Rufe muttered, masking his nerves with sarcasm. He rattled his glass and signaled an oblivious server. "Another?"

"I won't say no," O'Brien agreed, his hands shaky. "The mind that can command eight of those things…"

"Quite," his companion agreed, as he gathered the tumblers and trash. "And there they go…"

The patrons drifted to the stairs in a mass exodus. Rufe snorted.

"They came for the show," O'Brien deduced.

"Dietricksen probably advertised — reminding the plebs what to expect from the mercy of the court. Stay — yours is GlenDronach Allardice?"

Eli: May 17ᵗʰ at Sullen Creek Farm

"Because," the girl, perched on the rail, watching little waterfalls gurgle down into the river below, explained in a fake-patient voice, "they need to fatten us up first! It's in all the stories. Here, read this part."

I recognized the green binding and swirling script — the Grimms. Of course. The brothers had seen fit to rearrange a few facts to make the stories more appealing.

"Why take care of us, then? Buy us clothes, bicycles," demanded the boy. The girl might be the talker, but the boy was the thinker. "They gave us cell phones!"

He threw some rocks in the water, his face screwed up like he might cry.

"Fattening takes time," insisted the girl. "People are educated. They read!" She waved the book at him. "The old tactics don't work anymore. Free-range eggs are better than the other kind — free-range children, too. They act nice to keep us here!"

"But there are lots of children here — fatter children, and they don't get eaten."

A rock disturbed a hellbender lounging in the shallows. The snot otter hissed, its color changing from mottled green to a glowy acid-yellow, before disappearing into the deeps.

"Yes, their children. They'll help eat us. Maybe a hand instead of a drumstick? New witches must come from somewhere. Look, we know that the stories are true. There are vampires, witches, and things. Why would we believe that they're misrepresented?"

"Because if all the stories are true, then that means I'm evil. I don't want to be evil."

"Pfft. Yours is a genetic evil — the insistence of nature. It doesn't count. They eat children. That's true evil!"

"She's right," I said, savoring their shock as they finally noticed me. I shut my book —*Hereditary Magic*, far superior to fairy tales — and peered down from the loft of the covered bridge. "Blood's a renewable resource if you're careful. Kids? Once they're cooked and eaten, that's that. That's why Mom and the aunts use scouts like Emmy — luring gullible children to the farm. We won't get to eat you, though. Once you're at a good weight, you'll be processed and sold for someone's solstice celebrations. Not all witches can afford to eat kids; some of us have to eat human food."

I recoiled for dramatic effect, and they turned a satisfying green. Despite her own arguments, the girl wasn't convinced.

"Why tell us?"

"I'm the spawn of evil, remember? If I'm not even going to enjoy a nicely roasted hand at Summer Solstice, at least I can have the fun of telling you that every wicked idea you've had is absolutely true. You'd be so much better off running away now."

I turned back to my book, letting the suggestion settle.

"Then...they are witches," said the boy.

After the initial flash of anger — my family were practitioners, not witches — something unpleasant squirmed in my middle. I ignored it. The boy was too naive for his own good, and the girl was blatantly hateful. They needed to be taught a lesson.

"Practitioner is the proper term," I corrected.

"And they only want us here because we're...food?"

The question hit harder than expected, swelling sour and sharp in my gut. The boy was newly risen — still new to our world, where every shadow could hide a monster. I recognized the look — on kids and even some adults hiding on the farm — swallowing every word told to them. It wasn't his fault, even if it was dumb. The girl glared, daring me to keep the lie going. Tempting, but the fun was gone.

"No," I grumbled, climbing down from the loft, sneakers thudding on the planks. "I made it up. She ticked me off, so I lied; it was stupid. We are practitioners, but no one eats people. And if we're reported, we'll be the ones running. Mom and the aunts are good. They rescue people — kids like you, who were raised by norms. Once you've adjusted, they'll offer you a choice — stay here, move to Wenen, or join another guild."

The girl chose that moment to elbow the boy, nodding toward the green book.

"It's weird when tons of stories match up. What happened to the books that said something different?" I grumbled, chucking out a few verbal breadcrumbs and watching a firebird soar past, its light flickering off the trees.

Chapter 18: Sweet Relief

May 19th in Chicago, Illinois

Veritas watched — again — as his brocade coat smoldered, withering into ashes. His death's head mask taunted him as the ifrit pranced around, looting his unprotected corpse.

He wasn't dead-dead, of course — just temporarily dead. He'd taken the precaution of refreshing his Elysian tattoo, good for fifteen deaths, before embarking on this ill-fated crusade. This investigation was pushing him toward bankruptcy.

Weaver's success pointed toward a deal with the creators — motive, means, and opportunity. No other theory offered as much. He'd emailed the authors of Egress to see if they would sit for an interview with The Simulator, the digital magazine he'd freelanced at for twenty years.

While waiting for their reply, he tried replicating Weaver's wins. Getting the timing and moves right proved to be an aggravating proposition. Veritas memorized her keystrokes. He had equipped with the same, or similar, weapons and spells. His Mameluke wasn't quite there, but his Falx was in a different class altogether. He had made it farther than ever before, banking experience like it was going out of style, but still died.

"Damn it, it doesn't make sense," he groused. She fought like her ship was on the line; he died like it was a speed run!

The Ifrit was a no-go...just like the dragon, siren, and vampire hamsters before it. Maybe the mistake was starting at the top of his wish list. The Flame of Kaga's Tor was the only quest where he could read Ehlidantus's grimoire. Oh, the things he could do with Ehlidantus's Wrath…and, if he had the Fluted Cockle, he could command the Dancer from anywhere in the Realm or in Wenen!

Veritas stopped fantasizing and flipped through his notes. He would aim for a more modest target...a quest that he'd won through shortcuts.

Ah, yes, that would do.

In-game, he resurrected in his cabin aboard the Dancer, naked, and four pounds lighter. Only a few possessions remained on his person. The ifrit had added his Mameluke sword, tricorn hat, and a few other fripperies to its hoard. It was to be expected — he had exquisite taste. Opening his inventory, Veritas switched out weapons and restocked his potions.

Purpose lending him drive, he strode to the transmitter. "New coordinates, Mr. Maitland. We're for the Shewi Khewew. I'm going duck hunting!"

The magnificent blue-tipped green-spangled crimson-crested Milnederian duck soared out over the flaming sea, disappearing into the sunset. Veritas had defeated Edmutt Spite, the smuggler helping himself to Wenen's endangered birds to sell to the Realm's elite. He was a placeholder, though — a liaison. True victory required taking out the leader of the enterprise.

"That was a mistake, lad," a gruff, yet oddly genteel voice assured him.

Veritas gave the therianthrope pirate captain a bow. "Guinness the Menace, I presume?"

"Aye, and who might I be 'aving the pleasure of killin'?" inquired the Menace.

That was his cue. Veritas scampered up the rigging like a white-handed gibbon. The enormous frigate had nets strung between the booms of the foremast, mainmast, and mizzen mast. It was completely illogical and an idiotic stage for a swordfight, but Weaver had defeated the duck-smuggling Menace there, and so would he! Veritas heard a flintlock discharge — a miss.

He pulled himself over the edge of the net and rolled twice, evading another bullet. Pulling his pistol, he fired through the net, knocking the pirate's flintlock into the ether.

"You 'ave a thirst for pain, boy. If ya doona want ta die quick, I'm willing ta kill ya slow."

The captain's hands shifted, deadly claws sprouting and, with a rip, a scaled tail burst out the back of his breeches. The cold-blooded fiend ascended with blinding speed. Veritas fired again, but the Lacertian darted out of the way, landing in front of him. Veritas drew his sword and slashed. Menace leaped high, flipping in the air, landing behind him.

Veritas heard the whisper of a sword leaving its sheath and dropped to his knees, stabbing beneath his armpit. A blade arced over his head, followed by a grunt — first blood. Veritas twirled, elated to see the wound wetting the pirate's thigh. His triumph was short-lived, however. Foot-long spikes erupted from the lizard-man's spine and tail, shredding his clothes.

The captain swung his lethal tail, lunging as Veritas hopped to avoid the appendage. He managed to twist out of the way and parried a sword thrust, but the blow knocked him back. A series of powerful maneuvers followed, causing Veritas to retreat further. Frantic, he skipped some command phrases, desperate to riposte. He tried taking the offensive, earning him a stripe along his ribs. He remembered to breathe and pushed himself faster...harder, struggling not to pound his keyboard into splinters.

He was losing.

The Menace nodded, chuckling. "You understand, lad. This is where you end. You were mildly diverting. If you 'ad recognized your mortality sooner, you might 'ave made me break a sweat."

He was going to die. After everything he'd done...the risks he had taken! He'd broken the law for this shit! He had to do something!

Recklessly, he battled on, feinting to the right and sailing over another tail swipe. The lizard-man, watching his every move, took the bait, protecting the wrong side. Veritas lunged, committing everything to the move.

His blade sank into scaled flesh, spearing through the pirate's ribs. Menace looked down in surprise, then up at Veritas.

Shit!

He'd missed the heart. Veritas yanked the sword free and delivered a brutal onslaught of thrusts and slashes, fear driving his sword.

The bleeding Lacertian wheezed from a collapsed lung, slowing by the second. Veritas, unwilling to trust the role reversal, kept up the barrage while sliding a throwing knife from his wrist guard. Between breaths, he flicked the blade end over end. It punctured Menace's left eye. Veritas lunged a second time, his steel blade sliding straight into the pirate's black heart.

The universe ground to a halt. After five seconds, Veritas allowed himself the luxury of a deep breath.

He'd won.

Death had stalked him, tangible and terrible. He had shaken hands with mortality.

The heavy weight of the dead Menace dragged his blade down, and the ruined body slid off the tip.

Veritas gasped, his body reeling. He felt...strange. He panted, breathing fast but without pulling oxygen in.

A whine broke through his panic, and Veritas looked from the screen to Russell, who, although curled up on his doggy bed, was alert and concerned.

He was alive. It was a game. Not real.

Sweet air filled his lungs.

Veritas set his lap desk down, not even saving, and called the pretty pittie, patting the sofa, "Come, Russ."

Russell barreled over, licking Veritas's hands and face, calming his frayed nerves.

"Relief," he murmured, hugging the good boy. His brain and body were taking their time exiting the fight or flight mode.

"That's how she does it, Russell. It's real. For Weaver, it's real. She lives it. Every second. What an awful way to play."

It took longer than planned to get back to the Phantom Dancer. Even after taking Russell for a long walk, Veritas's hands shook.

The idea that Weaver would go to that bleak desert where there were only two options: live or die… It was too much. Why had she harnessed the fear of her mortality for a game? It didn't make sense.

Was he wrong? Had he followed the mesmerizing swamp lights into a mire he wanted to believe in? Was Weaver one of several avatars for Kenny Jones, but the one she used when she knew that she would win?

No! He would have found them when he'd hacked the game. But...they could be registered under a different name. Kenny must be short for something — Kendra, Kendall. It was more likely than the thought he only dared consider inside his head — that this game, some version of it, was real. That Kenny Jones was a pirate witch irl.

There was another possibility, though.

Maybe the game was only hard for him.

Sure, he ranked higher than millions of players, but he'd dedicated his life to gaming. Perhaps they would crush him if they expended the same effort. Perhaps he had reached the level of his incompetence. He would see the gamers he had led as guild leader succeed where he had failed. His friends would ascend on the leader board while he remained stagnant...and then, inevitably, fall further and further behind. The moth-heads would realize that he was less...if they thought of him at all.

What if he were a fraud?

Chapter 19: The River Flows

"This is what I've turned into," Milo shouted, shoving a battered paperback in my face.

I reached for the lines, searching for turbulence and peril, blood and ruin, but found only calm. The wards, too, were quiet. Adrenalin churned in my veins; acid licked my throat. I set my pestle down and gripped the counter, just breathing.

Usually, it was Mouse who ambushed me, sneaking up and scaring the daylights out of me, grilling me over some fresh outrage, but Milo had found his voice. He'd lambasted me four times in the last week. I didn't know whether to rejoice or be annoyed.

Reaching a place of relative serenity, I caught his arm and read the title of the book. A familiar, uber-attractive couple stared at me from a rain-slicked street, seen through a blue filter. I noted the woman's fangs, plump lips, and enormous eyes, and the way the man loomed over her with a barely contained possessive protective rage and a jawline that could grate cheese. Niamh and Darius.

Oh...no.

"You didn't tell me about this! You made it sound like I was still normal and not...a...a…"

"High-handed mansplaining alpha dude-bro waiting for the perfect unlike-any-other woman to reform him," supplied Mouse, casually leaning against the doorjamb of our pantry, arms crossed.

Her Pulitzer Prize for poetry was due in the mail any day now.

What was so wrong with a man finding a woman unique, anyway? Sure, it was a line, but that didn't mean it wasn't true.

"That!" Milo jabbed a finger at Mouse. "Be honest. Am I going to sparkle?"

"Do you want to sparkle?" I shot back.

His eyes bugged out, then narrowed. "I'd like it to be a choice."

"Mouse might scoff, but there's nothing wrong with being strong and using it to protect others."

I yanked the book out of his hand and held it up.

"This," I said, shaking Deymienne Devereaux's — total pseudonym — urban fantasy classic, *The Cold Rush of Darkness*, "is fiction — as in, adult entertainment only. It is not a resource on preternatural beings. As it happens, there are vampires with a sparkly sheen; it usually indicates a nutritional deficiency. With as little Elixir as you drink, you'd already be dazzling us with your otherworldly radiance if you were one of them. Stop starving yourself and decide who you want to be. That choice is yours alone."

I continued pulverizing lavender, neglecting to mention Devereaux's eerie accuracy. If the Covenant agreed to my scheme, she and those like her would be in trouble. I'd need to find a way to manage the fallout.

"Grow your hair long, drive a beat-up truck with three-day stubble and a bad attitude if that lights your fire — you do you. If you want to practice standing half-engulfed in shadow as you mysteriously lurk outside a...coffee...bar — have at it! If you want to develop an encyclopedic knowledge of folklore, train as a ninja, reestablish an ancient craft, and overthrow a corrupt government — fantastic, but it's on you to make it happen! Sparkle, don't sparkle; nothing and no one gets to choose for you."

"Those were strangely specific," observed Mouse, peering through a dark glass bottle. The light made it glow like a trapped ember. "Is this poison?"

"No, that's chili-infused olive oil. See the label? Only edibles are allowed in this room. Anything toxic is kept in my stillroom. Don't go in there. I'll know," I warned.

"What's that say?" Mouse demanded, pointing up to a framed handkerchief on which my paternal great-grandmother had embroidered a river scene, surrounded by script in Blue Tongue. "The letters look like lace."

"Sheb ylmoora fohsha. It translates to, 'The river flows.'"

"What else would a river do?"

The sarcasm had lessened over the last week or two, but Mouse was still fluent and idiomatic.

"A river can stagnate or dry up. It's a creed; a call to live in balance. Creation and destruction are not opposites, nor are chaos and order. They're ingredients for the continuation of life. When you live a life of balance, you'll naturally avoid a lot of problems, and good habits will anchor you through those you don't."

"Huh…"

"Now some bad news."

Both children eyed me warily, as though I was about to explain that Darius's younger, but no less dangerous, brother would break scores of hearts before he found the girl he wanted to live for, and, instead of a satisfying conclusion, their happily-ever-after would be dragged into a ten-book series. Or worse — Milo would transform into a hog-sized bloated leech like those I saw in my peripherals, jump-roping with their proboscises.

I ought to wear wrap-around glasses. Leeches were vile…but it felt weird to be completely blind to the other planes. Besides, I was vain and wraparounds only worked on certain people. I was not one of them.

"This book is kept in the locked bookshelves because it is not suitable for children. It's going back. If you have any more like this, turn them over now. I'll know if you don't. Be ready in twenty minutes; we're going to Eli's school to get you both enrolled in their summer program. It's time to lay the foundation for your future."

Something happened.

The pair exchanged a look — a variety of eye movements and head shakes. I couldn't tell what they were thinking. Something important that I ought to understand. I was crap at this. I checked the time, frustrated that Maggie would still be working for a couple of hours.

"Does that mean you're keeping us?" asked Mouse, eyeing our collection of spices with curious indifference.

The question had weight. Were they unhappy?

"Do you want to stay?"

It had been nearly three months since they'd arrived. I had no illusions as to how they felt about me, but they adored Maggie, liked Déjà, and got along with the rest of our household. They'd gained some much-needed weight. They had chores, played with the animals, and explored the grounds. They were accepting lessons on the Community and preternaturals with steadily decreasing suspicion. I'd thought they were reasonably happy, but maybe not?

"It's all right — better than the streets," Mouse shrugged. "We don't have to worry about food, police, predators, or someone noticing Milo's fangs popping out. Enrolling in school sounds official, though — like you've made up your mind. There will be paperwork and stuff. It's a hassle if it's temporary."

I loathed paperwork with the burning passion of a million dying suns. Occasionally, when it didn't pertain to my own largely fictional history, I could dump it on someone else. Ironically, when it was someone else's mess, I wouldn't have minded doing it myself nearly as much.

They waited, expectant.

Oh, right.

"You need stability, an education, and people who care. We can provide that, but a home is something you build for yourself — relationships, memories, investing in yourself. I hope you build that with us."

It happened again. Was I nailing this or traumatizing them?

"Cool, I guess," Mouse said, shrugging.

Okay, then.

"Speaking of paperwork, I'll need your full names for enrollment," I announced, as deadpan as Miss Mouse.

She'd dodged the question before, but it was worth a shot.

"Dhriti Navdeep Nair."

My shock sent a jar of mint crashing into the sink and its herbal sharpness into the air. So Mouse was named for a goddess of courage. Sounded about right.

"No, Milo — don't touch it. I'll clean it up."

Toweling off, I offered Mouse a hand.

Perplexed, she accepted, and we shook.

"A pleasure, Dhriti Navdeep Nair. I am Hazel McKenna Jones. Welcome to the Sheta Djew."

I held out my hand to Milo.

"Milo Ignacio Ruiz Pereira..."

His grip was limp.

"People are dynamic, but at their core, there is a constant — something indelible. No one will interpret or experience existence the way you do. Terrible, unfair things have happened to you, but you are still Milo Ignacio Ruiz Pereira. What is the other name living in your head?"

His eyes widened, meeting mine.

"Miguel Emilio Molina Juárez. Which am I?"

A big question.

"We don't fully understand vampirism, but I will tell you what I know and what I believe. We know ley lines connect everything — flora and fauna, stars, planes, us. It's the nervous system for the universe. Parallel planes exist alongside ours, like pages in a book where the ley lines are the spine. Alternate universes exist — realities that mirror ours — where different versions of our lives are played out and the individual is the binding."

Were they following? Hard to tell, but they were listening; I'd take it.

"The pages in our books sometimes stick together — words bleed from one page to the next and, when pulled apart, the ink transfers. It's frightening; confusing. The brain protects itself, stimulating physiological responses — the predator that exists in all of us emerges."

I paused, but Milo nodded for me to continue.

"New vampires often believe that they've evicted another soul from their body, leaving them to wander. That's not what happened. You are Milo Ignacio Ruiz Pereira, and Miguel Emilio Molina Juárez is part of Milo Ignacio Ruiz Pereira — two names, two sets of memories, but the same person. Your body is yours alone. I am the sole occupant of my body, but I am both Hazel McKenna Jones and Enid Eileen Carter."

"It's crazy," he murmured.

Too right, it was.

"Just remember — you are in charge of who you are; you're also responsible for who you are."

His face hardening, he offered me his hand again.

"Milo Ignacio Ruiz Pereira. Nice to meet you, Hazel McKenna Jones."

"Back atcha, Milo. But, please, for the love of Deymienne Devereaux and her horde of preternatural lovers, call me Kenny."

Chapter 20: Bosom Buddies

June 12ᵗʰ in Chicago, Illinois

"I shouldn't be here. I should walk out those doors," Rena Amano murmured. "Why do I let you talk me into these things?"

A crush of inflated egos, beautifully outfitted in outrageous glad rags, swept them along, deeper into the Chicago chapter house of the TC — Therianthrope Council. It was a challenging bit of architecture — a spaceship that landed in Lincoln Park — all stark white walls, glass, and concrete with nary a straight line in sight. The furniture required an illustrated manual to sit, and more than one guest mistook a sculpture for a chair. The art was, as often as not, more comfortable.

Rena's question was rhetorical, but O'Brien couldn't resist answering. The warmth of her arm on his elicited an electric, terrifying joy — love combined with a heady dose of derealization.

She was exquisite — his equal in height at six-naught, delicately curved, with vulpine bones, henna-hued eyes, and a thick mane of strawberry blond layers cascading to kiss her collarbones. The minimalist, burgundy gown she wore emphasized her graceful form.

A rake of side-eye sent a frisson of lightning coursing through his skin. It wasn't magic. She and her kin were deadly, even in their benevolent incarnations, but her absolute faith in him held him captive.

"Early conditioning," he croaked, clearing his throat.

"Darragh, this is stupid. Why am I here? Why now?"

"Indulge me, love. We'll leave early, but you'll soon see why it's worth the risk."

"It isn't conditioning," she grumbled. "It's your bloody accent. You make a few pretty sounds, and I follow along like a simpleton."

O'Brien grinned, smug.

"Folklore is full of horse shit," she quietly continued. "Men fall for sirens, mermaids, víla—"

"Vixens," he suggested.

106

"—and succubi," she went on, ignoring him, "but for a hefty percentage of straight women, leprechauns are the most beguiling of all beings. Well-groomed, funny, flush, and they do their own mending? Then there's the brogue — lethal."

"They're also noted for their poetry," he teased.

"Do not recite any limericks!"

"You seem to forget that being Irish doesn't make me a leprechaun."

"You do your best, I'm sure."

The crowd thinned, and a very correct usher confronted them.

"Your invitations, please."

O'Brien presented their card, and the usher, after peering at it through a loupe, bowed.

"This way, Chairman."

A pear-shaped dais occupied the center of the domed ballroom, ringed by tables. Theirs turned out to be in the outer ring, among the lesser mortals whose existence couldn't quite be ignored, and was occupied by a blond woman in a black column gown. She gave the impression of being both very bored and mildly livid.

"Good evening, Isolde," O'Brien said with a knowing grin. He held Rena's chair before seating himself.

"Hallelujah! Someone sane at last! I didn't expect to see you, sir."

"I didn't expect to be here, but variables shifted. Rena, this is Senior Special Agent Isolde Gerahty. Isolde, this is Rena Amano — the love of my life and my tether to reason."

The ladies exchanged pleasantries as O'Brien surveyed the room, observing a smorgasbord of political intrigues in progress.

"I wouldn't have thought this was your scene, either, Izzy," he remarked amiably.

Gerahty scowled. "Senator Balbay requested my presence — not as his date, praise be."

"That honor seems to be taken," observed Rena, nodding toward a front-row table.

"Ah ha," murmured O'Brien, eyebrows shooting up as the senator seated his plus one.

"Nice dress. Who is she?" inquired Special Agent Gerahty. "She doesn't look desperate, dim, or deranged."

O'Brien chuckled. "Representative Hazel McKenna Jones — Kenny to her friends. As I've not had the opportunity to join that number, I can't answer for her mental state."

"Who is the woman speaking with them?" Rena asked.

"Judge Mara Dietricksen of the Heliaia."

Isolde inhaled deeply, squinting suspiciously. "What's Jones's Origin?"

"You can't tell?"

She sniffed and shook her head. "Not in this crowd. Mind you, nothing could mask Balbay's stench. It's enough to gag a troll in a hazmat suit."

"You don't like him much, do you," Rena noted.

"Nope," growled Gerahty, crimson flaring in her eyes.

"Several years ago, Rufe said something...indiscreet...about Izzy that may have cost her a promotion. Suffice it to say, they'll never be bosom buddies."

"He accused me of favoring hybrids after an agent came under suspicion of selling information. I thought she was being framed and said so. He told the brass that my fae-shifter pride skewed my perception, though they only had circumstantial evidence. In the end, the agent quit — days before she was proven innocent. She sued and settled out of court. One of the suits upstairs hadn't bothered to pull his blinds, and some nitwit with a telescope in the adjacent wing decided to cash in. But I'm not bitter."

Her voice had risen, drawing sneers. Izzy smiled back, a charming simper displaying her carnassial teeth.

"That explains it," Rena murmured.

The lights dimmed, the stragglers scampering to their seats as an immaculately groomed man bounded onto the stage, a spotlight highlighting his sublime features.

"Ladies and gentlemen, welcome! Welcome to the Therianthrope Council's 186th Annual Gala!"

"You've been quiet."

Rena stared out the window into the inky depths as they drove home, her voice hoarse.

"I don't understand."

O'Brien nodded, mentally castigating himself.

As soon as Rena had seen Representative Jones, he'd been fixated on her reaction, desperate to know if his theory held. Although she had chatted and watched the performances with apparent pleasure, Rena's mind was at the other table — a raw ache buried in her gaze. His promise to leave early was forgotten.

Jones had glanced in their direction without any reaction — not a look, no remonstrance, no hasty exit. Surely that meant he was right?

"I should have warned you."

"No," she murmured. "That would have been worse. I would have questioned my certainty. How did you know?"

"That it wasn't she?"

She nodded, pain twisting her face.

His breath hitched, and he tried not to condemn himself for forcing the experiment. "I didn't. I see possibilities, nothing more. Rena, love, this is vital — at any point tonight, did you see or sense her?"

"No."

It wasn't she. Questions smothered any sense of triumph. Where was the real Hazel McKenna Jones? Who was imitating her? Why? Was she weaving this trickery or caught in someone's web? Did Balbay know? He was close to finding her — had to be. He just had to dig a little bit deeper and nudge her into position before time ran out.

"To see someone so like her and still completely different... It's surreal," Rena whispered. "Like a dream."

"I'm sorry, love. I was nearly certain it wasn't she but we're at the point where nearly isn't good enough."

Kenny: May 22nd at Sullen Creek Farm

"We're doing things differently today," Déjà said.

"I'm game."

I sank into the oversized, heated sloth chair, its velvety arms wrapping me in a hug, chin resting on my head. It purred! The ridiculous thing dominated a third of Déjà's funky living room — her client space, sitting in front of a white-and-orange geometric accent wall. A curvy mid-century sofa and coffee table were set against tambour paneling and floating planters. It was both stimulating and comforting.

Déjà set up a laptop so that we could both see. "Muma Pădurii's joining us on Zoom."

"I'm out."

I was unwrapped, up, and opening the door when she hit me with, "It's not like you to be cowardly."

I spun back, glaring, but it faltered. Despite a ten-inch height gap, she mirrored her niece, my bestie, Nore. Same forehead, dark eyes, flaring nose, and smooth ebony skin. Nore wore her curls in a voluminous lob while Déjà's changed each week; today, it was in a braided fauxhawk. Thirty years apart, but they looked like twins. I couldn't stay mad at either of them.

"It's not cowardly to avoid someone who intentionally hurts others; it is a healthy awareness."

"Pădu had reasons for her actions, and she wants a relationship with you," Déjà replied. "I think she's earned it. She is your mother."

"She's my genetic donor. Vivienne Ritter-Vine is my mom! Giving birth to me doesn't entitle Pădu to my time, my emotional labor, or my thoughts."

Déjà gave an exaggerated sigh, and I could feel the mental slap to the back of my head. "True. But that isn't all this is, is it? You're angry that she left you for a fight she knew she might not win. Isn't that what you do? She ensured your safety and training — and left, setting an example you've followed. Croía endured three decades as a helot. Doesn't she deserve a chance?"

"You're right," I said, "If those were the only facts, you'd be right. But she demanded a magically enforced promise from Mom to love me as she would. It sounds natural, and you can bet Croía meant it to be taken that way. Mom knew, though; she agreed anyway."

Déjà sat motionless, sensing trouble ahead.

"Mom is less demonstrative than Croía, though she loves every bit as hard. Because of the sacrifices my parents made, she agreed, knowing Evy would pay the penalty. Mom and Dad tried to make it work, but Evy felt the difference and resented me for it. I was hugged and kissed for every little thing."

Déjà raised an eyebrow, well aware of my aversion to being touched. My adoptive parents adapted, but it took a while before I could believe I was genuinely loved.

"The geranium," she murmured.

The plant was weeping petals all over the back of the sofa. I capped my leaking energy.

"Evy craved it, but I received it. She was ordered to use her talents to aid in my training. Then, Kuwako bonded with me instead of Evy. I felt like a thief — unworthy of love. Therapy rebuilt us, but that promise wrecked our childhood and broke Mom's heart. She couldn't balance it without it feeling forced, fake. It was cruel, pointless."

My ire vented, I felt deflated.

"Evy's spent two decades atoning for childhood tricks, but there's not a damn thing I can do to make up for what Croía did."

"It's cathartic to cry, Kenny. Don't fight it," Déjà murmured.

I laughed, but it was devoid of humor. "I would if I could — I think I'd enjoy it."

Déjà nodded, understanding my emotions better than I did.

"Is it possible that, while Croía knew the promise was a manipulation, she didn't understand the ramifications? She wanted her baby to feel her love — her only legacy. She chose your caretakers carefully; punishing them for protecting you would have been counterproductive. If you were unhappy or scared, you might have run away. She would never have risked that." Her calm voice cut through bullshit like a hot knife through butter.

I glared at Déjà, unwilling to yield. She stared back for three seconds, then pulled a fish face — a literal catfish face, whiskers included.

A breathy huff escaped me despite my best efforts.

"I won't make you talk to Pădu today," she said. "But think about this: estrangement doesn't help Evy or Vivienne — it hurts you, your family, and the Covenant. It isn't often that we get one of ours back from the dead; don't waste it because of a misunderstanding."

Ouch. Her words stung. Every one of our people had lost someone; Déjà was no exception.

"I'll tell Pădu plans changed. Burrow into your sloth; we'll pick up from last week."

As she disappeared, I obeyed, hating myself. Déjà never let her history leak into a session, so I did it for her. My thoughts only got louder while I waited.

"Peace offering," she announced, returning with two Knoppers. She tossed one to me and scolded, "Stop thinking whatever's in your head. We're not comparing tragedies."

"You tricked me," I accused without heat. "You wouldn't have sprung Pădu on me. You wouldn't do that to me or her."

She nodded. "I hate lying. Whenever we discuss Croía, you shut down before we can make any headway. It's affecting your work. Others have mentioned it. I couldn't leave it, or you'd be taken out of the field. I decided you would prefer a pry bar to shackles. I'm sorry, Kenny."

I toyed with the sloth's claws, miserable.

"Are we good?"

I sighed. "Yeah, we're good."

"Okay. Tell me about the nightmares. Any improvement?"

Chapter 22: Stalking Horse

July 1ˢᵗ in Chicago, Illinois

Veritas had lingered in a funk, indifferent to food and games alike, for days. The creators of Egress stonewalling him hadn't helped; they refused to talk to anyone after the magic storm wrecked Halberd Krog's palace. And his alien expert had testily explained that intergalactic visitors would not be interested in MMORPGs. Very short-sighted of them, in his opinion.

Guinness the Menace had taunted him — then Veritas killed him, survival instinct directing his actions. But…it didn't prove anything. Adrenaline could sharpen or ruin a player's game.

He paced his cabin — naked again because he'd missed one toothy hamster. The vicious pest had looted his bloodless corpse, snagging his backup-backup tricorn hat, brocade coat, and his last pair of black breeches. No doubt, his gear would make a handsome nest in which to rebuild the vampire hamster population; nothing said rodent romance like brocade. Without his trademark garb, he felt as bare as his pixelated skin, though the game's "clouds of confusion" spared players' modesty.

Veritas couldn't shake the pirate's taunt — bosses didn't trash-talk. Moderators tweaked games for flair, but mocking players? Had he caught some conspirator's eye, earned a death mark? No, that was absurd. If they'd cottoned on, he'd have been arrested. He flicked the transmitter's horn.

"Mr. Maitland, back to the Mulberry."

A disguise was in order—no need to broadcast yet another hamster humiliation.

"Elessar38! Might I interest you in an elfstone?" wheedled an elderly wizard vendor.

"Another time."

"Hail, Longstrider!" bellowed a stout, cigar-chomping dwarf.

Veritas pulled up short, wary of the dubious honor being paid him. Windstone Church, the Mulberry harbormaster, spelled trouble when he appeared. It wasn't certain whether he was an NPC or a stalking horse. Politeness couldn't hurt, in any case.

"Well met, Windstone Church. How may I be of service?"

"Ship? I've no entry for an Elessar38 logged," the dwarf barked, puffing on his cigar as he waved a logbook.

Veritas waved the acrid smoke away from his face.

"The Phantom Dancer."

Total cooperation — nothing to see here!

Church made a note in the leather journal. "I see...Mr. Elessar38. Been some odd goings-on; mind yourself," warned the dwarf.

Veritas shrugged, unsettled by the interaction. A surreal itch lingered...like he was on a train and the points had switched when they shouldn't have. It was probably nothing. He just needed a walk with Russell, fresh air, sunshine, a bit of reality.

He turned down a narrow alley and entered a decidedly uninviting, dingy storefront —depressingly threadbare for a tailor supply shop.

"What the *hell* have you done to yourself?" demanded a shrill voice in horror.

From behind a counter twice his height ran Beppe of Beppe's Bobbins. The gnome gingerly clasped the corner of Veritas's cloak and examined it. "Are you doing penance for some fell deed?" Beppe shrieked, then in a flat, suspicious tone, "Were you robbed? Are you...indigent?"

Veritas chuckled.

Fashion trumped all but Beppe's bottom line. "Fear not, friend Beppe. It is only my apparel that has fallen on hard times. Do you have black brocade frock coats, black breeches, and tricorn hats in stock?"

Beppe was not appeased. "If you're not stony broke, then whyyyy? Where is the polish, the gravitas?"

"Didn't want to be recognized! Everyone knows I shop here. Would you want me to be recognized in anything less than the best?"

"Fine," conceded Beppe, eager to purge the gauche ensemble — mind you, it did coordinate with the dusty shelves. "Divest yourself of those filthy...vestments. I shall assemble the necessaries."

Veritas parted the dingy curtain, entering the pink marble palace beyond. Beppe trailed him, snipping a pair of shears aggressively and towing a burn barrel.

"Strip," snapped the tailor.

Some minutes later, Veritas emerged, scrubbed raw and with five upgraded ensembles. He wore Beppe's shadowy teal-on-black pick — lending him a sinister sheen, a malevolent phantom under lamplight or moonlight.

After bidding farewell to the peerless Beppe, Veritas restocked his supplies and weapons, then hit the Cocoon. A fellowship of halflings, rangers, wizards, and a few orcs nearly had him cornered, but he evaded all of their goodwill. Stupidly, he'd forgotten to switch back from alias mode, and Beppe had neglected to remind him. Even with his chimerical suit, the mummers were eager to adopt him.

As there were no illegal activities planned, it hardly mattered. Veritas disappeared into the back hallway, changed modes, and headed for his office. He wanted to test Weaver's consistency. Guild-specific quests ranged from beginner levels to expert, but Veritas rarely assigned them unless asked to do so.

That was about to change.

He entered a request for Weaver to undertake Atlas's Burden. No player had ever attempted it. Success would boost the Saturniidae's rep and cement Weaver's legend. If she took the bait, she would have one day to complete the challenge. Veritas would be ready and watching. Maybe, then, he'd prove he wasn't the fraud; she was.

Chapter 23: Subject to Change

July 3rd in Parkville, Missouri

"Ghost, I've got something," announced Special Agent Brandon "Hatter" Young, the APA's hacking whiz. A nice trilby or a rakish fedora never mussed his curls; however, his talent for code and discrete mathematics, rivaled only by his preternatural ability with beard oil, earned him the nickname.

Dorrit peered at Hatter's screen, focus hardening his already stern expression. They were short on time but had to do this just right.

"The probability of a cluster-strike spiked above twenty percent. I've marked the potential targets — red for victims, blue for practitioner baubles. The projections are subject to change as new information comes in."

"Good work," Dorrit murmured. "We concentrate on the living targets. Brings us down to…thirteen. Crow will take the West and Pacific Northwest regions. Gemini the South-Southwest. We'll take those in the Midwest, Mid-Atlantic, and Northeast."

The program chimed.

"Another ping," Hatter murmured, "Artifact. Probability is up…three percent and rising."

Dorrit stalked to his desk, barking, "Ridel, one sensitive per detail — top-tier. Call in favors, blackmail the Quorum if you must. Eyes on every mark, cameras in their homes within twelve hours."

"I've just the thing," the fae nodded, his wide mouth curling into a happy grin. "Senator Thrasher's little princess got caught selling pixie dust three days ago — and Thrasher owns Pest-Ex."

"MacDonnell, four agents per shift, including a warlock — exclude us; we stay on Jones. Outsiders are on a need-to-know basis. Sarduy, gear up for the worst-case scenario. Blake, scout vantage points — homes, jobs, schools."

"Our girl's on the move," reported MacDonnell, turning her laptop.

A yellow Beetle purred outside Jones's home — with Jones, Davy Moran, and three kids climbing in.

"Are those…"

The familiar half-starved waifs had filled out and looked...happy. Excited. How kids ought to look — and not what he would have expected.

"Representative Jones, Davy Moran, Eli Moran — Davy's son, Dhriti Nair, and Milo Pereira — Caterham's runaways," MacDonnell confirmed. "We got the school records today."

"Right. The children's safety comes first. If they're in danger, move in." Dorrit's eyes blazed with manic energy, but he calmly murmured, "Recruit someone in the school. Thoughts, sir?"

O'Brien's head, suspended like an unsavory specimen in a jar, peered out of a glass orb set on Dorrit's desk.

"Watch how you approach any members of the Sheta Djew," he warned. "A fanatical lot — Serrecold's sniffed around Jones's backyard for years with no luck. I'll be out of contact, tonight — the Quorum's peacocks are prancing."

The Agora in Chicago, Illinois

"You're doing it again."

"What am I doing?" O'Brien asked brightly, stowing his phone, a bare thread of relief in his voice. He'd baked every night for a week, yet no visions had come to him. But Dorrit had finally seen the kids. That, at least, had gone right.

"Smirking." Agent Gerahty squinted at him. "Something went right, didn't it?"

O'Brien raised his eyebrows, his baby blues dancing, and let the smirk widen.

"That's a yes," she said, grunting as the lady behind her scooted into her chair. Gerahty waved off the woman's apologies, glaring at the lasagna splattered across her crisp, white blouse. "What is going on today? It's a madhouse!"

The sixtieth floor of the Agora buzzed with unusual life. Sæhrímnir — or the Cafeteria, as most called it — claimed half the floor, its geometric partitions of stylized flora and fauna framing intimate dining rooms. Open 24/7 to cater to the Community's split of day-dwellers, night-owls, and twilight-denizens, it rarely saw this kind of crowd.

Gerahty sneered at the sea of new tables clogging the rooms.

"The amendment on the Shunned Protocol Omnibus Act is up tonight," O'Brien said, picking cilantro from his curry. He loved the dish, loathed the herb. "Everyone's picking sides. Over there," he jabbed his fork over his shoulder, "Senator Rufus Balbay, the Correctionists' heavyweight champ, pushing for truth, justice, and a preternatural U-turn."

Gerahty's eyes flicked to the indicated corner, where power players traded barbs and backslaps.

"And in this corner," O'Brien nodded across the room, "Tisiphone Shepherd's crew resides, ready to spit fire for the status quo. Ironic, isn't it?"

"Ironic because?" Gerahty muttered, dabbing at the lasagna stain with a damp napkin.

"Her name — Greek Fury, punisher of oathbreakers. Warlock originally meant 'deceiver,' and the first were, indeed, traitors, apprentices that stole secrets. The Community spun some PR and made 'em into heroes."

His eyes lit, waiting for Izzy to appreciate the humor.

Gerahty, consumed with her own ideas, chewed her lunch, eyeing the room's imaginary dividing lines. "So, the middle is neutral?"

"Just so," O'Brien concurred, glancing at Judge Dietricksen indulging in a luscious afternoon tea in the dead center. "Scavengers, mostly, except her. An Unrelenting, but the most sensible of the lot."

Dietricksen looked up, catching his stare with a wolfish grin.

"Scavengers," Gerahty echoed, clocking the exchange.

"Someone has to pick the corpses clean."

O'Brien raised his Perrier, toasting Dietricksen. She mirrored him with her teacup.

"Does any of it matter anymore?" grumbled Gerahty.

"Should any government be allowed to outlaw an entire people? If they do it once, they'll do it again. This isn't Stardew Valley; it's Gladius!"

Gerahty raised her eyebrows — as though he'd started speaking in tongues.

"Sorry, they're PC games. Did some research to understand Sandy's prophecies better. What I meant was, an authoritarian government is never benevolent."

His companion's eyes widened, surprised.

"You're a Correctionist?"

Beside them, a rumpled suit stumbled through the crowd, nearly clipping their table.

"That was fast! Good news?" his buddy greeted him.

"No. She's stuck in Missouri, and the signal's crap. Line disconnected three times. She's off-grid indefinitely."

"That's bullshit. Agency cases take precedence."

"It is the Agency — for her, Hewlitt, Aubert, and Kua. Gotta be a warlock assignment..."

The rumpled suit froze, spotting O'Brien and Gerahty as his buddy waved him quiet. Jaw tight, he sat.

"I'll deal with 'em, sir," Gerahty said, rolling her eyes as she stood.

"Thanks, Izzy," O'Brien hissed, staring the agent down, grabbing blindly for his buzzing phone. "Shit! Melisande had another vision."

Chapter 24: First Test

Kenny: July 4th at Sullen Creek Farm

"Baked beans?"

Mel stayed calm, unruffled by the tension in my voice. I scanned the buffet, sweating, teetering on panic. No Fourth of July was complete without baked beans — caramelized edges, spicy sauce sopped up with cornbread. It was a necessity!

I slowed my darting eyes: potato gratin, cheesy squash casserole, hashbrown casserole.

"Check," Derringer said, pen pointing to a turquoise dish brimming with bubbling beans — directly in front of me. I'd brought it out not two minutes ago. "The messier sides are up front, making shorter spoon trips."

I clucked in breathless relief, scanning the spread. All good...

"Potato salad?"

Potato salad was almost more important than beans.

A soft breeze brushed my face as I sweated doubt on the screened-in porch. Heirloom tomato salad filled a small turquoise bowl, pan-fried okra was heaped in a big coral one — spelled crisp, and a white bean salad sat in a medium yellow bowl.

"Check."

Derringer pointed to the largest coral bowl, standing proud among lesser options.

I exhaled.

"B...b...."

"Breathe," he said gently, "try again — slowly."

I inhaled deeply.

"B...barbecued chicken."

"Bravo. Check."

He nodded to cookie sheets heaped with burgers, hot dogs, and barbecued chicken set on warmers.

"Armand's grilling more."

"Fruit salad? Corn on the cob? Mac and cheese? Watergate salad? Strawberry shortcake," I blurted, racing against my jumbled thoughts.

Derringer's metallic mustache quivered as the robot smiled, putting a gentle alloy hand on my shoulder. "This is a feast. Perhaps you haven't thought of everything, but you have thought of enough. The celebration will be perfect, not because of the food, but because we're with our friends. Everything's delicious. No one needs three kinds of coleslaw. Others will bring things even though you tell them not to."

The knot in my chest eased, Derringer's Charleston drawl soothing me — an echo of my biological father.

He was right. Our unity mattered, not the minutiae.

"Thank you."

"That's why I'm here," he said, squeezing my shoulder. "Check on the beasties while I handle paper plates and napkins."

"Good idea. I mean, Oscar is perfectly capable, but..."

"But you need to know. I understand."

I smiled at him. He always did.

With a lighter heart, I marched to the horse barn, Mel dogging my heels. Even with my glasses on, I could almost see the strong sound barrier arcing over the building. The ward danced against my skin as I passed. Inside, all was calm and slightly unnatural. Dark, liquid eyes peeped out of the stalls at me. I murmured to the equine occupants, finding only clean boxes, gleaming coats, fresh hay and oats, and contented mounts as I handed out carrots and apples.

The little prairie, gardens, grove, our absurdly cheerful Sullen Creek — which was, in truth, a fair-sized river, the house, and petio were all sheltered by excellent wards. Fireworks wouldn't scare the animals or litter the fields.

Returning to the house, I spotted guests heading for the dining porch, each carrying something. Derringer had called it — our barbecue was officially a potluck. Why did I always fret about a potential shortage? If anything, we had too much.

Go bags!

Anxiety stiffened my limbs. I'd forgotten pub containers! Davy was still at work. Hands trembling, I dialed her number.

"Roll for charisma."

Armand rolled and grinned — dimples on display and teeth bright against his dark skin. "Twenty-three — dirty," he purred, his lyrical voice weaving seduction into three words.

Nore rolled her eyes. "Fine, the mine entrance swooned at your spiraling horns. The door didn't so much creak open on its rusty hinges as cooed. You managed to beguile a few planks and an unlocked latch. Next time, maybe try the knob."

His glow flared, brown eyes melting in invitation and thick lashes slowly blinking. Trouble was brewing. It was apparent that Armand had come up with something witty that would, inevitably, lead to disaster.

Nore arched an unimpressed eyebrow and pursed her lips — a warning shot.

Colt, placed between the combatants, looked uncomfortable, embarrassed, and uncertain of what was going on. Maggie, Davy, and Lou leaned in, grinning in wicked anticipation. Déjà smirked. Lon's eyes flicked to Oscar, who nodded — a bet. Oscar glanced at me. I winked and settled back to enjoy the show.

My money was always on Nore.

Music blared from my pocket — Lana Del Rey's cover of "Season of the Witch". All eyes swung to my musical butt, Armand's flirtatious downfall forgotten.

I sighed, tugging my phone free.

"Notification. Padǔ says... Oh, hell."

Mel's ears twitched.

"Go on," grunted Oscar.

"Things just got real. The Source reported that a warlock team with an attachment of sensitives has been assigned to investigate us. They are already here and watching. Anyone heading to the Mulberry leaves tomorrow." Glancing at the clock, I corrected myself, "This morning at eleven — side door. Drop-offs will be in Savannah until further notice. The main door stays locked; side door for emergencies. My proxies will be active, and the ads for Punk Bunks remain live. Business continues as usual."

You could have heard a pin drop. Sixteen sets of eyes regarded me solemnly. A few were anxious, some angry, but all were determined.

"The door shuts behind you, leaving you with the inexplicable sensation that the knob goosed you," continued Nore, her tone wry. "What do you do?"

Three seconds later, chaos hit. Oscar howled like a hound, crying. Davy's face hit the table, her neck red and blotchy, her shoulders shaking. Armand flipped his chair over; Lou choked; Lon snorted Zingiberaceous out his nose...which launched fresh hysteria.

Nore allowed herself a smirk before changing the tone. "I'll alert the cadre, but I can tell you right now, no one's going to miss this."

"Let 'em come. We're ready," Lon concurred in a dignified sputter, massaging his abused sinuses.

Goosebumps broke out as my team showed their mettle.

"There is no one that I would rather have standing beside me than the people in this room. That said, we cannot approach this as Covenant operatives. We protect the Sheta Djew," I said, nodding solemnly to Oscar. "They've risked everything because they believe in our mission. Let's prove ourselves worthy. We're guardians first, practitioners second. Nore-"

"Communication and muster drills — on and off the farm," she cut in, saluting. "The kids will be under constant watch."

"Wards and armory," drawled Lon. "We've already passed the first test. Found some cameras set up outside the borders two days ago. They won't be seeing anything suspicious."

"Excellent," I said with a nod.

"Morale," Davy and Déjà chorused.

"Medical supplies. No overtime at the clinic; everyone wears a tracker," Oscar grunted, "including you."

"Our footprint is tight, but I'll review our cybersecurity with Lady G," Arlo volunteered.

Armand assured us, "We're stocked for a siege."

"I'll fortify the sentinels," added Maggie.

"Good job, everyone. Just don't get complacent," I warned. "Our guild's lost seven this month. Let's not lose anymore. Outsiders, particularly guests, see nothing odd. Our housekeeping must be flawless."

"Oh!" A gasp came from the doorway. "We're doomed!"

Everyone jumped, gasped, or — in Arlo's case — shrieked...except Mel. He chortled.

Two faces peeked through the door at us — one pale with black curls and one smooshed and drooling nearer the floor.

If the Agency employed any soft-footed, fae children, we might be in trouble.

"Not that kind of housekeeping, Professor — ley tidiness."

"Eli," Davy scolded, scurrying over to her son. "You're supposed to be in bed. Take Mr. Spacely back upstairs this instant."

"If we're facing an invasion, shouldn't we all sleep while we can?" the eight-year-old countered.

"Fair point," Oscar grunted, rising. "Representative Jones, my fangs are yours to command. Night."

"And my axe," Lou quoted in a growl, trailing him.

"Goodnight, everyone," I replied, yawning. "Someone note that Armand took his turn."

July 30ᵗʰ in Chicago, Illinois

Denied.

Denied?

Why?

Why would any serious gamer turn down the chance for eternal glory? To become a legend?

Veritas stared at the screen, certain that some bizarre mistake had been made — a glitch in the game or a bug in an update. It made zero sense. He calmly logged out of the guild's administrative network, then the game. He serenely logged back in, closing his eyes as the page loaded while breathing composedly. Calm, calm, tranquil. He was an endless pool of placid water.

He opened his eyes.

Denied.

Weaver had turned down Atlas's Burden.

Well, he'd see about that!

Two clicks and the Saturniidae's muster roll popped up in the corner of his screen. Weaver was logged on and currently on the Mulberry. He'd talk with her face to face...so to speak. The fastest path to the wharf where the Wicked W'yatch'ch was moored was straight through the training grounds.

Excellent! He needed six points to level up and could accomplish that by running Griffin's Tail on the way!

Moments later, he barreled out of the Cocoon, dashed across a swinging bridge, and swung on a rope over open air — Indiana Jones's style — to the first few obstacle courses baby moth-heads ever navigated. Clicking on the spinning icon for the Griffin's Tail quest as he dashed through the entrance, Veritas climbed the first few nets with familiar ease. He'd run this course so often, it was effortless. Muscle memory was good stuff.

Veritas vaulted from a crow's nest onto a sail strung horizontally. Far below, he spotted Windstone Church marching through the maze of boardwalks and bridges, gazing up at him with a distinctly predatory look.

Unease stole over him. Church never left the harbor.

With additional care, Veritas leapt lightly from perch to perch until he saw the magnificent griffin silhouetted against the cloudless sky, sticking her butt up like a cat and stretching her powerful back legs in her enormous nest. He couldn't have timed this better!

Ignoring any lingering apprehension, he calculated the remaining jumps and closed the distance. With the agility of a galago, he scampered up the Mulberry's central mast, just under the nest.

Climbing into the aerie was not easy. Every handhold was a camouflaged tiger trap of jagged metal, hooks, and broken spears. Veritas took his time, moving gingerly.

He stopped in awe.

He'd forgotten how large the griffin was — all sleek, wind-ruffled feathers and razor-sharp beak. The graphics in the game were the stuff of legends.

Silently slipping over the flotsam and jetsam, he stretched out his arm and just caught hold of a flawless plume. With a quick jerk and a twist, the feather came loose.

So did something else.

Something...large...was expelled from the griffin's nether regions with tremendous force. Veritas could do nothing; fifty pounds of poo hit his head like a cannonball. His neck snapped, and the momentum swatted his body right through the base of the nest. His body bounced off crosstrees and spars, the camera angle dancing with every blow. The lowest level of the training deck flew up to meet him.

As long as he lived, he would never forget the whack of his brocaded body hitting the boardwalk — bloodied and buried in excrement. His life bar trickled down to nil.

The camera panned out as a crowd materialized around him — but not too close. The stench had quite an adverse effect on avatars.

A woman in brown leathers elbowed through the crush and stared down at him, her baffled expression melting to pity.

Weaver.

A cheerful jingle announced that he had leveled up.

Weaver had witnessed him getting vanquished by an epic shit on the noobiest of noob quests, but, hey, he'd leveled up! Fantastic.

Beside her, Windstone Church puffed smugly on his ever-present cigar, a creepy, satisfied little smile molding his mouth. He held the cigar up as if toasting Veritas, turned on his heel, and walked away with a spring in his step.

How could this have happened? No one ever died on Griffin's Tail. If asked, he would have said it wasn't possible! Since when did that griffin poop? He'd never seen any animal or construct in the game take a dump, not even a horse!

A half-memory rose, then fled. Veritas took a deep breath and chased it. Something he'd heard...in the tavern... A slurred voice… 'Forget all you've heard about that vamp queen.'

The Geralt wannabes! One had mentioned an update — Queen's Folly and Griffin's Tail.

Was this just a humiliating coincidence? Dying on the first quest most Saturniidae ever completed?

No. He couldn't accept that.

Gilded letters swirled onto the screen, announcing his demise, accompanied by an oddly upbeat dirge. Would he like to try again, beginning from the last save?

No, he would not, thank you! He would like to use one of the thirteen remaining lives on his tattoo.

Veritas searched the screen, but that option was strangely absent.

He clicked on the tattoo itself.

Zero lives remaining.

That...wasn't right.

He knew it wasn't right! He had only died twice since he last refreshed it!

Frustrated, he clicked on the list of saves. The last recorded was dated five years prior. Nearly all of his gaming history had been erased.

Cold, trembling fingers covered his mouth.

This proved it. His death had been deliberate — a publicly humiliating and premeditated murder! He had raised enough concern that someone reacted with reckless haste.

This...was awesome!

Chapter 26: Tornado Watch

August 25th in Parkville, Missouri

"Need a hand?"

John Dorrit jerked, dropping the socket wrench on his face — barely missing an eye. It made a thunk you could feel in your bones.

"Sorry! Didn't mean to startle you!"

He sat up and studied the menace above as he gently probed his cheekbone. Even silhouetted against the fading sunlight, Representative Jones was recognizable. Her dreadlocks, pulled back in a braid, coupled with her customary tank-jeans-sneakers combo, were a dead giveaway.

"No harm done," he muttered dryly. "Thanks; I'm just making an adjustment. I'll be set in two minutes."

"Good. Just…there's a tornado watch. If it takes longer than expected, the pub up the hill has a cellar. Be careful, okay?"

His flinty eyes warmed by half a degree. "I will, ma'am. I appreciate the heads up."

She smiled and nodded, turning toward a Chevy Cameo several spaces over.

Leaning on an elbow, Dorrit watched her go, waving as she pulled out.

"Keeping watch, huh?" he needled. Something teased his ear — like the crunch of fresh snow. He closed his eyes, focusing. A cool, burning, energetic sensation feathered over his senses. It tasted like mint, he decided, watching Jones signal to turn. Her truck had custom wards — good ones. Either she knew a guy, or she really was a skilled Ipseita Dualis.

"I didn't know she was coming over! She might have forgotten where she parked! By the time I twigged, she'd have heard me," O'Brien's bluster poured from Dorrit's cell, propped against a tool kit. "It doesn't matter, anyway! You're glamoured."

Dorrit wiped his hands on a greasy towel and stowed his gear. "Good thing you have baking to fall back on — if the whole soothsayer thing doesn't pan out."

O'Brien declined to dignify that with a response.

"Nice of her to mention the changing weather."

Dorrit hummed as he mounted the phone on the dash. "An unaccompanied woman approaching a strange man in a parking lot? She's either naive, reckless, or has a good reason not to be afraid. How dangerous is she?"

"Very, I would say. She's a rising star within the Quorum! No one achieves that without stabbing a few backs. However, she's still just a person of interest. It's possible to be both nice and dangerous at the same time. I've managed it for centuries."

"Sure; nice, dangerous, and treacherous," Dorrit deadpanned. "Forget baking. PR's your true calling."

O'Brien ignored him. "You weren't very chummy. Befriending her might help our cause."

"I'll get right on that."

Dorrit turned west on Mill Street, leaving downtown.

O'Brien sighed and shifted conversational gears. "This robot of hers...is it sentient?"

"Seems self-aware."

"What would that be like? No sarcasm, ineptitude, or leaks — unlike my secretary; she's been reporting to Hersch for years and still can't make decent coffee. Does Jones take custom orders?"

"Why not get a cat like the other villains, Blofeld?"

Dorrit was in a mood!

"Has Hatter wriggled past their firewall?" huffed the Chairman, changing tracks again.

"We have reservations for the twenty-eighth. Ley energy was integrated into their anti-virus software, firewalls, and VPN. Highly sophisticated. Jones takes security more seriously than it originally appeared."

Dorrit shifted his hands on the wheel, adjusting for the winding hills. Centrifugal force pulled him out of the cell's frame for a moment.

"We were forced to inconvenience some people — the kind who would make noise over a lost reservation. Ridel implied that the TC would be unhappy if they did. If you could smooth things over with the marshals, that could prevent some unpleasantness."

"I'll take care of it," O'Brien promised.

"There's our girl," murmured Dorrit, slowing.

"You caught up?"

"Near enough. She turned south — headed home," he reported. "We've found a spot just east of the farm — the drive to someone's honey hole. Good vantage point."

"Anything more on Martin's death or Caterham's disappearance?"

"Dead ends, no pun intended." Dorrit sighed, goading himself into action. "Rena's worried, sir."

His tires squealed, and the cell tumbled to the floor.

"John? You good?"

"Deer," Dorrit barked, "Stupid beast. Rena says you've been dreaming. And attempting phyllo dough."

When the warlock's eyes flicked down to the phone, the Chairman was lost in wonderment.

"What did I do to deserve her?"

Dorrit backed down a gravel lane, nearly concealed by scrubby trees and foliage. "Excellent question."

O'Brien chuckled, but it was forced. "I can't tell if you're being sarcastic or earnest."

"I'll have to work on that, sir. Effective communication is important," murmured Dorrit, sighing. "She's right, isn't she? You're plotting something."

"'Plotting' is a step too far. I've seen possibilities, John — markers indicating where we're headed. The plague of seers is that, when gifted part of the whole, we feel entitled to all of it. I admit I've been playing the augur — digging for some fragment to add to the picture. Senator Park's death signaled trouble. Now Elinor Keatling and Judge Sicotte have been assassinated — two shots to the head."

"Why didn't you tell me?"

"You'll be in the thick of it, John, and one false move..." O'Brien's voice grew harsh with frustration. "I haven't seen what I need to see — only flickers of ruin!"

The silence stretched, taut as a tripwire, as they waited for the world to explode around them.

Instead, the phone bleeped, going silent for half a second, then repeating the tone.

"A moment, sir," Dorrit requested, his voice cracking as he plucked up the cell.

"Righto." The Chairman launched into his version of elevator music —
some old ditty about bananas.

Dorrit snorted and took the call, returning moments later to 'I Am the
Very Model of a Modern Major General'.

"Sir?"

"...Ah! Yes, John?"

"Sarduy's en route; she'll babysit Jones. There's activity in Smithville. As
soon as she's here, I'm heading over. Probably a false alarm, but I want to be
on-site in case it isn't."

"I'll pop off then. Good luck! Oh — Rena and I will be heading out of
town for a few days, but I expect regular reports. And, John — don't die."

Chapter 27: Side Quest

Kenny: August 25th in Smithville, Missouri

A shiver, hot and electric, chased through my bones, along with a zing of anticipation. The combination was hard to ignore. I shot a look at Mort. His expression — like a house cat confronted with its first capybara — confirmed that it wasn't just in my head.

"The lantern was relit," I explained, pulling the mic on my headset back down. "Oscar, side quest; roll call!"

We hadn't left anyone behind; I was certain.

"Thekwane," Oscar snapped without preamble.

"Here," replied Armand.

"Gimli?"

"Yo!"

As he rattled through our call signs, I rebuilt the door — my fifth for this outing, and it felt like it. The throbbing in my head had blunted when we got back to the bridge. Buried in the in-between, I could see the ley lines but not the otherworldly beings, giant bugs, or alien hellscapes that populated the planes.

As I spindled more power, lowering my already depleted reserve, the migraine flared back to life — in technicolor splendor, pulsing a militant tattoo against my skull in case I'd failed to notice its demure presence. Kaleidoscope vision; brilliant colors and flashing patterns painted the inside of my eyelids. Some people collected stamps; I had nightmare headaches.

The peephole solidified; I went belly-down and peered through. Shadows, mist, and the Las Vegas lights dazzled me. I concentrated, willing my vision to focus. It worked as well as you'd expect.

"My vision's fried. Tell me what you see," I barked, rolling out of the way.

There was a rustle of movement as Mort flopped onto his stomach, flexing the anchor to get a good view.

"Lantern's lit," he confirmed, "There's two...no, three men dressed like us. No invisibility."

Form-fitting clothes embedded with charms and accessorized with ski masks, goggles, and gloves, in other words — bank robber chic. More likely another coven than APA.

"There's a body! A man's down. The other three are working a spell."

"Everyone is accounted for," Oscar grunted in my ear.

"Acknowledged." I tapped the kid's elbow and asked, "Are they facing in or out?"

"In."

"Move back," I commanded, shoving my fingers through the membrane. Power oozed around my fingers, nipping with needle teeth as the lines buzzed anxiously. A storm of energy was being funneled in the same direction.

"Oscar, get here. We have a complication," I snarled, urging the door to expand at an imprudent rate. "Mort, seal off the corridor and complete the quest. We'll meet back at the Cocoon."

Mort didn't move, fighting his instincts. I was debilitated, but he was only allowed to observe quests on the condition of absolute obedience.

Two seconds passed...three. He jumped to his feet. A moment later, magic swirled behind me — the walls began to compress with Mort on the far side.

Harried footfalls heralded Oscar's arrival. He hurtled over the growing barrier and dropped beside me, staring through the door.

"Unidentified man down. Lex Talionis' infiltration is suspected. I'll fetch, and you catch."

Without waiting for a response, I scurried through the slapdash gate, dropping to the floor from the middle leaf of the Ayari's dining table. I couldn't see crap, except the lines. It would do. The three practitioners had constructed a repercussion ward, dampening the resonance before it flowed into other lines, and a closed circuit, to build up energy. They intended to put on a big production, which bought us a few minutes.

Oscar joined me, his hands finding mine.

We don't have to do this: he signed.

We do.

If a warlock were killed in the home of a nice Djinn family, already suspected of harboring one of the warped, there would be a literal witch hunt.

Oscar's concern was valid. Messing with other covens was always questionable. Messing with Lex Talionis...they tended to express their displeasure in permanent ways. Still, we had to do something. Warlock or not, we couldn't let them kill the man. We couldn't let the Covenant be implicated.

A direct assault was out — too long and too loud. Warlocks never traveled alone, and I didn't fancy explaining to the APA that I'd been trying to help. Gingerly, I wove an illusion with only the lines to direct me, hoping it covered the body. The rogue practitioners, caught up in their manipulations, didn't notice the energy shift.

Sometimes, smaller magics trumped more spectacular efforts.

Does it look right?

Oscar signed: *It'll do.*

I nodded and climbed back onto the bridge. The clawed hand scraping at my brain loosened its talons, and the kaleidoscope vision cleared. The first thing I noticed was the primitive wall sealing us off from the bridge. It was an ugly effort, full of lumps and divots, and I couldn't have been prouder. Mort had shaped space in the field for the first time. I grinned and started weaving. Maggie was right; the kid was beating every metric.

Oscar pulled himself onto the bridge.

"Nearing the pinnacle," he reported, dismantling the original portal.

We worked in silence, racing the clock. My head went numb. I could hear my heartbeat, see my pulse in the veins in my eyes, and taste adrenaline on my tongue. Oscar smoothed reality back into place and took a position by the new opening. The eyelet would open below our mark. Gravity would be our friend.

Seconds ticked and the hole grew —— first, to the size of a melon, then a New York-style pizza. The man's torso flopped through, arms akimbo. I gasped even though I had expected it. Oscar locked his forearms around the fellow's chest and hauled him through. Our mystery man was a big guy — on the short end of tall and heavy with muscle. His boots caught the rim. Exasperated, Oscar dropped him. We each grabbed a leg and lifted, freeing Igor's feet.

He seemed like an Igor...likely being an evil henchman and all.

Light exploded around us. We dropped Igor's legs and dove, huddling half on top and half beside the big guy, expecting to be incinerated. The corridor burned white as biting waves of energy beat against the slender membrane separating our two ends of existence. Intellectually, we knew we were safe-ish. As flimsy as that last, thin layer was, only another hedge witch could force ley energy through it.

Once my brain accepted that I wasn't about to be burned out of existence, my skin prickled with a different sort of awareness — tingly and…weird. I put it down to relief until I noticed how hard and defined Igor's chest was. A broad, warm hand smoothed up my back, tripling the tingles.

"Morning," he moaned, his voice full of gravel. "Ow."

I glanced up, seeing red spots float across the room. The white-out had receded ten degrees. Igor was rubbing the side of his head, but his gaze was locked on the door in the wall.

This was bad.

There wasn't much to see, but if he understood any of it...

My vision went swimmy, and nausea swirled through my stomach. The man's face refused to hold still.

He turned his head, and it smeared — a kinetic glamour, used to distract, confuse, or disguise movement. And to make me seasick. I considered changing his name to Toxic Avenger.

"Witch."

His voice was still rough, but whatever had knocked him out seemed to be wearing off...unfortunately.

"Warlock," I replied on autopilot.

Talking while staring at him was not working. My reservoir was low, I was tired, my head ached, and I didn't want to get reacquainted with the buffalo chicken salad I'd had for lunch.

Most glamours were fae-made, and his appeared to be of high quality. It would be a bugger to unravel, and we had a door to close. I was in no shape to unstitch the illusion, and Oscar's considerable skills didn't fall in that arena. Igor's identity would remain a mystery for now.

Oscar's thoughts ran parallel to mine. His face was unreadable as he climbed to his feet.

"One thing at a time," he grumbled.

I nodded and stood.

"Why," murmured Igor, allowing his head to fall back to the floor, "haven't...you killed...me?"

"There's still time," Oscar observed, ambivalent. "Now please shut up. We need to concentrate."

By the time the light cleared, every magical marker on the other side needed to be gone. I tried not to think about the thin protection and the malicious forces polluting the lines on the other side. The curse wouldn't get through. I just needed to dissolve my illusion and siphon off my fingerprints. It only required one finger. Losing any would suck, but I'd live. Warding myself, I slipped a finger through the membrane.

Oscar worked around me, readying to seal the door.

"Don't...die," Igor mumbled.

Perplexed, I glanced at Oscar.

As clueless as I, he shrugged.

Shaking off a dark foreboding, I mumbled, "No promises, Igor."

August 26th at the Agora in Chicago, Illinois

O'Brien knocked softly on his office door, cracking it open, and peeked in with a hand over his eyes.

"John? It's me. Are you awake? Decent?"

"Why wouldn't I be?" Dorrit grumbled, lifting his head from his hands with effort. He slouched on the settee, elbows on knees, looking as miserable as fried pickles without ranch. "What'd you think I was doing?"

O'Brien peered around his hand before letting it fall. "Decency isn't just about clothes. No one likes intrusions when they're vulnerable."

"That's exactly why I called — so you wouldn't barge in while I quietly expired."

"Excuse me for being considerate," O'Brien pouted, shutting the door and thrusting a glowing paper sack at Dorrit. "Explain."

"I was too late. The house was empty. I'd swept every room," he said, pulling a potion from the bag. He read the label, ascertaining that the brew was what he needed — and wouldn't turn him into an iridescent, bubble-burping unicorn. Popping the cork, he downed the vial in one go.

"Did you think it would turn you into a blueberry? I know where to get a decent healing potion!"

Dorrit ignored him.

"There was a lantern on the Ayaris' mantle, ornate, warm to the touch. It was… familiar…but I can't place it. I lit it and…" He shrugged, frustrated. "I woke up in an orange grotto. Everything was searing white. Two people fell on me...a man and a woman. It was silent, but I could hear the world dying."

"What?" O'Brien prodded as the agent scowled at nothing.

"I don't know what was real."

"Assume it all was."

"It wasn't. I saw a star being born. I heard time speak. A river flowed through me." Dorrit shook his head. "Must be a concussion."

O'Brien knit his brows. "Maybe. Maybe not. Let me see your eyes. Who were they — the man and the woman?"

He knelt, shining a pocket light in Dorrit's eyes and directing him where to look.

"They didn't have faces."

The Chairman rocked back, perturbed but intrigued. "Kinetic glamour?"

"No. Invisible."

"No concussion, but get checked anyway. How'd you determine their gender?" O'Brien asked, pulling a chair over.

"A pair of anatomical differences was evident. We talked," Dorrit grunted, shifting on the short sofa.

"Well?"

Dorrit recited the conversation to the best of his memory as O'Brien paced the small room.

"Promising. Very promising! Maybe," murmured the Chairman.

"What is?"

"That they didn't kill you. Be careful, John; you'll get yourself obliterated and I'll do something stupid and follow right behind...," he murmured, moving to look out the window and down at the city's clogged arteries — normal people doing normal things. He almost envied them. "We're lucky MacDonnell wasn't with you. Even one more miracle and we'd all be headed to Sanctuary."

Dorrit stiffened. It had been his call, and if they didn't pull this off, he'd damned them all.

"The Ayaris' house burned down — the ground's smoking. Why? That's not their MO. Why not leave you inside? They know you're a warlock. Such nerve — leaving you steps from the Peregrine Gate! So cheeky. I love it!"

"Terrific. Maybe we can all go camping together."

"Could someone else have been there," O'Brien mused, ignoring him, "A greater threat?"

"Can a witch have a greater threat than a warlock?" Dorrit grumbled, an arm over his eyes.

"Certainly, John! The APA only wants them dead or contained. Duchowa pułapka are still being manufactured; most would prefer death to having their souls trapped and used by their enemies. Consider Sanctuary — why is Jones willing to execute practitioners rather than condemn them there? Angels of Mercy, John — death's not the worst fate."

Dorrit grunted, then added, "The Curator's murdered. We can't overlook that just because they spared me."

"But that's the point — this muddies things. What if we're wrong? Someone entered that house unseen. The outside cameras showed nothing; the cameras inside were on a loop. Backup was seconds behind you when a ward activated, blocking them. Burning the place down only makes sense if they meant to kill you — or lost their temper."

O'Brien beamed, apparently delighted at the possibility of being wrong.

"If they were destroying evidence, you'd be dead. Logically, there must have been two parties. Now, the question is, how long have both been involved and what drives them?" His glee swiftly shifted to calculation and then dismay. "We got lucky. For two hours, John, we thought you were gone."

Dorrit sat up, his mind whirring, and shook his head.

"I'm willing to admit the theory as a possibility, but if you're right, everything needs to be re-examined. How do they both know where to go and when? Why would they..."

His voice faded, and his eyes narrowed, fixed on some distant notion.

O'Brien huffed. "Two hours, John! I thought you were dead. An acknowledgement would be nice; a hug's too much to ask, I suppose."

Dorrit didn't hear.

"You might be right," he whispered, awed by the very idea. "Maybe we have misread the case. Sir, I need the file — the photos."

O'Brien pulled a face but unlocked a desk drawer and dug through it. "Here," he said, handing over a heavy packet.

Dorrit grabbed it, slid to the floor, and rifled through the images with frenetic energy. "Vessel. Vessel, vessel, vessel."

Two stacks emerged — one with three images, the other hundreds. The last caused a small landslide, sending pics of arcane gadgetry sliding across the wood floor.

"Not a collector," Dorrit proclaimed. "An Angel of Mercy. The stolen artifacts are pułapki duchowe, and Jones is freeing trapped souls. She wants to save souls? Let's offer her another."

"No!" O'Brien snapped, horrified. "Our budget doesn't stretch to high-end black-market goods!"

Dorrit stared at the Chairman, momentarily speechless. "I was thinking of MacDonnell, sir — not a spirit ripped from its body!"

"Oh… Oh, I see! Right. That would work — if you're certain. Once you've acted on this, there's no turning back, John. The pair that saved you might not even belong to Jones."

"You don't believe that any more than I do."

No, he didn't.

"You think we can sway her?"

"She saved me, didn't she?"

August 26th in Chicago, Illinois

Veritas knew he was playing a fool's game — reason demanded he stop. There was no doubt some dull explanation for everything, but he had to know. He'd tried to walk away. He knew there were real-world stakes — prison or worse. If these villains could kill an avatar with such ease, what wouldn't they do? No, this was the hill he would die on; there was no room for cheaters in gaming.

He gazed at Vindicta, his dark elf warlock, created solely to obtain particular objects from the warlock storyline, with resigned sorrow. She was stunning — mysterious, dangerous, clad in top-tier armor, level thirty-eight — a masterpiece deserving of a better fate than he could provide. She would never have her day in the sun. In his heart of hearts, he would always be a pirate sorcerer.

His avatar's humiliating death had ignited a fire — proof he'd rattled someone powerful. No one else saw it, but he did, and as a gamer and journalist, he was honor-bound to expose the corruption.

Galvanized, Veritas nestled deeper into his sofa, consulted his notes, and searched for Kenny Jones's address. A map and photos of a bizarre farm, minutes from Kansas City, popped up on his smart TV. The house was a fusion of styles — industrial, gothic, Craftsman, and drama queen — with Shou Sugi Ban siding, mullioned windows, and a witch's cap for a roof. It should've been creepy, but glowing windows and verdant gardens turned it into a forest haven.

Outbuildings dotted a circle drive — brew house, tasting room, greenhouse, garage — half-swallowed by lush foliage. Arresting and unexpected, it was a perfect backdrop for a scandalous scoop. It photographed well.

Veritas scrolled the search results, locking onto Sullen Creek Brewing Company and Brewpub. He clicked, skipped the fluff — About, Calendar, Menu — and hit the Brew Crew page. Scrolling by Leonore Drew, Miigwan Cloud, and Davida Moran, he zeroed in on Hazel McKenna Jones. Another click and a photo blazed across his screen.

Veritas gaped.

It was Weaver! The in-game Weaver come to life! The clothes were different, and her dreadlocks were swept up into a crown, beads and feathers framing her face, but it was her! Dark eyes gleamed under flying brows; a dimpled smile offset her sloping nose and mixed skin tone. Lovely, unnerving, and soul-piercing — even in the photo, she saw too much. She was too much — too animated for a static image, radiating determination. Piercings and tattoos softened the effect, changing the context. She was a bohemian artisan — not the villainous captain of a rag-tag crew.

Still recovering, he read her bio — California roots, college in Kansas City and Dublin, world traveler. She was a partner in the brewery, brewpub, and other ventures, including a hotel: Punk Bunks. Veritas clicked the Nubivagant link — a vacation rental platform. Punk Bunks was a 5-star Neo-Victorian micro beer hotel. He skimmed the gallery — fantastical rooms and proportionate rates — before hitting a wall: there was no calendar or booking options.

Ah ha! His spidey senses buzzed. Hands twitching with anticipation, he dug in.

Minutes later, a jolt penetrated his fixation, code unravelling like magic — he'd hit the motherlode. And Egress, Hooligan, and Nubivagant shared a unique dialect. The same programmer had built them — he'd bet Russell's squeaky Groot on it. Searching their calendar, he saw only one room, the Keeper's Sanctum, available.

It was fate.

Veritas snagged the Keeper's Sanctum for the entire eleven-day span it was available — exorbitant, but two meals were included. He punched in his payment, hit confirm, and grinned — until a questionnaire popped up.

"Please specify your Origin," he read, flummoxed. The options were therianthrope, vampire, fae, dverg, hybrid, or opt out. Something near his heart tightened painfully, and his breath stuttered, joy overwhelming him; it was a *themed* beer hotel! A shrill sound escaped him that should only ever come out of ball-gowned, six-year-old birthday girls presented with their first ponies.

Veritas bolted to his guest room, dug his custom fangs out of the dresser — Halloween relics — and tested them with a chomp. Not bad. He recited the *Jabberwocky* with only minor lisping. Perfect. Darting back to the screen, fangs still in, he entered "vampire," opted out of the cadre question, nixed blood but claimed a garlic allergy for authenticity. Blackout curtains, yes; sunlight issues, no. Daylight hours, sure. No aichmophobia.

Giddy, he erased his tracks in a rush, overlooking a sample of his patois still buried in the code — a ghost in the machine.

"Clotheth," Veritas gasped, turning to Russell, who'd shuffled in through the doggy door. "How doeth a vampire dreth for thummer?"

He snickered, picturing a fanged fiend in a Hawaiian shirt sipping a Bloody Mary from a coconut with a pink umbrella — sporting flip-flops and a fanny pack!

Springing to his cosplay closet, he flung open the doors and mourned — it was too hot for leather. Finally vindicated in his hobbies, he rummaged through two decades of costumes. Did vampires wear socks? They must. They wore boots, and boots without socks were just nasty.

A soft whimper brought his attention back to Russell, gazing at him with anxious eyes.

His chest tight, Veritas knelt and scratched behind the dog's ears. "Thorry, Ruthell. Where I'm going, you can't follow. What I need to do, you can't be part of," he murmured tenderly — lisping in his best Bogie imitation.

Russ buried his face against Veritas's leg.

"If you're snogging the dog again, I won't be kissing you for a month," a feminine voice shouted.

"I'm not thnogging the dog," he barked. That had only happened once, and he'd meant to kiss Russell's head. Russ had looked up, open-mouthed and panting at the wrong moment. In a gentler voice, he murmured, "Be good, thweet boy."

"There's a new bottle of mouthwash in the bathroom. Use it!"

Veritas yanked the fangs out of his mouth. "I am not snogging the dog, nor is the dog snogging me!"

Kenny: August 26ᵗʰ at Sullen Creek Farm

"Kenny," Maggie shouted.

I crashed through the underbrush, chasing her voice, expecting the worst.

"What've you got?" I demanded, wiping sweating palms on my jeans. The APA was onto us, and I was the weak link. I should have listened to Oscar. If Igor suspected hedge witchery… Evacuating meant betraying my promise to the Sheta Djew — even if they came with us, setting the Saturniidae back years, and abandoning hundreds we might have saved to their fate… But my people would be safe.

"Naabek was right," declared Maggie, her voice rusty as she presented their find. "Dead."

Relief hit first, then disgust.

A dead body was no problem. Living, breathing, reporting warlocks or APA agents, on the other hand, were much more troublesome. I battled past the bracken to the bloody wreck at her feet. No one should view the dead and feel grateful.

"Call Oscar."

Maggie grimaced but yanked out her radio. "Call off the search — body on the east boundary, quarter-mile south of the creek. Send Oscar and supplies," she hissed as I searched for a pulse — a faint flicker, weak but steady.

The uncooperative bastard was still alive! Nothing marked him as an agent, though, and letting him die felt gutless. I shoved my glasses up, seized a ley line, and forced power into his reservoir. The man didn't react. He wasn't feigning injury; ley transfusions hurt like hell. It wouldn't mend bones or knit flesh, but it would keep his heart pumping and brain active when nothing else could.

The patient was tall-ish, black, and fit. Blood crusted his clothes, but there were no visible wounds. Depending on his hereditary magic, they might have already closed. I squinted. Judging by size, he was a match for the warlock — but had Igor had it in him to navigate the Peregrine Gate, find our farm, and get into this much trouble in the time available? I'd be a fool to rule it out.

Our latest rescue — such a bad habit — hadn't been robbed. He still had his wallet, keys, and phone.

"James Darrow," I gleaned from his driver's license, "Forty-one, six-foot-one, two hundred and seven pounds, address in…Highland Park."

"Where's that?" Maggie hissed.

"Chicago." I blew a raspberry.

"Shove him in a hole," she advised.

I considered it. Foe or fluke? I couldn't do it. Enough ghosts were haunting me already. Besides, someone had dumped him here. Trouble was looming either way.

"We're saving him," I growled.

"You sound like Oscar."

"You sound like a Parselmouth."

"I am a Parselmouth," she sneered, exaggerating her sibilance. "Are you a trauma nurse named after a grumpy puppet?"

"No, I am," grunted Oscar, vaulting over a fallen tree. Mel followed, giving me the evil eye. I'd ditched him, but he'd forgive me, eventually.

Oscar dropped his backpack and checked Darrow.

"What?" Maggie asked.

"Brain trauma — concussion, possible bleeding. He can't be moved like this. I need a boost," he barked, looking at me. "Don't bother being gentle. We don't have the time."

I cut the link to Darrow and put my hand on Oscar's neck. Maggie's went on mine. Power punched like a shot of boiling vodka. Oscar's shoulders tensed with the raw energy, but he worked through it. Ley lines played double dutch at the healer's command, creating blood and rebuilding cells.

A burgundy-skinned being with two extra arms and a greedy leer drifted into view, eyeing me like prey. I gave him a one-fingered salute and put my glasses back on.

"Hypovolemia due to blood loss. Blue nails — he's not getting enough oxygen. Shit — he's waking," Oscar grunted, fiddling with the lines as Darrow clawed at the dirt. His body stiffened, glowing red eyes popping open, before collapsing.

Oscar flexed the lines, huffing, "Definitely preternatural — and that still shouldn't have happened. I've done what I can. He needs fluids, quiet, constant monitoring."

I conjured a stretcher under Darrow. Maggie took the far end — dude was built like Optimus Prime.

"If he has blood loss, why isn't he lighter?" demanded Maggie.

"He is," groused Oscar, helping us over the tree.

"Bet he fudged on his license," I rasped.

The forest trek dragged — fifteen minutes felt like forty — until Lon and Armand, along with a farm truck, came into view. The boys slid Mr. Darrow into the bed. Maggie and I braced him while Oscar monitored his patient. Mel chose the cab. He preferred air conditioning, and he was still miffed.

"Big house or bunk house?" Armand called through the back window.

I raised my eyebrows at Oscar.

"Bunkhouse," he murmured. "The kids."

Ah. Darrow was still a possible danger and a possible corpse. Best not to have kids around either.

"Will he be a guest?" Arlo inquired with false solicitousness. "If so, I'll need a Visa, Discover, or Mastercard."

Ignoring him, I looked at our availability. Darrow needed space, calm, and something on the main floor — a family suite, in other words.

"Cancel the reservations for the Ethos Suite for the next two weeks. Comp the guests' next stay due to the short notice and inconvenience," I told the albino giant. The look Arlo gave me was very teenager, belying his twenty-five years. His deep-set hazel eyes were ideal for expressing petulance, as was his wide, full mouth.

"That room's a gold mine! There's a waiting list! People plan their trips around our availability," he argued. "Put him in your guest room! Please!"

"The kids."

"Then the Orbit City suite."

"And if he wakes up only to have a heart attack?"

Rosy, the android concierge, could disturb the unprepared. She was intended to be quiet, not silent — although her Roomba impression was always a hit. Coupled with her tendency to sneak up on people, Orbit City was the heavy Halloween favorite. Our haunted house packages were sold out months in advance.

Arlo remained unmoved. I widened my eyes, allowing my bottom lip to tremble.

He huffed, spun to his desk, and updated our calendar. It wasn't the money; Punk Bunks was his baby. Unfortunately, it was more useful as camouflage than as a legitimate business.

"Thanks," I called, making for the stairs as he slipped Mel a biscuit. My guard dog chuffed and padded after me.

"Yeah, yeah," Arlo grumbled.

Oscar had Darrow stripped, washed, gowned, and hooked up to an IV. He was nothing if not efficient.

"Anything I should know?" I asked.

Oscar shook his head. "He stirred again — whispered, 'Stupid'. We've done what we can."

Interesting.

"I'll report him to the Agency," I decided.

"Is that wise?"

"Yes…if he survives."

Chapter 31: Strange Work

Kenny: August 26th at Sullen Creek Farm

"Proceed."

The clipped voice struck like a whip.

My eyes met the icy gaze of Judge Dietricksen, her expression hard, discontent. A sliver of distant pity, however, was impotent.

Why was she here? Once a guilty verdict was handed down, the judges never descended to the lower levels of the Agora to observe, let alone preside over, an execution.

I quit stalling. There was a job to do.

Seven-year-old Imani Curtis's large brown eyes locked on my hands. She didn't cry. She didn't beg. She was already beyond human fear; I didn't apologize. We both knew she deserved better.

Despising myself, I sang — a lullaby laced with subtle energy. Doing nothing to shield herself, her eyelids drooped, and she gradually fell asleep.

The seal on the syringe snapped loudly — the observers, safe behind enchanted glass, flinched — a small revenge, but better than none.

Focus, Kenny. Finish it.

I prepped the needle and, without letting myself think, injected the lethal mix into Imani's plump arm. Five times, her chest rose and fell — then stopped.

It was done.

My eyes stinging, I turned away from her angelic face and ripped the gloves off my hands. Sick of myself and sick of the world, I hurled them and the syringe into the waste bin. The syringe bounced off the rim, making a pitiful ting — just as useless as my anger.

A joint popped.

Something shifted behind me — the audience buzzed anxiously. I turned; Imani was on the bed, just as I'd left her...but her face was angled away. Her body jerked like a puppet. I flinched, then scoffed at myself — postmortem spasms.

148

The tiny corpse continued twitching, the movements blurring. The flailing arms elongated. Imani Curtis was gone. Levi Wilton lay still just long enough for me to clock his face, then morphed — Fareeha Nore, Eric Lopez, Beverly Clayton, Cheri Shannon, Michael Shore.

The remains cycled through a decade of faces. Dimly, I realized I was dreaming, but it didn't help. I would see all ninety-seven faces before I woke. Every victim got their turn.

After the first...visitation, I called the dream logical, possibly even a healthy response. Eventually, I would become desensitized. Time would dull the horror, and the nightmares would end.

Instead, I eventually accepted the dreams as fair payment for this farce.

Harriet Stevens, three hundred and six years old, wrestled with the sheets. Her eyes bulged — blind, milky orbs. She grinned at me, toothless. Harriet hated her dentures. They had never fit right.

As if some divine being had pressed fast forward, her flesh flaked away like ash, leaving behind a surprisingly tidy skeleton. Thanks be for small mercies.

"Kenny. How you been, doll?" Harriet's grinning skull clacked. "A spook of another sort's arrived to pester you."

The last bit was a new addition — both the skeleton and the message. I couldn't say I relished either.

"Thanks, Harriet. I'll be on my guard."

I wasn't clairvoyant; true sight was plenty generous enough...but I didn't doubt Harriet's exhortation. The universe was a strange place. Prophetic dreams weren't that unusual.

Staring up at the timbers bracing the sloped ceiling of my bedroom, my heart attempted to pound its way out of my chest — tachycardia. Nothing new.

I closed my eyes, grounding myself in the present and fishing for my glasses on top of the nightstand. Cartman's plump warmth pooled around my head. Cinnabun, a little brown rabbit, was half-under him and my locks. Little feet scampered through the walls. Gidget whirred, and the wards emitted a calm, unending hum. My hand snaked out and clutched my glasses like a talisman.

A soft whine had me looking to the left. Natasha, Gorg, and Mel were tangled in a puppy pile, hogging the bed. My faithful guardian put his paw on my hand; try as he might, he couldn't protect me from everything.

I squeezed his big, puppy paw and whispered, "It's okay. Just a dream."

My legs were too warm. Some opportunists had wedged themselves between my knees. I pushed back the covers, curled my legs, and rolled off the side, landing on my feet.

Mischief and Ms. Anthropy — properly, Mystery — were the feline culprits taking advantage of my warmth. Ms. Anthropy had earned her nickname — she hated everyone except her human familiar. It was highly unusual for her to snuggle up to me. It had only occurred once before — a terrible night. Fresh apprehension stole my breath.

I snatched up my phone and fired off two text messages. The first received an automatic reply — Aunt Gregg would get back to me when she was able — and the second, after an eternity lasting forty-two seconds, received a thumbs-up emoji followed by some rude suggestions. Relief warred with amusement — profanity was always preferable to silence.

So, just an off night.

I glanced at the cuckoo clock — a few minutes past two. Little wonder I'd been told off.

I yanked yesterday's clothes out of the hamper, tugged them on, and hung my glasses from the collar. The ley lines leaped to fulfill my will. Practice makes perfect — and this particular door was effortless, even across planes. I wriggled out the other side on my stomach.

The bunk above my portal was occupied...which meant I would need a new entrance for my illicit workings. Sealing the door and nudging aside a large pair of cleats and what I dearly hoped were a clean pair of boxers, I slipped from under the bed.

A harsh gasp froze me — Levi, eyes wild and teeth bared, bolted upright and was primed to scream bloody murder.

"Just me," I whispered.

It took three seconds for the words to translate.

"Why were you under Kyrie's bed?" he whisper-shouted, muttering something about demented, long-haired, monster-women under his breath.

Kyrie's? Since when?

I stood and studied the sleeping boy, watching his chest rise and fall. I touched his warm hand. My kids were safe. His box braids were gone; he'd fluffed his hair out into a crazy cloud, hiding his adorably over-confident face. His cast was off his arm, but now a thick layer of bandages wrapped his left ankle. Ley healing didn't work on him. It didn't stop him from making poor life choices, but it did explain why he wasn't in the top bunk.

Levi came over, studying me with concern. I hugged him hard and held up a finger. I was willing to explain, but I needed to check on my other kids. Green-eyed Michael Shore, now thirteen and growing like a weed, snuggled into his pillow; eight-year-old Ben Hojnowski snuffled as he dreamed — a lingering cold, poor boy. Felipe Zambrano, Jack Devi, and Kyle Everhart all slept soundly — safe, warm, and far from the Community's reach.

Levi followed me down the curving hall to a massive, wooden door. I held up a hand to indicate he should stay in the hall, and then a finger. One more minute. He nodded and took a seat out on the balcony.

In the girl's dorm, precious little Imani clutched a doll and, quiet as a mouse, stared at the ceiling. I breathed. I hadn't murdered my kids. Only simulacra had been injected — flesh golems that felt no pain, had no awareness, and possessed no soul. I'd known, but the intellect didn't always conquer the testimony of the eyes.

I took a couple of steps up the ladder to Imani's bunk and smiled. My little angel smiled back.

"Trouble sleeping?"

Imani nodded, her braids chattering.

"Come," I whispered.

I checked the other girls, all snug, as she climbed down. We joined Levi on the balcony and gazed at the strange panorama — a terraced city inside a transparent mountain. Imani curled up on my lap, head tucked under my chin.

"So, why were you imitating a ravenous shadow beast bent on eating Kyrie?" Levi pressed.

Imani giggled — ravenous shadow beasts were comedic gold.

"Portals in the hall attract attention."

"Right. Much better to terrorize sleeping children. What if I'd attacked you?" he demanded.

"She'd deserve it," a dry voice cut in.

A petite, Latina woman with long hair and belligerent eyes strode out from the darkened hallway, rust-red robes rippling in the breeze.

"Morning, Marisol," I greeted, blowing a raspberry on Imani's cheek. She giggled again. "I'm just visiting."

"Visiting hours are over! You're damned lucky I was on duty. Suppose Xandre had caught you?"

"Dr. Feyrer said a bad word," Imani observed.

"She did. Naughty, naughty Aunt Marisol!"

"Kenny," Marisol pleaded.

"Bad dream," I admitted, caving.

Her next words died on her tongue, and she sat down, sighing. She didn't have the heart to scold me.

"I'm sorry."

I shook my head, not wanting to discuss it. "Why's Xandre on rotation? I don't want her near my quarters."

"A team was attacked on the mainland. They're fine. Natalie's having recurring episodes of vertigo. We'll figure it out, but we're stuck with Xandre. No one told you?"

"Nope," I grumbled.

Her lips thinned. "You have your detractors — same old, same old."

"Why are visiting hours over? Aren't you the leader here?" Levi cut in. "What's the deal with Xandre?"

Imani braided my dreads, comparing my beads to her own.

"Kenny leads a team and a Community cadre; she's only a member of the Covenant. Her cadre, the Sheta Djew who harbor the Saturniidae, are being investigated. Not the first time; won't be the last," Marisol assured Levi, nudging his shoulder. "But Kenny isn't supposed to visit until things calm down. As for Xandre… Well, our girl has had an adventurous life, which some people hold against her. If she's caught here, there'll be trouble."

Levi frowned, trying to read between the lines.

"Practitioners require balance — they favor creativity but acknowledge that destruction is necessary. A while back, I went through a destructive phase. Some say I went too far — that I'm out of balance. I stood trial and was exonerated, but a few weren't appeased," I explained.

Levi glanced at Imani and realized no specifics would be forthcoming. "I get it."

"It's not just that, though," Marisol added. "Carter, the leader of the Saturniidae, favors Kenny. Some folks are jealous."

"I thought everyone in the Covenant was supposed to be equal," Levi asked. "There's a council, so there's a hierarchy."

"The Council and guilds govern institutions, not people. Through meritorious work, guild members can rise through the ranks. Kenny has done so within the Saturniidae. They..."

She looked to me for help.

"We steal things."

Dr. Feyrer glowered. Apparently, that wasn't the description she was looking for.

"Kenny is very skilled and influential because of her track record. But it's late. Back to bed."

"I don't want to sleep," murmured Imani, huddling into me and breaking my heart.

"I'll give you a potion so that you won't dream. Kenny, too," Marisol promised.

Imani wasn't thrilled, but she agreed and let the doc coax her inside.

I turned to Levi. "Sorry for scaring you. I'll make my doors in the hall."

A school of angel-winged fish flew by, just visible outside the mountain.

"Your dreams...they're about us, aren't they?"

Levi was too bright by half.

"I don't want to get you into trouble," he murmured.

"I can handle Xandre. Don't worry about me."

He nodded. "Any word on Talia?"

"Nothing new," I admitted. "We know she's alive and on the move. Your charms are holding — if we can't find her, no one else can."

He stared at the alien horizon — he'd traded his family, home, and safety for friendship, uncertainty, and a view. "Yeah. Bedtime."

I watched him go, felt the ache that slowed his stride, the fear that threatened to consume him — the same pain ground at my bones. Talia should have made it to the farm by now.

Alone, I stared up at the strange, green stars and two moons — one fiery red and the other a hazy blue-gray. Far below, beyond the ocean waves beating at the mountain, another moon was visible — massive and far too close. I could see strange earthworks on the indigo surface.

Wenen was a broken realm, discovered by accident. There was sky below the ocean and rivers winding through the ether above. Here, things didn't always work the way they ought. It was dangerous, and our geomancers agreed it had only three hundred years of stability left — a short-term solution for a long-term problem.

"Here," Marisol barked, thrusting a bottle filled with a thick, ice-blue liquid at me. "Kids get the yummy stuff. You get this: one tablespoon every night. I'll know if you're not taking it."

"Thanks, Doc."

Dr. Feyrer grunted. "Oscar?"

"He's good. He enjoys tormenting — I mean, teaching — apprentices the healing arts. Brandon? The kids?"

A tender smile escaped her. "We're well. Ramona took her first steps. Oscar didn't show you the video?"

"Must have slipped his mind," I replied, accepting her phone. I watched a dark-haired, chubby baby pull herself onto her feet and take her first, wobbling steps, wonderment filling her little face.

Off-screen, a man announced, "Mama's home! Mama, come look at your brilliant daughter!"

Ramona, excited to see Mama, clapped and had to take an involuntary step backwards. I knew the moment she saw her Mama. She gurgled joyously and took three swift steps before falling on her bottom. Ramona looked back at her daddy as if to ask what had happened.

"Precious!"

"She is. Matías and Tomás are the best big brothers, too!"

"Oh, I'm so telling on you!"

"Good! If my brother valued the title, he'd visit more," she returned, worry lining her face. "Keep him safe for me, Kenny. Keep yourself safe."

Chapter 32: New Arrivals

I loathed alarms.

If my life didn't revolve around my phone, I would beat it with my boot until it gave a little warble of apology and fell forever silent. It was four. In the morning. I had a total of two and a half hours of sleep. I was not ready for a new day. Neither was Cartman, who was coiled around my head, nor Chesney, Rogers, G, and Oreo — burrowed against my sweat-slicked side. I rolled off the bed, landing on my butt, and considered staying there. It was cold, though. My room held the peaceful, eerie silence of a heavy snow.

Maggie was in charge of the thermostat. Crawling into my closet, I dug my way into a forest green robe and furry, clawed slippers — a Christmas gift tagged with a "layer up or I go skyclad" ultimatum. Stupidly, I'd called her bluff…then layered up after it became awkward for our businesses. I grimaced at my slippers. The claws danced when I wiggled my toes, and I escalated to clogging until Skyfall blared through the room.

Custom alarms kept me somewhat organized. I opened my calendar. Sunday — a full day. Chores, training, breakfast, and checking on the patient. Our cycle ball team — soccer on bikes — was playing against Drifting Shadow. There was a finance meeting — always good fun. Our Sudoku Samurais were in a qualifying round for the state championship. I had to review cadre applicants (AKA — sort out the spies), set up for Stupid Cupid and Karaoke Night, and then play Capture the Flag. I wasn't going to make it to the brew house, but I had to squeeze in a few errands, and two deliveries had to be inspected upon arrival.

What was life without unrealistic expectations?

I yanked open the nightstand drawer, revealing a neat row of potions, ointments, and serums.

Was I doing this? Magical solutions were risky with the APA hunting us, but exhaustion was worse.

Ignoring the enticing lemon-yellow potion, violet serum, and periwinkle ointment — and my second thoughts — I grabbed the Edwician, a viscous, yellow-brown sludge. It tasted like it looked. I popped the cork and knocked back the slimy vial.

Sinking onto the rug, I braced for the kick. It was best to lie flat for this. Keeping my breathing controlled, I waited two minutes…then my veins combusted. Cold fled; sweat beaded on my forehead. My robe clung as my muscles seized, locking my limbs at sharp angles.

"Normal reaction," I grunted through clenched teeth. I knew every side effect, but doubt always crept in.

"Breathe through it," Derringer urged. "Panic never helps."

I jerked. I hadn't heard him enter or climb the loft stairs, but his advice registered. It was easier to obey than think. I forced oxygen in, then out. My muscles relaxed. I could move — albeit slowly.

"Almost there," Derringer soothed, grabbing a sports bra, ribbed tank, and yoga pants from my closet.

He dropped the clothes on the bed. "I'll meet Colt. Take it slow. Let him handle things; consider it a show of trust. Ditch the Edwician. Being alert isn't worth half-killing yourself."

Excellent advice. I even considered taking it for thirty seconds. I hauled myself up, dressed, and limped to the stairs. Colt was a paragon, but he lacked experience. I trusted him to do his best, but his best wasn't always good enough. Well, it had been up to now, but someday, it might not be. And Edwician didn't half-kill me — a third, at most. A hefty third that felt like a lean half. If it kept us alive, it was worth it.

Halfway down the stairs, the pain was gone, and I moved fluidly. By the door to the hall, I buzzed with more juice than Loco, the warehouse manager's levitating chihuahua.

With the horses fed, exercised, and paddock-bound, Colt handled water buckets, mucking the stalls, and laying fresh bedding. I milked and fed the cows. The goats got their supplements, and the petting zoo got tidied.

The work dulled my buzz; a hot shower soothed my muscles. By the time I made it to the kitchen, Lou — Davy's short muscular indigo-haired dwarf girlfriend — and my tall pale housemate simpered and brushed against each other as they poached eggs and sliced fruit. Copper arms zipped along tracks, frying polenta, sausage, and potato crowns, stirring up salsa verde. I breathed it in — Tex-Mex Benedicts were my jam.

Eli perched on the counter, phone in hand. He glanced up as I walked in and pocketed it; he'd been waiting for me.

"Mom says I can't have a phipthere as a pet," the pixie child solemnly explained, his puckish features at odds with his old soul.

"Oh? Why's that?" I asked, hunting in the fridge for my chai concentrate. My pitcher was gone. Davy caught my perplexed expression and rolled her eyes.

That was odd. She'd never scoffed at my chai dependency before — not when she relied on unhealthy amounts of caffeine to battle insomnia and get Eli to school on time. Of all people, she ought…

"Wait—what's today?"

"Sunday," Lou reminded me, smirking as she handed over my spice caddy and a clean pitcher. I mumbled a thank-you and reached for the grinder.

"Because they're native to other realms and aren't trainable. The norms don't know about magic or phiptheres and would freak."

Phiptheres… The dots connected; Davy's eye roll suddenly made sense. Edwician helped with sleep deprivation, but it did nothing for attention regulation. We did not require any magical constructs in this menagerie. I was Team Mom all the way.

"All excellent reasons," I said, plugging in my milk steamer. No eight-year-old really needed a flying serpent. They could get large and ate everything in sight — phiptheres, not eight-year-olds. Well, some did. Eli *was* tall for his age.

"They are," he allowed.

"I sense a 'but' coming."

"Hold on." He hopped off the counter and darted down the hall.

I shot Davy a look, pointing my spatula after him.

"You'll see," she sighed, brushing curls out of her eyes and smiling indulgently after her child.

"He'd better not be bringing a phipthere in here."

Lou's smirk did nothing to reassure me.

I dumped my ground spices into a steeping bag and filled the Dutch oven with hot water. The spices would steep before I added the decaf Assam. I nabbed my favorite mug and tidied my space.

Eli returned, cradling a cross between a twelve-pound cream-colored fennec fox and a Pomeranian. Its muzzle was slender and elegant, its ears large, and it ended with an oversized bottle-brush tail. The fluff ball gazed at Eli with adoring, jade-green eyes. Tiny, curling horns grew from its head, and neatly tucked wings sheathed its sides.

"He arrived this morning. He's dog enough that he wouldn't scare the norms if his wings and horns were glamoured. He's used to this plane. He may even have been born here," Eli argued. Both his blue eyes and the pom-fox's pale beauties pleaded with me.

I glanced at Davy.

She shrugged. "He's not wrong. Maybe add in the eyes? It's your call."

Oh. Her calm surprised me. After twenty years of friendship, I guess she'd become accustomed to the oddities that followed me home. There'd been a few daimons in there. Still, this was her child. It was one thing for her crazy pal to take in every magic-touched critter in the known universe and another for her baby boy to adopt one. She was surprisingly chill about it. Of course, compared to a wild construct, this fellow might as well have been a dog. This was a teachable moment for me.

I shifted my glasses and peered at the pair. A mess of ley lines connected them; they had already formed a familiar bond.

"Do you see how he's looking at me?" I asked Eli.

He looked: the creature shifted his attention to Eli, licked his chin, and then back to me. Twin tears pearled in its enormous eyes; it looked adorable as hard as it could.

"Yeah," he replied, cautiously.

"He understands what we're saying. We don't know anything about the practitioner he was bonded to, but he is intelligent. Don't show him off. He's your familiar, so his care's your responsibility. He won't be added to the automated system until you've demonstrated your ability to care for him. If he's neglected, we'll revisit this discussion," I said before looking at the pom-fox thing. "As for you, try to blend in. Don't work any unnecessary magic. Don't fly unless you're alone. Your place is with Eli, and I expect you to protect him. Understood?"

It yipped excitedly and bathed Eli's face in earnest. Sighing, I dug in the junk drawer until I found a precast glamour and flicked it at the pooka. The astonishing eyes dulled, and the darling horns and wings disappeared. I turned back to my spicy water, adding mesh tea balls and cackling over my cauldron.

Eli offered up a rare grin. "Thanks, Aunt Kenny!"

"You are welcome. What's his name?"

"Boruta, but he said Boris is acceptable since that fits our naming conventions."

"He said?" Davy asked sharply, dropping her paring knife.

Eli, Boruta, and I stared at her, confused by the shift in her tone.

The pom-fox thing was a sophisticated creature. What would be more natural than him speaking? Daimons often spoke.

"Many magic-touched creatures speak," I said slowly, getting an inkling that I'd grabbed the wrong side of the stick.

"You're sure he's safe," she demanded, crossing her arms.

"Nope, nope, nope. You're not putting this on me, little mama. You green-lit the daimon if I agreed *before* consulting me. If you had, I would have reminded you that he's an unknown commodity. The only thing I can definitively say is that he hasn't tripped any wards — but you knew that."

"Demon," she gasped.

Really?

"Oh, come on. Daimon, Davy. A helpful spirit! Imp, hobgoblin, puck, sprite — they're all the same family! Some words sound a little scary, some sound cute — that's how folklore works. Something bad happens — blame the imps. Something good happens — thank the brownies. Look, he's not a demon, and he doesn't intend any harm. Besides, it's too late anyway."

I grabbed the almond milk and poured enough for a monster chai into the steamer. I was going to need it.

"Might I weigh in?" Boruta interposed in a shrill but comprehensible voice. The pooka was older than I'd thought. Centuries older.

Interesting.

"Thank you, but now's not the best time," I told him.

Davy blanched, and Lou stifled a snicker.

"Boruta will be good for the other familiars," I argued, waving a hand behind my back at Eli. "He'll keep them in line, make sure no one gets bullied. He can help Eli with homework. He'll provide incredible insight into history and literature. Don't get me wrong — Eli's brilliant, but he's all prose and no poetry, if you know what I mean. Boruta might get him interested in things beyond science and math."

Davy gaped, her mind processing. I risked a glance around. Eli and Boruta had scarpered.

"Give the little guy a chance," I suggested, putting my mug back and hauling out the big tumbler. "He might surprise you. In a good way."

He had better surprise her in a very good way, I thought, spooning allulose into the chai.

"What did you mean by 'it was too late?'" Davy asked. I had never heard that suspicious tone from sweet Davida Moran. I was proud…and flabbergasted that it was directed at me!

"They've bonded. Boruta wasn't in mourning, Davy. He'd been called. Your son sent out the bat signal, and Boruta took the red-eye! The real decision was made when those two clapped eyes on each other," I explained, feeling a thickening in my throat. "I hadn't even realized that Eli was tapping the lines. They grow up so fast... My first familiar was a bumblebee — Archimedes. I haven't thought about Archie in a long time. Anyway, Eli is going to be a handful, drawing a pooka!"

I glanced up, sampling my concoction, and choked. Davy's eyes were bulging, and there was a thick pulse near her temple.

"Right. Not important. Just… let's remind him to be mindful. I don't want to put him off, but, wow, now isn't the best time for a new practitioner to emerge!"

Lou abandoned the eggs and hugged Davy, murmuring soft, comforting words.

Guess I wasn't the only one who'd missed the signs. I dumped my beautifully frothed milk into the tumbler and filled it up with the chai concentrate.

"You okay?" Lou asked, tapping my hand where it rested on the counter.

Static jumped from her fingers to mine, providing me with an excuse to pull back. I didn't mind Lou's show of affection. She'd earned my trust. But...the topic she'd nudged at came with its own rules. I couldn't handle sympathy.

I closed my eyes and shook my head...then smiled and forced a laugh. "This is a good thing. This...this is happiness."

Davy looked miserable. "I didn't even think..."

"You were concerned about your baby. Don't you dare feel guilty."

Davy gave my hand a quick squeeze. "I'm not, but…"

"It's okay. I'm okay," I assured them, feeling cowardly as I turned and fled from their compassion.

The real heartbreak hit in the pet parlor, where our predators slept. Generally, all of our critters got on, but they still had instincts. The prey animals were more comfortable sleeping in the conservatory. The exception to the rule was my room. All of the displaced familiars had access through a network of internal tunnels, and all were welcome.

Tiny, little Spook wound around my ankles as I entered, mewing with purpose. Gorg, a pit-mix, was also on hand. Seeing them both gave me a clue to prepare — they helped newcomers land on their paws.

A tortoise, a mink, and a rat hesitated just inside the petio door — orphaned familiars. More and more arrived every week. I recognized Tyrone, the tortoise, and a new pain gripped my heart. Warlocks had found Clan Bruin. There were eight fewer practitioners alive and free in the world.

I had to inform the Covenant, but they could wait ten minutes. Setting aside my chai, I lay down on the hardwood floor, slowly stretching one hand toward them but not making eye contact.

"I'm so sorry."

I could empathize. I could care for and protect them, but there was no justice for their loss. "You're safe here. Rest. Mourn. I promise that no one will hurt you."

Tyrone was the first to move forward. With some trepidation, he approached and, when I didn't make any sudden movements, he nuzzled his head against my hand. Tears were in me somewhere, but they never quite surfaced. They just stung my eyes and faded.

'Familiar' could refer to either party in the bond. Childhood bonds usually didn't last long. My bond with Archie extended my bee buddy's life many times over, but after two years, he was tired and ready to move on. The first time I witnessed death, it was welcomed with contentment and purpose. The second, the same year, was very different.

A bond formed as an adult usually lasted a lifetime. A shared purpose — a quest for knowledge, a desire to serve, or a search for meaning — drew two beings together. The lines tethering the bonded told them when the other was asleep, sad, angry, or in pain. When one half of the pair died, the other frequently followed.

Tyrone, sensing my loss, crawled over my arm and huddled against my shoulder. He curled up in his shell and communed with me. His courage was enough for the mink and the glossy brown rat. They spilled over my arms and curled up. Gorg flopped against my right side with Spook between his paws. A raucous dirge rose, the animals venting their anguish — a requiem for the fallen.

August 27ᵗʰ at Sullen Creek Farm

"Tell me that wasn't the finest beer you have ever tasted," the indigo-haired server demanded, stacking dishes onto her tray.

Veritas smirked, meeting her lurid, green, cat-slit gaze. The beer was good — great, even; top five in his life, and the food didn't disappoint, either. He decided to humor her.

"The very best. I'd like another."

"Oh, no, you wouldn't! We brew twelve spectacular beers, thirteen with our seasonal brew. You've had one. You want to walk out of here without having tried at least one more? No! No, sir, you do not! What you'd like is either a Beerista with a slice of bourbon pecan pie or a Frigid Witch with bread pudding topped with cinnamon whiskey sauce," she declared, balancing her tray above her shoulder with a fist planted on her hip, daring him to deny it.

He was powerless before such good-humored bullying. "Does the pecan pie come with ice cream?" he wheedled.

"Does a quokka fart pralines? You bet, it does! Sold?"

"Sold," he declared.

"That's the right answer," she said, grinning as she weaved back through the tables.

Lou's brashness might have irked him in his hometown, but in Parkville, he felt only exhilaration. Adventure thrummed in the air. He downed the last of his Golden Retriever and sighed contentedly. Indulging was unwise — though not drinking beer at a brewpub might raise a few eyebrows, too.

His gaze roamed the restaurant's saloon-birdcage mashup — the old building clung to the hillside through sheer cussedness. The interior was a patchwork of millwork, polished floors, wrought iron rails, and a riot of plants. High-backed booths lined the red brick walls, while flower-decked tables angled down the center.

His fellow patrons were an interesting mix, too — a knitting circle by the window, six ladies and one beaming man; teens three tables over, cajoling a beer from their server (an old hand at this game); two plainclothes cops behind them, snorting at her quips. Near the back, a tall woman in a vintage skirt suit, platinum tresses in victory rolls, coordinated with the staff before disappearing down a hall.

Two tables stood out: one with four twitchy figures in hooded capes and mud-caked boots, and a group of seven identical women — raven-haired beauties with bold eyes — at the other. The sisters accessorized their tailored slacks and sleeveless blouses with James Smith and Sons sun umbrellas, Lesca sunglasses, and wide-brimmed hats. He felt a stylistic kinship with them and was entranced by how they consumed their meal in neat, synchronized movements.

A thump brought his attention back front and center. A frosted snifter brimming with a dark brew, thick foam embellished with a stylized cup of joe, stood before him. Veritas had never seen beer art before. Beside the beer, a caramel-brown slice of pie, oozing ice cream waterfalls, basked in a stray ray of sunlight. The staging was on point.

Lou dropped her elbows on the table and cradled her chin in her hands.

"Get on in there! This is the moment when everything changes."

"Voyeur," he teased. "You talk big."

"It's the path to enlightenment," she half-sang, not disputing the accusation.

"Well, then." He toasted her, took a good sniff, and sipped — notes of coffee, roasted malt, vanilla, and a wisp of orange danced over his palate. It was a complex, beguiling brew, unearthing a yearning for cigars and smoking jackets. Memories were pulled from forgotten places, like an old film reel, and projected across the backs of his eyelids — happy, comfortable moments he rarely thought of anymore.

"There you have it, folks," Lou crowed, deservedly smug.

He held up a hand to delay further commentary and forked the tip of the pie. The custard was rich and buttery, the crust delicate, and the nuts crunchy. He chased the lingering sweetness with another pull on the snifter.

"And?" she demanded, eyebrow cocked.

Veritas nodded, conceding, "The scales have fallen from my eyes. I have seen the light."

Lou popped upright, beaming. "New regular?"

"Unfortunately, I'm just here for two weeks — might see me daily, though."

"A pilgrim! Sullen Creek Farm's a must for tastings!"

"I'm staying at Punk Bunks," he confessed, elated by his happy circumstances.

Her grin faltered, then snapped back. "Lucky duck! In that case, I'll see you at dinner. I live on the premises. Do you have directions? GPS can get squirrelly in these hills."

She whipped out a brochure with a map, offering a few tips involving a grove that resembled a high school diva clique casting shade and a large boulder shaped like the Czech Republic. Veritas was all gratitude.

"There's your bill, but don't rush," she said before drifting over to her other tables. "Holler if you need anything!"

A few minutes later, the seven sisters rose and exited in a uniform line just as a long-haired man with an eyepatch attempted to enter. The newcomer held the door, smirking when the seventh sister gave him a saucy wink. Veritas lost sight of him when a couple of servers began rearranging tables, making space for the bussers, carrying an enormous dartboard with a cupid skewering a red heart, to pass into the billiards room. The swirling script on top read, 'Love Hurts'.

He waved Lou over. "What's happening in the game room?"

"Stupid Cupid every Sunday! It's darts with a twist. Competitors vent about their dating experiences before taking a shot. If they're funny...or pitiful enough...they may be awarded additional points. No names, foul language, or underhanded tactics are permitted. The winner gets a gift card to a local business."

"Interesting," Veritas murmured in the same tone he would adopt to admire a colleague's overweight pet slug.

Lou snickered, grabbing a calendar from the napkin holder. "Here. We have a variety of events throughout the week — something for everyone. Although Stupid Cupid might surprise you. We have several regulars who are hilarious. They'll start in about an hour."

"I'll take it under advisement," he said, catching sight of Kenny Jones breezing out the front door purposefully.

"Ah," murmured Lou, looking troubled. "New arrivals."

Veritas didn't understand until he saw Jones kneel beside two ragged pups.

"She takes in strays?"

"Let's put it this way — Sullen Creek Farm's four-legged residents outnumber the two-legged variety four-to-one. I hope you're not allergic to any critters."

Chapter 34: Fangs for the Memories

August 27th at Sullen Creek Farm

A brass bell trilled as Veritas entered the lobby of Punk Bunks. He'd scoured its online gallery and reviews so he'd know what to expect. Online, it had been an atmospheric, neo-Victorian lantern. In person, the architecture was rather more imposing; despite the brilliance of the afternoon, the edifice loomed over him — tall, dark, and evoking the heavy oppressive feeling of being watched. Icy needles pricked at him when a dog howled, and cloud cover blocked the warmth of the sun. The next second, he shook off the dread and unloaded his bags.

A curious bit of mechanical engineering proclaimed the name of the establishment. Punk Bunks, letter by letter, was spelled out on metal cubes — copper, iron, bronze, and brass. Randomly, with a puff of steam and a hiss, a cube would rise and, upon reaching the track's apex, flip and fall to the bottom, displaying a new font.

Inside, his boots clomped against a marble checkerboard floor. His fingertips slid down textured, light-emitting paper — microchip wallpaper! To his left, an Art Deco console table sat nestled beneath a frosted, sliding partition — reminiscent of a hard-boiled detective's office door — and displayed three transparent wireless tablets flashing advertisements. To the right, there was a library in the same style. Beyond the lobby, a grand staircase wound around an old-school cage elevator.

"Be right with you," a voice boomed from nowhere.

The glass partition glided open, revealing a pale, broad-featured face. The albino receptionist's smile was polite, generic, and slightly unctuous until he'd taken in Veritas's ensemble. With that, his demeanor instantly shifted. He stood, eyes shining and a shy, joyous smile making him look younger than he was. But, good grief, the man was tall!

"Honored one, welcome to Punk Bunks," the fellow politely thundered, bowing deeply, a hand held to his heart. "My name is Arlo. How may I be of service?"

Honored one? Veritas considered the title, finding it agreeable.

"I have a reservation," he explained, masking his nerves. Arlo's look was perfection — a vampire from another era. His claret zoot suit was custom, and a handsome fedora hung in the corner of the tiny office. "It's under Vitruvio — Luke Vitruvio."

"Count Vitruvio — yes, right here. Please verify that all the details on the tablet are correct."

"Certainly," said Veritas, straightening his sleeveless ankle-length Matrix-style jacket. Count Vitruvio sounded so...diabolical!

"All correct," Veritas announced after a glance.

It hardly surprised him when two of the seven sisters from the brewpub skipped down the stairs, nodding politely as they exited.

"Wonderful," exclaimed Arlo. "I'll just need your credit card and a photo ID."

Veritas supplied both, ashamed that he hadn't even considered what his character's wallet ought to look like.

Arlo hummed, running the card, then returned it and Veritas's driver's license. "You're all set, Count Vitruvio. You're in the Keeper's Sanctum, room three — an excellent choice. Allow me to show you the way."

Without waiting for a response, Arlo closed the partition, emerging from around the corner a moment later. He collected Veritas's very vampiric duffel bag and a small trunk, effortlessly hefting the latter up on his broad shoulders.

"Would you prefer the stairs or the elevator, Count Vitruvio?"

Veritas glanced at his skirted legs. "Uh — the elevator. And, please, feel free to call me Luke."

Arlo grinned and pushed the call button. "Oh, I couldn't do that, honored one. It wouldn't be proper."

Ensconced in the brass cage, they rattled up to the second floor. The wide hall had hardwood floors and walls papered in a historic Nouveau damask print — gold herons on a navy field.

"Room three," Arlo declared, stopping before a door with an engraved three. Arlo deposited Veritas's luggage on the runner, unlocked the door with a flourish, and stepped aside.

"Wow," Veritas breathed.

Ancient timbers haphazardly framed limestone walls. Tall, arched windows allowed sunlight to flood over the room's cluttered surfaces — globes, books, art, and plants were strewn about like confetti. The oak headboard stood ten feet high, and the bed was heaped with gorgeous linens and furs.

A gift basket with a gold bow sat on a small dining table. He could make out two bottles of beer, a snifter, and cigars.

"The colors of the Sheta Djew," Arlo murmured, uncertainly, indicating the faded turquoise, melon, and dull gold tapestries hanging from the walls. "If you want them taken down or replaced, it would be no trouble."

"They're fine," Veritas promised, wondering if the Sheta Djew were part of some game he'd missed — but that was absurd. He'd written the book on games.

Arlo moved his bags inside the door, then hovered on the threshold. "I...hope I'm not overstepping, Count Vitruvio, but it's so rare that we have a guest who truly embraces the spirit of Punk Bunks. No one has ever arrived in costume. A vampire wearing fake fangs... Incredible! Most members of the Community... They're so conscious of their dignity, aren't they? I mean, no one in the forums is going to believe this! Could I possibly get a photo?"

Veritas blinked...and blinked again.

"On the contrary, Arlo, I appreciate your candor," he murmured and struck a suitably vampiric pose.

Arlo, quite overcome, took the selfie and bowed. Stumbling backward over his feet and incessantly thanking Veritas, he eventually made it onto the elevator. Veritas was left to meditate on the receptionist's strange words — and meditate he did, unable to shake the most peculiar sensation of déjà vu.

Chapter 35: The Long Game

Kenny: August 27th at Sullen Creek Farm

"Lon," I yelled, scanning the treetops. Not a leaf fluttered, but I knew they were up there. Lon ran the apprentices through confidence courses on Wednesdays and Sundays — ropes today per the schedule. "I need Colt for a few minutes."

Crickets.

He was testing me.

I rolled my eyes and grabbed an acorn, imbuing it with magic. "I have two hands but no fingers."

The wind whistled through the canopy, but all else was silent.

Closing my eyes, I listened closely. "I run and stop, but have no legs. No eyes nor ears, but I have a face. What am I?"

There!

My eyes popped open, and I met Lon's gaze through the foliage.

"Don't," he begged.

I threw the acorn. It smacked the stocky man in the forehead, erupting into a cloud of dust and spelling "I started it" across his brow.

"If you ever need to find a hidden sphinx, offer him a riddle, then listen. They can't leave it unanswered. If they're very disciplined, they can delay... Three...two...one."

"Clock," Lon growled, scowling.

"But even the best hold their breath to resist. If you have good hearing or use a charm, you'll find your cat when he inhales. Then, he'll one-up you."

Lon gritted his teeth. "I hate you."

"Don't be like that. It'll fade before Maggie sees it."

Snickers and a chorus of "Maggiiieeee" rose from the trees.

"What month has twenty-eight days?" Lon shot back.

"Every month. Colt, on the ground."

"Ebersol, take five. Restart when you return," instructed Lon.

Colt, halfway through the course, barked, "Yes, sir!"

He skipped across the balance beam forty feet up like it was nothing, swapped carabiners, and rappelled down.

"I hope you don't have any big plans tonight," I said as he landed.

"Why? What's happening?"

I handed him my phone, and he read the notification: *Oath approved. Witnesses on the Mulberry at 7.*

"I'm taking the oath? It's only been five months!"

"You're ahead of schedule." I shrugged, conflicted. I was proud of him, but our losses were higher this month; the average lifespan for operatives was dropping. "We're running out of course material. You either take your oath or enjoy three weeks of busy work. You'll be joining the team for training afterwards. Now, up the tree. Get a shower before the ceremony."

I'd need a shower, too — it was stupidly hot. My tank had sweat spots, and I wasn't the one climbing trees.

Colt nodded excitedly and bounded back to the course's start.

I caught Lon watching and held up three fingers, whistling like Katniss.

He snorted, waving me off, and barked at a student, "Demirci, when Jì Yuè is swinging, you gonna wait for the perfect moment to jump? Move your ass!"

The Mulberry

"You look weird."

Maggie scanned me from head to toe.

"Yup. You get used to it," she agreed, hissing more than usual.

"Thanks," I murmured, nudging my glasses up to study the lines. No movement. Trust our witnesses to be fashionably late.

It was Colt's first time on the Mulberry, but his curiosity was curiously lacking. He barely glanced at the glass wall hiding the Saturniidae's nerve center — the biggest Covenant base serving the Midwest, fifth nationwide, and eleventh globally. Most apprentices gaped at the futuristic, sci-fi bustle below — hundreds of practitioners analyzing data and coordinating with operatives across the globe — but, for Colt, the changes in my appearance were more arresting.

"Not bad-weird. Just…different," he clarified.

Didn't I know it.

I adjusted my dark red robes as the wall in front of us began to twirl. We weren't sure who the witnesses would be or what agenda the Covenant would pursue. Something would happen. Despite having a united cause, people were still people.

"Mmhmm." I resituated my glasses and whispered. "They're here."

Oscar, Nore, Maggie, Lon, Davy, Lou, Derringer, and Armand were in attendance...casually spaced so they had room to maneuver. It was overkill; the Covenant would not countenance a coup — just a nuisance.

The wall rippled, like a rock hitting a pond, then dissolved. Ancient trees with golden-gray trunks braced the opening, our conference room on one side and a primitive sun-dappled city on the other. A few burgundy leaves blew in as a regal woman with brown skin and cascading black curls stepped forward, her teal robes swishing against the floor.

My shoulders tensed, then relaxed as a blond woman with a dimpled smile in robes of pale gray and a smug Asian man in brilliant yellow followed: Doyenne Muma Padŭrii, Arachne, and Doyen Phi Thale — the Covenant's Midwest liaison, the top counter-intelligence operative, and the Voice of the Erebidae — the Council of Elders — respectively. Phi Thale was over three hundred, looked forty, and generally behaved like an evil, crotchety, twenty-year-old in terms of mood and stamina. He'd recruited me...after we nearly murdered each other.

It could have been worse.

"Kiybib mee nah Purinahmi, teylnim byi nah Tsidyaska," I greeted in Blue Tongue. *Welcome to the Mulberry, home of the Saturniidae.*

The Covenant's chosen entered, and the door sealed behind them, graphite-gray once again. We bowed as one, and I motioned our guests to the stone table.

"Please take your ease." The round syllables of the language fell off my tongue with an awkward splat.

Arachne snorted, hugging me. "So formal, baby girl!"

Padŭ hesitated, searching my face, and when I didn't snarl or bite, hugged me, as well.

Phi Thale cut in, "Yes, yes, a happy reunion. This is the postulant?"

Horrible word — made apprentices sound like weeping blisters.

Phi Thale, sensing my distaste, turned and smirked at my get-up. I'd anticipated some puppet of Xandre's, not one of the Erebidae. Our elders rarely left Meshrew Hepet. They must want something.

"This is my apprentice, Mort," I said. "Mort, this is Doyen Phi Thale, Voice of Erebidae; Arachne of Immoidae, my adoptive mother; and Doyenne Muma Pădŭrii, my biological mother — also of Saturniidae."

Pădŭ smiled knowingly as Colt gulped, valiantly meeting her gaze.

"You'll do," she said, patting his shoulder.

Sitting down and placing a rough, ice-blue stone in front of Colt, Phi Thale explained, "I am here as the Covenant's unbiased advocate and witness. We need to ensure that you fully comprehend what you're signing on for and that you are not being coerced in any way. Please pick up the rock. It will testify to the veracity of your answers."

Mort shot a quick, questioning glance my way but obeyed.

"Mort of Biloxi, are you here of your own accord?"

"I am."

The stone glowed nearly white.

"Good," said Phi Thale. "The oath is permanently binding. If you part ways with the Covenant, you will still be subject to our ley laws. Understood?"

"Yes."

The stone glowed.

"We enforce laws with an enchantment cast by the original collective, strengthened by each oath," Phi Thale said. "Break them, and your spell will rebound. Understood?"

"Yes."

More of the pretty light poured out.

"Our laws evolve with us — we do not vote in the manner of norms. The enchantment handles that. It's done without our knowledge; the magic cannot be corrupted, tricked, or bribed. The laws are summarized here." He shoved a booklet in front of Colt. "And can be found on our website. They're updated every six months — next in November — and should be reviewed at that time. When the Community is broken, it will have a seismic effect on the way we govern ourselves. In all probability, half these laws will be abolished. Now, read carefully."

As Colt read, I toyed with my fox keychain; Arachne eyed the glass wall. Others fidgeted — humming, thumb wars, recipes exchanged in sign language — while Pădŭ, Oscar, and Phi Thale sat rigid. Twenty-five minutes later, Colt set it down.

"Done."

The stone did its thing.

"Will you abide by these laws?" inquired Phi Thale.

"I will."

More light.

"Excellent. The enchantment is not rigid. If you are fighting for your life, it will not condemn you, unless the collective disagrees with your actions — sixty-five percent, you're fine; between sixty-five and forty, it stalls; less than forty, it backfires. The verdict is instantaneous, and the collective is unaware of the survey. All clear?"

"Crystal," Mort replied, showing the illuminated rock.

"Then it is your wish to take the oath?"

"It is."

The stone washed the room in searing white.

"Very well. Does anyone have anything to add?"

"I do," I said.

"By all means, Doyenne," Phi Thale oozed graciousness, using the title that matched my robes.

Grimacing, I said my piece. "If you need to kill someone who is not an immediate threat to you or someone else, don't use magic."

Padǔ made a sharp comment, but it was drowned out by Phi Thale's barking laugh. Arachne sighed and gave me an anxious smile.

"Okay," Colt mumbled. "Why?"

The stone warbled as if confused.

"Good. He's not as bloodthirsty as you," cackled Phi Thale. "The Doyenne, however, is correct. We are responsible for our conduct beyond magical applications — balance, purity of the soul, all that rot. However, a human jury will always have more potential for leniency, or manipulation, than an enchantment. The Doyenne will explain the nuances. She's well-versed in them."

I rolled my eyes at the jab.

"You're every bit as bloodthirsty as I am. Worse, probably."

"True, but I hide it better," he agreed cheerfully. "And I space out my kills. More than twenty in a decade and tongues wag; less than ten, and they think you're getting old. You went for quantity. No one likes that — draws too much attention."

"It wasn't sport. I don't enjoy dispensing death."

He gave my hand an indulgent pat in case his condescension was too subtle.

"You enjoy competence — both in wholesale slaughter and global chaos. It's not criticism; on the contrary, I admire your proficiency. The elders appreciate such things. But we are neither good nor decent. You strive to be both." This was criticism. "A disappointment and frequent topic of discussion for the council. Historically, those with a conscience have died very quickly. I lost thirty grand assuming you'd follow the trend."

He sighed, confused by his thoughts. "I do not understand you...but you've given us hope. I know you appreciate irony, but don't go get yourself killed just to be contrary."

"I didn't know you cared," I snarked, tired of the game.

He smiled, displaying a forest of sharp teeth and inhuman eyes. I could have counted his age by the shades of otherness in that gaze. "I thought I was past such foolishness, but you have revived many forgotten things. You possess an uncanny ability to make people listen to you — to consider the most naive and reckless of ideas...."

He paused, looking almost wistful.

"Vampires have a peculiar custom...when bored, they manufacture a new identity for themselves — new name, new home, new history. I should like that," he murmured dreamily. "The Erebidae are in agreement; we will support your proposal. We don't know if it will work...but we don't know that it won't."

He dropped the bomb with the same apathy Maggie displayed when plucking weeds, leaving silence in his wake. Padŭ gave me a probing look; Arachne, with admirable resolve, maintained her smile. Neither had been informed of the proposal that the Sheta Djew had been debating for the last two years.

"How?" I didn't recognize my voice — a hard, cold command.

Oscar settled an ankle on one knee, eyes communicating caution. Lon appeared relaxed, slouched in his chair. He would have the councilman subdued before the rest of us left our chairs.

Phi Thale cackled, enjoying the tension.

"The elders see all, Doyenne," he murmured in sepulchral tones, doing his best to appear otherworldly. "Now, Mort of Biloxi, if we haven't crushed your noble delusions, read that out loud. The magic will only take if you're sincere and certain."

Colt, anticipating fisticuffs, scanned the slip of paper. "That's it? I thought there would be a spell or an artifact..."

"The spell was cast a thousand years ago. All that is required is your oath," I explained absently. How did Phi Thale know? We hadn't even reached a consensus. A mole on the base was beyond absurd; it was next to impossible — magically, if not morally — with one possible exception. "With ley energy, less is often more."

A new Seer must have emerged — specifically, a foresight or hindsight.

We were protected from augurs, scrying, oneiromancy, and all the lesser forms of divination. If the elders had discovered a real seer, however, that was another matter. It was impossible to block a seer. The elders wouldn't be allowed to keep such a boon to themselves for long. A skilled foresight could change destinies. Technically, I suppose, an inept one could, too…just not for the better.

Colt took a deep breath and, dreadfully earnest, declared, "By our will, I will abide."

A click rippled through the Covenant; the enchantment, and a sense of rightness, grew by a sliver.

"Now what?"

Phi Thale snorted. "Your witch brews beer, boy. Now, we party!"

That was fine for some, but the workday hadn't ended for a few of us.

New Orleans, Louisiana

I sprinted until the shadows swallowed me, crashing into the warehouse's stone wall after vaulting the scaffolding. Momentum carried me into the unyielding surface. The cool rock soothed my abraded skin as I caught my breath.

Jake jogged my elbow, handing over a tin of ointment — he had a talent with herbs. I signed blessings on the swarthy dwarf, his someday wife, and the many children they would surely have, then stripped off my damaged gear and smeared the goop on my acid-burned face, chest, and arms.

Watching Phi Thale and Oscar get smashed and sing bawdy songs had been the highlight of the evening, maybe even topping Colt's oath.

We had now reached the low point.

Our mission was less about artifacts and more about sending a message. The target was in the burnt-out husk of a warehouse that somehow managed to have four standing walls after decades of neglect and several hurricanes. Our intel was limited, but we knew the new owner planned on restoring the wreck. Security was tight, and both the fenced grounds and the structure were riddled with traps; we'd discovered that the hard way.

The use of personal magic was prohibited. Precast spells were acceptable — provided that no Covenant practitioner had been involved in their making. That limited us; we didn't use the trash that came out of Sanctuary. What we had available was weak, of short duration, and temperamental — but better than nothing. High-tech, ley-enhanced gear was recommended.

A two-hundred-foot stretch of wasteland lay between the eight-foot fence and the warehouse's bones. The place looked like an industrial graveyard. Dodging around heavy machinery and boom lifts abandoned in seemingly random places, Jake and I had been sprayed with some ward-eating concoction in the first twenty feet. A few steps further, and I triggered an acid trap. Jake had sacrificed one of our precious pre-cast spells to wash the corrosive fluid off of me. It worked, but left me drenched.

Another fifty feet and Gaia had fallen through an illusion into a tiger trap. Jake snagged her fatigues just in time. When we hauled her out, she'd gotten sprayed with some pungent agent.

It takes a special kind of fixation to rig a trap within a trap.

In our final sprint, Jake missed a tripwire, nicking his ankle. A minor injury, but blood drew predators as surely as Gaia's stench. We needed it sealed fast.

Gaia stripped, bagged her ruined gear, and dug for deodorizing supplies. I tossed her a neutralizing spray and activated a new warding amulet. It clung to my skin, sticky and foreign — precast aegides were always uncomfortable. I swapped out my wet stuff and crouched by Jake. He'd triggered his amulet, cleaned his cut, and cut away the bloody cloth.

I smeared antibacterial salve on the wound, slapped a ley graft over it — it melted into his skin, sealing it — and wrapped a black bandage around his leg. Good to go. We moved deeper into the industrial jungle.

At the southwestern corner, Gaia raised a hand. We stopped, listening. I shut my eyes, hearing only a distant car alarm.

"Blood," the humid breeze seemed to sigh, thick with longing — like some B horror flick.

Through my night vision goggles, I saw something shift. I couldn't understand what it was. I pushed them up, and a humanoid shape seemed to spring together from bits and pieces of shadow. Light avoided the creature, bending around him as if his touch was toxic. He had to be security, but not standard issue. A black, textured bodysuit covered him like a second skin and distorted his face. He must have been melting inside that thing.

His head swiveled, the lumpy latex rippling like muscle. He lifted his chin, sniffing the air like a canine. Therianthropes would sooner die than exhibit any behavior the least bit animalistic, but shifters weren't the only ones known for their keen sense of smell.

Vampire: I signed. *Move!*

Gaia bolted around the corner. Jake and I followed. We scampered up into the scaffolding, staying low as we climbed onto the second-story platform.

Jake nodded toward a hole in the wall, but I shook my head, pulling my goggles down again. Rubble hid traps better than a few wooden planks would. Besides, anything could be lurking in there. Eventually, we'd have to enter, but I wanted more intel and to take out a few guards before it became necessary.

Clear. Smells safe: Gaia signed.

I'll take care of Bat-Boy: Jake volunteered.

A boom, followed by three streams of billowing smoke, erupted from the front of the building. A massive jet of flame shot straight up into the air.

Team two had arrived.

I grinned at Jake and shook my head. Pulling three pods of the Elixir from my belt, I nicked them with a knife, squeezed until a dribble of blood oozed out, and chucked them and the knife, far off into the darkness, each in a different direction. Gaia readied a dart gun.

Vampires were quick and silent when they wanted to be. Without Gaia's ears, Jake and I, even with boosted hearing, were easy prey. We held our breath, letting her listen.

She aimed and paused.

"Two teams," the guard murmured. "Back and front. Unknown numbers. One's bled, one's been sprayed — nettle tea fertilizer. Scents have been confused."

"Yes, ma'am," he added after a beat.

Gaia fired. The dart slipped past his pulsing ward, hitting his neck. I tensed — his super villain suit might be too thick to penetrate. He clawed at the dart, snarled, and lurched two steps toward us before dropping.

Seconds ticked by before Gaia gave the all-clear; the vampire was out. She sprang up, sprinting along the platform, eyes probing every stray leaf and shadow.

I followed, Jake at my back. Halfway up the west side, Gaia leaped, grabbing the edge of the third floor. She peeked over, toes twitching left and right — guards either way — then oozed up and over.

We waited, listening in case she'd been spotted. I nodded left; Jake shadowed me. When our cover ended, I peeked out and raised a finger. A guard — pale and fae — stood fifty feet off, her face dominated by sharp angles and sunken eyes. For her sake, I hoped it was a glamour and not genetics.

Jake, dropping low, scuttled out and placed a series of obscuration charms. Dwarves were naturally resistant to magic; he could take a couple of hits and keep moving.

The gaunt woman turned on her heel, and a pleasant, electric buzz tingled just under my skin. I aimed a dart gun at her neck, two inches below her left ear. She yawned, stopping five degrees short of catching my partner in her peripheral vision.

Jake slithered back to the wall, and we waited for the charms to engage. A stream of distortion bubbled out of each ball, silently piling higher upon itself until an invisible curtain cordoned off the area. I slipped out, climbing the ladder welded to the edge of the platform. When I looked back, Jake jiggled his hand and grimaced. The cover was patchy.

Feeling my way out along the floor above, I attached a series of charges. They would activate in six minutes.

Out of the corner of my eye, I glimpsed a hooded figure strolling outside the fence. The owner of the warehouse had saturated the place with enough spells and wards that there was no danger of the uninitiated noticing anything odd. My eyes followed the man's progress. It was late, and not the best neighborhood.

I shook myself. Not my problem.

Thinking team two might benefit from a distraction, I lobbed a fist-sized sphere toward the front yard. The fae's eyes immediately latched onto the silver ball as I climbed down. The mech-moth unfurled its wings and darted around, setting off snares and causing as much mayhem as a volleyball-sized moth could.

The guard spoke into her headset. We could see her jaw move, but neither of us could hear what was said. Jake picked up one of the charms. It was sputtering, nearly exhausted after a pathetic twenty seconds. We crept closer.

"— a drone. It's too maneuverable. No, ma'am… Yes, ma'am."

Once it was clear that the conversation was over, I tranqed her.

We retraced our path back, past where Gaia had ascended, and back to the southwest corner. Jake kept watch as I scaled the supports and peeked over. Twice now, we'd been reported. If reinforcements didn't arrive soon, I was going to take it personally. Charges secured, I climbed down, feeling antsy. We hadn't run into a single trap in the scaffolding.

Something's off. I signed.

Jake nodded. *We need to be louder.*

There aren't any traps up here. Why?

Jake didn't have an answer for me. We stuck to the plan, returning to the southern midpoint. Jake boosted me up.

Gaia was tucked down by some bins six feet away. She signed for silence, then held up three fingers, then two…with her right hand. Gaia was left-handed.

"Trap," I shouted, pushing away from the building as I let go.

Something huge dropped down right where I'd been.

Falling, four long, slender legs registered — each leading to a dust-colored, bulbous thorax, crowned by eight glowing eyes. Four legs rose above the beast, manipulating a thick cable of silk.

Spiders.

I hated spiders; more than six legs was just an unnecessary indulgence.

I mean, yeah, sure, I had a few arachnids in terrariums at home, but it was different once I'd gotten to know them a bit. And none of mine were larger than a fist, let alone a car.

My air-light amulet slowed my descent, bouncing me onto my feet. I tucked and rolled, landing right in front of a small opening in the wall. A serendipitous, dark hole to dive into? I didn't debate the issue, knowing, as likely as not, it would lead me straight into more trouble.

The first of our charges went off, causing the structure above my head to shake. Dust drifted down. I hoped I wasn't about to be buried alive — I didn't have an amulet for that.

Chapter 36: Perish the Thought

Eli: August 27th at Sullen Creek Farm

"Okay," announced the girl, flopping down across the table. "We're in."

Milo settled beside her, grimacing apologetically as he did. Everything he did was quiet. I liked quiet. Quiet was good for thinking.

The night was soft, and with the ceiling fans on, it was very comfortable on the dining porch. Crickets were singing, and a pair of owls were having a conversation. It was the sort of evening where sharing secrets came more naturally. The girl and Milo's timely arrival wasn't accidental. Two days ago, Boruta had urged me to foster a few assets — to let go of a bit of control in exchange for aid. My pooka was clever at managing people, me included.

"In what?" I asked, closing my journal. There was no need to make it easy.

The girl rolled her eyes.

"We're not stupid. We see things, hear things. We know that bad people are trying to get the Sheta Djew in trouble. We know you're..." She glanced around with narrowed eyes and whispered, "witches…but you're — well, not good, exactly. You're kind of a wart, but we know you're not evil. You and the talking dog are protecting Kenny. We're cadre now, too, and we want to help."

I glanced at Boruta, recognizing his wide-eyed innocent look. When I used it, it never fooled anyone except my mom — but only when she wanted to be fooled. Carefully, I wove a sound barrier around us. It was tricky; ley energy was slippery, but I was improving.

"As it happens," I admitted, "I can use your talents. No one can know — not Kenny, not my mom, definitely not outsiders. Any responsible adult would send us away to safety, which would be a disaster. I'm going to need a Solemn Vow of Secrecy if you're serious."

Milo tensed, but Mouse pressed on. "What is it, and how's it done?"

"It's binding magic." It was nonsense, but they had to mean this. "Say, 'I vow to maintain the secrets entrusted to me, or I'll painfully perish a thousand times in a thousand ways before I move to the next realm.'"

Mouse wanted to call my bluff but wasn't sure it was one.

"It's more stable if you face each cardinal direction," I said, pointing north, west, south, and east, "or it might zap you."

Call me a wart, see what you get!

She clenched her teeth and stood, facing north. "I vow to maintain the secrets…" Turn. "…entrusted to me…" Turn. "…or I'll painfully perish a thousand times…" Turn. "…in a thousand ways before I move to the next realm."

Good enough.

All three of us stared at Milo. He sighed, rose, and glumly echoed her.

"Bravo," Boruta trilled. I snorted when they jumped; they knew he could talk, and it still scared them. "First, we must polish your skills. You'll need familiars — luckily, there are plenty about."

Kenny: August 27th in New Orleans, Louisiana

Charges rocked the crumbling warehouse, each blast shaking the ground and dusting my eyes, but the walls held. With every bang, another mech-moth, lizard, or squirrel was freed. They harried guards — hopefully — as my compatriots slipped to relative safety. Battle sounds leaked through shattered walls, hinting that might not be the case.

Stay positive, Kenny! Maybe Jake and team two were absolutely crushing it. Four rescuing one was so much better than one rescuing four.

I crawled ten feet through another jagged opening and into the warehouse's guts — a dilapidated atrium, open to the sky. An attempt had been made to clear the debris, but pockets remained. Wires dangled from the walls, some humming with a live current. A genetic quirk made me sensitive to their ceaseless droning. Harsh lights blazed from above, carving pools of brilliance from languishing shadows.

The silence was unnervingly thick. I needed to think. I needed a hideout and a plan; guards would find me on the ground, and spiders hunted from above. I bared my fangs and started climbing, each crumbling stone or pipe handhold threatening to fall or inject me with tetanus.

Past the ten-foot mark, webs appeared — first cute, little cobwebs in corners, then silk nets cordoning off entire sections. I avoided them, wary of vibrations raising the alarm. Footfalls whispered below; there was no turning back.

At the third floor, an illusion ended. Thick funnel webs, concealed before, blotted out the sky, obscuring everything — the ground from me and me from the ground. Dark shapes — hundreds — slid through gossamer tunnels, smaller than the scaffold's eight-foot horror but bad enough.

Huddled against the wall, I caught my breath and watched the eerie shapes…slowly realizing that I'd been had. Spiders don't march and certainly not in sync. A squad scuttled overhead in perfect formation, ignoring me despite the thunder of my pounding heart. They saw me and didn't care — they were constructs and lacked the capacity to think.

Ley lines occasionally shed energy — big bursts spawned storms or sinkholes, small knots birthed chupacabras, hydras, or other wild constructs, magic mimicking life with exuberant flaws. Mythology was filled with some stunning examples. But these uniform spiders? They were too consistent to be wild; they had been farmed.

I crept through the webbed maze, contorting myself as I searched for purchase, muscles burning. I was gifted a rhythm — the twang of the Delta Blues — and, somehow, it helped. The music pulled me toward the source like a moth to flame. My vision filled with white, agitated tunnels — spider rush hour — with one giant funnel at the core.

Leaning out precariously, I glimpsed a massive leg — four feet of iron-gray shell marked with dashes of luminescent yellow — tapping to the beat. Climbing higher, I peered from a different vantage — a bloated arachnid, dwarfing all I'd yet seen, lounged in the web, watching music videos.

Big Mama was the original, the anchor. Take out Mama, and her spawn would vanish like smoke.

I plotted my move when a charm plunked into the woven den, leaking ley energy. Mama faded, leaving just her dancing leg visible. Black silk unfurled, held in place by a metal squirrel — glad someone found a use for them — and a small woman slid down headfirst and grinning. Edra-Rae, my favorite bartender. She was only ninety-seven but looked older — having aged normally until joining the Covenant at seventy-nine. Ley manipulation reversed aging — erasing disease, reducing inflammation, revitalizing cell growth, sparking vitality, and fueling Edra-Rae's passion for parkour.

My plan evaporated — ER, as we called her, was closer and was better suited for the job. She dropped onto the funnel's roof, denting it slightly.

Mama's leg froze.

Oblivious, Edra-Rae started slicing at the silk layers.

The giant spider scuttled forward, listening.

I was going to regret this, but we had to play the game if we wanted to win. I launched off the wall. The tunnel I landed on, flimsy though it certainly was, knocked the breath out of my lungs. The web buckled, trapping a frantic, chittering spider beneath me. Sharp elbows jabbed into my gut.

I shifted, attempting to free the offended party. The silk tore, and I, along with several beach-ball-sized monstrosities, landed on another tunnel some feet below. Much sturdier than the last, it appeared to be a main thoroughfare. I gained my feet and punted the overgrown arachnids off my perch.

"Kenny? Is that you?" Mama peered down from the edge of her funnel, pedipalps clicking with glee. "It is you! I hoped you'd drop in!"

Mama had jokes.

"Sous la Colline, knives out! Sheta Djew's here!" she yelled.

Another spider barreled down the chute, scuttling at the air. I bashed it aside with my pack, a snarl escaping me. "Giant spiders, Kodi? Really? Did I do something to piss you off? Lon's traps never have this many legs!"

Three more tumbled at me — I kicked, sickened by the resulting crunch.

"All the best stories have them — *Lord of the Rings, Harry Potter.* Your call sign's from *Perdido Street Station*, right? A good quarter of the dungeons have them. Spiders are a no-brainer."

Sadly, they were a fan-favorite.

"Like I've got time to read," I snapped, clawing at the sticky silk clinging to my hands. I hated things sticking to my hands, too.

"You need to make time. A healthy work-life balance is important!"

"My work-life balance is healthy. Without my work, I wouldn't have my life. Being lifeless is as unhealthy as it gets."

Edra-Rae finished hacking through the web and poked her head in. "Golly, look at that silly fae pretending she's an ugly-ass spider!"

Kodi's eight eyes bulged, then shriveled — her glamour unable to survive Edra-Rae's skeptical stare. All the webs and another tumbling spider dissolved like melting snow, dropping us. The cold, hard, concrete below grew at an alarming rate.

Had I put my air-light amulet back on after changing? I fumbled at my medallions — aegis, check; sensory booster, check — and the third? My thumb brushed the rune marking it, but my mind couldn't make sense of it. Hopefully, Oscar had sobered up by now.

Kodi flipped mid-air, morphing into a lanky, gray-skinned woman with eight yolk-yellow eyes nestled in a dainty face.

"Gross," I opined as we slapped the floor, bouncing like it was a stiff trampoline. Her tablet cracked between us.

"Like watching cheese mold on fast-forward," muttered Edra-Rae.

"Delicious, isn't she?" Kodi grinned, springing onto gray thigh-high boots paired with a grimy, yellow romper. "After trouncing Shiroi Tsuki last week, I figured no one'd show up to see her."

"Kodi, you look like a Tim Burton pin-up."

She twirled and curtsied. "Thank you!"

With a flick of her gnarly nails, she smirked, "Now, let's discuss your options. My sweet little pawns are gone, but your knight, bishop, and rook," guards hauled out Gaia, Jake, and Taylor, each bound and looking pissed, "are mine. There's no need to waste the evening, though. How about a little, friendly knife practice? One-on-one, Sheta Djew vs. Sous la Colline. If any of yours beat mine, we'll award them thirty seconds with no interference."

"Before the game is called," I added.

She grinned, flashing a fine set of dimples, and nodded.

"Out loud, Kodi."

She hooted, amused, but it paid to be cautious around Kodi.

"I, Kodi Carrington, défteros of Sous la Colline, swear to you, Hazel McKenna Jones, Representative of the Sheta Djew, that if any of the Sheta Djew triumphs over mine in a one-on-one knife duel, we'll give 'em thirty seconds, free of interference, before chasing after your witchy asses. May I never pop another boil if I lie. Happy?"

"Ecstatic."

She tossed me a blade, and we paired off.

"Right. Come on, then, Tiger. Let's see what ya got," my bartender grunted, nodding to the vampire in the ropey bodysuit.

One by one, the rest of my people were released from their bindings, which was an unexpected bonus; I hadn't negotiated for it.

Kodi's excitement was palpable. She faced me, eight transparent inner lids blinking, licking wetly at her eyeballs.

That was new, but the special effects were not. Who needed trash talk when you could turn your entire body into a cloud of flaky, dead skin and threaten to hug your opponent?

I crossed my arms, waiting for the show to close.

Her lurid, yellow eyes swelled before bursting like blisters, tracing rivers of ichor down her filthy cheeks. Dark lashes fluttered over brown eyes. The dimples never dimmed as ashy, cobweb hair gave way to flowing honey-brown locks. The romper was swapped out for a dusty coverall.

"All set?"

"Bring it on, buttercup," she invited.

We measured our battleground, assessing each other, feinting to test reaction times. She lunged, but I wasn't there. I sailed over her low strike, twisting to nick her shoulder.

I landed; my fatigues had deflected a thrust that would have bloodied my hip. I'd only been concerned with the knife I'd seen — my mistake. Our agreement hadn't ruled out magic or multiple blades.

Kodi smirked, teeth pointed despite her human shape; I grinned, suddenly feeling lighter. We made a tight circle, trading slashes, parrying for an edge. She wanted to end things fast, impatient to humble us, while I fought for time.

"Anniversary dinner Thursday," she grunted, almost missing my arm.

"RSVP'd. Port of Call, no gifts."

She snorted at my facetiousness. I let her mark my throat in exchange for slicing the tendons in her left elbow.

"Son of a Saturday morning cartoon," she swore…sort of. "I know you did. Xandre did, too."

I winced.

Kodi's sympathy flashed as she spun me, stabbing under my armpit, piercing a lung. "I get it, sweetie; I do. But Carter has to make a showing or Xandre will claim she was sent in her stead."

I nodded, gasping. Kodi's coveralls ran red — my fatigues matched. Silence fell as we clashed, my chest screaming. I slipped into a sterile haze made of muscle memory. With Kodi, I didn't need to hold back. I didn't need to be concerned about accidentally killing someone. My focus was so absolute, the world retreated. Bliss, until an elephant stomped on my chest.

My back thudded against a concrete wall, and I crumpled to the floor.

Across the room, Kodi stared uncomprehendingly at me from where she had crashed.

The room was silent — our people fixed on the same shadow. Oscar emerged, looking grumpier than usual — or hungover. He couldn't heal himself, more's the pity.

"Playtime's over, ladies. Kenny's got somewhere she needs to be."

"Spoilsport," I groaned, rolling until I could sit up. He prodded my ribs; I yelped, swatting him halfheartedly. His magic was already repairing my lung.

"We'd just gotten warmed up," Kodi whined. "Five more minutes?"

"You'd both be dead," Colette, Sous la Colline's medic, deadpanned. "Poor Antoine. All this blood and none of it drinkable."

Kodi sighed. "Draw?"

I blinked, too addled to fully appreciate her generosity. Before I could formulate a response, a body fell from the fourth floor, bouncing three times before lying still. The face was familiar even in my blurry vision. I blinked twice, and a name came to me.

"Laurent," I crowed.

I looked up and saw two American flags flapping from two poles on top of two buildings, slowly rotating. Standing underneath, his hood thrown back, was my apprentice — both of them, beaming like the gold-medal champions they were. I gave him — them — two thumbs up.

"Someone order delivery?" Colt asked, smiling so wide it had to hurt.

"Three teams?" Kodi screeched. "You sent your apprentice in here alone? Madwoman!"

"Oscar...I think you gave me a concussion," I whined. Shaking my head did nothing to cure my double vision.

"So, Sous la Colline's buying the drinks," Jake chirped, holding a wad of gauze to a bloody nose.

"No drinking. No drunk-casting," Oscar barked, adding, "My weaving might be a bit heavy-handed tonight. You'll live."

As apologies went, it was somewhat lacking. Before I could grumble about it, though, I remembered what he'd said earlier.

"Where do I need to be?"

"Lydia missed her check-in. Her sensor is active, and her vitals are normal. We're concerned that she might need an emergency pick-up."

What went unsaid was that if we left it too long, my Aunt Gregg would blow her cover saving my baby cousin, whether she needed saving or not. I whimpered and beat my fists on the floor in a mini-tantrum. All I wanted to do was go to bed. But, I couldn't. Family trumped all.

"Right."

I managed to stand up, mainly by using Oscar as an uncooperative ladder. "I'll keep. Have someone review her movements. Kodi, it's been a blast. I look forward to beating Sous la Colline again in a few weeks."

"Not a chance, pumpkin muffin, but you go ahead and dream."

Chapter 38: Clan Ritter

Kenny: August 28th in the In-Between

"Team one," Oscar barked into my ear.

"Ready," I replied, sweating around my gas mask.

Oscar insisted on slapping a little more life into me after Capture the Flag — the spit-and-duct tape special, due to time constraints. My chest still ached, and my head felt solid and heavy. It would have to do.

An intern had accused my cousin, working undercover in the Agora, of stealing office supplies. Lydia, knowing nothing of this, saw two security guards heading her way and, per protocol, tried to exit the building. She hadn't gotten far. Six months of planning had been washed down the drain because of jealousy. Worse still, Lydia's fake ID wouldn't hold up to APA scrutiny.

We'd been attached to a multi-strike mission — one bridge, three teams, three separate assignments, and only each other for backup. It was risky, but necessary.

"Team two?"

"Ready," Evy — Lady G that was — said.

"Team three?"

"Ready," Martin answered.

"Acknowledged. Anchor doors."

Four corridors branched off the bridge's hub, each leading to a different location. It was easier than building four portals — one for an escape hatch — and good practice for Flint, who was still inexperienced at jumping the lines in the field.

I channeled power into our eyelet, the peephole expanding in the bridge's green canvas wall — the tent-like construction manifesting from Flint's love of camping. We'd surveyed our drop-off. Breaking into the Agora's jail was new for me, and I'd rather have left Colt behind, but I needed a partner, and he was awake and eager while others were asleep. The job rated a four out of ten on difficulty — tight security, but we wouldn't be breaching the exterior. Colt wouldn't be allowed to pick and choose missions, so here we were.

The portal clicked, stabilizing.

"Door one anchored," I said.

"Door three anchored," Flint echoed, a fraction of a second behind.

Uh-oh. Evy'd hate being last — fieldwork hadn't come naturally to any of us, and though we'd adapted, some did better than others.

"Door two anchored," Lady Gelsemine reported calmly.

"Acknowledged. Watch your six. Deploy potions."

I ducked through the portal's membrane into the Agora's basement, emerging under a metal table in the guard room, boxed in by files. I snagged our marker — a business card for Zosime's Artifacts and Antiques, passed it to Mort to ditch, then set the automatic air freshener dispenser humming and pulled back.

"Team one marker retrieved. Potion delivered," I announced.

"Standby," Oscar said from the bridge's hub, his voice tight. He hated being support only; it was the nature of the beast, though. Tension coiled in me as we waited, visions of everything going wrong flooding my imagination. Two minutes. Three — the guard should be out.

"Team three marker retrieved. Potion delivered," Flint said.

Double uh-oh. Now Evy had something to prove.

"Acknowledged. Teams one and three stand by."

Four minutes. Five.

"Team two marker retrieved. Potion delivered," Lady Gelsemine panted. Relief hit like a battleaxe — Evy was safe.

"Acknowledged. Teams two and three, stand by. Team one, deploy."

"Deploying," I said, ducking through again.

The guard slumped in his chair, his bowl of popcorn scattered across the floor. I passed the air freshener off to Colt and stepped out from under the table. Bare concrete walls and a mix of off-white and yellow stained tiles — tea stains, no doubt; chamomile or hwangcha — surrounded us. I tossed the popcorn while Colt wriggled through. After a brief exchange in sign language, we lifted the guard, easing him to the floor. I hissed and shook my head as his head neared a stain. Colt took the hint, and we settled him on unbesmirched tiles.

Golden rule: I signed.

Mort grinned behind his mask. *Golden's about right. At least it doesn't stink.*

I grimaced, sat in the guard's chair, and plugged a zip drive into the computer, installing Acquire. Colt, fully focused, scanned the room. Silently, I cheered. He was wearing his aggregate glasses and wasn't fazed by a steaming hot spring formation filled with sixty or so muddy green, four-legged creatures, each equipped with a single opalescent eye, visible on a nearby plane. He was swiftly acclimating to true sight! The green guys' eyes remained glued to us like this was the premiere episode of season two following a season one cliff-hanger.

The app binged — it had worked its magic; twenty-three seconds, and we owned every security camera and surveillance spell in the building.

"Team three, deploy," Oscar ordered.

"Deploying."

Mort checked his mask, slid a gas tube under the door, and ducked through the portal to twist the tank valve. I checked my mask and installed Sesame on the computer.

"Team two, deploy."

"Deploying," Lady Gelsemine said, serene.

I watched the security feed as the gas worked, an unnatural stillness spreading over the prisoners. With a few clicks, I looped the recording back thirteen minutes — right after the guard ran checks — then deployed our get-out-of-jail-free card, unlocking cells twelve and twenty-nine. Colt slipped down the hall; I followed.

"Team two home. Package retrieved," Lady Gelsemine said evenly.

It had been less than five minutes! How had… Evy had used her magic — she must have. She had four people, two dogs, three cats, and a parakeet to retrieve. Unless the family just happened to be packed up and waiting, there was no other way. My stomach soured, but I bit my tongue. I bent the rules often enough; I did not restructure the ley network doing so, but I either trusted her or I didn't. She knew to scrub the scene. She was a team leader because she'd earned it.

There was a reason they didn't often let us work together. Fretting led to micromanaging.

"Acknowledged. Team two, stand by."

Mort hit cell twenty-nine; I entered twelve and found my red-haired cousin scowling in her sleep. Conscious or not, my cousins were spitfires. And inconveniently tall; Lydia was not a large person, but she had three inches on me. Shifting her into a fireman's carry was no joke. I got her up and turned to see Colt pass the cell with a young man draped across his shoulder.

We retreated to the guard's room and carefully unburdened ourselves. I slipped under the table and through the squat door. Colt shoved the man in after me. I grabbed his arms and pulled him through. Lydia received the same regrettably undignified service.

"Team one's package has been retrieved," I panted. "Someone let her mother know. Retrieval of zip drive in progress."

"Acknowledged. Team two, assist team one."

"Team two is en route." Lady G's voice was so determinedly free of smugness that she sounded positively smug about it.

Mort smirked. "Acknowledged."

Oh, Mort.

"Watch your mouth. We don't break protocol while our colleagues are still in the field," reproved Oscar.

"Apologies, sir," the kid said, chastened.

I darted back through and sat at the computer. I uninstalled Acquire and Sesame before uploading a third app — Expunge. It would erase any sign that we had been there and didn't need to be uninstalled. In just one minute, we'd be out — free and clear.

"Hey, Coltrane, unlock the door!" someone yelled, banging on the entrance.

"Crap," I hissed.

The furry, green things collectively leaned forward in their steamy pools, squirming anxiously.

I broke protocol and twisted magic to heft Coltrane into his chair as Expunge ticked down, forty-seven seconds left. Alarms wailed, lights flashed. I tossed the gas tube through the portal — twenty-nine seconds.

"Team three, home. Package retrieved."

A series of alarming clicks sounded from the doors — they were overriding the system. Eighteen seconds.

"Team three, assist team one."

Expunge hit full. I yanked the zip drive, dove through the portal, and Mort pulled me onto the bridge. Whipping around, I grabbed the air freshener dispenser and pumped six times, spraying the sleeping potion into the guard room. Lady G began dismantling the door.

"Team one home. Hot pursuit. Dismantling door one. Evacuate corridor one," I snarled into my headset.

The canvas roof over our heads sagged, then snapped taut. A nice recovery — just a few wobbles to iron out in Flint's concentration. Martin and his team reversed course, pale but outwardly calm as they quick-marched back to the bridge hub.

Tellus grabbed Evy and Colt and dragged them back. I stuck my head through the portal, needing to hear what was said.

"Coltrane, what the hell?"

They rushed over to Mr. Muscles, oblivious to the shrinking porthole under the table. My rapidly beating heart gave a funny little twitter in gratitude. Never had a door shrunk so slowly.

"Is he dead?"

"No, — he's been hexed. Alert the warlocks and check the cells. Call an ambulance!"

"I feel...odd..."

A guard dropped to the floor.

"Worstell! No, Mendez, don't come...in...here. Call...an......ambul..."

A second guard fell, and someone in the hallway barreled back the other way, their shoes squeaking against the ugly tiled floor.

"Oh, heck..."

The third guard dropped. I pulled my head back onto the bridge. When the aperture was the size of my fist, I halted its progress. Time to scrub my mess — the line I'd plucked to move Coltrane was humming like a guitar string. Three breaths, and my signature had been erased.

Through my abbreviated window, I saw one of the denizens of the outer worlds violently shake another, thrilled by the ley-infused suspense. I pulled off my gas mask and cackled, sealing the door.

What a rush!

I fiddled with the door's anchor points, feeling euphoric, energized! Like I'd eaten lightning and found it deliciously refreshing!

"Team one home. Door one sealed," I sang into my headset.

"Acknowledged," growled Oscar.

Lady G and Mort skidded down the hall, tackling me in their version of a gentle, affectionate squeeze. I assumed that's what it was. It could have been a pummeling, I suppose.

"I love you guys, too," I grunted. "Let me up. I need to pee."

"Gave me a coronary, you idiot," my sister ranted. "Oscar revived Lydia — she hasn't stopped cussing yet, and Aunt Gregg and Mom are waiting for us."

I slumped, my giddy buzz fading. I needed sleep! Sleep!

Evy's grin was sadistic.

Chapter 39: The Preternatural Dilemma

August 28ᵗʰ at Sullen Creek Farm

The strange and unexpected familiarity he felt at Punk Bunks hadn't dulled Veritas's appetite. He joined staff and guests for dinner on the screened-in porch linking the inn to Jones's house. Arlo played host, making introductions and keeping everyone supplied with barbecue, cold salads, and pie. Veritas, out of some sense of loyalty to Arlo, ate heartily.

The niggling feeling lingered into the night, always out of reach, though his soft, warm bed ensured a heavy sleep. The sensation followed him to breakfast and intensified every minute. He guessed things he shouldn't have guessed, knew things he had no way of knowing. The alluring man, lean and pale, with fangs and a curtain of black hair, making an acai bowl at the buffet wasn't a vampire; Tyson Groper was a goblin. And Veritas knew it without being told. He predicted that the guest sporting donkey ears — a Midasian from Anatolia in a rumpled monkey suit — would only take toast and coffee, and he'd been right. He'd also known to veer away from the sad-looking woman with long, colorless hair.

Breakfast, though lavish, was a casual event, with guests drifting in for light bites or full courses. Metal arms, unnoticed the night before, whizzed along copper tracks, keeping the sideboards stocked.

The previous evening, Veritas had become acquainted with Cully and Coen Haigh — two of the seven sisters favoring a Dark Academia look. On their advice, he took the ten-thirty brewery tour before the rush, then a leisurely lunch in the tasting room. Both proved thoroughly enjoyable, and the staff's enthusiasm sparked his own, prompting him to buy a home-brewing kit.

Aside from the odd fairy godmother, it all seemed so normal. Veritas nearly dismissed Arlo's strange remarks as part of the hotel experience when a young woman with glossy horns entered with two friends, one three feet tall, the other nearly eight.

"What's your problem?" snapped the short brunette with solid black eyes, catching his stare.

"I do apologize! It's just that my sister's horns never take a shine, unlike your friend's. I wondered if she had any recommendations," he lied, bracing for maximum embarrassment.

The horned woman, rightfully proud of her gleaming horns, had numerous tips to share — hydration, sun protection, and the correct waxing technique. Veritas scribbled them down and even ventured a question or two about extreme measures like sanding — half convinced he could publish the advice in Egress and make a tidy packet. The lady firmly instructed him to warn his fictitious sister against anything permanent until she'd done her research — some horns regrew, others did not.

After lunch, he strolled by the river, processing this brave new world. Egress was safe, coded, and predictable. This? He'd happened upon a bigger mystery than the one he'd expected. If supernatural beings were real, it would shift the very foundations of civilization. A great game…but off topic; was he really going to pursue this?

Maybe?

First, he had to prove it to himself. Especially considering the risk he'd be taking — not merely a prison sentence, but perhaps his life! There it was again — a half-memory teasing him. Why couldn't he remember?

On the hunt for hard evidence, he circled back to the hotel and browsed the library. His eye caught a handsome collection of naturalist illustrations scattered among the shelves — all moths belonging to the Saturniidae family.

On the coffee table, he recognized magazines like *Victoria*, *PC Gamer*, *Wired*, *BBC Gardener's World*, *Kill Screen*, and *Draft*. Other titles, such as *Bellwether*, a cultural guide to the Community, and *Vicissitude*, a journal focusing on the Lost Origin, were unknown to him. Both had articles following a string of robberies — lacrymatories, a Drebbel submarine, a set of hourglasses — with possible links to the Warped. Neither specified who 'the Warped' were. Zombies, perhaps? But why would zombies be interested in antiques?

A few books caught his eye — *The Preternatural Dilemma* by Edmund Slate, *A Criticism of Slatian Philosophy* by Dr. Evelyn Vine, and *The Anthropological War* by Dr. Vine and Enid Carter.

"Heavy stuff," remarked a gray-eyed woman with red hair and pointed ears, considering the Punk Bunks merch. Veritas, despite his weighty concerns, snagged an Arlo bobblehead for his dash.

"It's funny. I only read serious stuff on vacation…or for work," he admitted.

"Same," the redhead replied. "It's the only time I'm not too exhausted."

"Have you read these?"

She nodded, lifting *The Dilemma*. "Take time to think critically with Slate. Many call him narrow-minded, tossing around phrases like 'agents of chaos' and 'negative progress.' He incorporates a lot of historical symbolism and gets misinterpreted. He doesn't say chaos is evil, though people choose to take it that way."

"And Vine?" he asked, curious.

"The courageous daughter of the late, great Senator Vine. I used to think she was a pampered princess who wanted to be admired for her acumen. She got her doctorate in anthropology and put in her time as a grunt in field research. Now, she's the leading expert on the old powers. Vine doesn't think much of Slate, but they have a lot in common. They agree on the necessity of the creation-destruction cycle, organic change, and the dangers associated with any consolidation of power. What she really objects to are his criticisms of the Shunned — and even there, I think it boils down to semantics."

"Luke Vitruvio," he said, offering his hand.

"Angie Donahue."

"Will you be around for a few days? I'd love to discuss these after I've read them."

"Ang, we're set," a dark-haired young man called, pocketing a receipt as he approached.

"Blake, this is Luke Vitruvio," Angie said, her tone very older-sisterly. "Luke, my brother Blake. We're here for a few weeks; we'll have plenty of time to debate the merits of Slate and Vine."

"Edmund Slate?" Blake grimaced. "The torch-wielding, Warped-hating, pseudointellectual philosopher? That Slate?"

Angie just rolled her eyes, ruffling her brother's hair. "Everyone has an opinion on Slate."

Chapter 40: Living the Dream

James Darrow opened his lovely brown eyes, inhaled deeply, and realized he wasn't dead. This confused him — as it should. The first day had been touch-and-go, needing constant care; the second wasn't much better. Oscar stepped forward, but I held up a finger — letting Darrow get his bearings.

He ran his hands over his body, searching for wounds, finding only smooth skin and the tug of an IV. Perplexed, he studied the medical equipment, the seamless white stone ceiling — elna quarried in Wenen — above and pondered his miraculous survival.

As his expression and gestures grew increasingly agitated, I felt some pity for him. Ethos had a distinct new-age, temple-like aesthetic — drenched in light and draped in a jungle of plants; Maggie used it as an auxiliary greenhouse. Propping up on his elbows, Darrow gaped at the utopian city beyond the curved glass windows, eyes wide, wondering if he had crossed through the pearly gates.

"We call it Ethos," I murmured.

He leapt straight up like a startled cat, landing on his feet — good reflexes. His legs buckled, but Oscar caught him before he hit the floor.

"I didn't mean to startle you," I lied, holding up a stack of laundry and wondering if his reaction had been genuine or an excellent performance. He was tattooed with the marks of the Mwindaji wa kimya, a shifter cadre, but it could be fake. There was nothing in his expression to suggest deceit, though — only intense wariness. "We brought your clothes – washed and mended."

"Thanks," he grumbled, his voice rough as he reluctantly accepted Oscar's assistance. His eye tracked my movements as I set the clothes at the foot of the bed. He was weak and underweight, yet still dangerous — like a caged panther, biding his time.

Once he was settled on the bed, and neither Oscar nor I had displayed any aggression, he jutted his chin toward the window.

"The city is Ethos?"

"The artwork. It's not real — a collaboration between Davy Moran, a local artist and, coincidentally, one of your nurses, and me. I'm Kenny Jones, Representative of the Sheta Djew. Welcome to Sullen Creek Farm."

He licked his lips, mind whirring.

"How did I get here?"

"We hoped you'd tell us. You were found unconscious and near death on our eastern border. Oscar," I gestured to that man of mystery, "is my second and our chief medic. You wouldn't have survived the trip to the Clinic, so we treated you here."

He nodded, lost in thought. "Thank you both."

"You're welcome."

He stared out the window. "The people move. It looks…real."

"Yes," I agreed, watching a woman leap from a solarpunk skyscraper, wings unfurling as she glided over a waterfall. The work was Davy's interpretation of Cartref Afon — a fabled practitioner city and a dream we hoped to realize. "I'm an ipseitatum dualis — I enchanted Davy's artwork."

He nodded, eyes on the woman's flight. Oscar's gaze sharpened — Darrow had held his breath for two beats, a subtle flinch we weren't meant to catch. IDs were controversial; many in the Community, Unrelenting and Correctionist alike, frowned on tampering with the lines.

"You've been through quite an ordeal, and I'm afraid it's not completely over."

Darrow's stare hardened, daring me to start something.

You'll know if and when I threaten you, pal.

"You're healing, but slowly. A curse clings to you — fatal, if we can't lift it. We're close, but it would help if we knew its source and nature. Who cast it? Why?"

He turned back to the winged woman lazily looping in the sun, and shook his head. "I don't know."

My eyes flicked to Oscar, who subtly shook his head. We both thought Darrow was lying.

"No worries — we'll crack it one way or another. You're stable enough to go to the Clinic now, but you're welcome to stay if you prefer."

He snorted, rubbing his face. "I hate to impose further, but I'll stay till I can walk if that's all right."

"It's no imposition. We found your medical card in your wallet; the farm's an Emergency Medical Station. Payment was prompt."

He laughed, genuine and bright. "One less weight on my mind."

I glanced at Oscar, who shrugged. I didn't know what was going on with our Mr. Darrow, but…he didn't seem malicious. Still…

"Would this be a good time to introduce your med team?"

"Please."

The doors whooshed open as I neared. Davy, chatting in the hall, turned. I waved them in, signaling caution. I didn't trust our patient, not yet.

"Mr. Darrow, meet Davy Moran."

Davy grinned and waved, jubilant at his survival. "Nice to meet you!"

"Sawyer Jeong handles nights." Sawyer was better able to contain his joy. "Jenny Briggs, Breah Franklin, and Taylor Amsel fill in as needed."

He nodded to each, then inhaled deeply. "I'm a little rusty when it comes to gratitude, but thank you. If there's ever anything I can do for any of you, tell me. I pay my debts."

Chapter 41: All Right

August 28th at Sullen Creek Farm

The bastard Triumph's engine settled to a low chug as Aiden Benilde eyed the sculpture over the pond — a rustic composition of beer barrels. Water gurgled out from bungholes and tumbled into the pool below. A patinaed copper sign read *'Sullen Creek Farm and Brewery'*.

He guided the bike onto the narrow lane, boots skimming just above the pavement for several feet. The road curved, and by the fifth bend, young oaks and sweet gum gave way to ancient pines and gnarled willows, the Missouri landscape fading into something else entirely. Trees arched overhead, glowing like stained glass in the afternoon light.

Atop a hill, the drive swerved, revealing two eccentric houses seated on a rise, like the dark lord and lady of the forest, surrounded by their small court. Shadows thickened as he parked, stretching toward him as the wind whispered dire warnings. The temperature plummeted, and a stench, sweet and rotting, drifted from the forest — which Aiden ignored. With something like a shrug, the trees relented, and the wind ceased its dark prognostications. Sunlight filled the clearing again, and what had seemed almost ominous a moment before became downright cheerful.

Nudging the kickstand down, he shed his helmet and grabbed his bag. Aiden stalked up the porch steps, passing a spare figure in a rocking chair picking at a guitar, and entered the hotel.

"En garde, you peach-faced, cookie-stealing chipmunk," menaced a pale giant, wielding a limp rubber chicken.

"En garde, you bleach-bellied giraffe," a tiny redheaded child roared back, brandishing a sturdier bird.

The faux fowl clashed with a frenzy of chilling clucks.

Aiden's weekender thumped loudly on the marble floor. When that failed to quell the uprising, he swung the door, setting the brass bell jangling.

"Oh! Sorry," Arlo bleated, his cheeks tinged with color. "Minelli Paper, we'll settle this later, once and for all! Welcome to Punk Bunks, sir! How may I assist you?"

The girl stared up at Aiden with large, cornflower blue eyes and sighed, her fists on her hips. He nodded by way of an apology for the interruption.

"Reservation under Benilde."

"Absolutely! One moment," Arlo chirped, vanishing around the corner.

Minelli Paper stepped closer, examining him with frank curiosity, then sniffed. Aiden pondered her with no less interest.

"Are you a pirate? You don't smell like a hunter."

"Not a pirate, not a hunter. May I?" He indicated the chicken.

After some deliberation, she gave him the bird. He set his helmet on the table and adjusted her grip. "Better for slashing."

The girl's smile was angelic.

A frosted glass panel slid open.

"Here we are," Arlo said, knocking a tablet off the console table. "Oops! Oh…uh…thanks. Please verify that our information is correct and…um…I'll need a photo ID and credit card."

After assuring the concierge that he did not require assistance with his luggage, Aiden climbed the stairs. The door to room seven, Port Dejima, was in the center of the hall on the third floor. The room he entered, however, was a spacious corner bedroom with adjacent plate glass walls overlooking a post-cyberpunk metropolis glowing with candy-colored neon lights and holographic hover-signs.

Aiden checked the hall — rooms to both sides — then shut the door again, an eyebrow arched in consideration. He tested the glass: cool, solid, normal. Tiny vehicles slid through the neon-lit cityscape below, aerials ferrying people and androids between rooftop bars. The opposite building had fifty-eight floors.

All right.

Turning away, he noticed that there were no fingerprints on the glass. He touched the window again — nothing. A burly man in a suit and sunglasses, arguing with an aqua-hued hologram on the next-door balcony, stole his attention. The faux-hawked projection winked at him; Sunglasses glanced over and gave him a hard stare before storming back inside. He half-expected an angry knock on his door — the ley work was that convincing.

He unpacked, stowing clothes in the closet dresser. Aiden strode over to what he assumed was the bathroom door, pausing as the slick, black panel automatically slid into the wall.

"Shit," he muttered, staring into the washroom with its angled plate-glass windows. A sexy, black tub sat a mere twelve inches from the edge of oblivion.

Chapter 42: Delaying the Inevitable

August 28th at Sullen Creek Farm

Books about games and movies usually admit that their subjects were
fictional. *The Preternatural Dilemma* did not.

Nor did *A Criticism of Slatian Philosophy*. Both tomes accepted vampires,
ghosts, and zombies as verified races. Eight chapters into Slate's opus, and
the author's conviction (delusion) was undeniable: things went bump in the
night. Slate even claimed to be one — a born vampire, as opposed to made.
Yet Veritas lived in the real world — realistic-looking fangs and elf ears were
a click away.

"They can't be real," he insisted.

There was a knock on the door. "Housekeeping," called a feminine
voice.

"Later," he yelled back, closing the laptop and opening the door long
enough to put the 'Do not disturb' placard on the door — squeaking when
he noticed the red robot silently rolling down the hall. Its head swiveled
back toward him. She — it — scanned the placard and grinned. He slammed
the door shut and locked it.

The staff and guests seemed normal…more or less. Words, horns, and
sourceless knowledge were not proof. Yeah, some things were decidedly
off…like a cosplayer who thought Paul Atreides was a hero. But…if he was
wrong…if supernaturals existed, then he was the ignorant cosplayer. A
misstep was inevitable — he hadn't had access to the source material! What
then? No wonder he'd had to hack the hotel website — they were hiding
from humans.

Shit. He'd hacked their site!

He couldn't let them find out. Even if everyone he'd met seemed nice,
not all supernaturals would be. Fairy tricks, hag appetites, bogle malice —
the legends came from somewhere! But…he couldn't walk away. Every time
someone disappeared, he'd wonder if he could have prevented it. No —
humanity needed him. He had to do something!

He sat down at the carved desk and opened his laptop, searching the dark web for The Contingency Plan — a journalist and PI haunt he'd never needed before. A dead man's switch. It would keep his evidence safe and, if he failed to check in, send it wherever he chose.

Swallowing hard, Veritas entered his email address…and was informed that an account matching that address already existed. He stared at the screen for several seconds, seeing his déjà vu in a new and terrifying light. It wasn't possible… There were no gaps in his memory…but he'd always been nosy, even as a child.

"Mo-oom, the fart-face was using the office phone to listen in on my calls again," his *sister's long-ago voice echoed in his head. "We heard him giggling!"*

This was crazy…but not unbelievable.

Hands trembling, he typed in a password.

Incorrect.

Veritas never used the same password twice. He had a system for their creation — sixteen characters, no words, in an order that only made sense to him. If he could determine when the account had been made, he could unlock it…assuming he had made it. Veritas grabbed a legal pad, using notes on his phone to work backwards through his password history.

Forty minutes later, he had gone back three years and was climbing the stone walls. He had nothing. Veritas gave up and pressed the "forgot password" option. He knew the site wouldn't use the typical security questions, or there would be a twist.

There was. He had selected, if he had truly been involved in the creation of this account, a laundry list of chemical notations for the first challenge question. Not having a strong background in chemistry, he skipped to the next question. A map filled his screen. The Southwest US… With a surge of excitement, he clicked on Roswell and…was booted off the site.

"You have merely delayed the inevitable," he murmured, vowing to crack this mystery — later.

Navigating back to the website, he created a new account and began uploading pictures of Slate's Dilemma and his clock-punk hotel room.

Chapter 43: Hold My Beer

"...and the elevator," trilled Davy, waving down the hall. Darrow buzzed behind her in an electric wheelchair.

When we'd presented it, he had sneered and tried standing. We caught him — again, but only just. He graciously allowed us to heft him into the chair.

"An EMS with clinic-grade equipment," he observed, glowering at the device that made him mobile. "Unusual for a farm."

"We buy lemons cheap and Kenny fixes them," Davy explained, then grinned at me. "Care to explain why it's necessary?"

Darrow's eyes sharpened.

"It's not that interesting. I've represented the Sheta Djew for only ten years. My relative anonymity and new-kid status drew out the challengers. The first year, we were hacked, blackmailed, harassed, ambushed, assaulted, and finally three members of our cadre were kidnapped and murdered."

Darrow's nod was suitably grim. It was a common enough story — and a load of tripe. The Covenant staged it, providing cover for consolidating our people and building our reputation. It was true, however, that we lost three people.

"I'd made the mistake of trying to negotiate over the lesser offenses, and my people paid the price. A statement had to be made. With the Quorum's blessing, we hunted down those responsible, executed them, and disbanded their cadres."

Davy huffed.

"You're not telling it right! The Sheta Djew petitioned the Quorum for retribution rights against seventeen individuals and three cadres. The cadres claimed the attacks had been perpetrated by rogue members and petitioned for immunity. There was a six-day trial. Othello York spoke for Sinnihte; Mallory Engel for Boswachter; Anthea Saelim for Jug-eum-ui Nolae; and Leonore Drew for Sheta Djew. Nore cleaned their clocks. Nineteen hours after permission had been granted, it was over."

Davy held her hand to her head like a gun. I rolled my eyes as she concluded with two words, "Double-tapped."

With her thirst for violence, it was a wonder Eli hadn't turned into a psychopath. Only one person died — and at our healer's hands. We hadn't been friends in those days, and his protective instincts had surprised us both.

"Our culture had to change," I jumped in before Davy could vent her imagination further. "Everyone learned defense, and it grew from there. We participate in survival exercises and extreme sports all over the world. In the last five years, we've not lost a soul to cadre warfare. Ninety-one percent of our injuries are from training."

"And seven percent because we are now the proud capital of 'hold my beer and watch this,'" Davy added. "You can't cure stupid. We've tried."

"That's not fair."

"Stoo-pid," retorted Davy.

"Inexperienced. It may take two or three injuries — and a dire warning from Oscar — but eventually, they learn."

A door ahead opened, and a guest exited his room. We waved as the Michael Caine look-alike tipped an imaginary hat and disappeared down the stairs.

"Another patient?" James inquired.

"No, Punk Bunks is part beer hotel, part staff housing, and, when required, part recovery ward. Oscar is in room ten if you need anything."

His expression was eloquent — he'd rather die than call for help. Davy was right; sometimes you couldn't cure stupid.

She pressed the call button.

"Opening a hotel seems an odd choice," the patient observed, entering the elevator.

"A dare," I explained, a small, hard smile curling my mouth. "We're prepared now."

Darrow looked dubious, as well he might.

When the cage doors opened, Davy launched her tour, leading us into the atompunk kitchen and dining room.

"Breakfast and dinner are served on the screened-in porch unless there's bad weather," she explained. "There's always beer and snacks in here, but until Oscar gives the all-clear, no alcohol."

"While you're recovering, we'll provide lunch. Let the medic on duty know if you want to join us on the porch," I chimed in. He'd be on a strict Mediterranean diet for a while, but he needn't be isolated.

Davy tugged the red retro fridge open and scanned the interior. "Toffee cookies," she announced, grabbing three for us.

Darrow examined the misshapen lump dubiously, then took a hesitant bite. They didn't look like much, but they melted in the mouth.

"I thought I heard someone," a voice boomed like thunder.

Darrow glanced to the right but, otherwise, displayed no surprise at our receptionist's arrival. His gaze continued to travel up until he reached Arlo's pretty face.

"Basketball?"

The young Goliath smirked and replied, "Underwater rugby."

"This is Arlo Freeman, our concierge," Davy explained. "Arlo, this is James Darrow."

After the two men exchanged courtesies, Arlo was all business. "When you're up to it, Mr. Darrow, there's a questionnaire for you. It helps us ensure a pleasant stay for our guests."

"Arlo," scolded Davy.

"It serves an important purpose," Arlo insisted, red-cheeked and self-conscious.

"What kind of questionnaire?" inquired the patient.

Arlo whipped a paper out from nowhere and presented it.

"No problem. Do you have a -"

Arlo handed him a pen. Mr. Darrow stuffed the rest of his cookie into his mouth and began writing.

"Sorry about Arlo. He's…enthusiastic," Davy murmured as we rolled out onto the dining porch. Mismatched sideboards guarded each set of double doors. Five long farm tables, with assorted chairs, ran end-to-end down the center of the room. A stone fireplace divided the space; the far side hung with sleeping swings.

"He's dedicated. It's admirable," observed Darrow.

"It is," I agreed, liking him for defending Arlo.

Davy opened the door, and he rolled into our quirky kitchen. The room ran the width of the house and was lined with stained apothecary-style cabinets. The countertops were soapstone, and a long wooden worktable served as an island. Two people, one in a flame-colored pant suit paired with a kiss-the-cook apron and the other in a suit straight out of Dickens, a short top hat, and a ruffled apron reading 'Whatever happens, we're eating it,' sang "Kyrie" into carrots.

Davy joined in.

Half-bemused and half-amused, Darrow watched the performance. He gave a start when he realized that the background music wasn't a recording. Maggie's hanging plants — a philodendron and an ivy — had been outfitted with small drums which they periodically whipped with their tendrils. A trio of parrots danced on the back of a chair and sang backup. Two mechanical arms hanging from the copper piping above the cabinets wailed on a guitar.

"Mondays are bake day. We all get a little excited."

Such displays of ley manipulations were unusual within the Community, but IDs did show off. With this many practitioners living in close quarters, it was inevitable that a few innovations would emerge. Too many beers, and bang, we had a golden pothos that unicycled all on its own — although the unicycle did most of the work. It made home home.

Darrow stared at Gidget, tracing the copper piping to a contraption resembling an old punch card machine mounted to the wall. Tracks and clockwork ran above the upper cabinets and along the V-groove backsplash. The arms washed dishes in the apron-front sink, boiled ears of corn, expertly frosted a cake, and shredded cabbage on a stand mixer.

Davy tugged Déjà and Derringer over for introductions. Darrow stared, his eyes locked on my personal assistant.

"Mr. Darrow, allow me to introduce Ms. Florence Theriot, better known as Déjà, and this handsome fellow is Derringer," Davy enthused, half-hugging the automaton and playfully flicking his metal mustache. The ensuing ting vibrated through the air.

"Ms. Moran, you're too kind," Derringer declared, bashful but pleased. A timer sounded, and Derringer jumped. "The cornbread!"

"It needs another minute," Déjà called after him, adding privately, "He doesn't understand cast-iron cookery, Kenny. Remember that the next time you upgrade his circuits."

"It needs another minute," Derringer called, and she rolled her eyes.

"So, Derringer is...," Mr. Darrow began, trailing off because he didn't know what direction to go in.

"I am the Representative's personal assistant and steward of the main house," the automaton proudly reported.

"And an absolute treasure," added Davy.

Derringer waved off the compliment, blushing.

"That sounds like it ought to keep you busy," Darrow observed tactfully, still unsure of the correct etiquette.

"Not so much as you might think," the mechanical man said, gesturing to the pipe network. "Most of the housekeeping is as automated as I am, and the Representative is a hands-on leader. Much of my time is spent reminding her to slow down, delegate, and take care of herself."

"And cooking," purred Davy, sniffing the contents of a pot.

"Derringer is a gifted chef," I agreed.

"Oh, but Déjà supervises," he interjected.

"Not really," she laughed. "I end up singing with the birds and punching out recipe cards."

She waved a hand to indicate a stack of stiff blue cards on the worktable.

"So that machine..."

"The cards tell the system what to do. Some sequences are performed automatically, such as taking out the trash and washing the dishes, but recipes require more precise instructions," I explained. "And some demand more intuitive handling than Gidget can provide."

Darrow turned back to the automaton. "So, you're a gourmet?"

"I do not require nutrients; however, the Representative was my creator, and much of her personality passed to me. She loves to cook, so I love to cook. Although I'll venture that my results are more consistent."

Davy bit her lower lip, clapping both hands over her mouth, failing to disguise her snorting. Déjà just grinned.

"Why is that?"

"Because if she isn't hyper-fixated, her attention span is five seconds long — on a good day," Eli explained, entering through the hall and heading for the fridge, Boruta close on his heels. "Aunt Kenny gets halfway through a recipe and remembers that the Great Buttinsky and Petal haven't had their medicine. She'll rush out, never remembering that a glorious mac and cheese casserole's in the oven. Burnt macaroni and cheese is very disappointing."

"Buttinsky?"

I cackled. Eli's nonchalance killed me.

"Goats," Déjà offered. "Sullen Creek Farm has a petting zoo."

"Sullen Creek Farm is a zoo," Maggie rasped, banging through the back door and plucking a beer from the fridge. She was two swigs in before she spotted Darrow.

"Oh, the stiff survived. Congratulations. When's dinner? Do I have time to order parts?"

Chapter 44: A Guessing Game

Kenny: August 29ᵗʰ at Sullen Creek Farm

"Hazy, love, how's your paw?" I asked the Flemish Giant rabbit while examining said paw. "You tried to get into the littles' warren again, didn't you? Your paw won't heal if you keep digging at concrete. Salome? Ah, she's hiding. Mr. Spacely, don't rub your butt on the rug. Goodnight, Spacey, what did you eat today? Whoof! Remind me to burn this! I can taste it! Ughh! Mystery, don't stalk Clovis."

"And that," Nore announced from above, "is our distinguished Representative Jones."

Oh, glory.

"Hello!" I chirped from the living room floor, buried in animals, up to where Nore and several guests peered down over the mezzanine rail.

An elderly couple gawked. The most handsome man on Earth tried not to smile while brushing his luxurious curls out of dark, mysterious eyes. Three daughters of Clan Haigh snickered while the eldest, Raleigh, gave me an exuberant thumbs up. A brawny fellow with long golden-brown hair tied in a ponytail stood behind her. He alone didn't react — absorbed by his phone.

"Paul and Beatrice Galanis; Luke Vitruvio; Rhian, Briony, Greer, and Raleigh Haigh; and, last but not least, Aiden Benilde, meet Kenny. Kenny, meet our guests. We were discussing home-brewing," Nore explained.

The sound of his name brought Mr. Benilde's head up, stealing my breath. The man looked exactly how I imagined a warlock ought to look — dangerous, disciplined, and like a block of ice. Taller than average, his burly body was a carved wall of "you cannot pass". Despite a dusting of stubble, there was a hint of military correctness in his posture — a mentality that extended beyond tucked shirts and shined shoes. A slender scar bisected his eyebrow and stretched down to the corner of his jaw. Ironically, the eyepatch covered the other eye.

If it hadn't been so ridiculous, he would be my front-runner for the enemy among us. But that would be too absurd. He was too big, too masculine, too intimidating, too obvious. Something painfully stupid and feminine in me fluttered her eyelashes when he glanced my way. It was probably best that, after his good eye had its fill, his attention returned to his phone.

"It's a pleasure," I said — not at all disappointed — and shifted my glasses to take an unobstructed gander at our guests. I studied the lines while stroking Cartman as he clawed his sizable behind onto my torso and curled up like a fluffy nautilus. My big boy found a tender spot with his kneading, and I keened, trying to unhook him. Vitruvio had the most ley activity gathered around him, but that meant little. Maybe he had the least control or attracted the most energy.

"I suggested we take a look at your library."

"Do any of you have experience with brewing?" I asked.

"I'm a novice. Thought I'd try a batch and see how it goes," Aiden Benilde replied without glancing up. His voice was not as deep as Arlo's, but I could still feel it rumble in my chest. Or that might have been Cartman. The ginger had an impressive purr.

"I'm a noob, as well."

Vitruvio's voice was a pleasant baritone.

"Bea, here, made some bang-up cider, and last year we tried our hand at a Porter," boasted Paul Galanis, making his wife blush happily. "Turned out all right, too!"

"Wonderful. A Porter is an excellent brew to start with — they're more forgiving than some. John J. Palmer's *How to Brew* is great for beginners. The gift shop has some solid starter kits and books. Feel free to read anything from our collection during your stay. Lon, the manager of our brewhouse, and I would be happy to answer any questions. Cartman, sweetness, your tail is — puugh — in my mouth!"

"I take it you're an animal person," Greer Haigh observed, chortling as I battled the plumy tail. She knew very well what kind of person I was. The Covenant and Clan Haigh had been neck-deep in negotiations for two months and had a history that spanned nine years.

Cartman reluctantly repositioned himself.

One of the younger Haighs, Briony, shifted her eyes, first to Vitruvio, then to Benilde, before wagging her eyebrows.

The last thing I needed was a pack of high-spirited Haighs flirting with guests. I might have to be polite to them, but there were boundaries — especially with the APA interested in us.

I tried to sit up, but something caught my locks. A short investigation revealed The Stig and Jezza trying to weave my hair into a literal rat's nest.

"What gave you that impression?" I asked, freeing myself.

"They certainly think so," drawled Nore, nodding to my beasties. "New arrivals show up most weeks. We rehouse those we can and those we can't..."

"I adopt," I finished, rubbing behind Mel's ear as he blocked Mystery from pouncing on Clovis. "They're my babies."

A clanging outside alerted us that dinner was served.

"Shall I bring a plate in for you since your babies are all comfy now?" suggested Nore with slightly more than the required sarcasm.

"No, thanks. Cartman would think it was for him, and he's quite fat enough."

The tables had nearly filled when I made it onto the porch. I ended up squeezing between Aiden and Luke, who Arlo introduced as Count Vitruvio for reasons known only to Arlo. Rhian Haigh eyed the seating arrangements with satisfaction and whispered something to her sister, Monroe, who only shook her head.

Apparently, one of them minded her own beeswax.

"Red bowls have beans in the chili and green bowls have none," Derringer announced, making himself heard above the din.

Mel parked himself under my chair as I recovered from such close proximity to Count Vitruvio. Upon review, I stood firm in my analysis. He was a work of art. His dark brown curls looked like he'd missed a haircut, just a touch long and sinfully soft. His olive complexion glowed with health. He had prominent cheekbones, a square jaw, and a cleft chin — the works. It was a wonder the Haighs hadn't claimed him for themselves. Liquid eyes regarded me solemnly as I completed the survey, his mouth curving in forgivable smugness.

"Do you prefer Luke or Count Vitruvio?" I asked, passing a bowl of chili down the line.

"Luke is fine," he mumbled, blushing. I hoped Arlo hadn't embarrassed him. "Coleslaw?"

"Please! Coleslaw, Aiden?"

"Nobody move!" hollered a voice from the far end of the porch.

One-third of the room froze — two with their hands up; the other two-thirds had acclimated to the recurring pretense. Three police officers and two firemen made their way through the door at the far end of the porch and over to the table.

"You're not funny, Dad," Gaia called to Dave Coinin.

A few people seemed to disagree, chuckling as their neighbors realized that the vice squad wasn't raiding us and cautiously began filling their plates.

"Just in time," Armand hollered, passing them bowls.

It was several minutes before every dish had made it around the table, and a few more before conversation resumed. The farmhands took food seriously.

"Aunt Kenny has a motorcycle, Aiden," Eli informed my neighbor. "Aiden has a motorcycle, too."

"What make?" I inquired, noting our guest's lovely table manners. He held his fork in his left hand — European style. I briefly considered feeling ashamed of my own, but gave a mental shrug. I was what I was.

"It's a mutt — mostly Triumph. You?"

"Aunt Kenny has a Gremlin," Eli informed him.

"Not quite, Eli; her name is Gremlin. She's a Honda CB400F. Colt, would you hand down the jalapeno cornbread?"

Eli shrugged. Somehow, he'd never caught the vehicle bug. His mama was nuts about vintage V-dubs, though.

"If motor sports interest you, you should come racing with us," Armand suggested to Aiden, his light South African accent flavoring his words.

"After signing a waiver," I put in, pointing my fork at Armand.

"Of course," he agreed, wide-eyed and innocent.

"Motorcycle racing?" Aiden inquired, showing a degree of enthusiasm for the first time.

"Uh, no, not quite. Lon, what's next on the docket?" I asked the bear-like man sitting opposite me.

His eyes rolled heavenward as he struggled to remember, "Dry boat racing Mondays; trials riding Wednesdays; and skid plate racing Fridays," he rattled off. "I'd have to check the calendar for any one-offs."

"What is dry boat racing?" inquired Luke, spooning himself a second helping of the cucumber salad.

"Dry boat racing isn't a traditional race," Armand clarified. "The shell of a boat — larger is better — is hitched without a trailer to your vehicle, preferably one where the front bumper has been reinforced. Competitors drive around a dirt track attempting to disconnect their rivals' boats from their vehicles. Whoever has the most intact boat, still connected, wins."

"Why would anyone do that?"

"We'll try anything at least once," I told Luke. "It makes life more interesting and prepares us for the unexpected."

Aiden's stormy gaze pierced me and swept away.

"Sometimes we get a little too caught up in things. Grilled peaches, Aiden? Kenny, remember Two-Nine-Oh-Two-Nine Everesting? 'Leave me! Take the penguin and go on without me,'" Lon wailed in an appalling imitation.

Pity he was too far away to kick.

"First off, I do not sound like that," I retorted, pointing my fork at him now. "Second, it wasn't the penguin. This year was the polar bear."

"In Snow Basin? A gigantic, four-foot stuffed polar bear?" James Darrow demanded, looking rocked. "Halfway through and two-thirds up, you slipped and twisted your ankle. Made a horrible sound! Lon took the polar bear but stuck around as another guy and I helped you limp to the first-aid station. I thought you were out, but I saw your final ascent thirty-three hours in."

I stared at him open-mouthed and, for some inexplicable reason, batted my lashes.

"I still have the penguin," grunted Oscar from further down the table. "Looks real nice with the polar bear."

"And both look adorable in your post-apocalyptic bedroom," snickered Maggie from way, way down the table.

The post-apocalyptic theme of Oscar's room was misleading. Bill Murray's house in *Zombieland* had inspired it, and it was extremely comfortable, if a trifle flamboyant. The penguin and polar bear did look rather out of place on his crimson and gilt sofa.

"I still say you cheated, old man," accused Lon.

Oscar smirked, showing off his fangs. "We'll find out next year, son."

"Hey, that is the baddest post-apocalyptic décor the world will ever know. Giant polar bears and penguins fit in seamlessly," declared Arlo.

I couldn't see where he sat, but no matter. He made himself heard.

"If I — uh — didn't say th...thank you before, thank you," I half-stuttered.

James smiled, little creases forming in the corners of his mouth. "You thanked me, and you're still welcome. I'm glad you were able to finish. I thought your ankle was broken. And...I'm sorry, but Lon's imitation was solid."

"Vindication," Lon roared, pumping his fists.

"Calm down, you overgrown pillock," hissed Maggie.

"Kenny, it's time," hollered Nore. I couldn't see her, either, but that was typical for our dinner conversations.

"Derringer," I called, standing up and searching for my assistant. He nodded and rose from his perch between Eli and Lou, ducking back into the kitchen.

"Everyone, if I could have your attention, please! Today is a very important day!"

The table fell silent.

"Oh, no," moaned Olivia, one of the few Maggie trusted with the care of our precious hop crop. She hid her face behind her hands, but with her auburn hair, she was easy to identify.

"Shut up and take it, birthday girl," crowed Mags as Derringer arrived with the candlelit, three-tiered cake.

"Today, Olivia turns twenty-nine years old," I announced.

"Last year you said thirty," Eli reminded me without looking up from his chili.

He got considerably more laughs than Dave had. Olivia was fifty-two but looked about thirty-five — roughly the age she had discovered magic.

"Yes, well, Olivia is peculiar that way. Next year she'll be twenty-eight," I misinformed him. "Anyhoo, Olivia has been a vital part of our story for six years now. She is diligent, knowledgeable, and above all, she puts up with Maggie."

"Here, here," enough voices chorused for Maggie to be uncertain who to glare at. She settled for everyone.

"Happy birthday, Olivia!"

Derringer set the glowing cake in front of her, and everyone sang the Happy Birthday song. Breah held back her hair as she blew out the candles.

"Speech, speech, speech," chanted Davy.

Olivia stood, unsuccessfully trying to push her radiant curls back behind her shoulders, and motioned for silence. She looked around at us and, eyes a little moist, said, "I just want y'all to know...how much I hate every last one of you! There had better be ice cream!"

Chapter 45: Wenen Rome

August 29th at Sullen Creek Farm

"Did one escape?"

Hazel McKenna Jones whirled around, dreadlocks slapping against the carved chest belonging to Aiden Benilde. He was fresh from a run, glistening under the pre-dawn lamplight of the parking lot.

The Representative gasped, startled.

"Sorry. You got it?" he asked, smirking.

He'd caught the base of the cage she carried, steadying it. Inside, three rats protested the bumpy ride.

"I've got it. Thanks," Jones murmured. "Scamp, Gigi, and Hibiscus would never forgive me if I dropped them."

"Well, I'm glad Scamp, Gigi, and Hibiscus have come to no harm."

Her mouth twitched. His tone was teasing, and she didn't know quite what to do with it. This was the fourth time she'd bumped into Benilde since last night — and the second time without any conspiring Haighs to blame.

"My fault entirely," Benilde told the rats.

They believed him and began berating him instead.

"I don't think I'll make their Christmas card list."

Jones tucked the cage into the mint green Chevy Cameo, speculative.

"That's…an idea," she murmured, then shouted, "Davy! Christmas cards with fur babies in Santa hats, paw-print signatures? Might boost adoptions!"

"Brilliant," Davy Moran hollered, handing a crate of guinea pigs to Armand Dlamini.

"Sorry," Jones said to Benilde. "Shameless theft. And the babies don't mean what they say. Tuesdays are just stressful. We partner with the local rescue for a Shelter Safari in the pub lot."

Alonzo Cowfer zip-tied a crate of chinchillas into the truck.

"No, Kenny, don't take Babbage!"

A young girl darted through, nearly upsetting a cage of kittens. "Please, please, please, Kenny, let me keep Babbage! I promise I'll look after him! I'll do extra chores! I'll stop making sure that all the center brownies get handed out before Dylan Johnson can get one when I'm on KP at school because he's a bully and they're his favorite and he deserves the dried-out, crusty edges if you'll let me keep Babbage!"

The child collided with the Representative, knocking the wind out of her, and continued to plead her case. Jones stared down at the head burrowed into her as if unaccustomed to being mauled in this fashion. When she looked up, Benilde's mask of distant disdain had cracked — he was chortling.

Jones pushed her glasses onto her head, then glanced at the crate of chinchillas. One very round, very sad, pale gray rodent clung to the bars, whiskers trembling.

"What is going on here? Must be something in the water." She bent to the girl. "Mouse, calm down. You can keep Babbage, but the same rules that apply to Eli and Boruta apply to you and Babbage. You need to learn how to care for him. Chinchillas are nocturnal and sociable, so he'll need to be let out into the Conservatory garden at dusk with the others. He's not the type of critter who'll be happy curled up next to you in bed at night. If he gets neglected, we'll revisit this conversation. Deal?"

"Deal! Thank you! Thank you! Thank you! Um… do I have to stop handing out the center brownies so Dylan can't get one?"

"Is he still making rude comments about Etienne Knowles?"

"Yes. And Charlotte Viglianco, because of her glasses."

Jones's tea-colored eyes spat lightning. "Then no, he doesn't deserve a center brownie. Derringer, remind me to have a word with Dylan Johnson's parents." She glanced left, where a boy materialized as if from thin air. "If Mouse made a fluffy friend, I'm sure you did too, Milo. Which one?"

A blond dog barked wildly as Milo's solemn expression split into joy. "Duke Sigmund! I promise I won't neglect him!"

"See that you don't."

Dlamini let the Labradoodle loose. It skidded off the tailgate, righted itself, and bowled Milo over. Babbage, upon release, tried to do the same. Mouse scooped him up and cuddled him.

"All right, you two, school…doesn't start for two hours. Why are you dressed? Never mind. Breakfast first, pets later."

As they ran off, Jones whirled back to Benilde. "You asked if one had escaped. Which one, and where?"

"A long-haired gray cat with a murderous expression. Over there." He pointed toward a massive rhododendron covered in peach flowers. It was out of season, but that meant little with Maggie around. Two soulless, green eyes glowed underneath.

"Miss Anthropy," Cowfer, Moran, and Dlamini chorused in a macabre grumble.

No one wanted to retrieve her. It was inevitably a bloody assignment.

"You named a cat Miss Anthropy?"

Benilde's expression suggested he was revising his assumptions about Sullen Creek Farm.

"No, that would be a horrible thing to do," Jones retorted, more to her friends than to him. She reached into the bush, hauled out the struggling cat, and clamped her to her chest, wincing as claws scored her flesh.

"One of my cadre is boarding her and her sister. Their real names are Mischief and Mystery. Cute, but Mystery hates everyone except her owner — so she's earned the nickname. All right, all right, I'll put you down."

The cat went rigid, yowling like the world was ending.

"If you don't want down, stop shredding my skin."

Mystery yowled louder.

Benilde approached and offered his hand. The cat sniffed, fell silent, and pressed her head into his palm, purring.

"Do cats usually like you?" Jones murmured, struck by the unlikely event.

"Or do you moonlight as an exorcist?" Alonzo asked.

With a demonic screech, Mystery clawed up Benilde's chest, vaulted over his shoulder, and vanished into the bushes, leaving a bloody trail behind.

"Neither, actually," Benilde said mildly. "I've never owned a pet. Perhaps for the best."

"I'd like to say she doesn't usually behave that way, but I'd be lying," Jones admitted, holding her own scratched arms out for display. "I've got antiseptic and bandages in the truck."

"I was warned," Aiden said with a sardonic smile.

Feeling he ought to behave like a tourist for a bit, Veritas spent the morning in town — a music shop, a vintage watch dealer, lunch at a little French restaurant. At the Strong Distillery, he sampled cave-aged spirits and invested in a few bottles. By mid-afternoon, though, he was impatient to make progress on his quest.

He intended to search the main house. For what, he wasn't sure. It just felt necessary.

Back at Punk Bunks, he stashed his purchases, waved to Arlo, and strolled off toward the river, in full view of the windows. Once the outbuildings hid him, he looped around the barn and cut through the gardens.

Most of the household was busy with school or work; only Derringer was a risk. Slipping in through the kitchen's back door, Veritas eased it shut. The automaton was mercifully absent. He peeked down the hall.

Clear.

He crept along, noting the layout. The large room to his left looked like it belonged to Jones's menagerie, but a closed door on his left looked highly suspect. Beyond it was a staircase. Up or down? Upstairs, he was more likely to bump into the residents of the house.

He tiptoed down, where another door opened onto a surprisingly serious gym. The ropes course, heavy with vines and stuffed snakes, tempted him, but the racks of weapons were sobering. Why would beer-brewing vampires need to be proficient in a thousand weapons? Weren't fangs enough?

Reconsidering his life choices, he pressed on. Two more doors lined the wall. The first revealed a bathroom. The penny-tile was arranged like a rug, and the old bicycle-cum-sink was cheerfully whimsical.

As soon as the next door swung open, he was rooted to the floor.

Stone walls, Gothic windows, a rough-hewn floor, and in the center: a banquet table for sixteen, topped with an acrylic honeycomb grid. A mossy miniature world sprawled across it — ruins wrapped in kudzu, mounted travelers of many races facing down a goblin horde.

Veritas shut the door behind him and approached the shrine to tabletop gaming with reverence. Each place had an ergonomic chair, a tooled leather journal, multi-colored pens, and a stack of cards. Two ceramic bowls held familiar velvet bags. He picked one up, smiled, and returned it. Dice! Above the table, four glowing amber dragons undulated in lazy flight, lighting the room.

The dungeon master's station was a masterpiece: a carved screen with dice towers and drawers, a laptop, a whole series of journals, an initiative tree, and a cart of exquisitely painted monsters. This wasn't a casual game. It had been running for *years*.

Three walls were lined with a continuous live-edge desk and eighteen computers. Each monitor sat between privacy partitions, with copper plaques overhead. Asibikaashi must be Maggie, judging by the jungle of air plants and ivy. Nebthu, he didn't know. Aibell was familiar, but he couldn't place it. OGGimli. Thekwane.

Veritas choked.

Oscar's player name was *Oscar*. Ridiculous!

He found Weaver.

Her desk looked like the others — only far messier. Kenny Jones, it seemed, was allergic to paper organizers and the multiple wastebaskets provided. Sketches of tiny houses and travel vans spilled over fidget spinners, framed photos propped up intricate battle plans (real or imagined?), meeting reminders mingled with carved balsa-wood animals and a utility knife — all buried under a thick snowfall of wood shavings.

He nudged her mouse. The screen came alive with what looked like a real photo. A pale mountain island rose from a crystalline sea. He knew this place. The Seba Rewed — the mythic Star Stairway — towering behind it. It was Wenen.

It was glorious.

A shiver ran up his spine.

This room was underground. The Gothic windows…shouldn't let sunlight spill in. He peered out at the same impossible landscape as Weaver's background — an alien jungle with cream-colored mountains to one side and a pale sea to the other. For the first time, Veritas wondered if Wenen might be real. Absurd…but where had supernatural beings come from? Were they aliens? Was Wenen their world?

A password prompt popped up.

What would Weaver use? Something sentimental. The dog — what was his name? One syllable. Mel!

Rejected.

Maybe the hiking challenge thingy — Everest 29029. Rejected. He started a third guess, then stopped. Better not risk getting locked out. He needed to leave no trace.

He turned — and froze.

The last wall was covered in bookshelves, floor to ceiling, crammed to bursting with gaming ecosystems and lore. Swamps, cathedrals, deserts, oceans — miniature worlds ready for battle. Memorabilia and the greatest sci-fi and fantasy books crowded for space.

It was the most comprehensive collection he had ever seen. The influences of his youth, the muses of his ambitions, the joys of his soul — gathered here, honored.

His eyes stung.

Stupid allergies.

August 29th at Sullen Creek Farm

James Darrow watched the other guests and most of the staff depart with a subdued expression. If yesterday was any indication, even those staying behind would scatter to the far corners of the farm.

He hadn't wanted lunch but forced enough down to keep his nurse — Jessie, Jill, whatever — from fussing. He waited impatiently for early afternoon, when the house finally emptied, save for Arlo.

Taking the steak knife he'd pocketed the night before, he made a shallow cut on his forearm and squeezed. A dark, rune-etched pebble, slick with blood, popped free. He cleaned it, eliminating all scents attached to it, then directed his wheelchair over to a snake plant and tucked it among the decorative rocks at the base.

A glance confirmed the wound had already healed. New vigor and a sense of urgency surged through him. He stood slowly. The curse had drained him — twenty pounds gone in two and a half days, much of it muscle. Still, he was alive.

He slipped past Arlo's office, noting the shut slider, and stepped into the sunshine, silencing the bell as he exited.

It was a perfect day — not a cloud in the sky.

He followed the river path down to the bank, his nose catching a trace of vanilla.

There.

He retrieved a dark green waterproof bag from between a log and a rock. A quick shuffle through turned up what he needed. Zipping it shut, he returned it to its hiding place and headed toward the main house.

The screened-in dining porch was empty, save for a sleeping dog. Slipping in through the back door, he dropped a small gunmetal-gray ball and let it roll under the table. Without watching its path across the terracotta floor, he moved into the kitchen and dropped a second ball onto the runner.

He grabbed a beer from the fridge — a Golden Retriever, Sullen Creek Brewing Company's IPA — twisted the cap off, peeked into the pantry, and headed down the hallway. He took a swig. Not as bitter as a British IPA — more West Coast: malt, citrus, and just enough bite.

Lovely.

He passed a laundry room, sweeping for occupants. On the right, a cased opening framed a formal dining room — a dark plate rail and herbarium fabric clothed the walls. French doors led back to the dining porch.

Next came a half bath. The door beyond it squeaked open under protest. When no one appeared to intervene, he stepped into a strange little room filled with jars of herbs and less pleasant specimens floating in liquid. A mirror of bubbled glass seemed to watch his every movement.

The living room had a cathedral ceiling, wall-to-wall bookshelves, and a massive fireplace drowning in millwork. Leather chairs flanked a green velvet couch — improbably free of fur. The gleaming copper pipe network explained the immaculate surfaces. He felt a flash of envy. Dust made him sneeze.

He dropped another ball as he admired the eclectic library and natural history collection, then peered through one of two arched doorways along the western wall. The conservatory was unlike anything he'd seen — verdant greenery enclosed in an ornate cage that also housed snoozing chinchillas, rats, mice, hedgehogs, hamsters, vibrant birds, and capering guinea pigs, each section with a pint-sized breezeway leading outside. At least eighty animals lived there.

James inhaled. Lemon, rosemary, and mint. No trace of animal funk. What was this magic, and how could he obtain it?

"Come on in and sit a spell," squawked a magnificent green parrot, watching him with friendly curiosity.

"Yes, yes, do," seconded a Quaker parrot. A quartet of smaller birds swooped over and cooed in encouragement.

"That's kind, but I'm afraid I have a standing engagement. Another day, perhaps," he politely demurred.

"Does a seraphic star-nosed mole fart sticky toffee pudding?" the green bird replied cheerfully.

"It's settled then. Until next time."

He bowed and backed out, noting the second arched doorway also led into the conservatory.

At the far end of the living room, a staircase climbed to the gallery. He checked the time — safe enough to go up.

The second floor mirrored the first, with two halls splitting off from the balcony. Darrow took the western hall and found an unoccupied guestroom on the right, a bathroom on the left. The next door was locked. He dropped another ball and moved on. A second door on the left revealed a second staircase.

He reached for the copper knob on a door at the south end of the house but froze as energy prickled against his palm. The sensation lingered even after he pulled back. Curious, James dropped a ball. It unfurled, releasing a brood of tiny droids. The shell reconfigured itself into a slightly larger spybot, which — emboldened by its size advantage — led the charge. As soon as its legs touched the threshold, it liquefied.

James blinked.

No heat. No melting; the small droid instantly converted from solid to liquid. Silver droplets dotted the sill like tarnished rain.

The other bots stopped short, scanned the remains, and turned to James for instructions. They weren't sentient, but they were programmed for self-preservation.

He pulled out a handkerchief and wafted it forward. Two inches from the door, magic caught it. He let the cloth fall, hoping it would cover the evidence; it didn't. The fine lawn burned to ash before hitting the floor.

"Right. Next door," he muttered, taking a fortifying swig of beer.

The droids slipped beneath it unscathed. James tried the handle — locked.

He continued on. The two halls looped together with the bathroom and staircase, a dumbwaiter, a linen closet, and storage closets occupying the center of the house.

He met another locked door, dropped a ball, and moved on to a child's bedroom. Two children — it was clearly occupied. Twin beds sprouted from a gnarled tree — one tossed and buried under books and clothes, the other neatly made. Soft green wainscotting split the walls; above it rose a mural of the countryside. The ceiling was blue and hung with biplanes, balloon lamps, and kite mobiles.

His fingers toyed with a spy ball, but he exited without dropping it. There were limits — or there should be.

As he left, a door shushed open. Darrow froze, listening as quiet steps moved north. He silently closed the room's door and moved south.

A second door opened and closed. The steps reversed, retreating south. Darrow rolled his eyes and moved north. He slipped across the balcony and crept downstairs.

So…who else was wandering about — and why?

Veritas crept up to the main floor but paused at the sound of voices. He might have succeeded in slipping out unnoticed, but why risk it? Instead, he tiptoed to the second floor and quietly opened a door into the hall. To his right, the mezzanine overlooked the living room, with another staircase leading down.

The hallway on the left held two doors on either side — a moody, masculine guestroom, a similarly handsome bathroom, and a linen closet. The last door was locked. Pity.

Turning back, he crept toward a fifth door tucked in the corner. The moment his hand touched the copper knob, power jolted up his arm.

Not painful — just disconcerting.

He tapped it again. The current was stronger. Ashes and gray liquid droplets flecked the threshold. Carefully, as though he might melt, he let go. The fizzing in his palm lingered. It wasn't electricity. This sensation defied explanation, insistently pinging off his nerves. Then it hit him.

Magic.

He had experienced magic. Real, bona fide magic! Elation swelled — until panic set in.

What if he'd tripped an alarm? What if he was marked!

Tiptoeing at top speed, he made for the mezzanine. He peered over the railing. Clear! Down, down, down.

His descent was swift but quiet, his skin still tingling. At the base, lightheaded with adrenaline, he stopped to rest against a barrister's case.

"Count Vitruvio, were you in need of more books?" inquired Arlo, rounding the corner.

Veritas jumped straight up like a cat spotting a cucumber. The tall man stood in the hall beside the barrister's case, his expression unreadable.

"Yes! Yes, I do," Veritas squeaked. "Reading helps with the insomnia. Any recommendations? Fiction, perhaps?"

"If you're leaning toward Urban Fantasy," Arlo said, gesturing to the shelf Veritas had been leaning on, "you might enjoy Deymienne Devereaux's *Chicane*."

"The *Apocryphal* series? I haven't read that one yet. I generally like her stuff. *Junque* wasn't my favorite, but that's because Ione picked Vashti over Orson and I... Uh, have you read it?"

Arlo's impassive look dissolved in an instant.

"Yes — and I completely agree. Vashti's fine, but when you're going up against the Aberration, you need firepower."

"Exactly! Vashti made no sense in that context — and look what happened."

"Thank you! Someone finally said it!"

Chapter 47: It's All Relative

Kenny: August 29ᵗʰ at Sullen Creek Farm

I sipped the honey-gold fluid and grimaced. "Flabby. What's the pH?"

Lon stirred the meter through the brew. "Three-seven. Top of the range."

"Our sours need to be sour, not sour-ish." I watched the brewers. "Hey, Danielle — remember to remove the oxygen."

The tall, black woman nodded and waved, leaving off the sealing process to head for the CO_2 tanks. I glanced at Lon. He'd looked too, but kept his expression neutral.

"Henry made contact half an hour ago," Lon murmured. "He's home — safe. Feral Moon retrieved him and dropped him off at the side door. I told her to take off, but she insisted on working. Doesn't want Henry to know how much she worries."

Then louder, "What's the golden number, boss?"

A flash of anger surged, then faded. Most days, it felt like we were just treading water. We knew our work mattered, but it could unravel in a second. Right now, I could make a small but real difference for four people I loved.

I marched over to Danielle and waited for her to finish with the tanks.

"I'm sorry, Kenny. My brain's just—"

"Preoccupied with your husband. You've got nothing to apologize for."

She nodded.

"We love you. You're indispensable — but go home! I know you don't want Henry to see how hard this is for you, but he does. We all do. That's why we're here. So, go. Tell your husband you love him. Take tomorrow off. Be with Henry, Minelli, and Harper — for me, if not for yourself."

She closed her eyes, drew in his lips, and nodded. "Yeah... yeah."

Danielle turned and had her hairnet off before the door swung shut behind her.

"Think she'll be okay?" Lon asked, stepping up beside me.

"Relative to what? Let's get this sealed. Drop the sour to three-five and we'll see. Madison has some lambics for us to try. Don't let me drink more than a sample — even if I beg or bribe."

A few minutes later, we left the brewing room and stepped onto the fermentation floor. Open tanks lined both sides; three long metal tables punctuated the center aisle. A team was busy punching down foam to prevent mold. Taylor saluted us with his paddle. We waved back and headed into the tasting room.

It was a converted horse barn — concrete floor, skylights, one wall stacked to the ceiling with barrels. Live-edge tables, floor-to-ceiling windows, and living walls softened the space. Ella Fitzgerald crooned in the background, and the scent of fresh bread lingered. Displays of snifter, stange, and pilsner glasses towered behind the gleaming bar.

Madison, the pretty brunette who managed the tasting room, waved us to a corner table. A few minutes later, she joined us.

"We're starting with the strawberry lambics and crossing our fingers," she said, setting six tiny tulip glasses down, followed by a glass of ice water. "This first one's been sitting for eight months."

"Still has that rubber smell," Lon noted after a sip.

"Better flavor than the last batch," I added.

"Second one's three months," Madison said.

I sniffed. "Oh."

Lon nodded. "Smell it, Madison."

She did — once, then again. "The odor's gone."

"And the taste is better," I said.

"Good. The third's been sitting six months."

The aroma…wasn't strawberry, but it had a pleasant fruitiness and subtle nuttiness. I took a swig.

"It's money," I purred, draining the glass. "Rack it."

"Yes, ma'am," Lon drawled, grinning. If I told him he sounded like his ol' cousin Nore, I'd probably get pummeled at our next training session.

Madison set out six more tulip glasses. "This is the peach. We'll start with the three-month batch."

It passed the sniff test with flying colors and tasted lovely.

"Next is the six-month lambic," Madison said.

"Some bitterness has set in, but it's kind of nice," I murmured, rolling it in my mouth.

"Nice enough," Lon conceded. "But I prefer the first."

"And this one sat for nine months."

"Okay, yeah, we're going with the three-month peach," I coughed, nearly gagging. Lon didn't comment — too busy chugging water. Bitter, combined with tart, wasn't our thing.

"Madison, hand out a few of the winners to the guests and get their feedback. Send the notes to my office."

"Kenny."

It was never a good sign when Maggie sounded gentle. She was allergic to gentle unless something that grew roots, made chlorophyll, or flowered was involved.

"What happened?"

"Abigail… There was no warning. We don't know what happened yet. Her body was moved. They did find her. She's being prepped for the exequy, but Mystery—"

I was already moving.

"Where?"

"Hiding in the workshop. Mischief's with her."

I ran, propelled by fast and tangled emotions. How many friends had I lost? How many had to die before we earned peace?

I was going to find that warlock and make him explain why.

I forced myself to slow down and open the workshop door quietly. It was dark. No one was working.

I grabbed an apron from a hook, looped it over my head, and tied the bottom corners with the waist strings — a makeshift pouch.

I pushed up my glasses and traced the lines to two clusters near the planer.

Mystery was hunched on the floor, motionless. Mischief stopped bathing her sister and looked up at me, mewing plaintively.

"Come, sweet girls. Let's get you home," I whispered, eyes burning.

Even for Abigail — or her cats — the tears refused to come. Maybe when I had a solution, when I could tell them no more would follow.

I scooped up Mystery and settled her in the apron. She didn't fight.

"I'm so sorry, sweet baby. I'm so sorry."

The words sounded trite.

You're her Doyenne — the one she pledged herself to. You should've saved her. Why didn't you?

I shut the intrusive thoughts down. Abigail had always done what she believed was right. She believed we'd find a solution — provided we were brave enough to try.

I scooped up Mischief and nestled her beside her sister.

"I know what this is like," I whispered. "I've felt it, too. Like the best part of you is gone. No warning. Suddenly, you're only half of what you were."

I stroked Mystery gently.

"For Abigail. For Mischief. For me. And for yourself, please try to get through it. Please, try."

I hugged the pouch close and carried the babies back to the house.

<h2 style="text-align:center">Chapter 48: Barking Mad</h2>

August 29ᵗʰ at Sullen Creek Farm

Veritas, deciding he'd had enough espionage for one day, slipped out the back of the main house with his borrowed book and followed a forest path. He glanced at his hand — still tingling from his first brush with magic. Real magic. He pulled out his phone and tapped a few notes into his CP account. Pity he had no proof of what he'd experienced — only questions.

Supernaturals weren't relics; they were adaptable. Their cybersecurity was airtight. And even with heightened senses and strength, they obsessed over fitness and sports. He paused at a clearing to watch a Sepak Takraw match — volleyball, but with feet. The players moved with inhuman precision. No one watching could deny what they were.

He moved on, musing.

They read urban fantasy.

He chuckled. What must it be like to read about your kind, framed as myth or monsters? Did they cheer when writers got it right? Rage at the stereotypes? He shuddered at the thought of a real vampire catching him with fake fangs.

One thing was clear: the whole 'Punk Bunks' theme was not really a theme. Even the Wednesday Addams look-alike twins didn't seem like they were playing dress-up. He glanced down when something tugged on his clothes. His Jedi robes were tangled in some bracken. No one had mocked his getup, but now it felt foolish — inauthentic. If he could feel the difference, surely they could too.

Veritas freed his tangled robes and was too preoccupied with straightening them to notice any obstacles ahead — until he walked straight into the bear.

He bounced off a wall of shaggy belly, barely keeping his feet. Regaining his balance, he looked up. And up. Ten feet, his brain shrilly calculated. The massive bear stood on its hind legs, looking just as startled as he felt. Veritas's limbs twitched as instinct battled between freeze and flee. He took a few slow steps back.

The bear, curious, dropped to all fours and sniffed at him. Veritas closed his eyes and prayed.

"You must have some experience with Kodiaks," Maggie observed, standing a few feet behind him. "Most people panic. This is Naabek. He polices our borders. Oh, look — he likes you. He's usually more reserved."

Veritas remained frozen as the bear nosed his pockets. He wished Naabek had remained aloof — or even standoffish, but he nodded. "He's...very handsome."

"Isn't he? Most in the Nooke dodem prefer black bears or grizzlies, but it was love at first sight for me. Do you have something in your pocket?"

Veritas cautiously pulled out half a blueberry muffin. "I guess berries are okay, but should he eat the muffin part?"

"He'll eat anything. Thank the nice man, Naabek. No pretzels with lunch," Maggie added.

Naabek padded forward and gently bumped noses with Veritas before taking the treat.

"So...does Naabek..." Eat intruders? LARPing tourists who get in too deep? "...provide security?"

"Not really. He's too sweet to hurt anyone, though he's scared a few trespassers. He alerts us if someone's somewhere they shouldn't be. But anyone with a pastry in their pocket can wrap him around their finger. We're headed to my dad's houseboat now; want to come?"

"Sure," Veritas agreed, beginning to adjust to the bear's presence. "Can I...uh...pet him?"

Naabek flopped over and stretched out, paws in the air.

"I guess that's a yes," Maggie said. "He loves tummy rubs."

Still a little wary, Veritas knelt and gently rubbed Naabek's massive chest. A soft vibration rippled through the bear's body. Encouraged, Veritas tried a firmer stroke. The vibration grew louder.

"Is he...purring?"

"Yup," Maggie confirmed. "He's a big softie."

After five minutes of belly rubs, Maggie gently urged them along. Naabek chuffed, clearly reluctant, but lumbered to his feet. He gave Veritas another affectionate nose bump. Veritas huffed in return, a little dazed, and patted the bear's shoulder.

"You're good people, Naabek."

They followed a narrow, well-trodden path through the woods toward Sullen Creek. Veritas heard the water before they began descending toward a small dock and a plant-covered houseboat.

"Niniijaanis, who have you brought with you?"

Veritas glanced around, unsure where the voice had come from, until a small man seemed to emerge from the rocks themselves. Broad-cheeked, with deep sienna skin, black eyes, and shoulder-length black hair, he looked both familiar and ageless. Veritas had seen him at meals, but hadn't realized he was Maggie's father.

"Dad, this is Luke Vitruvio; he's a guest at Punk Bunks. Luke, my father — Waabaanakwad. Or Wayne Cloud."

The man extended a rather hairy hand and beamed. "Easier to remember, eh? Like Eeyore and the little cloud that follows him?"

"He likes puns," Maggie said with a resigned eye roll. Her father just chuckled.

"Nice to meet you, Waabaanakwad," Veritas replied, shaking his hand. "You have a lovely home."

"Thank you! I don't stray far from the water. My Miigwan is the brave one. Speaking of — Naabek seems to have found something."

They turned to see the bear at the riverbank, stretching his neck toward the houseboat. He waded in, circled the vessel, and barked once — sharp and alarmed.

"You two talk. I need to send a text," Maggie murmured, face tightening.

Chapter 49: Age and Perception

Kenny: August 29ᵗʰ at Sullen Creek Farm

"Questionnaires from the new arrivals," Arlo muttered, swiveling in his chair and slapping a stack of papers onto the only empty corner of his retro desk.

I gave him a thumbs-up but stayed focused on Lon's status report. A few cameras, listening devices, and spy bots had been found and collected. Same old, same old. We didn't have surveillance inside the main house, but Punk Bunks' public spaces, the brewhouse, and the parking lot were covered. Even when the Agency wasn't sniffing around, someone else always was — rival cadres, curious factions, or one of Nore's jealous exes.

Lon's team had already handled the matter. The culprits wouldn't even know we'd caught them.

A few minor energy spikes had hit the saturation ward during check-ins, but that wasn't unusual. People often weren't what they claimed and sometimes had strong emotions about us; it didn't mean they meant us harm. The wards would catch anything serious, regardless, but we'd keep an eye out.

The thought of trouble reminded me of Maggie's text. Naabek had smelled something...wrong...near Wayne's houseboat. And Naabek had a better nose than any bloodhound.

It would have to wait, however. I noted which guests might need closer watching and turned to the questionnaires. They were usually half-filled, inaccurate, and boring, but occasionally something surprising surfaced.

"Did anything arrive today? A small package from Louhi?" I asked, flipping through the pages. Aunt Gregg hadn't called me back, but there'd been murmurs on the Mulberry about unsanctioned activities. Nothing that indicated my aunt, but...we shared a gene pool — and an aversion to asking permission.

Arlo jolted, spun in his chair, and started rummaging through the paper stacks, uniforms, and rubber chickens cluttering his desk. I didn't comment on the chaos. Unlike me, Arlo's mess had a system that worked — most of the time.

A small white envelope slid off the edge and hit the floor. Arlo dove after it, presenting it with a flourish.

The envelope contained a zip drive and a short note.

"I can't believe I forgot this. Gidget already updated the records," Arlo said, beaming.

"You've read the files? Anything in there tell us who we're dealing with?" I asked, pocketing the drive as I flipped through his guest surveys.

"I skimmed the profiles. Nothing jumped out."

I looked up. "Then why are you making that face?"

He was chewing on something — brows scrunched, mouth corners pulled down. Classic overthinking.

Arlo slid the frosted partition open, glanced around the hall and lobby, then shut it again. He activated a precast sound barrier and finally blurted, "I thought all warlocks would be…"

"Evil, twisted, bloodthirsty, remorseless monsters," I offered, perplexed by Jeff and Lindsey Pye's preferred room temperature and listed allergens.

"Well, yes. Some are. But some…aren't so bad," he said, shrugging awkwardly.

I laughed — not because it was funny, but because it was just too much. Danielle and Henry. Abigail and Mystery. And now Arlo, sweet Arlo; he looked guilty for not condemning every warlock in the stolen files.

"I'm sorry," I said, still chuckling. "You're just so apologetic about it! But that's the point. If we don't want to be judged for the worst among us, we can't condemn everyone in the Community for being there. It's not the Community that does evil, or practitioners, or warlocks — it's evil people who do evil. They use whatever excuse is handy."

"Huh," Arlo murmured.

Poetic and succinct, if I said so myself.

"Ah," I added, finding something of interest — though maybe not importance.

"What've you got?" he asked, leaning closer.

"Our Mr. Darrow filled out every question. Claims to be a werewolf."

"Is he not?" Arlo asked.

"Undetermined, but... I'm inclined to believe him. I startled him when he woke up. You know how hard it is to sneak up on a wolf. At first, I thought he was playing us — but maybe not. He'd been gravely injured, and he jumped straight up. High! Good thing that room's got high ceilings, or we'd be installing a skylight." I shrugged. "He's holding things back, but his secrets may be none of our business."

"So…you don't think he's the warlock?"

"Don't go down that road, Arlo, or we'll start seeing suspects everywhere. We're not suspicious — we're prepared."

"I hope it's not Count Vitruvio," Arlo sighed.

"Why's that?"

Catching the wistful look on his face, I was reminded how young twenty-five could be. Preternaturals matured slowly — perhaps because we lived longer, or maybe because magic and instant gratification stunted our emotional growth.

"Because he is ah-mazing!"

Arlo reenacted the Count's arrival, playing both parts with flair and detailing every inch of the honored one's attire. No surprise he'd developed a man-crush. The Count had drama, humor, and enough confidence to pull off the robe-and-sandals look. Eccentric guests were common, but committed cosplayers were rare. Then again, fashion trends in the Community never really died — they hibernated.

"And he agrees Ione should've chosen Orson, not Vashti."

The smugness in his voice...

I smiled at Vitruvio's questionnaire but refused to take the bait — not today. All the guys thought Orson was the better choice, but for literary weight and crew integrity, Vashti was the only acceptable option. Ione owed Vashti that confrontation. It was a matter of honor. Facts were facts — even in fiction.

"I hope it's not him, too," I said, "but…if he's telling the truth about being a vampire, I'd bet he's old — possibly ancient."

"Like ancient-ancient?" Arlo leaned forward, reading over my shoulder. Probably unwise to feed the crush, but I'd opened the door.

"Ancient as in fourteen hundred–plus years."

"An ancient vampire who cosplays? That's so badass. But… he didn't seem old. He seemed…young-ish."

I turned toward him and let go of my humanity — just for a moment. No warmth, no connection. I viewed him like an object — a toy. Then I smiled.

"Don't do that," he whispered.

"Do what?" I tilted my head like a bird, letting a faint red glow flicker through my pupils.

"Don't look creepy! Seriously, Kenny, stop. You're freaking me out!"

I raised my eyebrows.

"How old am I?"

"Thirty-seven," he grumbled.

"If you didn't know?"

He gave me a 'you're insane' look. "So…because he acts young, you think he's old?"

"Vampires know the mystique they carry — both in norm culture and the Community. Young ones play it up — for protection, seduction, status. But older vamps don't bother. They've learned the value of going unnoticed."

I flipped a page and tapped Vitruvio's name.

"Ancient vampires? They turn it into an art. And Luke Vitruvio gives off the strongest foolish-human energy I've ever seen."

"Wicked," Arlo murmured dreamily.

"Indeed."

"What about Aiden Benilde?" he asked, fishing out the questionnaire. "He doesn't act otherworldly, but he's not as dour as he pretends. He showed Minelli how to grip Waffles better. Look." He turned to show me a welt on his upper arm.

I couldn't stop the cackle.

"Yes, yes, it's hilarious that a five-year-old beat me black and blue with a rubber chicken. Answer the question!"

"So bossy." I snatched the form. "Prefers not to say…prefers not to say… Not much to go on. I can't trace an Origin just by peeking at the lines, but he does have an interesting relationship with ley energy."

"Is he the warlock? Or maybe a witch?" Arlo asked, wide-eyed.

"We don't suspect anyone—"

"—but we're prepared for trouble from any quarter," he finished, prodding. "But…"

Practitioners from other covens had stayed here, but we avoided hosting them. They played by different rules — and were more dangerous than Agency warlocks. Unaffiliated witches showed up now and then, sometimes looking for help. We didn't advertise, but word got around in the right circles.

Benilde didn't fit any of those. He was too confident.

"Ley energy moves through him with almost no resistance. In and out, clean. He could be a warlock or practitioner, but more likely, he doesn't interact with the lines much. It happens — usually after trauma. Physical or emotional. People like that tend to age faster and often have health issues. It's rare for preternaturals, but not unheard of."

Arlo was quiet for a moment. "Can it be fixed?"

I sighed. I wasn't a psychologist, and my ley knowledge was highly specialized. But sometimes, fixing something wasn't about restoring it — it was about changing how you looked at it.

"Anything's possible. Someone just needs to figure out how."

August 29th at Sullen Creek Farm

"Marshal Sampson Reid is one of the Representative's guests, sir."

"Oh, fun! I seem to recall the two of you got on rather well. Business or pleasure? Did he recognize you?"

Dorrit sighed. "Yes, he recognized me. We've had a beer or two, swapped war stories. I respect him — he's dedicated, and damn good at his job," he said wearily. "He's here on business — undercover. Jones's people were celebrating a birthday, and while the others were at the bonfire, we caught up."

"He's investigating Representative Jones?" O'Brien asked, tension creeping into his voice.

"Not directly. He's hunting a serial killer."

A beat of silence followed as recent headlines came to mind.

"Of course. Because that's all we needed. This killer — he's connected to Jones's people, or just in the area?"

"The latter. He was here recently. Scent's fresh."

Dorrit heard O'Brien murmuring to someone off-screen before asking, "Have you figured out the wards surrounding the property?"

"There's a diagnostic component. When I arrived, the farm seemed forbidding — sinister, even. Then the mood shifted. Reid and MacDonnell experienced it too. Blake didn't. I think the wards assess potential threats but only react to active danger. No visible guards, but some of the animals… They're either magic-touched or higher-level beings. Possibly part of the security."

"Interesting! Any indication she has a familiar?"

"There's a dog that follows her constantly, but from what I've seen, he's just loyal. Any pet could be a familiar, but none are treated with special significance."

"And Jones? Have you met her again?"

"We were introduced. She's hospitable, uninhibited — watchful. Keeps busy. They all do. At any time, someone's training or competing in obscure sports — bossaball, cycle ball, sporthocking. They're talented. Everyone in the cadre seems to be in peak condition."

"What's your impression of the cadre as a whole?"

"Hardworking — whether it's work or play, I doubt they see the difference. They're purposeful. Happy. Conscientious. Welcoming. Eager to share knowledge and interests."

"You like them."

"It's difficult not to. They work with each other. Beyond Jones, Mendoza, and Cowfer, I haven't identified a clear hierarchy. But they're organized. They know where they're going, why, and what to do when they get there. I've gone undercover in struggling cadres before — Second Shadow, Bent Tree. I know the symptoms of dysfunction. This isn't that."

He paused.

"We've overheard budget meetings, disciplinary hearings, EMS inspections, an education board session, and a general assembly. They have a cultural unity that's rare in a group that accepts new members so often. The sports help — but it's more than that."

"Like a military base?"

"Possibly. Or a well-funded summer camp."

"And for our purposes — useful?"

Dorrit considered it. "If we're right, we won't find a better option in time. But any threat or coercion directed at the Sheta Djew will be resented, whether it's effective or not."

"So don't use force. Persuade her. Seduce her. Use reason."

"Perhaps," Dorrit murmured.

"Incidentally, have you been able to keep eyes on Jones throughout the day?"

"No, but we've tracked her. She's been in the brewpub office, hotel office, farm workshop, or the main house."

"What about between seven and eight this morning?"

"She and Alonzo Cowfer were demonstrating Krav Maga in the main house gym. It was open to guests. With waivers."

"Ah. So, however Jones is involved, she's not always active in operations. Someone burgled Senator Schultz's library this morning — fourteen books of poetry and folktales were taken. Keep an eye out for anything along those lines."

"They wouldn't leave stolen books lying around."

"Criminals make mistakes, John. As for Marshal Reid — if he suggests exchanging intel, weigh your options. This investigation was already complex. Adding a serial killer and other agencies doesn't help. Keep your people close."

"MacDonnell and Blake are a floor up. Surveillance is running smoothly. Ridel, Sarduy, and Hatter are nearby in town — we've got regular check-ins. With your permission, I'll give Sam my contact info and Ridel's. If nothing else, we can watch his back."

"Granted."

"How's Rena?"

"Ask her yourself. Here."

The line paused as the phone changed hands.

"John?"

"Hi, Rena. How are you? Enjoying the trip? Keeping the boss out of trouble?"

"Don't ask for miracles. Darragh does his best. I've basically moved into the hotel spa. It feels amazing to just relax. How are you? Working too hard?"

"I'm fine. Glad you got some time off. If the Chairman doesn't need me, I've got a blacksmithing class in ten minutes."

"Blacksmithing?" she laughed.

"A good agent seizes every opportunity to develop new skills. I believe we'll be making coat hooks."

He was rewarded with a delicate snort.

"Darragh says to have fun and be careful."

"You do the same."

August 29th at Sullen Creek Farm

John Dorrit gazed up at the strange house bathed in moonlight. It hadn't stood up on chicken legs like Baba Yaga's, but with what he'd seen so far, he wasn't ruling it out. He ghosted through the front door into the shadowed living room.

The space buzzed softly, like a beehive. Metal arms zipped along tracks, dusting shelves, sweeping floors, vacuuming cushions. The only living things present came with roots.

The labeled bookcases were just readable in the dim light as mechanized limbs whirred past: autobiographies, natural history, anthropology, art history, music theory. The residents had eclectic tastes. The barrister's cases held curious stones, fossils, crystals, sculptures, pottery shards, a collection of athames, and a surprising number of mildly smutty, well-loved paperbacks.

He mapped the ground floor, then descended into a cavernous basement set up as a gym. It was divided into four sections: endurance, balance and mobility, weight training, and martial arts. Plants filled every available space — even vines and flowers trailed around a ropes course. The effect was jungle-like...and tempting.

Murals covered any wall space not devoted to gear or greenery. The gym was stocked with speed bags, jump ropes, beams, weapons, wooden dummies, breaking boards, and agility ladders — all well-used. Speakers dotted the room, top to bottom. They hadn't skimped on the sound system.

He found a bathroom and a game room. Enchanted windows looked out on a gorgeous but forbidding fantasy world — terrifying in its realism. A long-limbed, transparent dragon-chimp fusion leapt through the trees, snatched a beautifully furred, lemur-like creature, and devoured it in three bites. The mind behind the illusion was brilliant — and savage.

Plaques above the computer stations lining the walls made little sense to him, except Oscar's. He studied the photos on each desk and gradually matched Davy, Nore, Maggie, Lon, Kenny, Lou, and Armand to their usernames.

Weaver was an interesting choice.

On Kenny's desk, a group photo showed her, Nore, Maggie, and Davy in their college years — fresh, innocent, and already plotting trouble. Beside it rested a picture of the late Senator Charles Vine, his wife, a blond girl, and a much younger Kenny, and, in a carved mahogany frame, was a photo of twenty-three children and a middle-aged woman holding a baby. Dorrit recognized Eli in the front row, but no one else. A silver locket-style frame lay beside the collection. He flicked it open.

It was a strange phenomenon — knowing he was in shock before his body reacted. Intellectually, he knew. The symptoms were en route, slow as a train easing into a station. He felt himself cooling, then shivering. His stomach turned. If he had a mirror, his pupils would be dilating.

"Representative Jones, why do you have a photo of Rena Amano?"

His hollow voice echoed in the room.

Hands trembling — a challenge when he wasn't fully present and his body was compromised — he undid the back of the frame. His form flickered between amorphous and solid, and he dropped the photo three times. On the back, handwritten: Kuwako Yamane, May 22, 2009 – San Francisco.

Not Rena.

He sighed aloud, relieved. It wasn't her. He turned the photo back over and studied the young woman. Now that he knew, the differences were apparent — rounder face, fuller lips, darker eyes, different hair texture. The resemblance was remarkable, but it wasn't Rena. Clumsily, he reassembled the frame and tucked the photo inside.

If it had been her…and it wasn't…he'd have to reconsider the Chairman's motives. Was O'Brien assisting — or playing him?

Dorrit ignored the couple murmuring on the bed as he examined the room — for the most part. After the shock in the basement, he'd drifted up to the second floor and was now exploring the occupied bedroom. Dark teal walls were hidden under a curtain of plants — hanging, potted, climbing, and sprouting from seashells.

He wondered if Ms. Cloud liked plants.

Wooden shelves with gold accents climbed the wall behind the bed, creating a waterfall of green. Each shelf was its own garden, dotted with gold, animal figurines. Ten feet up, the greenery met the loft railing, where more plants spilled from containers. Dorrit floated closer, peeking into crooks and crannies. He found plenty of tchotchkes but nothing unusual.

"Do you remember Ahriman Masoumi?"

The woman's soft, hissing voice barely registered. His memory regurgitated the name before her words even sank in. A jolt of cold ran through him. He stopped rifling through Maggie's tax records and listened.

Ahriman Masoumi had been a djinn — and not the wish-granting kind. Nearly thirty years ago, he had been a slaver.

Lon moved to comfort her.

"No," Cloud admonished. "Not yet."

The brawny man relented, his expression morphing into a stoic wariness.

She lay back on the pillows, eyes fixed on the cathedral ceiling. The same rich timbers lined both floor and roof. A tall, pointed window stood opposite the bed.

"Masoumi raided our dodem. He captured four of us."

"Why?"

"Children don't fear memegwesi. Our instinct is to protect them. Turned into a helot, we make perfect tools for slavers," she whispered.

Lon stroked her arm.

"You don't have to—"

Maggie cut him off, covering her face with her arm. "At the time, I didn't understand. Masoumi took me to parks and shopping centers, had me watch. He told me lies — said my father hated me, was replacing me. I believed him. By the time APA agents killed him, I was a vicious thing. Feral. Everyone was an enemy."

"You were protecting yourself," Lon murmured, though his golden eyes glowed with rage.

Dorrit knew Lon, like his Cousin Nore and Aunt Déjà, was a sphinx — changed, not cursed. The moon didn't move them, but strong emotion did. If a threat entered now, Cowfer would reflexively shift and eliminate it.

Maggie shook her head. "Dad was convicted of trafficking. By the time the APA took Masoumi down, Dad was already known as his associate. After Masoumi died, the tether dissolved. No one believed he'd been a helot. Not even me. I was put into foster care, bounced around until I was thirteen, then landed with Todd and Jenny Briggs, in Minneapolis."

She smiled. It was the first time Dorrit had seen her smile. Tears clung to her lashes, but her joy shone bright. "That's where I met Davy. I pushed everyone away; she pulled the whole world in. She needed someone to love; wanted it more than anything — and she chose me. I gave her every reason to hate me, but she wouldn't give up. It took three years. I think she saved my life."

"We met Kenny and Nore in college and bonded over our sob stories. They talked me into therapy. We all needed it. I started reading the letters Dad sent me. Then, the year Kenny became representative, she got his sentence revoked. I think the Quorum just gave in to shut her up. She lectured them fifty times in ten months — on helots, on the memegwesi."

Maggie suddenly rolled onto her side, away from Lon, the warmth in her voice gone. She sounded very small.

"When you're a helot…you know what's happening. The whole time. Dad knew, and he couldn't stop it. You can't love your way out of it — not like in the movies. Masoumi told him he'd make him kill me eventually. Dad said that thought kept him sane. If he ever had a chance to fight back, he had to be ready."

Helots.

The word echoed in Dorrit's mind, settling beside pułapki duchowe. Though highly illegal — and publicly denounced by every Quorum member — the practice persisted. Both practices.

"You know none of it was your fault," Lon murmured.

"I know."

"You know what you've survived won't scare me off. It took me five years to work up the nerve to ask you out. I'm not about to walk away."

His smile was soft and distant. "The day we met…you terrified me. I knew I'd only been hired because of my baby cousin, so I had to impress my new bosses. Then you opened the door, and I stared. You waved me in while threatening Kenny with a child harness. Everyone laughed — even her. It was obvious you were a team."

He chuckled, self-deprecatingly.

"How I made it through that meeting... It took three weeks and two days before I could speak to you. That was a major victory. Nore didn't help — she kept telling embarrassing childhood stories."

"I thought I annoyed you," Maggie whispered.

"Not even close. I did two tours in South Korea and one in Guam, no problem — but my cousin's beautiful friend? Utterly petrified. I knew you were the woman I wanted to spend my life with. It wasn't until you started dating that nitwit, Deacon, that I realized I had to do something."

"Deacon's nice. Too nice," she muttered.

"I'm not?"

Dorrit moved on — he'd heard all he needed — and checked the anime-themed Jack-and-Jill bathroom.

"You're as much of an asshole as I am," Maggie said. "I can argue with you without worrying about bruising your petal-soft ego. You don't smother me or get weird when I need space."

"So your ideal man is an occasional jerk who gives you room."

"Who makes me laugh," she added.

"Oh, I'll make you laugh, baby," Lon said, bouncing to his knees and tickling her.

She squealed, slapping at his hands, breathless. She grabbed a pillow and smacked him in the face.

He caught it with one hand, trying to yank it away while still attacking.

"You're absolutely right. I'm the perfect balance of confidence, charm, and wit."

"That's — hehe — not — hehehe — what — hehehehe — I said."

Dorrit dove through the wall.

"This can wait," Davy wheedled. "Eli doesn't have school tomorrow — we're spending the whole day together. I should get to bed early. And I don't see Déjà until next Monday! There's plenty of time later."

Dorrit agreed, drifting through the shabby chic bedroom. Smaller than Maggie's, it lacked the vaulted ceiling, but felt cozy — simple, cushy furnishings, sumptuous bedclothes betraying a deep abiding love for all things pastel yellow, blue chinoiserie, and objets d'art in the form of vigilant, life-sized, antique porcelain dogs. The latter guarded the dainty fireplace.

"Hands," said Lou.

"Lou," Davy whined.

"Do you trust me?"

Davy sighed and held out her hands. Lou tied them with a silk scarf printed with pastel dragons and princess-hat-wearing poop emojis. A blindfold followed.

"Are you comfortable?" Lou asked.

No, Dorrit thought, rifling through Davy's closet.

Costumes. Pirate, Renaissance, Star Trek, a lurid purple coat with fringe — every day was Halloween in Davy's wardrobe.

"Does a coruscated caracal fart cappuccino creams?" Davy chirped, sitting up, straight as a poker.

"Relax," Lou coaxed. "You're home…with someone who loves you. If it becomes too much, we stop. You may feel out of control, but you are in control. You're choosing to lend someone else authority that you can reclaim at any time."

Davy gave a jerky nod, stretched her legs, and leaned gingerly against the headboard. She crossed, then uncrossed her legs. "Okay," she announced, crossing them again. "I'm ready."

"Truth or mystery snack?" Lou asked.

"…Tr… snack."

"Open wide," Lou commanded, lifting the tray cover and picking up a raspberry.

After a moment's hesitation, Davy opened her mouth. Lou popped the berry in. Davy chewed.

"What is that?" Davy gagged. "It's squishy!"

"Raspberry. You were very brave. Now it's your turn — truth."

Davy's grin would strike terror in many a lesser server, Dorrit reflected.

"What's the most embarrassing thing that ever happened to you?"

"Right out of the gate," Lou snorted. "Freshman year, I told my best friend, Julia Frinkman, that I liked girls. She thought she could 'fix' me. She told Brandon Koontz I had a crush on him — she knew he liked me. Brandon believed her. He asked me out over the intercom during morning announcements. I had to tell him — and the whole school — that I didn't like him that way. He argued with me, only backing off after I said that I was a lesbian. The school called my parents. That's how they found out."

"Oh...! That's…awful," Davy keened, stricken.

"Mmmhmm. I survived. Mom gave the principal a world-class butt-chewing, and that was that. So, truth or snack?"

"Truth," Davy said, hands trembling slightly.

"Why did Kenny take over as staff manager the day I was hired?"

A shy smile sketched across Davy's lips, pink flushing her cheeks. "Because this gorgeous woman with mint green hair and a unicorn t-shirt came in for an interview. I wanted to ask you out, but that would've been unethical if I were your supervisor. So I begged Kenny to swap duties — we'd hire you, she'd manage staff, and I'd take over inventory and ordering. I threw in a Rococo-punk portrait of Mel. That's why the interview started seven minutes late."

Lou rose to her knees and kissed her.

"I'm proud of you," she murmured. "I transferred after reading an article about Representative Jones and her brew crew. In the interview, you said her favorite animal was the mystical, magical unicorn. I was already looking for a new cadre, and that sealed it. I applied that day."

Dorrit realized he'd been staring at an ugly purple jacket for five minutes. Shaking his head, he phased through the closet wall into a short, wide hallway. Straight ahead would be the main corridor. Left led back to Davy's room. On the right was a narrow staircase.

He flowed up into a space-themed bedroom with a slanted ceiling and a triangular dormer window rising from the floor.

The room was mostly dark, lit only by a globe casting constellations onto the ceiling. A lump under the covers suggested a boy reading by flashlight when he should've been asleep. A smaller lump, nestled beside him, had a twitching tail.

"I've journaled since I made the first attempt; he said that was imperative. That was…" Eli murmured, thumbing through pages, "May twenty-fifth. See? I noted my initial findings. I knew I wouldn't get much, but I think it was a promising start."

"Very promising," a shrill, excited voice replied. "Most first attempts fail. We'll need daily practice. Remember: what we observe will change or evolve over time. You are the constant — everything else varies."

What the hell?

Dorrit scanned the room and spotted a tablet perched precariously on a desk. He solidified a finger and nudged it. It fell with a soft thud onto the rug.

The covers flew back. Eli and his long-nosed floofball scanned the room with a flashlight.

"It was just my tablet," Eli said, uncertain.

"Probably," murmured the not-a-dog, clearly skeptical.

A daimon.

The child had a daimon. How long had it been since a sighting was reported? A century? Dorrit had thought they were extinct.

What did it mean that one had bonded with Eli? Was it safe? Did Moran know what it was?

Reeling, he tried to waft through the wall — and slammed into a reactive ward. He'd been so fixated on the talking dog, he'd missed it entirely. To be fair, it didn't disturb the lines much — until something touched it.

The impact inflated his consciousness, painfully. It took a moment to recover. He backed off, keeping a distance from the magical barrier.

He studied it. The field traced the room's dimensions, rising with the slanting ceiling and stretching to shield the oriel window. Subtle. Expertly done. It didn't retaliate — just drew on the ley energy Dorrit had borrowed to project himself.

Still, this wasn't a casual defense. It was created for a specific reason.

Dorrit held out a hand, stopping when the magic prickled his skin. Yeah. It had a purpose. He should move on.

The next door was unwarded. The walls were papered in pale fawn grasscloth with a faint motif of birds and magnolias. Sepia-toned photos, matted in French blue and framed in black, hung in tidy clusters — residents of the house, staff, Déjà, Lon…a few unfamiliar faces. Kuwako Yamane appeared once or twice, though she barely resembled Rena Amano here.

A wrought iron four-poster bed stood against the interior wall, dressed in crisp white and a rich blue duvet. A fainting couch piled with pillows sat at its foot. Matching nightstands bore simple gold lamps and assorted trinkets. A window seat flanked by filmy ivory curtains and heavy brocade drapes overlooked a large rug in French blue, ivory, and gold. The room felt traditional, Southern, restrained.

Armand — decidedly not traditional — lay sprawled across the bed, shirt undone, long braids splayed in all directions. One elegant hand massaged his temple.

Nore, wrapped in a pale cyan kaftan, sat cross-legged on the window seat, absorbed in her phone. Armand glanced at her, then flopped back to stare at the ceiling.

Dorrit moved efficiently. The tension in the room was suffocating; he didn't want to linger. If the conversation didn't relate to his concerns, he'd leave.

"She's home," Armand said flatly. "In the next room over, Nore. You don't have to worry about her."

"And Breah? Gaia? Jake? Where are they? Are they safe?" Nore snapped. "Why haven't we heard from Gaia's mother in over forty-eight hours? Abigail was murdered. We're under investigation. I'm sorry — but when a notification comes in, I have to check."

So much for a discreet retreat, Dorrit thought, sinking onto a velvet chaise.

"Has the notification provided answers?"

Nore's eyes flashed. "No, it hasn't. But let's pretend it did. If they made it home safe, we'd all sleep well. If a call for help came through, you, Kenny, Lon, Davy, Maggie —everyone — would move heaven and earth to reach them. And me," her voice broke slightly. "I'd be stuck here, waiting. Hoping. Helpless, because even magic has its limits, and checking my damn phone. Do you know what that's like? No, you don't."

"And do you know what it's like," Armand countered, "to sit here while the person I love stares past me, waiting for an unlikely peace? We still have lives, Nore. Waiting and worrying won't save our friends. But finding joy, together, now — that's something no one can take from us. Only we can ruin that."

"I'm sorry my concern for our cadre is ruining your joy," she said coldly. "I didn't realize you were so...self-absorbed."

Armand stood and buttoned his shirt. "This isn't about spondylosis. Forbidden or not, painful or not — if you knew they needed you, nothing would stop you. Not even the Council. We both know it. They know it. The truth is, you're afraid. Afraid to lose more people. But be honest—" he paused in the doorway, voice low, "—denying love doesn't keep you from losing it."

He left, the door clicking shut behind him.

Dorrit sat with the echo of it, weighing what had and hadn't been said. Jones didn't stoop to the Community's petty games, but she'd have an intelligence network. 'Council' could mean the cadre's advisory board, the Therianthrope Council of the Midwest, or something else entirely.

He glanced at Nore.

Still on the window seat, still regal, silent, with tears streaming down her cheeks.

Chapter 52: Unmasked

I studied the ash and metallic droplets at my threshold.

The surveillance servers had glitched for twenty minutes, and someone had broken into my stillroom. Too serendipitous to be a coincidence. With our ley-integrated system, I'd hoped our security would stump even the APA — but clearly not.

Oddly enough, the breach was almost reassuring. It meant the warlock was investigating, not just condemning us out of hand. Within the Community, a warlock had a license to kill. Sometimes it was the only way to stop a rogue practitioner.

The intruder had disabled sixteen cameras across two systems, bypassed three containment wards, evaded three ley-cyber snares, fooled Lon's biometrics lock — face, voice, and fingerprints — and slipped through the saturation ward without alerting my beasties. All to tamper with backup surveillance.

The store of knowledge housed in the Agora's library, from which warlocks were trained, was extensive and a legitimate threat to the continuation of practitioners. We'd accounted for that when designing our security. But this? Not possible.

I brushed my hand over the door, waking its enchantment and drawing the pins-and-needles prickle of magic into my palm. The intruder had tried the door — and left a trail. I would get Lon a name, and we'd find out how this happened.

I stepped inside and, with a twitch of a line, cleared the debris. Humming, I climbed the stairs to my loft, soothed by the sounds of home: Gidget assembling precast spells, soft scurrying in the walls, Cartman snoring on the duvet — a rare, quest-free night.

"Brrrur," Malkin announced from atop the bookshelf wall.

"Brrrrruuurrrrr," echoed Widdershins, unwilling to be outdone.

The cats trotted across the beam spanning the shelves to my loft. Oreo and Carrie lolloped out of the tunnels, noses twitching. Inaba was already bounding up the pet ladder beside the bed.

My dream team had arrived.

"Hello, beautiful babies! Oh, such good floof-floofs! Who is the pinnacle of floofiness? You are," I cooed, opening my bedside drawer and retrieving the violet serum. It wasn't often that Canal de Rêve was called for. Disappointing, considering how much effort went into brewing the stuff and laying the enchantments.

After my usual bedtime rituals, I settled in. Three drops in each eye, right then left, from the delicate glass dropper. The vial went back into the drawer. I nestled under the covers and pressed a tingling palm over my eyes.

Call it intuition. Call it ESP. Either way, I knew this was going to be bad.

The beige mobile home sat trim and quiet beside a picturesque lake, all white accents and curb appeal. Something was off, though. I raised my nose and inhaled, sifting through the scent-stream: grass, pine sap, charcoal, pesticide, algae.

Nothing.

No sweet-sour stench of death. No roses. No human musk. Not even the cauterizing tingle of active magic. Yet magic had been present. That was the only way to explain the absence of more scents.

Tension prickled down my spine. I drew my phone and sent a quick text — in case this went poorly.

I advanced slowly, listening for the hum of a ward. Nothing. The front door stood open. My hand slid to the HK45 in my waistband. I drew it and stepped inside.

The living room was bright and empty. The kitchen the same — unscented air and cheerful pops of color. The hallway had been painted a uniform rust, a choice that narrowed the space, making it feel like the walls were closing in.

The carpet had been freshly vacuumed.

I knelt and pressed my hand into the pile. There it was — the faint buzz of ley energy. The ward hugged the space like a sausage casing. It wasn't pre-cast; warped work. My jurisdiction was murky there...but I was the one standing in it, not the APA.

The ward unsettled me, but a lack of evidence was worse.

Portraits lined the wall: an elderly woman, her son, three grandchildren. A paint-smeared thumbprint marred the glass over the eldest boy's face — same rust-red as the hallway.

Bile burned my throat, but I forced myself to move.

The first bedroom held a futon and bunk beds, each topped with elaborate quilts. The hall bath was littered with clothes; a damp towel had fallen from the rack. The second bedroom was tidy — books on a nightstand, clothes on a chair — but no heartbeat met my ears.

The primary bedroom was as neat and smelled aggressively clean. A sewing machine and fabric cluttered a table in the corner. Opposite, near the en suite, stood a queen bed under a quilt of embroidered flower pots.

I didn't step into the bathroom, fixated on the contents of the tub — buckets, a metal strainer, a half-empty box of latex gloves, paint trays, and rust-red rollers.

Confirmation.

I didn't need to ask why.

The only other sign of violence was a set of four clean, parallel slashes carved into the tiled surround — sharp, slicing marks. Like claws, but surgical.

Against the wall, four pairs of shoes: faded floral house slippers, black sneakers, cherry-red ballet flats, and electric blue kids' sneakers.

Four. Not five.

This was a message. A hidden-object puzzle left by a murderer who'd taken their time — who'd enjoyed staging their scene. Confident — maybe cocky. I needed to get inside their head. That was all I could do for the victims now.

I finished clearing the house. Nothing more.

Outside, overlooking the lake, I found four fresh plots of earth.

After the grisly display inside, burial didn't track. Incineration or dissolution would've been more consistent. Burying the remains implied respect. Or attachment.

I turned toward the garden — but the sunshine and roses dissolved. Now I stood outside a cookie-cutter suburban home, the kind with barking dogs, slamming car doors, and the distant shriek of playing children.

It should have been comforting. It wasn't.

The raised ranch's front door yawned wide, and dread prickled along my arms. Another atrocity waited inside.

I inhaled, hoping — praying — only one killer knew how to cast that scent-smothering ward.

The world blurred, then ripped.

Suddenly, I was expelled from the mind I'd been riding. Gagging, nausea overtook me. The dreamer — probably male — marched on without me. At first, I was relieved. Then logic caught up.

He thought of himself as a professional — but a professional what? Were these scenes nightmares? Or memories?

I had to go in. I needed to understand.

My guide was a sketch of shadow, a blur dark enough to mark where he was and what he was doing. He moved quickly, cautiously, methodically, preserving evidence as he cleared the house.

I wanted to sink deeper into his thoughts, to see what he saw. But delving too far into another's psyche was risky. Here, he was in charge — whether he realized it or not.

The house mirrored the mobile home. I tried to ignore the bloody décor and focus on the family photos on the mantel. Familiar faces stared back at me.

Their deaths had dominated Community news for the past three weeks. A lovely, normal lycanthrope family. Therianthropes.

Their deaths fell under the jurisdiction of the Therianthrope Council.

I fled the dream.

A marshal had tracked a serial killer to our base — someone targeting therianthropes. My people were in danger. Any refugees arriving on foot were in danger.

The Covenant needed to know. Now.

I bypassed Nore and texted the Mulberry directly; no time to lose. People had to be warned.

As I waited, I stroked Oreo's soft black-and-white fur, mind racing. Should I evacuate the farm? Send everyone back to Wenen? Just the kids and the shapeshifters?

I was halfway to panic when a knock sounded on my door.

I jumped, then cursed myself. At this hour, it could only be a housemate. Although Maggie wouldn't have knocked.

Untangling myself from my bedding was delicate work. Malkin whimpered when my ankle slipped out from under his velvet cheek, but he didn't fully wake. I padded downstairs and opened the door.

The entry was thick with shadow.

A chill climbed my spine.

He didn't step forth from the dark — he seemed spun from it. The tall figure wore a tailored suit of black brocade, its haunting teal sheen catching the light along the broad line of his shoulders. A plumed tricorn hat cast deeper shadows across the hammered silver disc of his mask.

"Veritas," I blurted.

But…he was dead.

"In the flesh," he smirked, dangerous, predatory. He tipped his hat. "May I?"

I backed up three steps, my dressing gown catching at my ankles. That voice… Had I heard it before? Surely not. I'd remember. It was hypnotic.

"What are you doing here?" I asked, though it didn't matter. The guild leader of the Saturniidae was in my home — and I hadn't cleaned. There was laundry on the floor — underwear!

His presence thickened the air, transforming…well, everything.

I pushed my dreadlocks back, wishing I'd looked in a mirror before opening the door. How had I never noticed how mysterious he was? Always masked. Always veiled. Was he scarred beneath? Or was he someone I'd recognize?

The curiosity dug deep, visceral — but I would never ask. It had to be something personal.

"I…it's an honor, s-sir, but…why are you h-h-here?" I stammered, light-headed and flushed. My deference wasn't natural. Wasn't mine.

He took my hand and bowed with elegance.

A waltz began.

"Shall we dance?"

I felt—

Off. Uncomfortable. Wrong.

Why? The most powerful man in Egress had come to me. The honor smothered all doubt.

He spun us into motion, perfectly in sync with the rise and fall of the melody. We glided across the floor like the Phantom Dancer across the sky—effortless, precise, envied by all…

And still, I squirmed. Trapped. Cornered.

I needed space.

I needed out.

Frustration coated my esophagus, curling tight in my chest. I growled under my breath — but the music, soft and surreal, drowned everything but his rhythm.

We drifted, perfectly matched, around my chamber.

Only...it wasn't my room anymore. Gidget was gone. No wheeled bins of spell supplies, no beams, no bookshelves. My worktable, my laptop — vanished. Instead, we sailed across an elegant ballroom, just one of a thousand couples. But that barely registered.

He led us through the open window, the snowy drapes fluttering as we glided onto the balcony.

His hand around mine, the other at my back, made my stomach curdle. The feeling worsened with every step.

Moonlight framed his silhouette as he launched me into a twirl, my velvet robe flaring. For a breathless second, I thought I might spin right off the balcony and into the churning sea below.

The danger thrilled me. My adrenaline surged.

"Tell me your secrets, Weaver," Veritas murmured, his dark eyes locking mine, magnetic...enthralling.

"Secrets..." I echoed, my mind blank. "I... I..."

He tugged me back. His hands clamped down on my shoulders — strong. Inescapable. His eyes blazed behind the mask.

But why escape? He was the Hero of Wenen.

No.

He wasn't. He was an avatar. Egress was a game. This wasn't real. And I wanted his hands off me!

"You've been cheating," Veritas whispered.

I stomped on his foot — hard.

He yowled and stumbled back, more startled than hurt.

"Get your hands off me, you presumptuous toad!" I snarled. "I'll turn you into a toad!"

I threw a right cross.

Veritas hit the floor like a sack of bricks — and stayed there.

Cheating?

How had Veritas entered my dream? Was this my dream? Why was I wearing a dressing gown so heavy it could be used as ballast?

"What the heck? You do realize it's summer," I snapped, glaring at the yards of embroidered persimmon velvet clinging to me. "And a balcony on a frigate? Your mind is a strange place. I mean — what the what?"

Mouse was rubbing off on me.

The thought of Mouse brought the rest of my consciousness snapping into focus. We had bigger issues than seasonally inappropriate loungewear and nautical architecture.

The serum hadn't worked right.

I wasn't supposed to see, touch, or interact with the dreamer.

How had this happened?

I cheated.

He was here. Because… I cheated.

Could Veritas be the warlock?

I studied the man crumpled on the floor. No. We ran background checks on any players joining the Saturniidae. Only a few norms were ever admitted — and only for cover.

Still…Veritas must have noticed something off about Egress.

But how?

How had he found us? Had he hacked the game? Was he stalking me? Or was it just an eerie coincidence?

He had to be preternatural. There was no other explanation.

The blood in my veins turned to ice.

If the guild leader of the Saturniidae belonged to the Community…

We had a problem.

Evy was going to lose it. She and Arlo had sworn that our cybersecurity was unbreachable. Just like the Titanic.

I scanned him again. With the dream's enchantment fading — and how was he casting in his sleep? — Veritas remained frustratingly well-made. Tall. Fit. Graceful.

I tried to lift his hat. No luck. Same with the hammered silver mask. It wouldn't budge.

Ugh. Touching him was just as unpleasant as being touched by him. We didn't have that kind of relationship.

I searched for any clues and came up with diddly squat.

Sure, several guests were tall enough to match Veritas — assuming this was an accurate representation; a big assumption. The dream had gone off the rails, and anything I gleaned from it was suspect.

Whoever was behind this…they were powerful.

Perhaps ancient-vampire powerful? One who gave off strong foolish human vibes? I looked down at Veritas and imagined Count Vitruvio. Growling in frustration, I dismissed the thought. It was too neat.

Veritas's body was all business. It belonged to a man of action. Luke Vitruvio kept his physique hidden under lightweight cloaks, but he didn't move like a fighter.

Was I getting ahead of myself?

Veritas might be a sixty-two-year-old customer service rep with a half-paid mortgage and a chubby cat named George, but in his head, he was a pirate Casanova with the physique of an MMA fighter. Maybe he was so out of touch with reality that his dream-self bore zero resemblance to the man behind the mask.

I weighed two possibilities — a member of the Community discovered our use of Egress, bypassed security, infiltrated our online ranks, and studied us for years before making a move. Or…a norm hacked our system — magic and all — passed as preternatural, and plotted vengeance because he thought we'd cheated at a computer game.

As much as I trusted Evy and Arlo's firewall, my gut pointed to the former.

Still, I had to keep an open mind. Veritas could be a woman, for all I knew. How many men waltzed in their dreams? Either way, I had to report to the Covenant. The situation was now officially dire.

Time to wake up.

The presence considered me.

This was it. The end. I'd finally gone too far.

But — wait — I hadn't woven a door in over twenty-seven hours! Why now? What had I done that finally crossed the line?

Panic warred with anger, both sneering at reason.

Maybe this visit wasn't because of anything recent. Maybe bureaucracy in the beyond was as slow as Earth's. Perhaps it took decades to push a file through. Maybe time didn't move the same way for them?

Right.

The Watcher watched as my thoughts spun in every direction.

Defiance snapped my spine straight. If he thought I'd bow before his silent judgment, he had another think coming. I wasn't a child anymore.

I would not cower.

"Well?" I demanded, fists on hips.

The darkness stirred — then took shape. An impossibly tall silhouette emerged.

I'd had enough of darkness, shadows, and the men they became. Taking a quick mental check, I was reasonably confident I was free of beguilements. Whatever came next, my reactions would be my own.

The Watcher made no move toward me, nor did I feel compelled to submit. A glance down confirmed, praise be, I was back in my clothes — oversized Brew Crew tee and ancient but beloved plaid shorts.

Though…in retrospect, the persimmon robe had covered more skin.

I watched the Watcher. He loomed, all strength, purpose, carrying the silent authority of someone used to being obeyed.

Oscar did it better.

Why did you save my life?

The hollow voice echoed inside my skull — powerful, unearthly, and…unexpected. That…was not the Watcher's voice. And not a question the Watcher would ask.

He had saved me, not the other way around.

"Who are you?" I demanded, though I knew. The warlock.

Not Veritas. Someone else. Something else.

A headache bloomed, sharp and hot, as I tried to untangle it all.

Why did you save my life?

The creepy voice in my head gained a sinister edge.

I didn't bother denying it; denials were weak.

"Who are you?" I stood tall, arms crossed, with cold steel in my voice. "And why did you attempt to enter my room?"

The shade stepped forward — slowly, deliberately. I didn't flinch.

He took another step. I held my ground, though I regretted it almost immediately. Funny how much braver I'd felt with a few feet between us.

When only twelve inches separated us, he stopped — finally satisfied — and studied me like a bug under a microscope.

I scowled, even as the silence clawed at my skin. Confusing. Irritating.

I know—

An impossible force seized me — compressing every molecule.

I screamed.

I knew what was happening; I just couldn't stop it.

The warlock reached for me — whether to help or harm, I never found out.

I was torn from the dream and flung down a well in eternity. The beyond spun around me, a cyclone of fractured color and motion too fast for my eyes to focus. Just as I began to dissolve, a new voice sliced through the chaos.

You light up the void like a beacon, and there are worse things out here than your warlock. Stay in your own dimension, little practitioner.

I fell.

And fell.

And fell—

My back slammed into my own body, drenched in sweat and freezing.

Around me, the babies stared with wide, silent eyes.

"I'm all right," I told them, breathless, shaking. "Just a bad dream. A bad, bad dream."

Hoping the dreaming was done for good, I reached for my phone with a weak, trembling hand. I had a report to file with the Covenant — if they believed me.

Eli: August 30th at Sullen Creek Farm

The screen door murmured, and someone stepped onto the dining porch. I knew who it was…sort of. Their walk was unfamiliar.

Mom had a quiet walk — too quiet. She didn't mean to sneak up on people, but it happened a lot. Preternaturals generally moved quietly and were prone to startling each other. This wasn't Mom, though; she was teaching a Cocktails and Canvas class at the brewpub.

Aunt Lou clomped or made an entrance. She liked attention. Aunt Mags could go either way — if she was annoyed or restless, she went quiet until it was too late. If she was happy, she hummed or chatted with plants as she moved. Aunt Kenny smelled like fresh herbs and vibrated like a wall of repressed energy. Aunt Nore had a sarcastic gait.

This walk didn't match anyone I knew.

I glanced at Boruta. He looked just as tense as I felt, but gave me a nod. I looked up as the newcomer passed the two-sided fireplace.

For a moment, we just stared at each other.

"Oh," I murmured. "I thought you'd be older."

"Likewise," he replied, visibly perplexed.

His words made my stomach twist. What if he didn't believe me? He had to. He just…had to.

"Did you have visions of an old man with long gray hair, a staff, and a pointed hat?"

He was teasing me — or, more likely, testing me. How would Aunt Kenny handle this…

"I'm trying to keep my family safe," I reminded, but without anger. I knew things about him — scary things — and I didn't want to upset him. "I know your names — all of them. I expected your age to show, or that you'd look tired, is all. Most adults look tired."

His smile suddenly looked tired, and his shoulders drooped. "I've learned to hide it better than most. I thought you'd look older, too. Such a common mistake — confusing competence with age. You'd think I'd have learned more humility by now. C'est la vie."

He clapped his hands lightly. "Well, shall we get down to business?"

Boruta exhaled beside me, nudging my ribs, reminding me to breathe. My word had been accepted.

We had help. Experienced help.

Everything would be fine.

Hopefully.

We exchanged zip drives. He nodded toward my journal.

"May I?"

I nodded.

He picked up the spiral notebook just as the screen door from the main house creaked open. Derringer elbowed his way out, a large rectangular basket cradled in his arms — restocking the Punk Bunks fridge.

"I'll get the door," I offered, by way of a distraction.

"Bless you, Eli. You'd think Kenny would've programmed Gidget to open doors when our arms are full, but nope."

"She will, if you remind her during an update."

"I'll do that."

Derringer scuttled into the kitchen, setting the basket down with a relieved sigh. He smiled and waved me off. I let the screen door close behind me and returned to my new friend.

He was several pages in when I got back and looked...pained.

"You have an extraordinary talent, Eli, but this is cruel work for children. Is there someone you can confide in?"

He did believe, then. I bit my tongue as fear and relief choked in my throat. I didn't want him to think I was a baby.

"Aunt Déjà, Uncle Oscar, Colt, Milo, and Mouse."

Boruta had advised me on whom to confide in. It was hard sharing my visions — and scary. Telling the wrong person could ruin everything, and even the right person wasn't guaranteed help. He was right, though; the stakes were too high. I couldn't do this alone.

My friend smiled the tired smile.

"Good. Never take the trust of another for granted, Eli. It's precious — especially for us."

Chapter 54: Constructive Interference

Kenny: August 30th at Sullen Creek Farm

I'd advised both my cadre and the Covenant on the situation. They took it better than I expected — too well.

The Sheta Djew trusted me. If I said 'evacuate,' they would; if I said 'stay,' they'd stay. That was the problem. I didn't know what the right call was. I was terrified of losing people — or destroying everything we'd built by jumping the gun.

The Covenant decided for me: a warning had been issued, recommending that therianthropes and families with children evacuate. Everyone else? Business as usual.

Evacuation had been our knee-jerk response for centuries — and why we'd survived, but it was also why we'd never built a stable society.

I urged my people to take the warning seriously. Davy, Lou, Eli, Milo, and Mouse flat-out refused to leave. I considered strong-arming the kids, but settled for tagging them with trackers and assigning bodyguards.

I spent the morning with Lon's team, summoning every foreign bug, camera, and surveillance charm on the property. Kyle — Lon's apprentice — botched his summoning, and our resident tarantulas, Matilda and Jeepers, were magically yanked from their terrarium. The spiders were not speaking to me. I hadn't cast the spell, but I was management; the buck stopped with me.

At least I got a new paperweight: I'd soldered the spy bots together into a single lump with twitchy legs. And because I fixate, we spent two more hours reinforcing wards, testing snares, and scanning for magical and mundane surveillance. Everything came back clean. Which made me more nervous.

After breakfast, I tried to focus on work, but I was making the brewhouse staff jumpy. I handed the reins to Lon and retreated to my hideout.

The forest was full of green, spicy scents and the rustle of leafy conversation. Quiet, but not lonely.

At the covered bridge, I climbed onto the old railing and up into the trusses. Near the far end was a little loft where I kept some treasures — things I didn't want destroyed if the house was attacked. One of many hidey-holes on the farm, just in case.

It wasn't paranoia if they were really after you.

I crept across the bottom chords until I reached the loft's uneven floor. An old steamer trunk, enchanted until it repelled moisture, pests, and fire, filled most of the space. I unlocked it and pulled out a case.

My biological father's banjo. I rarely played it, but the feel and sound always pulled me out of my head.

Sitting with my legs dangling off the platform, I fitted my picks and tuned the instrument. When I was satisfied, I channeled Mean Mary and let muscle memory take over. Sound danced under my fingertips — stark, moody yarns spun in rhythm. I lost myself in faithless lovers, wild creatures of the night, and dark, wordless beats.

An hour passed too fast.

I didn't want to go back, but too many pieces were in motion. With a sigh, I tucked the banjo into its velvet-lined case and packed it away.

"That was unexpected."

I jumped off the rail and eyed James Darrow, standing on his own two feet. I hadn't heard him approach.

Now I needed a new hideout.

"Look at you, up and about. Did Oscar clear you?"

He grimaced. "Not quite. The curse is contained, not broken. A day or two, they think. But don't change the subject. Why didn't you play with the others at the bonfire?"

I waved him along as I started toward the house. "The banjo belonged to my father. He was murdered when I was five. When I play...it's not a celebration."

"I'm sorry."

I shrugged. "It is what it is."

"May I ask how it happened?"

The memory surged forward, all too eager to mug me. I was transported to a little white cottage clinging to a rocky bluff with a dark ocean beyond. I heard my mother's sharp voice as she helped my dad activate defenses. I watched through wooden blinds as half a dozen people surrounded our home. One woman had copper curls that trailed in the wind beneath a sickly, green-gray sky. None of them looked evil. They didn't even look angry.

"Practitioners," I said.

"But—"

"But I'm a correctionist," I finished. "Titus Quade's helots. My family wasn't the only casualty."

Quade was what happened when an Ancient snapped — three hundred dead, forty-two bound as helots. The APA needed six years to put him down.

"I'm sorry," he repeated.

He didn't argue; didn't explain that helots no longer existed. He just accepted it.

The wind shifted, and for a moment I thought I had been transported back to Maine. It was something I'd done as a kid whenever I was frightened — I'd scared my adoptive parents more than a few times. But beneath the trembling boughs, I caught the song of a sweet, elusive voice.

Darrow had stopped a few steps behind me. His eyes glowed bright. He swayed, still weak, as fur sprang up over his hands. I marched over and slapped him hard.

He blinked, then intelligence snapped back into place.

"Run," he snarled.

I ran.

Weakened or not, he kept pace as we sprinted toward the Missouri River. I scanned the skies for the uninvited singer, but she remained hidden.

"In the water! Look!"

I didn't know who shouted, but I saw the body getting swept downstream — no struggling, caught in the siren's grip. I hesitated.

"Get the siren!" Darrow barked, stripping down and diving in.

He was right; the siren had to take priority.

Tapping the lines, I flung a blazing sigil over the water. I leapt, toe-tapped the symbol, and launched into the air. I threw a second sigil mid-fall, caught it, and sprang again. I paved my path, eyes searching for the music's source.

A second voice joined in — deeper, soulful, weaving the melody in a new direction. Clouds churned and parted under Nore's command, revealing a terrible beauty: half woman, half bird, and all malice.

The siren lifted its face and sang, too preoccupied with Nore to notice me.

At level altitude, I launched, wrapping my legs around its waist and slapping a silencing ward over its mouth. It jerked in surprise — so lifelike; I almost apologized. Then it raked me with filthy talons.

I drove my thumbs into its eyes. It silently screamed, body reverberating like a tuning fork. Our flight path shifted. Wings beat against my ribs while it clawed at my arms and legs, fighting blind.

I needed to unravel its heart — the twist of malevolent energy holding the construct together. We wrestled midair, and it tried to buck me off while I tapped a tattoo and summoned my kunai, careful not to impale myself. Ikita Kawaki's magic was as deadly to me as anything else. It was not a smooth fight.

Something struck the bird-woman square between the eyes. Its head snapped back into my nose, jerking my hand. Burning ice scored the curve of my forearm. Another missile flew up. Someone below was helping.

"Stop throwing shit!" I shouted, projecting my voice as I wiped blood from my eyes.

The wound on my arm filled with bright crimson, its edges blackened. Not venom — ley absence. True death.

I gave up on finesse and stabbed near the construct's sternum, where the lines thickened. Wind and its thrashing made it nearly impossible. It craned its neck and bit my wound.

I screamed, barely maintaining my grip as we tumbled through the air. I tossed the weapon to the other hand and stabbed wildly. Over and over, I stabbed — until I heard the screaming from below getting louder.

I flung out a sigil and clung to it.

My fall was arrested; the siren's was not. With its teeth still sunk in my arm, its weight yanked hard. The earth slammed into me, and my vision went dark around the edges.

"Get that thing off her arm," Oscar snapped, already working.

"Witnesses," I mumbled, unsure if it was audible.

"Occupied with rescuing Count Vitruvio," he grunted, cleaning me up. "Benilde found him after he stopped surfacing. He looked like a goner, but once you tackled the construct, he started struggling. Everyone's watching him now."

"Nore?"

"The Haighs covered her. No one saw or heard her. Now shut up and let me work."

Oscar had my broken nose healed before Lon navigated the speedboat off the river. Anything more would have to wait.

Ignoring all protests, I got to my feet and boarded before they were tied off. Lon was dry, looking grim. Armand, Darrow, Benilde, and Vitruvio were soaked — three of them scratched and bitten like me. The Count looked bemused but unharmed.

"Hold still," I ordered, pushing him down when he tried to rise. I scanned him for stray magic. I prodded a suspicious twist, and he lunged forward, knocking us both overboard.

Cold water closed over my head. A silhouette blocked the sun, and strong hands gripped my throat, pushing me down. I panicked, lost hold of the knotted line, as the river flooded my mouth and nose.

Someone yanked him off, and I surfaced, gasping.

"Hexed," I rasped. "He doesn't know what he's doing."

Armand caught me before I went under again, setting me on my feet and holding me upright. My legs wouldn't cooperate.

"If I hold him, can you fix him?" Benilde grunted, grappling with the Count. His good eye was wild, his expression livid.

I shoved my glasses to my forehead and scanned for the hex. It pulsed — a dull red.

"Yes. Armand, help him."

Armand didn't let go until I'd proven that I wouldn't topple over. It was a two-man job, though. Even dazed, Vitruvio was putting up a fight.

Once they had him pinned, I flushed the spell. As I drew it into my reservoir, malevolence surged through me. The desire to rend, to destroy, was overwhelming — until my defenses crushed it. I unraveled the nasty tangle and learned two things: the construct hadn't come by accident, and Vitruvio had drawn the short straw. There had been no specific target. If I hadn't slapped Darrow, he'd have needed rescuing, too. I was grateful it hadn't claimed anyone else.

"I'm sorry! I'm sorry!" Vitruvio babbled as the others dragged him onto the dock. "I didn't mean to!"

"We know," Lon said, rolling him aside so Armand could climb out. "Just rest, buddy."

Benilde scooped me up and tossed me to Darrow like a sack of potatoes. I gasped — more from surprise than pain — as the werewolf caught and eased me down. I didn't even try to stand — I was exhausted and didn't have any pressing engagements.

"You're sure you got all of it?" Benilde asked, ignoring any offers of help as he clambered up.

"Yes. Didn't settle deep." Complete sentences weren't worth the effort.

He slumped beside me, scowling at my torn arm and bruised throat.

"Was that typical behavior for a wild construct?" Darrow asked as Addison cleaned a bite on his neck. It looked…off.

Lon's, too. All of them were bloody and bitten…and something about it was wrong.

"Wild constructs don't cast hexes," I huffed as Oscar rolled me sideways and started disinfecting wounds, muttering under his breath.

"Someone brought it here. Lent it power — ID or practitioner. If I see that magic again, I'll know it."

Chapter 55: Motives and Macaron

Kenny: August 31st at Sullen Creek Farm

Rwack-rwack-rwack.

I was going to kill that alarm. It was the only reasonable thing to do.

Groaning, I rolled onto my side and blindly reached for my phone —
sleep mask still on. A lazy finger swipe silenced the infernal device.

Another morning, another injury. The painkillers had dulled everything,
including my brain. I felt stupid — stuffed with cotton. I tugged off my
sleep mask and blinked blearily. Too bright. Too…

"Umm…hi…everyone," I mumbled.

A few hundred furry, feathered, and scaled faces stared back. Mel sat
upright beside me, his floofy tail under my hand. The rest of the babies filled
the bed, the beams, the bookshelves, and the floor below. Word had spread.

"I'm all right. I'm alive. I love you. Please go about your normal
activities. No suspicious behavior, okay?"

Not a whisker twitched.

"Ahem."

I knelt and scanned the sea of faces. Found him — at the foot of the
bed between Orpheus and Pascale.

"Yes, Boruta?"

"I've been appointed spokes-familiar for Sullen Creek," he announced.
"We're aware of several recent threats, though we were not informed of
them at the time. Nore's skills could have been exposed. An apprentice
might have reached for the lines. You might have died. We've reviewed our
security with Lon and determined that better aerial surveillance is needed.
We are concerned that we are not taken seriously as a resource and that our
communication channels urgently need to be improved."

"I'm sorry. The oversight wasn't intentional. And, you're right. This
could have been prevented."

Communication channels? Maybe something with pet buttons…

"Thank you. There will not be another air assault. We won't permit it."

I'd wronged them. I thought of the farm's familiars as wounded babies
needing love and care, but here they were, ready to defend their home.
Courage came in all sizes and shapes.

"We further request a distribution of treats as recompense for pain and suffering."

A shake-down.

"Breakfast first," I said firmly. "Then treats."

After five minutes of wheedling, the fur brigade realized I wasn't budging and shuffled out in a graceless exodus. They were clever and brave, but most still hadn't figured out how to take turns crossing suspended beams. Luckily, the only accidents that occurred could be solved with paper towels and disinfectant.

Eventually, only Mel remained…and Cartman, who'd slept through the whole thing, the precious boy.

I looked at Mel. Mel looked at me. I twitched like I was going to blink. He didn't. I faked a sneeze…then really sneezed and blinked. Mel chuffed and assumed his on-duty stance.

"What on earth is that?" Nore demanded.

Fair question. I eyed the tower of ten gold filigreed boxes tied with a ridiculous turquoise velvet bow.

"Delivery for Hazel Jones," the driver announced, wheeling it up the stairs. The tower came up to my waist.

"That would be me. Nore, help?"

We hefted the stack onto the bench. After I'd signed for delivery, I pulled a turquoise envelope off the top and read it.

"So?" Nore prompted.

"Chairman Darragh O'Brien heard I'd built myself a personal assistant-bot and would like to commission a baker-bot. This," I gestured to the monolith, "is a bribe. His words."

"O'Brien? The Chairman of the Union of Seers bakes?"

"Apparently. He included a guide: Paris-Brests, Tartelettes aux fraises des bois, Tuiles, Tartes au citron, Figues, Canelés de Bordeaux… Even as tall as it is, I'm not sure how they all fit."

Nore looked stricken.

"Lon will have a fit if we eat them. What are the odds they're compliant?"

"Excellent. The Chairman included a list of ingredients, although I have other concerns." I cast a detection spell, and the boxes pulsed with active magic, but nothing hostile. "All safe. He even added a neat little charm for freshness. I wonder if the Haighs could reverse-engineer that."

I needed to speak to the sisters anyway. I'd failed to replicate the enchantment on my kunai, and after the siren, I wanted my people appropriately armed.

We brought the tower to the kitchen, repacked the treats so each box had a mix, and took them out to the porch. As folks gathered, Nore explained their origins.

"Are you going to accept the commission?" Colt asked, already inhaling his third Madeleine. He argued with no food.

Conscious of our guests, I considered my reply while helping myself to bacon. "Unfortunately, no. I wasn't the only one who worked on Derringer — I can't volunteer other people's time."

"How did he hear about Derringer?" Oscar growled, eyeing his Paris-Brest with suspicion. One bite later, he moaned aloud — cutting off abruptly when he realized others heard.

Aiden and James — apparently fast friends, now — found seats further down. Luke was already wedged between Davy and Madison. All three guests looked groggy from yesterday's mess.

"We run a beer hotel," Maggie said with a shrug. "No mystery. A guest told him…or he's spying. Or both."

"Why not ask the others?" Colt pressed, grinning as he played devil's advocate. "If it's for a Quorum bigwig, and they'd be compensated. Why wouldn't they help?"

Derringer turned from the hash browns he was refilling.

"What Kenny is too considerate to mention is the ethical component. Am I just advanced code — or an intelligent being? Kenny chooses to treat me as more than a thing. Would Chairman O'Brien do the same?"

Chapter 56: Good Faith

Kenny: August 31ˢᵗ at Sullen Creek Farm

"Enter," I droned, barely looking up from my calendar. I was busy deleting appointments. Derringer would scold me for interfering with his domain, but I didn't care. If another emergency struck, I needed to be here.

When Raleigh Haigh opened the door, with Monroe right behind her, I snapped to attention and shut my laptop. They weren't on the docket, which meant something had gone wrong, or they'd made a decision early — or both. Either way, the surprise visit made me nervous.

Monroe locked the door and wove a sound seal. Redundant — the room was already warded — but telling. Raleigh placed a sleek, forest green briefcase on my desk, opened it, and silently handed me a flash drive and a slim file. She sat without a word. Monroe dragged over a chair with a screech of metal on concrete and shot a glare first at her sister, then at me.

I got the sense Monroe was here under protest. She looked like Evy when she was in a snit.

"I apologize for the intrusion," Raleigh murmured, still keeping her voice low despite the seal. "Please read this and tell us if it's possible."

"What's happened?"

I'd spent eight years courting Clan Haigh, trying to form an alliance. Most independent clans were vulnerable — targets for the remaining seven covens. Many stayed hidden, isolated, either for peace, ideology, or sheer survival. The Covenant offered protection without demanding fealty. For most, that was tempting.

But not the Haighs.

They were the exception: neutral, powerful, and fiercely independent. Research specialists with the size, knowledge, and resources to stay unaffiliated. They didn't need us and knew it.

Instead of courting them with the usual perks — access to the Covenant library, training, protection — I'd built a slow, careful business relationship based on time, reliability, and mutual respect. A few favors traded. A few crises solved. They'd had ample time to see we weren't interested in controlling them.

Three months ago, I'd floated the idea of an alliance to Callum Haigh. He'd agreed to consider it — after some of his daughters had spent time at our base. For Raleigh to negotiate anything early, something seismic had shifted. For her to refuse the offer after only three days? We must have made a terrible impression.

"Read and you'll understand," Raleigh said.

I did.

It was a contract — but not the one I'd expected. The sisters watched as I flipped through the pages, trying not to scowl. The document was a masterpiece of understatement: glossing over manipulations, chock full of weak justifications, and minimizing both the reckless choices they'd made and the threat of devastation they had raised. It wasn't a proposal. It was a confession.

The final page hit like a punch.

I took a breath. Maybe three.

"Well. That makes for interesting reading."

"You don't sound surprised," Monroe dryly observed, with a thread of suspicion in her voice. Suddenly, I realized the years I'd invested in building trust with Clan Haigh meant nothing. They wouldn't trust me — not unless their backs were to the wall.

In hindsight, I should've seen it. They were an ancient bloodline and self-reliant — survivors conditioned to be skeptical. Callum Haigh was nearly five hundred years old, the oldest practitioner on record. Even fifty years of loyal friendship wouldn't have cracked that shell.

But even the untouchable make mistakes. Sometimes, they stumble across something new and forget the caution that's kept them alive. Callum's behavior was out of character — but then, practitioners are unpredictable creatures.

I pushed my glasses up and rubbed my temples.

"By what, exactly?" I asked, sarcasm bleeding in. "That your father never intended to ally with the Covenant? Or that playing with portal magic went sideways? Because neither of those is shocking. That he's still alive? Now that's nothing short of incredible. He's beyond lucky not to have gotten stranded on a plane he couldn't survive — or lost in the in-between."

"That contract doesn't say who we lost," Monroe said tightly.

"Portal magic is a lost art. No one knows what to expect," Raleigh reminded me, speaking calmly over her sister.

"For good reason!" I snapped, not heeding the implied warning. "Every practitioner who thought they were clever enough to mess with ley doors eventually walked through one too many. Most never came back. The ones who did usually died shortly after — in agony. Every single one brought it on themselves."

I winced. I was saying too much, sounding too familiar with the hazards of hedge witchery.

I turned to Monroe.

"And yes, it did specify who it was. There's only one member of Clan Haigh arrogant enough to land himself in this mess and still have the rest of you lining up to get him back. You're giving up your independence — for a hundred years! You're sacrificing your freedom, your nieces' and nephews' freedom. Who else would you do that for? Certainly not one of your brothers-in-law. You barely acknowledge them as family."

"And you're not arrogant?" Monroe shot back. "You really thought we'd ally with you — a thief and a murderer?"

She gestured broadly. "Look at this place! You're using our crisis as an excuse to live in luxury."

I glanced down at my tank top, then at her silk blouse. She didn't take the hint.

"What have you even changed?" she pressed. "What lasting good have you done? Stop buying your own press! You're not an Angel of Mercy; you're a coward. A fraud."

She wasn't pulling her punches.

"We wanted to believe in you. We were ready to back you, but Dad said to wait. And we did wait — for years. I thought you were audacious, strutting around with magically manufactured fangs, convincing the Community that you were one of them. You held your cadre. You earned respect. You convinced the Quorum to make you an Ipseita Dualis. But what's it all for? We're still dying — only now you're the one administering the injection."

"This isn't helping," Raleigh cut in, sharp now. She tapped the contract. "Can this be done?"

Neither of them noticed the portal behind them — wide and ominous.

I'd twisted the lines without thinking, angry and afraid. I'd never done it with my glasses on. I hadn't known I could.

Was Monroe right?

I wasn't a coward. I'd saved lives. But I hadn't changed the game. Everything we'd accomplished was temporary. If there was a real solution, did I have it in me to seize it?

I stared into the swirling mists beyond the portal and waited for the Watcher to intervene.

Nothing.

I gave it a few more seconds.

The last time I had used a gate to frighten someone — Oscar — to make a point and take a little revenge; it had been satisfying in the moment...and even for several days afterward. But, ultimately, it had reinforced his initial bad impression of me and his distrust of practitioners in general.

It took years to rebuild what I'd broken.

I learned from my mistakes. I unraveled the door.

"Of course it can be done," I snapped, pulling out my phone. "Jake, send Lon, Jonathan, and Breah to the brewhouse office. Wake up both of my proxies. The Doyenne needs to be at the reunion. The other are on standby."

I hung up and made a second call. "Nore, please come to my office. Bring Oscar, someone from Legal — Sean or Sherri — and a notary."

Raleigh went pale. Monroe's jaw dropped.

"You're going to sign?" Raleigh asked softly, her voice ghostly.

Funny how success can shock people more than failure.

"No. We're going to write a new contract. Similar, but with some important differences." I waved the old one. "First, this says the agreement is between me and Clan Haigh, not the Covenant. That's not going to fly. I'm not vain enough to hold this over the Covenant, nor dumb enough to let you build a loophole around my death. I'm not dying for your father. So don't count on this being voided if I kick the bucket."

Both sisters looked disconcerted. Monroe recovered first.

"What else are you changing — and why would we agree?"

"Good faith," I said, answering the second question first. "A concept I suggest your clan get better acquainted with."

I tapped the contract. "I'm adding a clause: any hostile action toward me, any Covenant member, any cadre member, our guests, property, or innocent bystanders will immediately dissolve Clan Haigh and mark every one of you as a self-confessed warlock — whether the rest of the contract's fulfilled or not."

Monroe reared back, ready to unleash more vitriol, but Raleigh laid a firm hand on her arm.

"No more," she said, then turned to me. "Anything else?"

"Yes. But it'll have to wait."

Three minutes of bitter silence passed before a knock came.

"Come in!"

Oscar entered, giving Monroe's sound seal a dry look before waving it away.

"Welcome to the party."

He grunted. "Nore's on her way."

"Good. While we wait, read this."

I rose and handed him the file, motioning for him to take my seat. As he read, his expression shifted from bored to murderous. I poured myself a glass of water from the fridge pitcher, took two sips, then reached for a sticky pad and scribbled down the amendments I had in mind.

"No," Oscar said flatly, glaring at the Haighs. Monroe squirmed under his stare.

I stuck the mint green note on the file's cover.

Oscar read it. "Perhaps. If you think they're worth the effort."

Another knock.

Sean — slight, sharp-eyed, smiling — stepped in and bowed slightly.

"Excellent timing."

I was closing the door when Lon, Nore, and a pale, raven-haired Lizzy Coinin rounded the corner. Suddenly, my spacious office felt claustrophobic.

"Nore, Sean, take this," I said, pointing to the file. "Analyze the binding magic, rewrite it with my amendments, and add anything else you deem necessary."

"Fun," Sean murmured, already absorbed by the document.

Nore raised a brow, questioning what was going on. I shrugged. This wasn't ideal, but it was workable.

They left just before Jonathan and Breah arrived. We played musical chairs until everyone was settled.

"Lizzy, Raleigh and Monroe need to sign standard NDAs," I said. "If they walk, the information stays protected. Afterward, stick around to notarize."

Lizzy booted Oscar from the desk chair and got to work. It took a few minutes to enchant and print the documents. Once ready, she handed them over.

"I'm not signing that," Monroe snapped, lip curled.

"If you don't, there's no deal," I replied.

Raleigh read and signed, then passed the pen to her sister. Monroe hesitated, arms crossed, then finally accepted it. After three reads, she signed.

"This better be worth it."

Yes, it had.

"Breah, Jonathan — for the benefit of our guests — what's Lon's favorite counterintelligence maxim?"

Lon crossed his arms and gave Raleigh a cheeky eyebrow waggle.

"Control the flow of information," the operatives chorused.

"At some point, there's going to be a leak," Breah added. "So we control who, when, and what gets leaked."

Raleigh looked resigned. Monroe tried for bored.

"And how does he apply that?"

"We stage a slow-burn scenario," Jonathan said. "A few folks appear disgruntled or in trouble — only works if we know the target's watching."

"How much has Clan Haigh paid you over the last decade?"

Jonathan grinned. "Nearly four million. Boss loves it when Haigh calls."

"Thanks, kids. Back to the grindstone."

As the door shut behind them, Raleigh met my eyes.

"All right," she said. "You controlled the information we received. But why let anything negative slip?"

Lon barked a laugh. "Would you have believed perfection? We gave you bits of truth — neutral things. You saw what you wanted to see."

Oscar grunted and glanced at me. I nodded.

"We'll fill in the blanks soon. Each Covenant guild has a specialty. Clan Haigh's is reverse-engineering rare magics and artifacts," he explained.

"They already know mine is theft and murder," I added, with a vapid smile. Lon choked beside me. I met Monroe's glare. "Odd strategy — antagonizing a murderer."

"We understand why you offer to execute those who were caught and convicted of warped practices. It's better than the alternative," Raleigh soothed, giving Monroe a warning look. "Clan Haigh does not condemn the Angels of Mercy for the service they provide. Some of us are ashamed that we cannot do as much."

"The Saturniidae specializes in rescue operations," Oscar corrected sharply, "establishing new identities, and covert relocation. And theft."

Chapter 57: Essential Witness

August 31ˢᵗ at Sullen Creek Farm

Veritas found himself in an untenable position. His hosts — rather than calling the police after he'd assaulted Weaver… He shook his head, confused. They were falling over themselves to make amends for his near-death experience, and ignoring the bit where he'd tried to crush the life out of their leader.

He had tried to kill her. He'd wanted to.

He didn't even like killing the ants that got into his kitchen, let alone a person! None of this made sense.

Weaver had explained that the siren — apparently not a living creature — had hidden itself in the clouds at the edge of the property and bewitched him with its song. It had also hexed him. That accounted for the impulse, the rage, the blank spots in his memory.

The wards hadn't caught it because the siren wasn't alive — with no malice to detect. Just song and sabotage.

But…he'd seen the body. It looked like something out of myth: a perfect meld of a breathtaking woman and an enormous bird.

His absolute ignorance of constructs, bewitchments, and hexes hadn't fazed Weaver. Maybe the trauma was excuse enough. Maybe supernaturals were ignorant of each other.

His hosts had insisted he witness the siren's unraveling firsthand — proof that he was safe. The unraveling was the strangest experience of his life. Well, second to accidentally strangling someone.

Weaver had chosen her ground and walked a slow circle around it three times. No salt. No chanting. No chalk. No blood. She tripped over a rock on the first pass, but it hadn't seemed to matter.

Lon brought out a red collapsible camp chair and set it in the ring with a perfect view of the…remains. He stepped in and out of the boundary like it was just another Thursday and walked over to Veritas.

Only then did he realize that the chair was meant for him. Lon half-coaxed, half-carried him over, ignoring his objections with polite firmness. So, Veritas sat — mere feet from the arcane carcass. If anyone had given the slightest indication they were going to eat it, he would have been gone.

The staff — and several guests — stood in a wide circle around the boundary. Weaver sat cross-legged on the opposite side of the...dead object.

She didn't touch it — just pushed her glasses up and stared. No incantations. No wind. No spirit guides or glowing lights. No hand gestures. No drama.

Nothing.

He was nearly faint with gratitude that it hadn't been more horrific. And still, he hadn't known it was possible for something to be both deeply unsettling and achingly dull at the same time.

After a few minutes — just when he'd convinced himself the whole thing was a colossal hoax — Veritas noticed the remains had blurred. His first thought: concussion. But the murmuring around him confirmed that others had noticed, too. Cold sweat broke out on his forehead as the siren slowly dissolved before his eyes.

If Weaver could do that to a construct, could she do it to him?

He needed to leave — without raising suspicion. But they knew his real name. He'd need an alias. How did one hide from the supernatural?

When the last feather had vanished, the crowd erupted — cheers, congratulations, replays of the attack. Veritas could hardly process it. No wonder supernaturals had been able to remain hidden! They could vaporize bodies in minutes — by staring.

Was this legal? Did they have laws? Was bloodsucking and casual cannibalism normal? He knew so little. And needed to know everything.

A couple of nearby teenagers had latched onto the bit where Veritas had attempted to kill their beloved representative and were taking turns choking each other. They rather overdid it, in his opinion. A little went a long way. Several adults agreed with him and eventually hushed their antics.

Oscar, Aiden, and James escorted him back to the hotel — apparently done with the spectacle as well. Once in his room, Oscar left a few grumbled instructions: no stress, no alcohol, hydrate, rest.

A few quiet hours followed. Veritas processed what he'd seen — and began to appreciate what he'd learned. He logged into The Contingency Plan, recorded his experiences, and drafted a list of questions. Supernaturals wrote on philosophy and ethics. They had to have laws. Enforcement. Trials. Everything. The answers were out there. He just had to be strong enough to find them.

Later, Weaver stopped by to check in. New security measures had been put in place. His bill had been fully refunded, and she apologized for failing to protect him. While he stammered, she handed over a thick envelope of vouchers — beer flights, balloon rides, and more.

Veritas hadn't been able to formulate a coherent refusal, or Weaver had refused to hear it. He wasn't sure. He still felt like he was existing in a haze — The Twilight Zone, but real...and so achingly familiar. He wished he could understand why!

Weaver had just patted his shoulder and advised a hot bath, rest, and a good dinner. She'd even had a tray sent up.

Thanks to the don't-sue-us vouchers, the next morning, Veritas found himself watching qualifiers for the Community's Midwest Chess-Boxing Championship — hosted by Sullen Creek Farm. He'd never heard of chess-boxing, but it had a fervent supernatural following. And since sports were integral to most cultures, it was an opportunity he couldn't ignore.

A massive, air-conditioned tent covered three boxing rings, a concession stand, and a slew of bleachers. Despite the crowd, one of Weaver's staff — Saffron, a lovely girl with long brown hair — spotted him immediately and brought a menu. The staff had been instructed to cater to his every need and ensure that he didn't so much as stub a toe. The fear from yesterday had dulled just enough that he could enjoy the attention — even if it vexed him, too.

Two hours, three beers, a boat of nachos, and another of lasagna fritters later, Veritas was hooked. He bobbed and weaved in his seat during matches and barely stopped himself from calling out chess suggestions. He'd picked favorites and even had Saffron place a flutter on one fighter. The guy was favored, but Veritas still won a few bucks.

"Your dulce de leche pie, Count Vitruvio — with churros and a side of honey-banana compote."

"Ah! Thank you, Saffron," he murmured, wincing as Desmond the Destroyer took a brutal hit. "That looked like it hurt."

"Anything else I can get you, sir?"

"No...yes! A water would be nice."

"No trouble at all," she smiled.

He hadn't finished his first bite before she returned with a towering ice water in a commemorative tumbler — service with a smile. The VIP treatment was growing on him. Maybe tomorrow he'd try a massage.

Past the ring where Buzz the Baleful was dismantling the Destroyer, Weaver and Lon entered the tent. They made their way through the crowd to the contestants' section, deep in discussion. Lon frowned, replied, frowned again, then finally nodded.

Something about the exchange — or Lon's reaction — pinged Veritas's radar. He scraped up the last drizzle of honey, grabbed his water, and casually headed for the exit.

It was time to show his mettle.

"I can take care of that, Count Vitruvio," Saffron said, hurrying over to take his plate. "Did you enjoy the chess-boxing?"

"Very much, and the exceptional service. But just so we're all on the same page," and so helpful busybodies wouldn't shadow him, "while I appreciate having every whim granted, it isn't necessary. I'm grateful for the part Kenny, Lon, Oscar, and the other guests played in my rescue. I don't hold anyone here accountable for the attack and won't be pursuing any legal action. It couldn't have been foreseen. It was their quick, selfless actions that saved me. I am in the Sheta Djew's debt."

Saffron smiled. "There are no debts between friends. But if there's anything we can do to make your stay more comfortable, please let us know."

He promised he would, then exited, stretching naturally as he scanned the area. He spotted Weaver just slipping into a distant outbuilding — one he vaguely recalled as a workshop. Plotting a casual route, he sipped water and acknowledged well-wishers as he drifted that way.

Congratulating himself on his growing skills in skullduggery, he bypassed the building entirely, ducked into the woods, circling back to the east wall. About ten feet out, a familiar buzz washed over him — like a limb falling asleep. Some kind of magical security, no doubt, similar to the one on Weaver's bedroom door. She must've spent a good bit of time staring at the place to erect something so wide.

When no one stopped him, he crept under a window and listened. He heard nothing. The window was closed.

Edging to the north, he noted glass-paneled garage doors and strolled past them, peeking in. Several people were working on carpentry projects, but there was no sign of Kenny inside. Still, she might be out of view.

Around the corner, he tried the door. If caught, he could claim confusion — the many outbuildings, the trauma from yesterday. Believable enough, he reasoned.

The knob buzzed — sharper this time — but turned easily. The space was a single large room, with a trussed ceiling overhead, full of workbenches, machinery, and shelving that divided it into functional zones.

Veritas had no real experience with crafting or woodworking — beyond painting minis and assembling terrain tiles — but he recognized a saw when he saw one. He hadn't known there were so many types, though. And…the place was silent. From outside, it had been bustling. Inside, the utter stillness was giving him serious slasher vibes.

He didn't know how to account for it.

Perhaps Kenny had slipped out when he'd looped through the trees…but not all of the workers could have left unnoticed. He continued, reaching the back wall. To his far right, near a garage door, sat a pair of glasses beside a canvas tote on a worktable.

The floor was thick with sawdust — easily a couple of inches deep. Veritas crept closer, not leaving any prints in the mess. A glance at the floor behind him told him that ship had sailed, but his weren't the only set, at least.

The glasses — slim metal frames with squarish lenses — looked like Weaver's…as best he could remember. There was no reason to assign any particular importance to them. Still, they were here, and Weaver wasn't.

Leaning forward, using whatever prop was handy, he stretched out and snatched up the glasses. The retreat wasn't as graceful — one hand short — but he managed.

Copper frame. That matched his mental picture. Hers were understated. Nothing flashy. He unfolded the arms and peered through the lenses.

"Yack!" he squealed, flinging them across the room.

They clattered to the floor but didn't break. He stared at them like they were a venomous snake. But…they were evidence.

Grimacing, he leaned again, awkwardly scooped them up, and slipped them on.

The world flattened — like a drawing packed with detail but missing depth. He could see shadows, but everything was two-dimensional. Veritas watched his hand close into a fist and open again in fascinated disbelief. It was like living inside a comic book. He glanced up, half expecting a thought bubble to form over his head.

None appeared.

Why would anyone wear these? Even the fog looked flat. It was trippy as heck and...

Wait. Fog?

He removed the glasses. The fog remained — bleeding from a small ring suspended in midair.

The haze spilled to the floor and inched toward him. He took a step back.

Time to go.

Veritas didn't waste another second. He scuttled out of the building, circled the back, darted through the woods, and made a beeline for Punk Bunks like his butt was on fire.

He had some urgent typing to do.

Kenny: August 31st at Sullen Creek Farm

"Agreed," Raleigh said, setting the contract down. "Pen?"

I shook my head with a small, bittersweet smile.

Of all the Haighs — and they were legion — Raleigh was the one I distrusted the least. I believed she intended to honor the agreement. But she wasn't the matriarch or the patriarch. Later, someone could argue she lacked the authority to sign anything.

"I'm sorry, Raleigh. That's not good enough."

Monroe scoffed but stayed quiet. She'd been oddly subdued since signing the NDA. I didn't expect it to last, but I was enjoying the reprieve.

"Ottilie signs, or I don't."

"Utterly useless! By the time Mom could get here, Dad will either be dead or a mindless drone," Monroe snapped.

Her bloodshot eyes were fixed on Gidget. The machine was eye-catching. Twenty slender copper arms whirred, tapping the ley reservoir and manufacturing precast spells. The basalt vessel was topped off by the adult Saturniidae members once a week in a rotation. The limitation helped prevent burnout and, as a bonus, the mix of ley energies muddied the magical signature. Warlocks could trace precast magic, but not as easily.

Once the legal team had done their thing and the ink on the new contract had dried, I'd brought the two Haigh sisters to my private spelling room. It was the most secure space on the property — and housed the only fixed portal to the Mulberry.

If Ottilie Haigh signed, we'd be using it.

I doubted Monroe saw Gidget. She just needed somewhere neutral to focus.

"And what do you suggest instead?" Raleigh demanded. "Raid the Agora ourselves? Our allies refused to help. Mom tried before she contacted us — they all said it was suicide. Why else would we offer our clan as an esne to the Covenant?"

She turned to me, eyes dark with apology. "Would you be willing to expedite our travel?"

A glance at Monroe suggested she hadn't noticed the question or grasped its implications.

"Of course. Nore, if you would," I nodded to my bestie, who sat on the steps leading up to my sleeping loft.

Nore's enormous eyes smoldered like coals as she regarded the Haighs, arms folded under her ample chest. Then she started singing — "Born Under a Bad Sign." Swaying to a beat only she heard, she turned her face upward and put grit into her usually velvet voice. The ley lines quivered in response.

The relationship between a practitioner and the lines was unique. For me, the lines were a loom — I wove intent into being. It was controlled, deliberate. Nore's bond was different. For her, the lines were an instrument, as responsive as her voice. She connected through rhythm and emotion — coaxing where I commanded. Her process was fluid and intuitive, but the results were just as potent.

A soulful strum filled the room — guitar-like, but not quite. The sound startled both Haighs. Monroe traced it to a spark near the window, pulsing with the music. As the shape grew clearer, she rounded on me.

"You've had a hedge witch this whole time!"

She made it sound like a personal betrayal.

"She's been a hedge witch all this time," Nore sang, without missing a beat.

Monroe swung between us, mouth working like an indignant, confused fish.

"What, Monroe," I asked, laughing. "Did you think you were omniscient? That no truth could remain hidden from you? Why is this such a shock?"

She found her words.

"You've been gifted this incredible power! It could save us all... Why—" her voice dropped, barely audible, full of loathing. "Why haven't you used it? Are you such a coward?"

"Oh, for crying out loud! She has used it," Raleigh snapped, shocking her sister and earning a delighted cackle from me. "The Covenant has saved tens of thousands. They just don't advertise it to you."

Nore's song faded, and she rose to her full height, towering over the petite Haighs. She paused, ensuring their full attention.

"Go, while there's still a chance to save your father," she said, voice low and serene. "And if you can't refrain from parading your ignorance, don't bother coming back."

Raleigh shoved her sister through the gate before she could offer another insult.

"Thank you both. Clan Haigh is grateful," she said quickly, stepping through the thin film separating our two realities.

"Peace, at last! Now, let's plan a prison break," I chirped, clapping my hands.

Nore shook her head and trudged after me.

Rumor was the wicked queen trope was based on Ottilie Haigh. It might even be true. She was three centuries old, ridiculously beautiful, vain, cold-blooded, and a skilled practitioner.

That's where the similarities ended.

Ottilie didn't bathe in virgin blood — she preferred essential oils. She was devoted to her husband, fiercely loved her daughters, and made a point to get along with her many stepdaughters. She would — and had — committed atrocities to keep her family whole.

Which was why, when Raleigh and Monroe returned, she came with them.

Like her daughters, she wore her dark hair long. Unlike them, she let it trail in loose waves. They favored linen pants and sleeveless silk blouses. Ottilie wore a vintage summer dress, pearls, and a smile. Hope, humility, and gratitude curved her lips.

I had to fight not to gag. I'd seen her gut a man while wearing that same expression.

"I'm not taking the very pregnant matriarch of Clan Haigh into the Agora," I told her. "We can't guarantee your safety, and I refuse to give the covens a reason to accuse the Covenant of conspiring against you."

That, and I didn't trust her.

"Then take one of my daughters," she offered in a rich 'see, I'm reasonable' tone.

"No."

She sighed, eyes closed, like she was mustering the patience to deal with a willful child. "Clan Haigh mus—"

"No. Sign or don't, but stop wasting my time."

The smile vanished. Cold, reptilian eyes met mine.

"If my husband dies, I will hold you personally responsible. Once the contract is fulfilled, I will dedicate my life to erasing any trace of your existence."

It wasn't a threat or a warning. It was a desperate woman's vow. Whatever Callum's faults, he loved her, and she loved him. I envied that. I'd never been in love and probably never would be. Even if I did, I couldn't surrender to it. I had other obligations.

With that thought, envy turned to fury. I had no doubt Callum had meant to do good. I refused to let another family be torn apart just because the Community considered us abominations to be controlled or culled.

Comforting her would've been pointless. She would've met it with suspicion and spite, so I didn't bother.

"Then hurry," I said, "so the warlocks don't execute him before I have an opportunity to save him."

She considered me a moment longer, then signed. She pushed the contract across the table. I signed and passed it to Lizzy. Without a word, she began a litany of tests, confirming the magic worked as intended. Once satisfied, she notarized it.

At her nod, I turned to the Haighs. "This is the Mulberry — our nerve center. We use an MMORPG to observe operatives, assign missions, and store intel. You'll be able to monitor the quest progression from this room. Please don't leave before the mission ends. Nore is available if you need anything. You'll be under surveillance. In-game, your father will appear as NPC Auley Drever. My avatar is Weaver. Once he's tagged," I held up a clear sticker, "you'll see his vitals and location."

Eight sets of haughty Haigh eyes studied me — and each other. We'd corralled the younger sisters earlier and filled them in. Saying they hadn't taken the news well would be a gross understatement.

"Once your father is in our custody, he'll be seen by our med mage, debriefed, and released into your care. We're deploying shortly. Please make yourselves comfortable."

I exited and walked down the hall. Lon and Arlo moved to flank me.

"Is this wise?" Arlo asked.

"Nothing we do is wise. It is necessary."

"You'll be walking into a trap," Lon added, eyes sparkling — not to dissuade me, just acknowledging the fun ahead.

"Yup."

"You know that contract's worthless," Arlo added. "The Covenant doesn't hold vassals. What's our motivation here? They wouldn't lift a finger if our roles were reversed."

"Is that how we do things? Only help those who help us?" I turned into a narrow, arched corridor alive with clockwork clicks, pumping pistons, and the hiss of steam valves. Five steps later, we were back in my room. "We'll have a lot more free time if that's the case. I thought we were trying to change the status quo — not reinforce it."

"Clan Haigh will offer polite noises that sound like gratitude and be twice as quick to use us later," Arlo argued. "They might prioritize our projects, if it's convenient, but there's no real benefit for us here."

Halfway down the steps to the kitchen, I turned to face them.

"Does Callum Haigh deserve to live as a helot?"

"Callum Haigh is an egotistical bastard who wants to use us."

Fair enough.

"Is he an egotistical bastard who deserves to live as a helot? Do his wife and daughters deserve to lose him? Should the Community imprison practitioners for existing?"

"No."

I continued down the stairs and through the kitchen.

"We don't shop among the Community's victims, weighing perks. We save who we can. We know the Haighs — and we know their faults. If they were strangers, we wouldn't be having this conversation; you'd be all in. I need you to back me on this. Can you look past the who and focus on the what?"

"Fine, but I still don't like them," Arlo grumbled, taking the lead so he could open the back door. "Yes. What do you need?"

"Verify the teams are ready. Monitor the game. Make sure no one traces this back to us. We leave in ten. Lon, you have to compete in the chess-boxing tourney as planned. If you forfeit and vanish, people will notice. Deathblade and Fife's teams are briefed, but we'll need three more on standby in case things go sideways."

Arlo, calling our people, saluted and used his absurdly long legs to eat the distance to Punk Bunks. Lon and I headed for the marquee where the hopefuls were duking it out.

"Done and done. Tellus wants her team on standby — her dad's going into that pit. Novak's team came off rotation three nights ago, and they're restless. Flint's isn't due for another week. Anything else?"

"I'm going to show Callum Haigh what his bribes have funded."

Lon paused, pulling back the tent flap and searching my face.

"You think he'll agree to an alliance?"

"No, but it's only fair to give him the chance."

He nodded, and we stepped inside. The noise hit me like a fist. The audience wasn't huge — but they were bloodthirsty.

"Would make one hell of an announcement at the anniversary dinner," Lon mused. "But it's not worth losing you. Be smart. Don't take risks. Come home, Kenny."

"Scout's honor," I promised, saluting with three fingers.

"And listen to Oscar," he added dryly.

"Always."

Chapter 59: Disarming

Kenny: August 31st at the Agora in Chicago, Illinois

"Visitors to the queue on the left. Next," the woman called, eyeing my sensible outfit before waving me along. Her crisp burgundy bellhop uniform looked stuffy.

I'd wear a suit to the Community's seat when they recognized my right to live free. Until then: broken-in jeans, ribbed tank, lightweight kimono, and boots.

"Representative Jones of the Sheta Djew. Here on business," I said, smiling as I held up my ID. My fangs may or may not have snicked out.

She scanned the badge with a slender brass cylinder. It chirped, flashing amber.

"So you are. The Quorum's not in session. Purpose?"

"I'm visiting the APA."

Her eyes rounded.

"Have fun with that," she muttered, feeding two slips through a brass slot. "Sticker goes on your ID. Give the other to the gate attendant on your way out. Have a good day, Representative Jones. Next!"

"Thanks. You too," I said, peeling the sticker and tossing the backing into a brass bin.

I moved away from the Peregrine Gate, focused on placing the sticker without covering my face.

"Kenny!"

I looked up at a sea of suits, haloed by the sunlight pouring through the glass roof. It dazzled my eyes — I momentarily thought I'd forgotten my glasses.

"Kenny," the voice repeated — clear over the din. A tall man cut through the crush and seized my hand, pulling me into an alcove of tropical plants.

"This is unexpected. What brings you to Chicago? I don't suppose it's me," Senator Balbay said with a crooked smile. The self-deprecating twist of his mouth was at such odds with his somber appearance that I automatically returned the smile.

His flirtatious manner, however, threw me. We weren't friends — barely acquaintances. The last time I'd seen him…right. I'd been his date at the TC Gala. Well, my proxy had — I wasn't a fan of formal dinners, but the unexpected invitation had made me curious.

She'd made more of an impression than I'd realized.

"Nothing so pleasant. A wild construct — siren — showed up near my property. It attacked a guest and nearly drowned him. I want some assurance that the APA is taking this seriously. Up until this year, we hadn't seen one. Now we've had sixteen. I know this isn't a localized issue."

"Ah," Balbay murmured, brow furrowing. "That may present some difficulties — there were two incursions into the Agora this week. It's been all hands on deck. I believe the Director is handling it personally."

My jaw dropped. "What were they after? If they came back, they must've failed the first time."

He shrugged. "If the Agency knows, they're not saying. No one's told me."

The tide of foot traffic swelled around us, nudging us backward. His hand landed on my upper arm, shielding me from a woman's emphatic gesturing. It was…considerate. I waited for the nausea from being touched to hit, but it never came.

"Will you be in town for a few days? You might have better luck tomorrow or the next day. And perhaps I could claim the pleasure of your company for dinner?"

Rufe Balbay wasn't exactly suave, but a foreign thrill rippled through me. His expression — open, wistful, almost…vulnerable — caught me off guard.

I liked him.

It had happened only twice before, this bone-deep conviction of compatibility. The first time, I'd been right, though it still hadn't worked out. The second…was absurd. Both experiences had unsettled me. They didn't align with what I believed about myself.

Balbay was handsome, no question. But formal. Tidy. Not my type.

I'd never been good at forming relationships of any kind without a social framework — leader, mentor, landlord, colleague.

Still…he was asking for an evening, not a lifelong bond.

"I'm afraid not," I said, nearly mumbling. "I only have a few hours. I'm heading to New Orleans this evening for a family thing — anniversary dinner."

"My loss." He smiled, a little sad.

"Perhaps..."

My phone rang, making me jump. I declined the call and shot off a one-word text before pocketing it.

"Yes?"

This was madness.

But I liked him. He was a Correctionist. Kind. Probably liked reading. Didn't matter what — fiction, manuals, cookbooks. A man who reads...yum. Balbay was passionate and dedicated. Compelling.

"If I do end up having to wait...or if no one finds time for me, since I'm already here...would you have time for a drink in Holy Water, maybe?"

It might've been my imagination — or ego — but something euphoric lit his face. He suddenly looked taller. His eyes twinkled.

What would he look like if he laughed — a real, deep belly laugh?

"I'd like that," he rumbled, his voice deepening. "Let's go check if there's an opening."

I nodded and quickly learned to appreciate the perks of navigating a crowd with an imposing companion. With his warm, dry hand wrapped around mine, he guided me through the crush to the bank of elevators along the far wall.

While we waited in line, he studied my face with something like wonder, thumb brushing my knuckles. My cheeks burned. Eye contact became impossible.

I felt hot and cold at once — flustered. I couldn't decide if his hand in mine was comforting or...strange. Things like this didn't happen to me. I'd been told it was because I didn't 'put myself out there,' whatever that meant.

"No one move," a harsh voice shouted — and a warning shot shattered a large pot. The tree inside slumped sideways.

This kind of thing was more familiar.

More shots. The beautiful glass ceiling exploded overhead, showering shards on the lobby. Chaos erupted. Screams. Scrambling. People dove for cover or collapsed outright.

Eight masked men, loaded for bear and wearing bandoliers of precast spells, blocked the exits.

Between one breath and the next, I primed a circuit and stepped forward, catching motion at the edge of my vision.

Something heavy slammed into my temple.

Somewhere distant, as if underwater, I heard a voice say, "Now, don't try anything heroic."

"Umph," I whimpered. Something was wrong. The right side of my face throbbed. I was hot and limp as a waterlogged noodle.

"Shut her up or I will."

"She needs medical attention. Your...colleague...assaulted her. She could have bleeding in her brain. Without proper treatment, she could die."

"Shut her up or she will die," the first voice replied, slow and sarcastic.

The second voice was familiar, though I'd never heard it so vicious. My brain revolted, trying to place it. A strange feeling dragged at me, threatening darkness. Acting on instinct, I scrambled from the arms holding me and dropped to my hands and knees.

I dry-heaved — couldn't breathe.

A warm hand smoothed up and down my back.

"Breathe, Kenny. With me — in...and out. In...and out."

By the third repetition, my lungs obeyed. I collapsed onto the cold floor — it was glorious. The chill grounded me.

The voice continued to murmur comfortingly, calm and steady, as I panted.

"I told you to shut-the-bitch-up!"

A whoosh and a grunt.

The warm hand was gone. Fingers knotted in my hair and yanked me upright.

I screamed.

"You're going to be quiet one way or another," the man growled.

I opened my eyes — and stared down the barrel of a Sig Sauer P320. Cracked lenses blurred everything but the blue-gray eyes behind the gun. He was enjoying this.

Fury tore through me.

I drove my shoulder into his gut and wrapped an arm around his legs, dragging him down while shoving the gun hand up. It discharged twice. Screams erupted — but my ears rang too loudly to care.

I threw my weight onto his wrist.

Balbay was suddenly beside me, hammering his fists into the guy's face.

I winced as the gunman's skull thunked against the floor — felt it in my bones — but clung to his arm. He let go of the gun to protect his head.

I grabbed it and rose to my knees. Aimed. Bile burned my throat as I pulled at Balbay's arm — and fired twice.

The silence that followed made the ringing in my ears worse.

Balbay mouthed something. When I didn't respond, he yanked me down.

More shots. The door burst open. A masked man entered.

I fired. And kept firing.

The intruder's head snapped back. He stumbled, hit the door, and slid to the ground. Blood pooled out in a silent, elegant curve, stretching across the stone floor.

I was mesmerized by its slow progress.

Rufe's hands shifted on my hips.

Focus. We had things to do.

"Where are we?" I mumbled. There was bruising around his eye and mouth, and I stupidly asked, "What happened to your face?"

"I tried to be a hero. Hearing better," he asked. "We're in the conference rooms near the library. Can you stand?"

"Yes."

It wasn't pretty, but I managed to get upright. Rufe steadied me. When I didn't immediately collapse, he turned to check the second body.

"Dead. T-box. Your aim's fine," he said, dragging the corpse out of the doorway and stripping it of weapons and spells.

"They'll be guarding the elevators and stairs," I muttered, shaking my head — bad idea. Nausea rolled over me. I froze, breathing slow and deep. "I can't think. They'll have heard the shots. How do we get everyone out?"

"This high up? We don't. We barricade."

He scanned the room.

"Okay," he muttered, grabbing a chair and wedging it under the knob. He barked orders. "You four — push the table against the chair. Everyone else, stack chairs on top of it, then move to the left side and stay low. Any cords?"

I helped, trying to ignore the guilt that hit every time I met someone's eyes. They were terrified — politicians, guards, tourists clutching kids. I felt personally responsible.

Minutes later, the door was tied shut and barricaded. Rufe and I crouched in the front corner, guns trained on the door. Then we waited.

And waited.

And waited.

"As second dates go, where does this rank?"

I tried to suppress the giddy, bubbling hysteria. Tears leaked from my eyes.

"Rufe," I wheezed.

"Comments? Critiques? What worked, what could improve?"

"Please stop."

"Of course."

A few minutes passed. Gunfire. Screams. Silence.

I shivered and kept my eyes on the door.

"We've already survived a Community dinner and masked gunmen. I was thinking we could disarm a doomsday device for the third date. Thoughts?"

"I appreciate the effort, but don't peak too soon, honey. How would you ever top a doomsday device?"

The words came out rough. It didn't sound like my voice.

"Don't underestimate me," Rufe murmured in my ear. "I have a few ideas."

Twenty minutes crawled by, broken by gunfire and other unsettling noises. Our people huddled against the wall, doing their best to comfort each other.

It was hell.

Fifteen minutes passed before we heard a thump from outside. Rufe shifted in front of me, careful not to block my line of fire.

"Don't shoot," someone called from the window with the bullet hole. "Special Agent Wladyslaw. I'm coming in."

A man in black tactical gear, suspended by a cable, kicked at the glass and climbed through.

"Senator Balbay. Ma'am," he greeted, detaching the cable. It slithered back up the side of the building. "Any wounded? Dead?"

"Representative Jones has a head injury. That gentleman was grazed. The hostage-takers are dead. What's the status?" Rufe asked, still shielding me.

"Five intruders down — including yours. No captures. Seventeen injured, none life-threatening, no fatalities. We've retaken all but two conference rooms. I've got first aid. Use it. We'll be here until we get the all-clear."

He waved off further questions and reported into his headset.

Two hours later, I got my meeting with the APA — with Director Serrecold himself.

I'd been patched up, but as the fae's ice-white eyes swept over me, catching on every bruise, I still felt flayed. My nerves were raw and I itched to escape his scrutiny.

"I wanted to thank you personally, Representative Jones," he said. "Your actions saved lives — yours and others." He chuckled, eerie and whispery, yet unexpectedly hearty. "I've never heard Balbay speak so effusively."

"Senator Balbay's the hero. I don't know what he did — I was unconscious — but he stopped them from killing me, organized the barricade, reminded me how to breathe...and kept putting himself between me and danger."

I scrubbed my face, trying to shake my unease.

The Director smiled, revealing the whitest, sharpest teeth I'd ever seen. "There's no doubt you both showed remarkable courage. Now, as I understand it, you came to follow up on a wild construct report?"

I shifted in my seat. It wasn't an interrogation room, but it felt like one. The spartan office offered no comfort. Even seated, relaxed, legs crossed, Director Gilles-Eugene Serrecold cast a shadow — as if he were a great, white-blond mountain: beautiful and treacherous.

With everything that had happened, why was he even here? I didn't rank high enough in the Quorum to warrant his attention.

I took a deep breath and fought for a reasonable level of control. My hands shook, and focus was a beautiful myth. Everything was fuzzy, my head ached, and throwing up sounded wildly indulgent.

"It hardly seems important now. But, yes — a siren attacked one of my guests. Lured him into the river. My staff and several others saved him. I reported it — just like the fifteen other sightings this year. If anything's been done, no one told me. I've lived on that land for over a decade without seeing a single wild construct. Now it's sixteen. Maybe it's minor, comparatively—"

"No, Representative Jones. Your concerns are valid." He leaned forward slightly, voice deepening. "Sightings and attacks are rising exponentially. It's a real, growing problem. Unfortunately, you're one of the lucky ones. You've seen fewer than most, and you're better equipped to respond."

He sighed — a soft, human sound that felt wrong coming from him.

"It's the same old story. Warlocks are the only agents trained for this, and there are too few of them. Even post-Cleansing, there are too few. Their life expectancy is poor, and the dangers rarely justify the rewards."

He shook his head. "Of those who do qualify...only a fraction should ever be trusted with knowledge of ley manipulations."

The old boy, despite feigning solemnity, was practically giddy. Fae didn't adjust themselves for comfort or politics — they just leaned into their weirdness.

Serrecold chuckled. It wasn't a soothing sound. I didn't want to know what amused him.

"We've started an initiative — training agents who meet strict prerequisites in the untwisting of rogue magics. Demi-warlocks, I suppose. Even if successful, the problem will worsen before it improves. It'll be years before we see meaningful change."

His mouth was too pink — almost red. That's what made him look so creepy. All that pale-on-pale skin, and then a mouth like a bloody blossom — more vampiric than most vampires. Like he'd just had a liquid lunch.

"My best advice, and I don't mean to sound cavalier, is to treat this as an opportunity." His mouth twisted in apology, but his eyes were cold stone. "Keep doing what you're doing — but do it with greater intent. Educate your people. Teach them the forms, the tactics, the weaknesses. Run drills. Become experts. Encourage your neighbors and allies to do the same."

I shivered, wondering what hid behind those glacial eyes.

"We'll do that, then."

He stood, smiling faintly. "We could use a few more like you, Jones. Hours after tackling an armed man, and you're already focused on the next problem. If you ever tire of politics, come see me."

"Thank you, sir," I said, then hesitated. "What were the shooters after? Artifacts? A grimoire?"

"Ah...painting us as fools, more like."

"Sir?"

"Confidential, I'm afraid. Suffice it to say — they were successful. My only consolation is that it cost them eleven lives."

Kenny: August 31ˢᵗ at Sullen Creek Farm

"Well, that wasn't so bad, was it?" Nore said, humming as she passed out water bottles and trail mix.

The Haighs gawked at her.

"I need my backup glasses," I grunted as Oscar checked my head. No repairing my main pair — ley energy had its limits. Or more accurately, our knowledge of it had limits.

"They're missing again, not on your workbench. Colt's checking your usual hiding spots — window seats, the fridge, feeding bags, your laundry hamper," he said dryly. "Did Mercutio have to wallop you so hard?"

"It had to look real."

"Mission accomplished. It was real enough to fracture your skull. The Agency medics jump-started your healing, but there's more to do. Without anesthetics."

"I don't get why you had to be there at all," Ottilie said, not sure whether to be aloof, contemptuous, or grateful. She landed on cool but curious.

"The Agora has eighty-six stories," Nore said. "Even assuming Callum was in the building, finding him would've taken too long — we'd be caught. We needed intel, fast. Senator Balbay, formerly Special Agent Balbay — is head of Internal Investigations. The foundation for his career is his service record and efforts in getting the Genocide Laws rescinded. He's cozy with the APA, championed Serrecold's appointment after Lester retired, and he's a Correctionist — a solid source for information."

She sipped her water and dug through her trail mix, not mentioning that our usual source still hadn't made contact.

"He keeps office hours eight to ten. We timed Kenny's arrival to intercept him. She was ready to enthrall him, if needed. Since Serrecold handled the interrogation himself, we knew what room Callum would be in. His methods…require certain preparations."

Callum, looking feverish, snorted.

"The Genocide Laws weren't rescinded. Just amended," Coen said. Cully nodded, backing her up.

"True," Briony replied, "but Balbay fought to end them entirely. That was seventeen years ago. You two were toddlers."

"So playing kissy-face with the Correctionist golden boy was part of the plan," Monroe said. "Was personally shooting two of your own men — sacrificing Mercutio and the others — part of the ruse?"

Shockingly, her voice was almost neutral. In fairness, she was distracted by her father's condition. The APA hadn't been kind.

"Yes — an expensive one. And they're not dead," I said, eyes closed, fighting instinct. Oscar growled a warning as I flinched under his hands. Bone knitting hurts both healer and patient. "To be dead, they'd have to be alive. Mercutio and his crew were simulacra — flesh golems. Anatomically human, but still only an imitation. It'll take six months to replace those we couldn't recover."

"Thank you," Callum Haigh rasped, voice hoarse, eyes intense.

It was the first thing he'd said to me since Dave Coinin's team fished him out of Serrecold's tank. Torture was illegal in the Community, but not magical persuasion. And sometimes that was worse.

Serrecold's method was unique — hydro-optical perception, a hereditary talent that let him read memories through water. No physical harm, so it was legal with a warrant.

I'd counted on Callum shielding against psychic intrusion. He hadn't failed me. Serrecold learned only that he was hunting an ancient artifact: the Clamare Vero — aka Veritas Clamat — and roughly translating to "truth cries out".

The mirror revealed truth in its own warped way.

Serrecold hadn't learned who Callum was, how he got in, why he wanted the artifact, or anything about his family, the Sheta Djew, the Covenant, or me. That was a win.

"You might want to see what your wife signed to get us to go after you," I said, pushing the notarized contract across the table. I expected to feel smug satisfaction. Instead, I just felt tired. He looked terrible — even after Oscar's help.

"Must we do this now?" Ottilie snapped.

"Yes," Callum and I chorused.

I studied him. He held my gaze — dignified, resigned. Pity melted into respect. His shaved head was ringed with dark stubble, his tan skin pale, eyes haunted. He twitched at stray noises — and hated it. He was broken but not beaten, still in control.

Serrecold's toxins had been purged, Oscar had healed him, and he'd showered and dressed. He'd refused food until he saw his family. After hugs and tears, he'd devoured broth, mac and cheese, and was now attacking a pudding cup with gusto.

The lines surrounding him were scrambled and frayed, explaining his diminished appearance. It wasn't down to Serrecold's efforts. Callum had done it to himself.

Practitioners faced three known ailments. Ley burn occurred when energy was forcibly ripped from a reservoir, with consequences ranging from mild irritation to death. Burnout was damage caused by overuse — common and painful, but usually manageable. Ley febrility was a craving that mutated into dependency. Lines deteriorated, behavior destabilized, and death followed — either by the shock of abstinence or unraveling reality until killed. It was usually terminal.

Callum set down the pudding and read the contract.

"You should have let me rot."

His wife and daughters protested, but he looked only at me.

"Thank you."

How long had he been edging toward febrility? A man who'd kept his family safe for centuries didn't act rashly. Charging through an unstable portal into the Agora wasn't like him.

"You're welcome. The Covenant holds no vassals, esnes, or helots. You owe us nothing. A door will be constructed so you and your family can return home."

The contract began to smoke and curl into ash.

"What was the point of that, then?" Ottilie hissed.

Callum met my eyes and murmured in bitter sing-song, "The race has begun; the door yawns wide. One must live and one must die; The mirror of truth can show you why."

"Some time ago, I consulted an augur," he said.

He was farther gone than I'd realized.

There were seers, and then there were augurs. The latter rarely had true psychic gifts. They mined for answers using tools and rituals. Even when they hit something real, there was no telling who it was meant for…or what it meant. The field was thick with con artists and the deluded.

Callum chuckled at my expression.

"Chimere Mahagna."

I grimaced. Chimere Mahagna was the exception.

"Frustrated by my research, I sought help unlocking portal magic. I could hold a rift for seconds — no longer. Chimere gave me only the rhyme. She begged me to stop — said the obsession was destroying me. I refused."

"Why would she say that?" Ottilie asked sharply.

They didn't know.

Monroe bolted from her chair, pacing in sharp strides. Raleigh stared at her hands. Some of them hadn't known.

"I believed 'the door' referred to hedgecraft. And the 'mirror of truth'? The Clamare Vero. I happened to know where it was. By mid-morning, I'd convinced myself to try for it. Best time to break in, I thought. The prophecy said it was a race. I acted impetuously and nearly banished myself. The Covenant paid for my arrogance. I am in your debt."

"There is no debt," Lon said, avoiding eye contact. He'd noticed Callum's condition — and was trying not to pity him. "This is what we do."

Callum nodded — not in agreement, but acceptance.

"Clan Haigh would be honored to pursue an alliance with the Covenant."

Since Colt hadn't found my backup glasses and I'd neglected to restock my null contacts, I got to enjoy the anniversary dinner through a haze of psychedelic horror.

A giant, carnivorous hummingbird — also gifted with true sight — was trying to eat Avery Johnson's kidneys. Gorgeous plumage.

It was hard to focus on the Doyen's speech, recounting our proud history, while a shimmering bird on another plane kept lunging for his organs.

"…against the warlock Deidamia and slew her, saving their clans and the village of Cardine, at great personal cost…"

I bit my lip, trembling with suppressed laughter, as Davy elbowed me.

"...mortally hexed, they did not give in to sorrow or pain..."

Thrust, thrust, thrust.

Colt glanced at me, confused. I tapped my eye. Cautiously, he dug out his glasses and slipped them on.

An iridescent forked tongue pierced the Doyen's chest, trying to shred his pink flesh.

Colt's face was priceless.

"...honor our heritage and renew our vow to that cause, though death may take us ere the battle is won. Together, we stand strong! Together, we shall prevail!"

Avery Johnson was a powerful orator, and he must've delivered — judging by the applause. It was loud enough to mask my cackles from everyone except those at my table.

"What was it?" Lou whisper-shouted.

"A giant hummingbird trying to eat the Doyen's kidneys."

Lou's smile vanished. The others looked grim. I blinked. They usually enjoyed beyond-the-veil oddities.

"Hazel," came a calm, firm voice.

Oh.

Only two people used that name.

"Doyenne," I replied, twirling in my seat and serving up a big smile.

Enid Carter made me feel short even when I was standing. Sitting while she loomed over me in three-inch heels felt like crouching under a Loblolly pine.

Nore and Davy were taller, but Carter had more impact. Ageless and commanding, she wore a steel-blue pantsuit with matching heels, curls bouncing in a Rezo cut. Graceful. Imposing. Impeccable.

"Walk with us," she murmured, already moving.

Another woman — her equal in height, with wine-red hair in a severe French braid, flawless pale skin, and ice-blue eyes — waited for me.

"Xandre," I greeted.

"Hazel."

She motioned for me to lead. It felt like an execution.

At the back wall of the dining room, Carter tapped the paneling. A hidden door opened, leading us into a dim corner of Port of Call's public dining room. Once the door slid shut, Xandre wove a sound barrier while Carter studied me.

"The Agora was breached today. Seventy-two hostages. It was held for three hours. There were fourteen assailants. We don't know by whom or why. In a few minutes, I have to deliver a report on our current status. I don't want to be ambushed. Was it you?"

"No."

Xandre twitched at my answer. Carter exhaled slowly, tension leaving her shoulders.

"I was one of the hostages."

"Hazel," the Doyenne chided, somehow growing taller. "You've served admirably for a decade. The Saturniidae love you, and the Sheta Djew have flourished. I will take that into consideration. Explain why you launched an unsanctioned mission that left eleven dead."

"Because rules don't apply to her," Xandre said flatly. "Discipline's just an occasional hobby."

"Because she brokered an alliance with Clan Haigh — and when my life was in danger, she and her people upheld it," barked Callum Haigh from behind them, hand-in-hand with Ottilie, radiant in a 1940s green evening gown.

No one bothered asking how they'd breached the sound barrier.

"Hazel," Xandre said slowly, pointing to me, "brokered an alliance with Clan Haigh?"

Callum gave her an unimpressed once-over.

"Yes. And rescued me from Serrecold's dunk tank. Should I assume my new allies would've preferred that she left me there?"

"Hazel should have reported the alliance. She should have reported your capture. A quiet extraction could have been organized. One that wouldn't implicate the Sheta Djew," Xandre countered.

"If she had, I'd be a widow," Ottilie snapped.

Xandre had no response to that.

"No one died, Doyenne," I said. "But we lost eleven simulacra. Two bystanders and some of the Saturniidae sustained minor injuries."

I gave thanks again that none of the Agora's guards or APA agents fired on civilians. We'd gotten lucky. But Ottilie was right — if I'd waited for permission, Callum would've been too far gone.

Carter's smile returned — broad, gleaming, and hard to read. It always looked a bit carnivorous.

"Be welcome, Clan Haigh. We're honored by your presence. It seems I lacked the full picture. Thank you for your testimony. Hazel is one of our most capable operatives. Losing trust in her judgment would be...unfortunate. Another time, Hazel, I want a full report. For now — it's time to celebrate."

She tapped the paneled wall, reopening the hidden door.

"Would Clan Haigh approve of announcing this alliance tonight?"

"I believe that was the point of Representative Jones's kind invitation," Callum said smoothly.

"Excellent. Come, Xandre."

The redhead said nothing. But her frosty glare landed on me as she flicked something in my direction. I dodged, and a black zip drive skittered across the floor. Callum picked it up and handed it over with a questioning look. I shrugged and pocketed it.

Xandre didn't usually stoop to petty revenge. She aimed for the jugular. Next time I went off-script, she'd report it — with just the right tone of gleeful disappointment.

Chapter 61: In a Tizzy

August 31st in Parkville, Missouri

Night had fallen gently. After a day of trying to be everywhere at once — followed by reviewing hours of Agora footage from every possible angle — O'Brien wanted nothing more than to sleep. Unfortunately, that wasn't in the cards. An old acquaintance required his attention.

"Was it a coincidence your intriguing quarry showed up today, or is there more to her than meets the eye?"

The bloodless face of the APA Director bobbed unbecomingly in the Seer's orb O'Brien had placed on a folding tray.

"There's definitely more to her," O'Brien said. "But, to your question: I'm not sure. The Union isn't hunting her. I'm no Hound, and she'd be very uncooperative prey. She's a wild card. What she chooses in the next few days will shape much of the future."

The lamplight obscured the nuances of Serrecold's eye roll, but O'Brien got the gist.

"You've monopolized my best warlock and his team for months — while the Community's in need. She'd better be worth it," the Director rumbled. "What is it about her that has everyone in such a tizzy, anyway?"

"What do you mean? Who's in a tizzy?" O'Brien yawned, tidying up the hotel room — hoping someone might take the hint.

"You, for one. Even Ghost—"

"Ghost? Did he say something?"

"Cool your jets, Lestrade. He hasn't slipped me any secret overlays — though I am his employer; something you both seem happy to forget. But, since you asked: no. Neither in passing nor in reports. He suspects her, but doesn't want her to be guilty. Usually means an agent's gotten personally invested with the...wild card."

O'Brien rocked back on his heels, mulling it over.

"I'm not accusing him of any impropriety, but it's more than due diligence. He's read her college essays and pored over her high school transcript. She was homeschooled, so he's relying on standardized tests to build a picture. He's obsessed. It happens. But in the end, Ghost will do what must be done. It's a good reminder — we're all human."

O'Brien poured himself a whiskey and dropped into a chair a few feet from the orb.

"Hypothetically, if there is a crime involved, how do you know he doesn't want her to be guilty? Maybe he likes her for the job but can't make it stick."

"You sound...concerned. Like you had a plan, and it's not going your way." The Director's voice softened, distant. "Is that it?"

When O'Brien didn't answer, Serrecold chuckled.

"Ah! You can't explain, or we'll all meet with calamity and perish in some horrible way." He blew a raspberry. "Seers! Still, now I'm intrigued. You're all dancing around her like twitterpated peacocks, and I want to know why she's so bloody important. You're always in the middle of these webs, so—"

"Who else?"

O'Brien studied the russet spirit in his glass, eyes downcast, as if the question were trivial. Serrecold, the conniving bastard, wasn't fooled. He chuckled again — darkly.

"The TC requested access to her file. Someone on their team's got it nearly as bad as Ghost — though they were content with her college transcript, travel history, and social media history from the last twenty years."

"Oh? Is that all? You had me thinki—"

"Then there's Balbay. I've known the man thirty years — not as long as I've known you, of course — but it's long enough to learn what a man isn't, if not always what he is."

"And what isn't he?"

Serrecold smirked, enjoying the disdain in O'Brien's voice.

"I know you're not a fan, but Balbay's one of the good ones. Logical, patient, methodical — not at all fanciful. And yet, now he fancies himself in love with your wild card. He claims otherwise, but it's plain to see. The way he watches her...talks about her... Completely fascinated. Used to go for untouchable ice queens, but..."

"Oh no, please — do go on. I'd love to hear more about what Balbay fancies."

Serrecold's strange, cold eyes lit with amusement.

"You're jealous."

O'Brien laughed. "Don't be absurd. Rena is the reason I breathe. Representative Jones is lovely, but not a temptation."

The Director's grin didn't fade; if anything, a calculating glint entered his eye.

"Don't try to steer me, Darragh. There's more than one kind of jealousy. Jones is attractive, certainly, but that alone wouldn't entice the men we're talking about. A Farsight Seer, a warlock, a marshal, and a Senator who heads II? That's quite the resume. One or two, maybe — but not all four. She's intelligent…struck me as wary."

"Same thing, when it comes to you."

"You flatter me. Financially, her cadre is impressive, but within the Quorum's structure, she's small potatoes. Not influential. As an ID, though — there's an allure. And she handles a pistol like a veteran, doesn't shy away from violence. She put seven bullets in two bodies — each a kill shot — while suffering a cracked skull. And then there's the Angel of Mercy bit. She takes the hard jobs. Determined, well-trained, a risk-taker. Actually…that does sound fun. Maybe I should throw my hat in the ring."

"I wouldn't think you'd be compatible."

Serrecold beamed. "That's part of the fun. Not all of us are romantics waiting to be tamed."

"Then there's the age gap."

Serrecold's roar of laughter broke like thunder — sudden and overwhelming.

"If we're talking women of an appropriate age, there are, what, seven, maybe eight women in the country within seventy-five years of us? Beguiling creatures, too. Thyrsa de Alne's survived fourteen husbands. Lucy Flaxton will be released from prison in the next decade. Melisande Waites is crackers. Mathilda Grace and I had a thing back in the 1870s. She tried to kill me three times — and nearly succeeded. Exciting, but a man can't always be on his guard. Women our age, with the possible exception of the exquisite Ms. Amano, are too dangerous to dally with. They're the ultimate survivors."

"If you're concerned for your longevity, then as a friend, I'd warn against disporting yourself with Representative Jones."

Some of the glee drained from Serrecold's face, replaced by comprehension. He studied O'Brien's earnest expression and sighed.

"I suspect this current intrigue traces back to one of your blasted journals — visions from the baker's boy. Very well, oh great Seer; I have enough respect for your gift and just barely enough humility to take your warning to heart. I won't pursue the lady, but I won't avoid her either. Does that satisfy your compulsion?"

"It eases the burden," the Chairman murmured dryly. "Thank you."

"Do me a favor, Darragh. Whatever this is — when the lines are drawn — give me a heads-up on which will be the winning side, eh?"

"Certainly...so long as it doesn't end the world."

Chapter 62: Chasing Squirrels

Kenny: September 1st at Sullen Creek Farm

I jerked upright in bed, a claxon sounding a long note before abruptly cutting off. It didn't repeat.

Cartman, who'd been draped over my chest and throat, grumbled as he crawled out of my lap — where he'd landed when I bolted upright. Wrinkle and Tug, a pair of Cú Sidhe who'd arrived while we were in New Orleans, occupied the left side of the bed, snuffling in their sleep, with Spook, Mittens, and Steve nestled under their big, floppy ears.

So, the alarm had only been in my head.

Someone with benign intent must've crossed the boundary. The wards were more sensitive at night, especially to trespassers avoiding the driveway. If it had been malicious, the sentinels would've blocked their path — and the whole farm would've heard it. As it was, only Spook stirred, poking her nose out from under a borrowed ear, her eyes glowing green in the dark.

I held still, listening. The only sounds were the familiars dreaming and Gidget whirring below.

"The sentinels stirred," I told Spook. "Nothing to worry about. Go back to sleep, honey."

No one listened to me.

Spook climbed out, stretched, and took her spot on the nightstand. I knew she'd been spending too much time with Mel. His work ethic was rubbing off on her. He sat tall on the floor, looking like a proud papa.

The clock read 3:23.

I'd gotten home with the worst migraine I'd had in five years, taken painkillers, massaged my neck and shoulders, strapped on a sleep mask, and buried myself under a quilt. Now, only a few hours later — too soon for more meds — my headache was alive and well.

And right above my bathroom door, a mile-long line of hairy, brown-violet amoebas waited their turn to enter something that looked like a white metallic car wash.

As the next guy stepped in, I realized it wasn't built to clean anything. Gauntlets clamped its limbs while forceps grabbed what might be its head and pulled it off like a mask, revealing a carmine knob.

Reflux licked up my throat as a new, vaguely humanoid, heavily whiskered head was installed. At the next station, the body was clamped in a mold and matched to a humanoid frame. It was spray-painted greige, tucked into socks, coveralls, and boots.

I shook my head — remembering too late that it was a bad idea. The creepy assembly line hit uncomfortably close to home.

Still, leaving my soft, warm bed to investigate the alarm sounded better than staying with the amoeba-walrus men.

By the time I reached the kitchen, Lon, Oscar, Mel, and Maggie had already gathered. They stood by the sink, quietly discussing the matter, while mirror zombies loitered in the breakfast nook. Mirror zombies mimicked whoever they saw on other planes — except they looked several weeks dead. This batch was confused. There were five of us and three of them, but they had two dead Maggies.

I missed my null glasses.

I'd rush-ordered three new pairs, but who knew when they'd arrive.

"Plan," Maggie croaked, her eyes swollen from the rude awakening.

Lon turned as I approached.

"You and me?"

I boosted myself onto the worktable in the center of the room and nodded, yawning. "I suspect our new guest may appreciate discretion."

A loud clatter came from the stairs, like someone had pushed a pair of small elephants down them. Lou, Nore, and Armand spilled into the hall. The world paused as our group blinked at theirs.

Lou grinned. "Davy stayed upstairs in case the kids woke up."

Armand looked smug and said nothing.

Nore folded her arms and dared anyone to comment.

Lon's gaze ping-ponged between his best friend and baby cousin. He opened his mouth, closed it, and looked totally lost.

I empathized. She was my best friend. How had I not known? Last I'd heard, she had no patience for Armand's long-lashed nonsense. Or pretended she didn't.

Whatever.

"Lon and I are going out to find our guest," I chirped, cutting the silence.

Oscar shot me his hard stare, and everyone else looked away.

"After you find them and get them settled, you're going to lie down and rest with a mask on so your brain doesn't leak out your ears," he growled.

"Sir, yes, sir," I barked, saluting.

"If any other emergencies pop up, the others will handle them."

"What if…"

I trailed off as he loomed aggressively.

Unfair. I was taller on the table, but he still managed to be an immovable object.

"Sir, yes, sir," I muttered.

Colt stumbled into the kitchen, tripping over his bootlaces.

"What was that?"

"I'll fill him in," my défteros said. "Go."

Our property stretched across ninety acres in a long, narrow rectangle, but roughly a third — especially near the borders — was dense with trees, bracken, vines, and kudzu. It took us fifteen minutes to reach the northwest boundary where the disturbance began. A kindly tree branch pointed us back south, and Mel picked up an unfamiliar scent. He led us about five hundred feet, staying close to the boundary.

Even in the dark, the trail was obvious. Someone had trampled the grass, broken through thorny brambles, and left clear footprints.

It must've rained while I was asleep. Mud squelched beneath our boots with every step.

Look: Lon signed, pointing across the boundary.

A second set of boot prints ran parallel to the first. I had only a moment to register them before fog rolled in from the river, swallowing everything beyond ten feet.

On your guard.

Lon nodded.

We pushed on through the woods, tearing through brambles that clawed at our clothes and skin, until we broke into a clearing.

A mirror zombie crouched in the fog, curls matted to her scalp, tear tracks streaking through the grime, defiance burning in her hollowed eyes.

Lon stared — but he wasn't wearing his aggregate glasses. She was real.

Recognition slammed into me. She had changed — she was starved and dirty, but still the same girl.

"Talia Davis—"

She rose, trembling, fresh tears falling as she spat, "You can't have me!"

From the fog's cover, she lifted a knife and set the blade to her throat. The metal glinted in the moonlight. Her burning gaze met mine — and she smiled.

The entire Covenant had searched for her for six months. The trail had long gone cold. We thought she'd been caught or killed, and that if we ever found her, it'd be a body.

I was not going to lose her now.

Mel barked, buying me half a second. There wasn't time for anything clever. I dropped to my knees, pressed my hands to the earth, and shoved my energy down.

"Rise," I commanded, pleading.

I'd criticize myself later for verbalizing the command — a novice move. It wasn't necessary and only told an opponent what to expect. In this case, it told Lon, which was good, but that wasn't why I'd said it. I was begging physics and my magic to work fast enough.

Lon moved, tapping into his therianthropic speed.

The earth in front of Talia exploded as a large steel plate — part of a system that could raise a twelve-foot wall around the farm in two minutes — shot out of the ground, knocking her off balance. She flailed, trying to stay upright. Lon knocked the knife from her hand and caught her before she fell, pinning her arms.

"Talia Davis," I said quietly. "No one is going to hurt you. If anyone tries, we'll kill them."

It would upset the Covenant — but looking at her, bones jutting out and spirit all but broken, I meant every word. She didn't turn at my voice. Her eyes stared through me, empty. Her earlier defiance had been the last spark she had left. At my nod, Lon gently lowered her until she collapsed to her knees, weeping into her hands.

We're being watched. I signed. *My magic will draw notice. Take her to Wayne's. Portal back. Send Maggie and Oscar.*

Lon nodded and swept her into his arms.

"I was hunted," she whispered. "One of their freaks…"

So there was still something left inside her.

Go.

He blurred into the trees, vanishing fast as a shadow.

Alone, I pressed my hands to the ground again and shut my eyes, searching the darkness through our sentinels. Nothing within our borders. But beyond…maybe. A flicker of motion. I opened my eyes and caught the suggestion of a face — but…perhaps just leaves.

Beside me, a ley line hummed — inaudible, but vibrating against my skin. I hadn't touched it. Someone else had. Either someone had tapped a line and the vibration traveled all the way to this exact spot, or there was some subtle art at work that I didn't understand.

"I think, Mel, it's time to go back to the house."

Mel chirruped in agreement.

At Oscar's insistence, I skipped my morning chores — poor Colt picked up the slack — and my usual workout. After a bland, low-acid breakfast under Mother Hen's watchful eye, I wandered into the living room and face-planted on the sofa.

"Rough morning?" came a sardonic voice.

Aiden.

I hadn't noticed him. For a relatively large, piratical man, he had an uncanny knack for blending in. Then again, I'd been distracted by a clump of ottoman-sized, fanged toadstools lurking near the biography section. Even though they were on another plane, I gave them a wide berth. They looked slimy.

"You could say that," I mumbled into the velvet upholstery.

He didn't reply. That suited me fine. I wasn't about to volunteer anything. Arlo had already told the guests that I'd been one of the Agora hostages and that my glasses had been broken.

The silence stretched. I flipped onto my back. The darkness behind my eyelids helped with the ache, but I was restless. I sighed, feeling both grumpy and guilty. Maybe I was being rude. Surviving Chicago didn't give me a pass on basic manners. I hadn't even asked how his morning was going.

I was a bad hostess.

"How about you?" I asked — two minutes too late. Conversational genius, right here.

A bowling ball landed on my stomach.

"Who's a good boy?" I wheezed. "Cartman, love, please don't knead my bladder."

Aiden chuckled — a rich, dark sound.

"You can tell which cat it is without looking?"

"They have distinct personalities. Cartman outweighs the others by at least ten ounces. We've tried putting him on a diet, but it never works. He's determined to remain a chonk. He's also got a mid-length coat, and he's a determined cuddler."

"I can see that," Aiden murmured, turning a page. "I've had an excellent morning. Slept well, breakfast was fantastic, and now I'm debating between an altbier and a dubbel for my first homebrew."

"Ooh, good choices," I said, brightening. "Either's great for a beginner. I love a dubbel — pairs well with roasted meats, beef stew, cheese, and bread pudding. Just be careful with the sugar selection."

"I'm writing this down."

I waited, listening to his pencil scratch across the page.

"Please proceed."

"Altbiers are more versatile — they pair with everything a dubbel does, plus fish and desserts like apple fritters. They're hybrids, neither ale nor lager, and use a cold fermentation process. The flavor profile can be fruity, floral, or peppery, usually balancing hops and malt. Lots of great recipes — some true to Düsseldorf, some less so. If you're detail-oriented, it shouldn't be too hard, though fermentation can be tricky. I'd start with an altbier. We begin our training flights with one for folks looking to develop their palate."

More pencil scratching. "Good…to…know…"

"Aiden? Oh, there you are! Blake and I are ready whenever—" A woman's voice cut off. She'd spotted me and my massive, orange cat elegantly sprawled on the sofa like a pair of swooning princesses. "Oh, hello, Representative Jones. You look comfy."

One eyelid popped open, noting the alluring redhead behind my velvet bower, and closed it again.

If Aiden's presence had irked me, Angie Donahue's turned that into a full-fledged mood. And it wasn't just the headache. I didn't like her, but I couldn't even say why. We'd never spoken. I'd never seen her do anything weird, rude, or remotely shady.

This was why I didn't like socializing with strangers. I always ended up cross or confused.

"Please, just Kenny. And we are very comfy. Where are you three off to?"

"Weston," Aiden said. "Supposed to be some good hiking. Angie wanted to visit… What was it?"

"The Celtic Ranch. I promised my dad a cap made in Ireland."

"Love that shop! Gorgeous sweaters. If you've got time, the McCormick and Holladay distilleries are worth a tour."

"Sounds good," Aiden said, standing. "Thanks for the brewing advice."

"We'll see you at dinner, Kenny. Bye," Angie cooed.

"Have fun! Bye," I cooed back — definitely not fantasizing about unleashing Miss Anthropy on her.

I smiled, all teeth, and listened to them walk off. This was Oscar's fault. Half an hour with the punching bag and I'd have been sweeter than Babbage when he tried to cute some rosehips out of Mouse. We'd had to limit Mouse's access.

"Mrffph," said Cartman, booping my nose.

"I'm fine, buddy. Just irritable," I mumbled, scratching his head.

It was rare for Cartman to demonstrate enough awareness to show concern, but when he did, it was always easy to convince him that everything was A-okay. A head scratch and chin rub, and he was back to snoring and chasing dream-squirrels. Funny — he never bothered chasing anything when awake.

Chapter 63: Unauthorized

The episode ended with Kara and Nate teasing their next big adventure. I was hoping for Elafonisi in Crete. After the whole wingsuit incident, Kara had earned a spa day and a few cocktails.

"Flying the Nest," I suggested.

"Are you going to stop peeking?" Oscar grouched. "I can treat a migraine, but if you keep opening your eyes, it'll just come back."

He was grumpy because he wanted to catch up on Matt's Off-Road Recovery, but I'd already watched their latest video.

"I'll be good."

"Fine…"

He shuffled through my subscriptions. "Nothing new posted."

"Drat. Travel Beans?"

"Nope."

"How to Renovate a Chateau?"

"Nada."

"I'm not sure I believe you. The power of the remote has gone to your head."

"Says the woman who wouldn't let me watch Matt."

"What about Urban Rescue Ranch?" James asked, slipping in quietly. "Sorry if I'm intruding. Davy lost track of time and asked if I could sit with the invalid for ten minutes."

We didn't ask guests for favors. I was about to apologize when Oscar barked, "Thank you," and ran.

"Really? I'm not that annoying."

Oscar was the one who decided I needed babysitting in the first place.

James made a noncommittal sound and sat down.

"Just start Urban Rescue Ranch and hit play all, if you would. Despite Oscar's fussing, I'm not in any real danger."

"Don't forget — I'm recovering from a mysterious curse. I need someone to remind me to take it easy."

"In that case, have some popcorn," I said, offering the cheese and caramel blend.

"Don't mind if I do."

We made it through three episodes — still no Davy.

"Seriously, if there's something you'd rather be doing, I'll be fine," I said.

"I'm having fun…unless you'd prefer I leave."

Way to go, Kenny. Another guest offended. Hopefully, I'd get it out of my system before tomorrow.

"I'm not trying to get rid of you. I just don't want you to feel trapped."

"I don't. How about some old episodes of Roadkill?"

"Sounds good."

We were debating whether Stubby Bob or the C-Body Roadrunner was the better build when a loud thump came from upstairs.

"What was that?" he asked.

I pulled my mask off, wincing at the light and the lurid desert that had replaced the fireplace. Just cloudless poison-green sky above miles of black dunes. It would've made an amazing heavy metal album cover.

"Good question. I'll check."

"I'll go. You have a headache," James offered, slipping his phone into his back pocket. Had he been playing Wordle, or would I find an unauthorized tour of my house online?

We both went.

The hall was empty. So were the guest room, hall bath, and closet. A twist of unease coiled in my gut.

"Please stay here while I check the bedrooms," I said, hoping it wouldn't offend him.

"Of course."

Nothing was out of place in Milo and Mouse's room…at least, nothing I cared about. Milo was fastidious, treasuring everything he received. Mouse was every bit as messy as I was — maybe worse. I was delighted to add another member to our very small club.

Nore's room looked fine.

My room...

Gidget was calmly humming away, but a heavy book had fallen from the lectern. Spook sat beside it, looking neither guilty nor innocent. Just purposeful.

"Maybe it is good you've taken to hanging out with Mel," I murmured, returning the book to its place.

When I picked her up, she turned her tiny head toward the loft. Heart thudding, I climbed the stairs and set her on the bed.

A sticky note clung to my pillow.

"Time to talk," I whispered, reading the message along with a place and time.

A goose walked over my grave.

Someone had gotten past my wards without setting them off. An hour ago, I would've said that was impossible. Even portal magic shouldn't have bypassed my protections.

"You all right in there?" James called from the hall.

No!

"Sure. Everything's just great!"

Chapter 64: Known Unknowns

September 1ˢᵗ in Parkville, Missouri

"What's eating you?"

O'Brien leaned back in the porch swing, eyes closed, feet propped on what he had been told by a reliable source was a rattan pouf. It didn't look poufy to him, but it did fine as a footrest. The antique fan above sang a creaking tune. It was pleasant to sit and be, sipping iced tea and listening to the distant bustle of downtown.

"Why would a woman have clothing in two different sizes in her closet?"

O'Brien snorted, eyes still closed.

"I didn't realize we needed to have this discussion, but better late than never. At a certain time of the month, the female of the speci—"

"Don't be an ass. This isn't about bloating or minor fluctuations in weight. I'm talking two distinct wardrobes — one for a petite woman who dresses casually, one for a taller woman in tailored suits and embroidered robes. Not bathrobes. Ceremonial robes."

"The simplest explanation is they belong to two different women who share the closet for some reason."

When the silence stretched, he recrossed his ankles on the pouf.

"I know your silences. This one has weight. What else is bothering you?"

A heavy beat passed.

"This isn't going to work."

"Of course it will. Once you've gathered enough evidence—"

"Caterham's runaways are here. Leonore Drew changed the weather by singing. We can't prove it, but we know it. Our recordings are worthless — likely due to the wards. Eli Moran has a pet daemon. It looks like a fluffy dog, but it speaks and has glamoured horns and wings. Davida Moran's dreams manifest in paintings in her bedroom. They're disturbing — to her and anyone else. Maggie charges her fields with ley energy — not enough to trip alarms, but enough to show up in a thorough test. Kenny performs manipulations not found in any Agora grimoire. Evidence isn't the issue."

"Then what is?"

"The Sheta Djew. Some are practitioners, some aren't — but they're unified. Zealots. They'd die for Jones. Seduction, coercion, or threats won't work and could backfire spectacularly. We'll have to reason with her."

O'Brien looked at his phone like Dorrit had suggested hand-feeding a crocodile.

"You want to convince Representative Jones it's in her best interest to teach ley manipulation to an APA agent? Say your goodbyes first."

"These people are good, Chairman. The more we learn, the more I think they're doing the same thing we are. They should be our allies."

O'Brien rose from the swing and stepped inside for privacy.

"Serrecold thinks you've fallen for Jones."

Dorrit exhaled, chuckling darkly.

"I'm not in love with her. Or sleeping with her or anyone in her cadre. They're the kind of people I joined the APA to protect. And they've got more enemies than we realized."

"What enemies?"

"A secondary ward protects Jones's rooms. It stains intruders — she can trace the mark and enter their subconscious. She dream-walks."

O'Brien stilled.

"You let a practitioner into your mind?"

It was a rare thing for O'Brien to sound dangerous, but with the intensity of his power, age, and anger resonating in every syllable, he no longer sounded human.

"Answer."

"Of course I did," Dorrit replied. "I appreciate the concern. But this is my job. And Jones isn't a threat."

"HOW COULD YOU BE SO STUPID? People lose their minds doing shit like that. They go crazy; their psyche gets lost. Your job is to investigate magical threats and act accordingly — not commit passive suicide!"

He gestured so wildly that he cracked his hand on an antique console. A brief examination told him that it would leave an ugly bruise.

"She was forced out of the dream."

O'Brien took a deep breath to blast the warlock further — but choked when Dorrit's words registered.

"How?" he demanded, coughing.

"Some entity, with no physical form, reached into my mind and tore her out. I couldn't stop it. I tried to breach the wards on her room, but only figured out how to get past them this morning. We were certain she'd be found dead. But...she survived. I don't know how. When she was in my head, Darragh, I felt her terror."

The Chairman said nothing, processing.

"There's more. Talia Davis showed up early this morning looking like death — starved, filthy, and desperate enough to attempt suicide. She was being pursued by a white man: dark hair worn long, dark eyes, young to middle-aged, preternatural — origin unknown. Representative Jones and Alonzo Cowfer reached her first. They signed to each other — I couldn't catch what was said — but Cowfer picked Davis up and ran. Jones stayed behind in case anyone tracked the magic used. Whether she saw the man or not, I don't know."

"You're going to get yourself killed, John," the Chairman sighed. "So...Talia Davis ran from some unknown threat and, for six months, chose not to contact her very wealthy, very concerned family. Jones was at Levi Wilton's trial — a convicted practitioner and Davis's friend. Now Davis turns up at Sullen Creek, which is haunted by a powerful being we can't identify..." He exhaled. "I don't know what the hell this is. Find out what she was running from. Be careful how you approach Jones, and if you don't want me there breathing down your neck — don't be so reckless."

Chapter 65: Unforeseen

September 1ˢᵗ in Parkville, Missouri

"Any news?" Rena asked, humming as she set up the chessboard on their little dining table.

"Things are coming to a head," O'Brien murmured, pouring her a tumbler of crisp Assyrtiko before sitting. "The boy's taking risks, as usual. Which house?"

"Ravenclaw. You go first."

As Rena sipped her wine, O'Brien scowled at the board, weighing both his opening and the intel he'd just received. After a minute, he moved.

"How've you liked the town?" he asked absently.

"I love it! Life moves slower here — or I do, I suppose. Every day, I walk through the park with an apple cider latte — like liquid apple pie — and watch the world go by. I sleep in, shop, and eat pizza. It's heaven. I see why she chose it. There's something magical here."

"Yes — her," he snorted, moving a student.

"Darragh."

"Hmmm?"

"Look at the board," she said, sliding her ghost to h4. "Fool's Mate never works on you. What is going on?"

He stared, then chuffed quietly. Checkmate in two turns. No hiding his distraction now.

"Blind spot," he sighed, leaning back and covering his mouth. He didn't speak again for several moments. "No matter how many seers, no matter the type, or skill, there will always be a part of the crossroads that remains obscured. Some shadows cannot be penetrated — just the way it is. What's coming…is different. I've not had a vision since that day we met in the park. It's not just me. In a matter of days, we'll have passed the events relevant to that last vision. Every farsight and foresight will be flying blind."

He toyed with the pieces.

"The typical blind spot lasts an hour, maybe a day. Rarely more than a week. Usually, it falls somewhere insignificant. Not so this time. And I've no idea how long it will last — certainly days, probably years, possibly decades. The futures I've seen, or heard from others. vary so wildly, they feel like separate worlds. The only constant is that the next few days…matter."

The sentence ended lamely, O'Brien's baritone trailing into silence.

Rena paled, reading more into the confession than he'd meant to reveal.

"This is why you've been playing augur — dreaming, baking, scrying… You're looking for anything that might fill the gap."

He shrugged. "The life of a seer is full of futile endeavors."

They sat in silence, imagining what might come.

"Rena, love…the night of the TC Gala — when you said Balbay's date wasn't her… what did you mean?"

"Exactly that!" She blinked, startled. "That woman wasn't Kenny Jones. She looked right — her face, gestures, even her scent — but it was not Kenny Jones. I thought you knew. That's why I assumed you brought me. Why? What did you think I meant?"

O'Brien stood and paced.

"Darragh, you're worrying me."

"I think…I made a mistake," he whispered, sitting down. "I thought she was being impersonated, but now…I think your Kenny Jones has found a way to be in two places at once… And I didn't account for that."

They sat quietly while the maid next door sang Danny Boy in a soft soprano.

"Most people," Rena murmured after a few minutes, "have no idea what the future holds. Healthy minds don't dwell on uncertainty — they live in the present."

She smiled, and it was the sun spearing through the clouds after a heavy rain.

"So don't worry," she said, offering her hand. "It's not your job to determine the fate of the world. That's too much for anyone to bear. You've seen that there's hope and you've worked to shift the odds in that direction. That's enough. Now it's time to live. Come — I'll show you my favorite spots around town."

He let her pull him to his feet and out into the world, her touch a reminder that the best things in life were unforeseen.

Kenny: September 1st at Sullen Creek Farm

Davy's foray into glassblowing wasn't going well. She'd guilted Oscar into relieving James, and he'd reluctantly returned, irritated at finding us upstairs. James, wisely, made himself scarce after muttering something about the tasting room. I considered feeling abandoned, but with chill wafting off my défteros, I could hardly blame him.

Oscar was in a mood.

"I need to send a notification," I told him, having endured his lecture on the dangers of my condition — particularly when treatment was delayed or refused — all the way back to the living room. The trip took four times longer than usual. He'd insisted I wear the eye mask again, then directed every step while quoting grim statistics. I stubbed the same toe three times and I didn't think it was an accident.

"Tell me what to type, and I'll send it," he grunted. He'd confiscated my phone, claiming that I couldn't be trusted.

I knew I wasn't going to win this one, so I conceded with what dignity I could muster.

"Fine," I said calmly, with the absolute bare minimum of mutterings about high-handed, self-righteous, busybody healers under my breath. "I need our people to keep the bridge cleared from three-thirty to four. Post a sign or some cones. Anything that makes it obvious."

"Why?"

Ignoring a prickle of irritation, I fished the sticky note out of my pocket and slapped it down onto the coffee table. As my second, it was his job to know what I knew, question, and advise me, after all.

"Because I have an appointment."

When he leaned to retrieve the note, I nudged the corner of my eye mask up — just enough to peek. He'd left his phone on the end table. I snagged it, slipped it into my pocket, and adjusted my mask.

"Where did you find this? Who wrote it?"

"My room. It was left on my pillow — I'm assuming, by the warlock. That's why James and I were upstairs. Spook noticed something off and knocked over a book to alert me."

"You're not going."

Think serene thoughts...

"Actually, I am."

Oscar's teeth ground hard enough that the enamel squeaked.

"How many times have we had to reconstruct your bedroom ward?"

"Never."

"Exactly. Lon has a standing challenge. Anyone — operatives, staff, apprentices — who manages to bypass or disable that ward and retrieve a specific book from your shelves gets bragging rights *and* gets to play drill sergeant for two weeks. Lon takes their place in drills. They get to boss *him* around for a change."

I knew. Lon had been forced to explain after I found *Knitting with Dog Hair* shelved between my Martha Wells novels. Sure, I was messy, but my books were organized. And I loved Lon like a brother — but the chance to spit insults in his face while he melted under the sun or froze in the winter? Priceless.

With the caveat that I couldn't simply dismantle the wards — or order someone else to — I'd been allowed to participate. So far, I'd tried ninety-three times.

"Do you know how often someone tries to win that prize?" Oscar asked. "It's slowed since the contest began five years ago, but we've had fifteen attempts this week. I've made nearly seventy. Whoever got through every layer without tripping a single ward or trap is death in a body. Don't go."

Logic and genuine fear? Unsportsmanlike. There was only one response. I leaned over and hugged him.

"Thank you," he murmured, squeezing.

"I love you, Oscar, and I appreciate your concern. But I'm going."

"Kenny—"

His phone vibrated in my pocket. Mine, wherever he'd stashed it, remained silent.

"Did you tell Nore to cut me off from notifications?" I demanded. I was properly pissed now.

"Where is my phone, Kenny?" His voice was calm, but his eyes sparked with a malignant light.

We had reached an impasse.

Oscar was faster and stronger, but I'd had ten years to adapt. When motivated, I could compete. Rolling back on the couch, I kicked off his chest, while ripping off my mask and typing in his password.

"How do you know my password?" he growled, knocking my leg aside.

"Dien19cephalon34? That password?" I ducked his lunge and backflipped, giving myself some space. "Because I see you type it fifty bazillion times a day."

As I scrolled through the notifications I'd missed, one caught my eye. "What does this mean? James's curse is gone, but you didn't cure him?"

I jerked away as Oscar moved. His elbow clipped my shoulder, staggering me into a bookshelf. I dropped low, swept his legs, and darted behind the couch.

"It means what it says," he snapped, springing up. "Either the one who cursed him removed it; James broke it, intentionally or not; or he was never cursed and just carried a cursed object — on or inside him — that is now gone."

I refused to dwell on how one might carry a cursed object inside themselves — or why.

I feinted right and dove under the coffee table. Oscar anticipated me, grabbed my ankle, and started dragging me out. I wrapped an arm around a table leg; it slid with me six inches.

"Would most healers know if they weren't the one who cured a patient?" I huffed, still scrolling, when I accidentally kicked him.

An exasperated grunt escaped Oscar when my foot hit his face.

Oops.

His fault, really — for withholding information. At least it made him let go. I scrambled forward and got back on my feet, skimming the next update.

"No. If I hadn't trained in ley manipulation, I'd have congratulated myself on unraveling the damn thing," he said, climbing up and rubbing a mark on his forehead, checking for blood.

So, we'd likely been played. The question was why?

"That's why you came back! You were worried the babysitter you left me with was a threat," I said, feeling warm and fuzzy. I proceeded to the following alert. "Lon says there's been an uptick in activity along the west border."

It took a moment for Oscar's silence to register. When it did and I looked up, I was just in time to see the precast spell coming. It was house-made and hit my chest with enough force to knock me flat on my back.

"I haven't felt any incursions — not since this morning," Oscar said, sauntering over like he hadn't just sucker-spelled me.

"Cheater," I hissed through paralyzed lips.

"Mm-hmm," he said, plucking the phone from my limp fingers. Our suspended manipulations were top-notch, which was some consolation.

"Ah. Not incursions — agitated wildlife. Something's stirring up squirrels and birds to sniff out sentinels."

"Not good," I rasped, unraveling the hex. La Mort Respira — death breathes. A theatrical name for what amounted to full-body stiffness and pins and needles.

Oscar stooped to refit my eye mask on me.

"No, it isn't. Lon's changed their parameters — it'll mask them for now, but we need to figure out who's attacking and how they know what to look for."

The hex withered. I yanked the mask off and, in a flash of poor judgment, snapped it over the sofa. Light was evil.

I swept Oscar's legs a second time and tackled him. I used my weight and knees to pin him and reached for the phone. Tried to, anyway. I was strong, but not enough to hold down a full-grown vampire without magical assistance — and unlike some people, I didn't cheat.

He rolled with an exaggerated grunt, took me with him, and slammed me into the floor.

I glared up at him.

"Kenny," Colt called. "Where are—"

He stepped into the room, saw me flat on the floor with Oscar pinning my wrists, and froze. His eyes tripled in size. Without a word, he turned and walked out.

"It's not what it looks like!" I yelled. "We were just fighting!"

Crickets.

"He stole my phone!"

"Hey, no sparring in the living room," Nore shouted from the mezzanine. She leaned over the rail, one brow arched. "Not my business, but y'all tried that before, remember? It really did not work!"

Oscar lost it — snorting, wheezing, hooting.

I bucked. "Get off!"

He rolled onto his back, still laughing. I scuttled behind the sofa to escape both the migraine and the sound of his mirth. I grabbed the mask — now proudly sporting the only two dust bunnies Gidget had missed — and slid it back on.

"I'm not leaving the farm, Oscar."

The laughter stopped.

"You're not meeting with a warlock."

"If he wanted to kill me, I'd be dead. He didn't ambush me. He picked a location on our property. He didn't even say to come alone. He's given every concession we could ask for — before we asked. It's embarrassingly polite — and demonstrates that we can't protect our land."

"No."

"He's investigating us. If I run, it looks guilty. We need to make this feel like a nuisance, not a threat. I'm just the annoyed Sheta Djew rep, wondering why he's wasting my time. We need to know who he is."

"No."

"Oscar!"

"You don't even have your glasses!"

"That won't change if I run. I'm safer here, with backup."

"We'll vote."

"Give me my phone back and include me in all notifications," I said sharply. "That breach of trust doesn't fly."

"Yes, *my liege*," he muttered, handing it over.

A moment later, the phone buzzed with votes.

Nore, Davy, Lou, and Oscar opposed the meeting.

Lon, Arlo, Maggie, and Armand were in favor.

"I break the tie," I announced. "I'm going."

The bridge was empty when I arrived, sawhorses guarding either end. My footfalls were loud, making the uneven boards creak and complain. I made my way to the center, leaned against the rail, and watched the current ripple past a fallen branch — until the light and motion forced me to shut my eyes.

You're uninjured?

I gasped, spinning—

Nothing. Just Mel, ever dutiful, watching me like I'd lost it.

No one stood behind me, no shadow, nothing but a subtle tremor in the lines and that eldritch voice inside my head.

A hedge-rider.

The warlock was a hedge-rider — someone who could push their consciousness through the lines.

The universe had a cruel sense of humor.

Technically, hedge-riding was the simplest skill in a hedge witch's arsenal, but I'd only managed it once unaided — and I'd gotten lost. Only dumb luck had brought me back.

But a warlock?

The library in the Agora housed around ten thousand grimoires and a small but significant collection of practitioner manipulations and lore within them. It was enough to make those granted access a danger to us, to themselves, and to the continued existence of mankind. It was not enough to resurrect portal magic within the Community.

He'd been lucid in the dream — awake and aware. High mental discipline. Walked through walls like...

Ghost.

The codename echoed in my head like a gong.

I knew who he was. I'd read the file. Even outside Agency records, he was a legend. *The* warlock. The oldest still living and the most dangerous. The one Arlo had felt guilty for admiring. The one who quietly removed the worst of my kind — our bogeyman.

And now he was here.

I white-knuckled the rail, trying to convince my heart that a cardiac episode wasn't required.

I didn't mean to startle you.

A warlock with a sense of humor. Great.

"That might be hard for you to avoid," I rasped, the implications settling in. How much had he seen? Heard? Sound barriers could no longer be trusted. Why was I still alive?

You weren't hurt? When that thing ripped you from the dream?

"Why does it matter?" I snapped, venom masking fear. "You don't respect my privacy. Why the concern for my health?"

I'm not your enemy.

I snorted and rolled my eyes.

Rogue witches are a danger to everyone — even other practitioners. Someone has to stop them. That said, I'm not hunting you.

I'd buy that for a dollar.

I need your help.

A thin laugh slipped out before I could stop it, edging toward hysterical. Beside me, Mel shifted his paws, clearly uncomfortable. I couldn't help it. Of all the outcomes I'd imagined — failure, death, maybe convincing him he had the wrong witch — a request for aid hadn't made the list.

It had to be a trap, but I couldn't see why he'd need one.

Pulling myself together, I asked, "With what?"

Though I still couldn't see him, I could feel him weighing each word.

A member of my team manipulated the lines — accidentally. I've taught them everything I know, but it hasn't helped. There have been no accusations, but questions have been raised. We're on borrowed time.

My mouth dropped open.

"Wow... Wow."

It must seem hypocritical. I can't prove otherwise without endangering others, but we don't kill indiscriminately.

Hypocrisy might have been on the list, but it was so far down that it made little difference. He had just put his life and the lives of his agents in my hands. Just by knowing that one of their people had engaged in warped practices and not turning them in, they were guilty in the eyes of the Quorum.

If he was lying? Then, he was after a bigger target...like the Covenant. An outright refusal would carry its own consequences. I needed time to think.

"Why me?"

To my knowledge, you're the only practitioner who's ever saved a warlock's life.

Maybe it had happened before, but I didn't have any names to offer.

"I'll...think about it," I said. I braced for pressure — but he surprised me.

Talk to your people. I'll answer what questions I can. If you need help, call me.

I nodded and saved the number he gave me.

"This doesn't mean—"

I looked up, but he was already gone.

Just as well. Denial seemed pointless at this point.

I held out my hand. Still trembling. I stood there and listened to the Sullen Creek bubble and chirp and flow beneath me. The sounds were so busy and carefree, as if fear and doubt were as unknown, insubstantial, and temporary as a stray wisp of cloud blocking the sun.

I had a warlock's number in my phone. Under the name Igor — to remind me, he was still an enemy. He captured and killed people like me. Some had earned it — but to him, we were a blight. Authorities were allowed to lie to suspects. He was using me.

Then I felt it—

A ward stretching. Tugging, as if it were trying to keep someone from leaving the property.

Talia...

I cursed as I ran. Why the hell would she leave the grounds?

Didn't matter. She had and if anyone saw her...

Thorns whipped my arms and snagged my hair as I tore through the forest, lungs burning, legs screaming. I aimed for the western boundary, dread sharpening my focus, certain that I was already too late even as desperation drove me.

I released a spray of sparks, my energy sinking into the forest floor. The roots of the sentinels stirred. Trees, half-asleep by nature, were loyal when roused — and my agitation jolted them awake.

As I reached the edge of a gully, a willow branch bent low. I caught it, and it flung me skyward. My body arced, but before I fell, a thick oak limb slid beneath my feet. I landed running, more branches weaving a path through the canopy.

I spotted her.

And Levi Wilton—

Only it couldn't be him.

She must've seen the doppelgänger from Wayne's window. But Maggie or Wayne would've stopped her from chasing swamp lights.

She'd crawled out.

The windows were spelled to keep things out, not to lock anyone in. She wasn't a prisoner. We'd been so focused on hiding her, we hadn't considered...

Yeah. We hadn't considered.

"It's not him!" I yelled. "Glamour!"

She turned at the sound — confused, and vanished.

Both of them were gone. Only a will-o'-the-wisp hovered where they'd stood, bobbing once before drifting away.

No. I'm not losing her.

The boundary rushed up. Outside our ward, Maggie had tamed the trees — but they wouldn't listen to anyone but her.

I'd have to drop.

Panting, I sketched a sigil mid-stride, hurled it through the ward, and leapt after it. Cool magic slid over me — followed by something foreign and sticky. Something shiny.

I slammed into a hard, curved surface. I bounced, tumbled, ricocheted inside a spinning shell. I rolled up the wall, over the floor, eyes watering, clutching my battered ribs.

Thunk.

Everything stopped.

"That worked rather better than I'd anticipated."

A distorted face peered through the curved ceiling. Massive. Hairy. Warped by the convex glass.

"Still alive?"

"Debatable," I rasped.

My nose was bleeding. Hopefully, that was all.

"Yes. I imagine that was an uncomfortable ride," he said. "I wish I could say it gets better from here, but I won't lie."

He offered a slight, not-quite-sincere smile.

"My apologies in advance. I'll do my best to make your stay in there brief."

The roof turned opaque — an antiqued, mirrored finish, warped and imperfect. My reflection stared back at me: long-limbed, distorted, tarnished. I blinked, trying to make sense of the chaos.

Movement knocked me off my feet again just as a clawed forearm of some monstrous, indigo-skinned creature reached out of a water stain and tried to find some purchase on the mirror's slick surface. I froze.

Swirls of impenetrable darkness billowed in, filling the sphere. Through it, perfectly distinct, I saw two unblinking, white eyes gaze malevolently out of the reflective surface.

Something, I don't know what, made me look up. The same white eyes stared down at me — an infinite number. A reflection within a reflection within a reflection. I didn't know which one was real. I didn't know which to fight!

I curled tight, eyes shut, trying to vanish.

Behind my lids, faces bloomed — bright and awful. Normal people. People I might have passed every day on the street — now swinging bats, clawing, biting, smashing my dad's head in with a rock.

I tore my eyes open.

The Watcher's gaze had crept closer. He'd come to claim me.

Not like this. I wouldn't die curled up in the dark like a child. I wouldn't make it easy.

I gathered every ounce of fear, rage, helplessness — and hurled it.

The magic slammed the wall and rebounded.

I barely caught it — by the tips of my fingers, and pulled the energy back into myself. The abyss flickered, just for a second, and I saw my reflection.

Just me.

I was the white-eyed monster. And I understood.

When the darkness returned, the white eyes scowled hungrily at me before fading into nothingness.

Laenat Alijini — the curse of the Jinn.

I collapsed against the cool floor, breath ragged, and made plans to abuse myself for not having worked it out faster — because the confined space for extensive self-reflection was a dead giveaway. The greatest monster we would ever face was the one we carried within ourselves.

In the meantime, I had a curse to unravel.

September 1ˢᵗ at Sullen Creek Farm

"Rise," the strange man bellowed at the sky, arms thrown wide like he was catching an oversized beach ball.

That couldn't possibly be a good sign.

Veritas reflected on the last six days of his life and the widening rift between what he'd known and this new reality — one where nothing felt certain. It didn't even surprise him that his hosts were under attack by what appeared to be the preternatural incarnation of Darryl Dixon. With unwashed shoulder-length hair, studded leather armor, and gauntlets bearing gleaming blade-like knuckles, the man looked ready for a zombie apocalypse...or an encounter with Sabretooth. A silent, slightly hysterical snicker shook Veritas's shoulders.

He'd obviously stepped into a parallel plane — one where he watched bossaball matches, used vouchers for indoor skydiving, gave nunchaku demonstrations at Arlo's request, and rushed off to battle monsters. What was even stranger was how quickly he'd adapted...and how quickly they had accepted him.

No one cared about his nunchucks back in the real world — his world.

"I'm afraid you'll have to stay out of the action, Count Veritas," Arlo murmured, as they watched fangs — actual fangs — drop from Aiden Benilde's upper gums as he snarled and charged the intruder. Veritas made a mental note to stay well out of Benilde's way; no one that muscular should be that fast, and the man had no absolutely qualms about biting people. "Kenny will kill me if I let you join the fight without signing a waiver."

Veritas frowned as a desiccated hand punched up through the forest floor. He took a large step away from the tree they were crouched behind when a textured, but unmistakably shapely, leg kicked out from under the bark. The ghoul and the nymph worked themselves free with unsettling speed.

Three small, glowing phantoms — will-o'-the-wisps, his memory supplied — floated past their hiding place and into the fray.

He recognized this. He'd seen these beings in Egress. They were Corruptions: magic warped by ley lines into pitiful, often grotesque semblances of life.

Maggie Cloud, perched atop a towering oak, shouted orders to the trees like a general on the field of battle. They swung their heavy limbs like giant golf clubs, launching three imps and a kelpie skyward.

Alonzo Cowfer grappled with two trolls — one held in a headlock and used as a shield while the other tried to pummel him.

Wayne Cloud vanished into mist, crept up behind a goblin, swallowed it, and spat it out with its head turned around backward. The goblin appeared alive...but disoriented.

James Darrow had also jumped into the fray — shifting into something that was not quite a wolf. He didn't wait for his nymph to emerge fully; he caught her by the neck and shook her hard. Veritas winced at the crack.

Aiding their hosts was obviously the done thing. Old-world rules of hospitality had always appealed to him. Symbiosis was the backbone of civilization. Kenny Jones and her household had offered him their roof, their table, and the warmth of their hearth. Now they needed his skill as a warrior.

Doing less would feel shameful — and might blow his cover. Besides, when else would he get to fully live as Veritas, Count Vitruvio, battling the minions of the underworld?

"Would a verbal agreement suffice?" Veritas whispered, slightly breathless as a ghoul got birch-slapped into a troll's backside. The result wasn't pretty.

Arlo considered. "I'm afraid it wouldn't be legally binding without a witness."

The violated troll, understandably irked, grabbed Lon and hurled him like a football — excellent spiral — roughly sixty yards, just missing the larger trees. Lon shifted midair into something between a man and a sleek, dark lion. The creature bounced off a sweet gum and dashed straight back into the fight.

"Screw it," muttered Arlo. "I'll take it. Count Veritas, do you promise not to hold Representative Jones, Sullen Creek Farm, Punk Bunks, or any subsidiaries or affiliates, staff, or residents liable for injuries or death resulting from this encounter?"

"I do."

"Excellent! We welcome your assistance and thank you. Let's go!"

Wings erupted from Arlo's back, and he launched into the air, immediately targeting a large, gnarled imp harassing Maggie.

"Whoa," breathed Veritas. He'd assumed Arlo was a vampire. Maybe, in this world, some vampires came with eagle wings? Or maybe Arlo wasn't a vampire at all.

Snapping out of his awe, Veritas spotted a skeletal fae woman in a lacy black gown sidling toward him. He'd always considered hitting women reprehensible — until this one's maw gaped wide to reveal a mouthful of piranha teeth and lunged for his neck. This instance, he decided, didn't count. Twirling his nunchucks with expert grace, he walloped her across the face, then the temple.

She dropped like an anvil in a cartoon.

Veritas allowed himself a small, triumphant smile before squaring off with a spindle-fingered nymph who liked to stab people through the back mid-battle. She could dish it out, but couldn't take it.

A burst of light and thunder erupted from the leather messenger bag worn by the Darryl-wannabe. Shards of glass sprayed outward, pelting anyone within twenty feet. The blast knocked the villain, Aiden, and James to the ground.

Weaver, having sprung out of nowhere, hovered above them — her bloodstained skin aglow with eerie light, eyes swallowed by shadow.

"Where is she?" she demanded in a voice not of this world.

Veritas thought of Galadriel wrestling the One Ring or the Erinyes — except this goddess wore old jeans. Of course, the Furies were supposed to be ugly, but who knew? Maybe their victims had been both stupid and spiteful.

The bad man crab-scrambled backward until he hit a tree.

"Impossible," he rasped, both fascinated and afraid. "That spell imprisoned jinn for millennia. What...are you?"

"Where is she?" Weaver repeated, cracking a bolas spun from light — because, of course, she did. That's how supernaturals rolled. The weapon flew from her hand, striking him dead-on and binding his arms.

Kenny stepped forward, a ghostly kunai in hand, and stabbed it into his chest. The iron seeped through his leather armor like the earth drinking in rain. The metal glowed. The man screamed, slashing with his bladed fists. His limited movement should have been enough, but somehow, he missed the weapon entirely.

"Tell me," coaxed Weaver, her soft voice grinding against the enemy's will.

Evidence, Veritas's brain screamed. Memories weren't proof. He yanked out his phone and, ducking behind a blackberry bush, began filming. Even if video meant little in a world of deepfakes, he'd get enough that no one could deny what he'd seen.

The wastrel laughed — a choked, broken sound. "Oh, someone's not going to be happy! Shown up twice! Clever witch! But indulge me...how did the warlock get past your pretty wards? Did you tame him?"

Weaver gaped at the rogue, stunned. The light beneath her skin flickered and went dark. Veritas could see her mind turning over the question, unwieldy as a hydra. He wished he understood it.

All at once, the Corruptions turned like puppets, abandoning their opponents and charging her. Aiden and James leapt to defend her. The others, shifting from defense to offense, were on their heels.

"Where is she?" Weaver roared, recovering and driving the kunai in deeper.

The villain keened, writhing in the dirt as the weapon did its work. He swiped at it wildly, his bladed fingers passing straight through the handle — nearly slicing off Weaver's hand. His mouth opened in a silent scream. Seconds ticked by slowly. His thrashing slowed, then stopped. He whimpered now and then, moaning or twitching, until at last she yanked the kunai free. A shrill whine accompanied the motion.

Dirty Darryl looked different. Diminished.

For a moment, Veritas feared he'd just filmed a murder — but to his relief, the man gasped. Pale and nearly skeletal, he looked ill...but less manic. Calmer. Veritas couldn't define it.

"Free," the man wheezed.

"Where is she?" Weaver repeated, quietly — almost gently. The darkness drained from her eyes, leaving them full of pity and suspicion.

The man turned his head toward the troll.

Weaver's gaze followed. Her feet touched down, and she stalked toward the corrupted beast, who looked like a dog caught chewing up the couch. The hulking blue-gray giant spun around, searching in vain for somewhere to hide.

"Thank you," the man rasped as she passed — and then stilled.

Weaver's stride hitched. Veritas could've sworn she whispered "Thank you," in return — but that couldn't be right. No one thanked their assailant.

A chimera dive-bombed her.

Without looking, she flung the kunai. The creature vanished in a flash of lightning. The kunai fell — and Weaver caught it midair without even breaking stride.

So badass. This video was guaranteed to go viral.

Faced with certain death, the troll did what any troll would do — grabbed her around the waist and tried to bite her head off. Weaver tossed a copper-colored ball into its open maw. The monster froze.

She pried herself out of its grip and climbed up its thick arm.

Veritas nearly puked as she wriggled headfirst into the troll's disgusting mouth. Did trolls even brush their teeth?

Its craggy throat undulated as her hips shimmied inside.

After a good thirty seconds, Lon — alerted by Weaver's excited kicking — finished off the last of the imps, shifted, and sprinted over. He grabbed her ankles and gave a fierce tug.

Weaver slid up the troll's larynx, her denim-clad legs emerging damp and...discolored. Lon yanked again, and she popped out with a wet squelch, both hands clamped around the ankles of a young woman, who landed hard on top of her.

A teenager, Veritas corrected. The girl gasped, looked around at the carnage and unfamiliar faces, the whites of her eyes too visible — then curled into a ball and screamed bloody murder.

A reasonable response, all things considered.

"Hot showers and therapy all around," Weaver groaned, shaking a sticky strand of...something off her hand. "Lots and lots of therapy."

Lon and James — now human again — along with Aiden and Arlo, who landed elegantly, closed ranks around the two women, holding off the last of the Corruptions. When the fae woman Veritas had knocked out earlier stirred and skittered toward them — jaw broken but alive — the girl bolted past her would-be rescuers.

"Talia!" Weaver shouted, crawling, then sprinting after her. She tried to drag her back to safety and got a pointy elbow to the cheek for her trouble.

"Where is he?" the girl — Talia — demanded, unknowingly echoing her heroine.

The fae woman leered, her bulging eyes fixed on the girl like a snack on legs. Her jaw unhinged grotesquely — pop, pop, pop — opening far wider than it should.

Talia grabbed her tongue and yanked her head into a tree.

The Corruption gurgled, dazed.

"Where is he?" Talia shrieked, slamming her again, dodging her hands with desperate fury.

Thunk. Thunk. *Thunk.*

Light burst from the fae woman's face. She crumpled — dead or unconscious — as Weaver stepped up behind her, tucking the kunai away to wherever all good magic weapons go.

"It was a glamour, Talia," Weaver said softly. "He was never here. But I swear to you, he's safe."

"I don't know you," the girl shouted. "He said...he said you were like them. That you make monsters...!"

"It wasn't him," Weaver replied calmly. "He was never here. Those hunting you don't want you to trust me. If you run, they'll catch you."

"I can't trust anyone," Talia howled.

"Look around," Aiden barked, punting a will-o'-the-wisp into a tree. "Generally speaking, if someone jumps down a construct's throat to rescue you, she's fairly trustworthy. Now she's taking time to reassure you while her people are bleeding. The hunters? They'd toss a freeze charm at your head and feed you to another troll."

"Well said," Maggie hissed as she descended from her perch — just as one of her trees swatted the final Corruptions from the air.

Veritas glanced around. Angie Donahue and her brother stood silently over a pair of decapitated ghouls, bloodied swords in hand. Evidently, they'd joined in at some point — before the battle had ended.

Perhaps...he'd gathered enough evidence. Yes. Time to stop recording.

Tears streamed down the girl's face as she turned in a slow circle, taking in the consequences of her flight.

"I... I..."

"You're not the cause of this, Talia," Weaver said gently, though her voice was thick with exhaustion. "Other people chose to hunt you. We chose to fight them. You're not wrong to be cautious about who you trust — but you do need help. All we're asking is that you let us supply it."

"There are other matters to consider," James interjected, his voice calm, eyes flicking between Aiden, Talia, and finally resting on Weaver. "Like reporting the discovery of the runaway — who might be the catalyst for all this," he gestured broadly at the wreckage around them, "and the many manipulations that have been flung about like confetti."

Lon stepped forward, bristling, but Weaver held up a hand.

He stopped, grudgingly, though his expression made his displeasure clear.

James, oblivious or unconcerned, turned to Maggie. "The trees?"

"They're part of the defenses Kenny set up," she muttered. "They'll obey anyone she's told them to obey."

"James Darrow," Lon growled, voice low and cold, "welcome to the Sullen Creek Forest. Forest — greet our guest."

The trees answered with a deep, rustling bow, the sound like the ocean surf crashing against a jagged shoreline — ominous and ancient.

"The mist?" James asked, pivoting to Wayne.

"Hereditary magic," Wayne replied with a shrug. "Would you ask the shifters by what right they shift?"

James nodded — not out of agreement, but in acknowledgment. "*Laenat alijini?* No ID can evade that curse."

"When it's done right," Weaver grumbled. "He's a hack."

That earned a small, reluctant smile from James before he pressed on. "Your weapons?"

"The bolas is just a bolas," Arlo said. "The kunai's an artifact from a dig site near St. Augustine, Florida. It's registered with the Quorum." He rolled his eyes. "Are we done? Kenny's got a mess of constructs to unravel, and I, for one, would like a bath."

He held up bloodied talons and clicked them together with a grimace.

"Almost," said James, eyes still locked on Weaver. "Practitioner artifacts usually don't bond to new owners. They're decorative relics, not weapons."

"I'm likable," she said.

James chuckled, flashing human teeth. "And you — and the kunai that likes you — dispatched the fae?"

"Of course. No one here is warped except him," She jabbed her thumb over her shoulder toward the bad man's body.

Or rather—where the body had been.

"Shit," James cursed, followed by several more colorful phrases. "I have to go after him. This will have to be reported — assuming someone hasn't already called it in. Talia's a known associate of a convicted practitioner. Some may see her as a threat instead of a victim."

He looked directly at Talia. "I'm assuming there's a reason you haven't contacted your family?"

She blanched and gave a mute nod.

"The APA will want to speak with her," James continued, eyes back on Weaver. "But as you're a registered representative and an ID, and she was found in your territory, no one — not even her parents — can remove her without a Community Service Advocate or an APA agent with a warrant."

Weaver nodded.

"I don't know how long this will take," he added, "but I'd appreciate it if you'd hold my room."

"Do you need backup?"

"Can't accept it. But I appreciate the offer."

"Call if you need anything," Lon said gruffly.

James nodded once, then, shifting back to four legs, he vanished into the trees.

Parkville, Missouri

"She's a blinking witch," Special Agent MacDonnell grumbled, dropping into a chair.

"Pots and kettles," Ridel admonished over speakerphone.

"This is different, and you know it. Ghost knows it. I know it. Blake knows it." She nodded first to Dorrit, then toward Special Agent Dakota Blake. "Everyone who was in that forest knows it!"

"And?"

She opened her mouth to tell him exactly what he could do with his 'and,' but just managed to refrain.

Dorrit waited for the exchange to end before turning back to the seer's orb on his desk, where O'Brien's disgustingly handsome mug observed them.

"Talia Davis is in grave danger. Her parents and others have been experimenting with harnessing a wild construct's energy inside a human's ley reservoir to boost their power. To our certain knowledge, they've succeeded with a practitioner and a fae. Representative Jones was able to at least partially — perhaps fully — reverse both. The fae, Fabienne Poels, was a homeless woman beguiled into the experiment. The practitioner, Carrick Levisay, the serial killer who's been targeting therianthropes — including his own family, escaped."

The admission cost him. He schooled his expression, took a breath, and went on.

"According to Ms. Poels, their orders were to capture Davis and set a second trap — the Laenat alijini curse — to imprison Jones. It worked, but Jones's people, along with myself, Sampson Reid, and Luke Vitruvio, prevented the suspects and their minions from fleeing. At the time, we didn't know either target had been captured. When her people responded to an alarm, we followed and found ourselves in a fight. Jones escaped the trap on her own and immediately set about rescuing Davis."

His tone shifted, sharpening as he lobbed a verbal grenade.

"In my opinion, the safest place for Talia Davis is in Representative Jones's custody."

His team held their breath, waiting for the explosion.

"How?"

"How…what, sir?"

"How did Jones escape Laenat Alijini?" O'Brien inquired dryly.

Dorrit's Adam's apple bobbed.

"I…suspect Jones is true-sighted. When I spoke with her on the bridge, I was projecting but not manifesting. She heard my voice in her head, but when she replied, she faced me directly — as if I were physically there."

"And you trust her? Not just her motivations, but her judgment?"

"I do."

"You believe she's innocent of all wrongdoing — that the kidnappings, theft, and murders were either committed by someone else, misunderstood, or justified?"

Dorrit didn't reply right away.

"I trust her. I won't swear to her innocence, but she's not guilty. Not according to what we know. She does everything she can to protect others, not just her people."

"Ridel," O'Brien queried. "Do you concur?"

"They're careful — no signs of ley addiction. Without Ghost, we wouldn't have noticed any rogue manipulations. In a fair trial, our testimony might not guarantee a conviction. They're practitioners, yes, but disciplined and loyal. Under the circumstances, doesn't that serve our purpose?"

"MacDonnell?"

The redhead grimaced.

"I was out of line calling her a witch. Dorrit and Ridel are right, sir. Jones puts others' safety before her own. She'll guard Talia with her life, and her people will follow. Even with more time, I don't think we'd find a better option. If she's willing…I suspect she could train me."

"Hatter?"

"She likes MMORPGs. A lot. And their footprint is tight." He shrugged. "Their movements rule them out for most thefts and kidnappings. We haven't found anything that condemns them. They've got secrets — like Ridel said, they're careful — but I don't see them kidnapping for fun. And murder? Not without a damn good reason."

"Sarduy?"

"Dogs are a good judge of character, and they adore her," said the dour Latina.

"Blake?"

The younger agent pressed his lips into a line and glanced at his teammates, apology in his eyes.

"I agree, Talia's safest with Jones for now," he said slowly, "but we have a lot of unanswered questions. Half the guests are black holes. We can't find any information on them. Who are the Haighs? What cadre do they belong to? Why do guests appear and disappear during the night? And the animals! New ones show up every day, but the total number always seems to be about the same. Where do they go? Why is the workshop enchanted to look occupied even when it isn't? Why does Jones spend hours in there every day? She's a representative! She has better things to do than make freaky machines. Why have they had only a third as many wild construct attacks as every other cadre in the country?"

O'Brien raised his eyebrows and turned to Dorrit, who nodded to Blake instead.

"They're good questions," Dorrit admitted. "We don't have all the answers. But you've said Talia's better off with Jones. Why not another cadre or a service advocate?"

Blake looked down at his shoes, searching.

"The Sheta Djew…feels more real," he said finally. He shook his head. "The Quorum keeps itself distant. They insulate themselves from the consequences of their decisions. Jones could rule from Chicago like others do — trade favors, build clout — but she stays here. She works with her people. They're…happier."

Dorrit raised his brows and met O'Brien's resigned gaze.

"I see. I'll remind you — Jones has a knack for turning rivals, even enemies, into fanatical allies. Almost like magic." O'Brien sighed, raking a hand through his hair. "I don't need to tell you what hangs in the balance. John, I trust your judgment — but be sure. Doing the wrong thing for the right reasons will get us killed."

The orb turned clear.

"Are we?" MacDonnell asked, arms crossed. "Are we doing the right thing?"

"Yes."

"Then what's the plan? The Chairman's right — if this goes sideways, we can't disappear her. We can't make a whole cadre — thousands of people — disappear."

"We won't need to. She'll protect Talia. She'll help us."

MacDonnell quirked a brow, but he offered nothing more.

"Sooner or later, someone else is going to take a hard look at the Sheta Djew and find what we did — they're steeped in warped practices."

"You don't believe they're a threat to the Community any more than I do."

"I'm worried we're in too deep. That she'll pull you in farther than you meant to go. I'll look the other way when someone grabs the lines in a crisis, but these people court disaster. They were lucky we were the ones investigating…this time. What happens next time?"

The lines of Dorrit's face sharpened, hollowing his cheeks and hardening his good eye, but his voice stayed gentle.

"The Quorum was made to serve the Community, not feed its worst instincts at the cost of basic humanity. I'm all in. How deep do you want to go? All of you — decide where you stand."

Chapter 68: Bulletproof

Kenny: September 2nd at Sullen Creek Farm

"How is she?" Maggie murmured, scaring the pants off me. I'd been jumpy ever since learning that our wards weren't infallible. "Has she eaten?"

I clutched my chest and let my head thunk against the floor, my foam eye mask and thick skull absorbing the blow.

"Sorry," she whispered.

"It's okay," I muttered, pulling off the mask. "She's eaten — barely. She's...waiting."

Maggie watched Mischief groom her unresponsive sister, concern etched across her face. I'd made a blanket nest in the closet, and there the cats remained. Mystery allowed herself to be coaxed into a few bites, tolerated chin ointment, and had entirely given up hissing, scratching, and biting. One way or another, it wouldn't be long.

"What's she waiting for?"

"A purpose. She's holding on for Mischief — for now. Choosing a new familiar would feel like a betrayal. She needs a quest. Something only she can do."

Mystery didn't lift her head, but her lantern eyes flicked to me. I stroked her soft fur, silently begging her to remove a chunk from my hand for taking such liberties.

She didn't.

"Oh," Maggie breathed, clearly brainstorming missions for a once-hateful fluffball. "I thought I saw mice droppings in the barn."

Mystery closed her eyes and tucked her face into the blankets.

"Thanks, Mags, but I don't think that's gonna cut it," I whispered, smoothing down a few tufts Mischief hadn't reached yet. "Keep thinking. We have to come up with something."

"I will. Evy's here — with your new glasses. We should hurry. She's interrogating the guests."

I nodded, eager for migraine relief but reluctant to leave the babies.

"I'll be back soon, angel-kittens," I said, scrambling to my feet. "I love you both. I need you both."

Evy had Angie Donahue, Blake Donahue, and Count Vitruvio cornered in the breakfast nook — literally. They were crammed onto one side of the banquette, looking unsure how they'd ended up there, while she held court at the other end of the table.

"— been absolutely terrifying! I'm so glad none of you were hurt! And Talia Davis is alive after all? Where has she been?"

Dodging monsters while walking from Chicago to Kansas City without money or magic to ease the way.

"Sis," I said, "I think my guests have donated enough time to our concerns for today."

Evy turned in her chair and stuck out her tongue.

Yes, yes. I ruined everything.

"There you go," she said, handing me a small periwinkle shopping bag with *Eyes by Iris — Custom Frames* scrawled in a loopy white font. "Just remember, I'm not your personal courier."

I passed her a zip drive. "Here's your tip, Evy-Applesauce."

Her smile was bittersweet. Our dad had given her that nickname.

Inside the bag was a matching drive and three pairs of null glasses, identical to my old ones. Aviators were forever. I slipped on a pair and watched a whole city of bouncing iridescent blobs vanish. I could feel the swollen tissues in my brain retreat millimeter by millimeter.

"What will happen to Talia?" Angie asked.

"I don't know," I said, pretending to misunderstand. She wasn't asking what the authorities would do — who could guess that — but what I intended. I was going to ignore that question until I couldn't. Then I'd lie. "It's up to the APA to find enough evidence against her parents to press charges. Until then, the poor kid's not safe."

Evy, back still to them, smirked.

Talia was as safe as we could make her. Last night, we'd staged settling her into Déjà's spare room, then portaled her to Wenen. It took fifteen minutes to convince her Levi was Levi, but the reunion was still the highlight of my week.

"And the fae woman?" Blake asked.

"Fabienne will be turned over to the APA. I've submitted a report, including testimony that she wasn't in her right mind. They'll investigate. If she's released, I've invited her to return — at least during recovery, if not longer."

"That's nice of you," Luke observed, snagging a warm peanut butter cookie from the plate Derringer passed around.

"It's practical. What was done to her is unconscionable. Even so, I doubt the Community will crack down on such vile experiments. If enough cadres band together, though, we might gain traction. Her testimony will be vital. Which means she'll need protection. We have the healers and the strength to keep her safe."

"A fair exchange, then," murmured Angie.

I'd set myself up for that, so I didn't bother disputing it.

"We appreciate your help yesterday," I told her. "The skirmish ended faster and cleaner because of it. These disturbances are — were — unusual for us, but Director Serrecold tells me that with the rise in wild constructs, things will get worse before they get better. We'll do everything we can to avoid further interruptions. Evy, could I get your opinion on something?"

With a wave goodbye, Evy followed me onto the dining porch.

"That was Dr. Evelyn Vine?" I heard Luke whisper. "She doesn't even look old enough to drink."

"Small world, isn't it?" Angie replied.

We cut through Punk Bunk's kitchen and headed for Arlo's office. I knocked once and pushed the door open.

"By all means, Eternally Patient and Ever Correct One, enter. Oh! And what a treat — her sister, the Cyber Sea Boss!"

Evy arched a brow at me.

"He's miffed because he got scolded for taking Count Vitruvio's verbal liability waiver instead of getting a written one — right before your email about the Egress hack landed. Turns out, Punk Bunks got hacked, too. The wonderkid is fallible."

"I get your nickname," she said. "But Cyber Sea Boss?"

"You're one of our cyber experts, you live near Lake Erie, and you're bossy," I said. "Arlo, I need the warlock files."

He stopped what he was doing and logged in to the private network.

"It's because she rules the Mulberry like a harbor master, while the rest of us are her underappreciated minions," he grumped. "Now, can you imagine how Count Vitruvio would've felt if I hadn't accepted his word? Benilde and Darrow were already fighting — and Darrow's still recovering from a life-threatening curse. Did they sign waivers? No. But you wanted a seasoned and ancient warrior benched over paperwork? His honor *demanded* he defend his hosts. And he took down multiple foes without a scratch — which is more than the rest of us can say. He certainly didn't get trapped in a Christmas ornament. Here."

"I'll be hearing about that for a while," I told Evy, steering her into a chair and spinning it toward the screen. "We couldn't stop Benilde and Darrow from jumping in. But Vitruvio asked for permission, and you granted it. I'm grateful for the help, but more grateful no one got seriously hurt. You know how vulnerable we are. A lawsuit, even a nuisance one, could expose everything. Okay — Ghost, aka John Dorrit — active for the last thirty-four years. Read his case history."

"You had Arlo hack the APA? Are you both nuts?" Evy hissed. "Wait — don't answer. Stupid question."

"No…well, not recently. The APA doesn't keep this stuff digital. I asked Aunt Gregg to photocopy the files."

"Uh-huh. Sounds like something Mom ought to hear," she sang.

"Blackmail won't work. Shut up and read."

She gave an exaggerated sniff and turned to the screen.

"He's exonerated more suspects than not... Cleared Montague Bodwin — *our* Bodwin — of warped practices? So is he lenient or incompetent? Hmm. Lenient. This guy's got a hell of a resume. He took out Dáinn Korhonen three years ago. And executed Naberius Stallings...and the year before that, he rid the world of Blossom Pomeroy...and... Dear God. This...this is the guy! The reason the Community believes practitioners are gone! Please tell me this isn't who they sent..."

"He is."

"Arlo, tell Nore to evacuate. Kenny, you're coming with me. Now!"

"Arlo, ignore her," I said. "Evy, he's here. He's a guest. He hasn't triggered the wards. Levisay asked if I'd tamed him. We've got six guests flagged as potential but inactive threats — Luke Vitruvio, Angie Donahue — but not her brother. James Darrow, Tyson Groper, Bianca Foss, and Aiden Benilde. John Dorrit's clearly a man, so we're down to four suspects — none of whom mean us harm."

"Well, the warlock's not Count Vitruvio, so make that three," Arlo chimed in. "He was generously demonstrating his nunchaku skills while you were on the bridge."

Evy made a derisive noise and flopped into a Cubist Art Deco armchair, crossing her legs. She flicked a hand like she was tossing her blond mane over her shoulder — even though it was pinned into a complicated bun.

"See, this is the problem with saturation wards," she said. "They make you feel bulletproof. You think you know things you don't. So you let people get close, build relationships — and then bam! The wards expel them, and it feels like some arcane glitch. Not them! They can't be evil — they're a friend! Kenny, come on! He's not an active threat now, but that will change!"

"On paper, Dorrit looks as honorable as warlocks come, I'll give you that. He's taken out real threats to humanity — and pronounced harmless people guilty of nothing. But that doesn't make him safe. And it sure as hell doesn't mean you can trust him. He's still a warlock!"

She was right, of course. That admission hit hard — like reason slapping me across the face.

"Are you able to stay a day or two?" I asked, sighing as I pivoted. "Or do you need to get back to Ann Arbor?"

She stood and pulled me into a hug.

"I can stay for dinner. Then I need to head back. Lon said Oscar got recalled to Wenen by the elders — something urgent. Addison's a good healer, but she's not Oscar. I know you don't want to hear it, but don't wait to evacuate until it's too late. You can rebuild everything here. But human lives? Those aren't replaceable."

Chapter 69: Start Talking

Eli: September 2nd at Sullen Creek Farm

"How am I supposed to get in there?" Mouse asked, shaking paws with Babbage before feeding him another rose hip.

After a spectacularly gross digestive incident, Aunt Kenny had finally convinced her to slow down on the treats or let Babbage forage for them. Cleaning the mess off her bed had been enough to make Mouse stick to the recommended diet.

We'd gathered on the rug in the pet parlor, which gave us some privacy without actually hiding. As long as we looked comfortable and stayed visible, grown-ups ignored us. Mom, Derringer, Armand, three guests, and maybe five members of the cadre had passed by without suspecting anything.

What I didn't plan on was how much attention the animals drew. Boruta and Duke Sigmund — Mundy, as he preferred — tried to distract with a bad case of the zoomies, but everyone wanted to stop and pet Babbage or watch him munch papaya. Babbage only wanted to stay protected in Mouse's lap, chewing his toys and napping. It was like inviting a rock star to switch careers and become a secret agent.

I still wasn't entirely sure why Boruta thought Mouse and Milo needed familiars. So far, Mouse had only developed a talent for stealing chinchilla treats off the high shelf, where Aunt Kenny had stashed them, and Milo had gotten very good at throwing a frisbee. At least Mundy wasn't fat. They ran around outside for hours unless it rained.

I pointed over my shoulder to a small door in the wall, leading to the pet tunnels. "Same way the warlock did; through there."

Mouse's eyes narrowed. "I won't fit."

"Not as you are, no."

She glared at me. "Who else knows?"

What did she expect? She called herself Mouse!

"No one, as far as I know. Aunt Kenny might suspect, but she won't pry. She'd want you to tell Déjà or Aunt Maggie." I widened my eyes. "Once you're inside, wait for the portal to open. Not many people use that route, but tonight they will. You won't have to wait more than twenty minutes. And you absolutely can't get caught."

"I won't. You're sure he'll show?"

"Yes. You won't see him right away. Take your phone and, at exactly twelve-eighteen, start talking. He'll be there. You'll have ten minutes to convince him to leave, or neither of you will make it out in time. Milo, your job is riskier," I said, locking eyes with him, "but there's no other way. She needs to know she can trust him…or Kenny will die."

He nodded solemnly.

"I won't let you down."

Chapter 70: Don't Worry

Kenny: September 2nd at Sullen Creek Farm

I stared in the mirror and wondered about the woman looking back. I felt itchy, like I'd outgrown my skin. Maybe I needed a new quest, too — something to stretch into.

Just…not tonight.

"These," Mouse declared, holding up wood-cut earrings in one hand and strappy sandals in the other.

She didn't know the earrings were spelled to boost hearing or the sandals for comfort. The former were great for patrols — not ideal for a noisy night at the bar. My eyes were still recovering from two days without null glasses; I wasn't eager to put my ears through the ringer.

"And wear your hair down," she added.

"You don't think—"

"No. These." Her tone brooked no argument.

I silently chuckled; if it made her happy, I'd wear them. If it got too loud, I could always take them off.

"I'm not questioning your taste, but why the dress?" I gestured to the deep red maxi I hadn't worn in years. It clung in the right places yet breathed, which was crucial in this heat. "A Haigh hasn't bribed you, have they?"

Clan Haigh had only stayed overnight, despite Oscar's best efforts. He'd told Callum he couldn't travel for forty-eight hours. Callum and I made a deal: they would reverse-engineer the enchantment on my kunai, manufacture and sell enchanted weapons — after providing us with five thousand — and I'd weave a door so they could go home. They'd make millions, and folks would have a chance against the wild constructs.

Though the window was small, I still wouldn't put it past Briony, Cully, or Coen to bribe my kids into causing mischief.

"No one bribed me," Mouse grumbled. "You have these dresses and never wear them. Every girl should feel pretty sometimes."

"Fair enough."

"Besides, the others are dressing up. Nore's wearing that gold dress."

Something sharp and unpleasant slid through me.

"Nore's wearing the gold dress?" I repeated.

That dress meant business. Nore only wore it when she was serious — devastatingly serious. But she and Armand weren't... Were they? We hadn't had as much time together lately, but we still lived in the same house. Our rooms shared a wall.

How had I missed this?

"So...can I?"

Could she...? I'd completely spaced out while Mouse kept talking.

"Sorry, hon. Would you repeat the question?"

She grabbed my hands and seesawed back and forth, wheedling — no eye contact. I braced myself.

"Lou told me about her roller derby team and how there's a junior league. Katie used to be on it, and Gwendolyn and Onora still are. I want to join! It'd be so cool to be part of a team — and it'd help my coordination. Can I?"

Valid points...

"May I," I corrected, buying time.

Roller derby was rough enough in the norm world — our version added spells, charms, and not-quite-lethal hexes for flair. On the other hand, if Mouse decided to join the Covenant, her training couldn't start too soon.

"Have you ever skated before?"

"No, but I can learn. How hard can it be?"

Ha!

"With a few people trying to knock you down? Hard. And dangerous. There's an age limit — I'll have to check what it is. Let's try skating first. If you're still standing after that, we'll revisit this discussion."

She collapsed into me with exaggerated resignation. "Okaaaay. I guesssss. Tomorrow?"

Too easy. Had this been the goal all along?

Didn't matter. If she wanted to go roller-skating, I had no problem with it.

"We'll make time."

Word had spread: Nore and the Hoppy Endings were performing at the brewpub, and Sullen Creek was showing up in force — along with several guests.

Angie — resplendent in a sky-blue T-shirt dress I reluctantly admired — and Luke, nearly swallowed by a sage-green hooded mantle, chatted near the door. Blake Donahue was charming Gaia. Tyson Groper, James Darrow, and Bianca Foss stood nearby, watching the crowd gather.

"Lon, we're going to need the Bad Decisions Bus."

"Arlo's pulling it around now. Davy's making a list of who's riding." He gave my outfit a skeptical once-over. "You look...nice. What gives?"

Funny guy.

"Backatcha. Mouse picked my outfit. She also mentioned Nore's wearing the gold dress tonight."

Lon ran a hand over his buzz cut and grimaced. "Yeah. Armand and I talked. They're serious. I've given my blessing. It's a good thing, but...yeah."

I patted his shoulder. "We grow or we stagnate."

"Guess so."

"Everyone shut up," Maggie barked. "We've taken everyone's names. If we missed you, talk to Davy. Pick a buddy for the ride. When you're ready, get on the bus!"

A slim figure with ginger curls sidled up beside me.

"Be my buddy," Olivia asked.

I linked arms with her. "It's you and me, kid."

We shuffled into line with the others.

"Representative Jones's night off," murmured a sardonic voice. "Who's watching the kids?"

"Sounds like a comedy," Angie said, standing close to, but not quite touching, Aiden Benilde.

Benilde's eyes flicked over me, a hint of amusement tugging at his mouth. I didn't get the joke, so I ignored it.

"Deja and Dave have arranged entertainment for the kids," Olivia said smoothly. "Wayne will be on patrol, and our security's been reinforced. The local police department has sent over a couple cruisers. We're ready for anything."

"Famous last words," I muttered. I didn't like leaving, but the Covenant insisted we stick with our usual routine.

Lon had tripled the guards. Arlo had rigged a pet button-to-phone alert system at Wayne's and the parlor. The farm was as secure as we could make it.

September 2nd at Sullen Creek Brewpub

Veritas, tucked in the dark corner of the brewpub patio, signaled for another *Pie in the Sky*. The frenetic music seemed to hold back the night. He could feel the beat in his chest. His body itched to move — but he also wanted to maintain a certain mystique. Some vampires did not dance.

His buddy for the night, Arlo — less encumbered by deadly secrets — was letting loose with Pheona Bell. Their exuberance established a three-foot buffer zone around them.

When the song ended, Lon, looking petrified, stepped onto the stage.

"Good evening, everyone. I hope you're having a good time. We've had a rough few days of it. It's good to be able to relax with a few friends, take a moment to recover. Things are moving, changing — some good, some bad. The best thing to do is surround yourself with good people. I've…uh…I've been lucky to have all of you in my life, but especially one of you in particular."

Someone adjusted the lighting, blinding him until they got it adjusted.

"Maggie…I'm no good with words, but I love you and I want to spend my life with you. Will you marry me?"

His lady strolled up and took the mike from him.

"I will…as long as you don't say 'good' for the next ten minutes."

The eruption of cheers was stunning. Covering his ears, Veritas laughed and watched Weaver fling herself at them. Lon, being taller, caught her full weight and staggered. Armand pulled a champagne bottle out of a hat, popped it, and sprayed the crowd as Nore reclaimed the mic and sang *At Last*.

"Hoppy endings abound," Veritas teased as Weaver, forced by the crowd to give way, dropped into the chair beside him.

She snorted. "About time. They've kept us waiting two years. How about you? Enjoyed yourself, Count?"

"Very much. Good beer, good company, good music."

"Good to hear." Her contented smile gave way to something more serious. "May I ask you a question? Something personal?"

"Certainly."

"The day you were attacked by the siren...while under her hex, you bit James, Aiden, and Armand. Several times."

"I didn't know what I was doing," he reminded her, shifting uncomfortably.

"I know. It was a potent hex. The bites were odd — bloody, but there were no punctures. The skin had been torn, not pierced. Then, in the woods, you didn't bite the wild constructs. You used your nunchucks and your wits. You're not a vampire, are you?"

Veritas stopped breathing.

So this was it — the end of the line. And the worst part? He didn't even believe the truth would come out, or that anyone would avenge him.

Weaver pressed her lips and nodded, as if he'd confirmed her suspicions.

"I won't ask what you're hiding or why. Vampires are the easiest origin to fake. You're not the first, and you won't be the last. But...maybe don't tell Arlo," she added. "At first, I thought you might be one of the Ancients. Honestly — and I mean this as a compliment — you often feel like a norm. You're free from the usual constraints of the Community. I mentioned my theory to Arlo. Between that and your style, humor, and fighting prowess... well, he's a fan."

"I won't tell him. And...may I ask—"

She seemed to read his mind.

"I'll keep your secret. You came to our aid when you didn't have to. I've granted each guest who fought beside us a favor. Call on us in a time of need, and we will come."

He felt it. Her words carried power. It wound through him, settled in his skin. But, instead of fear, he felt comfort; safety. And...he felt conflicted. Veritas could hardly believe his luck — against all odds, he'd landed on his feet. He owed the Sheta Djew and their guests his life. He had seen their humanity, their compassion.

"Your kindness shall not be forgotten," he swore. One way or another, he would do as he must *and* repay their generosity.

"Come on, you two!" Olivia called. "Everyone's on the bus!"

Veritas turned, surprised to see the patio was nearly empty.

"Shall we, Count Vitruvio?" Weaver asked with a smile.

He rose and offered her his arm.

"About the siren—" he began, lowering his voice as they fell in line.

Tick-tick.

Weaver stiffened. Her fingers brushed her earring as she stared into the trees backing the lot.

Aiden Benilde, halfway up the bus steps, moved.

Tick-whoosh.

"Down," Weaver screamed.

Benilde covered twenty feet and slammed into her, knocking her to the ground.

Veritas stared, confused.

Benilde's bulk shielded Weaver completely — only her head was visible — but he wasn't moving. A long, forked prong was buried in his back, and blood was seeping through his shirt.

Tick-tick. Tick-whoosh. Another prong materialized — hovering inches from Weaver's neck.

"Down!" she screamed again. "Everyone down! Lon! Lon!"

Olivia kicked the weapon, making it skitter and scrape across the asphalt, before dropping.

A dark lion sprang from the bus and charged into the woods. A massive black-and-white bird followed close behind.

"Arlo — drive! Lock down the pub!" Weaver shouted, struggling to free her arms. "Luke, Olivia, stay close. There's a ward around us. Help me get up!"

The *Bad Decision Bus* roared out of the parking lot and down the road.

They lifted Benilde's torso just enough for Kenny to slide out from beneath.

"What is it?" Olivia rasped as Weaver examined the prong.

"I don't know. Call Oscar — no, Addison," Weaver barked, staring hard at the thing embedded in Benilde's back, her face straining and turning red.

The matte-black, five-sided spike resisted her every effort. Veritas watched helplessly as she took a breath and studied the weapon more closely. The tip had hinged claws.

Veritas's déjà vu sucker-punched him. His skull throbbed. He knew this. He'd seen this before.

"Lóng yá," he hissed.

"What?" Kenny asked, looking up at him, then back down. "Shit!"

"What?" echoed Olivia, not understanding.

Weaver's expression was grim. "Dragon teeth — used when you want to take something or someone alive. It's loaded with sedatives, potions, antidotes, whatever might be needed, and it monitors the victim, adjusting the dose and making sure they don't have a bad reaction. Originally, they were used to subdue and relocate sea serpents. The APA uses them for magically resistant targets."

A wave of images, sound, and pain crashed through Veritas's mind. It hurt. It hurt so bad… The shackles binding his memory snapped, and he fell to his knees.

Weaver's hands trembled over Benilde's back. The prong twitched — then retracted with a thick, wet sound. She grabbed it and hurled it across the lot. Wading up her skirt, she packed it into the bleeding wound.

"Olivia — check his pulse," she whispered, now staring hard at Benilde's back.

The redhead grabbed Benilde's wrist.

"He's alive. It's steady."

"He can stay that way — if you come with us, Representative Jones," a voice murmured.

It was like the night itself had spoken. Veritas whipped around, seeing only pavement and trees.

Three figures were just suddenly there, under a streetlamp. Veritas didn't believe in ghosts. Well, he hadn't a few days ago. These guys, although silent and fluid in their movements, were shaped with a weight and purpose not associated with wraiths.

"Stay close," Weaver said. "They can't breach the ward."

"No ward is infallible," said the voice, the three figures suddenly much closer. His voice was soft, reasonable. "We will break it, and then people will get hurt. Or, you could surrender yourself, Representative Jones, and we can be on our way. Surrender and we'll leave the others."

"You can't have her," Olivia snarled, climbing to her feet and standing in front of Weaver. Veritas rose and joined her.

The speaker raised a modified Glock long-slide. It spat red lightning at Olivia's head — three shots. She didn't flinch. The energy splattered against the ward, flickering out like tentacles.

"The offer stands…for now," he murmured. "You're channeling magic in two directions, Jones. You have, maybe, ninety seconds. After that, you'll watch your friends die. Clock's ticking."

Veritas watched the red lightning slither across the ward, probing, hissing, searching for weaknesses.

"They've caught the impundulu," another voice reported, a finger pressed to his ear.

"That would be Armand Dlamini — Nore's lover. Good. Kill him."

There was a soft murmur, and a gunshot cracked in the woods.

"Do you suppose the sphinx — Alonzo Cowfer — heard that? Think he understood what it meant? That his best friend's dead, and you didn't even try to save him? Will it make him reckless? You can save him, Jones. Haven't they earned that? Save your...remaining friends."

Veritas glanced at Weaver. She hadn't stirred — she just stared at Benilde's back and pressed against the wound.

He turned back and shrugged. "I think that's a no."

The speaker tilted his head. "You — I don't know you. You're not one of hers. Yet here you stand. Why? Do you know what she is? Warped. She's not even human anymore; just hunger trapped in flesh. She'll protect you...until the ward breaks. Then she'll abandon you and save her skin."

The red lightning etched into the ward, finding purchase.

"You're just full of happy stories, aren't you?"

"Don't be too harsh, Count," Lon called from the trees. "He doesn't know her like we do."

The sphinx threw something large at them, too fast to identify, and the three men whipped around and fired at it. The body hit the ground with a thump and a groan — they'd shot one of their own.

A massive black-and-white bird dropped from the sky, nabbed a baddie, and soared back up before the others could react. It dropped the guy from thirty-five feet. Veritas shuddered at the crunch.

"Armand's alive," Olivia softly reported to Kenny.

A siren wailed in the distance, all but drowned out by a lion's roar, real, close, and foretelling imminent death. The black beast was on the two remaining villains. One fired their third and final prong. It missed. The lóng yá punched a crater into the parking lot. A giant paw swatted the miscreant's head into the ground.

The ringleader lined up a shot...and got struck by lightning. It lifted him eight feet into the air before releasing him.

Kenny dropped the ward.

Olivia dashed forward and kicked the ringleader in the kidneys — hard — then confiscated his weapons and searched his body.

Veritas stood guard over Weaver and Benilde. He didn't even use his phone to record Armand the bird landing as Armand the man, or Lon the lion struggling to handcuff the other evil-doers.

The sirens were closer.

Weaver's mint-green Chevy Cameo screeched around the corner, nearly flattening Lon, and skidded to a stop. Arlo tumbled out, tripping over his own feet. A pixie-cut brunette with glasses leapt from the passenger side, followed by James Darrow.

The woman ran to Benilde.

"He's alive," she confirmed. "Nasty wound. No idea what they injected — doesn't smell like anything. I'll pack it, then we get him to the farm."

Three police cruisers ground to a stop out on the street, expelling officers who crouched behind their doors, guns up.

"Kenny, what did you do?" demanded Dave Coinin.

"It's a bar, Officer Coinin. Sometimes things get rowdy."

"It was an ambush," Lon explained, shifting. "They didn't care about witnesses, collateral damage, or noise. They were well-armed and knew our names and origins, but not what to expect. This needs to be kept quiet until we learn who they are and why they wanted Kenny."

"Right," sighed Coinin. "Boys, you know what to do — ward, tape, and document everything."

"Why not the clinic?" Darrow asked Addison once it was clear the Sheta Djew weren't being arrested.

"Someone's after Kenny. We're not handing them a hostage," Olivia snapped. Then, softer, "Sorry. It's been a rough night. We're going into lockdown."

Kenny, having been shooed away from the patient, turned to Arlo.

"I know what you're going to say," he preempted her, raising one hand and pulling a crumpled paper from his pocket with the other. He shook it open and handed it to her. "James signed the waiver in the truck."

Kenny stared at him for a second, then burst into laughter. She collapsed to the ground, covering her face.

After twenty seconds — when she could breathe again — she flopped on her back.

"No. I mean, yes, well done — of course," she began, shaking her head and giggling, "I was going to ask if anyone canceled Capture the Flag for tonight. We're supposed to be there in…three minutes. I'd rather not have the Yets'eḥālyi Lijochi showing up en masse to rescue us."

"Oh. Right… I'll call Tigest."

September 2ⁿᵈ at Sullen Creek Farm

"They're running tests… No, Addison says when something comes back positive. Until then — what? We don't have a — I know the infrastructure can't support a full evacuation — I'm not — let me finish! We *are* evacuating the children to the Mulberry, ten at a time, every fifteen minutes. From there, they're being sent to secure bases. No one is going to Wenen, so the plane won't fracture! You can take… Yeah, well, good luck with that! Meanwhile, I've got real problems. Sheb ylmoora fohsha, asshole."

Mouse's whiskers twitched as Kenny's lower fourth stomped past the oriel window. From behind the drapes, she couldn't see much. That was fine. She just needed Kenny to finish her calls, leave the portal open, and leave the room.

"Mothmaid? It's Weaver. The Saturniidae will be practicing formations for the next few days. Please make sure they're not bumped from the server… Yes. That's all. Thank you. *Sheb ylmoora fohsha.*"

A series of wet squelches and the soft thud of multiple feet signaled the arrival of guests. Mouse inhaled deeply. Six people…four men, two women — one of them smelled like chinchillas.

Good people.

"Doyenne," a man greeted. "Representative Banerjee has welcomed the children to his home and to the Dhana Nadī. He regrets he cannot offer support in person, but sends us in his stead. We are yours to command."

"It's good to see you again, Dhairya. The Sheta Djew thanks Representative Banerjee and the Dhana Nadī for their generosity. We won't waste it. Please follow me — Lon's our security chief and will direct you."

Finally.

Mouse listened as the door opened, and seven people left. It shut with a soft click. She counted to fifteen, then scampered out, dodging Gidget's arms, weaving through books, and springing off baskets of pre-cast spells like a furry ninja.

Following Boruta's advice, she paused at the portal and scanned the odd space beyond — an arched hall lined with steam-puffing copper machinery. A few robed figures passed by the mouth but none turned down the corridor.

Now or never.

Mouse slid through the gelatinous portal covering, fur bristling at the slick sensation, and stepped onto the Mulberry. She crept down the steamy hall, giving the pistons plenty of space. It opened into a bright passage with silver-white walls and sun-drenched skylights…even though it was nighttime…and the Mulberry existed in between worlds.

From the central passage, dozens of smaller halls branched off, each stranger than the last — one like a library, one pulsing with moist red fibers and pink-blue cords, and one intricately folded from paper.

A tall man in dark green robes swept past. Mouse slipped behind him, tail low, shadowing him past a hall of white stone, then one glittering with rhinestones. He continued past a staircase, but Mouse paused, checked her surroundings, and scurried down.

The lower level was quieter — but that only meant stealth mattered more. A stray sound could get her caught. Moving in short bursts, she hugged the shadows in open doorways. Closed doors were risky; someone might walk out.

Two hallways later, she was tempted to check the cell phone tucked in her fanny pack, but that would be stupid. She wasn't there yet. Until she was, time didn't matter.

Slow and steady.

Listen. Move.

Listen. Move.

Turn. Move.

Listen.

Another turn. The hallway widened. On the left: forklifts — thirteen…fourteen…twenty in a row. On the right: a wall of hand trucks.

This was it.

Mouse darted between two forklifts and unzipped her pack. The phone slipped out and hit the floor with a sharp clatter. She froze. Waiting for sirens, alarms, and armed guards.

Nothing.

She snatched the phone — 12:07. Eleven minutes. She shoved it back into the pouch and glanced around.

The forklift next to her hummed to life and rolled away.

She choked down a squeal, belatedly realizing it was automated.

Footsteps echoed from around the corner. Without thinking, she leapt onto the forklift's pronged front and crouched low. Ahead, the hangar doors began to open.

If anyone in the warehouse saw her — game over.

Heart pounding, she peered back. Four people had rounded the corner. If she hadn't hitched a ride, they'd have seen her for sure.

The thought cheered her — briefly. Then she realized the corridor had no turnoffs. The four practitioners were headed for the warehouse too.

Mouse would have to ditch her ride as it passed the doors. For a brief moment, she'd have no cover. She just had to time it right. Stay low. Easy-peasy. She'd done this kind of thing plenty when she and Milo were living on the streets. Finding them food had been her job.

She perched on the fork, fluffy legs dangling, and counted down. Three...two.. one — go. She somersaulted off, landing in a crouch, and darted behind the door. No time to check if she'd been seen. She needed to hide.

The walls were stacked with metal scaffolding three stories tall, each shelf cradling large transparent tubes capped at both ends.

Eli had warned her the tubes held people — but she hadn't expected them to look real. There were hundreds, maybe thousands of them.

Shaking off her shock, she climbed over the first tube and peered down. A pudgy old man, with a beer belly and smile lines, lay inside like he was napping, as if he might wake and see her.

Mouse shuddered and moved on, crawling across three more tubes before ducking into the gap between them.

Just in time.

The forklift had stopped, and two of the practitioners jogged in. The other two followed with a cart.

"Number three-thirty-nine," a woman read. "Toby Kettlewell. Thirty-six, five-seven, one-fifty-one, dark brown hair, brown eyes, attractive."

"Yep, he's a cutie. We've got a match."

Mouse listened as the machinery buzzed, scraped, and hummed. The selected tube settled onto the cart.

"Good morning, Mr. Kettlewell," one of them cooed. "Let's get you to your orientation."

As they rolled past, Mouse dared a peek at her phone. 12:16. Too close.

She willed them to hurry, but they moved at a relaxed pace.

She started counting — Boruta's advice.

Counting was supposed to keep the panic at bay.

It didn't.

Thirty-five feet away, the hangar doors began to close.

She kept counting. The lights flickered out.

12:17.

Counting, counting, counting.

12:18

Before nerves could take over, she turned on the phone's flashlight and began.

"Hi, there. I'm Mouse — Kenny's little girl. You're the warlock who's been following her, right? You're probably thinking this room is super creepy. It is. *Totally*. But the people in the tubes aren't real. They're simu...simu..." She wrinkled her nose, releasing a thin scream-hiss. "They're fake."

She took a breath.

"I came down here to explain, because there's a team of seers trying to stop bad things from happening. They knew you'd be here. And when you saw all these fake guys, they figured you'd think Kenny was doing something awful. She's not. She doesn't want to hurt anyone. She just wants to keep people safe."

A cold, stern voice replied — not out loud, but in her head: *Yet she sends a terrified child into a dark, hidden room to explain simulacra to her people's ancient enemy.*

Mouse straightened, even as she shivered. She wasn't terrified!

"Huh…you really are there," she squeaked, then firmed up her voice. "I wasn't sure you would be. Kenny doesn't know I'm here. Only the seers — and a few others. We had to do it this way because Eli's the Foresight. People know to trust seers, but they still don't listen. If the vision came from a kid? They definitely wouldn't listen."

She rechecked the time.

"The portal's closing in a few minutes. We have to be on the other side, or we can't get back — not even you. Not unless someone opens it again. No one can know we were here. If we don't make it, really, *really* bad things will happen. Please help."

Silence.

Then, a sigh.

What a mess. Hang on while I check the hall.

Kenny: September 3rd at Sullen Creek Farm

I paced the floor, uncertainty twisting in my gut. This was my fault. I should've been paying attention. I should have—

My phone buzzed. I nearly tripped over the rug, yanking it out of my pocket.

"Yes! Have you found them? Are they safe?"

"Not yet. I'm sorry."

The words echoed in my head before they sank in.

"What if they've been taken?" I whispered, my throat closing, trying to fend off the words.

"They couldn't have left the farm without us knowing. They're probably hiding — didn't want to evacuate with the other kids. Just focus on what needs to be done and trust us. We'll find them."

Easier said than done.

I exhaled. "Okay. Thanks, Colt. I know you—"

Footsteps pounded overhead.

"Kenny! Kenny! Milo's sick. You have to come! Please! He's sick and I don't know what to do!" Mouse shrieked.

"Milo collapsed!" Eli shouted, overlapping. "He's pale and his skin's really cold! You have to come!"

I looked up. The kids leaned over the rail, terror filling their eyes. It infected me.

"Colt, they're here. Milo's sick," I panted, running up the stairs. "Mouse, where is he?"

"Eli's room! Hurry!"

I'd searched the house, but they must not have been in there yet — they probably had been avoiding all adults, fearing evacuation. I was so grateful they'd been together. The three of them had been getting along better, but they still weren't exactly besties.

"They're in Eli's room. I have to go!"

I reached the loft seconds behind them, breathless and nauseous. A pale hand dangled past the foot of the bed.

"There," Eli pointed. "He wasn't feeling well all evening, and then he just sort of crumpled."

I stumbled past them, weaving through heavy tomes, star charts, and a pack of six-inch, hyper-realistic dinosaurs — my hands cold and trembling.

I could feel Milo's pulse — barely.

"He's alive," I croaked, already hoping for more. "He's in stasis. He hasn't been taking enough blood."

I looked up. "Eli, go to my room. Grab as many Elixir pods as you can carry. Mouse, keep his arms from flopping while I lift him."

They bolted into action. Eli thundered down the stairs like he was trying to bust them. Mouse and I got Milo onto the bed without adding a concussion to the mix.

"I'm going to breach his subconscious," I explained to Mouse with forced calm. "If I don't respond when Eli gets back, it's okay — don't panic. Break open a pod and trickle some into his mouth. Massage his throat like this — he needs to swallow or he could choke. Yes, that's it...feel that? Good. No more than three pods, or he'll throw it up. I'm going in. When Colt gets here, don't let them wake me."

Her nod was solemn. My brave girl.

I knelt beside the bed, took off my glasses, and set them on the nightstand. Gripping Milo's hand, I found one of the ley lines that tethered us. I fed my consciousness into it, slow and steady — drip by drip, until I slipped past the surface and into his mind.

It had been a long time since I'd done this. Hedge riding wasn't my strength. The first time—

Nope. Don't go there. Focus.

Milo? Can you hear me?

Nothing but a faint echo, a rippling tease.

I hadn't expected a response yet. I was still on the fringes. The skull might be small, but the psyche was vast — and protected. I pushed deeper.

Milo? Please, baby, answer me.

A barrier! It was smooth and glassy, faintly trembling with half-formed thoughts — his classes, catching lightning bugs with Mouse, rappelling with Lon, trying out new recipes with Derringer and me — innocent, bright memories. The trauma would be buried at the core.

I couldn't smash through, not without hurting him. We had time to be delicate — five to seven hours. I'd find a way in.

My fingers brushed the mental wall, searching for thin spots.

Milo, sweetheart, I'm here. I'm so sorry. I should've seen it. Mouse is beside herself. You have to come back to us.

The surface held. Impenetrable. Solid. Shame lived in walls like this — and fear. Guilt pooled in my chest. He'd been carrying so much pain. Not even Mouse knew how deep it went.

Please.

Let us keep him.

Milo, you're not alone. Please say something.

There was nothing but silence — thick, cold, numbing. Except…

A presence.

Not Milo.

It lingered out of sight, in the dark, watching. I considered bargaining — but stopped myself. Beings from the beyond were rarely kind. I wouldn't beg for Milo's life just for him to be kept as a curiosity, trapped in another realm.

I had to surface or I risked losing myself. Again.

I shuddered and yanked myself back into my body.

"Kenny?" Mouse's voice was small, pressed against my side like a cat curling close for warmth. "Did you find him?"

"No," I whispered, sliding an arm around her. "He's shielded too deeply."

I glanced around the room. Colt, Lon, Nore, Davy, Maggie, everyone had packed into every square inch — perched on the floor, crammed into corners, slumped against furniture like grief-struck statues.

"How long was I gone, Professor?"

"Three hours," Eli said, voice raw. He looked worse than I felt — sheet-white, eyes bloodshot, haunted. Guilt had hollowed out his face.

"Addison's given him another three pods," he added.

Addison confirmed with a grunt. "At this point, the problem isn't in his body; it's his mind. Get that back online, and we're golden."

I nodded, facing the truth: I wasn't going to reach him — not in time. But maybe someone else could.

"Mouse, sweetheart, I need to get up." I eased her off me. "I'm not giving up — we just need to try something different."

I stood, addressing the room. "I know you're worried, but I think the next attempt will go better in private. Please wait in the living room."

Too many eyes. Too much noise. If he agreed to help, I didn't need distractions — or arguments.

"Come on, Mighty Mouse," Colt murmured, holding out a hand.

She followed, shoulders trembling. If we lost Milo, it would destroy her.

I couldn't face that. I didn't know what the cost would be, but I'd find a way to pay it and keep my people safe.

Slowly, giving myself time to figure out what I was going to say, I made my way downstairs.

I crossed the hall to the guest room and knocked once. No response. I knocked again, harder.

After a pause, he grumbled, "Come in."

I slipped inside and shut the door behind me. The room was dark — until a lamp snapped on, making me jump.

Aiden lay on his stomach, leaving the bandages on his back undisturbed. His hair had been teased into outlandish shapes. One arm dragged back from the lamp, the other curled beneath him. As he turned to look over his shoulder, the sheet slid down, revealing far too much skin and a frankly distracting torso.

Um.

I looked away, self-conscious. When I finally glanced back, he was watching me — his good eye glittering, amused. His mouth tugged into a smirk.

Fantastic. He was laughing at me.

He rolled to sit up, dragging the sheet with him, but not nearly far enough. Another two inches of muscled chest was revealed. My face flushed hot.

That grin — wide and unapologetic — grew darker, sharper. Gleeful.

He was having way too much fun with this. And it was getting us nowhere.

"Thank you," I murmured, laying the groundwork, "for protecting me."

"You're welcome," he purred, tilting his head like a cat sizing up a twitching mouse. "Although I've since been informed that it was unnecessary — and spectacularly stupid — because every member of the Sheta Djew wears a personal ward. Also, that I'm fortunate the cocktail they pumped into me was only meant to knock you out and keep you weak."

My mouth twitched. Addison had a way with gratitude.

I nodded and held up the amulet. "I'd be dead a dozen times over without an aegis."

I took a breath.

"I have no right to ask you," I said, "but I need… another favor."

I bit the inside of my lip. My firstborn was off the table, but I was open to other suggestions. I'd train a dozen warlocks and their teams. I'd spend the rest of my life in Sanctuary. I braced for whatever it would cost.

"You protected me, too," he said, his gaze sharpening. He was reading me — pulse, posture, breath. Every flicker of tension in my body was catalogued and measured. I felt exposed. Shaky. A breath away from fainting.

"Tell me."

"Milo's in stasis," I whispered, closing my eyes. "I can't reach him."

The words cracked something open inside me. Tears spilled, cutting fast tracks down my cheeks. This was supposed to be a calculated negotiation, subtle and sharp. But desperation had me by the throat. My control was shot.

"I've tried," I said, barely audible. "I can't reach him! Please-"

"Take me to him."

I gasped and opened my eyes. He was standing, inches away, fully clothed.

We hadn't discussed terms. It didn't matter.

I led him into the hall, up the stairs.

Milo lay still, ghost-pale, barely tethered to this world. Aiden knelt at the edge of the bed and studied him.

He closed his eyes and drifted away.

I watched his face — eye twitches, little involuntary movements. His lashes trembled. The fine muscles around his mouth jerked once, then again.

And then...stillness. The wary vigilance he wore like armor slipped away. Something softer settled in.

I held my breath.

Please.

Minutes passed. Enough that time lost its meaning.

I stood, silent and tense, too restless to sit, too afraid to pace. The floor creaked if you breathed wrong in this house. I didn't dare risk disturbing Aiden.

Instead, I closed my eyes and whispered prayers — breath after breath, wordless, desperate.

Somewhere between one inhale and the next, it hit me — he'd trusted me.

Aiden trusted *me*.

This could've been a trap. He hadn't asked questions, hadn't bargained — just stepped into the fire without flinching. Whatever else he was — arrogant, smug, terrifying — he'd laid himself bare for someone he didn't owe.

The thought stunned me.

He shuddered.

I snapped to attention.

Aiden gasped, dragging air into his lungs like he'd been drowning. His body jerked as he came back. I turned to Milo.

Please.

Some color had returned to his cheeks, but he didn't move. His eyes remained shut. No twitch, no shift, no sign of life but the faintest breath.

Still gone.

A sob tore loose as my knees gave out. I slid down the wall and crumpled on the floor. I barely registered Aiden rising — until his voice reached me, a low, gentle rumble.

"Come on, buddy. Let's not make her suffer more than she already has."

My head jerked up.

He nudged Milo's shoulder with an almost reverent touch.

"Kay."

Milo's lip moved. His eyelids fluttered open — just enough to find me.

A broken noise burst from my throat, and the floodgates opened. I'd cried six times in nearly forty years, and now I was sobbing like a busted pipe.

"Sorry, Kenny," he whispered, his voice barely audible.

I shook my head fiercely. No. No blame. Whatever had gone wrong, we had missed it. I'd known he wasn't drinking enough; I thought he needed time to adjust. He had tried to keep it together. We were the ones who hadn't paid enough attention.

Aiden appeared in front of me like a conjuring trick and gripped my forearms, steady and strong. He hauled me upright.

I squeezed his arm. I couldn't speak. There weren't words big enough for what I owed him.

Then I stumbled to Milo's side, unable to look away from his face. I couldn't stop watching him breathe.

"I'm sorry, too," I whispered, hiccupping through my tears. "We'll do better. We'll talk. I'll be better. We'll figure it out, okay?"

"Yeah," he murmured.

I reached for Milo's hand, terrified he might vanish again.

His fingers curled around mine, weak but present. I was shaking now — my body catching up with reality.

He was okay. He was safe.

Soon, he'd be tossing frisbees for Mundy, pestering Eli with that relentless kindness, playing with Mouse, just...being a boy.

My boy.

Vertigo decided this was its big moment and punched through me. I locked my knees, fighting to stay upright.

"There are a lot of people who'll want to know you're awake," I said gently. "Is it okay if they come in?"

He nodded.

"Good… good." I kissed the back of his hand. "I'll be back soon, sweet boy."

Aiden had already opened the door, moving down a step to make space on the landing. I followed, my hand trailing from Milo's like I was leaving part of my soul behind.

"Thank you," I said, voice barely above a breath.

"You're welcome."

That was it.

No demands. No fine print. No deal struck. Just...grace. And patience.

"The others are waiting in the living room," I said. "Would you—"

"I'll tell them he's awake."

I bit my lip and nodded, but as he turned away—

"Aiden."

He paused, an eyebrow lifted.

When I hesitated, his gaze sharpened — amused again. Coward, it accused.

'Thanks' felt too threadbare. Too small to wrap around the gratitude threatening to break me. And maybe...maybe this was the last bit of plausible deniability I'd get.

"Aiden... I..."

I shook my head — and before I could stop myself, I pressed my palms to his chest, and kissed him.

Quick. Certain.

"Thank you."

His hand caught my elbow before I could retreat.

His expression flickered through shock, curiosity, the faintest flare of anger...and something else...

He crowded me, enough energy rolling off him to make the air crackle. He closed his eyes and leaned in, resting his forehead against mine.

I exhaled, my lids fluttering shut.

In that quiet space between breaths, I lived a thousand lives we'd never have. Couldn't have.

"Witch," he murmured.

"Warlock," I whispered back.

His hand slid up my back, cradling my neck, the other resting warm against my hip. And then his mouth met mine — hungry, deliberate, *real*.

Kenny: September 4th at Sullen Creek Farm

Nore found me curled in the window seat, hidden behind the living room drapes in the early morning hush.

She waved her phone at me. I had reported that Aiden Benilde was Special Agent John Dorrit. The Ghost. The infamous APA warlock. And that I had granted him a favor.

"You want to talk about it?" she asked.

I shook my head, but moved my feet so she could sit. Humming, she raised a sound barrier and nestled beside me.

I smirked. "Bit late for privacy, don't you think?"

"Can't make it any worse," she said. When I stayed quiet, she asked, "How'd you figure it out?"

"There were clues. I…didn't want to be right."

It took a second for my meaning to sink in. She choked on nothing, coughing hard. "Girl," she wheezed, "you don't make things easy on yourself. How did I miss—"

I snorted. "You didn't. We're not madly in love. I'm just mourning the possibility. In another life…maybe." I toasted her with my beer. "In a kinder, gentler world."

I thunked my head back against the wall. I'd been such a damn fool.

"My immediate need for a made vampire made it all click together. We had four suspects: Count Vitruvio, James Darrow, Tyson Groper, and Aiden Benilde. The Count is Veritas. He was investigating Weaver. Evy caught wind of his activities, staged an accident for his avatar, and here we are. His bite gave him away. He thinks he's a norm — he's going to have a hard time in the coming days."

"That explains the favors. Unnamed future favors aren't a currency you normally deal in."

"For good reason, it turns out."

"Is he a threat?"

"Oh, absolutely!" I laughed. "Which means we need to speed things up. I was hoping to make a few more edits, but...we should've sent it to the printer yesterday."

Nore hesitated. "So...we're really doing this?"

I looked out the window, searching the darkness for answers. "I don't know what else to do. We're barely hanging on. Either way, people will die. Either way, there might be another war."

I took a breath.

"We have to do something."

I didn't notice the silence until Spook jumped up between us, facing the room in Mel's classic, on-duty stance. Mel, two steps behind, took his position, chuffing.

Nore scratched the little cat's head. "What's up with Darrow?"

"Sampson Reid — a Therianthrope Council Marshal. Darrow was tracking Levisay. He found his scent — same as Naabek — down by the river. Levisay had been spying on us for days. Since we're an EMS, Reid parked himself on the edge of the property with a cursed pebble gnawing at him. He didn't expect it to take us so long to find him, but he didn't know about our extracurricular activities. He checked out a bit ago — back to the hunt. Offered to stay, but he's got his job. We've got ours."

"And Groper?"

"Tourist. We're a themed beer hotel. One had to come along at some point."

Nore snickered, then yawned. "How'd Ai — how'd Dorrit get into your rooms?"

"I've been wondering about that. It's not confirmed, but with his skillset? I think he used the pet tunnels. They're warded now."

"Good," she mumbled. "To bed! We might squeeze in a couple of hours. Carpe noctem."

Mel, Spook, and I followed her, though I didn't hold out much hope — definitely a murky yellow potion kind of morning.

"Mewr, mew mew mew! MEWR!"

Mischief met us at the top of the stairs. My heart stopped.

No. Not now.

But the fluffy cat didn't stop at my door. She pranced to...John Dorrit's.

"Mew mew mewr mewr!"

I looked at Nore, puzzled.

She shrugged.

I knocked gently.

No answer.

Nore nudged my elbow, pointing to a thin line of light beneath the door.

Hesitating, feeling like I was violating both his privacy and my innkeeper ethics, I cracked the door. Mischief darted past and inside.

John Dorrit had fallen asleep with the light on — a big spoon to Mystery's little spoon. Mischief jumped up and curled around her sister.

I shut the door, mind reeling.

"What was all that about?"

"I'm not sure," I said. "But it looks like Miss Anthropy has found herself a quest."

Kenny: September 4th at Sullen Creek Farm

It was strange, waking up in my bed, warm under the quilt Nore made me years ago, fur-babies nestled close — like it was any other day.

I moved on autopilot: sat up, texted Derringer to warn him I'd be using Edwician again, arranged my robe on the bed but didn't put it on, and checked my schedule as my brain spun through survival probabilities.

Several duels were on the calendar. I'd need to observe the apprentices' ley defense drills — ever since Count Vitruvio's arrival, they'd been using dueling practice as an excuse for cosplay. The Sepak Tractow team had practice. Two bartending classes were on deck, but Edra-Rae and Iosefina could cover those. Dryboat racing was tonight.

"Morning, Kenny," Derringer said gently, his concern evident as I stood beside the bed, staring at nothing.

"I want to invite Agent Dorrit and his team to a private breakfast in the dining room. We'll need extra wards, soundproofing, and the table extended. Nothing spicy — I don't want indigestion to be mistaken for poison."

"I'll handle it," he said.

I nodded and lay down on the rug — always left side down — before taking my medicine.

"But Moooom!"

"No arguments, Eli. This isn't easy for any of us, but it's necessary. I need to be able to focus on the Saturniidae needs; I can't do that if you're not safe."

Davy stood firm, hands on her hips, her sweet face set with rare resolve.

"Aunt Kenny, please—"

"Your mom's right," I said. "Our cover's blown."

"But the wards—"

"Wards aren't perfect. Relying too heavily on magic is how you get blindsided. Milo and Mouse will be with you, and Aunt Kodi's promised to spoil you rotten."

"You don't understand! I *have* to be here!" he shouted, hopping down from the counter and plowing through the back door.

Lou handed me a chai the size of my head as the last of my potion-induced sprightliness fizzled out. At this rate, I'd be begging Déjà for antidepressants by lunch.

Surely we were due a day off by now.

"Sorry about that," Davy sighed. "I'll talk to him."

"Let me," Boruta said, wheeling and prancing like he couldn't sit still. Watching him was making me queasy. "He's scared. Right now, there's nothing he can do to help, and that makes him feel helpless. And because you love him so much, he doesn't trust your judgment — he knows you'll choose his safety over everything."

Davy nodded and held the door open for him.

'Right now, there's nothing he can do to help.' Boruta's words echoed in my brain. Why was Eli so sure he had to stay? What had I missed? Or forgotten? Then it hit me — hard.

"Davy," I rasped. "The Bean Sídhe — they're always female, right?"

"Of course we are," she said, startled. "Why?"

"But sometimes…male children are born with special talents?"

"Every five to seven genera… Oh, dear Lord… You think Eli—? He almost never throws tantrums. Boruta... Phi Thale... You think Eli's—"

"Shit," Lou muttered, handing Davy a coffee — and the last three Madeleines.

The thunderous stomp of an agitated elephant came barreling down the hall.

"Kenny? Where's—" Arlo froze when he saw me. "You need to see something. Now."

Lou took my empty tumbler and handed me another monster chai. I hadn't realized I'd finished the first — or even started it.

"You're going to need this."

"You're an angel."

"I know."

Arlo ushered me into his office and spun his monitor so I could see. Four live feeds from inside the Mulberry flickered on-screen.

"Noelle just sent this," he said, pointing to the top right. "Watch here."

On screen, a set of electric doors slid open. Before the gap was even a foot wide, a supersized rodent in a fanny pack squeezed through and somersaulted out of frame like a fluffy ninja.

"That's the only clip they found of the beastie."

"Replay it," I said, scooting closer.

Arlo obliged.

"Freeze and zoom."

A few clicks later, the mouse filled the screen. Short, white-tipped tail. Badger-like gait. Cinnamon-pink fur. Soft, white belly. Mint green, pink, and white fanny pack.

I tilted my head, tapping a finger against my lips.

"Well?" Arlo prompted.

"Why did she need to meet him there?" I murmured.

I hadn't expected the warlock to stop investigating us — even after our liplock. He wanted something — either help, or the Covenant — and more information increased his odds. I was starting to think his request had been genuine…but a bit of friendly blackmail never hurt a negotiation.

If the idea left a bad taste in his mouth, he could always sweeten the deal — fulfill one of our many needs. Stabilizing a crumbling pocket plane took a lot of resources — machinery, crops, livestock, tools, generators, Teslin, ink, food, clothes, arms, manpower. We were desperate.

The scale of this incursion left me breathless.

He'd seen the simulacra. Who knew what he'd make of them? I'd been *criminally* stupid. I knew he could slip into my room undetected. I'd done nothing to close that hole in our security until this morning. It hadn't occurred to me that he might enter while injured and while I was inside the same room as the portal.

Thank the stars that — most— of the children were evacuated.

"What?"

Arlo's voice snapped me out of my self-recriminations.

"It's Mouse — our Mouse. See? Even in her second form, she's not fully grown. She's a therianthrope, and her shift is based on the grasshopper mouse. Predatory. They howl when they hunt. It suits her."

I leaned in, pointing. "That door was opened from this side. Look — you can see the keypad numbers depress as the code is entered. Some invisible entity let her out."

I took the mouse from Arlo and zoomed again. "As far as I know, we've only got one Ghost haunting us. So, did he recruit her or did she, and a baby foresight, recruit him?"

A chill settled between my shoulders.

"You wouldn't happen to know where the kids are, would you?"

I didn't believe Mouse would betray us — not knowingly. But if he'd tricked her? I'd…probably do nothing. Not with so much at stake. But we were going to have a serious conversation.

"Shit," Arlo muttered, which summed up my feelings exactly. "They're with Colt. By the rabbit warren."

"Call Noelle. I want every recording from last night reviewed, frame by frame. Same for any time the portal's been open in the last three days."

I rose, heart pounding.

"We have to assume he's seen everything. Every mission. Every secret. We're compromised — we just don't know how badly. But Mouse might."

September 4ᵗʰ in Parkville, Missouri

"Did we have a meeting scheduled, John? Has something happened?"

His head bobbed inside the orb, making the special agent seasick as O'Brien set aside his laptop.

"Yes, several things. Last night, four thugs tried to drug and kidnap Representative Jones outside the pub. They used dragon's teeth. I missed most of it — I'd been hit. Ridel later informed me that the assailants were well-equipped, remorseless, and chatty. He recognized one as Nocny Straznik."

"The Night Guard? Dietricksen's wolves…"

"The very same. When I regained consciousness — apparently ahead of schedule — I did a little reconnaissance. And I found something," Dorrit purred — signaling danger. "There's a portal in the Representative's quarters. She was busy alerting her cadre and didn't notice when I went through."

"YOU DID WHAT?"

"Save it. You're in this up to your gills, Darragh. The portal leads to a base crawling with personnel. I didn't see everything, but I recognized Novia Walls-ffrench and Emily Caterham — each either dead or asleep in transparent silicon tubes. A little girl, one of Caterham's runaways, appeared and warned me we had minutes before the portal closed. She'd known I would be there."

"How?"

"A seer told her. She said if we didn't hurry, we'd be trapped — and she was right. We escaped with seconds to spare. But her assumption that I'd be stuck puzzled me. The base had a skylit hallway, with sunshine pouring in, even though it was night here. I hadn't thought anything of it, considering the décor at Punk Bunks."

"You're saying…"

"I'm saying if Jones has — or is — a hedge witch powerful enough to create an intraplanar portal, why not one between planes?"

"But—"

"My theory was partially confirmed. Turns out Milo — Caterham's second foundling — has risen as a vampire but fell into stasis after refusing blood, unbeknownst to his caretakers. Jones tried to reach his subconscious and failed. She came to me — she knew what I was. Darragh, in that position, what would you do?"

"To rouse a strigoi child? Establish a blood connection."

"Jones didn't trade blood. She rode the lines. So, I did the same. I don't think she realized she gave herself away — or she no longer cares."

"So—"

"And now we come to the interesting bit. Mouse told me that Eli is the foresight who guided her. He's been working with another seer. This morning, that same boy came to me, demanding I contact you, Darragh — adamant, in fact. Imagine my surprise that an eight-year-old from a farm in Missouri knew who you were — foresight or not. He told me that Jones is evacuating the Sheta Djew's children. He'll be leaving soon, along with Milo and Mouse. He insisted that I pass along a message."

"Ah."

Dorrit let out a humorless chuckle.

"Indeed. His message was — and I quote — 'She knows. We're shifting to Plan E two-point-oh.' What the hell does that mean?"

Crickets.

"What did he mean, Darragh?"

"It means Jones knows he's a foresight. It will affect their interactions, but at this point, we're improvising anyway. We've entered a blind spot — neither of us has seen what's next. Eli doesn't understand what that means yet. It will be difficult for him because he is talented, if a bit literal. He'll adapt. John? John? Are you there?"

Dorrit sighed and softly said, "I'm still here. But I'm done. When this is over — and Annie's safe — I'm done."

"I don't follow."

"This is my last case, Darragh. I'm retiring. Done. Finished. Finis. We've reached the thrilling conclusion of my illustrious career."

"John, I... I didn't see that coming. Out of curiosity — this doesn't have anything to do with Representative Jones, does it?"

"It has everything to do with her. With her people. With the tactics we're forced to adopt — spying on decent people, arresting them for a single mistake. I don't condone using children. I don't enjoy being used — though you'll claim it's necessary. It can't be. There has to be a better way. Someone has to police the ley lines, but...not me. Not anymore. I need to get out before I do something I can't take back."

"John-"

"Look after my team for me...please."

"Of course. Please believe—"

"We're invited to breakfast," Dorrit cut in.

"I thought breakfast was included in the fee. Do we need to adjust your expense account? Serrecold will approve it. I won't mention your plans, in case he throws a hissy fit."

"The team, including you, is invited to a private breakfast. Jones wants to come to terms. We can set the seer's orb on the table so—"

"What time?"

After a beat of silence, Dorrit curtly replied, "Eight."

"I'll be there."

Kenny: September 4th at Sullen Creek Farm

"I can't! I'm sorry! I made a Solemn Vow of Secrecy!" Mouse wailed —
not crying, just shrieking at air-rending levels. "Please don't make me tell! I
don't want to perish a thousand times in a thousand ways! Please don't be
angry!"

Somewhere behind me, Colt snorted.

After checking to make sure my ears weren't bleeding — and giving
myself a moment to think — I switched tactics.

"There is no Solemn Vow of Secrecy. There's binding magic. It
wouldn't kill you, but it would stop you from speaking. So, here's what we'll
do: I'll guess, and if I'm wrong, shake your head. I promise, it won't kill you.
Sound good?"

Mouse nodded, jaw set.

I sighed. A part of her still believed whatever crap Eli had fed her. The
Professor and I were going to have words. I couldn't remember ever being
angry with him before — but this vow nonsense was a shit move.

"Eli is a foresight."

Mouse didn't move.

"He confided in you and Milo."

She squeezed her eyes shut; a vein pulsed at her temple. No head shake.

"Probably others too. Remember to breathe."

She'd be great at Red Light, Green Light — so long as she didn't pass
out.

"Eli explained how to enter the portal in my workroom and sent you to
meet Aiden Benilde."

Her brows twitched at the name, but she didn't deny it. So, she knew he
was the warlock. This is where things started to get shaky.

"Because Aiden needed to be available to save Milo."

Tears welled — silent and guilt-ridden — but she didn't speak.

Yes. Eli and I were absolutely going to talk.

"Milo stopped taking blood because Eli asked him to. For the plan?"

"It wasn't that," Mouse burst out. "Not just that. Milo already wasn't taking enough. It horrifies him. Once the thirst fades…he's tried to throw it up. Déjà said he must realize he can't live without it and that he does want to live. She said he needs therapy and that you needed to know his mental state. But Eli said if you were told, you'd be killed. And Boruta said doing what we did might save you both. Everything depended on whether you'd trust Aiden."

Déjà knew. She knew and hadn't told me.

They'd put my life ahead of Milo's.

The enormity of it… My lungs tightened. My hands went cold. Despite all my knowledge, training, and power, I felt utterly impotent.

"Has he decided to live?" My voice sounded almost casual.

"We think so. He believes he did something heroic. Please don't tell him otherwise."

He had done something heroic — utterly wrong, ill-advised, stupid, horrific, and maddening, but still heroic. How could Déjà have let him?

"All right," I murmured, biting my tongue. "I'm not happy about this. This conversation isn't over — but it'll have to wait. For future reference, I need to know when you, Milo, or Eli are struggling. Big or small. Life-threatening or not."

"That sounds like you're mad."

"I'm not mad. I'm…concerned." I was bloody livid. "I believe you acted with the best intentions. Eli is a young seer — that's a terrible burden. Boruta should have known better. Déjà did know better. She let fear blind her. We're all susceptible."

"We did it for you. Please trust us."

Inside my chest, something broke and shifted. Every breath hurt.

"I do, sweetheart. But I can't trust Boruta or Déjà. I'm supposed to be your guardian — not the one you guard." I hugged her tight. "I love you. I love Milo and Eli. We'll get past this. We'll figure out when to follow Eli's lead — and when I need to be told the truth, no matter the cost. It might be a steep learning curve, but we'll get there. Okay?"

"'Kay," she mumbled into my shirt.

"You three behave for the Sous la Colline. You're representing the cadre — your choices reflect on all of us. If Kodi tries to gross you out with her glamour, tell her she's got nothing on my baby vamp lessons. Then take a picture of her face and send it to me. I'll need every laugh I can get."

"I don't want to leave. This is our home."

Ohhhh. She was good.

I led her to a bench and sat with her.

"We get attached to places. They become symbols of safety, love, comfort — but they're not home. Home exists in the people you love. You and Milo, Eli and Nore, Lon, Oscar, Davy — all of you are my home. And we're yours. I won't promise that nothing bad will happen. I can't. But if you're safe, then home is safe."

Mouse, sentimentalist that she was, rolled her eyes — but hugged me again.

"Don't do anything stupid while we're gone," she barked.

No promises. Stupid was my middle name.

"It's time," Davy murmured, marching up with a bitter but resigned Professor at her side. Milo trailed behind them — quiet as usual, but more accepting of the evacuation.

Although...I no longer trusted my judgment when it came to him.

With their familiars leading the parade, we made our way back to the house and through the portal in my room. Davy, Lou, Colt, and I brought up the rear with their luggage.

"'Bout time," Oscar grunted. Arms crossed, he leaned against the wall between a carved chrysoprase corridor and another full of floating Holi dust in vibrant colors. Just seeing him settled something in me. He was my rock.

"We have a problem."

Of course we did.

I'd hoped to get the kids settled in New Orleans first. After the last few days, it felt more important than ever — but the universe had other ideas.

Kodi appeared down a side hall that resembled a ravine carved through red-violet stone. Her hair, currently pale blue, was Viking-braided. Crimson, cat-slit eyes and elf ears topped off a shredded Red Caps concert tee, buckle-covered black jeggings, and army boots. Her river otter familiar, Arcane Murphy, waddled along behind in a spiked collar.

Mouse instantly fell in love — with Murphy. Babbage was scandalized. Murphy was smug.

Oscar shifted behind me while Kodi's crew gathered my kids, their animals, and their accessories.

Milo hugged me first. When I gave him an extra squeeze, he offered a soft smile.

"I'm okay. I'll be okay. Davy says the world's falling apart, and you need to deal with that. Don't worry about us. We'll be waiting."

I kissed his forehead, blinking fast. Lately, tears came too easily.

"Easier said than done. I love you, kiddo. Look after yourself — and the others. We need you."

Eli gave his mom a squeeze, then turned to me. "Good luck. Don't die."

"I'll try, Professor. And don't let the visions drag you down. You're not responsible for saving us."

He nodded, though I doubted my words stuck.

Mouse gave Murphy one last pat before cuddling me quickly.

Kodi grinned. "Don't worry! We've got fun stuff planned — the Insectarium, beignets, airboats, gators!"

"She won't let an alligator eat them," Oscar growled when Davy's eyes went wide. He tapped my arm. "Come on. Time's running out."

He pulled me down a lesser-used corridor — polished marble floor, millwork, and portraits of pompous blokes in wigs. Geometric Art Deco chandeliers softened the stuffy vibe. We stepped through a portal into a bedroom that reeked of tasteful wealth: layered neutrals, antique craftsmanship, soft light, and the scent of French lavender. The sounds of a string quartet spilled from hidden speakers.

"Ah, there you are, Kenny," said Judge Mara Dietricksen, closing a book and setting it on a marble-topped table beside her chair. A cream blanket lay across her lap; an IV stand loomed on her right. "You'll have to forgive me for not rising. I'm a little under the weather, and we haven't time for formalities."

"Ten hours ago, the APA," Oscar said, nodding to a black man in a crisp white Oxford near the door, "received an anonymous tip about an unregistered vampire nest in West Pullman. They raided it and found fifteen prisoners — each one known in the Community, none reported missing. They also uncovered precast spell materials and seven unregistered vampires."

"Which explains why we hadn't heard from you for seven days," I said, noting the shadows under Mara's eyes, the bandages on her neck, and a fragile air I'd never seen in her before. Our 'Source' had been through the ringer.

"They were compelled," my défteros added, voice rough as he checked the IV. "Helots."

Red filled my vision — hot, furious crimson. This was the life we'd chosen. It wasn't easy or kind, but it was better than doing nothing. Mara had made the same calculation; she wouldn't thank me for pitying her.

She rolled her eyes, more annoyed with herself than anything.

"I'm not dead, dying, or bleeding, so stop fussing, Oscar. I don't need more pain meds. They make me lightheaded. Kenny, this wasn't some hovel full of feral blood junkies. They indulged," she said, gesturing to her neck, "but they were organized. No infighting, clear agenda, and plenty of money. They were careful. I only saw one of them, and I never heard any names."

"The Brána Tieňov?" I asked, uneasy. The Boston-based cadre specialized in intel — knowing everything about everyone and keeping the Covenant two steps ahead.

"They knew nothing," Oscar snarled. "These vamps sent their victims to work every day with precise instructions. No red flags. No odd behavior. No reports. Because of that, Lomax refused to activate a sleeper. 'No news was good news.' Then Judge Havelock barred Senator Chmiel from attending Brenda Budny's trial. Mara had been told to ease the way, but couldn't. The trial went ahead. Budny was found guilty of warped practices and chose execution over Sanctuary. Rep. Lilly followed protocol. After that disaster, Lomax tried to reach Mara. The neighbors said she was on vacation."

The scorecard in my head marked down the failure. Knowing we couldn't save everyone didn't make it easier.

"Why you? What did they want?"

Mara closed her eyes, bowed her head. "The Nocny Straznik and my Hounds. What else? The blocks you put in place," she tapped her temple, "held — for a while. Then they brought in this humming black box with blue lights. I don't know what it was. I'm sorry."

"Don't agitate yourself," Oscar muttered.

Her head snapped up, eyes blazing.

"I'm not agitated. I'm pissed! If my stool sample came back clean and you're out of tests, then sit down. Let me breathe," Mara hissed, swatting at him. "It's bad, but it could be worse. They never linked me to the Covenant, and if they hadn't targeted me, we'd never have found them. The Guard believes you're a traitor, Kenny — or they never would've attacked you. Under the vampire's influence...I told them you were."

She looked ready to tear her enemies apart with her fangs.

"Whoever did this — don't underestimate them. They will learn to control the Hounds. In days, if we're lucky, but don't count on more than a few hours. They're fixated on you, Kenny. If the Hounds have been released, they will find you."

I smiled and locked my knees, trying to hide the shaking.

Part of Colt's training would involve learning how to cope with and protect himself from magic burn — the sensation of having your native energy forcefully yanked out of your reservoir. It was painful and could lead to death or a vegetative state.

The Hounds, the last remnant of the original Wild Hunt, were devastating weapons for numerous reasons: they always caught their prey; their construction was strange and couldn't be unraveled; their weapons always struck true; if their master could wield the ley lines, they could, as well; and, although they sometimes ate their victims, they did not require food or sleep. The Hounds *did* require energy. They siphoned it from whatever source their master found acceptable. Practitioners were an ideal food source; those who practiced ley manipulations had larger reservoirs. The inflicted magic burn on steroids.

"You must run," Oscar barked. "Now."

I shook my head. "They tried to kidnap me, not kill me."

"You can't count on that."

"She's right," Mara said sharply. "Whoever this is, he's patient and smart. He hid an infected helot among the victims, tagged a siren, and sent Levisay with constructs. He's testing her. The question is, to what purpose."

Mara grabbed my wrist. Her eyes were fierce.

"The Hounds aren't limited to this plane. If you run, they'll follow. The Mulberry isn't safe. Wenen isn't safe. They'll flatten everything between them and their target. You're strong, but you can't beat this — go around, not through. Find the oldest, wiliest son of a bitch you can to wrangle with their new master and set a trap. Not Phi Thale."

"No!" I agreed with vehemence. "He's a sociopath."

Mara snorted. "He isn't; he just likes to pretend — keeps those he cares about at a safe distance. Not him because he's not an ancient. The mind we're dealing with would steamroll him."

If I lived through this, I would take a two-week vacation with my phone turned off. It would never happen — but I could dream.

"Yeah, that would be…bad. Thank you, Mara. For everything."

"Gaia…" Her voice broke off. Gaia didn't get along so well with her mother — Mara made Padŭ look like an angel — but she still loved her daughter.

"We'll do everything we can to keep Gaia, Dave, and Lizzie safe."

She nodded and let go of my wrist.

Oscar and I left the room.

"She's doing well, considering what she endured, but it'll be weeks before her mind fully recovers."

I nodded, contemplating our next steps. There weren't a lot of options.

"Whatever you're thinking — don't," he warned.

I checked my phone. "We're having breakfast with the warlock and his friends. I need you there."

"Why?"

"Because I can't escape or use magic. I'm effectively hamstrung. We need to make a deal before I lose all negotiating power."

He nodded and waved me on.

Kenny: September 4th at Sullen Creek Farm

"Hollandaise...sawmill gravy...red and green salsa...sour cream..."

"Check. We are fully prepared to make every variety of Benny ever invented," Derringer said, his accent thick with pride.

"Plus any spontaneous creations, should the muse strike," Maggie muttered, pouring herself orange juice. "Why are we trying to impress them? Will it make them less likely to enslave us for all eternity?"

"Is it too much?" I gulped, eyeing the long line of copper chafing dishes piled with meats, eggs, potatoes, sweet and savory breads, sauce boats, fruit bowls, and an army of drinks on the sideboard. I didn't know if all of John's team kept daylight hours, so we'd rolled out the bar cart, too.

"It is too much, isn't it?"

Why had I decided on breakfast? A ten o'clock meeting and a pot of coffee would have done. Hosting always gave me a panic attack.

"Now, see what you've done," Derringer scolded Mags. "It's just right, Kenny. Would you do less for any other guests? No? Then we're fine."

I nodded, somewhat reassured...right up until Lon poked his head into the dining room and whispered, "They're here."

My lungs weren't working. They alternated between exploding and imploding, like I was twenty-three miles into a marathon, having an asthma attack. And my right eye was doing that weird thing where I could see my pulse.

"This isn't a cotillion, Weaver," Derringer murmured sharply, snapping me out of my trance. "This is just another mission. Your people need rescuing. You've done this before. You'll do it now."

"What he said," Maggie added, sampling the breakfast potatoes and burning her fingers.

I hoped she'd washed her hands — Maggie'd been fertilizing the gardens, and our fertilizer came courtesy of the horses.

I took a deep breath. Then another. "I've got this," I agreed.

Nore sauntered in first, leading John Dorrit — honey-blond hair braided at the nape, dressed in a fusion of leather-clad biker and modern-day knight, ready to slay dragons...or practitioners. Six similarly outfitted hardasses followed, expressions ranging from curious to stone cold. Sweet of them to dress up.

Agent Dorrit's hard eyes landed on my lacy mint-green tank, and his mouth curled into a first-class smirk. When he cocked an eyebrow, I was sorely tempted to start a one-sided food fight. So, I had a crush on the bogeyman — so what?

"Shall we eat first or talk?" I asked. "Or are we skipping negotiations and jumping straight to the epic battle sequence?"

"Door two, please," muttered Angie Donahue.

Of course, she was here, already pouring gas on the fire. At least we were past the simpering smiles stage of our relationship.

"We're waiting for one of our party to arrive...although that shouldn't prevent anyone from eating. Perhaps introductions first," the warlock said, nodding to a tall, angular man with short, black hair and an air of calm competence. "Senior Special Agent Ridel."

Ridel shook my hand.

"Senior Special Agent MacDonnell, you already know."

Van Helsing's redheaded Celtic fantasy glared at me.

Special Agent Sarduy was a fierce Latina with dark, jaded eyes. Hatter had an olive complexion, sleepy amber eyes, and luxurious curls. Blake, with his dark hair and mischievous smile, gave me a friendly wave.

In turn, I introduced my people — more out of politeness than necessity. I mean, they had spied on us.

After the requisite number of suspicious glances were exchanged, a line for food eventually formed — Oscar leading with an eye roll when MacDonnell muttered something about the smell of bitter almonds. Ten minutes later, we were seated: agents on one side, Sheta Djew on the other. Thanks to Oscar, Ridel, Davy, and Blake, there was even some conversation — stilted and awkward, but sentences were exchanged.

It was a relief when the wards popped, admitting a newcomer. For a split second, Ridel's voice grew distant, and the dining room dimmed with malevolent shadows. Foreboding whispers tickled my ear, unseen eyes causing the hairs on my neck to prickle. I blinked, and everything was back to rainbows and sunshine.

I'd hoped John's last guest wouldn't register as a threat. Maybe they'd be a big-eyed, hemophobe retrocog who weighed a hundred and ten pounds soaking wet. You never knew.

"I believe your missing teammate has arrived," I announced, rising.

John grimaced, put his fork down, and joined me. We'd made it halfway down the hall when the front door flew open with an eerie creak, revealing a tall, masculine silhouette. The figure seemed motionless, but the door slammed shut behind him. My eyes failed to track his movements — he glided out of the shadows like a ghost or...

The theme from *Jaws* hammered in my head.

Shadows fell away like theater curtains, shattering my expectations.

The newcomer had careless black curls peeking from beneath a white fedora, merry blue eyes, and a half-bashful, half-infectious grin. He wore a Hawaiian shirt covered in tipsy flamingos, cargo shorts that showcased a spectacular sunburn, and flip-flops. Around his neck hung a white and green lei, and draped over his candy-apple-red arms were more in tropical hues. A heavy, syrupy floral scent wafted over me.

"Aloha," the ghost of vacations past sang, flinging his arms wide.

I scrambled for a rational response.

"A...aloha. Would you care for some aloe vera?"

Just looking at his lobster-red legs made my skin burn.

"A pleasure to meet you, Representative Jones. Have a lei," the man caroled, ignoring my offer and tossing a garland of yellow plumeria over my head. "And one for you, John!"

He scuttled past us into the dining room as my fingers brushed the petals.

"Who was that?" I murmured, half-expecting him to bounce back out.

"Darragh O'Brien, Chairman of the Union of Seers," Dorrit replied, voice carefully flat.

Ah. Seer fingerprints were all over this mess.

"Is he...um...has he...uh..."

Was there a polite way to ask someone if their friend was nuttier than squirrel poo?

Dorrit's mouth twitched, intuiting my question.

"Brace yourself."

With a light touch on my shoulder, he nodded toward the dining room. We entered as the famed farsight handed out the last of his leis.

"Yes, Sarduy, you have to wear it. We're all friends here, risking our lives in the name of revolution, and we should match. Unity! Here you are, Blake! See, Blake doesn't mind. And one for you! Might that be a bicorn motorcyclist on your shirt? Smashing!"

"May I present Chairman Darragh O'Brien of the Union of Seers?" I murmured to my shell-shocked colleagues.

The silence had a particular quality to it — one that promised to be long and awkward, but I'd underestimated the Chairman.

"Thank you for inviting me! Your home is most extraordinary!" he remarked before frowning at the others with mock consternation. "Now, I know you're all expecting the usual dog-and-pony show — sneers, passive-aggressive pronouncements, and eventually, but only when pushed, reaching some kind of accord. I've drawn up a contract, and if you'll all take a look-see, I'm certain we can speed things along."

He conjured a stack of leather-bound portfolios from thin air, confirming his Ipseitatum Dualis status with a single flourish, and handed them around.

"I believe I've covered everything — the Hounds are hunting Representative Jones."

"*They're what?*" John demanded, glaring at me over the table.

I shrugged and mouthed, 'recent development', as the Chairman continued.

"And she will require protection while the Sheta Djew lay a trap to catch the villain responsible; our darling Annie and the rest of the team must learn how not to manipulate the ley lines by accident…say, within three months? The Sheta Djew require a guarantee of secrecy, early warnings if they come under scrutiny again, and a workable cover should Dorrit be called to investigate them a second time; and we need to establish a pipeline to funnel exonerated practitioners to the Sheta Djew for training. Any questions?"

Davy hesitantly raised her hand, looking unnaturally stiff.

"Yes, Ms. Moran…oh, just a moment! I nearly forgot! That's for you," he trilled, presenting her with a wax-sealed envelope. My guess was it wasn't from Hogwarts.

For a moment, I saw Elena Romero's horrified face instead of Davy's. Her eyes narrowed, a reckless light snapping into them. I held my breath. If the Union had pegged Eli as a seer — if they tried to claim him — our dining room would be ground zero for the fifth preternatural war, and gentle Davy would strike the first blow.

Everyone watched as she broke the seal. Her eyes traced across the page, a furrow etched between her brows. Three lines down, a tulip-pink flush warmed her pale cheeks. By the end, a small smile curved her lips.

"That is acceptable," she murmured, twinkling at O'Brien like he was her new favorite person.

"What is?" I demanded.

"This letter certifies Eli as a foresight squire. Rather than inconvenience us with the usual formalities, the Chairman recommends that Eli train under Boruta and that both be assigned to the Sheta Djew for at least ten years. There are visions on record regarding our cadre — some two centuries old — and the Union feels a foresight spaeman and squire on-site is warranted. I approve this arrangement."

I sank into my chair as my insides turned to jelly.

Boruta was a Union Spaeman — a top-tier seer. I'd naively thought Eli had called a familiar and drawn a pooka, of all things. Calling was simple — a sort of ley beacon we taught our children. The bat-signal for practitioners. But the daimon had been assigned to him all along... It felt like the plate-railed walls were closing in on us.

"That's one less thing to worry about," observed Oscar, as chipper as I'd ever seen him.

Did he not grasp the implications? O'Brien probably knew more about us than we did! The Union was centuries ahead in the timeline.

"And another," murmured John, signing O'Brien's proposed contract. Catching Agent MacDonnell's look, he smiled. "Someone has to go first."

It didn't make sense. Why had O'Brien allowed John to investigate us? We might have killed him! Unless he already knew we wouldn't...but no seer was infallible. I wanted to grill that lobster for answers, but giving dear, darling Annie more ammo to sabotage this alliance was out of the question.

I glanced at Nore, who nodded — she found the terms, the binding magic, and the legalese acceptable. I read my copy twice. Everything was precisely as O'Brien had said, without a single flourish or word-dense quagmire to hide behind.

It felt too good to be true.

O'Brien was trouble — a world-famous, ley-trained seer who had, somehow, retained a semblance of sanity. Seers were compelled to help those in their visions, but compulsion was a slippery thing — shaped by their individual morals, perceptions, and knowledge.

The Chairman wouldn't have survived this long if he were easily swayed by propaganda or his vices. He would have his own agenda. Unfortunately...he seemed tied to our best shot at survival.

"Any objections or concerns?" I asked. I was going to regret this.

"Speak now or forever hold your peace," O'Brien sang, twirling when he spotted the orange-glazed sweet rolls. I'd added them for John. He seemed partial to them.

A strange notion sparked in my head as I watched the seer load a plate. I didn't know where it came from or why...but I couldn't dismiss it. I studied the back of O'Brien's head, then the warlock. I had to be imagining things.

One by one, the others signed in silence. I followed suit and passed my folder to Lizzy.

While the notary worked her magic, the Chairman settled at one end of the table, somehow balancing three plates and two bottles of Beerista. He held his fork in his left hand, prongs down. Not odd, exactly, but old-world. He had to be old.

"For weeks now, this lot has been regaling me with tales of Sullen Creek's food and legendary brews. At last, it's my turn to glut!"

His evil cackle was convincing...and a little too much like my own for comfort.

"Cousins?" The question burst out of me. Looking between them, the notion seemed more ludicrous than ever.

John choked on his hot chocolate, spitting some into his napkin. Ridel thumped him on the back.

O'Brien beamed at me as if I'd paid him a tremendous compliment.

"No," John rasped. "We are not cousins."

Relief washed through me — until the seer spoke.

"Cousins? No," O'Brien murmured, unwinding his sweet roll, smearing it with extra glaze, then rerolling it.

There was no inflection to those two words, but dread settled over me. It shouldn't matter... It wasn't like there was any real future there. I was being ridiculous — but they did eat sweet rolls the same way.

Following the Chairman's example, we resumed our meal. Conversation dropped to a murmur until Lizzy looked up from her work and announced, "We're set!"

Something tight in my shoulders eased. The general mood loosened.

"Too often," O'Brien began, unexpectedly somber, "people forget that history isn't always written in courtrooms and government offices. It's forged in dining rooms, coffeehouses, gyms, backyards, and everywhere in between. When people accept their differences and take pride in their commonalities, the foundation for change — for peace — is already laid. We're fortunate to live in a time that celebrates liberty; fortunate to have found like-minded allies in unlikely places. May I propose a toast — to sharing such great good fortune with the rest of the world."

Despite my distrust, a surreal hope threaded through my fears. I raised my mug, meeting John's intent gaze across the table. An embarrassed grin escaped me. *Change.* There was magic in that word — chaos, destruction, creation, possibility, order — all in one syllable.

Maybe...one day...

Maybe.

"John suggested something fabulous the other day," O'Brien added, exuberant again. "When things calm down, we should all go camping! A float trip! Ice chests, beer, cooking over a campfire. A real bonding experience! Thoughts?"

Maggie snorted.

"You're invited to my wedding."

"How kind!"

Kenny: September 4ᵗʰ on the Mulberry

Dorrit shook his head in frustration as he scanned me head-to-toe, twirling his finger for me to turn. Self-conscious, I obeyed, hands behind my head.

We'd moved to a Mulberry conference room — partly to interrupt my magical trail, partly for privacy.

"No taser," Dorrit concluded, narrowing his gaze as if x-raying me. "It wouldn't do anything against the Hounds anyway."

"Precast spells are more versatile," Lon put in.

"And where is she supposed to keep them? Stuffed down her socks?" MacDonnell asked dryly.

Everyone glanced down at my boots.

"Yes, I'm wearing socks," I muttered. "Boots without socks are gross."

"MacDonnell's right," Dorrit said. "It has to look like you were caught unaware. They'll search you, so we'll let them find something — cellphone, keys, wallet — but not everything. Your clothes are both a boon and a hindrance. A tank top won't hide much, so they may ignore it. The jeans and boots, though…"

"Or we could use ether pockets."

I tapped the white-capped wave tattooed on my bicep. A cursed trident shimmered into existence, radiating dark power.

The APA agents gaped.

"Right…hedge magic," Dorrit muttered. "How many pockets, and what can they hold?"

"Mags, chuck me our inventory."

I caught the three-ring binder Maggie obligingly hurled at me and set the beast on the table. Pocket after pocket was stuffed full of press-on tattoos.

"To answer your question, more than will fit on my body. Bigger or more complex tats hold more. My bumblebee could store ten precast spells, one enchanted weapon, or an AR-15 with six mags. Ley-infused items have more…mass, for lack of a better word."

"Forget camping. Let's get matching tats," O'Brien said, eyeing a collection of Norse runes.

Dorrit ignored him. "Okay. Ridel, Lon — grab every weapon Kenny's proficient with. Pretend she has to hold Helm's Deep solo. MacDonnell, Nore — survival gear, like she's trekking unknown terrain for three months. Make that rescuing ten others and their familiars. Oscar — first aid. Sarduy, Maggie — precast spells, potions, snares, whatever slows them down. Davy—personal stuff, backup glasses, meds, clothes. Something to pass the time — puzzles, fidget toys, pens. Armand — three months' food and water. Hatter, Arlo, Evy — electronics, drones, trackers, the works. Everyone else — fill in the gaps."

A manic gleam lit Dorrit's eyes as he turned back.

"Kenny — right-handed weapons on the left arm, left-handed on the right. Non-essentials go where your clothes cover them. You should be able to grab water, food, and a knife even if you're bound. Pick images you associate with the contents."

Over the next hour, gear was sorted by priority, each item assigned a tattoo and a body part. Lily pads circled my left ankle. A mandala bloomed across my right shoulder. Bees buzzed behind my ear, a four-masted ship sailed up my ribs, a Honda NSR500 engine wrapped my calf, and a ragged tear on my back revealed copper clockwork beneath my skin.

"Not too high," Davy warned. "They'll know your body art. Anything new or obvious is a risk."

"The bees?" I asked.

"They're fine. The mandala...maybe not."

O'Brien rose from his chair, a wistful look on his face.

"I hate to be a party pooper, but I need to be back at the Union in an hour. I'll try to catch up later." He pouted at his watch. "Could someone guide me to the right portal?"

"Agreed." Dorrit nodded to Davy, who escorted the Chairman to the door. "What's left?"

"Uh, Chairman, do you know any Ancients who would be willing to help? I was told we'd need one to recover the Hounds."

It was as if all emotion had been wiped off his face — the animation, the joie de vivre — it was gone in an instant as he pondered the matter.

"I'll see what I can do."

It wasn't the answer I'd hoped for, but I smiled in thanks, regardless. I'd take whatever help he found.

"Amulets, enchanted jewelry, decoy phone and keys, wallet," Nore read, clipboard in hand. "Arlo's prepped the bridge, Ridel and Lon are readying the teams."

Dorrit closed his eyes and ran his hands slowly down my arms, the roughness of his callused fingers making me shiver.

"The tattoos feel inert," he said, smiling at my reaction. At some point, the tables would turn, and I'd be smiling smugly at his obvious infatuation. "No one below a level six sensitive will notice. Hanging in there?"

"I'm fine. Just ready to do something."

"Good. It's showtime."

Sullen Creek Brewpub in Parkville, Missouri

"We need more maraschino cherries," faux-Davy chirped, "and olives!"

"On it," I called back, pushing through the swinging door into faux-Armand's domain. The kitchen was an orchestra of motion and sound — risotto plated with a flourish, bread baskets steaming, steaks searing, sweet potato fries hissing in oil, mixers and machines setting the rhythm.

"Crazy busy for a Monday," faux-Armand shouted as I passed.

"Sure is. Another bachelorette party came in — Jane Austen theme. Full Regency dresses, carriage, and all. You should have seen them coming down the hill! They want their beer in champagne flutes."

"And that last group was zombies! Guess it's Bride and Prejudice and Zombies tonight," faux-Jake hooted, waggling his brows. "Get it?"

Faux-Armand mouthed 'wow' and shook his head. "Lame, man. Really lame."

"I thought it was funny," faux-Iosefina soothed.

Laughing, I pushed back into the dining room. The roar of chatter and clinking glasses hit like a battering ram. I dumped my haul on the bar with a sigh.

Seven hours had passed since the contracts were signed, and we'd stuck to our routine — morning meetings, ley drills with Colt in the afternoon. But around three, faux-Caro, our manager, called: even with all the doppelgangers, the brewpub was short-staffed. Apprentices and teens — our usual bussers and dishwashers — had no doubles, and the pub was swamped. I showed up fifteen minutes later, sleeves rolled.

"Here we go," I announced, unloading cherries, olives, tubs of orange slices, and an industrial-sized box of Pop Rocks.

"You're a lifesaver," faux-Davy murmured. "Lou! Your drinks!"

"'Scuse me," slurred a petite blonde in a white Regency gown and pale blue shawl, sash reading *Bride*. She clung to the bar for balance. "Are you the one to talk to? Ladies' is out of toilet paper."

"Yes, I'll handle it. Sorry — we didn't expect this crowd."

She gave an indistinct burble and a thumbs-up.

"Maybe cut them off," I murmured to faux-Davy as the woman staggered back to her table, nearly tripping over her satin slippers.

"I did — half an hour ago. Even gave them two fig and prosciutto pizzas on the house to soak up the sauce. They must all have bottomless hip flasks tucked in their garters."

I grimaced and headed down the back hall to the supply closet. Fumbling with the keys, I finally found the right one — and was shoved hard from behind.

The light flicked on. A dark-skinned beauty in a rose-pink empire gown, sash in a darker shade, upended a wine bottle over my head. The liquid didn't soak me — it hovered, viscous and shimmering, eating through my personal wards like acid.

I tried to dodge, but strong hands clamped onto my shoulders. I screamed and yanked on the lines, blasting my assailants with magic. They stumbled back, but not as far as they should have. I clawed past a brunette in apple-green and wrestled the door open — Green yanked my ankles out from under me.

Pink struck — a syringe to the throat.

Green kept me pinned until the contents was fully injected — the chick was freakishly strong. In a last-ditch surge, I unleashed everything I had, letting power rip through the closet. Shelves exploded off their brackets. Pink hit the ceiling. Green left an Austenian impression in the door.

If not for the wards, the door would have been ripped off its hinges.

The needle's contents burned and thickened, flushing through my system. My legs crumpled, and my vision faded in a pink, green, and white swirl.

Kenny: September 4th at twelve thousand feet AGL

—that, I left. At first, I was too angry to go back, then too embarrassed. Only after weeks on my own did I realize how much he'd shielded me. And I'd paid his kindness back with contempt. He's still a high-handed, vain, lying bastard but—

"John?"

My voice came out thin, the effort leaving me weak.

Kenny?

Even in my head, he sounded relieved.

Don't talk or move. The Hounds took you — glamoured as drunk girls in historic dresses. We're airborne now.

The Hounds. That explained the distinctly male, naked nipple inches from my face and the cheap satin *Bride Tribe* sash. Frigid air tugged at my top and skated up my exposed arm. A jerking, repetitive motion made everything hurt. With every bob, my right arm flailed, and I felt weightless in the worst way. At least I'd been right — they wanted me alive.

We've been flying for hours. If they've stayed on course, we're heading toward Chicago. The houses below are getting closer together — probably nearing a city. When we land, if they sedate you again, don't fight it; we can't risk more injuries.

No problem. I wasn't sure I had enough strength to offer any resistance.

My eyes burned and felt gritty. They didn't want to open, I didn't want them open, but I had some perverse need to see how bad it was. Clouds smudged the sky, the earth was far away, and the land looked like a patchwork quilt in charcoal and indigo. I was being carried bridal-style — two arms between me and eternity. If they dropped me, I doubted John could save me. How did gravity affect him? Would I drag him down, too? Something we probably should've discussed earlier.

My ride had a dog-like snout, pale skin, and two great, leathery wings sprouting from its back.

It glanced down at me with eyes like shadowed caverns — empty and pitiless. A string of drool slid from its muzzle, wetting my tank.

"Ughh." My stomach lurched.

Fido chuffed, pitching me up to get a better grip on my thighs. I gasped, clutching at the creature as nausea and vertigo battled for supremacy.

We're okay, Kenny. It won't drop you, and I won't leave you. Once we land, the others will open a door. Between your people and mine, we'll wrap this up fast and be home in time for breakfast.

He kept up a steady monologue — opinions on motorcycles, combat techniques, and our brews (*Frigid Witch*, our eisbock, was his favorite) — plus ideas for stopping Mystery from attacking his feet at 2 a.m. Somehow, it helped. That a warlock could be this considerate blew my mind.

A breeze shifted, lifting my dreads.

We're descending. Remember, don't resist.

Not an issue.

That's Lake Michigan. We're north of the city. Winnetka, maybe.

I took his word for it. I planned to keep my eyes and mouth clamped shut.

Our host likes lakefront castles.

Couldn't care less. I had more pressing matters at hand — like my stomach drifting up my throat.

The Hound hit the ground running — great, shuddering clomps rattled through me until my brain fizzed. Even before the momentum died, I was heaving. I couldn't breathe, couldn't think.

Fido didn't notice. If I hadn't already known the Hounds weren't alive, this would've sealed it. The mess sprayed over both of us, and the sadist just trotted into the house.

"Well, this isn't good," a pleasant voice proclaimed.

Fuck off.

I tried to look up, but spasms wracked me, leaving me no control. Every nerve screamed as my core tried to purge — poison? Allergens? Head trauma? All three.

No!

"Take the young lady to the guest suite — the bathroom, if you please. Clean her up," the voice ordered. "I do apologize for the terrible journey, Representative Jones, but I needed to test my new pets' capabilities. You do look dreadful, but fear not; you will be well looked after."

The lust in his tone gave me all the One Ring feels. It wasn't sexual — at least, I hoped not. He was eager — almost giddy, and that scared me.

It's not possible.

I tried to ask John what wasn't possible, but someone switched off the lights.

The problem with arcane constructs is that they take instructions very literally, with just enough intelligence to make disastrous misinterpretations. I learned this firsthand when I woke up choking on water and gagging on a toothbrush.

The Hounds had draped me over a bathroom counter, ignored my soiled clothes, and proceeded with their own translations of 'clean her up'. One washed my dreadlocks in the sink with hand soap; another brushed my teeth with petroleum jelly. A third scrubbed my jeans with vinegar and a scouring pad, while the fourth clipped my peach-painted toenails with sewing scissors.

It was a massive bathroom with high ceilings, but still not enough space for all of them. Five through Eight had to wait their turn — armed with a mop and bucket, a wire brush, bleach, and a shop vac, respectively.

I screamed.

I kept screaming until the Hounds froze and stepped back. I fell off the counter, hitting the beautifully tiled floor — gray marble in a quatrefoil pattern — and jarred both an elbow and a knee.

"Put those things back where you found them and guard the house," my captor sighed. "I do apologize, Kenny. May I call you Kenny? Good help is so hard to find."

Strong, calloused hands pulled me upright, propping me against the wall.

"Nothing broken," he murmured, patting me down. "Ah…what's this?"

Long fingers scraped along my neck, finding a sensor there. I was too horrified to react. My glasses had fallen off and the ley lines…were all wrong. They didn't shimmer or pulse. A third of them looked waxy and dull; some had thickened, turning opaque white. Pockets of nothingness yawned where lines had vanished, and pinpricks of blue fire marked where reality had burned away.

I knew this. I'd seen it years ago when I began hedge-crossing; realities that were dying, blights where ley lines had been worn away. There were entire planes consumed by blue fire.

And it was happening here. In my world.

A mop of dark curls bobbed into view as elegant fingers stripped the sensor and fished out a tracker clipped to my jeans. I hadn't known either was there. He claimed my charm bracelet, then tore all three amulets from my neck.

"I suppose I should have expected this. You let yourself be taken, didn't you, clever girl?" He braced my head, tilting my face up. The brightest blue eyes I'd ever seen twinkled above a beautiful mouth built for smiling. It took me a moment, but the name surfaced: Darragh O'Brien, Chairman of the Union of Seers. "You do make it fun."

I didn't understand. The sunburn was gone, along with the tipsy flamingos. Had it all been a front? And for what purpose? John had hinted that odd behavior was…expected.

Had they both played me?

O'Brien released me, and I slumped to the floor.

The faint resemblance to John — the cut of the eyes, the hairline, the hands — hurt to look at.

"I'd almost suspect you of chundering on purpose. The stench really is too atrocious to be born, or we'd be on our way right off — never to be seen again," he teased, squatting. "Here. Rub that muck off your teeth."

He dropped a wad of toilet tissue in my lap and washed his hands.

I closed my eyes, taking several deep breaths as I scraped the petroleum jelly from my mouth. It wasn't going without a fight.

His footsteps retreated — harsh slaps against marble, softening on wood — and I sagged in relief. My mind kicked into gear. I dug a couple of painkillers from the nightingale tattoo, let them dissolve on my tongue, shoved my glasses back on, and rested against the wall.

As more oxygen reached my brain, my confusion deepened. O'Brien was a seer. It made no sense for a seer to kidnap me. Sure, a rare few were psychotic, but most were violence-averse.

Then again, I'd faked vampirism for a decade…but I'd never tried passing as Chief Justice of the Hall of Vampires. To be recognized by the Union, a seer had to meet at least three others at important ley junctions — and at least one of those seers had to be from a different subtype. Most seers didn't perceive ley lines the way I did; they saw ordered paths where I saw energy and chaos.

"—as possible. Strip her, search her thoroughly, wash her with something strongly scented, give her a toothbrush and mouthwash, and put her in these. Two Hounds will guard the door. Neither of you will leave until she's ready. Twenty minutes."

Pain ebbed, my tears dried, and my thoughts sharpened. Whoever he was, this bastard wasn't O'Brien. I was almost certain.

I forced my eyes open just in time to see the impostor set a bundle of clothes on the counter while a terrified maid in a black dress and white apron attempted spontaneous invisibility. It was a good effort, considering she wasn't using magic.

"If your staff's this afraid of you, I see why you wanted an automaton," I murmured.

For half a breath, his face stayed eerily still — the kind of stillness only preternaturals managed — then he grinned. "Like I said, good help is hard to find."

It wasn't conclusive, but I was convinced. This wasn't O'Brien. I bet he didn't even know what viennoiserie was. He did, however, look exactly like O'Brien. There were several possible explanations — glamour, a cryptic genetic transmutation talent, a doppelganger potion, or even a simulacrum. He could be a twin or a relative.

He turned his gaze on the maid. "Twenty minutes, Leah."

She nodded, eyes downcast until he was gone.

Whatever was good for this impostor was bad for me — and even if Leah seemed harmless, I couldn't trust her. Still, 'atrocious' was a generous description. I needed to be clean.

Using the wall and counter for leverage, I pushed to my feet.

Leah paled and stepped back.

"Um…"

"I can strip and wash myself."

"I'm supposed to…search you," she mumbled.

"Then keep your eyes peeled."

Chapter 81: Welcome Home

Kenny: September 4th in Winnetka, Illinois

The clothing provided was an unfortunate mix: a dark red skirt suit with a wrap jacket — no blouse, cami, or button-down; a black belt; a deep red agate brooch that felt odd in my hand; and almond stilettos that nearly matched my skin. The skirt was shorter than I liked and a size too big, but at least it was clean.

No bra. No panties; just a black one-piece swimsuit with a plunging neckline. Maybe the impostor hadn't planned properly, and these were the only women's clothes in the house? Whatever the reason, I layered up.

John hadn't said a word since I woke up, leaving me alone with Leah. She watched every move I made, but aside from gasping at the 3D underhousing tat on my back, she said nothing. Her ley sensitivity was weak — nowhere near level six — but I kept my distance anyway.

Worry gnawed at me as I dressed. I was tempted to knock Leah out, make a portal, and run — but I'd learned nothing useful, and the ley lines were in no shape to trust. Their weakened state probably accounted for John's absence.

No markers could be left here, but I slipped a few cards from the ether into the jacket's pockets. Just in case.

My dreads were still wet, and my twenty minutes were almost up. I tried tapping a line to expedite the drying time and got ley-burned for my trouble. The feeble lines sucked my power down before I'd managed to twist the spell, leaving my reservoir feeling raw and abraded. If I'd attempted a door, the starving lines would have drained me dry. Sighing, I French-braided twin plaits and pinned them up in a large bun at the base of my head. It wasn't ideal, but it would at least keep the damp blanket of hair from wetting my back.

Through the door, I heard the impostor's voice: "Follow your brethren and guard the estate perimeter. No one enters or exits without my permission."

The door opened.

"Ah. Much better," he murmured.

The impostor needed a name. 'The impostor' was too impersonal, and this had become deeply personal. With his Hounds, warped morality, and wild constructs, I settled on Jareth.

"A great improvement. Now, we depart."

I scowled, defiant, as Leah scurried out.

Jareth grinned, lips curling in satisfaction, and an opalescent sheen rolled over his eyes. Power swept through me — gentle, inexorable — tethering my will to his. We'd trained to resist compulsion, but Mara's words whispered in my memory: *Age and experience.* His mind brushed mine — textured, layered, shifting like the deeps. He was a leviathan, an Ancient.

If I stayed bound to him too long, I'd eventually lose the desire to escape.

Panicking, I instinctively lashed out…and he didn't even notice.

"Come stand beside me, Kenny. Remember to breathe."

A pressure rolled through me, coaxing my thoughts, massaging my muscles into warmth and compliance. My body obeyed.

"Take my arm. Very good," he murmured, almost apologetic. "Persuasion is not a kind tool, and I regret using it. Instinct demands resistance — futile though it is. I won't hold it against you."

How considerate.

"I'll keep the binding brief. We're going to the Agora. You will remain calm, not draw attention, and if someone speaks to you, you'll answer politely but give no sign you're in distress. Don't reveal our business or intent. Lie to others if need be — but never to me. Stay close and obey my every command."

The threads of suppression pinched, squeezing me into an unnatural shape. Still, nothing stopped me from dropping a card as I followed him down the hall.

Outside, a green Bentley Mulliner Bacalar waited — at least I was being kidnapped in style. As I climbed in, the whisper of calloused fingers brushed mine.

John!

I bit my tongue to keep it together. It had occurred to me that the broken ley lines might have trapped him, leeching him of energy, leaving nothing but a husk. But he was here. He was okay. He hadn't abandoned me.

I wasn't alone.

Jareth tucked a handkerchief into my palm. "I'm truly sorry. If there were another way, I'd have found it. Wipe your eyes."

The drive passed uneventfully. Jareth kept a close eye on me — no doubt waiting for me to shatter his net of coercion with a heroic flourish and launch into my good-guys-always-prevail speech. I'd have been delighted to oblige. Still, he hadn't ordered me to perform the helot ritual. The situation was dire, not hopeless.

"You've been remarkably calm," Jareth observed as he pulled into the Agora's parking complex forty minutes later. "Planned an ambush?"

A prickle ran up my spine. Best not to encourage that line of thought. The question was specific enough that I could answer truthfully — this time.

"No," I murmured. "I'm debating if I want to know your motives, or if ignorance is bliss."

"I'm sure you are." His roguish smile was maddening. "Seers' secrets, I'm afraid. I know it doesn't seem like it, but we're on the same side. If time weren't so tight, I'd have made my case without the psychic handcuffs."

His earnestness almost sounded genuine — but his behavior didn't back his words.

"Sure, you would. You just wasted forty minutes. Why not pitch it then?"

A thousand thoughts flickered across his bright blue gaze, but the moment passed.

"We need to move before your other admirers catch up."

I started, trying to guess his meaning.

He chuckled, getting out. "I'm not the only interested party, love, but I'm likely the most benign. Come."

The slam of the car door echoed through the cavernous garage. I considered dropping another card, but I dismissed the idea — there were too many cameras. Inside, we hit security almost immediately.

"Your purse," he murmured, handing me a small clutch that coordinated with the suit. "You'll need your ID. Give it to security when they ask."

When my turn came, the ID — complete with a photo of me that wasn't me — passed without a hitch. It had to be genuine: Teslin paper, microchip, all the right magical identifiers. Jareth's card was accepted just as easily.

With a hand on my lower back, he steered me toward a bank of gilded elevators. When our turn came, he gave me a gentle push.

The elevator wouldn't work for my team — too many cameras, too much traffic. I was getting desperate. Breadcrumbs don't help when they're still in your pocket.

"Chairman," a blonde woman in a sharp black pantsuit greeted Jareth, elbowing her way over. Her hair was coiled into a perfect French twist, gold square hoops glinting from her ears, and a matching bracelet dangled from her wrist. "Good to see you, sir. I didn't realize you were back from vacation."

She shot me a curious look, noting his hand still resting on my back. A fierce desire to disavow any connection rose — but the compulsion kept me silent.

"Just a quick drop-in, Izzy. Some things won't wait," Jareth said with a sigh that dripped with amused contempt. He was enjoying impersonating O'Brien far too much. "I don't believe you've met Representative Kenny Jones. Kenny, this is Senior Special Agent Isolde Gerahty — one of the APA's finest."

"Nice to meet you, Agent Gerahty," I said, offering my hand with a card tucked inside. Whatever she did with it was better than leaving none at all.

She felt the card and gave me a sharp smile. "Likewise, Representative Jones. You've become very popular in the rumor mill. I wonder if the scuttlebutt is true?"

"Likely some, but certainly not all," I replied with a rueful smile, trying not to fumble the paper she'd pressed back into my fingers. A clumsy exchange, but it worked.

"I heard the therianthrope serial killer attacked your farm and escaped?"

"True."

"And he's after Talia Davis?"

"It would seem so."

The elevator chimed.

"Interesting. I wonder what he wants with her. Oh…this is my floor. Nice bumping into you!"

As the doors closed, Jareth murmured, "Hand it over."

I gave him my clutch, but he shook his head.

"Whatever Gerahty slipped you. Now."

One of the other passengers shifted uneasily at his tone. I passed him the folded paper.

The doors opened again — a few people slipped out, one boarded.

Jareth read the note, grinned, and handed it back: *The LT does not tolerate interference. Put your affairs in order.*

Go figure. I wondered how they'd caught on.

"Making friends everywhere," he whispered, leaning close. "And who might the LT be?"

"Lex Talionis."

"The law of retribution?"

Retaliation, but close enough.

"I think I can guess, but why that name?"

"They're practitioners. They want revenge — in kind and degree," I said as the doors slid open again.

"Practitioners? And sweet little Izzy is one of them," Jareth murmured, sharp-edged glee in his tone. "Extraordinary! Turn over a rock, and you never know what pestilence will crawl out. Why would she risk her cover to pass you this? What did you do?"

"I don't know her personal motives, but I rescued Ghost when Lex Talionis tried to kill him."

The doors closed.

He looked down, puzzled. "Why?"

"Hate begets hate."

"You're not that naive. Hate won't be eradicated. It's far too useful."

The doors opened again.

"Down the hall, to the right. Have your ID ready," he instructed, ushering me forward.

I bit my tongue. The more I argued, the more likely I was to slip up.

We turned the corner and joined another line. At the center of the Agora stood Chicago's Peregrine Gate — one of only 300 surviving temples, carved millennia ago by hedge witches — before we were shunned. When they were unearthed 80 years back, the octagonal temples were painstakingly deconstructed and rebuilt inside government facilities around the world for Community use.

Each of its eight archways contained a programmable portal — and only the gatekeeper knew how to make it work. His identity was even more closely guarded than a warlock's.

Where was Jareth taking me?

As if sensing my anxiety spike, John squeezed my hand. We would be fine.

"Please remove all amulets, spelled items, and magical effects class three or higher," a guard called.

Beside me, Jareth waited calmly.

He wasn't a simulacrum. Being a class twelve spelled item, they wouldn't survive travel by Peregrine Gate. Any transformative elixir or spell effect was similarly out. The security guards would detect the manipulation, unravel it, and then boot us out of line, fine us, or some combination of the three.

Cryptic Genetic Transmutation and glamours didn't rank on the scale. They were considered low-level hereditary magics. The ability to glamour was more common. Nearly every fae and a hefty chunk of the hybrids could manage a personal glamour. Although less common in other Origins, the ability still popped up. Three of my cousins had the gift, tracing back to a fae great-grandmother. Made family reunions interesting.

"Next!"

Jareth nudged me forward.

"ID."

I handed it over.

"Destination?"

"New Arcadia — city center," Jareth replied.

New Arcadia? I'd never heard of it. Despite the name, I wasn't exactly in the mood for traveling to new and exciting destinations.

The guard, running on autopilot, glanced at us — hovering between curiosity and suspicion — before recognizing Jareth and settling back into comfortable routine.

"Oh, hello, Chairman," he grunted. "Any magic to declare?"

Once our IDs were verified — more or less — and we'd been scanned for contraband spells, another guard waved us to an empty queue.

"Lucky you! No wait," he quipped, unlocking the barrier. "Happy travels."

If Jareth were glamoured, it wouldn't survive the journey. The gates, being rather more demanding than my portals, were always hungry and accepted all offerings. If he were a lesser mortal, the beguilement would fail, too. It was good to be ancient.

"After you," Jareth murmured with a mock bow.

I stepped through the dark archway and emerged into sunlight. For a heartbeat, I thought I'd stumbled into Ethos — Davy's utopian, solar-punk dream. Towering, seamless glass buildings twisted together with dense greenery and vivid gardens. Orchards climbed dark skyscrapers like they were nothing more than rolling hills. The terrain's natural rise and fall had been conquered and reformed in a neat grid, as though the entire city had been stamped in a waffle iron.

The lowest tier was residential, with lush parks at the center. The second tier bustled with restaurants and public spaces. Above that were grand estates, theaters, museums, and sleek office buildings lining broad canals.

Despite the beauty, surreal dread clawed at me. A woman leaped across the skyline, her feet springing from blazing sigils. This…was a city of practitioners — the fabled Cartref Afon, brought to life.

Sanctuary.

My fingers trembled as I slipped another card from my pocket. Invisible fingers plucked it from my grip.

John.

He was still with me.

"Welcome home, Kenny," a familiar voice, charming and giddy, purred in my ear as two broad hands settled on my shoulders. "No, don't turn. Let me get my face on, and then we'll walk out — quiet, calm — and get you settled. You'll love it here."

September 4ᵗʰ in Sanctuary

The towers and terraces of New Arcadia rose around him like dark sentinels, their shadows cut by sunlit gardens and plazas. It was too beautiful — open to the sky, alive with color and motion — to inspire fear. The nightmare city whispered about in the Community was, in truth, a carefully curated utopia.

There were no roads, only wide plazas and bike paths. Floating pods traced golden arcs between terraces; discs of light carried people to higher levels. Families picnicked in the parks, office workers grabbed coffee from food stalls, and some residents skimmed the air on liquid-metal wings. Life looked effortless, idyllic.

And yet this place was the Community's most controversial prison — a fate so dreaded that many begged for death rather than exile here.

Dorrit was still reconciling that contradiction when Kenny strode out of the arched portal and froze, startled. Her horror soured his perception as she plucked a card from a bumblebee tat. For all its pretty trappings, New Arcadia was still a gulag.

He caught her hand, took the card — reminding her she wasn't alone.

A man in a beautiful suit and opaque mask stepped out behind her. His glamour was gone, but he'd come prepared. He gripped her shoulders with casual ownership, lowering his voice.

"Welcome home, Kenny. No, don't turn. Let me get my face on, and then we'll walk out — quiet, calm — and get you settled. You'll love it here."

Dorrit froze, recognizing the voice.

Gilles-Eugene Serrecold, Director of the APA.

Cold rage bled through his consciousness. He didn't doubt his ears — only every assignment he'd taken, every decision he'd made under Serrecold's command. Slowly, he reined himself in. He wouldn't endanger Kenny by losing control.

Dorrit had always known that every organization housed in the Agora was corrupt, but this was different. Serrecold, sadist and coward though he was, had never been reckless. Now the entire Quorum was compromised. Every vote, every verdict of recent years would have to be reexamined. It would cripple the government for months — if it recovered at all.

This was treason.

What had changed? Why now?

He must have been frightened, coerced, or convinced it wouldn't matter. Dorrit couldn't imagine Serrecold sacrificing his interests for any cause — moral or otherwise.

Absently, Dorrit turned Kenny's marker over in his palm, keeping it hidden as they neared the security desk. Once he knew where Serrecold was taking her, he'd find a safe, concealed entry point for their people. Then, they would end this.

The In-Between

"Turn him on his side," Oscar barked. "Has this happened before?"

"Twice," Ridel grunted as he rolled Dorrit's convulsing body over, while the healer drove an injector into his arm. "Both times, he blundered into a reactive ward but broke free on his own. Said it was like his mind dissolved, but he continued to exist, suspended in pain."

"Accurate enough," Oscar said. "It's a mental attack — likely a ward. Without his body present, there's no buffer. His brain's being overloaded. Time?"

The light vanished, plunging them into blackness. The bridge shuddered. People screamed, gasped, and then — beyond it all — a chilling, inhuman wail echoed in the distance.

Light suddenly returned. Aside from an overturned medical cart and one twisted ankle, it was as if nothing had happened.

"A minute forty-eight," Iosephina said evenly.

"Oscar," Mort called from across the station. "She's waking."

Oscar's jaw tightened. "Second injection at two-fifteen. If the seizure hits three minutes, shout. If he wakes, shout." He moved to the other patient.

Davy thrashed on the gurney, her gauzy shroud tangling on the handles.

"She's… disoriented," someone offered.

"Typical," Oscar assured, checking her vitals. "A bean sídhe's prophecies are never pleasant — especially for the bean sídhe. She's fine — just bruised."

"And the hair?"

Several feet of inky curls spilled off the bed, brushing the glass floor and blending with the chaotic void below.

"Also normal," Oscar said. "Thirty-eight prophecies since I've known her. Each time — hair and nails grow, skin pales, eyes go black, clothes vanish, and the shroud forms."

Davy's eyes fluttered open, flickering from blue to solid black and back.

"There we go," Oscar coaxed. "Don't fight it, Davy. It's coming. No one blames you for the message. Come on — who's it to be?"

Davy curled into the fetal position, sobbing as the lights vanished again. A chorus of distant wails — closer now — echoed her distress.

The light returned.

"He's awake, Oscar!"

"Addison, watch her. If she names anyone, yell."

Dorrit was already sitting up, arguing.

"—otic! How do you plan to find the ward without someone else stumbling into it?"

"If their field mage hadn't acted fast, you'd be dead," Ridel said tightly. "You need time to recover."

"Please don't agitate my patient," Oscar cut in. "Ghost, we'll run a battery of tests — think on-the-go EEG, but magical. If you're stable, I'll discharge you. If not—"

The light faltered again. The phantom chorus swelled, wailing their funeral song.

Davy shot upright on the gurney, her pale skin glowing like a pearl.

"Kenny!" she shrieked.

Silence followed — heavy, smothering — broken only by Davy's sobbing as the lights returned.

"Oh, hell no," Nore snarled, marching over to the commissary and snatching a uniform from the clerk. "Nebthu, I'm going."

"Both of us," hissed Maggie, grabbing another set of fatigues.

"Three of us," Mort added, daring the clerk to object.

Dr. Evelyn Vine jogged over to Nore, eyes bright with restrained fury.

"I can't go with you," she said.

"No."

Tears clung to her lashes, but her voice was steady.

"Don't hold back."

Nore nodded — everything else passed between them without words.

"Give him his uniform. Artemis, make the door," Oscar barked as Davy collapsed back onto the bed. Aides rushed to untangle her limbs and check her vitals.

The healer stepped aside, slumping against the wall and biting his fist.

"That was a prophecy," Dorrit murmured.

Oscar inhaled sharply. "It was."

"Davy's a bean sídhe. Kenny will die within three days."

Oscar's fangs snapped down. It was answer enough.

"But not today," Dorrit vowed. "Test me all you like after she's safe."

September 4ᵗʰ in Sanctuary

"What the hell is that?" Nebthu murmured, staring at the man-made slope cresting forty feet above New Arcadia's third terrace.

The Sheta Djew emerged from the manifold bridge into an orchard adjacent to their destination. A sheet of seamless, black glass carved into the hillside, concave and ominous, while a narrow waterfall thundered over its peak and vanished into the earth. Dorrit could hear it, yet the sheet of water hung suspended, unmoving. The grass lawn fronting the structure, however, did move — fast. It flowed like a green sea, every blade streaming up and over the hill away from a placid reflecting pool.

It was hard to look at.

"Elphame."

Nebthu's brows arched.

"There's a sign near the front entrance," Dorrit said, shifting his quest tote.

"Of course there is. How do we get in?"

"Serrecold went through on the west side. Beyond that, I don't know. First, we need to deal with the wards."

"Leave that to us," Nebthu said with a mirthless smile, sliding on wraparound shades.

"Oscar to teams: three, four, five, six — hold the bridge. One and two — shield. Nebthu, Onyx, Peridot — approach the gate," Oscar growled through the radio.

"Acknowledged."

"Nebthu, Onyx, and Peridot en route," Nebthu confirmed.

Peridot and Onyx weren't imposing, even in mottled fatigues. But when Lon barked a command and all three vanished, Dorrit decided not to underestimate them.

"How do we shield someone we can't see?" he muttered.

"You can't see them," said Tellus — also invisible. She tapped the eye-shaped patch on his borrowed fatigues, and his arm faded from sight, followed by the rest of him. "But we can."

"What's to prevent me or my people from stumbling into you?"

"This isn't our first rodeo, warlock. We'll be keeping tabs on your lot. Now watch."

He didn't know what to watch for until he felt the lines shift and weave. A ward formed over them, enclosing the whole of Elphame within its boundary.

"Teams one and two reporting: repercussion ward in place," a voice crackled.

"Acknowledged. Nebthu, Onyx, Peridot — break."

A moment later, dark green streaks crawled across the Elphame's ward. The magic sang sharply, drilling fissures into the aegis. Dorrit felt it shatter — energy exploded, lashing the air. Heat rolled over his face, tightening his skin and filling his nose with the scent of scorched ozone. The earth trembled underfoot as the ward-breakers funneled the excess power back into the lines.

"Nebthu reporting: wards down. Power subdued."

Dorrit waited for sirens, peace advocates to descend, or some sign of discovery, but the Saturniidae's ward did its job. He finally understood how they had gone so long without being caught.

"Acknowledged. Nebthu, Onyx, Peridot — hold. Teams one and two, take the south."

"Acknowledged," Ridel replied.

"Teams three and four, exit the bridge and hold."

"Acknowledged."

"Teams five and six, stand by."

Dorrit reached the fence — a strange mosaic of stacked metal plates with narrow gaps — and slipped through the gate. He half expected a trap, but nothing happened.

"Teams three and four holding," Kukri reported.

"Any movement?"

"Team one reporting; quiet as a tomb."

"Teams three and four; advance to the gate and move north," grumbled Oscar.

"Team one reporting: evidence of entry — tripwire yanked loose, two traps triggered. No casualties."

"Proceed with caution."

Dorrit moved deeper into the estate, the movement in the lines the only indication of those around him, aside from the occasional invisible hand redirecting him. Three more traps were neutralized. There were no guards, no dogs — only the creeping tension that each step could be the wrong one.

Two hundred feet in, Dorrit's senses flared. He paused, loosening his stance, scanning for movement.

Nothing.

He advanced three steps.

Nothing. But something in the lines caught his attention.

"Scout Three to Fox Leader — sector C cleared. Ward destroyed. Copy?"

The voice was faint, carried on ley-infused tech — *a sphaera nuntilus*. The sound formed a narrow column, audible only if you held the device or stood directly above or below it.

Dorrit searched the trees above.

"Copy, Scout Three. Bravo Zulu. Scout Four, report."

A figure crouched in a gnarled oak, masked like a ninja and whispering into a small glass sphere.

"Scout Four to Fox Leader — signs of intrusion. No rabbits in sight. Sector B cleared. Copy?"

"Copy, Scout Four. Any sign our rat has bolted?"

"Negative, Fox Leader. All roads lead to Rome."

"Copy. Stay lively. Charlie Mike," replied the familiar voice.

Senator Balbay; Internal Investigations had beaten them here. Usually, warlocks took jurisdiction, but Dorrit was willing to accept assistance, given there were hostages — assuming they were all on the same side.

He knocked on the oak's trunk.

"Fox Leader," he murmured, voice cold and echoing.

"Ghost," Balbay acknowledged, exhaling with something like relief. "What brings you to Sanctuary?"

Kenny: September 4th in Sanctuary

"Bumblebee, where's your mask?" Mommy asked as I dragged my giant stuffed rabbit, Sweet-Sweet, into the kitchen by her neck.

"Don't like it. Don't like the dark. It's dead," I whispered.

Mommy scooped me up, blowing raspberries on my cheek until I giggled.

"Hmmm. Let's try something. Close your eyes and no peeking,"   she murmured.

She carried me outside, the screen door banging softly behind us. Crickets, an owl, and something creeping in the scrub filled my ears as she sat us down in a rocking chair.

"What do you hear?" she whispered.

"Chirping...an owl...the trees."

"Good girl. Now open your eyes. See? It's dark out here, just like under your mask. But the night isn't dead — it's filled with life. Deer, raccoons, bobcats, even if you don't see them. Your eyes need rest sometimes. But when break time is over, all this will still be here."

There wasn't another car in sight except a gold Yugo blocking the inside lane. I shot the driver a look as I passed; she shrank in her seat. The Yugo vanished behind me, nearly sideswiped when a silver-blue Prius fishtailed onto the highway. I kept an eye on it, but as the hills softened, my thoughts drifted.

"Here," Evy barked.

She shoved a VHS tape into my hands.

"What is this?" I asked, already shrinking into myself. Nothing good ever came from Evy's 'gifts' — although...it had been a year since she'd given me anything. Not since the new doctor. Evy hated me; I didn't blame her. I hated me a little, too. I'd stolen her mom. Ruined her bright, safe home.

"An apology," she muttered. "Don't tell Mom."

She slammed my door, leaving me staring at the black VHS tape like it might bite. I couldn't ignore it — it might have a message from Mom, Kuwako, or Mrs. Ortez on it. If I watched it, it might hold something I wasn't supposed to see. Evy was like that.

Dad was at work; Mom was busy with laundry. I had to watch it, and this was my chance. I ran to the upstairs family room and slid the tape into the VCR.

I gasped.

My real dad lifted a younger me high above his head, spinning us around. Something sharp twisted inside, but I couldn't stop watching. I memorized everything — his navy shirt, his farmer's tan, the love shining in his brown eyes, the ruffles on my sleeves, my yellow pants, the bandanna over my eyes. I drowned in it.

Static flared, then a birthday party popped up — a pink cake with a green-and-white candle shaped like a '3' took center-stage, the table littered with half-eaten hot dogs and smears of potato salad, and a pastel pile of gifts. My parents and a gang of children sang as I blew out the candle.

A fresh terror filled me. I knew where Evy had gotten the video — she'd used her talent. Mom and Dad could never know.

It was my greatest treasure, and I couldn't risk them taking it. I ejected the tape without rewinding. I'd watch the rest later, in bits. Scurrying out to the attic access, I jumped twice to grab the cord. I hated the attic — dust, spiders, shadows — but no one would find it there. I shoved the tape into the bottom drawer of an old dresser, behind a few precious relics of my old life: Dad's banjo, Mom's loom.

When it was safely hidden, I found Evy in her room, hugging a pillow.

"Thank you," I whispered, voice hoarse. "Promise you won't go back for more. It's too far. If you got lost—"

Tears clogged my throat.

"I'll promise," Evy mumbled, "if you'll forgive me."

I nodded.

My sister hugged me, willingly, for the first time.

The squeal of tires snapped me back to the present. The Prius, a quarter mile behind me, slammed into the guardrail as a lime green Dodge Challenger Hellcat wove past. Idiot. The crumpled Prius limped back onto the highway. I checked the dash for my phone — must be in my purse. Just as well; I couldn't call 911 while driving.

The Hellcat roared past, its driver flashing a deranged grin and a one-fingered salute, skimming inches from my car. I memorized her license plate. When I stopped, I'd report her for reckless driving.

Ten miles later, my thoughts wandered to the day I first met Kuwako. Evy had been impossible that morning — accusing me of stealing her barrette, hogging syrup at breakfast, and shoving me into the wall on her way outside. When she was busy, I hid behind the shed with my wood chain.

An hour passed before a beautiful Asian woman found me. She didn't speak, just sat on the grass in her pretty clothes, watching me carve each link. Somehow, without speaking, we became familiars — one more thing I'd stolen from Evy.

A 1961 VW bus, cream and soft orange, merged onto the highway. Davy would have adored it. I switched lanes to let them in, earning a cheerful wave from the dreadlocked driver.

Then Danny Eisher popped into my head — my only college boyfriend. A sweet guy, but he'd quickly tired of my secrets, dumping me by mid-junior year. I'd drowned my heartbreak with Maggie, Nore, and Davy, eating pie until we were sick.

A scarlet Jaguar XKE Series II roadster — '69, maybe — sat pulled over, probably for speeding. I stayed in the left lane, smirking at the cop's posture as he lectured the driver. Evidently, the car wasn't the only beauty parked on the shoulder of the road.

College had been surreal. It was a miracle I'd graduated, with no one to micromanage me. I remembered Ms. Pringle, my tutor at age eight, telling Mom I daydreamed through lessons and talked to 'imaginary friends'. They hadn't been imaginary — but I'd been forbidden to explain.

Back in the right lane, a battered Humvee settled eight car lengths behind me. We became silent travel companions for twenty miles, cruise control holding steady at seventy-three. When it exited, I felt oddly abandoned.

Then a darker memory slid in. I was sixteen, and Mom's voice — calm but sharp — still echoed in my head as she called the emergency dispatcher. She blocked Evy and me from the living room. We'd just come back from a weekend at the beach. Dad had supposedly hung himself. We left California as soon as the police finished their investigation. I hadn't been back since, except for work.

A red and black Bugatti Veyron roared up, tailgating me hard. I slowed, hoping it would pass. Instead, it crept closer, backed off, and repeated the game three times.

Asshole!

My car shuddered as they clipped my corner, finally pulling into the left lane. I braced for a threat, a gun, some show of violence, but when I glanced over, I saw a curly-haired woman yelling desperately at me. I could almost hear her, even over the highway noise.

I didn't know what to do. If I pulled over, I might be attacked. I couldn't reach my phone without stopping. I tried slowing down, but the Veyron slowed with me, edging into my lane as signs for a construction zone started appearing. I sped up; she sped up too. Nothing for it — I'd have to stop. It wasn't like I couldn't defend myself.

A black 1950 Mercury M72A slammed into the Veyron's bumper. The driver — hair slicked back, sunglasses hiding her eyes — never looked away from me. I knew her.

I hit the brakes — nothing happened.

I was in the back seat of the Charger, hands cuffed behind me, a metal grill separating me from the front.

There was no driver.

Orange cones blurred past. We were in the construction zone. Something searing hot pressed into my chest, right between my breasts.

"It will hurt less if you accept it," Serrecold's voice whispered, strange and distant, like it was underwater.

I tried to scream, but my mouth wouldn't open.

Sunglasses rammed the Mercury against my door, a small, contemptuous smile flashing across her face.

Then foreign emotions flooded me — anger that Mom had made me wear a blindfold when I felt isolated and vulnerable; disdain that Evy thought she could buy forgiveness after years of torment; raw jealousy every time my foster parents cooed over Danny. For two years, I'd been their baby, adored and spoiled. Then that awful, wriggling boy arrived, and they forgot me. My plan could have worked. Leaving him in the woods had been smart — but not smart enough.

I fought the handcuffs, bruising my wrists. The ring of fire over my sternum burrowed deeper, eating into my flesh. I thrashed, tears burning my eyes, but the pain wasn't the worst part. Something essential — what made me *me* — was being twisted.

"This is who you were born to be, Kenny," murmured Serrecold. "Embrace it."

I hated that I couldn't accept Kuwako's love and friendship without feeling like I'd done something wrong. I felt only contempt for Annabeth Driscoll. This world beat you when you were down — anyone who tried to soften it was naive and deserved what they got. She'd fed me, given me a bed, and an easy grand. She never realized I'd planted the packet the police found the next morning.

I despised Danny Eisher for not accepting that my life was complicated. I was a practitioner; he was a norm. I'd protected him! So, I kept secrets — who doesn't? Did that mean I didn't deserve love? Why did shallow, selfish women find protective men, and I couldn't? Why wasn't there someone for me?

One by one, my memories stretched and warped. New, ugly ones shoved their way in. What was happening to me?

I'd been elated when Rick called to say Tess was in the hospital. If only she had died — then Rick would've realized he loved me, not her. She'd stolen him. Even after I relapsed and she barged in, demanding his attention, I'd thought he'd see her for what she was. But he hadn't, and I'd been forced to take other measures.

Ms. Pringle's smug ignorance came to mind — hers and others like her. I felt cowardly. Guilty. If someone could scramble my dad's mind so badly that he'd hang himself, what hope did I have? My adoptive dad had died, and I was afraid for myself? Weak. Selfish. Pathetic—

The Veyron braked hard, and the Mercury rammed it at full speed. Sunglasses was beside me, sneering — then gone. The crunch of metal and carbon fiber jolted me from the spiral. The false memories fell away, and I spun on the bench seat, staring out the rear window.

"You're delaying the inevitable," the Director scolded. "If you knew what I knew, you wouldn't resist. Preternaturals need someone they trust — a victim who rises as a hero. You're going to save us."

The Veyron, crumpled but still moving, weaved to block the Mercury. Both cars were shedding parts like confetti.

I could relate.

My eyes met the curly-haired driver's. Even from here, I saw her determination, fear, and…hope. I turned away, unable to face her emotions and my own.

There were more urgent things to consider. Why was the Charger still moving? How had I gotten into the back seat? Why was the Veyron driver protecting me — and why was Sunglasses attacking?

I glimpsed Curls in the rearview, swerving to cut off the Mercury before vanishing from sight. Judging by her movements, Sunglasses was bellowing in frustration.

For one brief second, I saw them both — different cars, different expressions, different hair — but the same face.

The Veyron shifted, revealing a passenger: the Watcher. He winked and was gone. I didn't have time to process how I knew him. I'd never actually seen him before.

The molten heat between my breasts pulsed savagely, dragging memories to the surface. The Hounds. Being kidnapped. The power suit and that agate brooch. The feel of the necklace hadn't matched the shape! It had to be an artifact. It felt like I was skimming files stored in memory, scouring for enlightenment, making it so much more complicated than it had to be.

And then clarity was gifted to me from an outside force — an invisible hand rearranging the puzzle pieces so that they made sense. Every driver I'd seen was me — a version in another life. Humbling…and disturbing.

Serrecold was turning me into a vampire. Using the broşă de creuzet.

The Mercury rammed the Veyron into a concrete barrier, shortening it by several feet and invalidating the warranty.

"Apparently, I have unresolved anger in several lives," I muttered. "And self-destructive tendencies."

I only noticed the handcuffs were gone when I found myself rubbing my raw wrists. My foggy brain grew fuzzier as I tried to come to grips.

Curls blasted her horn, dragging my attention back to the demolition derby. Sunglasses had the Veyron pinned, grinding it into the barrier. Curls's glare bore into me. Honk! Honk! Hoooonk!

Message received. This was on me.

The cuffs had vanished after I acknowledged two of my issues.

"We are what we make ourselves," I reasoned, thinking back to my therapy sessions and waiting for my belly to light up like a Care Bear. "And I don't want to be a self-absorbed psycho chick."

My hands landed on the steering wheel.

Seriously? This was an arcane intervention?

"Okay! Fine! I can be a selfish asshole sometimes," I growled, cranking the wheel. The Charger shrieked as it drifted, skidding until I faced the oncoming traffic.

Light flickered in a war dance on Sunglasses's mirrored shades as she stared at me. The Mercury reversed with squeals and crunches, lining up for a game of chicken.

Remembering that I was a hedge witch, I fixed on a point beyond my adversary. I had no plan, no marker, no idea what I was doing, just fear and instinct.

Speaking of which, it was probably time to feed the machine another token.

"I deal with my fear of rejection by hiding at the farm, letting my cousin run interference with the Covenant — even though she hates it. I've kept my mother at arm's length because I'm afraid she'll leave again. I'm…comfortable at Sullen Creek, but the need for me there is long past. Oscar has earned the Covenant's trust and then some. Using the full extent of my magic terrifies me. My friends enable me, and I let them; they put my welfare above that of a child! I…need to leave. If I don't, it'll get worse."

The Mercury gunned it, belching smoke; Sunglasses was all-in. She didn't care if she survived, as long as I didn't.

I slammed my foot down, and the Charger roared forward. Should I make a door and drive through it? No. I couldn't escape my problems that easily.

"I will be there when you rise," Serrecold promised, awe and conviction saturating his voice.

"It won't be the reunion you're imagining," I shot back.

The Mercury's hood filled my windshield. The instrument of death was a blunt metaphor?

I swerved left, clipping her bumper.

I never could get out of my own way, but I refused to keep fighting myself.

"I determine who I am. I accept and take responsibility for what I am. I'll leave Sullen Creek, and I'll take our solution to the Covenant. Right or wrong, I'll have tried."

The Mercury spun out of control. The driver's side slammed into the median. I braked, tires screaming, and ground to a stop. Sunglasses fought her door but couldn't get out. The way she was wedged, she couldn't even climb out the window.

We were done.

I got out, slammed the Charger's door, and walked away. I was going home — and exorcising my demons the old-fashioned way: therapy. With a new therapist.

Behind me, Sunglasses unleashed a scream sharp enough to cut bone. I ignored her. Energy gathered in my hands as I put the last touches on my door. A push, and it opened.

I glanced back just once and saluted Curls. She held up three fingers like Katniss, then hopped the median, heading off to wherever good alter-egos go. I stepped through the portal.

The world splintered. All the bright, brittle, broken pieces of my soul slammed back into place. Whether I was a vampire or not remained to be seen — but I was still me. Exhausted, but whole.

I yawned — and water rushed into my mouth.

My eyes snapped open, chlorine stinging. I was underwater.

Panic gripped me as I realized my ankles were chained to the bottom of a tank. My wrists were cuffed behind my back. The mask that had been feeding me oxygen was no longer working.

<h1 style="text-align:center">Chapter 85: C'est la Vie</h1>

Kenny: September 4th in Sanctuary

Forcing myself to stay calm cost a few precious seconds. A wailing siren and a gladiatorial brawl between a three-legged, sword-swinging, eyeless eel and a massive, acid-burping wad of snot on a nearby plane didn't help. I scanned my mental inventory for anything that could cut metal — only something magical would work fast enough.

A splash shattered my focus. Someone in dark clothes dove past me, inspecting the cuffs on my ankles and the chain pinning me underwater. I didn't see what he did, but the chain snapped. The cuffs still dragged at me, but he hauled me up, breaking the surface. I tore off the mask and gulped sweet oxygen.

Breathable air did wonders for my mood!

Rufe Balbay surfaced beside me, hair slicked back, expression grim. Not who I'd expected — but I was delighted to see him.

Despite my relief, my limbs wouldn't cooperate, and I slipped under again. Rufe caught me, but something small and hard was trapped between us. With a hiss, he yanked the necklace free. The agate brooch had morphed into two shallow bronze bowls welded together at their bases — the broșă de creuzet.

Why couldn't evil lost artifacts stay lost?

The Senator's face twisted in disgusted recognition, and he chucked it across the room.

"Are you hurt?" He spotted the ring of welts on my chest, which were healing fast — too fast. The swelling was visibly fading, angry red softening to pink.

I didn't heal like that — not without treatment. The ritual had worked.

"Are you—"

"I'm fine. Still me," I panted, a shaky laugh bubbling up. "Thanks for the rescue."

His gaze searched mine, and he grinned — his smile unexpectedly boyish.

"It is you!"

He helped me to the ladder attached to the fishbowl's side. I clung to it, my arms clumsy but regaining strength.

Distant explosions vibrated through the ladder's rungs.

"What's going on? Where's Serrecold?"

"He was gone when I got here."

Quickly, he explained that Internal Investigations had been surveilling Serrecold for weeks after an anonymous tip. When the Director shook their tail a few days ago, and when I'd shown up at the Agora with Chairman O'Brien — who was supposed to be out of town — it raised red flags. The II agents had followed us to Sanctuary. The Saturniidae and the APA agents had joined them just before Serrecold's forces had taken issue with their presence.

Rufe boosted me to the top of the ladder. He got the cuffs off my wrists and ankles, dropping them back in the water, and climbed up behind me. I swung a leg over the tank's edge, but his hand brushed my chin, turning my face toward his. He kissed me.

It warmed me from the inside out. His beard rasped against my cold, hypersensitive skin, every nerve sparking like a lightning storm bottled inside me.

It was…a great kiss.

My hands slid over the wet fabric clinging to his chest and gently pushed him back. He retreated without argument, reading the look on my face.

"Ah," he murmured, glancing past me. John stood in the doorway, bloodied and panting, a Staccato 2011 CS in his hand and a trickle of blood on his forehead. The warlock's eyes were locked on us, his face carved in perfect indifference.

"There's competition," Rufe observed.

That was a stretch, but I didn't correct him.

"I'm sorry, Rufe."

He gave a humorless chuckle, looking down before forcing a mild smile. "C'est la vie. Come. Let's get you dry clothes and end this."

"I'll keep. We need t—"

"You're not stepping onto a battlefield in a wet bathing suit," John cut in, holstering his gun and striding over. "Your eyes aren't even tracking. You need dry clothes and medical attention."

"He's right," Rufe agreed.

I nodded, embarrassed but grateful, and swung my legs over the ladder. John caught my hips and lifted me down, soaking his fatigues in the process.

"Sorry," I muttered, patting a wet patch.

His lips twitched, his gaze sharpening. I ducked my head, unable to hold his gaze.

"I don't suppose anyone knows what's behind these doors," I said by way of a distraction, crossing my arms and shivering in the air-conditioned room. Water pooled at my feet.

There were no windows, but each wall had at least two doors. The tank dominated the room — its smooth sides sank into the hardwood floor, and four leather club chairs were arranged on one side. An abandoned whiskey glass, a single finger left, sat on a side table. Behind the chairs was a billiards table. Serrecold liked to entertain in his den of iniquity.

My opinion of him somehow managed to drop.

The red suit and my glasses were nowhere in sight.

Rufe jumped down from the ladder, striding to the nearest door.

"Bedroom. Unoccupied. No clothes," he reported after a quick search, already moving on.

"Wrap yourself in that and sit," John murmured, pulling a woven throw from a side table and handing it to me. "Use the first aid kit Oscar packed. Even if Balbay notices."

I cocooned myself in the blanket and nodded. I retrieved my backup glasses and amulets from a bumblebee tattoo. After a few quick treatments — concussion, nausea, dehydration, and a poison flush — I felt almost human again. And restless.

I chose a door — another en-suite bedroom, larger and more opulent than the first. A kitchen, stocked for a Michelin-star apocalypse, was revealed — then a gym with sauna and plunge pool, four escape tunnels, and all the necessary amenities of a luxury bug-out bunker. The last door opened onto a third bedroom with a walk-in closet stuffed with men's and women's clothes in every size and style. I spotted the red suit and shuddered.

Wasting no time, I stripped out of the swimsuit, pulled my own clothes from an Atlas moth tat, and scurried into them.

"Clothes!" I called, randomly yanking outfits off hangers and stuffing them into a dresser drawer. Perhaps it was overkill, but Rufe would notice if every hanger were full.

The two men arrived almost simultaneously.

"In there. I'm using the bathroom," I said, waving them in as I made my escape.

By the time I reemerged — two granola bars later — Rufe wore jeans and a dark t-shirt while John had changed into a dry henley.

"Here," John murmured, handing me my original glasses as we returned to the common room.

"Where were they?"

John and Rufe exchanged a look of mutual disgust. The Senator finally said, "Serrecold kept a trophy case."

Charming.

"Shall we?" Rufe asked, nodding toward the main room.

A sphere of swirling fog, stretching from the platform floor to the concrete ceiling, waited at the top of the landing. Rufe fished in his pockets as distant noises — roars, blasts, percussions — signaled that we were just in time to watch the world end in a sensational fashion. The stairs had looked sturdy enough four flights below, but as each new volley shook the earth, they complained in ominous, droning creaks.

"I'll take point," Rufe said, palming a set of keys and turning to face us. "Serrecold's finished in the Community, but he'll try to take you, Kenny. If you're beyond his reach, this battle ends faster. Our objective is to get you to safety. Agreed?"

"We don't know tha—" I began.

"Agreed," John cut in, voice like stone. "Ending this quickly outweighs all that you'd bring to the fight. Our people are holding the line so we can get you out. Let's not waste that."

The building shook again. Something massive screamed overhead and detonated with teeth-rattling force. We clutched the railing, waiting for the floor to vanish beneath us. The stairs held.

"All right," I said, my pride bruised and my mouth tasting bitter.

If leaving made it safer for the others, that's what we'd do. I didn't have to like it.

Rufe, as if reading my thoughts, gave me a quick, commiserating smile. "We'll make for the Peregrine Gate. Kenny, on me. Ghost, you'll cover our six?"

John nodded.

"Stay low. Move fast."

Rufe pressed a black fob into the fog and murmured something in a language I didn't recognize. The mist collapsed with a hiss, revealing a steel hatch in the ceiling. He pocketed the keys and scaled the ladder.

I followed, bursting into dappled sunlight. The hatch opened into a grove. Around us, three Saturniidae teams — nearly sixty strong — were arrayed in a phalanx-testudo hybrid. The first row knelt tight, warding shields overlapping like scales. The second and third rows alternated offensive and defensive practitioners, wards held overhead, flashing as they repelled aerial assaults. A narrow channel cut down the center where we stood.

Rufe grabbed my hand and hauled me forward. John's warm palm pressed against my back — a silent promise that he was still there.

Through gaps between bodies, I glimpsed the enemy: at least six for every one of us, their formation bristling on a grassy rise. Beneath the hill lay the black, concave glass façade of a futuristic hobbit mansion, its long reflecting pool framed in stone. The grass itself rippled and chirped like a capricious stream. Classic fae architecture, in other words. Maximalist minimalism with a side of vertigo.

I tore my gaze from the bizarre mansion and fixed it on the advancing force. Mostly vampires — interesting in itself. They scrambled forward, firing precast spells while using landscaping for cover. They were well-armed but disorganized. No units. No signals. No chain of command.

Every man for himself.

No — every couple.

I froze, staring at the sneering faces, convinced my brain was lying to me.

"What?" Rufe barked, scanning for fresh danger as fireballs slammed into the aegis overhead, heat sucking the moisture from my skin.

"Madison!" I shouted, spotting the nearest shielder.

"Weaver?" she acknowledged without breaking ranks.

"Serrecold's recruited the parents and families of the convicted children! Look— Frank and Jenelle Wilton! We can't hurt them!"

Madison's jaw went slack.

It was one thing for Serrecold to gather mercenaries. It was another to turn grieving parents into his private militia. He couldn't have beguiled all of them…could he? What had he promised? *The warped who corrupted your children are still out there — help me stop them.*

Fae beauty and charisma had always been dangerous tools. Whatever Serrecold had said, it had worked.

"-identified," Madison murmured into her headset. "These aren't rogues or mercenaries. They're civilians. Coerced… Yes, sir. Ye—"

Something enormous dropped from the sky. The impact struck the shield wall like a bowling ball, throwing Madison into her neighbors. Rufe stumbled. I would've landed on John if a large, cold hand hadn't clamped around my arm.

I stared up at the tall, pale figure, tilting my head back until my neck ached. Conical ears. Translucent forelock. A Hound.

This one looked like a horse.

I'd been wrong about their eyes. They weren't empty. Deep inside the cavern, a pinprick of amber light burned — an intelligent, malevolent presence gazing back at me. Serrecold.

Then the Hound yanked me into the air.

John shouted, his voice fading under the rush of air.

We had our answers, though. Serrecold was behind it all. I was no longer obligated to stay on this pony ride.

For all their fabled history, the Hounds were merely constructs — sophisticated, legendary, nearly invincible constructs, but still just ley knots. Keeping my movements controlled and deliberate, I stowed my glasses back into the bumblebee and pulled the Ikita Kawaki from a stylized wave.

The thickest of the ley lines was coiled in its gut, so I drove the blade in there. The creature shrieked, convulsed, then bucked like a rodeo monster and flung me away.

The air punched from my lungs when I slammed into a snarling tiger, its smoky stripes writhing like oil in water. A dense knot of energy glowed inside its skull.

"Everything all right here?" called a trembling voice.

A man with molten wings and a battered leather briefcase flapped past, his wide eyes bulging like he'd flown into the wrong dimension.

I stabbed the tiger in the temple.

"No! Call the police!"

"Police? There are no police in New Arcadia!" he squeaked, flapping away through the clouds.

The tiger sank two-inch fangs into my shoulder.

I screamed, the muscles in my arm going numb, useless. I couldn't stab again — but I could twist the blade.

The cat shrieked, flinging me like a rag doll. I barely had time to register the blur of motion before I landed in the claws of a bear-shaped Hound.

I drove the kunai home — once, twice — before the bear ripped me free.

"Desist or die," it roared, spittle raining down.

"You first," I snarled, hacking at its arms. I wasn't aiming for finesse; even a shallow cut on a ley line would weaken it.

The bear dropped me. I scrawled a sigil midair and dropped it, tapping it and springing back up like a human slingshot. My angle was off. I missed the bear's heart.

Clinging to the beast, I corrected my mistake. Stab. Stab. Stab.

We spun, falling headfirst. Only then did I notice the bear Hound had stopped flapping. It was playing chicken.

I hated this game.

Its claws raked my back, but I didn't stop. Every punch, every shove to dislodge the kunai only confirmed one thing: Serrecold didn't want me dead. But I would sear every one of these Hounds from existence before I'd submit.

Chapter 86: First Salvo

September 4th in Sanctuary

Dorrit spat blood, swiping at his split lip as he searched for Kenny. He hadn't seen what had slammed him face-first into the dirt, but he could guess.

A whir cut the air. He looked up, snarling as a Hound — wings fanning — launched back up into the sky, taking his witch with it. More appeared — a dragon, an eagle, a stag — to guard its ascent.

"Hold your fire!" Lon bellowed, locking eyes with Dorrit and giving him a grim nod.

Dorrit returned it. The Saturniidae would hold the line. His job was to rescue Kenny.

"Make space!" he barked as the shielders reformed the columns.

He sprinted, then vaulted into the air, catching the ankle of a crocodile Hound. The construct bucked, thrashing its leg like a dog shaking water from its paw. Dorrit gritted his teeth, climbed higher, dodging spells Serrecold's militia hurled skyward.

There was no room for thought beyond getting Kenny back.

Fifteen feet over, Senator Balbay mirrored him — leaping high and catching the taloned foot of a griffin. A feral grin split the vampire's face as he scaled its body.

"Desist or die," the Hounds intoned, their voices a hollow chorus stripped of all humanity. Each reached into the ether and drew out a glowing spear of crackling light.

"You first," Dorrit snarled. He swung his legs, built momentum, and vaulted higher — grabbing the wings just as the crocodile jabbed its weapon backward. Fire seared across his forearm where the spear grazed him. He ignored it, tightening his grip, dodging a second strike. For a moment, he thought he'd escaped unscathed — until blood dribbled down his ribs.

"Gungnir," Balbay grunted, grappling for control as his griffin lunged near Dorrit's construct. "The spears don't miss. Not completely."

The Senator's shoulder was slowly soaking his shirt.

Excellent. Dorrit had worried this was going to be too easy.

446

But the spears were secondary. Control the Hound, control the fight. Snarling, he yanked the crocodile's head back, forcing its gaze to his. Twin bister flames writhed in its eyes. Dorrit bared his teeth and launched the first salvo in a mental war.

Chapter 87: Timing is Everything

September 4ᵗʰ in the In-Between

"Teams one and two reporting — we're surrounded by desperate parents we can't harm," Nebthu grunted, absorbing the recoil from a big gun. A beat of silence was followed by a distant boom. "We're out of sleep bombs. Ridel's people can't reach us and—"

A chorus of screams and detonations bled into Oscar's ear, Nore's singing rising above the chaos.

"Hold the line. Highwayman, get Peridot out of that crater. Oscar, we need immediate assistance. They've cast withering darkness, and it's working. The wards are holding, but when they fall, we're dead."

"Team six reporting. We've lost contact with five. We're pinned by possessed practitioners and constructs. Oscar, there are too many of them!"

"Teams three and four reporting," Novak barked over gunfire and a softer, crackling sound — like fire. "We're stable but can't reach the others!"

"Acknowledged. Assistance is en route," Oscar said, turning away from his pop-up clinic on the manifold bridge. In the center of the hub, forty-eight troopers stood in four neat lines, each column facing a glowing portal in the floor. Evelyn Vine hovered between the center fire teams, chewing her nails. Opposite the portals, twelve hedge witches stood, loose-limbed, ready to weave new doors at a moment's notice. Behind them hung one last portal, opening to a remote cabin filled with hospital beds.

"All units, activate stealth mode."

One by one, the troopers vanished.

"Deploy!"

Twelve soldiers — betrayed only by the ley lines connecting to them — quick-marched forward, dropping out of the bridge. Twelve more followed and so on until the hub felt unnaturally empty.

Time moved slowly.

"I can never stand this part," Vine muttered, rolling her shoulders.

"It requires trust," Oscar murmured, hand cupped over his mic. "Our people know their jobs — and what's at stake."

"It's not a lack of trust. Too many things can go wrong," she said woodenly.

A shorn head burst up through the fourth portal, followed by a limp torso. A hedge witch's hand twitched, but Oscar snapped, "Maintain position."

A humanoid web of ley lines climbed through, pulling the unconscious man onto the bridge. The soldier hefted him up and carried him through the cabin portal.

A head with box braids appeared in portal six, ginger curls in portal one. The process repeated, the bridge filled with comings and goings.

Ten minutes later, thirty-seven prisoners had been delivered to the cabin for holding. Oscar swept the now-reforming ranks of invisible soldiers, verifying everyone had returned, then nodded to the witches. They unraveled the old doors and wove new ones.

"My lady, it's your time to shine," Oscar told the chronurgist.

Dr. Evelyn Vine didn't answer. She frowned and shut her eyes, focusing inward.

The atmosphere warped — stretching, folding, condensing — before snapping back. The lights flickered at the surge of power as reality seemed to take a deep breath.

Everyone stood where they had been, but the net of ley lines marking the troops' presence had thickened — doubled, in fact.

"Deploy," Oscar barked in stereo, scratching his chin with a third arm.

Professor Vine had woven an overlapping time loop. Twelve troopers advanced, their transparent limbs swinging in a blur before vanishing through the portals all over again.

"Heard any good jokes?" she asked.

"No."

Silence stretched. Then the chronurgist started humming.

"Evy," Oscar rumbled, muting his mic.

"You heard Aibell. My sister dies within three days. I can't deal with that now. I have to distract myself or I'll go mad."

"I know. I haven't figured out how to cope either. But right now, we focus."

A shorn head popped up through the fourth portal…and a second —
blonde, bixie-cut — beside it. Two torsos spilled onto the floor, followed by
their legs. They were rolled aside as a thick web of ley lines, vaguely human,
climbed through and carried them toward the cabin.

Box braids emerged from portal six, ginger curls from the first. A third,
bald as an egg, flopped up through the third portal and nearly fell out again.
He buoyed back up right before his chin would have smacked on the floor.

Two clusters of ley lines reached the cabin's door at once. One waited
politely. The other, holding the curly redhead, didn't pause.

"Stillman, they're time shades. Nothing's there."

With a low growl, Stillman hefted his prisoner's feet while another knot
of ley lines grabbed the man's arms and dragged him through.

By the time the troops stood at attention, another sixty captives had
been delivered — with only three soldiers needing treatment for acid rash.

"My lady, it's your time to shine," said the Oscar-shade.

"What he said," Oscar echoed.

Dr. Vine closed her eyes and pulled the world tight around them.
Existence shivered — then snapped solid.

"Deploy," barked three Oscars, their voices overlapping in perfect
stereo. One scratched his chin as the soldiers — glowing like miniature suns
— marched forward. History repeated itself.

Three minutes later, three heads burst through the portals at once.

Static flared in the headsets, resolving into Lon's voice. "Teams one and
two reporting! The withering darkness has lifted. We're clear!"

Vicious satisfaction curved across Oscar's face.

"Teams one and two acknowledged. Stay alive!"

Twenty-one prisoners later, the Oscars — still grinning — announced,
"My lady, it's your time to shine."

"What he said," echoed an Oscar-shade.

Chapter 88: The Descent

Darragh O'Brien stepped out of the Peregrine Gate's security line and glanced up through the terminal's glass ceiling.

There were people in the sky.

He chortled — this was New Arcadia. There were always people in the sky: flying to work, playing aerial games, or taking a lazy flight after dinner. But this…this was not recreational.

"What is that?"

Huge, winged figures wheeled above, three of them larger than the rest. One hurled a woman — long hair streaming — and another caught her, only to fling her again.

"The warped love their infernal winged contraptions. Nothing to worry about, Chairman," the guard said, barely glancing up before returning to his phone. "I wouldn't trust an artifact to keep me aloft, but—"

"That's not a practitioner with wings," O'Brien snapped, shielding his eyes. "Shit! Those are Hounds. Call for help — now!"

"This is New Arcadia, sir. If the Wild Hunt wants a new chew toy, good on 'em. Plenty more where—"

"Idiot! Don't you watch the news? The Hounds went rogue days ago! That's Senator Balbay with the griffin — and Ghost! And Representative Jones! If you don't call backup, I'll feed you to them myself!"

The guard fumbled for his radio. "Yes, sir! Right away, sir!"

But O'Brien was already gone. He scanned the constructs' erratic flight, judged their heading, and bolted from the building.

He sprinted across the plaza to a ley lift — an open-air platform of consolidated energy — shoving past startled passengers.

"Hey!"

He didn't slow, leaping onto the lift as it rose thirty feet to the next terrace. Phone out, he barked into the receiver, "Oscar? Never mind how I found this frequency. We need aerial support — southeastern corner of Goswami Park."

He disconnected, vaulted from the platform, and tore down the promenade, dodging hovercraft and pedestrians. A staircase to the upper tier came into view. He took it at a dead run, pumping his legs, lungs burning.

At the top, he spotted the constructs again and veered toward a spiraling skyscraper shaped like a unicorn horn. Shoving through the flow of visitors, he searched for an elevator, a ley lift, anything that would move upward. There — a fusion between an escalator and a hover train.

"Welcome to the West Arcadian Business Complex. What is your destination?" a smooth, disembodied voice asked as O'Brien stepped onto an empty platform.

He glanced at the sky outside. "One hundred seventy-sixth floor — as fast as possible."

"Destination: one hundred seventy-sixth floor. Is that correct?"

"Yes. Move it!"

"For your safety, remain on the funicular glide platform until it stops. For a scenic tour, press one. For a swift ascent, press three."

He hit three.

A yellow-tinted dome formed over the platform. The glide clicked, detached from the others, and veered into a narrow, well-lit tunnel.

"Initiating hyperspeed in three…two…one."

O'Brien grabbed the safety rail just in time, narrowly avoiding being plastered against the shield. His lei tangled, but he managed to flip it over his head with one hand.

Seconds later, the glide shot out of the tunnel and slowed.

"You have arrived at the one hundred seventy-sixth floor. Thank you for visiting West Arcadian Business Complex. Have a wonderful day. Goodbye!"

He leapt off, spun, disoriented by solid doors, glass doors, and blank white hallways.

Impatient, he pushed through glass doors onto a balcony — trees, flowers, glossy bistro tables, all hugging the building's curve and climbing into the clouds.

He dashed up the nearest staircase, scanning for Hounds and listening for screams.

Halfway around the building, he saw them — the griffin wadding up Senator Balbay and flicking him away like a straw wrapper.

Balbay had managed to wrest the Gungnir from the construct, but as he fell, it was little comfort.

O'Brien's heart pounded.

Balbay collided with the Hound Dorrit held in a headlock two hundred feet below. The warlock's grip slid. Balbay's spear plunged through the crocodile's torso, with Balbay clinging to the shaft for dear life. Dorrit caught the beast's arm, but it shook him off. Balbay caught his wrist.

O'Brien's heart stopped, then ventured a cautious thump, momentarily relieved — until the spear slid out an inch. Under their combined weight, The Gungnir wouldn't hold. The crocodile gripped the weapon and spun into a series of violent barrel rolls, desperate to shake off both passengers.

O'Brien's eyes locked on a lion-headed Hound circling nearby. He ran, vaulted from the building's ledge amid a chorus of screams, and fell straight toward it. His aim was a hair off — he landed straddling its shoulders instead of its back. Locking his feet behind its waist, he seized its muzzle, wrenched its head back, and stared into its eyes.

"I can't allow this, old friend," he growled. "I did warn you."

Their minds clashed, writhing like snakes in a pit, striking, fangs sinking into thought. O'Brien knew, intellectually, that the pain was excruciating, but he felt nothing. He didn't dodge or shield, only grappled, strangling Serrecold's hold on the legendary constructs, praying that he wouldn't be too late. The Director jerked and flailed, but O'Brien refused to relent.

He felt it — a loosening. Serrecold felt it, too, and redoubled his efforts to buck O'Brien off the lion...to no avail.

O'Brien was unaware, at first, when the tether linking the Hounds to Serrecold failed. His desperation kept him fighting until he noticed the silence inside his head. Even then, he lashed around, stabbing blindly...but he was alone, staring into the lion's empty gaze.

Blood blurred his vision. He had no idea where it had come from. Releasing the muzzle, he wiped his eyes with a corner of his shirt. It came away red. As the mental haze cleared and the bleeding slowed, he sensed the eight Hounds' tethers — tangible, foreign threads — linked to his mind and awaiting his command.

He pushed his desire for the crocodile to land on the West Arcadia Business Complex's skydeck down the leash — and saw Dorrit and Balbay, still clinging to the bloody spear, fall.

"No!" O'Brien screamed, hurling frantic commands at the Hounds.

The crocodile tilted its head, as if some annoying gnat was buzzing around, and began descending — angling toward the spiral edifice — with half-assed flaps of its wings.

"No! Catch them, you idiotic lump of arcane Play-Doh!" bellowed O'Brien, frantically flapping his own arms. "Save my s—"

A streak of white and black thundered past — a massive bird of prey, lightning pulsing beneath its wings. A pale man with eagle wings followed, cutting through the air like a blade. Arlo, O'Brien thought, the name rising like a prayer — Arlo the lamassu and Armand the impundulu. The lightning bird and the eagle man dove, snatching both tumbling agents mere feet above the ground.

For several moments, O'Brien could only stare. Tears blurred his vision as he gulped down air. Finally realizing that Dorrit and Balbay had survived, he took up the tether on the lion Hound and urged it to land. The construct gave a single, uncertain flap of its wings, then tucked them and dropped thirty feet in a terrifying freefall before O'Brien's frantic pleas sank in. With a puzzled jerk, the creature fluttered just enough to stay aloft.

"Downward *and* flap, you idiot," he muttered, forcing the mental image into the Hound's sluggish mind. The ride smoothed — somewhat.

Relief loosened his chest when Armand swooped up, Dorrit clutched neatly in his talons, and curved back down to land. The warlock hit the ground running…until gravity reminded him who was boss, and he collapsed.

With the other two safe on the ground, O'Brien turned his focus to the rest of the Wild Hunt. He reached for another tether — only to yelp as it burned out of his mind. The sensation felt like being whipped with a chain of fire — brief but memorable.

He scanned the sky.

"Not the griffin…not the crocodile… not the lion," he murmured. Then he saw it — the stag Hound dissolving into mist, its antlers vanishing into the clouds. Something small and dark tumbled headfirst through the ether.

"Kenny," he rasped. The idiot woman had done the impossible! She'd unraveled the construct without realizing there'd been a change in management.

"Armand! Arlo! Get Kenny!" he shouted, pointing skyward.

Miraculously, they either heard or saw him. They followed the direction of his hand and shot back into the air.

O'Brien tightened his grip on the Hounds' tethers, simplifying his commands to sharp, visual bursts until they moved.

Arlo and Armand streaked past, Arlo in the lead. He flew up below her with his arms stretched out, neither hearing nor heeding Armand's warning squawks. Bones crunched. Arlo's unearthly scream rent the air. For a heartbeat, they spiraled, then Arlo forced his wings to work, Kenny clinging to his waist with her eyes shut.

Armand circled, ready if she slipped. O'Brien's Hounds joined in, cobbling together an awkward rescue effort. It was going well — until Jones drove her kunai into the dragon's eye. O'Brien let out a startled, keening hiss. It didn't damage him, but it sure wasn't pleasant.

After a few chaotic adjustments, everyone was on solid ground.

From the skydeck of the West Arcadian Business Complex, a wave of applause erupted, but Chairman Darragh O'Brien — rarely immune to an appreciative audience — didn't so much as wave. He was fully occupied with his own relief.

Chapter 89: Cleanup

September 4th in Elphame

"… the wards are holding, but when they fall, we're dead."

"Team six reporting. We've lost contact with five. We're pinned by possessed practitioners and constructs. Oscar, there are too many of them!"

"Teams three and four reporting. We're stable but can't reach the others."

"Acknowledged. Assistance is en route."

"Hold the line," Lon snapped, tapping Olivia out and taking her place. The wounded woman nodded and staggered toward the medic. "Steady!"

A volley of hexes cut off abruptly, fizzling out harmlessly against their weakening wards. The tarry darkness crushing in on them vanished, leaving clear blue sky — and spectators wheeling above on glimmering wings. It had only been a matter of time; the ward blocked ley agitation and noise, but it couldn't hide the explosions from the locals.

Their complete lack of fear was concerning.

Lon rose, scanning the battlefield. The deranged parents were gone — spirited away by the invisible fire teams. With his aggregate specs in place, Lon only saw a few shrinking clusters of ley lines. Twelve appendages separated from the clumps and waved cheekily. Lon waved back.

Lady Gelsemine's fire teams had cleaned up. He'd seen their work seven times, and it still freaked him out.

"Teams one and two reporting — the darkness has lifted. We're clear."

"Five and six — clear. Wounded incoming."

"Three and four — Portal B closed, approaching the elf house."

"All teams acknowledged. Watch your tails!" Oscar advised.

Lon exhaled. Everyone was still alive. The plan had worked.

"All right, kids — breathe. We hold here until Weaver's recovered."

Chapter 90: Few and Far Between

September 4th in the In-Between

"That's the last of them."

Dr. Evelyn Vine let her body go limp and collapsed to the floor.

Few took note, as she also appeared to be standing.

The time shades marched on, ferrying prisoners to the log cabin, returning to phantom portals, redeploying, and — one by one — completing the marathon mission.

A shade standing over the chronurgist dropped. She twitched as its timeline expired and the leftover energy snapped back into her reservoir.

"You okay, Lady G?"

She raised a shaky hand to signal she was fine.

"One thousand six hundred and three relatives of convicted practitioners, seven hundred possessed practitioners in…thirty-seven wrinkles. Lady, you beat your record by four!"

Another shade hit the floor.

"Great."

The rasp sounded less like her own voice and more like a chain-smoker who'd had their tonsils scraped out with a dull spoon. She felt all of two thirty-sevenths better than she had a moment before.

"So…what's next? Do we—"

"We stay right here," Oscar snapped, crouching beside Dr. Vine. "Do you understand every nuance of folding time? Neither do I. The manipulation's still in progress. Until the last shade is reabsorbed, we remain on the bridge. We'll receive wounded from the field, but no one leaves. Time is a finicky fluid. Look at her! There's a reason we swapped hedge witches sixteen times. Unfortunately, our chronurgists are few and far between. Even if you didn't notice her fading near the end, I did. One more loop could've been her last. And someone get her a blanket! She's shivering!"

Chapter 91: The Pigeon has Landed

September 4th in Sanctuary

"Bounced?"

It wasn't actually a question — more a horrified realization — but she answered him anyway, dark eyes soft and apologetic.

"Yes… I would have bounced. You were there when we loaded my tattoos, Arlo. When do I ever leave the farm without at least a portable aegis, sensory booster, and air-light amulet? I wasn't in mortal danger from falling. I'm so sorry you were hurt. You were very heroic…but…this is—"

"Don't say it!"

"—a teachable moment. Next time, control your protective instincts. Just let me fall."

Cradled in the tiger construct's arms, Deathblade winced, having tried and failed to cross his own.

The impundulu let out a shrill, warbling trill.

"It's not funny, Thekwane," Weaver scolded. "Imagine the pain he's in!"

"Out of curiosity…you had the amulet — why did you choose to hang on to Deathblade?" O'Brien asked, brows scrunched.

"It would've been ungrateful to let go after he was already hurt. I didn't want him to think he'd failed. Scaring him like that, after the damage was done…just felt cruel."

"Amulets aren't reliable," Dorrit grunted, riding his Hound piggyback with as much dignity as possible.

"Sanctuary's amulets aren't reliable," Kenny corrected, softening her voice as the airspace thickened with airborne gawkers. "Mine are. They've been well-tested. What's this?"

"Spectators," O'Brien murmured. "Residents rarely see this much commotion. When they do…"

Sirens blared from below. A loudspeaker boomed, "Halt! You are in violation of Title Eleven, Subsection Twelve, Section Four of the New Arcadian Ordinances. Return to the ground and present yourself to the nearest Compliance Facilitator. Resistance will be met with force. I repeat, halt…"

"Compliance Facilitators?" Kenny asked.

O'Brien grimaced. "No prisoners here — just brainwashed drones. And no police, just 'public aid attendants,' 'municipal orderlies,' 'compliance facilitators,' and 'peace advocates.' Attendants are resident bullies who scout for trouble. Orderlies send out tax notices and thinly veiled threats. Facilitators — Agency trainees who washed out — handle real disturbances. They disperse crowds and detain troublemakers. Peace Advocates…make problems disappear."

"A lovely city," she murmured as the Hounds began their descent, landing clumsily in the clearing Nebthu's team guarded.

"Team One reporting — the pigeon has landed," Lon said with a grin. "Nice of you to drop in, Weaver."

"Don't," groaned Deathblade, still in the Hound's arms, his face an alarming shade of puce.

Nebthu raised his brows and handed Kenny a headset.

"He — uh — caught me and broke both arms. 'Drop,' or any similar word, is *verbum non grata* for a while," she explained, adjusting her mic. "Chairman, could the tiger deliver Arlo to Oscar on the bridge?"

O'Brien's brows arched, his expression brightening.

"Not sure I can, but I'll give it a go. Hold tight, Arlo!"

Arlo's protests went ignored.

"O'Brien, we'll also have to square things with the Peace Advocates," Balbay added darkly. "No doubt they'll see this as an insurrection." He turned to Weaver and Ghost. "You're going after Serrecold, I take it?"

They nodded.

"If anyone challenges your right to be here, show them this."

He pressed a medallion marked with a gladiolus flower into Weaver's palm, leaving behind a blazing imprint.

"The symbol of the II. You're deputizing me?"

"Something like that. It lasts six hours. I suggest you hurry."

Chapter 92: The House Always Wins

Kenny: September 4th in Elphame

"The tunnels and grounds are clear. If he's still here, he's in the house."
Nebthu nodded toward the imposing structure behind the waterfall.
Through my glasses, I spotted human-sized ley clusters — teams two, five,
and six — holding position nearby. The rolling lawn made our jog
interesting. "And that's a problem."

"Meaning?" John demanded.

"Elphame is an active hummock — a faerie mound. The house doesn't
want us here, and we have the losses to prove it."

I bit my tongue. Time to mourn would come later.

Faerie mounds were conjurations born of a powerful fae's lingering
presence, each with its own rules, and prone to vanishing if their owner
flitted off. Fae dungeons were the worst — like Scooby-Doo, but with more
psychological torture.

"Has anyone made it inside?" I asked. "Alive, uninjured, and
conscious?"

Nebthu's pained expression was answer enough.

"The front door swallowed Novak after she suggested we bust the glass.
Anubis found a deadfall atop the parapet after climbing to the third floor.
He should've fallen straight through, right on top of team five. He didn't.
Neither he nor his body has been located. All sensors went offline — no
contact since."

We didn't know if they were dead or alive.

"He fell through a portal," I probed.

"Possibly. Or we're meant to think so. Hidden portals to who-knows-
what kind of fae hellscape, arranged at random, make a pretty strong
trespassing deterrent," Nebthu deadpanned.

"'Abandon hope, all ye who enter here,'" I quoted.

"Exactly."

"Okay. Who do we have who's uninjured and at least a quarter fae?" I
murmured, running through the list.

John's curious look made me flinch.

I wasn't unfeeling, but grief in the field was a luxury. A justification tumbled out before I could think better of it.

"There were ten on my original team. Six were seasoned vets, all highly trained. Three are still alive — hopefully. Six died in action, and the seventh took his own life — a contagion curse. By the time we identified the spell, the damage was done. His sacrifice saved twenty-three people. Our operatives last, on average, thirty-nine months. Grief is an indulgence we can't afford. I won't let that number drop because I'm too sad to function."

The warlock nodded, making no comment.

We passed the reflecting pool and were greeted by a tremendous cheer.

Nebthu's radio beeped, then Lazarus's voice crackled through: "Team two reporting. Ridel got the doors open. No sign of Novak. We've split into units to clear the ground floor. Team five has the basement; team six is holding the door."

"Acknowledged, team two," Oscar replied. "Good work."

Ridel cut in. "For the record, I didn't beat the hummock. It stopped fighting. Either Serrecold allowed entry, or he's already dead."

We absorbed that in silence. We were entering an already hostile, semi-sentient house that might collapse at any moment. If Serrecold had been killed, and by whom, was barely a consideration. Evy, I'd been informed, was tapped out. We needed to find Novak, Anubis, and any prisoners and get the hell out.

"Acknowledged. Be careful," Oscar said.

Fae tastes varied, but whatever they chose, they always overdid it.

Serrecold was no exception. His hummock's décor leaned modern Scandinavian — functional furniture, gray concrete, pale woods, creamy textiles, and enough art to suggest a fondness for Pollock and Rothko.

There was just so much of it.

No one needed this much space. Two steps inside, I saw three sitting areas, a conservatory of carnivorous plants, a glassed-in wine room, and a hallway guarded by nine disturbing, suggestively human, stone sculptures.

"Stay with your unit," Nebthu and I chorused as team one climbed to the second floor.

The staircase shifted from straight concrete to white-oak treads on concrete risers curving in a 180-degree arc. At the top, the treads seemed to float in space.

If I thought about it too much, I'd trip.

Team one split into four units. Nebthu, John, Puma, and I pushed deeper into the mansion.

"Left or right?" I asked.

"Left," rasped Lon. "Look at the painting — it's Novak."

I grabbed his sleeve, scanning the rippling plaster walls. There was no painting. Two tapestries, yes, but no Novak — just the same lantern-jawed face repeating through the shifting texture — but experiencing pareidolia was nothing new. When one winked, I'll admit to feeling a degree of concern.

I removed my glasses. No change. The lines were healthy, and the faces still watched me. There was no painting — but on another plane, a lilac snail the size of a baby elephant oozed down the toe of a leather loafer.

"Elphame's messing with us," I said. "I'm seeing a hallway, three doors, and two tapestries. The right's a mirror image. Puma?"

"Left's an antique door with a red light above," Madison reported. "Right's a cased opening, but I can't see anything in the darkness."

"John?"

"Left's a long, white hallway with a door at the end. Right's a wall with another sculpture."

"White hallway," Lon decided. "John, take point. Weaver, Puma. I've got our six."

I kept a hand on John's back, hoping to catch a glimpse of what he saw. No such luck — Elphame's magic didn't cut corners. Madison's hand settled on my shoulder as John tested each step. By the sixth, nothing had triggered, and I had to stop myself from urging him to hurry.

At last, we reached the door. I saw nothing, but John turned an invisible knob and stepped through. I followed, still touching him — until he vanished. Madison's hand was gone, too.

I stood alone in the absolute dark.

Reaching out, my heart pounding, I found nothing. I took a slow breath, willing myself not to overthink recent events.

"John," I whispered.

Silence.

Hands out, I took a blind step, then another. On the third, a heavy thump sounded behind me. A door swung open, spilling amber light across the hall, and a man stumbled out.

Blinding light swallowed me.

When my eyes had adjusted, I was back in a textured hallway. The lantern-jawed faces in the walls now looked both prim and smug — never trust a fae who looks like butter wouldn't melt in his mouth.

The man who'd tumbled through the door straightened, and I recognized my apprentice — in jogging shorts and a tank.

"Mort…why aren't you with Team Six? Where's your uniform?"

He jerked, trembling, mouth working silently.

I glanced behind me — just another statue blocking the hall. If the door hadn't opened, I would have plowed into it.

When I looked back, Colt was edging away, staring at me like I'd sprouted a second head.

"Put your glasses on," I suggested.

He hesitated, then pulled them down from his head. His magnified eyes blinked with visible relief when he realized the horror he'd seen was only me.

Bent over, hands on his knees, he panted for a few breaths, then waved toward the door.

"In there," he croaked.

I nodded, half-expecting him to morph into the lantern-jawed figure I kept seeing.

The room was an office, violently ransacked. Papers soaked in whiskey littered the floor, mixed with splintered furniture, shattered glass, and stuffing ripped from sofa cushions.

Serrecold sat dead behind the desk, his handsome features locked in bittersweet serenity. A hand mirror rested before him. Four parallel lacerations — thin threads of vermillion — marked his neck, arms, and chest. Duplicate slashes marred the walls and furniture.

This wasn't why I was here. But Elphame had an agenda. Defying the house wouldn't end well; humoring it might buy us time.

"Weaver reporting," I said into my headset, getting the distinct impression that no one heard me. "The house took me and Mort to Serrecold's office. The Director's dead, and the room's been ransacked. This is a code red — find our people and get out."

Mort huddled in the doorway, looking haunted as he observed my movements.

I studied the mess, pulling latex gloves from the lily pad tattoo on my ankle. I owed John and Oscar an apology for doubting they'd come in handy.

Serrecold had no pulse. Even his rose-red lips had faded to pink.

My gaze fell on the Clamare Vero. Of course it was here. Artifacts had no true sapience, but sometimes the will of their maker clung to them — and this one reeked of malice.

Gingerly, I picked it up by the handle, hating the warmth that seeped into my skin. The beasts etched into the silver melted, replaced by a thousand lidless eyes.

Daughter of my daughter's daughter, I greet you. I've waited long for this day.

The voice slid through my mind — slimy and cold.

"Not long enough, evil old crone," I growled, dropping the mirror into a trash can. The glass shattered on impact.

At least one good thing had come of this field trip.

I sifted through the debris on the floor, searching for answers.

I found a string — thick and white.

It was so unexpected, I tugged on it, following the movement as it shifted a photograph — a fit, well-dressed Asian man caught mid-step, scowling into a cell phone. The city was unfamiliar, but I recognized Senator Francis Dal Park of the Mul Wuiu Bich.

I pulled my phone from a tribal tattoo and began documenting my findings.

Following the string, I unearthed a receipt for two almond croissants and two coffees, the word *Văzători* — Romanian for Seers — underlined, bold journal photocopies, and a photo of Henrietta Scott, the late and infamous practitioner. Supposedly, she'd died of a stroke before the trial seventeen years ago. This photo told another story: she lay on a slab, sheet to the shoulders, with two bullet holes in her forehead.

Click, click, click.

The string led me behind an overturned sofa and up a pair of booted legs in chestnut armor. The torso was still there, but the floor had swallowed the head and shoulders.

Ah-ha.

"I see he threw quite the temper tantrum," I told the hummock, adding a touch of persuasion to my voice, and feeling stupid talking to a house. "But this man didn't kill Serrecold. If he had, there'd be more blood."

Faerie mounds weren't known for being reasonable.

I slipped off my glasses, scanning again. A shattered whiskey decanter glowed faintly with ley energy.

I raised the string.

"Serrecold was investigating Park's death. He had an evidence board and a lead. Someone murdered him — hexed the whiskey. This man, Carrick Levisay, is another victim. Release him, let us leave safely, and I'll hunt Serrecold's killer."

Mort shuffled further in, glancing down the hall furtively.

I held my breath, waiting for Elphame to reach a decision. I didn't know how a game of tug-of-war — with a body as the rope — would end between two practitioners and a haunted house, but my imagination supplied several vivid possibilities.

While a visceral pop played on loop in my brain, the floor regurgitated Levisay's head. Simultaneously, a thin line of power attached to me.

"It's a deal, then," I murmured, checking his pulse. Thready, but there.

The house shook — not in thanks, but warning.

"Will you return my other people?"

Another rumble.

A pity I didn't speak faerie mound.

"Mort, do you know how to get out?"

He shook his head, voice hoarse. "No. It sucked me in from outside and spat me out here… Kept my gear." He plucked at his undershirt.

"I'm making a door," I decided, warning Elphame and adjusting my mic. "Oscar? Nebthu? If you can hear me, I'm opening a door to the bridge. Elphame's collapsing — evacuate the grounds! Anyone inside, get out now!"

September 4ᵗʰ in Sanctuary

"Who's in charge here?" Balbay roared.

The crowd of residents and compliance facilitators froze for three seconds — until a short, black-haired woman in uniform marched over and snapped, "I'll be asking the questions. This assembly is unregistered, in violation of Title Eleven, Subsection Nine, Section Four of the New Arcadian Ordinances. You and your companion are persons of interest and will be referred to the Peace Advocates' office. Name and address?"

O'Brien's phone blared *Don't Rain on My Parade*.

"Apologies! I thought it was on silent," he grimaced, checking his notifications.

A figure in matte black dropped beside them, wings folding away. "That will do, C.F. Gupnik," he said coldly. "Return to your station and review the ordinances — and the members of the Quorum."

"They made it inside the mound," O'Brien muttered.

Gupnik sputtered as the masked man saluted. "Senator Balbay, Chairman O'Brien. I am P.A. Recker. Your orders?"

O'Brien's phone chirped again.

"Recker, advise your people that a joint operation between the II, APA, the Union of Seers, and the Sheta Djew is underway on the Elphame estate. Seal the perimeter. Gilles-Eugene Serrecold has been stripped of rank and is a fugitive. He must not escape. Have the facilitators clear a three-block radius and reinforce you."

"Yes, sir." Recker saluted and began issuing orders.

"The ground floor's been cleared," O'Brien reported, sliding his phone away.

Balbay frowned. "Who's sending you the play-by-play? The Sheta Djew? Neither the APA nor my team has shared updates."

"It's not the Sheta Djew," O'Brien admitted. "I have a private intelligence network. We cloned Ghost's phone, his team's, Representative Jones's, most of her circle's — and hacked the Sheta Djew's communication network. My people filter the data."

"You spy on your people? Do you trust no one?"

"I'm a seer, so no. I've seen people at their best and worst. For some, there's not much difference. On average, we all have the potential to be a hero or a villain."

O'Brien's pocket trilled.

"That's no way to live."

"Don't I know it," O'Brien grumbled. "They've recovered Anubis. Even the best intel has its limits. I didn't expect you to turn up."

The Senator looked sheepish. "About that…I may have read your message at Holy Water. Bad habit — reading other people's mail. We knew something was off: disappearances, stolen objects, odd behavior, ley spikes. Serrecold wasn't on our radar. Why didn't you tell me your suspicions? Unless…"

"Unless I had two suspects? Remember the Algernon Treatise? The week before, someone broke into my office, destroyed my security system, and accessed my journals. That single act may have altered the future. Whatever they read certainly did, and I've been playing catch-up since. It was either you or Serrecold. I haven't trusted you since," O'Brien admitted, shrugging. "The note was bait. If you were guilty, you'd frame him. If innocent, you'd track him. I apologize for doubting you, Rufe."

Balbay shook his head. "I…didn't realize. I suppose it wouldn't have made much difference if I had. We've worked together since, but I never wondered why we weren't allies. We vote the same, aim for the same ends — just with different methods. I should have wondered. Never mind, Darragh. No hard feelings?"

"None," O'Brien said, shaking his hand.

They turned back toward Elphame.

"Speaking of methods," Balbay said, "why the clown act in Quorum sessions?"

O'Brien shrugged. "That's just my glittering personality."

His phone chirped.

"I'd hate to call you a liar so early in our…friendship. Are we friends?"

"You'll need to develop a sense of humor, but yes. Incidentally, have you noticed how Acacia's nostrils flare like an enraged bull when I sing? Small pleasures help with the stress."

"I had wondered. You do sing quite often."

O'Brien smirked, checked his phone, and sighed. "Kenny's vanished again. No — wait — she's back. That young woman concerns me."

Chapter 94: Gone

Kenny: September 5th in the In-Between

"He's alive. He'll stay that way. Evy's fine — just needs time to recover," Oscar said, scribbling vitals down and hooking a clipboard to Madison's bed. "Madison will live. Sarduy will live. Taylor will live. You'll l—"

He broke off, took a breath. "So far, no casualties, but we're still missing a third of our people."

"Oscar, code four," Lydia called.

He turned to go, then paused to squeeze my shoulder — gently, terrifyingly. "Nore and Armand haven't returned yet."

I nodded and left Levisay to Oscar's care. Some things I couldn't control. Others, I could.

Team One was already assigning missing operatives and opening portals. Elphame was rumbling — but still standing.

"Put me in, coach," I murmured to Nebthu.

The bridge shook, straining to stay open.

"You'll alternate with Munmu. I mean it, Weaver; wait your turn. Everyone here volunteered. Don't disrespect that devotion."

Under the circumstances, arguing would've been bad form. I nodded, braced myself, and waited.

Fatigue-covered arms slid through the door. I grabbed warm, brown hands and pulled. Geraldine Patel spilled through, unconscious or dead.

Sasha smiled, reassuring me. Unconscious, then.

A raven-haired head popped through the door, mask down, invisibility off — standard recovery op procedure.

"Two more," Munmu said, and vanished again.

Danielle Paper — decidedly not a combat operative — walked through, cradling a ruined hand, determination burning in her face. We'd talk. And train. She'd done it once; she'd do it again.

Henry Paper followed, bruised but upright. Munmu came last. The door stayed open — for any still missing.

They handed me my assignment — third floor, south corner. I keyed onto the marker and began weaving.

Someone screamed.

Someone screamed every third minute. I ignored it. I had to.

"She's alive," I heard Nebthu rumble.

My eyelet was six inches wide when someone grabbed my shoulder and snarled in my ear like a rabid harpy, "You stupid, self-absorbed little bitch!"

I kept the door growing and muttered, "Missed you too, boo bear."

"What Xandre means," Padŭ said, peeling the redhead off me and patting my back, "is that we're relieved to see you intact — and we're here to help."

"Lovely to see you both. All help is welcome. Excuse me."

I anchored the portal and marched back into the faerie mound.

The bedroom walls undulated like water. A highboy toppled, shattering a ceramic lamp.

"Weaver!"

Gaia crouched in the corner, shielding her father. "He's hurt bad, and I'm out of juice."

Dave was conscious, but he didn't react to my presence or his daughter's voice.

"Help me get him through the door."

She nodded, rising awkwardly as Elphame bucked and heaved beneath us. We moved Dave Coinin as gently as we could. It was fine. We had time. Munmu caught him on the other side.

"Anyone else nearby?" I shouted as the house groaned and pitched.

"I don't think so."

I nodded, nudged her toward the exit, then hesitated. I remembered Lon's lecture, reached deep, and found some discipline.

The cacophony on the bridge lashed like a whip. Shouting. Weeping. Creaking. I barely made out Munmu's shout, "—vak! Trapped in a jewelry box!"

I scanned the bridge and spotted our pub manager locked in a reunion hug with her husband. It was distracting — not just the joy, but the six-foot-five vision of Caro Humboldt in toe shoes, tights, tiara, and a flower-laden tutu.

Her baby blues locked on me. "Don't ask," she mouthed.

She had a nasty gash and a new fragility in her expression — but she was alive.

I grinned and made an X over my heart.

Munmu and I cycled through four more doors before Oscar ordered the wounded evacuated to the Mulberry. The bridge was shaking too much for the med team to work.

"The third floor is—"

Six portals crumpled with a metallic shriek, one nearly trapping Onyx halfway through. Lon yanked her through right before the door imploded, spraying us with hot, glowing sparks.

"—collapsing!"

My ears popped. My stomach dropped like we'd gone down the big hill on a roller coaster. Someone screamed.

The floor reformed beneath us.

Fine. Everything was fine.

We'd cleared the third floor. There was still time.

I'd never seen a portal self-destruct. The bridge held. No one got sucked into the in-between. Even the turbulence had quieted to a modest shiver.

Someone shoved a new assignment into my hand. I read the business card: *Yildiz's Illustrations*. The words danced meaninglessly before my eyes. I reread them. Habit, instinct — or divine intervention — clicked. The marker pulsed: northwest basement. I moved.

A minute later, I stumbled through the door, tripping over Jake's body. The walls and ceiling were caving in. The floor was caving up! Distantly, I heard singing.

Someone screamed.

"Olivia!" I checked Jake's pulse.

He was gone.

"Kenny?" Her voice slurred. "I'm fine...can't move. Get... Jake first. Curse hit... him."

The ceiling flapped above us like wet sheets in a tornado. Bookshelves disintegrated into sawdust and vanished.

We were out of time.

I tapped a line and sent Olivia through the door on a surge of energy. I dragged Jake's body over, already weaving to lift him through. My back scraped against the sagging ceiling — ice shot down my spine, sucking power from my reservoir. I shoved him through and scrambled after, yanking his arms the rest of the way.

"Nore! Armand!" I screamed, trying to get to the bedroom door. It was pinched out of existence as my hand touched the knob. I made a run for the portal, Munmu pulling me through.

"—apsed. Elphame is gone."

"Nore?" I bellowed.

The question echoed.

"Get me her card!"

Someone screamed.

"Portal!"

I lurched upright, searching. Lon grabbed my arm and hauled me toward a tangle of filaments floating five feet off the floor.

"It stopped growing."

It had — but then it started again.

I held back in agony. Interfering with another practitioner's working — especially mid-manipulation — was asking for catastrophe.

The eyelet reached Frisbee size and fizzled. Seconds passed. A minute. It began again, growing to manhole size.

Lon shoved his head and shoulders through.

An eternity later, he backed out — dragging someone with him.

"She's alive," he rasped. Nore. Her face was slack, but her chest rose and fell.

I squeezed her hand before Oscar took charge. Whether she felt it or not — I needed it.

Lon was already waist-deep again. He pulled Pheona out, bloodied but conscious.

"She sang," she rasped, tears cutting paths through the dust on her cheeks. "Held the mound up 'slong as she could."

Last came Armand — naked from shifting, grinning like a lunatic.

"Found her," he declared…and passed out.

Chapter 95: Hedging

Kenny: September 5th at Sullen Creek Farm

It was very comfortable stretched out on the office couch, with Mel pinning my feet — he wasn't speaking to me — and Cartman massaging one boob. His claws were extended, but the little pinches of pain were oddly reassuring.

Oscar sat in my desk chair, stoic and grim, as he explained that I was going to die.

"Three days. Less now…" he murmured, not meeting my eyes.

"You're certain Davy said *Kenny*?"

"Yes."

He gritted his teeth and finally looked up. Staying on the bridge and out of the battle had been hell for Oscar.

I squeezed his hand. "It doesn't matter anymore."

Oscar shot to his feet and punched a hole in the wall.

"It matters to *me!*" he shouted at the sheetrock.

The dots weren't connecting.

"The race has begun; the door yawns wide. One must live and one must die; The mirror of truth can show you why," I recited. "Very *Harry Potter*. Callum Haigh thought the 'mirror of truth' referred to the *Clamare Vero*. It didn't — that mirror was just a bitter woman's last grasp at relevance. The one in the rhyme was metaphorical. I realized what it meant when Serrecold forced vampirism on me."

Oscar started. That bit hadn't reached him, evidently. I grinned and winked.

"I'm a bona fide member of the club now."

After a few basic tests, I'd determined that I was both stronger and faster. Whether I'd develop a taste for blood remained to be seen.

"I got to see what I might've been if my life had gone another way. It wasn't pretty, but it made one thing clear — it's on me to keep myself in check."

Oscar turned from the wall, listening.

"It's time for me to leave Sullen Creek," I said. "Past time."

"That doesn't sound like someone who's planning to die."

"I'm resigning as Representative of the Sheta Djew. We'll need to move fast to make the transition smooth. Time to stop hedging. Time for Enid Carter to be a full-time Doyenne."

"Shit," he cursed, understanding the implications. "Davy said *Kenny!*"

He paced the room, then stopped and looked at me.

"It won't be the same," he rasped — hissing like Maggie.

I hauled myself upright, upsetting the babies, and toddled over to hug him. Everything ached.

"I'll miss you, too, Representative Mendoza. But I'm only a door away."

He squeezed me tight enough to pop my back.

"They might not pick me, you know. Might decide Arlo's the man for the job."

"Twenty bucks says Arlo is the man for the job…in twenty or thirty years."

"Can't be a range. Man up and pick a number," he barked — though he didn't ask where I thought *he'd* be by then. I'd hoped he would. I had a theory…

"Fine. Twenty-three years. Arlo gets elected."

Oscar shook his head. "Fifteen. I'll mark it on the board."

I called out, "Colt," scanning the garden.

Rusty red stonecrop, blue dragonflies, purple Russian sage, and dusty pink coneflowers surrounded me, punctuated by the occasional flash of a green hummingbird — but without an apprentice in sight. The flagstone was warm beneath my feet. It was silly to be out without shoes, but after the last few days, I needed the contact — needed to ground myself. I wanted to memorize every scent, sight, sound, texture, and taste of my home.

I spun east — and plowed into a very nice chest.

Warm, calloused hands steadied me when I teetered. How could such a large man creep so well? I'd known John had survived Elphame, but he'd made himself scarce ever since we returned to the farm. I hadn't been sure I'd see him again.

"Hey," he said, sweeping his good eye over me before looking away.

"Hey, yourself."

He glanced back and caught me mapping his features. A smirk curled his mouth, the smug bastard. His confidence was irritating. And attractive. Unfortunately.

"We're packed," he said, dousing my hormones with cold water. "We'll head out after the exequy."

I sighed, closing my eyes and only opening them again once the pressure behind them had faded. It wouldn't be the last time we met, I knew, but there could never be anything more than a flirtation between us. Not the way things were. Maybe, one day.

"Thank you. For everything."

He nodded, a lock of his honeyed hair escaping his ponytail and wafting out on the breeze to tickle my ear.

"With Serrecold dead and the Hounds under O'Brien's control, what does that mean for Davy's prophecy?"

Absolutely nothing.

"The bean sídhe aren't precogs. They don't track time or calculate probabilities — they see endings. And only when they're inevitable. It doesn't have to be murder. I could choke on an ice cube or have an aneurysm. But...I *am* going to die, John. Soon. There is no escaping it."

"There has to be."

His voice remained level — calm and absolute.

What the hell.

I rose on my tiptoes and, one hand braced on his chest and the other tracing his face, kissed him.

His arms banded around me, crushing me to him as though he meant to meld us into one. His mouth was hot — ferocious.

"Don't give up."

The words were a heated breath against my lips.

"Goodbye," I whispered, and walked away.

Before I told him more than I should. Before he saw me crying again. This was already hard enough.

Something stung me as I rounded the corner — a wasp, probably. Bees loved me. I reached for the stinger and touched plastic instead. The dart fell, skittering across the flagstone.

Chapter 96: Helot

September 5th at Sullen Creek Farm

"Colt?"

Jones watched a murmuration of starlings overhead, pretending not to notice her apprentice disentangling himself from Katie, or Davy's apprentice's subsequent retreat into the trees.

"You called, boss?"

"I did. Got a minute?"

He fell into step beside her, glancing too often in the same direction. Not subtle.

"Tomorrow evening, I return to Wenen to resume my duties as Doyenne and Voice of the Saturniidae. Permanently."

Colt stumbled. Even after catching himself, he froze. She stopped too, breathing in the spicy scent of black walnuts.

"Sorry for the short notice. I'll understand if you choose to stay here. Oscar will serve as acting representative until an election is held. I expect he'll win, but I've been wrong before. Either way, he's well-equipped to finish your training…but I'd like for you to join me. Colt?"

He didn't answer — just stared past her, the air thickening.

Jones didn't see the movement. She heard it — a wet *snick*. The impact rocked through her, and she gasped like she'd been punched. Looking down, she saw the knife in her stomach — Colt's hand on the hilt. He braced her shoulder, yanked the blade out, and drove it in again.

Her eyes locked on his face — twisted, flushed, wet with tears.

"I'm sorry. I'm so sorry, Kenny. I can't stop," he panted.

She reached up and knocked off her glasses as he slashed her throat.

A bellow split the air, raw and animal.

"I remembered," Colt sobbed. "No magic."

John Dorrit tore him away, flinging him twenty feet. The warlock caught Jones as her legs buckled.

"Don't talk. Just breathe. Help is coming. Breathe."

She couldn't speak. Blood filled her mouth. So she signed, again and again, spending the last of her strength.

Dorrit flooded her reservoir with his power, trying to save her — just as she'd done for him. He watched her hands, frantic.

It didn't work.

She was gone.

He didn't react when they took her body; didn't flinch as someone wiped her blood off his skin, searching for injuries. But when Lon slapped him a second time, he punched back — hard.

They grappled. It was messy, violent, grounding. Eventually, Lon knocked him back into himself.

"What happened?" the sphinx panted, voice ragged — a roar barely contained.

Dorrit wiped his arm across his face as if to erase the last twenty minutes.

"He stabbed her…"

Saying it made it real.

"The kid. Colt. He stabbed her in the stomach, then slit her throat. I tried to hold the blood in. She tried to speak. I couldn't understand. She signed."

He mimicked the motion.

"What does it mean?"

Lon's brow furrowed. "Like this?" He mirrored the gesture, altering it slightly.

"Yes."

Lon's eyes flashed ruby-red. His voice turned lethal.

"It means someone performed the helot ritual on Colt."

Déjà's voice cracked through the silence, eyes wet with silent tears. "Then fix the boy before anyone else dies. And when you're done, send him to me."

She hooked an arm around Dorrit. "You," she said, "are in shock. Come on."

No one argued as the psychologist led him away.

And no one noticed the long-haired gray cat trailing behind.

September 6th in Wenen

"—defective leader. She bucked authority and ignored procedure. She put herself and our people in danger, selfishly pursuing her own ends. As Theorist Xandre said, we made a mistake — and this is the best possible outcome. We'll face similar temptations in the future: knowledge, services, goods we may not survive without. But at what cost? We may feed and clothe our bodies while auctioning off our integrity — warping ourselves into what we hate most. It's time to re-evaluate our standards."

The furious man sneered at John Dorrit and his team before storming off the dais, nearly knocking over a much shorter, much prettier woman who rose from a bench in the front row. She recovered, then stepped onto the stage, staring down at the elna plinth where Hazel McKenna Jones — dressed in her usual ribbed tank, plaid overshirt, and worn jeans — lay in repose.

"My name is Elena Ebersol Romero. Colt Ebersol is my son."

Her eyes scorched those who dared murmur, nearly setting them on fire.

"I met Hazel the night my first husband, Isaac Ebersol, died. Kenny and the Saturniidae saved my nine-year-old son and me — but not Isaac. He gave his life so we could escape. Colt, mourning his father and in awe of our rescuers, swore to Kenny Jones that one day he'd earn his place as her apprentice."

"He had no idea what that meant, but he was determined. He pushed himself at school and begged for extra homework. He delivered newspapers, mowed lawns, walked dogs — anything to pay for extracurricular lessons. I did everything I could to spare him from succeeding. I failed."

In the breath between those last two words, grief vanished. Pride lifted her head and steeled her voice.

"I will never like Kenny Jones," she said with brutal honesty. "I owe her everything — but she stole my firstborn from me. And told him to call me after every assignment."

"She found a place of safety for practitioners. She invited my family to make our home there. We no longer live in fear. But now, Julio and Rafael say they'll follow in Colt's footsteps. I no longer fear the Community — I fear my children's courage."

"In our new home, I heard terrible things. Rumors that our savior was strange. Untrustworthy. A murderer — tried and exonerated, yes, but a murderer still. That she tampered with the natural balance. That she used Angel of Mercy executions to placate sick urges. Kenny Jones was disgusting in every way."

The room shifted. Some fidgeted. Some froze. One man's face flushed with rage. Elena Romero named no names — she didn't have to. They outed themselves when they heard their own words repeated aloud.

"By happy accident, I discovered some key details were missing from those reports. No one mentioned that the twenty-nine people she 'murdered' were human traffickers. Or that they had kidnapped her kitsune familiar — her surrogate mother. I never heard it said that Kenny rescued ninety-three people from a life of slavery."

"No one told me she stood before the Covenant to be judged so that her vow would be accepted — a requirement before *we* agreed to help find Kuwako Yamane. Fear stopped us. It never stopped Kenny Jones."

"Her critics forget that every hedge witch we can boast of was trained by Kenny or one of her students. That she cared for thousands of displaced familiars and children. That she knew what was said about her and helped anyway. She was committed to saving others, even to her final breath."

"No one told me they owed Kenny Jones everything, too."

The air around her crackled like a live wire.

"Now, those same people call my precious boy a killer. They say he murdered the champion of his childhood — his mentor. His hero. Not that he was a helot, or a tool, or a victim. But a murderer."

The breeze that had cooled the crowd moments before grew heavy, agitated with magic. No one dared move. Only her children — a toddler burbling happily in Colt's lap, and his brothers — remained unfazed. They were used to the force of nature that was their mother. The rest of the room was not.

"Screw them," she spat.

Then she turned, fixing on a tall, curly-haired woman in the crowd while pointing to Kenny's corpse.

"Doyenne Carter. The person I trusted most to keep my son alive is dead. Take Colt as your apprentice. Do better by him than you did by her."

The Doyenne rose from her stone bench, the layers of her crimson robe rustling in the charged air.

"I shall," she said, "provided Colt agrees. And there is a place for you in the Saturniidae, should you ever wish to claim it."

Elena Ebersol Romero's righteous fire stalled at the unexpected job offer. Nonplussed but thinking, she stepped down from the dais and returned to her children.

The Doyenne approached the stage, a small, bittersweet smile forming.

"Hazel left a few words," she said, unfolding a letter.

> *"Here we part for a little while. I can only hope I went in a way that, were the consequences otherwise, would've earned a sound scolding from Padŭ, insincere threats from the Doyenne, and the usual gushing endorsement of Xandre.*
>
> *Oh, that my last words were, 'Hold my beer and watch this!' Tales would be told. Songs would be sung.*
>
> *Even if I inspire no legends, I ask you not to mourn me. Where I failed, I at least tried. I loved and was loved. What more is there?*
>
> *My companions, my brothers and sisters — it has been an honor. I'll say hello to our friends upstairs for you.*
>
> *Until we meet again: continue the search for Kuwako. Hold the line. Stem the tide. Give them hell.*
>
> *Yours ever,*
>
> *Kenny."*

The Doyenne looked away, drew a ragged breath, turned back, smiled weakly, and looked away again.

"I thought I'd be uniquely prepared to speak today. I've had to consider what I might say at Hazel's funeral a thousand times before. Second only to weaving doors, she was famous for cheating death by the skin of her teeth."

Her voice cracked. She rubbed her forehead and chuckled through a watery grimace.

"She always beat the odds. Always brought her team home. At some point, I suppose I started believing she always would. That there'd be some last trick. That she'd show up laughing — with a new lizard friend. Maybe a hedgehog."

She paused as if waiting for the deceased to comment.

When nothing of the sort happened, she sighed.

"A dangerous practice in our business. As others have already mentioned, controversy clung to Kenny like cheap perfume. Without intent or effort, she could divide a room instantly — usually into three distinct groups: those who thought she was dangerous, those who wanted to use her, and those who were loyal to her first, the Saturniidae second, and the Covenant a distant third. I was an overachiever in that regard."

She seemed to lose her train of thought for a few moments.

"I don't have any poetic words for you — no great wisdom or soothing platitudes to impart. *Stand strong. Chin up. Soldier on. She's in a better place. She's at peace now.* Anyone who knew her knows peace was out of the question. Just...for God's sake, make your life count."

Doyenne Carter inhaled deeply, drawing in the fresh, alien scents of Wenen. The Sleeping Bridge had been carved out of the *elna* below the pinnacle of the *Jazirat Mushriqa* — the Shining Island, by millions of trickling rivers. The cavern could only be reached by portal or a fearless and knowledgeable mountain climbing expedition. It was a miniature world unto itself. Sunlight poured into the gallery, lightly diffused and split into rose, peach, sunflower, and melon-tinted facets by the natural variations in the translucent stone overhead.

A forest grew inside the mountain — trees soaring three hundred feet or more. Blue vines curled lovingly around the ankles of anyone foolish enough to linger near the tree line, tugging playfully, and then insistently, to draw their victims deeper into the verdant wood. Escape was difficult.

The cool air vibrated with the sounds of life — the mournful cry of a massive cinnabar-colored maned tree frog with claws; the undulating whoop of an aubergine-hued cat-chimp perched high in the canopy; and the soft chorus of what sounded like crickets or locusts, but were, in fact, a flock of tiny, four-limbed, bird-like creatures with magnificent mallard-green plumage and iridescent wings.

It was an enchanting, bewildering microclimate — its flora and fauna strange and fascinating.

A death with a view.

Twelve pale plinths — each bearing a body, unblemished but lifeless — had been positioned on one of the many natural terraces to face the cave's mouth and the beautiful, broken plane beyond. Warded into stasis, the dead would remain undisturbed by pests or decay.

The arrangement was for the living. Mourners would have a year and a day to visit and make peace before the remains were cremated and interred beneath a tree, as custom demanded — generally an oak or hazel sapling. A smaller, more intimate ceremony would usher them to their final resting place.

Just as she had spoken over each of the twelve familiar faces, the Doyenne would do the same for them once again...in a year and a day.

"You're Kenny's...boss? Commanding officer? Supervisor?"

She pulled her streaming eyes away from where Olivia lay to confront John Dorrit, who looked like he wanted to thrash something but was reining in his temper and attempting to be civil. Politeness was quite out of reach.

"The Covenant's equivalent, yes," the Doyenne replied, wiping her eyes and studying the warlock with a quiet, fervid fascination.

It did not go unnoticed, but the warlock merely lifted the brow over his good eye and pressed on.

"What is being done to uncover how Kenny's apprentice came to be ensorcelled?"

The Doyenne's expression sharpened. Her head tilted, speculative. Something slightly predatory flickered across her face.

"What do you think I *should* be doing to determine the truth?"

"Hopefully, you've already had a high-level sensitive run a full analysis on the kid. If not, it's imperative — and urgent. Once it's determined that he's free from all forms of beguilement or mind control, he needs to be questioned — under the influence of a truth aid or by a telepath. He must have *some* information about where and how it occurred. If possible, analyze the site. Question everyone who might know something. Canvas the neighborhood. Find out where Kenny's dog was when it happened. Why didn't anyone see anything? Talk to your seers. Hire an augur if there's no better lead to follow. Ask questions. Brainstorm motives. Just...just don't let it go."

His pitch dropped lower and lower the longer he spoke, roughening with every word. By the end, it was nearly a growl.

The Doyenne listened in silence, then nodded, as if coming to some decision.

"Be honest, Agent Dorrit — even if I've done all those things and more, even if I presented you with the perpetrator wrapped in a big red bow, it wouldn't satisfy you. You wouldn't have *seen* the evidence. *You* wouldn't have drawn your own conclusions."

She paused. "You need to investigate Hazel's death for yourself."

His stormy blue-green eye locked on her with devastating focus. "Yes."

Enid Carter made her move.

"I'm willing to turn over the evidence we've collected and allow you access to Colt, the Sheta Djew, and anyone else you believe is relevant. You'll have access to Sullen Creek Farm. Hazel's quarters here in Wenen are still occupied, but during daylight hours, I'll allow supervised access."

"Occupied? By whom?"

The Doyenne arched her brows in bitter amusement and tilted her head toward a group huddled around Representative Jones's plinth.

Dorrit followed her gaze.

"You didn't think Hazel confined her collecting to displaced familiars, did you? Community children — though they've been victimized as much or more than the rest of us — have a hard time getting adopted. Hazel and a few like-minded souls take them in. Unless it interfered with a mission or her reservoir was low, she did her best to spend a few hours with them every day. Often she brought Eli, Milo, and Mouse. If she couldn't make it, some of her pets would visit in her stead. Now...they've been orphaned all over again."

He remained transfixed by the vignette for several seconds.

"You're working hard. But what are you selling?"

She smiled, appreciative of his bluntness.

"No one who didn't work directly with Hazel ever truly understood her." The Doyenne's voice trembled. "They thought she was reckless. A liability. Treasonous, even. I doubted her at first — she was so unpredictable. Her mind didn't work like most; her values, her priorities...were different."

She swallowed hard, tears welling again.

"Because of that, she found it difficult to trust others. She preferred working with a small, tightly knit group. And yet — after only a few days — she trusted you. I cannot overstate how curious that is. It wasn't Eli's influence, and it wasn't infatuation. It was instinct. Intuition. Something I can't quite name."

Doyenne Carter looked him over like a buyer at auction, measuring him.

"I've learned to trust her instincts. Join us. Join the Covenant. Stay. Train. Bring your team." She raised her chin. "It won't be easy, and it won't be fun. The guilds may put you on trial, as they did her. But—" she glanced toward the children gathered near Kenny's plinth "—together, we might build a kinder world."

Dorrit's eye narrowed.

"You're attempting to recruit us?"

"I am."

He paced a few feet back and forth, then paused.

"Why do you call her Hazel?"

Carter inhaled slowly.

"Names matter. They shape us in ways we rarely expect. In Hebrew, *Hazel* means 'God has seen.' In Celtic lore, hazel trees are sacred — symbols of wisdom and inspiration. Anyone who ate their fruit was granted insight. Nine hazel trees grew round the Well at the End of the World. Their nuts fell into the waters and were eaten by the Salmon of Knowledge. The fae revere the hazel. Hermes carried a hazel staff to guide him through the mortal and divine realms. In Old English, hazel means 'rod of power.' Sometimes it denotes a leader or protector. Druids often preferred hazel staves to oak. They made hazelmead to induce prophetic dreams. To fell a hazel tree was a capital offense. Hazel divining rods were used to judge guilt or innocence in murder cases. I call her Hazel because that's who she was — a leader who inspired visions of hope."

He listened — intently, even appreciatively — but when he spoke, there was no give in his voice.

"I owe Kenny a life debt. I'll repay it, even now that she's gone. I'll honor the contract we signed. But the trust *she* earned? That's not transferable. Not to you, and not to the Covenant. My loyalty lies with the Community — now and always."

She opened her mouth, but he raised a hand to silence her.

"I'm angry."

That was an understatement. He was incandescent — radiating fury, jaw clenched, eye burning.

"I want someone to blame for Kenny's death. She should have been better protected. She should have protected herself — valued herself more. After what I've heard today, the Covenant never deserved her and has no idea what it's lost."

His gaze bored into her — searing, soul-deep.

"I'm withholding judgment as far as it applies to you. For now."

"Fair enough," she murmured, drying her tears. "We haven't made the best impression."

As he turned to go, she touched his arm.

"Before you judge us too harshly, John — walk a mile in our shoes. What would you be like if you'd been hunted your whole life? Who would you trust, knowing a single mistake could destroy everyone you loved? The man who condemned Hazel — he trusted the wrong person. Because of that, his family was destroyed — not by the APA. By someone much worse. When we found his wife, his son, his two daughters, his brother, and his sister-in-law...we could only identify them with their trackers. He's broken. He's tried to kill himself three times — and three times, he's healed himself. For their sake. He's healed every one of us — even Hazel."

Chapter 98: Dissonance

September 6th in Wenen

Chairman Darragh O'Brien was uncharacteristically subdued as he steered his lady through clusters of side-eyeing practitioners. Let the Covenant revile him — he just needed to reach Kenny. He needed to know.

He deliberately didn't rush — any haste would draw a mob. Even so, the sight of the fallen slowed his progress further. Over three hundred were laid out on the sun-drenched terraces like a silent, sleeping army. No one could see them — arranged with such care — and not be moved.

"Darragh," Rena whispered, tightening her grip on his arm and leaning into his shoulder. "It isn't her."

Relief struck like lightning — there and gone — as he cradled her.

"Where the hell is she?" he murmured. He didn't understand. He hated not understanding. If John was going to flay him, he'd at least...

Rena's response got lost in his jacket.

"Didn't quite catch that..."

She looked up. Her hennaed eyes, rimmed in tears, were startling.

"She's here. Close. What if...what if she can't forgive me?"

A distinct possibility.

"She's alive. That was always the goal. We're immersed in the blind spot now. Our notions of success must be...flexible."

"How flexible? Will more die?"

They turned to the bodies lying in state.

"I hope not," he said. "But it's almost certain. Fewer will die — if my theories hold. I hope."

Rena nodded, not fully comprehending but trusting him, nonetheless. "And she was important to John? This Kenny?"

"Mind the vine," he warned, spotting one of the creeping blue nuisances. "She was never meant to be, but yes. Did that weed grab you?"

Rena had stopped short, staring at Dorrit and the woman beside him. The Doyenne spoke earnestly, touching his arm. Rena's lips parted as she stood frozen — spellbound — not hearing O'Brien.

Enid Carter turned, sensing something. Her eyes locked on Rena, and a small, pained sound escaped her. She shook her head, utter disbelief settling over her.

"I'm a fool," O'Brien breathed, noting the Doyenne's height and clothes. "A certifiable idiot. The robes. The simulacra… That little, winged mutt's been keeping secrets."

His brief triumph faded. The reckoning had arrived.

"She'll forgive you. She won't be able to help herself," he murmured with absolute conviction. "Don't stay away too long, love. I'm lost without you."

Rena jerked, as if tearing her gaze from the other woman took iron will. She laughed softly through her tears — all the more stunning for her strength.

"I love you, Darragh," she said, kissing him. "I'll come home soon. Promise."

"Home?" he echoed, hardly daring to believe he'd heard her right.

"Of course, home, ridiculous man."

O'Brien watched her close the distance, barely holding herself together, while Carter radiated with tormented hope and confusion.

"Rena Amano is Kuwako Yamane, then," Dorrit grunted, stepping beside him.

"She is," O'Brien said.

"And she returned just in time for Kenny's funeral. Incredible." The warlock hissed and stalked off, vanishing through the portal. His team followed in uneasy concern.

"Poor fellow," Boruta squeaked.

"Indeed. How much have you been withholding in your reports?" O'Brien murmured.

The daemon yapped — a high, wheezing giggle — three times.

"Plenty. We seers are not exempt from the rules. If I told you everything, it would have changed the path."

O'Brien scowled. He much preferred managing to being managed.

"How's your young charge holding up?"

They looked over to where Eli, Louise, Miigwan, and Alonzo attempted to comfort a sunken-eyed Davy.

"Better than expected. The young are endlessly resilient. Good thing, too — he'll need to be."

"And the mirror?"

"Destroyed."

"By Kenny?"

The pooka gave him a sly look. "Officially or unofficially?"

"Both."

"Officially, she took it from Elphame and gave it to the Doyenne of the Saturniidae — one of only two living descendants of the warlock Deidamia — who then destroyed it. Unofficially, it never left Elphame. But yes, it's gone."

"You've always been a repulsive little pest," O'Brien muttered. "Why can't you just say, 'Yes, Kenny Jones was an alias. Her adoptive parents changed her name to protect her. But now, unknown forces require her to go back to her birth name — Enid Carter.' Is that too much to ask?"

Boruta wheeled in delighted circles around the Chairman's ankles, clearly pleased with himself.

"Consider it overdue vengeance — lording over us poor foresights. 'We'll see, Boruta. Just wait a few centuries.'"

O'Brien rolled his eyes.

"How did they manage it? It's not a glamour — Ghost sees through them. Spells won't work for the same reason."

The pooka nearly levitated with smug glee.

"Hereditary magic! A cryptic genetic transmutation talent," the Chairman guessed.

Boruta froze mid-prance.

"Wonderful. I'll add that tidbit to her profile."

The Chairman yelped — drawing more attention than he liked — as the fluffy imp nipped his ankle.

"…hadn't, this day would've come thirteen years sooner and been far more tragic," Rena said, a pleading note creeping into her voice.

"So you've said."

"Can you forgive me?"

The Doyenne sighed, stepping down from the desk through the open window. She gathered her robes, careful not to catch her heels.

"I understand why you did it, but that doesn't make this okay. I'm furious. I'm relieved. I'm numb. And I feel like I've been split open and left hollow. There's nothing left in me, Kuwako. So no — I can't forgive you."

She let out a raw bellow, hurled a chair at the wall, and knotted her fingers in her hair. She wanted to cry — needed to — but the tears had abandoned her.

"I needed you. I killed for you. And all this time…it was a choice."

Rena flinched as though struck. She reached out, then hesitated, her hand trembling in the air between them. "When I look at you, I still see the heartbroken little girl behind the shed, whittling on her stick. I'd never felt such pain — such guilt — in a child so young. You always thought you could fix everything, and then blamed yourself when you failed. I know this wasn't the solution you wanted, but I could not bear to watch you die — knowing I could have prevented it."

"Doyenne!"

The double doors to the game room burst open. Arlo stumbled in — both arms fully healed, fortunately, because he tripped over his own feet in his rush.

"Just found it. Fallen to the floor — overlooked until now," he said breathlessly from the ground, thrusting up a white envelope stamped with a muddy boot print.

Carter sagged, exhausted and defeated.

"What is it?" she asked, accepting the missive with great reluctance.

"I haven't read it, but...I believe that's Count Vitruvio's calligraphy."

She glanced at the writing. Arlo hadn't exaggerated — it was calligraphy, with all the fussy swirls and flourishes. Usually, such excess would've amused her; now, it just irritated her. Biting the inside of her bottom lip, she tore open the envelope, unfolded the single sheet inside, and read.

> Dear Weaver,
> It is difficult to write this letter after the hospitality the Sheta Djew have shown me, when I owe you so much. The last few days have been the adventure of a lifetime. I will cherish the friends and memories I've made until the day I die. Thank you.

In a few days, the existence of supernatural beings — along with a substantial body of evidence — will be made public. Just as Egress led me to Sullen Creek, The Parallel Realm led me to Santa Fe seven years ago. There, I first discovered that humans are not alone.

Before I could share what I'd found, I was caught. The Quorum placed a lock in my mind. I remembered nothing.

At Sullen Creek, I began to experience intense déjà vu. Living among supernaturals, talking with you, reading your books, and being healed by Oscar created enough dissonance to break the lock. That's my theory, at least. In any case, I remember everything now.

I'm grateful it happened this way. I've learned that while some supernaturals can be cruel, others can be kind. I will try to be fair in my representation.

I know this is a betrayal of trust; I'm sorry. My loyalty must remain with my fellow humans. I only hope no harm comes to the Sheta Djew.

I had thought, in fairness, I should release you from the promise you made me — but I fear I will have great need of your help and soon. I want to believe you won't regret making that promise, despite what I must do.

If there is ever an opportunity to balance the scales without violating my loyalty to humanity, please believe that I will seize it.

Your friend,

Count Vitruvio, A.K.A. Veritas

Just the cherry on top.

"Arlo, fetch Chairman O'Brien. Bring him to the Mulberry portal. Tell him it's urgent. Kuw— Rena...we'll finish this later," she rasped, the letter clenched in her fist. "This won't wait."

Chapter 99: The Forfeit

September 6th in Wenen

"Warlock?"

Dorrit's jaw clenched at being addressed thus, but he kept his peace. Rather than being intimidated by the agent in their midst, the guild leaders of the Covenant ranged from openly hostile to indifferent to nearly welcoming. The slender man beside him — robed in tarnished gold, and one of two who showed their face — was particularly friendly. To the point of being creepy.

O'Brien was busy demanding an emergency session of the Quorum. He alone could be both persistent and obnoxious enough to get the Community's leaders to move when they did not want to move. So, Dorrit was on his own.

He held little hope for these negotiations — he didn't see how it would benefit them and had little skill as a salesman. It was imperative, however, according to O'Brien; as such, he would try. Taking Carter and the one she introduced as Phi Thale as the Covenant's spokespeople, he focused on them. If they could be convinced, the rest might follow.

"Although Luke Vitruvio was thwarted seven years ago and his memory altered, the documentation he gathered was never recovered," Dorrit began, enduring the belligerence of the gathered Voices with resigned equanimity. The sealed chamber, carved from dark stone and lit only by a floating white sphere, felt suffocating. The ley lines were agitated and snapping, curdling with discontent.

"He'd made enough noise that, even for the twelve hours the Agency had him in custody, his absence was reported to the police. Vitruvio — or Brian Malinconico, as he went by then — was well-versed in our methods. He's immune to persuasion and can outwit our best cybersmiths. Any attempt to seize his files was deemed reckless. Regardless, the APA tried — and failed."

That's right; paint the Agency as a pack of incompetents with a license to kill. That'll reel them in. Internally, Dorrit rolled his eyes and continued.

490

"No one knew he'd planted cameras in preternatural hotspots. He obtained footage of glamours being dropped, spells being cast, feedings, and pop-up markets. Forty-two hours ago, he released everything. DNA samples. Names. Art. Books. Music. Technology. Live streams. The wild constructs at Sullen Creek. It's a large and cogent body of evidence."

The ley lines coiled around him like a constrictor.

One Voice — Torticidae, he'd been informed — turned her gaze toward her left-hand colleague.

"Killing the messenger will do no good," she murmured.

"I've no intention of killing him."

"You intend to dishonor the Covenant. He is Saturniidae's guest. We are bound by parley." She jutted her chin toward Carter, who watched silently. "Warlock, continue."

Dorrit nodded, his gratitude tempered by frustration.

"Chancellor Ishaq Wasem, one of the named, hasn't waited to see if Vitruvio will be believed. He fled, abandoning his cadre. In the last seven hours, there have been twenty-three attacks on suspected preternaturals. Three were genuine. One was fatal."

"What would you have of us?" asked the gray-robed Voice of Nolidae. "We cannot undo what has already been done."

Dorrit wasn't convinced of that, but it would keep for now.

"Why do anything?" another snapped. "They made this mess. Let them clean it up. If the roles were reversed, the Community would lead the hunt."

"You forget — the Sheta Djew have been outed. Like it or not, we are involved."

"And we can mitigate the damage," Carter said calmly. "Neither side is blameless, but for the first time in three thousand years, the Covenant and Community share a common enemy: ignorance. If we present a united front — confirm what's true, dismantle the myths — we can limit the fallout."

"Turn calamity into opportunity," Phi Thale mused before anyone else could throw in their two cents. "There is wisdom in this...but how? Time is short."

Dorrit snorted quietly.

Too late, he realized that rousing the Quorum before this meeting's outcome was known was risky — unless the outcome was assured. O'Brien wouldn't leave it to chance. Suspicion crystallized into certainty; even if he was telling the truth about the blind spot, he knew something — enough to feel certain that, barring outright violence, even Dorrit's worst effort would be enough. It was both a relief and an irritant.

"The Covenant has achieved great things," Carter urged, "but our people are dying. Wenen is a reprieve, not a solution. If the current rate of mortality holds, in ten years, we will be forced to abandon Earth or perish. We must try something new."

She held up a flash drive.

"This was prepared by Saturniidae prior to Vitruvio's betrayal."

She stepped forward and dropped the drive onto the floating sphere. It vanished without a sound.

"Adidae," said Phi Thale.

A dwarf swaddled in blue stepped forward and plunged his hands into the sphere. A moment passed; he withdrew and returned to his place.

"Dalceridae."

The process repeated.

"Doidea."

One by one, Phi Thale called the guild leaders forward — saving himself for last.

When he stepped back, his hands slipping out of the stone, a flash drive rested in one, and an enormous moth — an Atlas moth, belonging to the Saturniidae family — clung to the other. It took flight and vanished.

"The Covenant has spoken," Phi Thale intoned, grinning. He tossed the drive to Dorrit. "We stand with the Saturniidae. Doyenne Carter will accompany you to Chicago, Agent Dorrit."

The Agora in Chicago, Illinois

"No need to be nervous," O'Brien assured the Doyenne as she wove.

She eyed his own trembling hands with an arched brow.

"He's not nervous," Dorrit explained, checking his weapons before they portaled back to the Agora. "He's excited."

"Excited?"

"Farsights live in two timelines — one slow, one fleeting. Most enjoy blind spots as a break — a forced vacation. Not Darragh O'Brien. To him, they're wild cards. A challenge. He's a junkie gamester at the end of a long play."

Dorrit's tone suggested he did not share in the thrill.

"No seer sees every road, John. Hers was never fully visible to me — it just overlapped with those I could see. If I'd known what would happen, I swear — I would have stopped her death."

Dorrit made no reply, turning instead toward the growing portal — except it had stopped.

Both men turned to the Doyenne, who covered her mouth, trying — and failing — not to laugh.

"I'm sorry. I just realized. You're father and son! Hazel was right." Her grin faltered. "My mother and I don't always get along either."

"My father was Elizeus Kenelm Dorrit," the warlock said darkly.

O'Brien's energy evaporated. When he met her gaze, he gave a slight shake of his head.

Pity nearly kept her silent — but not quite.

"Hazel was never a vampire, not before the Eliberarea Demonului ritual, not after. It was performed correctly, but Hazel recognized the entity she was contending with — she knew herself and became something other, possibly something older. Spontaneous vampirism isn't a clean split between good and evil, of course, but the fact remains — the invention of a secondary history is the psyche protecting itself."

Dorrit stared at the motionless portal. O'Brien watched the floor. Carter, satisfied she'd said her piece, turned her focus back to the spell.

It was a grim trio that emerged in O'Brien's office.

"You're sure about this?" the Chairman asked, eyeing the pretty bauble Carter handed Dorrit — a precast *Laenat Alijini*.

"I'm not about to demonstrate hedge magic in front of the Quorum. This is the cleanest way to smuggle me in."

"Ready?" Dorrit asked.

She met his gaze and offered a small, bittersweet smile. "Have at it."

He activated the curse and pressed it to her hand. She vanished without fanfare.

"Curious that she trusts you so completely," O'Brien mused. "You've only just met."

Dorrit stared at the copper bauble for a moment, then set it gently on the desk.

The Chairman consulted his pocket watch. "It's time."

A muscle ticked in Dorrit's jaw, but he nodded. He lay down on the settee — though it was too short for comfort — and fell out of himself. Manifesting briefly for O'Brien's benefit, Dorrit retrieved the Doyenne's glass prison, considered it for a moment, and pocketed it.

Let's get this over with.

"So, you're saying that no one — not a single member of the Sheta Djew — was ever a suspect? Nearly two thousand individuals, all read-in and assisting you and the APA?"

They'd been at this for hours.

"Yes," O'Brien said, smiling despite the Minister's sarcasm. "All but the children and those living or traveling outside Representative Jones's territory — closer to twelve hundred, all told. Of course, most were only informed that their cadre was assisting the APA and instructed to maintain normal routines. We weren't advertising our presence or the extent of cooperation. In any case, there's a more pressing—"

"And you can't explain how they helped you, because that might 'alter the future'? Convenient."

O'Brien's grin grew — smug and sheepish at once. It was good to be a seer.

"It certainly is, but that doesn't make it less true. I can say that Representative Jones's staff flagged a couple of odd hotel reservations. One for a Ted Marbel was canceled eleven days ago — exactly six months after it was made. Not unusual. But seconds after the cancellation, a new reservation came in. Same hotel, same window. That alone wasn't cause for alarm — small beer hotel, popular with tourists — but a minor cybersecurity breach was detected and reported to the APA. The new name on the reservation? Luke Vitruvio — the true name of Brian Malinconico."

The name stirred a murmur from the audience, enough to rouse the Magister for three groggy blinks before Morpheus reclaimed him.

"The APA contacted Jones. She agreed to assist us. Due to the investigation's sensitivity, we constructed a false case file implying she was tied to a long-running series of burglaries and disappearances. That can all be addressed later—"

"But she wasn't?" Pendragon interrupted.

"Wasn't what?"

"A person of interest. Despite the crimes being real."

"Correct. The crimes were real, but she was never a suspect."

"She was never suspected of warped practices?"

"Never," O'Brien replied, deadpan.

"Yet a warlock team was assigned to the case."

"The Sheta Djew take security seriously, Minister. The breach involved magic and a master hacker — like Vitruvio. We already knew he had access to ley manipulations — either via an accomplice or a stockpile of potent precast spells. Calling in the APA's top warlock team was judged prudent. There was an imminent threat to both the Community and the Sheta Djew. And it fit the cover story. Now, if we could—"

"Pity Serrecold isn't alive to confirm any of this."

Pendragon's glare, meant to shake O'Brien's composure, failed.

"If you say so. That's a separate matter. His notes should cover it. But this session is meant to determine our strategy moving—"

Aloysius Pendragon cleared his throat loudly, pursed his lips, stuffed his hands in his pockets, and rocked on his heels.

"And yet, despite all these precautions, Representative Jones was killed, correct?"

"Sadly, yes. But her death is unrelated to this case. There are two other active investigations involving the Sheta Djew. For all his sins, Vitruvio isn't a murderer — not directly. I've been instructed by both the APA and the Therianthrope Council to limit my comments to what's been publicly released: she was murdered by a helot. That said, a more recent death must be—"

A surge of murmuring drowned out the Minister's next question and DeWitt's gavel-pounding.

"But it was *because* of the Representative's death that Vitruvio escaped!" the dwarf bellowed once quiet resumed.

"We're nearing classified territory. Suffice it to say that a life-or-death emergency arose. The Sheta Djew requested aid, and the APA responded — as is required by law. Vitruvio used the distraction to disappear. He disabled all trackers, ditched his phone, and vanished. He's smoke. Regardless—"

"I think it's time we heard from the APA. We may return to you, Chairman, but for now, please step down. The Quorum calls Special Agent in Charge Ghost to the floor."

O'Brien rolled his eyes and returned to the Union's table.

Before he even sat, a form materialized in the witness chair. Male in shape, the warlock's true features were obscured — except for the fact that he was yawning.

I beg your pardon, Minister. It's been a long few days.

The eldritch voice echoed. No one wanted to volunteer a response — not even his questioner.

"Uh-uhm… We quite understand, Agent Ghost. Would you give us your impression of Representative Jones?"

A bold, determined, and loyal leader, beloved by her cadre.

"And not a person of interest?"

Ghost's voice dropped into a soul-burning register.

You've been told repeatedly — Representative Jones was assisting the APA. She was not a person of interest. She died protecting her cadre.

An uncomfortable silence followed. No one met his gaze, though several flinched when he turned his head.

"Were the…um…actions that led to Vitruvio's escape justified?" Pendragon slowly ventured.

Yes.

"Would you care to elaborate?"

No. I am legally and ethically bound not to. Why are we discussing this? There's an urgent threat to the Community, and you're too busy showboating to address it.

"Yes, Minister," snapped Senator Balbay, his fangs lowered in a rare show of emotion. "Your obsession with the Warped clouds your judgment. You didn't even call this session, but you're determined to slander someone who can't defend herself."

"As much as it pains me to agree with Senator Balbay," added Judge Dietricksen, "this can wait. Our response to Vitruvio's actions cannot. I'd love nothing more than to grill Chairman O'Brien over how my Hounds came to be in his care — but right now, that's a secondary concern. Especially with the APA being left rudderless. I propose that we appoint an interim director immediately."

"I second the motion," declared Irit Jackson, "And nom—"

"I nominate Senator Balbay," O'Brien interrupted.

The Senator, stunned, gaped for a moment. "I'm honored by the Chairman's nomination. Thank you, Darragh. That is…thank you. However, I must decline. I believe I serve the Community best by continuing to lead Internal Investigations. My cadre already gets too little of my time as it is. There is, however, someone I think we could all agree on. I nominate Special Agent Ghost."

Chief Justice Jackson, unused to and unappreciative of being ignored, hissed.

The warlock, still seated in the witness's chair, started — an oddly human reaction from someone so otherworldly.

"Twice in one night," murmured Dietricksen. "We do live in strange times. Do you accept the nomination, Special Agent Ghost?"

The silence stretched into something nearly unbearable before his flinty, spectral voice replied, "I do."

"Excellent. Magister, we need to take a vote," the Judge said, turning toward the podium. Dumitru DeWitt was, as usual, draped precariously over the lectern — sound asleep.

"Magister," she snapped, her voice like a whip.

DeWitt didn't stir.

An aide rushed forward and checked his pulse.

"Uhhh...it appears the Magister has...expired."

There was a beat of silence as the room digested this unexpected event.

"Wonderful," sighed Judge Dietricksen. "We'll vote on his replacement next. Please remove the body and notify his next of kin. Moving on — what the bloody hell is that?"

A thick, black fog slithered across the floor in jerky, insectile bursts — like a spider hunting. It crept from vents and under chairs, curling around ankles.

The click of heels sounded loud in the quiet hall.

Ghost tried to rise, but some invisible force kept him pinned. His ephemeral form jerked, straining against the chair, which remained bolted to the floor. Others tried to flee but found themselves equally restrained.

"Do not be alarmed," came a woman's voice — soft, gentle, and echoing from every direction.

A figure emerged from the fog.

She wore a sleek suit in a very dark green and a wide-brimmed fedora that shadowed her face.

"I mean you no harm."

"Who are you?" Judge Dietricksen snarled, her wolf fangs promising retribution.

"I am Enid Carter, Voice of the Saturniidae and Doyenne of the Covenant. I'll go ahead and assume most of you don't know what that means."

White teeth flashed beneath the brim.

"I am a practitioner."

A volley of precast spells launched at the intruder, bursting against an invisible barrier like fireworks and dripping onto the unlucky senators and representatives below.

Unbothered, the woman stepped onto the dais and approached the warlock.

"Mind if I sit here?" she asked, perching on the arm of his chair. Then, to the room:

"I only need a moment of your time. Practitioners have been forced to live in your shadow — silenced, hunted, erased — for millennia. We chose secrecy to survive, but we are no longer content to merely survive. We had prepared to out both ourselves and the Community to the uninitiated — to step into the light on our terms. Imagine our surprise…when Mr. Vitruvio beat us to it."

She gave a small moue of disappointment.

"Frustrating, yes. But Vitruvio didn't out practitioners — and he wasn't exactly flattering to the rest of you. This left us with a unique opportunity. As a gesture of goodwill, the Covenant is donating our prepared materials to the Community. Use them as they are, or not at all. They're magically protected, but you'll find we were both kinder and more accurate than Vitruvio."

"If you do choose to make a united announcement, a member of the Covenant will be in touch to coordinate dates and appearances. And possibly to discuss a more lasting truce."

She rose, smoothing her suit.

"But be advised."

Her voice sharpened.

"Any attempt to apprehend or harm any member of the Covenant will trigger the release of a second, far less generous edition — including details on the Cleansing, the use of *pułapki duchowe*, helots, and every other atrocity the Community has sanctioned. Thank you for your hospitality — I'll see myself out."

"Wait," snapped Dietricksen. But the Doyenne was already gone, swallowed by fog.

"Security! Where are the guards?" shrieked Senator Hersch.

Freed from whatever spell had bound him, Ghost launched from his chair with a bellow — only to stumble face-first into the mist, knocking over a stack of objects that hadn't been there before. A beat later, he remembered he didn't need to manifest and disappeared.

The fog began to dissipate, revealing hundreds of books — stacked just low enough to remain concealed.

"Don't touch them," warned President Bell as O'Brien bent to pick one up.

"The young lady just punked us in our own palace, Adam," O'Brien said, snorting as he read the title. "*The Faces of Humanity*. Sounds dry. If she meant us harm, there was nothing we could've done about it."

"Young? You don't think she was an old power? That swagger—"

O'Brien snorted again. "Exactly. The young ones are always so desperate to impress."

September 6th at Sullen Creek Farm

"Closet," Davy announced, dropping three boxes to mark her territory. The long, trailing hair left after her prophecy had been haphazardly hacked off. She was still pale, with bruised-looking eyes, but the curly crop suited her. Her native vim was returning — slowly.

"The right side stays. Everything between the drawers and the door goes — leave a robe and one suit. The boots on the left go, and those three pairs of heels go. Jewelry too."

"Bookshelves," said Maggie. "Lon'll get the uppers."

"Pack a mix of fiction — no Devereaux."

"Maggie, don't listen to her. Pack four," Déjà cut in. "No, Enid, I insist. I'll write a prescription and file it with the Covenant if I must. You children think love is some grand, fated torment. Devereaux knows relationships take work."

Carter flinched. She and Déjà had spoken at length the night before. The psychologist hadn't accepted her take on Eli's visions or Milo, but they knew where they stood.

For peace, Carter nodded. No one could make her reread the books.

"Oscar, mark any references you want. Don't skimp. I'll use the Covenant's library."

Representative Mendoza lifted a sheet of neon stickers. He didn't look at Carter, nor did she at him. He'd privately confessed his part in Kenny's death, and she couldn't forgive him.

"Tools," Lou sang, looking positively dangerous with the label maker.

"Leave a basic set. The rest goes." Carter kept her voice steady.

"I'll take the bathroom," said Nore, squeezing her shoulder.

She hadn't told Nore about Eli's conspiracy. Or anyone uninvolved. She wasn't sure she should. She was isolated — stewing in her fury.

"Thank you. All of you."

"Don't be a sad sap," Déjà said. "You'll be back. Wednesdays are now game night."

Carter bit the inside of her lip. Change was good. Her friends were adapting. But her haven was gone.

"Where's Armand?"

"KP. He insisted on making the pizza — even if beer and takeout are traditional."

"I-I'll g-go check on him," the Doyenne stammered, ducking out.

She made it three steps before a chill danced up her spine.

"I know you're there."

Eli and Boruta crawled out from under the desk in the hallway. Eli looked tearfully defiant; Boruta, half-hyper, half-subdued.

"It worked," Eli sullenly declared. "I know it did."

"It worked," she echoed.

The memory swallowed her — John's kiss, the sting on her neck, the dart falling to her feet, the encroaching darkness, and Oscar's whispered apology as he caught her.

She'd woken up in her room, feeling as wilted as dirty laundry. Déjà sat beside her, pale beneath her dark skin, stroking her hand and silently crying. Colt, leaning against the wall, had been the first to notice that she was awake but said nothing, his eyes flat and empty.

She didn't need to ask what they'd done. Betrayal had a taste. Rage bloomed sharp and vast. Kenny had, indeed, died.

"It was the only way to keep you safe," Déjà had murmured. "To be certain."

Safe. She hated that word.

"It doesn't matter if they're simulacra. I was thirty when I killed my first. Colt is nineteen. You *know* what that does to the psyche — the dreams, the torment. To the eyes, it's real!"

Her shout had echoed.

"I volunteered," Colt had said quietly.

She'd stared at him, mourning what he didn't yet recognize but had already lost. His innocence was gone; the beautiful clarity with which he'd seen the world, even after enduring tragedy, had blurred. She knew this had always been inevitable, but she'd never stopped hoping that something would prevent it. He wasn't just a man now; he was a warrior.

"I was supposed to protect him."

Déjà's jaw tightened.

"I know it hurts. But this is bigger than you, than him, than the Covenant. We're unraveling global biases. That takes a symbol. You are that symbol. Sacrifices must be made."

Eli's plump hand wrapped around her cold one, grounding her.

"It *did* work," he repeated, red-eyed and trembling.

She was furious — and this brilliant child had helped cause it. But, for a moment, she was back on that lonely highway, choosing who to be.

She picked him up.

"I'm alive, Professor. I'm me."

"But you're leaving."

Even with his arm collaring her neck and his face buried in her shoulder, the accusation rang clear.

"I must. A house with a cracked foundation falls. When I joined the Covenant, I thought they might accept Deidamia's descendant — or an assassin — but not both. So I split the difference, though neither was whole. That's not fair to anyone. I need to fix things. You'll still see me."

"It won't be the same."

"And us?" Mouse asked, dragging Milo with one hand and cradling Babbage with the other. Mundy wagged his tail, simply happy to be with his people. Carter hadn't even noticed he wasn't Mel, who'd been sent back to Vivienne, lest his diligence give the game away.

"You have a choice. Come to Wenen with Colt and me — or stay here. I'll love you either way."

Mouse and Milo traded exasperated looks.

"We've packed."

Chapter 101: The Quest

September 6th in Chicago, Illinois

"Thank you," Carter's soft, melancholy voice echoed in his memory.

Freshly freed from her glass prison and deposited into the relative safety of O'Brien's office, she'd stared up at him expectantly.

He'd nodded — just enough to acknowledge her — then floated past, rejoining his body without a word.

Dorrit unlocked his apartment door and slammed it behind him, slamming it again after it bounced back at him. Turning the lock, he slumped against it, remembering how her tea-colored eyes raked over him as he'd opened his own, rejoining the land of the corporeal. She looked so much like Kenny...but not. She was taller. Hair darker. Eyes a tint lighter.

He'd *seen* Colt slash Kenny's throat. She was gone, and wishing otherwise wouldn't change it. He was a fool — grateful for Carter's existence and resentful of it. They'd have to work together, especially if his appointment as APA Director became permanent.

He had stared up at her, knowing he ought to say something...but what? His raised brows told her the burden of conversation was hers.

She'd gotten the message.

"Right. It's been a long night," she'd murmured, dismissing the Chairman's sputtering apologies. Her easy grace only deepened his self-disgust. "Thank you both."

Dorrit shoved himself off the door and wandered into his apartment. Functional. Industrial. Monochromatic. Sparse but cleverly arranged to feel twice the size. It was too quiet after Punk Bunks.

And empty.

Sullen Creek had felt like a living, breathing entity — a home.

He punched the wall, relishing the pain when his fist found the stud. It helped — just that split second of distraction; so, he did it again.

Perhaps it was because he'd missed the stud, or maybe the universe loathed him, but the second time wasn't as good. He went and rinsed his bleeding knuckles under the faucet in the kitchen, promised himself a long session on the punching bag, grabbed the first-aid kit from under the sink, and did his best to imitate a mentally stable adult.

He had let her walk through the portal without rising from the settee, each heel click a warning. The sound had an ominous finality about it. When she was gone, he'd watched the circular door shrink. He'd considered going after her — saw his fingers circling her arm, and begging her to be someone else.

She had trusted him without a thought, without effort.

But maybe it wasn't about him at all. Maybe Carter trusted him because Kenny had.

There had been two sizes of clothing in Kenny's closet. The larger fit a taller woman, one who wore tailored suits and stilettos.

He'd lost his mind.

He opened the fridge and grabbed a beer. Not a Frigid Witch — which was probably for the best. He could handle unhinged. Maudlin? No.

One long pull later, he surveyed the material evidence of his life — a flatscreen; the saddle-brown couch he'd gotten second-hand for his college apartment and had reupholstered; the only three books that weren't work-related were stacked on a small, sad bookshelf; the snake plant Ridel had given him as a housewarming gift — that only got watered when his colleague reminded him; a large forested landscape with a Dark Mark fading into the sky because the bare wall had needed something and the unexpected detail had caught his fancy; his cat with her cold, assessing eyes looking like she'd sooner murder him than offer a head nuzzle; the vintage gramophone in the corner that hinted at hidden depths but had never been repaired. His old jazz records were still packed away in a box, somewhere.

It all felt like it belonged to someone else.

His eyes roamed back to the floofy gray cat giving him a death glare.

He didn't own a cat.

He flipped up his eye patch, revealing a perfectly good eye with a metallic brown iris, and studied the feline. It wasn't a glamour, construct, or illusion.

And — bizarrely — a smile cracked across his face.

"Yeah, that's not creepy at all," the cat observed, chewing between her toe-beans.

Her voice was classic noir: sultry, jaded, with a gun in her clutch and blood on her claws.

"And you talk. Excellent," he said sincerely. "Why are you here?"

Just like that, the beer had flavor. The apartment's light warmed. His antique cameras, Schuco cars, and black-and-white street photos made the space feel eccentric — cozy. Streeterville shimmered beyond his windows.

The cat nudged a folded paper at him.

"For you."

"Thanks." He unfolded it with trembling hands. Read it twice. Then aloud, "Ground Wagyu beef, Sockeye salmon, pheasant, two automated litter boxes...sixteen squeaky mice, four velvet cat beds…a window hammock…and a climbing wall?"

He sank onto the couch, laughing softly. It was either laugh or start pounding drywall again. He bit his knuckle, shaking his head.

"Four velvet beds," he wheezed.

Had he really thought enlightenment would come in the form of a cat? Yes. Yes, he had.

"Of course, four," she repeated. "Two here, two in the gym. One for me and one for my sister. You're lucky your mattress is adequate, or it'd be six. I'm making do with the bare essentials."

Something in her voice cut through his fog.

"Why will you be staying here at all?"

She sat up, eyes glassy, voice light with forced nonchalance.

"I want to hire you to investigate my familiar's death."

Surprise, pity, and something darker flickered across his face.

"Try to comfort me, and you'll *need* that eyepatch. You've never been a familiar — you don't understand. I *felt* what she felt. Abigail discovered something, and she died trying to get the proof to Kenny. The Saturniidae found her body in a dumpster — two bullets to the head. No trail. I know what she found, but no one will believe me without proof."

"Mystery, I'm an Agency warlock. Not a PI."

"And I'm a *cat*! I don't have a credit card, a job, or a bank account — but I *can* pay you. Emily Caterham, Dunia Azan, Neveah Howard, Sylvia Ewens — simulacra. All of them. Dr. Feyrer is the Covenant's monster-maker, and she uses *living* tissue to build from. That's just a sample of what I know."

He considered her.

"Isn't that a bit disloyal?"

"It might be — if Kenny hadn't trusted you. But she did. The little seer made sure of that."

He rose, pacing.

If he could find out who killed Kenny — if he had something to chase — it might stop him from imploding.

"Is there a way to differentiate between a simulacrum and a real person?" he asked aloud.

Mystery smiled. And said nothing.

Smart cat.

"Very well. Do we shake or—?"

Five bloody stripes bloomed across his palm.

"We sign in blood," the cat purred.

Chapter 102: To Your Health

September 20th at the Agora in Chicago, Illinois

"—bone broth, kale salads, no flour, no sugar," the Chairman whined, closing his laptop, "water, water, and more water. No scotch or wine! Workouts at four in the morning, five days a week! You tell me — does this need improvement?"

O'Brien stood, sweeping his hands down his frame.

The Doyenne wrinkled her nose, uncomfortable. "No comment. Actually, just one. You're welcome."

"It's your fault," he muttered.

"You'd eat your weight in grilled, unsalted fish just to hear him call you 'dad.' Besides, healthy doesn't mean boring. I'll send you some recipes."

"I think not! One of you is bad enough. I don't need both of you pestering me!"

A wicked smile curled Carter's lips, visions of roasted root vegetables and cottage cheese pancakes dancing behind her eyes.

"No," he said, pointing at her. "Whatever you're thinking — no."

The malice lingered, but her expression softened.

"How is John?"

O'Brien's expression shifted, eyes creasing with an age he otherwise didn't show. "He's…good. Busy. He hasn't reached out?"

"A few times. Mostly logistics — for MacDonnell's training."

"How's that going?"

"She's a natural. Her mishaps are entirely because she can control magic! Protective instinct takes over…and let's face it, that isn't something we want to fix. So, our lessons have switched to containment and scrubbing — housekeeping basics," she groused, adding, "He texts Kenny."

"Does he? What does he say?"

That Mystery had adopted him. That he'd found a lead on Colt's captor, that DNA from the West Pullman nest was problematic, and that things weren't as straightforward as they'd seemed.

She gave O'Brien a quelling look.

"That's his business. I only mentioned it because…well, it can't be healthy."

He shrugged. "We all cope in our own way. It *is* odd, though."

"What is?"

"This blind spot. Even when I see roads, I don't see all ends — I'd have gone mad long ago if I did."

He cut off her grin. "I'm not insane, missy. Not very. Because of the blind spot, I can't tell what John's going through. I *can* tell you he's not in love with Kenny Jones."

"Oh…that's good. Isn't it? He shouldn't be pining over a dead woman. I'll…I'll stop worrying."

"Good."

"But…why isn't he moving on?"

O'Brien smiled indulgently. "How's Rena settling in?"

Carter grimaced, her head turned away, but allowed the subject change.

"She's trying. She asked me to create a training schedule for her. After years of subsisting entirely on delicacies, she has no muscle tone. She hates the morning workouts, foraging hikes, sports, and the local fauna. Rena bribes Arlo to smuggle in beer, takeout, and pastries, hiding them in her room. Now she's infested with horned ambush nixies. But she's determined, so I'll give her a month before *she* bails."

"I am not going to bail! I'm going to whine until your ears bleed. Now off with you — I've got work to do."

"Unfortunately, so do I." Carter gathered up a map and several folders. "Same time next week?"

"I look forward to it."

As the portal cinched shut behind her, O'Brien leaned back, contemplating the mysteries of the near future. How long his reverie lasted was anyone's guess — until a stack of manila files *thwacked* onto his desk.

Bad news, Chairman. Senator Whaley was found dead this afternoon. Two shots to the head. Close range.

O'Brien composed himself and dusted off his suit, eyeing the paperwork with disdain.

"How did you do that? You've never carried physical objects through walls before."

Concentrate, Chairman. Whaley — staunch Correctionist, growing Quorum influence — killed with the same MO as the others.

"Yes, yes. He's the one who found the glasses — the ones that reveal helot tethers. Bumped his voting weight up to twelve. The enemy's not even pretending to be subtle anymore."

No, they aren't. I've put Ridel on the case, and I'm joining the team in St. Augustine. There are reports that Vitruvio was spotted nearby.

"There are always reports Vitruvio was spotted nearby," O'Brien muttered, grabbing the top file. "What's this? An unregistered nest in West Pullman?"

Read the report. A trace of DNA was found there — a match to Serrecold. Hildebrand had walked the scene and found traces of multiple helots.

O'Brien looked suitably grim.

Dorrit summarized several more equally alarming reports before departing for a meeting — he had hopes of obtaining Dietricksen's support for a Mandatory Mind Manipulation Testing bill, requiring all members of the Quorum to submit to regular check-ups.

The Chairman, after seeing his guest off, returned to his desk and sat twiddling his thumbs for several minutes. When no further interruptions occurred, he unlocked a desk drawer and pulled out a Magic Eight Ball, giving it a twirl.

'Reply hazy' floated to the little window.

O'Brien grimaced and turned to his laptop for comfort.

"Right, then. We have an appointment with a certain harbor master, Vindicta."

Chapter 103: Setting The Record Straight

Enid: September 20ᵗʰ in Wenen

"I saw your face. You weren't sorry; you were exultant!"

The words, despite my best efforts, came out harsh and landed with the grace of a nuclear strike. It was an accusation, not the calm, lucid observation I'd intended.

Padŭ closed her eyes and retreated into herself.

I looked away, guilt nipping at me, and breathed.

The elna ceiling emanated with apricot light, drowning us and the little room in an overly friendly glow. I had to wear sunglasses to avoid a headache. There were three refurbished armchairs arranged around a small coffee table, one overloaded bookshelf, several stacks of books that didn't fit on the shelves, and a few potted plants. Eventually, we'd add a desk.

Dr. Ira Bakirtzis, a norm and recent arrival to Wenen, bowed his bronze-haired head and scribbled something on a notepad. The lighting was kind to him, minimizing his hawk-like nose and broadening his cheekbones. In a less favorable environment, he had the face of a sad, poetic moose. When his colorless eyes bobbed back up, they landed on my mother and waited patiently.

In our first session, he'd informed us that he needed to see how we interacted. He hadn't said another word until the hour was up. It had ended in twenty, uninterrupted minutes of bitter, seething silence.

Shame, I suspect, made us return for round two. We were trying.

Padŭ's — Croía's… My mother's hands white-knuckled the arms of her chair, and she jerked her head in the affirmative.

"I'm not proud of it."

She studied the smooth, stone floor as if it held the answers to the universe.

"I extracted that promise because I needed to know that you would be loved. I had expected to die-"

Dr. Bakirtzis held up a finger and made a note.

"You knew you would be attacked?"

He had a gentle voice — detached and unhurried. His serenity annoyed me.

"No...I knew that Vivienne would raise Enid."

That was news to me.

"How," I asked, trying to make it sound like a request and not a demand.

She glanced at me, surprised. That I didn't already know or that I had sounded almost polite?

"Did Vivienne explain how we met? We were apprenticed to Doyen Umansky? Viv's parents thought she was a sender, like me, but that her aim was off."

My mother smiled slyly, and I snorted.

"Was it?" inquired Bakirtzis, glancing between us.

"No," Croía and I replied.

"Senders push objects through the ley lines, relocating them; the talent is the root of hedge magic," I explained. "My adoptive mom isn't a sender, though; she sends objects through time — a different branch altogether. If the world made any sense, my sister's talent would be more important than mine. Evy's aim is precise. Our mom's is even better."

It was Croía's turn to snort.

"After all they put Viv through, it had to be. Umansky was…a difficult mentor; her consistent failure infuriated him, and he routinely put her in isolation as punishment. It took him six months to figure her out, and everything changed overnight. Suddenly, she wasn't an embarrassing failure; she was a priceless commodity. I was sent home — no longer an object of interest and, at thirteen, Vivienne became a spy."

Her tone of voice was almost monotonous, suggesting boredom.

My mothers had been rivals. Vivienne, who couldn't handle noise or crowds, was shoved into a profession that ought to have killed her, and Croía didn't receive a complete education until she was an adult. Her eyes drifted to the right, seeing through the pale wall to a different time and place.

"I had forgotten all about her until, one day, years before handheld video recorders were commonplace, I saw a blond girl — the very image of Vivienne — filming us. She appeared nine times — sometimes years apart but always the same age. She vanished anytime I approached her. I told your father. We arrived at the same conclusion: something was going to happen to us, and Vivienne would be the one to raise you. We prepared…and you survived."

Croía cleared her throat, cutting herself free from the memories.

"After the Covenant rescued me and you told me about your life, I had a bad moment. My husband was dead, I had endured three decades in hell, and my beautiful daughter had been raised by someone else. I wanted to punish Viv for doing as I'd asked. That the promise caused problems... Yes, when you told me, for a moment, I felt...jubilant. It wasn't much, but it felt like the scales had been evened a hair. I immediately regretted the thought. After you, there is no living person I love more than Vivienne Ritter-Vine. I can never repay her."

I didn't know what to say.

The buzzer went off. Our time was up.

"That's a good place to stop. Give each other space for a few hours. Think about what we've uncovered."

I went back to my little apartment utterly drained. I didn't want to think. I didn't want to talk. I didn't want to do anything.

Our resident serial killer waved from the sofa, Cartman drooling in his lap, and the TV on mute. It was their favorite spot. After the helot tethers had faded, Carrick had demonstrated no violent tendencies or any desire to manipulate the lines. I didn't know what to do with him. He slept in the dorms but struggled with noise and social interactions. He went to therapy, worked in the gardens, and retreated here to cuddle with my big, ginger boy.

"Carrick," I murmured, aiming for my bedroom and peace.

"Lady witch."

He nodded to the flatscreen and unmuted the news.

"-ces of Humanity. Following on the coattails of supernatural whistleblower, Luke Vitruvio, this publication attempts to set the record straight. It details how the seven Origins originated, the ins and outs of the contemporary Community, and why magic is relevant to everyone. Officials are still debating whether this is a hoax, even as a supernatural registry, ley tax, and magic-free zoning are being proposed. Every day, the controversy keeps getting thicker. Rob, over to you!"

I stared at the screen.

"They did it."

I had been convinced that we'd failed…and relieved in that conviction. Preternaturals had already been outed, and my name…names…weren't attached to it. Now, Dr. Evelyn Vine, Doyenne Enid Carter, Hazel Jones, and Alexandria Gregg blazed across the screen. The toothpaste couldn't go back in the tube. We were forever a part of history.

I didn't want that responsibility.

The entire world knew I was a practitioner.

I should have negotiated for hazard pay.

"Congratulations," said Carrick, toasting me with his beer. "We're both famous."

Enid: October 3rd in Wenen

A solitary line of electric red traced the horizon, glinting off a trillion shards of glass and washing the twisted steel skeletons of five Las Vegas high-rises with the first blush of dawn. They'd been obliterated. News cameras stalked the first responders as they climbed the rubble like ants. Darkness still clung to every chunk of concrete and stray armchair, concealing the dead, granting them a temporary dignity.

"A bomb didn't do that," Colt said.

He was right. Even without my glasses, I could see the buildings still standing, transparent, and haloed in gold. The wiring had been turned into a closed ley circuit, then filled to bursting. Someone had known exactly where to strike and how. Unless a team siphoned off the energy, the after-image would linger for years.

We wouldn't be allowed to. Practitioners had done this.

"You told them magic was involved?" Colt asked.

"I did."

"And they turned us down."

I didn't answer.

Even if the authorities had been kindly disposed, they had no idea where we fit in — consultants, agents, liabilities? If our people planted inside the government got us clearance, it would draw attention. One reporter, one influencer, one Joe Schmo asking questions, and our good deed would be used to hang us.

But if we hadn't offered, we'd be vilified too.

"You knew this would happen," Xandre snapped, slamming her mug down beside me.

Colt straightened — too quickly. Katie wasn't picking up, and his mom had just taken a post on the Mulberry. She ought to be safe, but nothing was guaranteed. All of that left him twitchy. And he still didn't trust my cousin.

"You were ready to release *Faces of Humanity* before Vitruvio came along — when it meant we'd be traitors," she hissed. "Don't doubt yourself. The world will adjust."

I smiled, bittersweet.

I'd apologized for leaving her alone to handle guild politics — isolated, flanked by detractors and simulacra. It had been necessary work, and she'd done it brilliantly. But the Covenant had grown. It couldn't be a one-woman show anymore. Saying she'd forgiven me would be a stretch, but she had my back.

"I knew," I said. "And if our luck holds, maybe it will. But someone is determined to undermine us."

Thirteen days had passed since the Community released *Faces*. Twenty-eight since Veritas redefined 'going viral'. Three thousand people — suspected preternaturals and bystanders — had been killed.

Double that, now.

There'd been fires, bombs, and a few mass poisonings. Forty-seven countries had outlawed our existence — and harboring us, both punishable by death. Vampire hunters, exorcists, and dragon slayers had sprouted from the woodwork and set up shop in every city. You couldn't swing a wild construct without hitting one.

And this was the best-case scenario.

Most of humanity was still reeling — waiting for someone to admit it was all a hoax. Instead, the world's leaders (the ones not jumping straight to murder) urged calm. The Chief Justice of the Hall of Vampires, the President of the Therianthrope Council, and I had met with the President and his cabinet. It was surreal but not unproductive. I'd done nine interviews — each some combination of short, awkward, and/or openly hostile. Still, I had to believe we were laying the groundwork for something better.

"Is it just hate, or is there more to it?" I asked, watching as another stretcher was carried from the rubble.

The door burst open. Evy marched in, waving her phone.

"New assignment."

Sia belted "Unstoppable" from my pocket — quest details incoming.

"A loxocosm," Colt read over my shoulder.

"Dr. Harrowell's our medic," Evy added.

"ETA five. Colt, make us a door. You need the practice."

He nodded and got to work.

"You sure you want Saul?" Evy asked.

He hadn't cared for Kenny, but he had no issues with Enid; said we didn't get to choose our relatives. I was still working up the nerve to let the Kenny-shaped cat out of the bag.

"I'm sure."

"I don't see it," Colt muttered, stepping back from the eyelet.

I removed my glasses. The other side of the portal revealed a dusty attic full of steamer trunks, dressmakers' dummies, faded bunting, a three-paneled Chinese screen, a ventriloquist's dummy on a carousel dragon, and three battered accordions. Fascinating and creepy, but no loxocosm. I twisted and stretched every which way — even climbed the worktable. I didn't see a clock of any sort.

Strange noises pulled me back to our side of reality.

Evy and Xandre were using their phones to document my contortions.

I rolled my eyes and folded back into a killer praying mantis pose, trying to peek through a gap between two stacks of boxes. Halfway there, a bronze being with four faces stepped into view — on another plane.

Chauncey!

I'd never seen an outer-world resident twice.

Hovering just above us in his garden paradise, each side-face grinned cheekily. The front face smiled beatifically and held up a gold coin between his thumb and forefinger. I waited for the magic trick, but he simply made the coin spin.

The point was lost on me — until he plucked up a gold gyroscope and set *that* spinning.

"A wheel," I whispered, reciting from Ezekiel, "within a wheel."

Chauncey was an angel.

A real one.

Angels existed.

"What?" Evy asked, reaching for her glasses.

I shook my head.

The enormity of what I'd seen was too much to unpack. Fortunately, there was something far more mundane I could fixate on.

I looked at Colt's eyelet with its one semi-flexible anchor point and felt very, very stupid. I reshaped it, forming a wheel within a wheel, and set them spinning with my finger. They moved with liquid grace.

"How?" Colt demanded.

Exactly.

How was I going to explain to the Covenant — and every hedge witch I'd trained — that I'd somehow overlooked the wondrous utility of *ball bearings?*

"Son of a...Saturday morning cartoon."

Finis

Thank you for reading *Blind Spot: The Covenant's Forfeit*.
If you enjoyed the story, please consider leaving a short review on the retailer's website where you purchased it. Reviews help readers find new authors, and they mean the world to indie writers.

Author's Note

It's been several years now, but I remember when I first visited Kenny's world. Hers is a noisy one and has only gained in volume — taking up space in my head and demanding attention. I'd once read about female brewers using twig brooms to mark their breweries for the illiterate and how they were sometimes accused of witchcraft. The true history remains fuzzy, but the notion of magic-wielding women who brewed beer became fixed in my imagination.

The first scene I wrote — Chapter 33 — instantly felt alive. I could see the Sullen Creek Brewpub, smell the food, and hear the chatter of patrons and pints hitting wooden tables. Originally, though, Kenny was the pushy server, not Lou, and John Dorrit was there instead of Veritas. Of course, in those early days, Kenny also went by Mickey. She has evolved quite a lot since then.

This book is a compilation of both new and old. Some of the terminology will likely be familiar, while other terms are pure invention. *Hedge riding, hedge jumping,* and *hedge crossing* are ancient — different names for the same practice: a technique used by hedge witches to enter the "Otherworld" through an induced trance. Having some personal experience with dissociation, I found the notion both fascinating and alarming.

I hail from a family that loves language, word games, and puns. If you're familiar with Tom Swifties, my father collects them and trades them with my uncle like baseball cards. He would be most grateful if you passed any along. With such a family, I've endured many a lecture on the devolution of the English language and how, the further we go, the closer we come to barbarism.

We're also drama queens.

Happily, I am not such a pessimist. I do, however, subscribe to the philosophy that language should change organically. Each age requires new words as technology and culture advance. Language is more than a tool for expression; it's a lever we use to change ourselves — sometimes for a moment, sometimes our very nature.

Perhaps you've noticed how that idea spills over here? O'Brien explains to Special Agent Gerahty how the term *warlock* has been corrupted by the Community. Once, it meant *deceiver* — referring to an apprentice who stole their mentor's work and/or reported them to the preternatural powers that be, often leading to the practitioner's death. They twisted the meaning until society saw a warlock as a trusted authority, like a firefighter or a teacher.

Similarly, the Community calls practitioners *witches* — much the same way people were persecuted in the sixteenth century in Europe and in the late seventeenth century in Salem, Massachusetts. The term has become so associated with evil in the Community that they don't like to say it. It's an absolute condemnation.

Until it isn't. For John Dorrit, it evolves almost into a term of affection — certainly into an acknowledgment of connection. It's a small redemption of sorts.

Edward Bulwer-Lytton wrote, "The pen is mightier than the sword." He was right.

Blind Spot serves as a reflection on many ideas — the complexity of human relationships, the weight of perception, and how conviction can often unravel greater powers — but most importantly, that words matter. They shape us in so many ways.

Thank you for joining me in this world.

— Thio Isobel Moss

Biographical Note

Thio Isobel Moss lives near Kansas City, Missouri, where the ley lines are strong, the DIY projects are eternal, and the rubber chickens are not to be trusted. She writes sly, genre-bending fiction full of conspiracies, magic, and emotional chaos. *Blind Spot: The Covenant's Forfeit* is her debut novel—and is only mildly autobiographical.

To learn more, visit www.thioisobelmoss.com

Upcoming Releases:

The Palmetto Predators:
Bump
(2026)

The Covenant's Forfeit:
Objects in the Mirror
(2027)